CHERISHED LOVE

It took every ounce of self-control Charles possessed to resist taking Thea into his arms and holding her until he confessed all that was in his eager heart. But their marriage, arranged by the government, denied all intimacy. And there was so much Charles wanted to tell Thea, to share with her. . . .

Thea felt there was no returning to a time when she and Charles were strangers, yet there seemed no other way for them to continue. She knew Charles's every mood and expression by heart. She slept in his bed every night, and was his wife in every way—except the one that was most important. Did she dare admit her love? And if she did, where would it lead their marriage?

EXCITING BESTSELLERS FROM ZEBRA

PASSION'S REIGN by Karen Harper (1177, $3.95)

Golden-haired Mary Bullen was wealthy, lovely and refined—
and lusty King Henry VIII's prize gem! But her passion for the
handsome Lord William Stafford put her at odds with the
Royal Court. Mary and Stafford lived by a lovers' vow: one day
they would be ruled by only the crown of PASSION'S REIGN.

HEIRLOOM by Eleanora Brownleigh (1200, $3.95)

The surge of desire Thea felt for Charles was powerful enough
to convince her that, even though they were strangers and
their marriage was a fake, fate was playing a most subtle trick
on them both: Were they on a mission for President Teddy
Roosevelt—or on a crusade to realize their own passionate
desire?

LOVESTONE by Deanna James (1202, $3.50)

After just one night of torrid passion and tender need, the dark-
haired, rugged lord could not deny that Moira, with her
precious beauty, was born to be a princess. But how could he
grant her freedom when he himself was a prisoner of her love?

DEBORAH'S LEGACY by Stephen Marlowe (1153, $3.75)

Deborah was young and innocent. Benton was worldly and
experienced. And while the world rumbled with the thunder of
battle, together they rose on a whirlwind of passion—daring
fate, fear and fury to keep them apart!

*Available wherever paperbacks are sold, or order direct from the
Publisher. Send cover price plus 50¢ per copy for mailing and
handling to Zebra Books, 475 Park Avenue South, New York,
N.Y. 10016 DO NOT SEND CASH.*

HEIRLOOM

BY
ELEANORA
BROWNLEIGH

ZEBRA BOOKS
KENSINGTON PUBLISHING CORP.

ZEBRA BOOKS

are published by

KENSINGTON PUBLISHING CORP.
475 Park Avenue South
New York, N.Y. 10016

Printed in the United States of America

FOR
*Kaylan Jester Riley
and her daughter
Rebecca Wright Riley
born 6 December 1981*

CLANDESTINE MARRIAGES

The clandestine marriage, this autumn, seems to have come into sudden fashion. Already only the month of September, and there have been three nuptial events of this kind, each of which has created a stir in fashionable life.

Now that Newport and Bar Harbor and Southampton and other seaside resorts have closed and there is a lull in gayeties, every one is asking 'who next?'

W. G. Robinson
Harvest of a Quiet Eye
Town and Country
September 17, 1904

The ladies men admire, I've heard,
Would shudder at a wicked word.
Their candle gives a single light;
They'd rather stay at home at night.
They do not keep awake till three,
Nor read erotic poetry.
They never sanction the impure,
Nor recognize an overture.
They shrink from powders and from paints.
So far, I have had no complaints.

Interview
Dorothy Parker

Prologue

The Presidential Train
St. Louis
September 6, 1904

I know how to work. I know how to impose a discipline on myself. But, if I do not want to do a thing, nothing and no one can persuade me to do it.

Chanel

In this life we get nothing save by effort.

Theodore Roosevelt

"Do you understand why we need you?"

There was no chance of mistaking the man seated behind the plain oak desk. His bluff, sanguine appearance was known all over the world, but this afternoon his usually hearty, genial voice was lowered to nearly a whisper, and his piercing gaze behind pince-nez spectacles was fixed on the young woman seated across from him on the hard, unattractive sofa upholstered in a dismal purple plush.

"The final decision is yours, of course," he went on as she made no immediate reply. "We certainly don't want to coerce you into this."

"Don't worry," she assured him, smiling. "I plan to think this thing through *very* carefully. It isn't every day that a New York interior decorator and antique dealer is asked by her President to go to Mexico and—how can I put it?—'look in' on the German Embassy."

Theodosia Harper rose from the sofa and crossed the floor, moving normally despite the motion of the train. They were in the President's private railroad car, speeding across the green, open plains of the Illinois-Missouri border toward St. Louis. It was a scalding hot, early September day and the shades in the car were drawn against the sun, leaving them in a state of semi-gloom. Which, Thea couldn't help thinking as she cautiously raised a shade to gaze out at the farmland they were hurtling through, wasn't such an awful thing considering the Spartan, utilitarian way the entire car was furnished. No rare tapestries or gold-leaf ceilings or antique furniture here. The American people wanted their President to live comfortably and well, but without any of the luxuries his millionaire friends and advisors travelled in.

"I should have known something special was up the moment Colonel Miles turned up in my office," she said humorously, not bothering to turn around. "Actually, he walked in at the perfect moment. I was just back from Europe and about to be buried under all my paperwork. When a dealer buys antiques abroad, she has to be very sure that all her letters of authentication are in order unless she wants to spend a lot of time with the men from Customs. When the colonel walked in, I'd just about had it and I begged him to take me away. I guess I got my wish."

Two months away from her twenty-sixth birthday, Thea Harper was well-educated, witty, attractive, and as tall as most men. Her glossy brown hair was swept up into a Gibson Girl knot and her figure was superbly suited for the clothes she purchased from Paquin, Poiret, and Lucile. There was a sort of breezy ebullience about her, which, combined with a basic kindness, inspired newly made millionaires' wives, who were either reduced to shaking nerves by the supercilious young male decorators who looked down their noses at them or struck dumb at the idea of patronizing the great firm of Duveen's even though they could easily afford it, to make Thea their confidant while she sold them antiques or gave them advice about decorating their new mansions.

Her firm, "Theodosia Harper: Antiques and Interiors," was just two years old, but had already created a hallmark for those who wanted coolly elegant but comfortable homes full of soft colors, good books, delicate bibelots, fine paintings, and no concessions to the heavy draperies, Turkish carpets and overstuffed Belter furniture most of her clients had grown up with.

Her suite of offices in a modern Fifth Avenue office building was its own best advertisement. Located a few blocks south of the Waldorf-Astoria, her out-of-town clients could walk over for their initial appointment with her after a late breakfast. Coming off the elevator and stepping through the double doors for the first time, they were greeted by Thea's secretary, who had her own small alcove with an oval satinwood desk, and were ushered into the reception room where, according to plan, Thea always gave prospective clients a few minutes alone to admire the decor before being shown into her office.

The large Limoges cache-pot filled with a lush arrangement of pale pink peonies, columbine, tulips, and statice made of silk, satin, and velvet that Fromentin in Paris had designed for her was the favorite. More than one lady had hurried across the off-white, powder blue, and taupe Chinese carpet to the Chinese Chippendale table with the English Chippendale gilt-frame mirror hanging above it to sniff the opulent bouquet before realizing it was false. After that embarrassing mistake, they usually went to the delicate Sheraton mahogany inlaid occasional tables where the real bouquets— arranged for Thea by Sarah Tucker and Alice Babcock at The Fernery, the fashionable florist shop and tea room on Thirty-third Street—were displayed, before sitting down on the black and gold stenciled Sheraton settee upholstered in taupe silk.

It was such a relaxing atmosphere that, by the time they entered her office and saw the haute-couture clad young woman sitting in the oval back George III armchair behind the Adam style mahogany inlaid writing table, they were certain that all their decorating problems would be solved.

When she had opened her firm, Thea made two rules

and stuck to them. Never take on a client she didn't like and, although her fees did run very high, never overcharge. In terms of personality and payment it would have been very easy to take outrageous advantage of these women (other decorators certainly did) but Thea was above that sort of behavior. She was open and honest with them on all subjects except one. After all, it was really no one's business that every so often she did a favor for the President of the United States. The first favor had started her on her own business and somehow, in a series of complicated twists and turns, the latest request had brought her here.

Colonel Hugh Miles was the second-in-command of Military Intelligence, and when he'd walked into Thea's office ten days ago, she should have immediately suspected he was in New York to do more than take her to lunch at the Waldorf after she'd helped him select a piece of porcelain from her collection for his wife's birthday.

"Has some prominent Republican friend of the President's unknowingly picked up a stolen Titian or some hot jewels in Paris or Amsterdam?" she inquired jokingly after they greeted one another and he was ensconced in the chair where her clients usually sat. "If the President needs me in Washington for a few days to smooth things over and facilitate the return, tell him I'll be glad to do it."

"No new clients then?"

Thea pushed aside the sheafs of paper that were covering her desk and held up several letters tied with green ribbon. "Would you care to pick one for me? So far, I have an offer to do an apartment here in town, a house in Albany, a small mansion in Wilmington, and a sweet inquiry from a woman outside of Oklahoma City who wants to know how much I'd charge to redecorate her ranch house. Honest," she said, seeing Miles' startled expression. "She read all about me in the 'Women of

12

Interest' series in *Harper's Bazaar.* Unless you, on behalf of T.R., can offer me something else, I may just accept." She made a sweeping motion at her desk. "Did you ever see such a mess? I got off the *La Savoie* on Monday afternoon and haven't seen the wood on this desk since."

Miles seemed to have acquired a sudden interest in the assortment of blue and white Oriental porcelains she kept in the glass fronted vitrine on the other side of the room. "Are you really interested in getting away for a while? I think we might be able to oblige you."

"Well, a couple of days in Washington is better than nothing. Sometimes I wish I hadn't been so successful in returning that diamond tiara in Budapest two years ago. Now the President thinks I'm the only one who can straighten out his friends' mishaps." She gave him a conspirator's smile. "What happened this time? Don't tell me someone 'accidentally' purchased the Mona Lisa."

But it hadn't been like that at all, and now she stood silently by the train window thinking everything over— all the possibilities, all the consequences.

Hugh Miles hadn't told her much of anything except that the President wanted her to take a trip to Mexico. She would need her best clothes and be prepared to remain away indefinitely.

After that basic bit of information had been delivered, he only wanted to know if she could conclude her business in time to go to Washington with him the following Wednesday so they could join Roosevelt on the Presidential train on Thursday morning.

For a second, Thea stared wordlessly at him across the flawless expanse of white damask tablecloth in the Waldorf. "But today is Friday. I have to put all my paperwork in order, close up my office and apartment, pack—not to mention little things like answering my mail and placating a couple of beaus who intend to take

13

me to some Broadway opening nights over the next couple of weeks."

Miles waved away a waiter who was hovering obsequiously nearby. "Anyone serious?"

"What? *No.*"

His normally reserved, hawklike face relaxed. "Well, then.. Thea, I know we're not giving you very much notice, but we really need your help in this."

Thea raised her eyebrows questioningly, took a sip of ice water, opened the elaborate, gold tasseled menu, and scanned the dessert selection before lifting her gaze to the colonel. "Tell me," she said in a deliberately casual voice, "what kind of weather can I expect in Mexico at this time of year?"

It was an impossible task to contemplate, and yet, in the space of four-and-a-half days, she had put her life in a state of near suspension. Potential clients were gently refused, the apartment at 34 Gramercy Park was returned to the dust covers it had been placed under when she'd left for Europe in June. Morgan Guaranty would pay all incoming bills for her, her secretary would come to the office every day to answer the phone and collect the mail.

On Saturday night she went to the opening of *Mrs. Wiggs of the Cabbage Patch* starring Madge Carr Cook— the only social engagement she hadn't cancelled. To her married friends who were already planning their fall dinner parties, and to the young men who wanted to take her to the theatre, she followed Miles' advice and told them she had to make an unexpected business trip out of town.

"It isn't far from the truth," he'd said when she asked. "I understand there are a lot of antiques in Mexico."

It had gone almost *too* smoothly. On Wednesday night she'd found herself in Washington in the new Shoreham Hotel with an uncountable pile of luggage, two letters of

14

credit (one personal, one business), no more information on what she was expected to do than when Colonel Miles had entered her office, and the odd feeling that a chapter of her life had been sealed off and would never be the same again.

It wasn't until Thea, the President, Colonel Miles and a Mr. Simpson from the State Department were in the private car and well on their way out of Washington, that she was told what they were considering and how she could be of help to them. They had retired to their rooms to pack and rest, leaving her and Roosevelt alone for one last conference and her answer.

"You haven't told me with whom I'll be working," she said, still looking out the window. "From what you've told me, it doesn't sound like something one person could handle."

"It isn't," he agreed. "You will travel with one other person and, of course, you'll have a contact at our Embassy in Mexico City. Major John Donovan will meet you in San Antonio and fill you in on the final details."

"Such as the name of my travelling companion?" Thea asked. And if it's some dried-up old duenna, you can put me and my luggage off the train right here and now, she added to herself.

"Yes." There was a subdued chuckle. "A good way of putting it. Travelling companion. You have the same way with words as you do with decorating, my dear."

"Thank you, Mr. President."

"Although I cannot name a name as yet, I can tell you that your . . . helpmeet will be male."

Thea wasn't sure if it was the train that lurched suddenly or her heart. Was she crazy? Were they *all* crazy? What was she doing here anyway? *The very idea.* Run on down to Mexico like a good girl, Thea, and eavesdrop in the German Embassy. And, oh, by the way, we're pairing you off with a man, only we can't tell you

15

his name yet. Would Ida Tarbell love to get her hands on this!

But through her rush of disbelief, anger and shock, whimsy was starting to poke its way to the surface and her natural curiosity was sparked. Young? Old? Dishonorable? Well-bred? What? Thea was a normal woman with a healthy regard toward men and she was intrigued by the mechanics of the male-female relationship. The natural distaste she'd felt at the thought of snooping on people—even if they *were* Germans—receded into the background.

"Well, Theodosia, we'll be in St. Louis in another hour or two. Have you made your decision?"

"What happens to me when we reach St. Louis?" Thea knew she was being exasperating, but she liked things spelled out in black and white. Muddy philosophies and half-truths didn't suit her and certainly didn't belong on an assignment like this.

"You will be escorted off the train by Colonel Miles and taken to the Jefferson Hotel. Mrs. Miles is already there, and the three of you will have a few days to enjoy the Exposition and do some sightseeing and shopping. When word is received that everything in San Antonio has been finalized, you'll be put on the Katy and Major Donovan will meet you at the other end. That will be your jumping-off spot."

Her eyes narrowed slightly. "From the Menger Hotel?"

"That will be your ultimate destination, but I think you'll like the first stop, since it's at the home of mutual friends of ours. My former supply officer from Cuba and his new bride," Roosevelt said as Thea finally turned around, a smile lighting up her face and relief flooding her before he even said a name. The President allowed himself a small sigh. "I'll never understand why the son of a United States senator decided his aim in life was to

16

found a woman's specialty store in Texas."

"But Morgan Browne has made a thriving success out of it," she countered, "and five months ago he married Admiral Dalton's daughter, Angela. If my stopover in San Antonio had meant I couldn't see them, I would have told you to go find someone else for this job. You know what great pals Nela and I are, and I haven't seen them since their wedding in San Francisco in April. You and Mrs. Roosevelt sent a wonderful telegram and a very handsome gift."

"Does that tip the scales in our favor?"

"Why me, Mr. President? Why me?" She took a theatrical tone, meaning to be funny, but Theodore Roosevelt took her seriously.

"You've shown great discretion and tact in handling the other assignments you've had. The people you've helped avoid scandal and the ambassadors you've dealt with, speak well of you, and Admiral Dalton recommends you highly. I trust Bruce Dalton. His European intelligence reports have proved as invaluable to me as they were to my predecessors, and will no doubt be to my successors, and his past two years in China were fruitful beyond our original expectations."

"Admiral Dalton and his new son-in-law are Democrats," Thea reminded him, unable to resist a bit of fun. "So am I, for all the good it does. Do you mind?"

"That is why I trust all of you. You have nothing to kowtow for. My dear, Europe is a time-bomb ticking quietly away, and we need all the information we can get before the explosion occurs. The Kaiser is turning his beady eyes on us, and Panama, now that we're going ahead with the canal. We're certain he'd like to cause trouble for us, either in the canal area or along the Mexican-American border. Once you start moving in the Embassy set in Mexico City, any information you can pass on will help us."

17

Thea reached behind her and grasped the ledge of the window with her hands, bracing her slim body against it. "I'll do it," she said recklessly. "It's worth a try, and the worst I can do is come up empty-handed."

The President looked at her, outlined against the window, the sun glinting on her hair. He thought for a minute of Saint Joan, ready to do battle, but immediately rejected the idea. This was a modern woman. The woman of 1904. Brave and forthright and ready to shoulder her own responsibility.

Thea moved away from the window, coming into the gloom again, her pale blue linen dress a pencil-slim streak of color. She held out her hand. "Shall we shake on it?"

Theodore Roosevelt took her hand and pumped it enthusiastically. "Bully," he said heartily, a great smile breaking across his face. "Just bully."

Part One

Healing is a matter of time, but it is sometimes a matter of opportunity.

Hippocrates

To fear love is to fear life, and those who fear life are already three parts dead.

Bertrand Russell

Great loves too must be endured.

Chanel

Chapter One

There was a huge, cheering crowd waiting for the President when they reached St. Louis. When Roosevelt stepped out onto the back platform to greet them, Thea and Colonel Miles left through the exit at the other end, and, as inconspicuously as possible, blended in with the other Pullman passengers streaming through Union Station followed by porters, their carts piled high with luggage.

"Are you sure you don't want to send some of your trunks thru to San Antonio?" Miles asked as they stood between the elegant brougham and the large, practical luggage brake that had been waiting for them when they emerged from the Market Street exit.

Thea shook her head. "I know there's an awful lot of it, but you *did* tell me to pack my best," she said as they watched the standing dress trunks, shoe trunks, suitcases, and hatboxes being loaded. "And if there's one thing I learned from being the daughter of an explorer it's to keep all your belongings with you."

"But do they all have to be Louis Vuitton?" he inquired, his steel blue eyes amused.

"Look at it this way: at least I don't have to worry that some absent-minded baggage master will mix up my luggage with someone else's!" she laughed as the last of

21

the eye-catching black and white striped cases was safely stowed away. They stepped into the brougham's taupe velvet-lined interior for the short ride to the Jefferson Hotel.

The Louisiana Purchase Exposition had opened less than four months before and was still going full swing with people from all over America and Europe arriving to enjoy the sights and swelling the city's population far beyond its normal half-million. Thea, like all normal New Yorkers, regarded crowds in *her* city as normal, but eyed the mass of humanity in downtown St. Louis with surprise.

"I certainly wasn't expecting to see anything like this," she said as they stalled in traffic near City Hall.

"I agree. Let's hope we're only caught in the overflow from the station. Lots of people wanted to get a look at T.R.," he smiled. "Gives them something else to write home about."

"I wonder what all those good people would say if they knew that an unmarried woman unaccompanied by chaperone, companion, or maid came along for the ride?"

Miles made a gesture of mock dismay. "Well, for starters, they'd call you something a lot more interesting than an interior decorator. Seriously though, there's little chance of that happening. You know that the servants who made the trip with us were White House personnel, not employees of the Pullman company."

She nodded. "And I noticed how the Secret Service made sure the car we walked through to leave the train was entirely empty. I'm aware that they're eager to protect a reputation—only I don't happen to think it's mine!"

"That's because we all know you're self-reliant enough to look after yourself without any outside help." Miles glanced out the window at the snarl of carriages, wagons and motor cars. "We should be moving again in a minute, and once we get to the hotel all of this won't seem quite so bad. Jane promised to have quite a welcome set up for us. She's looking forward to seeing you again."

"And I'm looking forward to seeing her. The best part of my assignment may turn out to be the time I spend with you and Mrs. Miles," Thea said tiredly, relaxing against the cushions and closing her eyes. She was hot, tired, sticky and although she usually managed a good night's sleep on a train, last night had been the exception. Worst of all, her brain felt as if it had been set down in a pool of sticky molasses. She wanted to think over every detail that they had discussed and plan how she would handle events when she got to San Antonio. Instead, it took all her strength to get out a simple sentence. She'd agreed to a plan whose final details were *still* unresolved because the idea of working with a man was too intriguing to pass up.

Of course, with my luck, he'll be some professorial sort who doesn't know that women have stopped wearing bustles. I'm going to the wrong city on the wrong mission, Thea thought as the brougham pulled up in front of the massive, fifteen-hundred room Jefferson Hotel. The commissionaire helped them out as a small army of bellhops ran to handle the luggage. Instead of going to Mexico City to join the Embassy set, I should be on my way to Vienna to start a series of consultations with an alienist!

Jane Miles had the knack that all good and wise women who marry military and diplomatic men have to develop if they expect to be considered assets to their husbands' careers. The first rule was to make whatever place to which you were assigned homelike and, in this, Mrs. Hugh Miles excelled.

Arriving in St. Louis two days earlier, she'd used her

time alone to make sure the huge, two-bedroom suite her husband had reserved for them was in perfect order when the two weary travellers arrived. Beautiful arrangements of fresh flowers were placed on the end tables, the windows were open to catch the passing breeze, silver framed pictures of family and friends, favorite books and treasured mementos placed at strategic points around the sitting room took the curse off the untouched uniformity that hangs over even the most luxurious of suites. While Thea and Colonel Miles were making their way across the crowded lobby toward the elevators, waiters were bringing in the tea things: a steaming pot of Prince of Wales blend, trays of small sandwiches and delicate pastries were placed on the low table flanked by two sofas covered in a brightly flowered chintz.

"Oh, Mrs. Miles, this is heaven," Thea said as she stepped over the threshold and saw the welcome waiting for them. "It makes that miserable trip worth it."

Jane Miles disengaged herself from her husband's embrace and hugged Thea warmly. "And here I was, ordering flowers and tea and envying you for travelling on the Presidential train!"

"I'm afraid it's a highly overrated honor and nothing to write home about," she said regretfully, taking off her hat, gloves and the jacket to her beige linen suit from Paquin as she enviously eyed Jane who looked cool and composed in a Worth tea gown of pale yellow chiffon. "You arrive at your destination just as worn out as you do when you travel in a Pullman car during the hottest week of the year. Not even the best service in the world and the honor of travelling with the President makes it any cooler!"

"Well, as the British say, what you need right now is a cup of hot tea. It will perk up the both of you, and in a little while all you'll remember is the fun you had."

"Oh, Jane, if you only knew," Thea thought as she

24

sipped her tea.

"I've booked a table for us in the restaurant downstairs at eight. Is that all right with you, dear?"

"Absolutely perfect," the colonel replied, accepting a steaming cup. "I understand they start playing dance music after nine, so I'll look forward to taking both you ladies for a turn around the floor. We're going to have an exciting time while we're in St. Louis, and there isn't a better way to start than with a good dinner and the latest dance tunes!"

Much to her own surprise, the hot tea *did* revive Thea. After two cups, several sandwiches, and a few of the little frosted cakes, she excused herself so that the Mileses— who were openly affectionate and still in love after nearly thirty years of marriage—could have their reunion in private. In her bedroom, she rang for a maid and gave her an armful of her lightest dresses to iron and, as soon as she was alone, she ran herself a nice hot perfumed bath.

To think it all out straight, she had to start at the beginning, Thea decided as she relaxed in the Guerlain scented water a few minutes later. All right, she'd already established the fact that the main impetus for accepting this not-as-yet fully explained assignment was her overwhelming curiosity about the man who was at this minute waiting for her in Texas. Fine. Take that for what it was and not go deeper into it. Even if he turned out to be the twin of Diamond Jim Brady—all three hundred pounds of him—she wouldn't renege after giving her word.

But what was the stumbling block—the thing that had annoyed her since she and Roosevelt shook hands? Had it been something he had said or, more significantly, what he *hadn't* said?

Thea almost dropped the bar of Jicky soap in the bubble-filled depths of the marble tub. *Why* hadn't she caught on right there and then? She was either to be the

25

first senile twenty-five-year-old or the heat had softened her brain. There was no other plausible explanation considering what had been said to her face and then gone straight over her head.

She couldn't remember a time when she didn't know Theodore Roosevelt. She knew the forceful, intelligent man with the exuberance, who enjoyed every word that was written about him no matter how exaggerated. The President's favorite expression when he was particularly pleased was "delighted." "De-lighted," he'd grin when something he had a personal interest in went according to plan. Yet, when they'd shaken hands a few hours ago, he'd said "bully." A word which, despite popular legend, he really didn't use that often—at least not in front of a woman.

He'd sent his intelligence officer to New York to bring her to Washington, spent very nearly the entire trip to St. Louis persuading her that she could do a great service to her country, and then, when she'd agreed to give it a try, he had been enthusiastic all right, but it was more from their good-natured parrying, *not* from her agreement to go to Mexico, she realized belatedly.

Thea leaned back in the tub, the perfumed water swirling over her shoulders as her heart sank with the certainty that the President hadn't said "bully" because he was happy but because he was relieved. Oh, dear God, she thought, what did I get myself into this time?

Chapter Two

September 6-17, 1904

There were times during the next week and a half when Thea wondered if the conversation on the train had actually taken place. Her natural apprehension that she had not been told the total truth wasn't helped by not being able to discuss it. Their conversation centered on the plans they made for doing the rounds at the Louisiana Purchase Exposition. No further mention was made of San Antonio or Mexico. The one time Thea *did* broach the subject—at breakfast two days after their arrival—the colonel only smiled and said that there were still a few snags at the other end and, until they were settled, she was to relax, enjoy herself and not worry.

"There's nothing to be concerned about," he told her as they sat at the table room service had set up in the suite's sitting room. "There'll be plenty of warning. We don't intend to bundle you off in the middle of the night." He poured himself another cup of coffee and handed Thea the city's Democratic paper, the *Republic*, while he took the Republican *Globe-Democrat*. "Now, as soon as Jane finishs dressing and joins us we can do the automobile exhibit this morning, then you and my wife can go shopping at Famous-Barr while I fit in a round of golf at the country club. We'll have dinner at Faust's and take in the vaudeville show at the Grand Opera. How does

27

that sound?"

Since she couldn't very well throw herself down on the carpet, kick her heels, and demand to be sent off to San Antonio on the next train, Thea said that it sounded very nice indeed.

In spite of the almost unbearable heat, Thea was enjoying herself. The Mileses treated her as one of their three daughters, and she loved them in return. Her own mother had been dead for nearly ten years, and she often thought her famous explorer-naturalist father might as well be dead for all she saw of him.

If there was one thing they weren't looking for, Thea mused wryly as she sat in the shade on a bench near the Grand Basin, it was a nice young man to introduce her to. But no plan—even when the President of the United States made it—ever runs without a hitch, and this one had taken on its own direction the very first night.

"Colonel Miles. It *is* Colonel Miles, isn't it? It's good to see you again, sir."

It was a few minutes before eight. Thea and the Mileses were enjoying cocktails in the Jefferson's Palm Court when the well-pitched, respectful voice broke into their conversation and Thea looked up to see what she thought *had* to be one of the best-looking men in the hotel—if not the entire city—standing beside the colonel's chair with his hand outstretched.

"As I live and breathe. Paul Merrill. What are you doing in St. Louis?" Miles questioned as he rose from his chair to grasp the younger man's hand. "The last I heard, you were giving some visiting French army officers the grand tour of our installations."

"All the way from Fort Myer to the Presidio and back again," he agreed, smiling. "And I no sooner delivered them back safe and sound to the arms of the French Embassy and the War Department when I was handed my

28

walking papers. My commanding officer was generous enough to suggest that I take the leave I had coming to me before I took on my new assignment," he finished as a waiter hurried over with a chair and a drink.

"That doesn't sound like any C.O. I had when I was at your level. I hope that means the army is taking a turn for the better," Miles joked as he resumed his seat and smiled at his wife. "Jane, darling, you remember Captain Paul Merrill. We met him last year when he was serving as our assistant military attaché in Madrid."

Jane put down her glass and extended an elegant, long fingered hand adorned with a flawless star sapphire and diamond ring. "Of course I remember the captain," she said warmly as Merrill bent over her hand before accepting the colonel's motion to sit down. "Have you been in town long?"

"Four days. I thought I saw you in the lobby yesterday, Mrs. Miles, but I didn't want to presume—"

During the perfectly polite, correct exchange, Thea relaxed against the chintz-covered cushions of her wicker chair, observing Merrill through half-closed lids as she savored the sweet-tart taste of her icy cold daiquiri and waited with amused patience for her hosts to remember her presence. It wasn't a long wait, and as soon as Jane finished assuring the young officer that he should have spoken to her the other day, she turned and bestowed a smile on Thea that sent her heart sinking. She recognized that smile. It held the twinkle of a woman who had just decided to play matchmaker.

"Captain, I'd like to present our guest, Miss Theodosia Harper, the New York interior decorator. Thea, dear, this is Captain Paul Merrill who is single-handedly—if all reports are correct—blazing a new trail in the field of military diplomacy."

He shook his head and smiled ruefully at the introduction. "All very boring. I push papers around my desk all day, make polite chitchat at boring receptions at night, and every so often attend a military maneuver. I think, Miss Harper, I'd rather learn about what an interior decorator does."

His voice was pleasant but Thea felt a warning signal ripple through her body. This man had heard of her, and whoever had done the talking wasn't spreading compliments. She managed a bright smile but was inwardly sighing. She was no stronger than any other woman when it came to looking at a man with carefully cut brown-blonde hair, sea-foam blue eyes, high slanting cheekbones, a straight nose and generous mouth supported by a lean, six foot frame in flawless civilian dinner clothes which, like the colonel's, displayed a military carriage that was easy and alert at the same time.

"The business of an interior decorator is to know her clients, Captain," she said at last. "Believe me, when I'm finished, they and their family like their new home."

"But what is it you *do* for them?" he persisted, and Thea gave him a smile of pure wicked delight.

"Anything I want, Captain. Anything at all."

It would be just her luck, Thea thought as dinner progressed, that her remark, aimed at putting off the handsome young officer, had boomeranged. Instead of turning stiffly polite and excusing himself from their company, he'd flashed a grin that transformed his face with boyish joy and said that it sounded like a perfect job, and if his taste wasn't military blue and long gray line with khaki accents, he'd give it a try himself.

After that, there was nothing else for Hugh Miles to do than invite Paul Merrill to join them for dinner, and then, as they studied their menus, to extend that invitation to include joining them when they began their tour of the Exposition.

"You can be our tour guide, Paul. Jane's collected all those leaflets they print, but she wanted to wait until

Thea and I got here before doing the exhibits," he said when they finished conferring with the wine steward, selecting a bottle of Mumm's '98.

"I'll be more than happy to, sir. The fair grounds are immense, and once you start wandering around you can go in circles if you're not careful."

"Then we'll put ourselves in your hands," Jane announced firmly, looking up from her menu to give Thea a significant look. "I hope you won't have to push off for your new assignment too quickly."

"I have at least another week."

"Splendid, Paul. Splendid. By the way, where is it they're sending you?"

"Mexico, sir. It appears that I'm to be the new assistant military attaché at our Embassy."

He spoke modestly and Thea, who'd been listening to the conversation with only half an ear as she perused the large menu, deciding on clear consomme, an entree of squab stuffed with wild rice, salad with French dressing, and one of those wicked looking Napoleons from the pastry cart to go with a lemon ice dessert, almost dropped her menu at his announcement.

It can't be, she thought, forcing herself to show no undue surprise. The plan is for San Antonio, but when was the last time *anything* went right? Oh, don't tell me I'm going to have an army officer for a partner.

Almost as if he had read her mind, Miles closed his menu and looked at Merrill with the best expression of surprise that Thea had ever seen off the stage. "Why, isn't this a coincidence," he said mildly. "That's where Thea here is headed. What's your route?"

"The scenic one. St. Louis to New Orleans, then one of the Wolvin Line steamers to Vera Cruz, then by train to Mexico City. Dare I hope that's your itinerary, Miss Harper?"

He's not the one, she thought with an unexplained

31

rush of relief. "Call me Thea, please. No, I'm afraid it's not."

"Of course, you may not make the trip at all unless your passport is issued," Jane interjected, and Paul gave Thea a surprised look.

"They're not required."

"No, but it's a good idea to have one, particularly since I'm going there on business. It'll give me more credibility as an antique dealer rather than just a tourist who decided to do a casual bit of plundering. I wrote to the State Department before I went to Europe in June and I expected to have it ready for me when I got home," she elaborated as the waiter arrived, creating a perfect pause. "Unfortunately," she continued a few minutes later when their orders had been taken, "there was a slip-up somewhere along the line and nothing was ready. Instead of having a very long and useless correspondence with State, I contacted the President and he very kindly said he'd see to it, and invited me to make the first part of my journey with him and Colonel Miles in his railway car."

It was all a lie—a total outright lie—and Thea listened to herself telling it as though it were gospel. Upstairs in her bedroom, locked away in a suitcase, resting in her business portfolio that Tiffany's leather department had designed for her, safely tucked away with her stationery, order book, checkbook, address book and business cards, was her passport. After briefing her on the customs and people she would be likely to encounter, Mr. Simpson had taken the official document from his briefcase and filled in all the necessary data. Later, she and Colonel Miles had decided that her cover story to Jane and anyone else they chanced to meet in St. Louis would be that she was on her way to Mexico City for a buying trip and there was a delay in issuing her passport.

Jane had accepted the story without question and, looking across the table at Paul's astonished face, Thea

32

remembered what Ethel Barrymore had told her when she'd asked the actress how she managed to hold theatre-goers in the palm of her hand with her performance. "It's all in your voice and your timing," she said. "Get that right and the worst skeptic in the audience will be at your feet!"

"But neither of your names appeared in the stories about the President's arrival this afternoon. They said he made the trip alone," he protested.

"In this one instance, I think what the public doesn't know isn't going to hurt them." Now that she was over her first qualms about lying, Thea was beginning to enjoy weaving fact and fiction in her tale. "I've known the President all my life and Colonel and Mrs. Miles for years. When T.R. invited us to make the trip with him, he suggested that St. Louis would be an ideal place to wait for my passport to catch up with me."

Their first course arrived, and for the rest of the meal the conversation drifted back to a discussion of the numerous exhibits awaiting them at the Fair and the sights of the city. "What do you think you're going to enjoy most about St. Louis?" Paul asked when he finished asking her about her life and preferences.

"Being able to paint my face again," she replied, resisting the temptation to see if any of the people at the tables closest to them had overheard. As it was, Jane's aristocratic nose was slightly pinched with pain and the colonel seemed to find great interest in his fruit ice, although Thea could have sworn he was trying to hide a smile. "It was so hot on the train all I could keep on my face was a light dusting of face powder. I never feel fully dressed without my eye black," Thea finished, gracefully lowering her gaze to the long-stemmed silver dessert in front of her. She could *feel* Paul Merrill's as they appraised her, taking in her perfectly coiffed hair, the discreetly made up face, the expensive diamond and rose quartz pendant and matching bracelets that set off her Paquin dinner gown of white crepe de chine and lace with a skirt of narrow tucks and a rose satin girdle.

Male admiration was nothing new to Thea. She'd begun to have beaus at sixteen, had collected eleven proposals of marriage and, as far as that old saw about a girl being permanently on the shelf as far as eligible men were concerned if she hadn't bagged a husband by her twenty-first birthday, Thea smiled triumphantly at that thought and lifted her gaze to meet Paul's.

He gave her his most engaging grin—the one that never failed to win over even the most standoffish of females. "Do you mean to tell me that face powder is the most important concern of a woman who has her own firm; before that worked for collectors like Robert Lehman and Benjamin Altman; started out helping curators at the Metropolitan Museum of Art; and graduated second in Barnard's class of '99—when she was twenty? And while we're at it, why *second?* What was the difference between you and the girl who graduated first?"

Thea let the last delicious bite of Napoleon melt in her mouth before she returned Paul's smile with an equally devastating one of her own. "I prefer men," she said, and for a second all movement and conversation—not only at their table but at the one closest to them—stopped as her soft, clear voice carried.

Jane turned a good two shades paler than her cream chiffon and lace Worth gown, and even the colonel's savoir-faire seemed a bit shaky at her statement. Respectable women didn't mention such distasteful deviations or, supposedly, know anything about them. While Thea waited for Paul's reaction, she noticed that the two couples at the next table—the men in old-fashioned, well-preserved dinner clothes and the women in gowns that would have been perfect for dinner at

34

Windsor Castle provided it were still Victoria's reign—were trying to be nonchalant now. But at first they couldn't have been more stunned if she'd stood up on the table and gone into a vaudeville routine.

"I asked for that one," Paul said as he began to laugh and the Mileses finally started to smile. "I really had it coming. Oh, Thea, you *are* a marvel." He was still shaking with laughter when the dance band that had been playing a sedate waltz finished their number, changed music, and started a rag-time two-step. "It's the 'Maple Leaf Rag'," he said as his composure returned. "Shall we dance?"

This wasn't at all the reaction Thea had anticipated his having, but all was fair in love and war and she knew how to be a good sport and carry on with the best of them. "Oh, Paul. I thought you'd never ask."

It would have been so much better if she and Paul Merrill had detested each other on sight, and better still if Colonel Miles had seen fit to tell his wife about her assignment, Thea realized as she continued to relax and watch the cool, sparkling waterways that ran into the Grand Basin. But there was no way she could change either situation and the only route open to her was to play it out to the end and hope Jane realized her rather pointed attempts at trying to make a match were falling on deaf ears—as far as Thea Harper was concerned.

Admittedly, it was difficult to find fault with a man who was good-looking, intelligent, and a fantastic dancer. He was respectful to the colonel and attentive to the ladies. He'd graduated in the upper ten percent of his class at West Point eleven years earlier, had seen action in the Philippines under Major General Wesley Merritt where he was decorated for conspicuous gallantry, and his flawless command of Spanish had been instrumental in his being made one of Arthur MacArthur's aides when

35

the general was made Military Governor and had led to his subsequent appointment to Madrid. All in all—if one depended only on outward appearances—he was every unmarried woman's dream of what an eligible bachelor should be. But, by the end of that first evening, Thea couldn't get rid of the feeling that if she ever got to know him better she wouldn't like what she found underneath his affable surface.

Nonetheless, she had to admit that they made a striking foursome. So far, there wasn't a maitre d' in St. Louis who failed to give them the best and most prominent table in his establishment and, Thea added silently as she scanned the crowds of people along the walkways to see if Paul were among them, he was a superb tour guide.

From the first morning, the Louisiana Purchase Exposition had, in equal parts, left them awed, annoyed, and amused. Built behind Forrest Park, the Fair's all-white buildings had earned it the soubriquet of the "ivory city," while the space it covered—twelve hundred and seventy-two acres—was thirty-five miles around and getting from one exhibition building to another required the stamina of a Swiss mountain climber. It was ambitious and grandiose and overdone. But, in spite of any discomforts, they loved it.

France had sent a replica of the Grand Trianon, Great Britain showed off with a copy of Sir Christopher Wren's Kensington Palace Orangery; and Belgium charmed everyone with Antwerp's Old Town Hall. China countered with the summer palace of Prince Lui; Japan had a traditional garden along with their displays of china, trinkets, and textiles showing off their technological advances; while Siam gave the peace of the temple of the Imperial Palace.

They saw Louisiana's statue carved in sugar; the one hundred-foot in diameter floral clock at the Palace of

Horticulture; and the Magic Whirlpool that ran along The Pike and the more serious Education & Social Economy and Electricity & Machinery Pavillions that flanked the Grand Basin. The Fine Arts Pavillion took a whole day and, naturally, they paid visits to the West Point and Annapolis exhibits as well as *The Detective* magazine's police display. Paul surprised them by being able to conduct a brief conversation in Tagaloq with one of the natives at The Philippine Village. The Olympic Games—newly revived eight years earlier—were being held at the Fair, and they had tickets to the best of the swimming and track events.

It was like living in a fantasy world, but reality had to reappear. This morning they had strolled through Floral Park to the Agricultural Pavillion, and visited Ceylon before repairing to one of the restaurants that flanked either end of the Terrace of States. As usual, they had the best table—one by the broad expanse of windows that looked out onto the fairgrounds—and they were in the middle of lunch when Thea glanced out, blinking at the bright sunlight, and found herself staring at the German Pavillion.

The building was big, white and ominous looking and she noticed that there were no other exhibition halls close to it. Her appetite seemed to ebb and she looked at the half-eaten plate of chicken salad with distaste. You're letting your imagination run away with you. If anything, Thea chided herself, you should have gotten nervous in the Mexican Pavillion. That hunk of white wood is no different from any of the other exhibits, and if you can believe what you hear, it's also one of the most boring. It was the best advice she could give herself, but it didn't stop the sickening lurch of her heart. And, to her own amazement, she heard her voice suggesting they make Germany their next stop.

As expected, it was as cold and correct as anything

connected with official Germany. The guards—no doubt aided by the massive oil painting of the Kaiser that dominated the entrance hall—kept the visitors in line and the mood of joyous conviviality that marked the other pavillions was missing here. It was all correct and in good order. Thea felt as though she were choking. Her original fear had somewhat faded but she couldn't shake the feeling that this . . . this unidentifiable *thing* was waiting for her in Mexico.

"Would you like to get out of here and get some ice cream?" Paul whispered, shattering the prescience that enveloped her. "You didn't finish your lunch and you've been pale as a ghost since we came in. Are you hungry?"

"Not really. But I never refuse an offer of ice cream," Thea replied brightly, tucking her arm through his as they came to the end of the chemical display. "Besides, it's a perfect excuse to get out of this burg. It's as bad as being in Berlin. The only thing missing is a couple of Death Head's Hussars in full dress uniform pushing you out of the way because you're impeding their magnificent progress down the Unter den Linden!"

"They sound like they can use a course in military deportment," he grinned. "Come on."

"The Mileses—"

"Are going to finish up here and go on to Nicaragua. We'll meet them back at the hotel. I know of a treat that'll cheer you right up. And besides, I've been waiting to have some time alone with you since we met."

So far, she was still waiting to see what it was that was supposed to make her happy again. Paul had settled her on the bench, disappeared up the path, and she hadn't seen him since. I wonder if he's making the ice cream or buying it, Thea thought. So he's been waiting ten days to get me alone. I'd give my best pearls to know what Jane's been telling him. Oh, well, if Mrs. Miles is trying to angle a social *coup* by getting me engaged to Paul Merrill, she has a big disappointment coming. Even if I didn't have some odd duck of a "companion" waiting for me in Texas, I don't think I'd want the good captain. It might be interesting to know what Colonel Miles thinks every time his wife encourages the captain and he has to sit there with a smile plastered on his face pretending we'd make an ideal couple! Her thoughts finished as she finally sighted Paul among the crowd and waved to him.

The idea that the cool, contained Hugh Miles who, in military matters, kept the upper hand at all times, had to watch his wife matchmake a rising young officer with his latest operative made her smile. Merrill approached her, carrying what appeared to be two cornucopias, like the ones Paris ice cream vendors sold in that city's parks except, as he came closer, she could see that the large scoops of ice cream weren't resting on cones of white paper but in some dark substance that looked edible.

"It's good to see you smiling again," he announced as he sat down and handed her an ice cream in its new receptacle. "A World's Fair Cornucopia for the lady in the big hat. A guaranteed cheerer-upper. Sorry I took so long, but these things have really caught on, and the line was a mile long."

"I should think so," she said as they licked back the fast melting ice cream. "Is this cylinder some sort of waffle? It looks delicious."

"It is. I had one last week. This invention is a real American success story. A fellow named Ernest Hamwi immigrated to this country from Syria and was given a World's Fair concession to sell zalabia. It's baked on something that looks like a flat waffle iron and when it's done they sprinkle powdered sugar on it. Unfortunately, as good as it tastes, it wasn't selling very well. However, the fellow at the next booth had an ice cream concession and was doing a land office business until one hot day when he ran out of dishes. Hamwi figured that if he took his pastries hot off the iron and rolled them into a cornucopia and let them cool, they got nice and crisp—"

"In other words, a perfect holder for a scoop of ice cream," Thea finished as Paul hastily went after the dark chocolate rivulets that were threatening to run down the side of the cone and drip on his immaculate Palm Beach suit. "I think this is a wonderful invention and I bet by next summer all the ice cream vendors in Central Park will be selling their wares like this. A whole new way of eating has been invented!"

"Do you realize that in ten days we've done nearly the whole fair?" Paul remarked a few minutes later as they nibbled at the crisp waffle and the remains of the ice cream. "All we have left are exhibitions like the Irish Village and Old St. Louis."

"I know. It seems incredible that we've done so much. A few months ago, I thought I'd never get to see it. My three best friends and their husbands have all been here and I was beginning to feel a bit left out. Because I hadn't been to the fair, not because I haven't a husband," she added rather needlessly and, to her own anger, felt her face color.

"Three best friends," he teased, taking advantage of her discomfort. "And all married. How does it go now? Are you supposed to envy them their secure state or do they envy your freedom?"

"Neither," she replied more coolly than she'd intended. But the tone of his voice was the same as he'd used when he inquired about her business and she felt a rush of annoyance. "We never think about things like that."

"Old school chums?" he inquired. Paul Merrill liked women and having fun with them. He found Thea's straightforward wit and clear intelligence refreshing after the usual run-of-the-mill young women he met who seemed to lack any clear will or opinions of their own.

40

Jane Miles had given him a brief run-through of Thea's life the first night: fine old New York family, impeccable background, an independent income. All the things, she'd hinted archly as they danced, that any personable and successful young army officer should take into account when it came time to consider getting married and, the hint continued, Thea Harper was more than worthy of this consideration. Unfortunately, he'd started off on the wrong foot by his patronizing question about her business and, without really meaning to, he was compounding it by asking about her friends.

"Strangely enough, none of us went to college together," she explained. "Oh, Alix and I were at Barnard together for a year—she was a senior the year I was a freshman. Nela and Regina graduated in '99 like me, but they're from Vassar and a year older."

"The nicknames you girls have. What are Alix and Nela short for?"

"Alicia and Angela." Thea could feel her blood starting to boil, but she managed to control her anger at his patronizing joviality. "Nela is Admiral Dalton's daughter and, before she married Morgan Browne and went to live in San Antonio, she worked at Thurn's in New York and San Francisco's I. Magnin as a sort of consultant, helping special customers select their wardrobe. Alix is a doctor—"

"Bet her husband loves those emergency calls at three in the morning," Paul interrupted, chuckling. He honestly wasn't used to women who took their friendships seriously unless they were too plain to attract men. It amused him to tease Thea like this, and never for one minute did he think that, for a man with all the right qualifications, he was making a pretty awful impression. "Or is he a doctor too?"

"No, very far from it. He's Henry Thorpe—Lord Thorpe actually, although he doesn't use his title in New

41

York—the very respected art historian and collector. Have you heard of him, Paul? You must have. He lectures at Columbia and was a consultant for the Palace of Fine Arts Pavillion here," Thea went on, her voice deliberately casual, grateful that her large-brimmed hat was effectively hiding her face. If this double-barred so-and-so thought that buying her an ice cream gave him the right to verbally pat her on the head and chuck her under the chin, did he have another think coming!

"Alix Turner Thorpe isn't practicing now, except for some dispensary work at the Henry Street Settlement. I don't think she'll do anything serious in the medical field for quite a few years," Thea continued. "Their baby is just a year old and she's expecting another next April. She says that a husband, a family, and a twenty-room apartment in the Dakota are quite enough for the time being.

"We all went out to San Francisco this past April to welcome the Daltons home from China and to see Nela and Morgan married. I had to come straight back to New York afterwards, but Alix and Henry wanted to see if the World's Fair people took his consultations and advice seriously, and Regina and her husband, Ian MacIverson, went along with them.

"Did you ever read her articles when Regina Bolt was a reporter for the *World?* Her Coronation articles were so successful two years ago that Ralph Pulitzer gave her *carte blanche* to go wherever she wanted the next summer and write what she pleased.

"Regina chose India, did a series of stories we're all still talking about, and met Ian. He'd gone to India fresh out of school and made a fortune there in less than twenty years. When he fell in love with Reggie he decided the time had come to pack it in and try his hand in America. They live in Santa Barbara in one of those beautiful mission-style houses. Regina's writing a who-

42

dunit while Ian buys orange groves and shipping lines," she finished triumphantly, caution advising her to leave out the reason that handsome, dynamic Ian MacIverson had quit England for India on his eighteenth birthday was that he was the illegitimate son of an English earl and a schoolteacher. He wasn't embittered, but he'd known that, even though by his thirty-sixth birthday he would be a millionaire in any nation's currency, it wouldn't give him an entrée into London society. Even his acceptance in India was limited, and when she met him for the first time, Thea knew instantly that Regina had captured him at the right moment—while his business success still delighted him and his love and generosity hadn't been spurned by girls who felt the stigma of his birth negated all else.

But Paul Merrill wasn't the sort of man she could tell this to. He might give lip service to the concept that every person had a right to make the most of their lives, but Thea felt he was really a subscriber to the status quo and probably thought anyone of base birth had no business ending up anywhere except the gutter.

They sat silently on the bench for several minutes, watching the cooling water swirling in the Cascades. Thea's anger had burned itself out but she was wondering if the difficulties she was experiencing with Paul Merrill were only a foretaste of what was waiting for her in San Antonio.

Whether it is or not, Miles and his bunch had better get a move on, Thea told herself as she stole a glance at Paul's impassive, disciplined profile. That excuse about my passport is wearing thin. Paul's no dummy. He knows those paper-pushers at State take their time, but not when the President's supposed to be keeping an eye on them! She sighed and relaxed against the bench's slatted back. Why do you complain so, Thea? she asked herself. You've had fun here in St. Louis, and whatever happens in Mexico, you'll do your best. As for Paul, well, face it, he's not the man for you and never will be. If he were, you'd know it by now. I just can't help wondering if there'll ever be—

"Thea, will I see you in Mexico City?"

Paul's quiet voice broke into her reverie, and Thea blinked at him, putting back together the facade she and Colonel Miles had erected around her assignment. "I'm not sure," she told him honestly, deciding a small evasion was the best tactic. "The way it looks now, I may not get there."

"You can come without one. The Embassy will look out and vouch for you."

She shook her head. "My father taught me never to travel to a country that's off the beaten track without proper identification from my government. Going to Mexico isn't like travelling to England or France. All the tour companies may be touting it as the perfect winter resort country, but it's not an accepted tourist spot yet."

"State could wire the information down to Mexico City and they'll issue your passport there," he countered. "As a matter of fact, I'm willing to bet if you took the steamer with me, the United States Consul would be waiting on the dock at Vera Cruz to hand it to you as you came down the gangplank," he said. His hand reached out to cover hers.

"I'm not in the habit of travelling on a liner I know nothing about with a man I've just met," she said, wanting to end *this* topic of conversation as quickly as possible. "My plans are made, Paul, and I'm sticking to them."

He withdrew his hand quickly. "For goodness sake, I wasn't suggesting . . . you mustn't think I was inferring . . . you said you loved ocean voyages and never got seasick, so I thought . . ."

The look on his face was so contrite—an expression

that Thea thought would have been completely alien to him—that her annoyance faded and she patted his hand. "I'm sorry, Paul. Really I am. Of course you didn't mean anything improper and I didn't mean to sound so snippy. It's the heat, all the excitement, wanting to push off for San Antonio and wondering what it's going to be like in Mexico City—"

"Must you go if you're so apprehensive about it? It's hard to think of Mexico as an untapped treasure trove of fine antiques."

"But it is. When the French quit Mexico they left an awfully lot behind. A rare book dealer friend of mine was down there last winter and he told me that a lot of the better pieces are finally starting to resurface."

"After thirty-odd years?"

"Isn't it incredible? I'm not expecting to find Empress Carlotta's breakfast set, but the market for anything in fine porcelain has never been better."

Thea hated lying. Normally she was a merciless teller of the truth and the elation at being able to weave a tale that two otherwise intelligent people had bought without question, had faded days ago. At least this much is true, she thought. Espionage, and the reasons for it, comes and goes, but the antique market will survive eternally!

However long she remained here in St. Louis or in San Antonio before crossing the border (if she did so at all) was anyone's guess, but Paul's leave was reaching its end. Before he departed, Thea wanted the answer to the question that had been in the back of her mind from the night they met.

"Paul, who told you about me?"

"Why, Jane, of course," he responded, a shade too quickly. "She's been singing your praises to the sky and thinks you're wise and talented and have all the qualifications."

To be an Army wife, I bet, Thea thought, but aloud she

said, "I mean *before* Jane. I know we've never met until ten days ago, and yet, when we were introduced I could have sworn you had heard some pretty—shall we say *interesting*—tales about me."

He flushed. "Was I that transparent?"

"Let's just say I'm sensitive to a lot of things. But you still haven't told me who our 'mutual friend' is. I've been going over my list of clients, but they all seem to like me, and it certainly wasn't one of my friends. Who was it?"

"I wish I'd never listened to her in the first place. Nancy Gilchrist is my cousin's wife."

"Damn and blast!" Thea said crossly. "I should have thought about her immediately, but I just pushed the whole incident with her out of my mind. An alienist would call it selective memory, I guess. But I think every person who has their own business should have a Nancy Gilchrist try to hire them when they start out. If nothing else, it's a good test of your integrity."

Nancy Gilchrist, to Thea's way of thinking, had walked into her studio (*sans* appointment which Thea, on her business card, insisted on) while the paint was still damp on the walls. Not really, of course. She'd walked through the reception room and into the office on a crisp fall morning at the end of October, 1902, insisting that Thea would be just the person to decorate the townhouse she and her husband had just purchased. "It'll make your business," Nancy Gilchrist declared, and insisted that Thea come with her right that minute to East Sixty-third Street to look at it. "I just know we're going to be the best of friends," she exclaimed as Thea put on her hat, locked the door, and followed Mrs. Gilchrist to where her gleaming new motor car was waiting to take them uptown.

Nancy Hadden Gilchrist was blonde, bubbly, twenty-two, newly married (they were just back from their honeymoon and were living in a suite at the Waldorf, she confided) to a handsome, prominent young man with a seat on the Exchange, and thoroughly spoiled. Her grandparents had been New Yorkers, she told Thea as they travelled north on Fifth Avenue, but like many fine old families they had suffered serious monetary reverses in the financial panic that followed the Civil War and had been forced to seek retrenchment in Ohio. The Middle West had been good to them; her mother had married into one of Cincinnati's leading families, and now, two generations later, the Haddens could once again be counted in New York society.

A determined gleam had come into her bright blue eyes and, looking back on it, Thea acknowledged that that should have been the moment she asked the chauffeur to pull up to the curb, thank young Mrs. Gilchrist for her offer, and get out. But she hadn't. The possibility of her first real client had been too strong to resist, and she had wanted to see the house. The handsome townhouse with its delicate Palladian facade was one of the few houses in the area she had never been inside and she was curious. It turned out to be a perfect jewel box of a small New York mansion with generously proportioned rooms spread over four stories; marble floors; a ballroom whose ceiling was a delightful shade of robin's egg blue; and lots and lots of sunlight coming through the large windows. It was completely up-to-date, ready to be furnished and, walking through the rooms, Thea felt like an artist with a blank canvas—she could create a masterpiece.

Located between Fifth and Madison Avenues, Thea recognized that it was located in a perfect section of Manhattan. No matter how many residential sections turned commercial, this part of town, with its close proximity to Central Park, would probably remain untouched for many years to come. For over a century, the Harpers had owned sizable portions of New York City real estate and, although Thea's father's life was centered around the natural sciences, he retained an active interest in the changes his city was making and passed this on to his daughter.

On the surface, it was almost too good to believe. Thea didn't have a real, full-scale client yet. Just the job she considered her "payment" for her summer "excursion," and friends of her and her mother's who purchased antiques from her private stock. It was a fairy tale come true. But, by the time they had finished lunch, it was collapsing. And, at the end of the week, Nancy Gilchrist and her new house held all the appeal of the wicked stepmother's house in *Hansel and Gretel.*

With great fanfare, Nancy plied her with lunch at Sherry's, Delmonico's, the Fernery, and the Women's Lunch Club where they were both members. They had met on Monday, and by Friday all her ideas for furnishing the house had been politely listened to, then totally rejected. Mrs. Gilchrist wasn't interested in the fine work that the pre- and post-Revolutionary cabinetmakers of Boston, Providence, Philadelphia, and Baltimore produced. She didn't care to discuss the merits of Sheraton versus Hepplewhite or hear how the delicate Chinese Export furniture in the mode of Chippendale and Queen Anne would look in their new home. Delicate striped silk, colorful chintz, and handsome damasks were of no more use to her than Impressionist paintings or Lalique glass.

Nancy Gilchrist wanted Fine French Furniture, and not the elegant charm of Louis XV which Thea would have gladly used. It was the unmistakable opulence of Louis XIV, replete with heavy brocades and walls of Fragonards and Bouchers that she wanted and, learning this, Thea Harper politely refused the offer.

No one in her whole pampered life had ever refused Nancy anything, and she was flabbergasted. How could Thea refuse? Here was the opportunity a decorator with a new business and no clients would get down on bended knees for, but Thea remained firm. In the face of her unwavering decision, Nancy switched tactics, and Thea became the recipient of notes, flowers, invitations to dinner, offers to introduce her to socially eligible young men; she dangled the prize of an all-expense paid trip to France to select furniture, but to no avail. Thea knew that if she took Nancy Gilchrist on as a client she would be marked as the kind of decorator she didn't want to be. And, by the end of their first luncheon, she knew she could never work with a selfish, spoiled, self-centered social climber like Nancy Gilchrist who was in such a hurry to find a decorator to carry out her ideas that she hadn't even bothered to find out Thea Harper's background and private life.

She had no intention of seeing her on a professional basis again, but certain social contact was going to be inevitable. And, with a certain sense of wicked delight, Thea found herself looking forward to it. It happened three weeks later, much sooner than she expected, in the glittering enclave of the Metropolitan Opera's Golden Horseshoe. Visiting during intermission was an accepted and popular form of socializing, and two of the many who stopped at Box 11, belonging to the popular Mr. and Mrs. Newton Phipps, were Robert and Nancy Gilchrist. The Phippses were a prestigious couple and, as they paused at the entrance to the box, Nancy was looking forward to making the acquaintance of their guests: the Earl and Countess of Tilmore, who were visiting from England; Henry and Alix Thorpe; Kathryn Neal, who figured among the city's wealthiest *grande dames;* and . . .

"I'll never forget the expression on her face when Esme introduced us," Thea told Paul who'd listened without comment to her story. "Nancy couldn't have looked more stunned if she'd seen me with one of Mrs. Jack's pet lion cubs on my lap," she said, referring to Boston's favorite eccentric socialite art collector. "We still see each other at parties where we nod politely from opposite ends of the room. Tell me the truth, did she really say vile things about me?"

"Only that you were obstinate, cold, and a snob. You injured her pride when you said no," he chuckled. "Nan doesn't like that."

"Too bad," Thea shrugged with a smile. "If you want my opinion, what really set her off was when she realized that I knew all the men she had offered to introduce me to. By the way, how did it turn out?"

"Not too bad. That is, if you like living in a version of the Petit Trianon. Nan said the decorators at Alavoine were very happy to do what you had refused. She said you had your gall, but after ten days of getting to know you, I'd say you showed an inordinate amount of good taste and wise judgment," he said consulting his watch. "Do you realize it's after four? I think we'd better see about getting back to the hotel."

"I hope you don't think I was too hard on Nancy," she said as they walked back to the main gate. "We just couldn't see eye to eye on anything. It doesn't mean the way she furnished her house was wrong."

"No," he replied, eyes twinkling. "It doesn't. But your mode of decor would have cost much less and looked a whole lot better. Nan put a whole lot of Rob's money into that house, and each time I visit them I can't help being thankful it wasn't my bank account she put a hole in!"

Paul left three days later. Thea and the Mileses gave him a farewell champagne dinner, toasting him both bon voyage and success at the Embassy before going with him to Union Station to see him off on the night train to New Orleans.

"Did you like him, Thea?" Jane asked her when they returned to their suite. The night manager had been waiting in the lobby for Colonel Miles when they returned and both women had gone upstairs ahead of him. "I thought he was quite taken with you from the first, and who knows what will happen when you run into him in Mexico City."

"Not too much, I hope."

"Oh, Thea, honestly!" Jane sounded annoyed. "I think you could work up a little more enthusiasm. It's not as if Paul were being shifted from one Western fort to the other. He's the cream of the crop and he's assigned accordingly. It was quite fortuitous, his meeting us the way he did, and I certainly tried to give the both of you *every* chance to be alone together. For a girl who has about as much use for a chaperone as an Eskimo does for an ice box, you turned very proper all of the sudden." She looked intently at her. "Did Hugh intimidate you about seeing Paul? Heaven knows, we both care for you as much as if you were our daughter, but whenever I mentioned what a nice couple the two of you made, he went through the roof!"

From the moment Paul had presented himself to their group, Jane Miles had decided to do a little planning and plotting. Thea, she felt, was far too casual about her life, running here and there as it suited her, decorating other people's houses when she should be doing one of her own, and not caring one whit about how much gossip swirled around her. Those fast New York girls—Angela Dalton and the rest—Heaven only knew how they managed to land on their feet, let alone find husbands. Paul, in his own way, was just as unthinking. A military man who wanted to advance with any style or alacrity needed a wife, and the right one. She'd counseled more than one young officer against becoming involved with a girl who could not pull her weight emotionally, intellectually, or financially. From that angle, Theodosia Harper was perfectly suited to be Paul Merrill's wife, but the girl's stubbornness had blocked her at every turn.

51

What was the matter with her anyway?

"Mrs. Miles, you know the colonel wouldn't meddle in my private life," Thea said soothingly, but couldn't resist adding, "Are you sure the reason you're so anxious that I find Paul attractive is that your girls didn't marry into the military?"

Jane looked injured. "Certainly not! I'm not one of *those* mothers. The only thing that matters in marriage is that a man and a woman be happy together."

"Which I don't think I could be with Paul Merrill."

"My dear girl, why not?"

"Oh, Mrs. Miles, I know you think he has all the right qualities, but there's something I just don't like. Paul Merrill thinks too highly of himself, and men like that set my teeth on edge!"

Jane was about to offer her illuminating words on the personalities of up-and-coming Army officers and how independent women had to learn to take them with a grain of salt, when a key turned in the lock and the colonel opened the door and entered the sitting room, holding out his hands to Thea.

"Well, my dear, I just had word from State. The telegram came while we were out. The problems about your passport have been straightened out. They'll send the information to the Federal Office in San Antonio and issue it to you there. Now that the last obstacle is out of the way, what do you say to seeing if we can get you space on tomorrow evening's Katy?"

Chapter Three

September 20, 1904

The surrey, driven by a sandy-haired youth who didn't look to be more than fifteen and was one of the "problem boys" the West Texas Military Academy took upon itself to educate along with the sons of officers, wound its way through the fashionable King William district of San Antonio.

Thea had spent the past two days travelling on the Katy, the crack luxury train of the Missouri, Kansas, & Texas railroad, alternately reading *The Sorceress of the Strand* and Ellen Glasgow's *The Deliverance* and watching the scenery as they hurtled along the route that followed the one which, until fairly recently, had been used by ranchers to drive their herds north to the markets of Dodge City and Abilene. The trip was no cooler than the one that had brought her to St. Louis, but Thea knew that whatever the discomfort, this was probably her last chance for any real privacy until the assignment was over. She'd better enjoy her solitude while it lasted.

If she'd learned anything during her St. Louis stay, it was that allowing her active, lively imagination think up circumstances that were far worse than any reality could be, was not going to help her situation one bit. Heaven only knew who her male "travelling companion" was, and she felt a sick sinking in the pit of her stomach every time she remembered the afternoon at the German Pavillion. But once she put all that and Colonel Miles' deliberate vagaries aside, Thea acted as any good businesswoman should and dealt with the problem that headed the list.

"How will this Major Donovan and I recognize each other?" she asked as she and Hugh Miles came out of the St. Louis' Wainwright Building. George Martin, the Katy's genial and charming General Passenger Agent, had reserved a Pullman drawing room for her and gave her the M, K, & T pamphlet "The Story of San Antonio" and wished her a pleasant journey.

For Thea, the whole morning seemed slightly unreal. Less than ten hours ago Miles had, in their prearranged code, told her that all was ready and waiting for her in San Antonio. And now, before noon, she had her travel arrangements made and Jane was back at the Jefferson supervising the maids as they packed her trunks for this evening's departure.

"I told him about your luggage."

Thea made a face. "Thanks a lot. Now, the Katy station can get pretty crowded, I imagine, and people miss each other all the time. How will *I* know *him?*"

Miles shot her an amused look. "Do you know how some Army men can wear civilian clothes without looking like odd ducks?"

"Like you and Bruce Dalton and Paul Merrill. So?"

"So Donovan doesn't."

In fact, Thea thought as she observed Major John Donovan, who was seated beside her in the surrey's back seat, he looks mighty uncomfortable. He was a tall, powerfully built, barrel-chested man whose tanned, unblinking visage hid an age that ranged anywhere from forty to sixty.

Neither had the slightest difficulty in spotting the other. In uniform, John Donovan would have been almost anonymous, but in civilian clothes he stuck out like the proverbial sore thumb. Thea had him picked out before she got from the steps of the Pullman car to the station gate. The major, at his vantage point near the main gate, took a bit longer to recognize Colonel Miles' latest addition to the service. There were any number of attractive young women getting off the Katy, but none carried the distinctive black and white dressing case he'd been told to watch for and, when he did see it and the woman who carried it, he scowled inwardly.

Where did Miles and his crew dig this one up? Some Fancy Dan Long Island country club, he'd bet. Women were supposed to travel in dark blue serge or something equally sensible that wouldn't show the dirt and dust of travel. Instead, she looked like she was ready for an afternoon's shopping in the kind of store no *truly* respectable woman would ever dream of patronizing. Well, so far, that was none of his business. He politely introduced himself, took charge of the thick packet of luggage checks she handed him, and saw to it that the porters brought it out to the luggage brake waiting with the surrey.

Probably, Thea thought as they drove away from the station building and headed along Laredo Street, he doesn't like any situation that isn't thoroughly masculine, and making small talk with a female agent definitely doesn't rate!

During the two-day trip, Thea had forced herself to start considering her status as an agent or operative. This isn't one of your usual favors, and just because the assignment won't be dangerous, there's no reason for not taking it seriously, she told herself.

For his part, once he had adjusted to the sight of a woman coming off a tiring, dusty train journey wearing a beige and white figured foulard dress with an embroidered belt of red and green silk, spotless beige gloves, and a broad-brimmed black taffeta sailor hat with rosettes of red taffeta created by the fashionable New York milliner, Henri Bendel, Donovan gradually relaxed and grew voluble, if not downright courtly, to Thea as he pointed out landmarks and places of interest.

"Are you and Mrs. Browne old school friends?" he asked as they passed a house of pale limestone that looked as if it might be more at home on Fifth Avenue than in the city that had been founded by a Spanish military expedition in 1718.

"No, Angela and I were at different colleges, but we always moved in the same circles in New York." She glanced at the large, elaborate houses they were passing. "Which one belongs to Morgan and Angela?"

"Right here," he said as the surrey stopped in front of a house that stood out from the Victorian gingerbread, gimcrackery and bastard Italian architecture that dominated the wealthy neighborhood.

Thea looked delightedly at the simple, almost severe three-story house that stood gracefully on the corner of Johnson Street whose lines were so pure it suggested the old Federalist school of architecture. The exhaustion of the hot, tiring train ride fell from her as she looked at the pale brick house, the shrubs and flowering bushes that surrounded it, and the large, green, well-tended lawn.

The surrey stopped and the front door, painted Chinese lacquer red, opened and a slender young woman with hair that was the color of expensive champagne and wearing an airy white dress, ran lightly down the front steps. Without waiting for Donovan's aid, Thea jumped down from the back seat and ran to meet Angela Dalton Browne halfway.

"Oh, we've been waiting *weeks* for everything to arrange itself! How was the trip?"

56

"Hot but wonderful. I read all day, and didn't talk to anyone but the porter and the conductor. Nela, you look beautiful!"

"So do you."

They hugged each other again, stood in the middle of the brick path that ran from the front steps to the sidewalk and tried to fill each other in on the events of their lives since they'd last seen each other. Finally, with their arms around each other's waists, they walked over to the surrey where Donovan was surveying them from his perch, a slight smile playing over his blunt features.

"My husband will be at the store until six or so," Angela said pleasantly as the major took off his hat and they shook hands. "If you don't care to go back downtown, you're more than welcome to wait in the library with a cool drink."

"Thank you, Mrs. Browne. I appreciate the offer, but if it's all the same, it's still early and I have some papers to check over back at Headquarters. I'll meet your husband at the store and we'll come back here together. I'm sure you and Miss Harper have a lot to talk about."

"We certainly do, Major. Please tell my husband we'll have cocktails in the drawing room at seven and dinner is scheduled for half-past."

The boy who'd driven the surrey, and the one who'd followed with the brake, carried Thea's luggage into the house under the direction of a white-coated servant who was introduced to Thea as Juan.

"He's our houseman, gardener, handyman, and he's taking driving lessons to boot. His wife, Consuelo, is our cook, and their nieces, Lupe and Maria, are the maids. You're our first guest, and they're thrilled to death."

"How do I live up to a welcome like that? Of course, they may not think so if they count my luggage. You should have seen Donovan's face when I gave him my baggage checks!"

"I can imagine. He knows you have no idea how long you'll be away and that once you're in Mexico it'll be party after party and he *still* doesn't see why you can't manage on two suitcases. Come on," she said as they mounted the steps. "I want to show you the house. Then we'll get you settled in the guest room and have a cold drink and something to eat while we gossip. I'm famished!"

Thea looked critically at her friend's waistline as they paused at the front door. "I really thought that with a man like Morgan you might have been too busy to eat on your honeymoon, but you look as though you managed stops at Rumpelmayer's, Demel's and the rest. If you don't watch it, your elegant waistline will only be a fond memory!"

Nela stopped, her hand on the ornately carved doorknob, and gave Thea a sidelong glance. "I'm very much afraid it's going to be a memory no matter what I eat or don't eat. For the very best reason, of course," she added with a smile as Thea grasped her meaning.

"Nela. Oh, Nela, *really?* How far along are you?"

"Nearly three months. We're so thrilled—"

"Well, I should certainly hope so! How do you feel?"

"Absolutely wonderful—I haven't been sick once. I've been taking it very easy of course, going into the store later and coming home earlier, and today I was here, getting everything ready for your arrival." Nela looked down at her figure in wry amusement. "God, but March seems a long way off."

"At least you won't be waiting alone, so to speak. You and Alix can spend the winter exchanging letters about the gradual disappearance of your waistlines," Thea suggested wickedly.

"Ohh—not fair!" Nela groaned, laughing. "I'm going to look like the side of a barn before this is over. But it's not only Alix and me in this condition," she added

58

gently. "I had a letter from Regina this morning and she and Ian are—as they love to say in England—planning their nursery."

"Why, how wonderful! But why are you so serious? Is she going to have a hard time?"

"No, not at all. She's perfectly well. I was only worried that you would. . . . That is . . ."

"Are you afraid that I might feel left out?" Thea suggested, amused. "Considering my marital status, isn't it better I *don't* join the rest of you? To think this is what's become of our little wrecking crew."

"I think we've all done pretty well considering. Come along, my dear Thea. It's time for you to see our home. Rosemary—you remember Morgan's sister, don't you? —came over from Dallas for the summer and watched over the painters and the movers," she said as they crossed the threshold.

Although San Antonio had recently become a popular place for tuberculars to pass the winter, Nela explained as they went inside, Morgan told her that the city eventually felt the cold. However, summer generally lingered long after its heat had disappeared in the northern climes and the house was still set up to defeat the broiling Texas heat. The rare Oriental and Persian rugs and silk draperies had been put away in April and would not reappear until November. The Austrian crystal chandelier was temporarily replaced by an electric fan whose broad white blades turned slowly as it kept the air moving in the large, square entry hall that Nela and Morgan had redecorated.

The walls were covered in a Chinese silk wallpaper depicting pagodas, mountains and elegant ladies in sedan chairs that they had discovered in a store in San Francisco's Chinatown. Just inside the door a mahogany Irish side table with a marble top was decorated with a famille verte covered incense burner and a Baccarat vase holding an arrangement of yellow tea roses and statice. An excellent mirror in a narrow gilt frame hung above the table. A selection of Chinese Export vases in varying sizes and designs were arranged beneath it and a pair of Federal-style side chairs upholstered in yellow and white striped silk—that Nela mentioned were attributed to Stephen Bedlam, one of the great furniture makers of Salem around 1790—flanked it.

"Morgan lived in Boston for two or three years after he finished college," Nela said as they finished their tour of the library, drawing room, and kitchen, "and he and Ellen began collecting antiques there. Those chairs, the table, and the mirror are three of their purchases. I brought along some of the furniture from my San Francisco apartment; Gran gave us some of her treasures; and, as you can see, Mummy was more than generous with her China plunder. Morgan thought it would be an interesting contrast—since San Antonio's main influence is Spanish—if we added some touches of Orientalia."

"I like the effect. But was it very difficult for you, Nela, coming into a house that another woman had planned and lived in and . . . and died in?"

"Ellen died in the hospital, not here. If she had, I think Morgan would have sold this house long before I met him, or would have put it on the market when we became engaged. Still and all, it was a little difficult," she admitted quietly as they began to climb the stairs to the second floor. "The hardest part was putting my own taste and imprint on the house without eliminating Ellen entirely. Christy knows her mother is never coming back, but I couldn't take away all signs that she ever existed. All her china, crystal, silver and some of the furniture has been moved to the attic for safekeeping. They'll be Christy's to do with what she wants when she's twenty-one. Our bedroom was done over from scratch," she

60

added as they went slowly up the stairs, pausing every few steps so that Thea could admire the series of ink and color on silk Chinese ancestral portraits lining the staircase wall.

The walls of the upstairs hall were painted white with lemon trim, and the area was dominated by an oversized black and gold Oriental lacquer writing cabinet—a superb antique with the modern incongruity of a telephone resting on it.

"It's the upstairs extension," Nela explained. "Right now, we don't need one in the bedroom."

"I certainly hope not."

"Mind your manners. What I mean is that this isn't New York where we're never off the telephone."

She showed Thea the large master suite, the room that would be the nursery come next March, her step-daughter's room, and finally led her into the cream and pink guest room where Lupe was setting out fresh towels in the adjoining bathroom and a pitcher of iced tea and plates of tea sandwiches and cakes were waiting for them.

Thea gave the young maid the keys to the cases that had been brought upstairs, unhooked the dress that had had such an unsettling effect on the major, slipped on a negligee, and curled up comfortably on the four-poster canopy bed while Nela stretched out on the chaise lounge. As Lupe unpacked they ate, gossiped, joked and laughed as they caught up on each others' lives.

"What do you think of San Antonio so far?" Nela asked as soon as Lupe left.

"Not at all what I was expecting. I thought I'd see a dusty little town, not a bustling city."

Nela poured herself another glass of iced tea. "My dear, this is San Antonio. The holiest of all holy Texas cities, consecrated at the Alamo on March 6, 1836, and fed on the legends of Davy Crockett, Jim Bowie, William Barrett Travis, and the one hundred and eighty-two men

61

that died with them. You can't describe this city in any letter, you have to live it. It's a state of mind as much as anything else. Even the poorest of the poor here have a special pride about this city. It's held its own through more wars and disturbances than you can count. The Union Army never got here during the Civil War, and all the Indian raids—Morgan told me the last one was only twenty years ago—never stopped it from growing."

"I'm impressed, Nela, I really am. But who holds the power here—political and the rest?"

"In Texas it's *only* politics," Nela laughed, "everything else is secondary. I think the real reason that Morgan decided to come here ten years ago was that he knew he wouldn't fit in with any of the three groups who run this city. No chance that either the Army or the Church—who divvy it all up—would come knocking on the door to see if the son of the late and respected Senator Browne would consider running for office. My husband is as interested in politics as the next person," she explained as Thea began to laugh. "But he was overexposed to it while he was growing up and all the glitter and prestige that's supposed to be connected with winning elective office is lost on him."

"For which you are, without a doubt, eternally grateful," Thea put in, knowing full well her friend's disgust of political maneuvering. "But you said there were *three* groups. Whom did you leave out?"

For a second, Nela looked as guilty as a child caught with its hand in the cookie jar, then she passed her hands over her champagne colored hair and looked Thea straight in the eye. "We have a pretty substantial German-American population here," she explained quietly. "The first German immigrants to arrive in this part of Texas were intellectuals and master craftsmen who wanted to get away from the famine and political problems they had at home. They came in 1845 with

Prince von Solms-Braunfels and established the community of New Braunfels. The second wave came the next year with Freiherr von Meusebach and founded Fredericksburg. The last major group came in 1851 and built Comfort which is northwest of here, and fifteen years later, Ernst Altgelt, who was one of Comfort's founders, came to San Antonio and planned the King William district. It's named for Wilhelm the First of Prussia, but if the *current* Wilhelm is looking for a nice little group of German sympathizers here, he can go bark up another tree," Nela added with unholy delight.

"And here I was, waiting for you to tell me that San Antonio, Texas, is a hot-bed of German spies," Thea said, feeling the hard knot of fear and apprehension that had formed in the pit of her stomach when Nela had said the word "German," start to dissolve. "Nela, what have they told you about what's going on? Not even T.R. told me much, and I get the feeling they're all playing it by ear." She made a disparaging face and settled herself more comfortably among the pillows on the Queen Anne walnut and maple bed with its softly draped cream silk hangings. "In St. Louis, when I'd ask Colonel Miles, he'd say, 'Wait until you get to San Antonio,'" she went on. "Well, I'm here and I'd like to know the details."

"After dinner," Nela replied, not wanting to admit that she knew no more than Thea.

"You know they're going to send me off with a man," she said, a terrible thought dawning. "Is it Donovan?"

"Good grief, no! He looks like a regular old army man and that sort is absolutely no good with women. It's someone else. Morgan knows who—I think they had lunch together today—but he's playing it very close to the chest and I haven't the faintest idea who it could be. Are you frightened?"

"A little, but the idea of it was too good to resist and I said yes. Do you think I was wrong?"

"It's a little too late to ask that question, isn't it? To tell you the truth, I think everyone has sabotage in Panama on their minds with the Germans supplying the TNT. All they want out of you is a listening post for a few months to find out if the Kaiser plans on stirring up trouble now, or will wait a few years."

Thea felt an inexplicable sense of relief slide over her. "Pretty routine, then?"

"More or less." Angela stood up. "Look, why don't you take a bath—it's all yours—and have a nap. The dressing bell is at half-past six and, if you need help, I'll send Lupe to you. That boor Donovan will dish all the dirt to you after dinner."

"I understand you're acquainted with Don Renaldo and Dona Imelda de Veiga, Miss Harper?" John Donovan said as he sat down behind Morgan Browne's massive Chippendale writing desk, taking care not to disturb the George III silver inkstand and pen holder, the set of matched Clichy paperweights, the Mark Cross leather-bound blotter, and the telephone, as he set out his own papers. He finally leaned back in the large burgundy leather swivel chair and observed the three people seated in front of him.

Dinner completed, the last drops of coffee and cognac consumed, the four of them retired to the library where Donovan took up his post, ready to give Thea the final pieces of her assignment. But, instead of beginning immediately, he seemed almost mesmerized by both the scene in front of him and its setting.

Until a few hours ago, his contact with Morgan Browne had been limited to strategy meetings, always held in some inconspicuous place where they were not likely to be overheard. He was well aware of the thirty-four-year-old department store owner's background and financial status, but this house and the people in it were enough of a surprise to leave him feeling like the proverbial bull in the china shop. A feeling he didn't like at all.

The dinner he'd just eaten, for instance; iced tomato soup, cold halibut with dilled mayonnaise, a lettuce and avocado salad, and a dessert Mrs. Browne told him was called *oeufs a la neige*—floating island. The food (for a man who considered bully beef and plum cake to be a swell meal), presented on Spode bone china; served by two pretty Mexican-American maids; accompanied by a dry white California wine; the excellent dry martinis they drank in the drawing room before dinner, and the warm glow produced by the cognac that followed the meal; was entirely lost on him. He was an officer whose roster of assignments in his years of service read like every pulp writer's dream of the American West. And this house, this high-ceilinged, book-lined room, and most of all, these people were anathema to him because he couldn't understand or compete with them.

He'd drifted into Military Intelligence almost by mistake ten years earlier when he'd been rotated to Washington for a tour of duty with the War Department, but he was not a social man and was eventually sent back to his beloved western outposts where his only covert activity was the tours he gave European army officers who seemed to descend on the forts like insects in summer since the American military victories of 1898. They were always full of questions and, more importantly, full of themselves—certain that the stolid rank-and-file officer they rode with, made inspections with, dined and drank with, couldn't understand anything they said in their own language. John Donovan's verbal command of foreign languages was atrocious. His accent and intonation amounted to butchery and his European visitors often had trouble hiding their smiles when they heard him speak. It is very much doubted, however, that they would have kept smiling if they knew Donovan read, wrote and understood Spanish, French, Italian, and German. Except for West Point, his education was best ignored. He'd learned a basic grasp of the first two languages at the Academy, improved on those and taught himself the others out of textbooks, novels and dictionaries ordered from New York and Chicago booksellers. It was the best way to pass the long winter and sultry summer nights at installations where diversions for off-duty bachelor officers were extremely limited. It was certainly safer than drinking rotgut whisky or bedding questionable women to pass the time. Last winter, at Fort Selden, he'd begun to delve into the intricacies of Russian.

In his own way he supposed he'd picked up and passed on as much information as all those eastern officers who'd as soon wear white tie and tails as their uniform, and even had *those* custom made. Not that he minded that they were were allowed to hob-nob with the embassy crowd while he stuck it out in hardship posts—what were hellholes to others, was home to him. They had their way, he had his, and as long as it all got put together, what did it matter?

Except for Colonel Miles' latest idea, he thought as his gaze slid beyond Thea and came to rest on the outsized mahogany octagonal library table on whose tooled leather top a large rose medallion bowl filled with white carnations rested. Espionage, even in its less dangerous facet of information-gathering, he felt, should be left to professionals, and in the case of women, whores. But Miles, being a card-carrying member of the upper strata himself, preferred to use ladies and gentlemen—such as the interesting number seated opposite him. With a sickening lurch, Donovan realized his mind had drifted so far off its course that if Miss Harper had answered him, he hadn't heard.

"Major Donovan, are you feeling all right?" Nela

inquired softly. She, Thea and Morgan had been watching with varying degrees of interest and annoyance as the major had slipped glassy-eyed into his own world. But, enough was enough, and it was time to bring him out of his little trance or else they'd sit here all night. Typical Army, she thought contemptuously as he blinked out of his self-inflicted state. If you'd pulled a stunt like this in the Navy, my father would have made mincemeat of you.

"Thank you, Mrs. Browne. I'm perfectly fine. It's only the after-effects of your fine dinner, it makes a man conducive to a little day-dreaming. It's not often I'm invited to such a . . . er . . . ah . . . *unique* home," he finished with a lame flourish.

I'll just bet, Thea thought coldly, all her instincts at full alert. No need to count the good silver after you leave, because there's no reason to show it off in the first place, she said silently as the major asked his question over again. She hadn't been fooled by Donovan's courtly attention on the trip from the station. He didn't like her, didn't trust her, and didn't know why Miles (and the President) had selected her. All the gentleman officer manners in the world weren't covering up that fact. Something told her that *he* might very well turn out to be the biggest problem she would have to face in Mexico City. She also knew that Donovan would love to catch her off guard with the news he carried. You'd just love it if I cried and fainted and begged to be let off, she told him in silent fury. But that's one satisfaction I'm *not* going to give you.

"I met them two years ago in Budapest," she replied at last, wondering where this particular line of questioning was leading. "They were travelling with all six of their children. They were quite a sight marching into the lobby of the Bristol Hotel. I was there with the Honorable Mr. and Mrs. Frederick de Noyer of London, and I'm sure your notes give you all the information as to why I was so far off the usual American tourist path," she added coolly. "Freddy runs the de Noyer family mills in England and, since Senor de Veiga is very interested in establishing a textile industry in Mexico, they were already acquainted. I was introduced to them and we saw a lot of each other during our stay. When I left they insisted that if I were ever in Mexico, I was to stay with them."

"Well, you will be, for the first part of your stay in Mexico at least. We contacted the de Veigas, and as soon as we mentioned your name and the name of your companion-to-be, they immediately agreed and assured us of their cooperation. You must have made an excellent impression on them."

"Are you certain? About their cooperation, I mean. I'm not disparaging the de Veigas in any way, but I always thought that a lot of the very old and aristocratic Mexican families have strong Royalist tendencies and portraits of Maximilian and Carlotta hidden in the attic."

Morgan Browne drew his fingers through his thick, tawny hair and shook his head smilingly at Thea. "The de Veigas are a very tradition-minded people, but they don't cling to a way of life that can never return. There'll never be any betrayal from that quarter."

Thea turned back to Donovan, who nodded in agreement. "The de Veigas will be instrumental in seeing you make the right connections when you reach the capital. Incidentally, it's not Mexico City. Just call it City of Mexico. Or Mexico."

"How long will I—that is, we—have to stay?"

"You should be home by Christmas, if not before. There has been a lot of activity at the German Embassy over the last few months and we'd like to know if it's their usual strutting around or if something is being cooked up. You won't have to do too much. Just listen in at all the right parties and report back to us."

"Colonel Miles told me you'd be there."

"Yes. I'm being sent to our Embassy there. We'll work out the best method for communication after your arrival."

Once again, he shuffled his papers. A technique Thea, relaxing in the large Queen Anne petit-point-covered wing chair, recognized as a move to buy time and find the proper words.

"You know you're to be accompanied by a man?" he questioned finally.

"Of course, and I have no objections. It's probably *the* best idea the government ever had. An unaccompanied woman in Latin countries has about as much status as a peon."

"We realized that, and since we didn't want too many impediments in your way, and at the same time wanted to provide you with the ultimate protection, we thought the best solution was to pass the both of you off as husband and wife."

Startled out of her cool facade, Thea caught her breath and looked at Nela and Morgan. Neither of them seemed terribly upset at the major's announcement. *So that's it,* she thought and, as his words sank in, Thea began to realize she rather liked the idea. If nothing else, it was certainly better than what her runaway imagination had been coming up with.

"Unfortunately," he continued before Thea could voice her agreement, "the Archbishop of San Antonio threw a fit when he heard about it. The young man is his guest, and His Grace considers himself to be his spiritual advisor for the length of his stay."

The refreshment Thea had gained from her bath and nap and excellent dinner was fading swiftly as Donovan dragged out this session with his hedging. She was tired and edgy and wanted it over with.

"Would it be terribly indelicate of me to ask at this point just who my mystery man is?" she said with poison sweetness.

"Charles de Renille."

"Is this a joke, Major? Or did someone in Washington actually think they had a good idea for once?" Nela's angry voice vibrated through the room. She sat bolt upright in the round backed Hepplewhite mahogany armchair, her ribbon-trimmed rose chiffon Lucile dress contrasting softly against the chair's cream and green patterned silk upholstery.

"I take it you have some objection, Mrs. Browne?"

"You're damn right, Major Donovan, I do. In case you haven't heard, Charles de Renille does not happen to be the most stable of men. He had a terrible nervous breakdown with all sorts of physical complications. It took him over two years to recover. Suppose he snaps again?"

"I don't think that's a likely possibility. We had lunch together today and he struck me as a very upright young man," Morgan remonstrated gently, his blue eyes grave. "A little too serious perhaps, but that may be all to the better. You don't want some remittance man who's going to play up to all the women he meets."

His gentle words had a soothing effect on Thea, but not on Nela who wasn't ready to give up the ghost. "Thea, did you know Charles was a priest—or at least trying to become one—until he had his breakdown?" she asked, playing her trump card. "A Jesuit, no less."

For one of the few times in her life, Thea found herself at a loss for words. She could feel her vocal cords working, but her mind had gone blank. Well, now she knew why Roosevelt had looked so relieved, why Miles had made her make up stories, why Donovan—who had all the sensitivity of an Army mule—had been so evasive and why Morgan Browne had not told Nela any more than was absolutely necessary. Had they really been so afraid that her reaction would be a duplicate of Nela's, and the only tactic they could come up with was to hold out on her until the last possible moment? It was all so patently ridiculous, so schoolboy-with-a-secret, that Thea felt an overwhelming desire to laugh right in the major's face.

I might as well laugh, Thea told herself as the others waited for her to break the silence. It's better than putting my head down on the desk and crying. An ex-whatever-he-was recovering from a nervous breakdown and we're supposed to pose as husband and wife. No wonder the Archbishop of San Antonio had a fit!

"I always thought being a priest was like being pregnant," she announced clearly. "You either were or you weren't."

As she spoke, Thea caught Nela's eye, unable to resist the temptation to see if her friend wanted to have a little fun at the major's expense.

Nela raised her eyebrows, an indication that she was willing and ready to play along. "Where the French aristocracy is concerned," she replied, "the rules—*any* rules—go out the window. And circumstances can always be *arranged.*"

"Speaking of breakdowns, rules, circumstances and men in groups, you don't suppose—"

"Oh, not at all! If he were, the old boys in charge would have booted him out without waiting for a convenient nervous breakdown. I'm afraid his *dépression nerveuse* was rooted in much more prosaic reasons."

"Well, at least the Jesuits are the *creme de la creme.* We should have some interesting conversations, if nothing else."

"My dear, your last two words may just sum it all up," Nela said, and both women began to laugh, oblivious to the men. For his part, Morgan Browne was used to the way his wife and her friends would suddenly carry on a cryptic conversation as if no one else were present, but Donovan was floored.

From what direction did these women come? he wondered, shocked not only at their casual speech but at their total disregard of the fact that their conversation was taking place in mixed company. None of the *ladies* he knew would ever carry on such an innuendo-filled conversation, even if they were alone.

Donovan's knowledge of women was gleaned mainly from the Army wives who followed their husbands to isolated forts where they made a home, raised children and never minded when their looks faded swiftly in the crackling heat of summer and bone chilling cold of winter. In his eyes, they represented a small speck of civilization, uncomplainingly endured all hardships, and never, never discussed—or even let on that they knew of—the intimate, physical, complex world of male and female relations in all its variations. His own marriage had been of such brief duration—less than two years from beginning to end—that he never found out that the company facade he saw and actual reality were two entirely different things. Women like Jane Miles and Evangeline Dalton, married to high-ranking officers and independently wealthy in their own rights, were as unknown in his life as the titled women of Europe. If a woman was a lady, she dressed conservatively and spoke modestly; if she was a prostitute, she dressed loudly, spoke crudely, and he paid them to take an interest in him. That was his world and, until tonight, it had worked just fine. But during the few hours he'd been in this house, he was suddenly exposed to the vast gray area between the two extremes where more women than he had ever dreamed existed, expressing their views, changing their conversations and speaking their minds just for the fun of it and with no more effort than it took to change hats.

He allowed some of the impassiveness to drop from his face as he got ready to deliver his final salvo. Thea felt a faint tremor of fear ripple through her as she saw his slightly sly, self-satisfied expression.

"I certainly hope so, Miss Harper," he remarked, gathering his papers together. "Because you'll have to get used to each other real quick. The only way we could get the Archbishop to give his blessing to the plan was if the two of you were right and proper married."

Chapter Four

The diamond pave hands of the agate, gold and rock crystal Cartier clock that Angela Dalton Browne held in her hands read half-past one. With a sign of resignation, she returned the clock (which, ironically enough, had been their wedding present from the Comtesse Solange de Renille—Charles' mother) and leaned back against the large pillows. The rest of the house was fast asleep, but she was wide awake and likely to stay that way.

Poor Morgan, she thought, looking lovingly at the sleeping man stretched out beside her. His face, with looks that were nowhere near handsome, and yet went far beyond it, boyishly relaxed as he breathed slowly and dreamlessly. He's had it these past couple of weeks—almost from the day we came back from our honeymoon—with Donovan popping in and out of the woodwork, pulling him away from the store for one meeting after another, acting as if he were the only one who ever had anything important to do. For every hour he was out of the store, there were two to make up and the strain was beginning to show on his face.

Nela had a theory that Donovan, for the sheer hell of it, had developed a secret antenna that told him just when to appear on the scene so as to cause the greatest possible disruption in other people's lives. She had nothing against military intelligence officers, having grown up on the Navy side of the game, but this was the first time she'd met someone who had so little finesse about the

74

matter, and that disturbed her more than the news he had imparted to them a few hours before.

God, but Morgan hated him! Loathed him, in fact, in a way he reserved for few other people. And Nela, seeing that emotion in him for the first time, was amazed, not at the depth of his feelings, but at how well he hid them. He was a Texan, a gentleman, a former Rough Rider and he wouldn't behave in a way that would disgrace his upbringing and what he believed in, he explained to her. No guest in his—*their*—house would ever go unwelcomed or unfed.

Nela had tried to go halfway in an effort to counterbalance Morgan's attitude (it was the right thing to do under the circumstances, she reasoned), but the major himself had defeated her efforts. Oh, he was polite enough (did they teach deportment at the Point?) but there was something *underneath*. . . . The way he looked at the house when he and Morgan arrived, and the way his eyes narrowed when Thea had come down the stairs, laughing and running, to fling her arms around Morgan, kiss his cheek and tell him how happy she was to be in their home. And as for dinner—Nela grimaced in the dark—Consuelo might as well have made the meal out of sawdust and library paste for all it meant to him. He blamed them for not living in a manner that was true, not only to his code of morality, but to the principles of the American West—or rather, its legend.

Beside her, Morgan stirred, said something unintelligible, and drifted back to sleep as Nela fixed the puffed silk comforter more securely over him. Poor darling—and while she was at it, poor Thea.

How would I feel if, instead of having fallen in love with Morgan on my own, I was told I *had* to marry him? she wondered. Suppose I were in Thea's place, doing exactly what she's about to do? Would I have been as cool and contained and agreed to it as if I'd known all

75

along that was the plan? For a minute she stared into the darkness, trying to imagine Donovan, seated behind the desk and shuffling his papers, saying "Morgan Browne" instead of "Charles de Renille" and picturing her reaction. But it was Thea's situation, not hers, and the transference wouldn't work. Except when she thought about the very first time she'd seen Morgan.

Nela grinned in the dark, remembering. If it were like that, if someone marched Morgan forward and said, "this is the man you have to marry," I'd do it without thinking twice, she told herself silently.

She was worried about Thea. Worried that underneath the cool, unshakable, faintly disinterested facade she'd managed to project all evening, was a woman in panic. The first shock must have worn off and the news sunk in by now. Suppose she was in a state of terror?

Oh, no, she's not, Nela told herself firmly, resisting the impulse to get out of bed, go to the guest room and check on her friend's emotional condition. Thea's not a hysteric any more than I am, or Alix, or Regina. However she feels about this, she's going to work it out by herself and come to terms with the situation. And whatever else happens, at least we've got Donovan out of our hair, she added, recalling how quickly he'd gotten out of the house once he'd imparted his news. In fact, he'd left almost immediately afterwards, gathering his papers with a speed and efficiency that had been noticeably lacking when he'd first sat down behind the desk. His part of the job was over until Mexico, he told them as they filed out of the library into the hall. He'd convey Thea's agreement to the Archbishop, and the next move would come from that quarter.

That had been over three hours ago, but Nela could still remember the sense of relief that had reflected on their faces when the door finally closed behind him.

* * *

76

"Thank God, he's gone," Morgan announced coldly as he locked the front door. "It's officers like him who ruin everything and generally give the Army a bad name. I swear we had more problems from his type in Cuba than we did with the Spanish Army. His sort aren't concerned about anything unless it's on a requisition form, or will bring them personal glory!

"When we finally landed on Siboney Beach, it was T.R. and Colonel Wood who kept us together," he told both women as they gazed at him silently, "and it was General Wheeler and General Lawton we gave our admiration and respect to. And if General Shafter had been any more superannuated than the misdirected figurehead he was, we would have all come back from Cuba in boxes!" he finished savagely.

And that's why he hates Donovan so much, Nela thought. These past few weeks I've been wondering *why*, and now I know. Every time he talks with him, Morgan remembers his Rough Rider days—and not the good times. All he can think about is the endless wait in Tampa, the shortage of transportation that made them leave some of the men and most of the horses behind and, worst of all, he dwells on the voyage on the *Yucatan*, and the night he spent throwing rotten tinned food overboard. He can't think about the good times during training in San Antonio; or that first night on Siboney Beach when he spent his time smoothing out the tift that "Fighting Joe" Wheeler and H.W. Lawton had when those two old, esteemed veterans from the Civil War—one Confederate and the other Union—had their all too inevitable rivalry; or even the adventure of the first day of the Battle of San Juan Hill when he'd dodged the Spanish Army's Mauser bullets as he took supplies up from the base camp at Kettle Hill. He looks at the major and his perspective is gone, and all that's left is the memory of all the things that went wrong and how they could have been avoided if the worst of the regular Army had kept their hands off.

"Morgan, do you realize that now Thea *has* to marry Charles de Renille in order to prove we all don't hate Catholics?" Nela asked archly, willing to try anything to get that look of pain and anger off Morgan's face.

For a second, Morgan stared at her nonplussed, and then, slowly but surely, his expression lightened. "That's the silliest thing I ever heard. The Army is Donovan's religion. I'll bet he's already put your outburst down to the ravings of a pregnant woman," he teased her.

"Why did you tell him about *that*, for crying out loud?"

"Mainly because I got the distinct impression he felt any man who couldn't find anything better to do with his life than run a women's specialty store didn't rate too highly on his masculinity chart, and I want as few problems from that man as possible."

"Well, let's hope the Archbishop's easier to take," Nela said, rubbing the back of her neck reflectively. "I'm sorry, Thea. I shouldn't have said what I did about Charles being unstable."

"You were only trying to protect me." Thea smiled, rousing herself from the all-enveloping numbness that had engulfed her in the library. "I got into this all by myself, and now I have to accept the consequences. At least," she added with a slight smile, "a temporary 'business marriage' with Charles de Renille sounds a good deal better than some of the other alternatives the government might have come up with!"

"You must have been having a pretty imaginative time of it," Nela smiled. "What do you think, darling?"

"I think I owe Thea an apology for the wine we served at dinner. It was a good, sound California vintage, but not the one I would have chosen to welcome you to San Antonio with. Unfortunately, I had the great misfortune to share a few meals with Major Donovan, and I swear a grizzly bear has a better palate," he explained. "It's bad enough I had to waste a snifter of Remy Martin on him, so you can be sure I wasn't about to decant a bottle of Mouton Cadet Blanc while he was at my table!"

As he spoke, Thea felt her equilibrium begin to return. She trusted Morgan Browne implicitly. Not only because he was Angela's husband, but because he was a man of high standards and unshakable integrity and, if for one minute he'd thought Charles de Renille was either unstable or unsuitable in some other way to be her companion, that scene in the library would never have taken place. Indeed, he felt Charles was so up to par that the only thing he saw reason to apologize for was the wine served with dinner, Thea realized, and gave him a conspirator's smile.

"Nela told me you wouldn't let her waste any of your special things on the good major," she laughed, hugging them. "Now lots of people would find purple and white Spode, Waterford crystal, and Reed & Barton silver all set out on an Irish linen tablecloth to be pretty special— and don't think for a second that I'm unappreciative— but you all had better remember that I know what's hidden away!"

"We'll make it up to you tomorrow night," Nela promised. "French wine, china and crystal—"

"And American food," Morgan put in. "A real welcome-to-Texas spread."

"And we have to invite Charles," Thea stated as the Brownes exchanged looks. "This might be a marriage of convenience, but I'm not going to wait until I reach the altar to see him for the first time. Besides, I have an idea that if he's a person of any sort of sensitivity, we might be able to put our heads together and keep Donovan from being too much of a bother. What do you say?"

"It sounds like a fine plan," Morgan replied, and

kissed them both. "When Charles and I had lunch today, I mentioned my map collection to him—I'll show it off to both of you tomorrow night. Nela, why don't you and Thea go on upstairs while I lock up and check the wine cellar for something that'll make our French visitor feel right at home."

"In case you haven't heard, you and Charles are in for a singular honor. Morgan's map collection is his pride and joy, and he won't show it off to just anyone," Nela told her as they climbed the stairs. "He began it as a boy, and some of the cartography he bought for pennies in Washington and Boston is now worth quite a bit of money."

"I've come to the conclusion that Morgan is one of this earth's great gentlemen, ranking right up there with your father and mine and Henry Thorpe and Ian MacIverson and—"

"And T.R.?"

"And T.R., and a very few others," Thea agreed as they reached the upstairs hall. "Men like that are born, not bred, and Morgan would be the same if his father had been a dirt farmer instead of a United States Senator. Good men, and men of integrity, aren't all *that* rare," she went on as they paused in front of the guest room door, "but unless there's a special something in their makeup to set it off, they can become the most God-awful bores. Morgan has *elan* and *eclat* and that not only sets him— and those like him—apart, but makes all of them very difficult to find!"

Oh yes, he had been incredibly difficult to find, Nela acknowledged with another glance at the clock. Funnily enough, Morgan Browne had become inextricably woven into the fabric of her life three years before they'd finally met. Even odder, two years before, they'd both been in London, knowing the same people and never meeting. It

80

was supposed to be that way, I guess. If we'd met then it might have been a disaster. We both had to reach a certain point in our own lives before we could begin to make one together.

Nela was finally beginning to relax and she closed her eyes, still thinking about the roundabout circumstances that had finally brought her and Morgan together. Strange to think that it had all begun for them with a letter written by Alix Thorpe in New York to Morgan's older sister, Rosemary Boyd, in Dallas seven months earlier. . . .

I really wish I could do something special for my friend, Angela Dalton (Alix had written Rosemary). When her parents went to China last October (her father, in case you're not up on the latest who's-who in Washington's Secret Intelligence, is Admiral Bruce Dalton, who has gone to Peking as Roosevelt's Special Naval Minister), Nela decided she'd had enough of being a walking advertisement for Thurn's, and is now in California, working for Mary Anne Magnin.

Although she's *succes fou* professionally, her private life is not what it should be for someone who looks like Nela. She apparently has no shortage of beaux (both casual, and those who'd like to make it otherwise), but she says that none of them are worth losing sleep over, and it's hard enough for her to spend an evening with them much less contemplate a lifetime together.

In her last letter, Nela said that she'd decided Ian MacIverson—who's married to our friend, Regina —and Henry were the last two gentle, decent, honest men left, and since Regina and I married them, there's no one left.

She's wrong, of course, but I know how she feels.

81

Until the moment I met Henry, I felt exactly the same way.

If Morgan ever goes to San Francisco, I'd love for them to meet. If nothing else, it would restore her faith that good men are still around. . . .

None of it had had any business whatsoever of turning out the way it had, and Morgan—as far as she knew—*still* didn't know about that letter, Nela reflected. But Rosemary had shown it to her, and together they had laughed and then marveled over how circumstance and fate sometimes combined when you were sure that all was lost.

Their path had not been straight and easy. But it might never have happened at all if Morgan hadn't been so worn down by the dual complexities of his fast-growing business and having to be both father and mother to his daughter.

Ordered by his family doctor to take a relaxing vacation or else, Rosemary had put together her plan of action, and almost before he knew it, Morgan—armed with a guest card to the Concordia Club, which had been provided by the theatrical producer-manager, Percy Lasky, an out-of-town member of the club who was in San Antonio checking up on one of his road companies, and happy to help out an old friend—was aboard the Southern Pacific train that would take him to San Francisco and to the private sitting room of an old friend—an Angela Dalton's favorite client.

Nearly everyone thought that Mary Anne Magnin, the only woman in America to have founded a department store, introduced Angela Dalton, whom she'd hired some sixteen months earlier as special consultant in charge of new clients who wanted complete wardrobes, to Morgan Browne, with whom she'd been carrying on a fourteen-year correspondence. Morgan had been a young trainee at Filene's in Boston with only the barest dream of returning to Texas to establish his own women's specialty store when they'd met.

In a manner of speaking, it *was* true. They were *formally* introduced by Mrs. Magnin in her office, but in reality they had met the day before—a meeting they had decided to keep their own personal secret. Neither of their meetings had any reason to work out. In fact, they should have hated each other on sight. But they hadn't, and that, as far as Nela was concerned, was enough to make her want to do something for Thea. People had a knack of finding each other and falling in love all on their own, but every so often it helped to work behind the scenes.

So I did sleep after all, Nela said to herself as she looked at the clock again. Seven-fifteen. Good—Morgan can sleep at least until eight. I wonder if the Archbishop will want to see us today? She watched the early morning sunlight as it filtered through the closed draperies.

Another hot day, she thought, and stretched luxuriously in bed, careful not to disturb Morgan. Slowly, methodically, her idea began to take shape.

It was idiotic, she told herself, and Morgan would absolutely *hate* it, but she had to try. It was as Rosemary had said when she'd shown her Alix's letter. Theirs hadn't been a premeditated meeting; just one woman's abstract wish that gave fire to another woman's solution for an overworked and distracted man. But they had been worthy of a chance, and, as Rosemary had said, if the human race didn't take chances, everyone on earth would still be swinging from trees, bananas in hand.

Quietly, Nela got out of the large Hepplewhite four-poster bed with fluted columns and blue and ivory silk hangings, and retrieved her negligee from the needle-point bench. Slipping it on, she crossed the antique

Peking medallion gold and blue and apricot rug that covered the floor and entered her dressing room. She ran a comb through her champagne-colored hair, went into the connecting bathroom to wash her face, and returned to the dressing room to sit at her desk.

For a long minute, she sat there, letting her gaze roam around the pale-colored, highly feminine room. Morgan's counterpart dressing room and bathroom were at the opposite end of the bathroom, done in a fittingly masculine decor.

You can't spend the day here, she chided herself and, opening a drawer, withdrew the letters she and Alix had exchanged over the past year.

She read them through carefully, and with her questions answered, she put them away and took several sheets of blank stationery from another drawer, and set to work. With a growing sense of enjoyment, Nela saw her plan taking definite shape. Even if there wasn't much time, a lot could still be done, she realized as her pen scratched on. All it took was proper organization and—

"Nela, what are you doing?" Morgan's voice broke into her reverie, and she looked up to see him standing at the door of the dressing room, looking boyish, rumpled and more appealing than ever in his pajamas. "Is there something so pressing that it couldn't wait until we got to the store? I want you to rest and take care of yourself—"

"Oh, I'm as healthy as a horse, and you know it!" Nela interrupted, laughing. "And to set your mind at ease, this isn't store business."

Morgan eyed the papers on her desk warily. "If it's not business, and it's not a letter, what is it?"

"Well, it's a guest list, a flower list, a menu plan and a few random thoughts—such as what champagne to serve," she said gaily, holding out her work to him.

He advanced cautiously into the room and took the proffered pages, studying the top one with great interest.

"The Wilders, the Stimsons, the Maurys, the Altmans, Colonel and Mrs. Forrest," he read from the guest list before gazing nonplussed at his wife. "There have to be at least twenty couples on this list. What kind of a party are we giving?"

"A wedding reception for Thea and Charles. If you'll check the menu, you'll see there's a wedding cake on it," she rushed on, hoping to forestall any objection. "Since we were married in San Francisco, Consuela only got to do that little cake to welcome us home with, and I know she's dying to create a real masterpiece."

"For a wedding that's going to be in name only?"

"Well, no one else knows that."

"Donovan's plan is to keep it simple."

"Which is exactly why we *shouldn't!*" Nela's voice was indignant. "Donovan's finally out of our lives, so why should he care *what* we do?"

"Oh, he'll care. His type has a perennial sore foot."

"Morgan, aren't you going to get angry?"

"I thought my calm attitude was admirable," he drawled with the last touch of Texas that all his years of New England schooling hadn't been able to breed out. "But anger? Let's see . . . Are you out of your mind? Has your pregnancy affected your brain? This is the worst idea I've ever heard of, and I've heard plenty." He stopped his mock tirade and grinned at her. "Is that what you were expecting?"

"Just about. But what do you *really* think?"

"Only this: is it really necessary to expose two sensitive people to the agony of a wedding reception?"

"Oh, Thea's pretty tough underneath it all, and I have an idea Charles is too. If they've survived all the government's machinations, not to mention the good major, they can stand a few hours of festivities. It's hardly as if the wedding party were going to camp outside the Menger's bridal suite for the wedding night.

Besides," she said, throwing in her final argument, "all of this is necessary for your business!"

"Really?" Morgan feigned innocence. "I thought I was doing rather well."

"Oh, Morgan, you never have to stop and think of the broader issues because you know whatever course you take, people will accept it. But I'm new here, and I'm seeing all of this . . . plan that's been cooked up through different eyes. This marriage can be kept *quiet*, but not *secret*, and sooner or later someone is going to ask us why our house guest and her fiance got married in such a hole-in-the-corner way. *Those* kind of questions will be a lot harder to answer and cause a lot more gossip than any reception we can give."

"We won't have to have any of the guests at the ceremony, will we? I don't think that would come off at all well."

"No," she reassured him, "it'll just be you, as best man, me, as matron of honor, and Christy as flower girl." Nela began to relax; this was going better than she had expected. "When I issue the invitations, I'll tell everyone that Thea and Charles met in New York, decided to honeymoon in Mexico, and since their families are so scattered, coming down to San Antonio to get married was the most logical thing. But they want to keep the ceremony *dans la plus stricte intimité.*"

Morgan consulted her plans again. "Apparently you've covered every possible detail. But do you think the two principles involved can carry it off? So far, they haven't even met."

"Then it's only because of the most twisted of circumstances that they haven't. Did you know that Charles has been staying with Alix and Henry in New York? I think that if Thea hadn't been out of New York for most of the winter, they would have been introduced by now. I look on this as completing a necessary task."

86

"I know Charles has been in New York—I was going to tell you at breakfast," he began, as comprehension of his wife's true plan dawned. "Nela, you're not suggesting that—?"

She gave him her most secret smile.

"If you want me to be angry, I am now!" he exploded. "Do you actually think we have any right to play games with their lives on the excuse that we felt like trying our hands at a little match-making?"

"I'm suggesting no such a thing, and if you'll think back, it was Thea who insisted we invite Charles to dinner tonight," Nela retorted. "Besides, Morgan, it's our responsibility to see that they get off on the right foot." Standing up, she quickly covered the few steps separating them and put her arms around him. "What do you say, darling?"

"We might as well," he sighed. "As you said, if we don't there'll be an awful lot of explaining to do. In the middle of our lunch yesterday, Dax Wilder came over to say howdy, and once he heard that Charles was in town to get married, he began making noises about throwing a bachelor party at the San Antonio Club."

"You see, it's just like I told you," Nela laughed, kissing him. "Besides, look at how long you've been involved one way or another with me and my friends. There are four of us, and somehow we've all been involved in your life, either for sorrow or happiness. Regina was here when Ellen died; sixteen months later in London you met Alix; and twenty months after that, we met in San Francisco." She looked seriously into his equally grave face. "One of us was a helpless participant in a tragedy, another of us gave you back some light, and you married *me*. Thea's the only one of us still unmarried, and this is a chance to complete the circle of our involvement with you. Look at it this way," Nela couldn't resist adding with a smile, "if the impossible does happen, at least they'll have a good start, and Thea will have a story she can tell in public. How can I tell anyone but our closest friends that I didn't see you for the first time in Mary Anne Magnin's office—that I met and fell in love with you in the private sitting room of Nell Tierney's Kearney Street cat house!''

Chapter Five

Charles de Renille sat in a comfortable armchair in the Archbishop of San Antonio's library, gazing unseeingly at his book. Once again, he tried to center his attention on the printed page, but the words refused to make sense. Resignedly, he closed the book, rose, crossed to the window, and stared into the garden of the Cathedral of San Fernando.

He blinked at the bright sunlight. Well, *maman*, he said to himself, you have your wish. I am to be married—at least temporarily, and if I didn't know better, I'd say our orders hadn't originated with the President of the United States, but with you!

He looked down reflectively at the abundant garden. How did anything grow in this heat? he wondered. A real end-of-summer Texas scorcher, he'd heard someone comment the other day, and now he knew what that remark meant. Strange to think he'd been in America for just over seven months, and not only had the weather changed totally, but so had his perception of himself.

If nothing else, Charles realized, he'd finally admitted to himself that at twenty-nine he was drifting, and that he didn't like it very much. The two years it took him to recover from the nervous and physical breakdown that nearly claimed his life and had turned him into a virtual recluse with no interests or activities beyond that of his family's Normandy stud farm. It was a life he might have gone on with indefinitely, except for his mother.

Even with seven months and six thousand miles separating them, Charles could still flinch at the memory of that icy morning and the words he'd exchanged with the strong-willed *comtesse*—his mother—who, had she but known the leitmotiv she was helping to weave, might have enjoyed besting him in their breakfast-room encounter that had been the first step in the sometimes circuitous journey that had brought him to San Antonio.

"Good morning, *Maman*. I see Guy has gone out already. We were supposed to ride together this morning."

Comtesse Solange de Renille—the widow of the late and greatly beloved Comte Adrian de Renille—looked up from the letter she was reading to see her youngest son standing at the threshold of the breakfast room. "No, *mon cheri*, Guy and Pauline have decided to enjoy their breakfast *solitude a deux* this morning." She smiled, extending an elegant hand to him. "Do you object to sharing this meal alone with me?"

"Never, *Maman*," he told her lightly, kissing her cheek. "Except that Guy, adoring husband that he is, has never been fond of breakfast in bed. Now, let me see what Martine has prepared this morning, and then we'll talk."

Like most of the great horse-breeding families of France, the de Renilles of the Haras de l'Soigneuse, had a great admiration for the English and the way of England's country-house living. To be sure, the de Renille *manoir*, with its twin salt-cellar turrets and three-story main wing flanked by spreading two-story wings, was the very essence of Norman architecture, and most of the spacious rooms were decorated with the finest of French antiques, but, as visitors often observed, the library, the gun room and the breakfast room could be lifted intact from France, carried across the channel, and set down in any notable country house without anyone guessing their previous home.

Feeling rather like an officer in the minutes before his first major battle, Solange de Renille, clad in a soft violet cashmere breakfast gown, sat back in her chair and watched her son standing by the Sheraton sideboard, lifting the covers off the row of silver chafing dishes to examine their contents. Love, apprehension, and determination mingled in her as she concentrated on his straight, slender back in the perfectly cut black riding coat.

His whole foray at the sideboard was mainly for show, she knew. True, he had put back nearly all of the seventy pounds he'd lost prior to, and just after, his collapse, but it had taken nearly two years to do it. His appetite had made a slow and grudging return, but it was still far too small, and often the sight of red meat would send him gagging from the table.

The doctors—eminent specialists, every one of them—had cautioned her that full recovery was a matter of that most fickle of all things—time. Still, Solange couldn't help reflecting as Charles rattled the silver covers, she couldn't be ungrateful. Not when she could close her eyes and remember precisely what he'd looked like the day she'd arrived at the seminary in Belgium, and been taken to the infirmary. He'd collapsed, was seriously ill, and possibly dying, the cable from the Rector had read. But nothing in those brief words could prepare her for the sight of the son she hadn't seen in nearly five years.

She suppressed a shudder as Charles turned back to the table. Just as she'd expected. On his plate was a small serving of creamy scrambled egg and half of a grilled tomato. Not starvation rations by any means, but hardly the proper breakfast for a man who intended to spend the remainder of the morning riding. Solange poured coffee into a Sevres cup for Charles, and then proceeded to refill her own. Ah, well, it would only be a few more moments before the first salvo was fired, and one had to be prepared—

"Is this my portion of this morning's mail?" Charles' teasing voice broke into her thoughts. "A gift, and an envelope without a name on it. How do you know it's for me?"

"Mainly because I purchased them," Solange replied, managing to keep her voice equally light. "Aren't you going to open them?"

For a countless second, he didn't move. The long white envelope propped up against his water glass, and the small rectangular package wrapped in glazed white paper resting next to it, suddenly seemed ominous. Something was wrong here. He could practically feel it in the air; and, like most people who've been ill for a long period of time, had the knack of knowing when a set pattern was about to be changed.

His eyes picked out the raised letters on the package's gold seals. *Brentano's, 37 Avenue de l'Opera.* "A book, *Maman?* Thank you very much," he said, quickly sampling his eggs and taking a sip of coffee before opening it. The seals gave way, and the glazed paper parted easily under his fingers. He stared at the small red book, its title stamped in gold on the cover and spine.

"Baedeker's Guide To The United States," he read. "Well, I suppose it's appropriate that I become an armchair traveller. But do you really think that a guide published in Leipzig can be very accurate?" he teased.

"Oh, I found my copy very useful on my visit. Yours, however, is a completely updated edition," Solange pointed out as a frigid February wind rattled the windows.

"Then why do we need two copies—?" he began as an icy shiver—as cold as the wind outside—snaked up his spine. He reached for the envelope, nearly overturning

92

the Baccarat goblet in the process. Some part of his mind already knew what the envelope contained.

Compagnie Generale Transatlantique
Le Havre—New York
First Cabin Outward Passage—Contract
Name of Passenger: Charles de Renille

Two pairs of topaz-colored eyes stared at each other over the length of the table, neither yielding an inch.

"No!"

"Yes!"

"You can send this ticket back to the *Transat, Maman*. I'm not going anywhere—least of all America!"

"Oh, yes, you are, Charles. You sail this coming Tuesday."

"The day before Lent?" His voice was horrified. "No, it's impossible—"

"You hardly need a dispensation to travel," his mother replied shortly. "And I've been assured there'll be a Lenten service on board. The *La Savoie* is hardly the floating palace of Babylon!"

"I wasn't suggesting that it was, Mother." His de Renille temper was beginning to boil now, and he found himself speaking in English, a habit everyone in his British-educated family had whenever the conversation became too heated. "I have no interest in going anywhere," he said coldly, tossing his steamship ticket on the table.

"That is precisely why you are going!" the comtesse shot back, also speaking in English. "I have had enough of your moping around!"

"I wasn't aware that I moped." His voice was icy.

"*Mais naturellement*. You wouldn't. No doubt you think that never leaving the grounds of the *haras*, not even to go to church because you fear exposing yourself to our neighbors, and always keeping to your room when there are guests, and refusing every invitation is perfectly normal!"

"Can you blame me for not wanting to see guests, or to visit London or Paris? Why should I give those friends of our family grist for the gossip they love so much? I have no intention of being a specimen for speculation, neither because I had a nervous breakdown nor because I was with the Jesuits!"

"And that is why you are going. America is the only alternative left. You'll either get better or turn into an anchorite," Solange de Renille remarked with her usual acid perception.

Now Charles knew why Guy—whose manifold duties as the Comte de Renille precluded leisurely, private breakfasts with his wife no matter how much he might enjoy them—was absent from the breakfast room this morning. All of this must have been planned well in advance, and his mother had decided that if there was to be a confrontation it was to be between the two of them with no third party to unexpectedly play devil's advocate.

His father, Charles remembered with a pang, had always told him that he'd inherited more of the Renille pride, temper and stubbornness than either of his two older brothers. When combined with the de Hautraviant determination of his mother, the final mix was potentially explosive and unremovable by any sort of tempering experience. Now, years later, he recognized that it was this combination that had sent him to the Church, kept him there long after he should have sought release. It was this selfsame combination that had eventually turned inward, nearly destroying him, and then kept him alive when someone with less strength of character might have died.

"I thought the last of my indignities were over," he told Solange at last. "Now you want to bundle me off like so much unwanted laundry. Have I really become that much of an inconvenience—or is it embarrassment—to have around?"

"We love you, and we want you wholly well," she retorted. "If you'd stop feeling sorry for yourself, you just might see that!"

"I do not feel sorry for myself, and I have no interest in crossing the Atlantic to sit in a hotel room!" he announced, and knew instantly that he'd played right into his mother's hands. Had he really been idiot enough to believe his mother hadn't covered every possible arrangement? he questioned himself wildly as the comtesse's look of anger and concern gave way to a smile of sweet victory.

"Of course you're not going to a hotel! That's absolute idiocy—and no way to spend a first visit to a city. You'll be staying with Henry and Alix Thorpe. They've written that they're moving into a twenty-room apartment, and will be thrilled to have you as their first guest. Now don't bristle and try to stare me down. You're going!"

And he went. With his mother there was no recourse or second appeal and, her sons always agreed, there were times it was simpler to go along. Particularly since she had the disconcerting knack of usually being in the right.

But not this time, he told himself as he strode from the breakfast room in cold anger. She couldn't be, but he was certainly the prize imbecile of all time, and *that* had made his mother the victor.

How *could* he have failed to see this coming? he wondered endlessly over the next days as the well-oiled machinery of the household began to function toward getting him ready to leave. Either he was as crazy as most of the outside world assumed him to be, or else his powers of observation had been destroyed, Charles decided grimly. What other explanation was there for his not seeing that his mother and brothers had planned out his exile weeks in advance? Or was it that he simply hadn't *wanted* to see all the signals around him?

But no matter how many times he questioned and searched himself for the truth, there was no one answer, and as the days melted away from him like ice before fire the preparations for his leave-taking became more and more complete.

His second brother, Andre, who handled the family's finances, accompanied by his wife, Janine, arrived from Paris, bringing with them Charles' letter of credit issued by Morgan's Bank, which, he was informed, would provide him with all the funds he would need in that expensive city. A variety of beribboned gift boxes, which contained presents for the Thorpes, made their appearance, an assortment of trunks and cases came down from the attic, and it seemed to Charles that every garment he owned was inspected before the best of the sorry lot was packed.

Except for the all-important riding gear, he hadn't had any new clothes in seven years, and while he could take Guy and Andre's scathing remarks about their condition, the remarks by his valet left him both hurt and angry. Louis had been his father's valet, and when Adrian de Renille died in December 1901, the old man had been lost without a male member of the family to tend to since his own son, Martin, looked after Guy. It wasn't until two months later, when Charles—then little more than a helpless vegetable—had been brought home from the seminary, that Louis, who looked upon retirement from his position with fear and loathing, was once again of service. He had as much pride as the men he served, and he didn't hesitate to speak his mind when he thought the family's good name was in danger.

"You are shaming us, Monsieur Charles, with the clothes you are taking," he protested as he packed.

"What the others on board ship—not to mention the Thorpes in New York—will say when they see you so poorly attired, I shudder to think about. And the servants! Those who serve on the *Transat* love nothing better than a chance to gossip about passengers who do not keep up the standards of the aristocracy. And for Lord Thorpe's valet, who will no doubt be attending you in New York—" The old man's bright blue eyes rolled heavenward. "Hodges is a worthy man, Monsieur Charles, I give him that, but he is a wily one, too, and when he sees that the garments on your back do not fit, and those he is unpacking are no more suitable, he will—"

"Enough, Louis. *Arretes!* Hodges will say nothing." Charles' voice was unnecessarily sharp. "The English servants—unlike some others—are trained not to notice or make a fuss," he said with a significant look. "And the wardrobe of a Jesuit seminarian does not include Savile Row suits."

"But you do not wear the noive's soutane now," the valet pointed out. "You are once again a private gentleman, and your clothes should reflect that."

"The Thorpes—and everyone else—will have to accept me as I appear."

"Which will not be to your best advantage," he sniffed. "These daytime suits are barely passable, yes, but as to your evening clothes—" Louis gestured at him with the wooden hanger he held. "I remember when *Monsieur le Comte* took you to Poole's for your dinner jacket and dress suit—you were at Oxford then, and *that* was ten years ago!"

There were a variety of responses on Charles' tongue, none of them very polite, but he restrained himself. *How ungrateful have I become that I would shout back at a harmless old man who has nothing but my best interests at heart?* he asked himself as Louis rambled on

97

indignantly as he filled the open trunk and suitcases around the room.

This time tomorrow, I'll be on board ship, he said silently, shifting his position in the armchair so he could look out the window at the barren, frozen garden, instead of at Louis toiling for him. The old, valued and trusted servant had done so much for him over the past two years that Charles was ashamed of himself for his behavior as he recalled how indispensible Louis had been in those first weeks after he'd been brought home. It had been Louis who had sat beside his bed night after night so that the English nurses who had been hired to tend him could get some much-needed sleep before resuming their duties in the morning. It had been Louis who cut up his food and fed him like a helpless child when his hands had been too weak to hold a fork or spoon. More importantly, it had been Louis who had bathed and dressed him and, finally, when the hair on his shaved head had grown back, it was Louis who trimmed the newly grown hair so that once again Charles looked like a normal human being instead of a circus freak.

"Don't upset yourself too much over me, Louis," he told the older man as he rose and came over to him, putting a conciliatory hand on his shoulder. "It will all work out, and I promise to write and tell you all the details."

"But your clothes—"

"Will have to do," he interjected gently. "It would be a waste of good money to have clothes made for a former Jesuit seminarian who has nowhere to go. The only new things I've needed were riding clothes," he pointed out with a sudden smile that lightened his usually grave features, "and they are so new that, however else I look at other times, you can rest assured that when I go riding in New York, I shall be the best turned-out equestrian in Central Park!"

*   *   *

If nothing else, his encounter with Louis finally managed to reduce some of the hostility he felt toward his family. For the remaining twenty-four hours before leaving for Le Havre, he was not only able to put on a good face, but began to formulate a plan for when he returned to France.

He was going with only the greatest of reluctance, but he had succeeded in overcoming the idea that he was being exiled. He'd stick it out until Easter, Charles decided. Dispensed once again from the usual Lenten penitence because of his health, he now regarded his upcoming voyage, and his stay in New York, as his sacrifice. But as soon after Easter Monday as possible, he'd catch the first boat back to France, buy a small house somewhere, and settle down with his books for life.

He didn't tell any of this to his mother and brothers, of course. He could easily imagine Guy's and Andre's reaction to the announcement that he intended to move to another part of France. As for his mother . . . To be sure, Solange de Renille made no bones about wanting to see him married. He could hear her voice in his dreams. He had been released from his vows, and he was fully recovered. At twenty-nine, she told him, it was time he picked up the pieces of his life.

But, no matter how well he kept his true feelings under wraps, or whatever tentative plans for the future he was now exploring, the next day, which began with the carriage ride in the frigid, gray pre-dawn Norman mist, that took them to the train at Lisieux, was hard on all of them.

Not until months later, when he had finally put enough time between himself and that day, would he be able to wonder about which event had been the worst. But until then, the entire day—from saying farewell to the servants, who had lined up at the front door to wish him bon voyage, to the train trip across the Normandy countryside—remained a blur in his mind. But, funnily enough, every detail of what took place from the moment the train pulled into Le Havre, was crystal-clear.

Possibly, it was the arrival at Le Havre itself that brought him out of his lethargic, dreamlike state, and made him realize that he was no longer going to have the loving buffer of his family to protect him. His life would, once again, be up to him.

The original harbor of Le Havre had been built under the direction of Francois I. And, although it was primarily a fishing village, in 1904 it was also the home port of the *Compagnie Generale Transatlantique*. But whatever great status that honor conferred upon it, the middle of February at the mouth of the Seine is no time to linger on the dock. The de Renilles hastily boarded the crown jewel of the Transat's fleet—the elegant *La Savoie*.

"Now this *is* a nice cabin," Solange remarked as she removed her sable cloak. "I think you should have a pleasant crossing here."

"I'm sure I shall, *Maman*," Charles replied a little stiffly as he looked around the handsomely furnished stateroom with adjoining bathroom. "And I'm glad to see there's a writing table. I promise you a long shipboard letter. Where is the rest of our family?"

"Oh, they said something about having to see the purser," Solange replied evasively as she moved gracefully around the room, making sure all was in order. "They should be here momentarily. Did I tell you Louis had a long conversation with me last night regarding your clothes?"

"He thinks I'm about to tarnish our family honor."

Solange's eyes swept knowingly over her son, taking in the dark suit that had originally come from Kilgour, but now no longer fit him. The same could be said of his fine white shirt from Turnbull and Asser. And, although his tie was new, the black cashmere topcoat tossed on a nearby chair could no longer be considered warm enough to keep out the cold weather.

"So he told me," she said, amused. "But I told him that as long as you didn't actually reek of mothballs, you'd be fine until . . . ah, here you are. Charles and I were beginning to think you'd all jumped overboard—"

Whatever Solange meant to say was lost with the arrival of Guy, Pauline, Andre and Janine, accompanied by two stewards and a stewardess, carrying champagne, trays of sandwiches and boxes of bon voyage presents.

During the next half-hour, the stiffness that had enveloped the family over the earlier part of the day gradually disappeared in the conviviality of vintage champagne, sandwiches of *paté* and smoked salmon and brotherly advice.

"Marcel and Marie are your steward and stewardess. They took care of Janine and me when we went over for Maurice's wedding," Andre informed him, referring to their cousin Maurice de Hautraviant, who was connected to the French Embassy in Ottawa. The superb young diplomat had been married in November, and Andre and Janine had represented the de Renilles, travelling with the rest of the wedding party to New York on the *La Savoie,* and continuing the journey to Ontario province from there.

"If you have any problems or questions, the purser is the one to see. There's very little that he can't handle," Guy remarked easily. "Now remember, you don't dress for dinner tonight, or Sunday night, or the last night out, but you will for every other evening including tomorrow, Lent or no Lent, and the Captain's Dinner is full dress. And since that's settled . . . open your presents."

They were really typical bon voyage gifts, he reflected silently as he opened them. A pair of Cartier cuff links

101

from his mother; a selection of new American books ordered from Brentano's by Guy; a black calf Hermes billfold filled with crisp American bank notes from Andre; the latest model Kodak box camera and film from Pauline and Janine; and a huge box of Debauve & Gallais chocolates packed in a cream-colored box decorated with the fleur-de-lis completed his bounty. Charles looked from one member of his family to the next, his eyes stinging.

There was Guy, who combined his love of their land and horses with an acute awareness of modern technology. Bold and dashing at thirty-three, he was the perfect Comte de Renille for the new century. It was Guy who had passed the long winter evenings of 1902 sitting by his bed, reading aloud to him. It was Guy who helped him up and down the stairs when he'd first become ambulatory again; who played tennis with him, taught him to drive a motor car; bullied and comforted him in equally generous doses when he felt he needed it, and, most importantly, had led him out to the stables on a frigid December morning fourteen months earlier and watched carefully as he began to ride again for the first time in seven years.

His gaze slowly shifted to Andre, no less important to his recovery because he and his wife lived in Paris. It was thirty-one-year-old Andre who sent him books, humorous letters and introduced him to the great American invention—the safety razor. On his monthly visits home, they played endless games of chess together, and Andre taught him every new variation in the game of bridge. And it had been Andre, holding a handful of new Charvet ties, who had strode into his bedroom one morning as Louis had been dressing him, pulled off the tie his valet had carefully adjusted, turned him in front of the mirror and, after selecting one of the new ties, proceeded to stand behind him and teach him once again how to knot his tie.

His sisters-in-law were equally dear to him. Pauline, at twenty-four, and Janine at twenty-two—both blonde, beautiful and intelligent—had seen to it that he kept his share of the social graces. Toward that end, they had had the servants roll back the carpet in the music room, wound up the gramophone, and endlessly instructed him in all the latest dance steps.

And then there was his mother. What he owed to her—and quite possibly it was his life—he could never put into words, much less say out loud. His anger at the high-handed way she had taken it upon herself to arrange—for at least the next six weeks—the way he lived his life, had nothing whatsoever to do with the unqualified love and respect he had for her, and no matter what the cost to his own pride, he had to tell her that now . . .

But Charles had run out of time. Just as he had made up his mind to speak, the page boys of the French Line— the *mousses* in their multi-buttoned uniforms—began to move through the corridors, sounding the musical chimes that were the Line's warning signal.

"All ashore that's going ashore. All ashore that's going ashore." The old cry, issued in both French and English, reverberated through the corridors and into the cabins, and the de Renilles began to gather up their wraps in preparation for going out on deck.

"We expect you to put that camera to good use," Janine laughingly warned him as Andre settled her mink cloak around her shoulders. "Andre and I are expecting to see photographs."

"And letters—good long ones about everything you see and do," Pauline added.

"But first you had better remember that no de Renille

103

has the reputation of being *un figaro* on this or any other lines," Andre warned him, using the *Transat*'s catchphrase for poor tippers.

After a final embrace, Andre, Janine and Pauline stepped over the threshold into the crowded corridor, and Charles turned to embrace his mother.

"I love you, *Maman*, and I'll try to have the kind of holiday you want me to," he whispered in her ear. "And I promise to come back with lots of adventures to tell you about."

Solange hugged her son wordlessly, for one of the few times in her life with no ready words. She knew Charles despised the idea of travelling, of having to expose himself to people who would greet him with a smile and then gossip viciously about him behind his back. There was no way to spare him from that possibility, Solange admitted as she kissed him and smoothed his hair. One could only hope and pray that the people she was sending him to would provide an atmosphere where such fears would remain unfounded.

It was Guy who moved to restore the humor of the situation. He wrapped his brother in an embrace as soon as Solange released him. "Here," he said a minute later, handing him a thick sheaf of American bills, "walking around money. And remember, in New York, if you tip the customs inspector, they'll put you in jail, and if you don't tip the longshoremen, they'll throw your luggage in the river. Which," he added disparagingly as they filed into the corridor crowded with passengers, visitors, officers and crew, "judging by the clothes you're taking, might not be such a terrible thing!"

By the time they were all together again in the embarkation hall, there was only time for one last round of embraces and kisses before they stepped out into the cold February wind.

From his place on deck, Charles watched his family make their way down the gangplank. This wasn't a gala summer sailing with a band playing and passengers and visitors happily shouting to each other as they waited for the ship to pull away from the dock. It was the dead of winter. The passengers and crew faced not only the channel crossing, but winter North Atlantic where the ship sits at its lowest point in the water, and dangerous storms are no longer a faint threat but a real occurrence. The preparations to get under way were both automatic and unemotional.

It seemed to Charles that it took only a minute for the gangplank to be lowered away and removed before the shouted cries of *bon voyage* that came from the dock were drowned out by the continuous blasts from the ship's whistle as the engines throbbed and the vessel began its slow, inexorable move away from the dock.

He stayed on deck as the *La Savoie* pulled away from Havre's docks, through the Avant Port, and into the English Channel toward Plymouth, its British port of call. His smiling, waving family had long since grown small in his sight, turned into specks, and, finally, vanished entirely. He walked the length of the five hundred and eighty-foot-long deck to the stern, waiting until the last sight of France had disappeared. Chilled to the bone, he turned and reentered the warm, secure confines of the ship and found his way back to his cabin where Marcel was busy unpacking the clothes he'd need for the next week, and eager to consult him as to which suit and tie he'd wear at dinner, and what time he'd want *cafe complet* the next morning.

Whatever else this voyage and his subsequent stay in New York would hold for him, the one thing Charles realized he could depend on was the service and total efficiency of the *Compagnie Generale Transatlantique*. He might be utterly alone and answerable to himself for the first time in years, but the buffer system that would cushion him crossing from the old to the new world wa already working as effortlessly as the ship's two four cylinder engines.

Certain questions were already floating through hi mind. But, as the gray, damp afternoon turned into an even darker night, he squashed them before they could form. It was one thing to be Charles de Renille, the proud possessor of an old and honorable name, who could accept his seat at the captain's table with the same automatic equanimity that he expected to put to good use over the next weeks, but it was quite another to wonder i the *La Savoie* was the bridge leading him away from hi old life and bringing him to a new one.

Information Slip of Landing Passengers

To be returned to the Purser

The following information is needed for the United States Customs House Manifest, as required by the Act of August 2, 1882, and the Regulations of the Secretary of the Treasury

Steamer: La Savoie
No. of steamer ticket: 96491
Embarked at: Le Havre
Passenger's Christian Name: Charles
Passenger's Surname: de Renille
Age: (years) 29   Profession: teacher
Final Destination: New York
Nativity (Country and Province): France
                                 Normandy
The country of which you are a citizen: France

106

Mail Address in America: 1 West 72nd Street
New York, N.Y.
in care of Thorpe

Number of Pieces of Baggage

1 Trunks	Baskets
Boxes	Satchels
2 Bags	Bicycles

Charles put down the gold fountain pen that had belonged to his father and reviewed the form he had just filled out. He'd hesitated a long time before listing his profession as teacher, but he really didn't have too many alternatives. "Former Jesuit seminarian" would have been the right answer, but he had no intention of having to discuss the past seven years of his life with perfect strangers, even if they were immigration officials. For a minute, he'd amused himself with the idea of putting down that he had no profession, imagining what his mother would say if he were denied entry to America on the basis of being an undesirable alien. Of course, he could always do what a friend of his family's had, and simply write aristocrat—technically, it was true enough. He certainly wasn't a student, horse-breeder wasn't correct, so he'd finally put down "teacher," remembering the four months he'd taught at St. Michel's in Brussels before his final deterioration and ultimate collapse . . .

A quick rapping on the door abruptly ended his reverie, and he quickly shook off the memories that were enveloping him. *"Entrez,"* he called out, and watched as Marcel entered, carrying a silver tray with his afternoon tea.

"If you have finished your form, Monsieur, I will bring it to the purser and collect your landing slip," he said, placing the tray on the writing desk. "It is best to be prepared in advance for tomorrow."

"You'll have to tell me the procedure—no, leave the tea for the moment—I want to know the details. Is it very difficult?"

The steward's old face regarded him wisely. "For those we carry in steerage and leave at Ellis Island, sometimes it is very hard, Monsieur. But for you—no, not at all. You will present the landing chit to one of the customs men. He will ask you a few questions that are of no particular consequence, and you will be free to leave the ship." Marcel permitted himself a small smile. "Please do not concern yourself, Monsieur. After all, entering the port of New York is hardly the same thing as preparing for holy orders!"

He couldn't know, Charles reassured himself as Marcel departed a moment later, carrying his information form. He merely saw it as a good comparison. And you have to admit it's a very apt one, he told himself, recalling his first days at the seminary which he and his comrades had spent in seclusion from the rest of the community as they were indoctrinated into the rules that would govern them. Odd to recall that his probationary period had lasted exactly as long as this passage. Except that tomorrow, instead of beginning the rigorous examination of his conscience, he would descend the gangplank to the docks of New York.

This was his first transatlantic voyage and, if he were the type susceptible to *mal de mer*, it might well have been his last, he observed as he drank his tea and ate a chicken sandwich, eyeing the pretty pink and white pastries in their frilled paper cups that awaited him on another plate. February was the worst month for an ocean crossing, and a good number of his shipmates had disappeared from the dining room on the first night out and had yet to reappear from their cabins. But whether e could credit his family stamina, his tough British ducation, his rigorous Jesuit training, or possibly a ombination of all three, he hadn't had a moment's ueasiness or missed a meal.

From *café au lait* and croissants at eight, to bouillon at leven, to lunch at one, to tea at four and dinner at seven, harles ate the specialties of the day (except for red ieat) and suffered no ill effects afterwards. Wisely, no ne had told him about the dire circumstances that ometimes surround a winter crossing, and he'd adjusted asily to the roll and pitch of the ship and the constant hrob of the engines.

Unfortunately, it was not only a stormy passage but, as ften happens in the dead of winter, a dull one as well. harles, who knew his mother entertained the hope that e might find a shipboard flirtation, wondered what the omtesse would make of his companions who seemed to e culled mainly from the business communities of Paris, ondon and New York. It seemed to him that the worst ours of each day were the ones spent after dinner in the rand saloon while the dance band played for the few ouples who were deft enough to navigate the floor, and onversation centered mainly around the weather.

All in all, it hadn't been a bad crossing, Charles decided s he finished the last pastry. It was ridiculous to have een so afraid of it and the people he would meet. It had een a paper tiger, and his real test was still waiting for im tomorrow afternoon.

It wasn't the idea of New York—that unknown, nenacing city—that filled him with apprehension, or ven seeing Alix again, but when he thought about Henry Thorpe, he cringed with the memory of their last onversation together.

It hadn't been their last meeting—that had been a year nd a half earlier when the Thorpes had been spending heir honeymoon at the de Renille *haras*, and he had come across them relaxing in the garden following his mother's *fete champetre. That* encounter hadn't gone particularly well—but it was the memory of the last time they'd spoken together which bothered him and, eight years later, he could still recall every detail.

It had been Paris in the summer of 1896 and, although it would be another year before Charles went to the Jesuits, he was already aware of the few alternatives left to the youngest son of an aristocratic family. He decided to try his hand at evangelizing on Henry Thorpe, not yet Lord Thorpe, and a year away from his first being mentioned on Queen Victoria's Honors List.

Henry Thorpe was then in his early thirties but somehow, he seemed much older—and almost bloodless. He was an old and cherished friend of the family, and whenever he stayed with the de Renilles, either in Normandy or the Avenue Dubois house in Paris, he was endlessly introduced to beautiful and available women. For Henry Thorpe was that rarest of all creatures—a very rich and highly presentable bachelor. He went to dinners, receptions, garden parties and balls; he met all the ladies he was supposed to, charmed them all—and never proposed.

"Face facts, Solange," his father had once said laughingly. "Henry Thorpe is a total and confirmed bachelor. And why should an art historian and collector of his merit want to marry? All he'd acquire is a wife who'd want to rearrange his paintings, and children who will destroy a placid existence."

"No, Adrian, you are missing the point entirely," had been his mother's reply. "His type marry—they almost always do—and generally in a very spectacular manner. You'll see."

Comte Adrian de Renille did not live to see that once again his wife had been right when it came to the mating and matrimony habits of their friends, but reflecting on it, Charles knew his father would have rejoiced as much as his mother had at their friend's marriage, particularly since the bride had been Alix Turner of New York, the daughter of one of Solange's dearest friends.

But that happy event was six years in the future when the two men had taken a long Sunday walk through Paris following mass at the Madeleine. Henry Thorpe had patiently listened to Charles de Renille try to convert him before letting him know, in no uncertain terms, what he thought of such goings-on.

"But you're so at home in our Church, I thought you would see the next step clearly enough," Charles stammered, totally taken aback at his rejection.

"I like to think I'm equally at home in Catholic churches, synagogues, Quaker meeting houses, Presbyterian chapels, Shinto shrines, and Buddhist temples. It's all part of trying to be a decent human being. I was raised to abhor prejudice of any kind, but I was born to the Church of England, and that's final!"

It was then he should have realized that, for all his scholarly attributes, he would never be a Jesuit causist, Charles acknowledged wryly as he went about the business of doing some preliminary packing.

Whether or not Henry Thorpe retained any memory of that conversation, he'd find out soon enough. But, by the time the *La Savoie* passed the Nantucket lightship in the early morning hours of the following day, Charles became so caught up in the events that marked his final hours at sea that his trepidation receded.

With one hundred and ninety stokers to keep the coal moving from its fifty storage bins into the eighteen boilers, the *La Savoie* kept to its normal speed of twenty knots through the rampages of the winter storms, and when she passed Sandy Hook and entered the Lower Bay of New York, the flagship of the *Compagnie Generale Transatlantique* was right on schedule.

Charles had gone out on deck as soon as he'd eaten breakfast. It was a bitterly cold morning with only a faint February sun filtering through, but he couldn't stand the inaction that shipboard life had imposed on him for the past week for a minute longer. And, reluctant as he was to admit it, he was curious about his first sight of America.

Neither Staten Island nor Brooklyn looked particularly imposing, he decided as they continued on through the Narrows, and he returned to the warm public rooms for lunch. This would be the most boring part of the day, some of his more seasoned fellow passengers informed him. During this time they would have a stop at the Upper Quarantine Station where the vessel would have to be cleared by the representatives of the Board of Health, and it was there that the Customs House inspectors who conducted the preliminary interviews would come on board.

Sure enough, during the meal, the steadily throbbing engines that he'd grown accustomed to, halted. When they began again, he returned to the deck for the advance up New York Harbor and his first sight of the Statue of Liberty, holding her torch aloft as she stood on her granite pedestal and welcomed all comers to America.

She was France's gift to the United States, commemorating the Centennial of 1876 and, designed by Auguste Bartholdi, she was put in her place of honor in 1886. Charles knew all of this, but nothing had prepared him for her stately magnificence. From the moment she glided into his field of vision, nothing short of a sudden typhoon could have persuaded him to leave the deck.

"Did I really convince myself I was so *blasé* that all of this would mean nothing to me?" he asked himself as the *La Savoie* passed Bedloe's Island and made the customary halt at Ellis Island. As a first-class passenger, the indignities and terror of the mass-immigration station did not apply to him. But, whether he was ready to accept

112

it or not, from the moment he saw the Statue of Liberty, he was really no different from the nearly four hundred men, women, and children who had made their crossing in steerage.

Equally enthralling to him was the spectacle of the skyline of New York Harbor. His Baedeker had informed him that the tall buildings which crowded lower Manhattan were known as skyscrapers. And, at his first sight of the Florentine-style tower of the Produce Exchange, the twenty-three-story American Surety Building, the twenty stories of 42 Broadway, the gilded dome of the *New York World*, and the rest of the many-storied structures which New Yorkers were rapidly learning to take for granted, Charles felt both an interest and a curiosity spark in him—two feelings with which he had long been out of touch.

The *La Savoie*'s actual docking was still a distant objective, and Charles finally tore himself away from the skyline to return to his cabin, wait out the last few hours and take care of the last details connected with his voyage.

Charles knew next to nothing about American money and, equally as bad, he hadn't handled any money—either French or British—since September 1897. From his more knowledgeable fellow-passengers he'd gleaned the information that the dining-room and smoking-room attendants—who rarely left the ship during the New York turnaround—preferred their tips in francs, while the cabin personnel—who got leave while in the city—were appreciative of dollars. The purser's office had told him the amounts that were generally correct, but with the memory of Andre's admonition about not disgracing the family name by bestowing poor tips, Charles added a few more bills to each envelope.

The wait seemed endless—and then it was over.

The tugboats had nudged the *La Savoie* into her New

York home and, even before the engines were turned off, Marcel appeared at his cabin door with the news that it was precisely the right moment to proceed to the first customs inquiry.

Charles bid farewell to Marcel, pressed an envelope into his hand and, with his topcoat over his arm, arrived in the Grand Saloon to find it had been transformed into a preliminary debarkation hall with three men from the United States Customs Office, each sitting behind a table piled high with printed forms, ready to process the passengers. By tradition, first-class passengers were interviewed first and, thanks to Marcel's warning, Charles de Renille was third in line to take his place in front of one of the tables, hand over his landing ticket, and state his name.

A middle-aged man placed a check mark next to his name and looked up to observe him carefully. "How long will you be staying in America, Mr. de Renille?" he questioned in a voice which told Charles that the inspector anticipated asking it many times that day.

"I'm planning on the next six weeks."

"I see. And you'll be staying where—?"

"With friends—at One West Seventy-second Street."

He nodded and made a few notations on the form in front of him. "Tell me, Mr. de Renille, what is your profession?"

"I . . . I teach—and write," Charles got out, a sense of uneasiness falling over him. He didn't care what this inspector thought of him, he hadn't even wanted to make this blasted journey in the first place, he fumed silently. So why was it suddenly so important that he successfully get off the ship?

"Do you teach in France?"

"No, in Brussels, at le College Saint Michel," he said, hoping the man had no idea that that strict and exclusive boys' school was run by the Jesuits. "I taught English."

114

"Did you now? Well, you *do* sound a little British to me. What did you write?"

"A biography of Saint Vincent de Paul."

He muttered a comment Charles didn't quite catch, and proceeded to question him about his luggage. "Sign here," he instructed a minute later, pushing the form at him and holding out a pen.

Thoroughly puzzled, Charles signed his name. "What do I do now?"

"Well, you take this form and your baggage-entry check, go down the gangplank, find yourself a customs inspector, and locate your luggage—welcome to New York, Mr. de Renille. Next, please!"

Of all the horrors New York City can offer the unwary and unsuspecting visitor in winter, none can be quite so bad as those first minutes spent on the unheated, shed-like dock with the February wind whistling through, and as Charles made his way down the open gangplank, he began to wonder why he'd been so eager to leave the warm, secure confines of the ship. The customs officer might have been a dolt, asking him questions already supplied on the form, but at least he hadn't forced him to open his luggage and have the contents examined.

Suddenly, the sympathetic *bon debarquement* that the master-at-arms had quietly wished him as he left the embarkation hall for the gangplank took on an ominous meaning as his feet touched solid ground for the first time in a week and he surveyed the horror scene that occurs on a freezing cold day when there are over five-hundred first-and-second-class passengers debarking, all of them wanting one of the too-few customs inspectors without delay.

For a countless minute, Charles stood rooted to the spot, looking at the long length of the pier where letters hanging from the ceiling swung in the wind and carts of

115

luggage were pushed by disreputable-looking men, and sour-visaged inspectors were appropriated by his fellow-passengers who were now coming onto Pier 42 in a steady stream.

Facing this thoroughly unexpected, utterly confused scene, Charles de Renille promptly forgot every instruction he'd received regarding this day—along with most of his Oxford-accented English. How did one snare a customs inspector? Where was his luggage? Was he supposed to be met, or had it been arranged that he would make his own way up to . . . to . . . *Mon Dieu*, where did Henry and Alix live? Some oddly named block of flats . . .

"Charles."

The sound of his name being called in a calm, level voice penetrated the din around him, and he whirled around to find Henry Thorpe standing three feet from him at the foot of the gangplank.

With something of a shock, Charles realized that he'd walked right past his friend. But then, *this* Henry Thorpe looked nothing like the perennially detached, largely unemotional man he'd always known. True, he'd seen him for a few minutes a year and a half earlier. But, caught in the first throes of his long recovery, Charles couldn't remember the incident very clearly, except for the fact that it had been one of his more bitter and self-reproachful days, and any memory of how Henry Thorpe had appeared had either long since vanished, or had never registered in the first place. Now he was left silently staring at the tall, slender man wearing an impeccably cut black wool melton topcoat with a cashmere muffler tucked in at his neck. His hat was tilted on his dark head at precisely the right angle to suggest the sensible, dashing man of the world he was. The handsome mahogany walking stick was planted firmly on the pier's floorboards and his hands, in expensive black leather gloves, were neatly folded over the stick's gold head. He radiated an air of total health and self-confidence—as well as giving the appearance of being able to rise above the cold and confusion on the dock.

"Henry, forgive me, I didn't see you," Charles said as Henry Thorpe closed the space between them to grasp his hand. "I wasn't expecting anything quite like this—"

"It can be quite a shock," Henry agreed with a smile. "It's good to see you again, Charles."

In spite of the cold, Charles felt his face grow warm. "After our last two meetings—"

"Water under the bridge. Now, let's see about rounding up a customs inspector to check over your baggage."

"I didn't bring much."

"Good—the less time we'll have to spend here. I swore to Alix that I'd bring you back to the Dakota in plenty of time to enjoy tea. Now where—" As he spoke, Henry Thorpe placed one hand on Charles' shoulder and motioned with his walking stick toward a walrus-moustached man in a gold-braided customs inspector's uniform. "Mr. Cullen!"

At the sound of Henry's voice the inspector, who'd been busy reading the riot act to two tough-looking longshoremen, cut short his conversation. "Yer lordship; and there be your friend! I was beginning to think he hadn't made the trip." With a smile, he took Charles' entry papers. "De Renille. That'll be R. Come along, and we'll have you out of here in no time flat."

"How have you been, Mr. Cullen?"

"In the pink, yer lordship. Oh, I have to tell you this. Yesterday was my day off, and I took the missus over to Knoedler's to show her that new painting you and her ladyship purchased," Mr. Cullen said as the three men walked the length of the pier toward their destination.

"Did you enjoy seeing it again?"

"Ah, that I did. Prettier than the day last month when

117

I cleared it. Liked the frame, too—tasteful, that's what the missus said. All those water lilies made us think of summer."

"Mr. Cullen—and a few of his associates—cleared Alix and me through customs the day we arrived in New York, and last month a painting we'd purchased from Claude Monet arrived," Henry explained as they reached the appropriate section. Charles unlocked his trunk and suitcases. "It's one of the new lily pad series, and Mr. Cullen was kind enough to admire it."

"That took no effort at all," the inspector chimed in admiringly.

"Knoedler's did the frame, and since we haven't room for it just now, they have it on informal exhibition until we're ready to take possession."

"No room for a painting? I thought you and Alix had twenty rooms in your block of flats."

"It's called an apartment building," Henry corrected gently. "And, no, we haven't moved yet. We've had quite a bit of renovation done, and the painters, plasterers and plumbers are still working on it." Henry Thorpe gave an understanding shrug. "In New York, when you move, it's almost never on time. Find any contraband yet, Mr. Cullen?"

"Not with any friend of yours, yer lordship. I'll stake a year's wages on it," Mr. Cullen replied, snapping shut and relocking Charles' luggage and handing him the keys. "Have a nice time in New York, Mr. de Renille, and all the best on your move, Lord Thorpe."

There was a quick round of handshakes, and two longshoremen arrived for the luggage.

It had snowed heavily in New York four days earlier, and the accumulation around the passenger terminal was primarily ugly black ice and slush as Henry Thorpe and Charles de Renille reached the doors of Pier 42 that led to Morton Street. On the best of days, it was not an inviting area, and on this murky afternoon no back alley in Marseilles could have looked less inviting.

"Which is your carriage?" Charles asked as he turned up the collar of his topcoat.

"Does that look like a carriage?" Henry smiled as he motioned. Charles beheld the largest and most luxurious motor car he'd ever seen outside of a newspaper or magazine photo. Proud and gleaming, it stood aloof from the other more mundane-looking autos and out-dated horse-drawn vehicles, much the way its owner stood apart from the rush and confusion on the pier.

"It's a Packard Model L," Henry told him. "The latest one on the market. And this is Pearce, our chauffeur," he added. "Pearce, this is Mr. de Renille."

"Pleased to meet you, sir." The gaunt-faced man in the gray whipcord uniform politely touched his cap and began to instruct the longshoremen in the disposition of Charles' baggage into the Packard's luggage hold.

As they worked, Charles reached for his billfold, but before he could withdraw it, Henry was handing crisp bills to the men as they finished.

"Henri, ce n'est pas necessaire," he protested.

"Think nothing of it," Henry replied as they settled into the Packard's burgundy leather tonneau and adjusted the fur-lined lap robe. "You're not quite used to American money yet, and I thought I'd save you a few problems. Also, Charles," he went on pleasantly, "I think the next weeks will be far easier for you if you speak English. Don't worry, though. Everyone in New York has *some* sort of accent," he added with a mixture of humor and comfort as Pearce guided the automobile away from Pier 42.

As they moved along Morton Street, Charles looked around him in disbelief and growing panic. Had the shining towers which enchanted him only a few hours earlier been only a mirage? All he saw now were delapidated warehouses and tough-looking people crowding the sidewalks. There had been some terrible mistake. This *couldn't* be the greatest city in America!

Just as he was about to voice his doubts to Henry, Pearce reached the end of Morton Street where it joined West Fourth Street, and turned up Sixth Avenue. Suddenly they were covered by a canopy of black iron, and whatever Charles meant to say was lost in the screeching din overhead.

"It's the Sixth Avenue Elevated," Henry said as the noise subsided. "Makes the worst racket, but it's one of the fastest ways to get around this city."

Charles looked around him. Both sides of Sixth Avenue were lined with tenement buildings—flats where the poor and disadvantaged of the city lived. It was dark and ugly and huge cinders floated down from the tracks above, melting into the slush of the street below.

"How do they stand it? All day and all night—"

"The Elevated Lines shut down at midnight."

"Lines! You mean there are more than one?"

Henry laughed. "Five, in fact. And they're busy building an underground system that should begin to be operational around the end of this year. Don't look so stricken. One gets used to it—in time. We're coming up to Tenth Street now, and I think you'll find the rest of our ride a fine introduction to New York," he added as Pearce made a right-hand turn, and Charles felt his shock recede.

Left behind were the frozen docks, rundown warehouses, dark tenements and rattling Elevated. Instead, they were passing a series of handsome private houses that lined both sides of the street and seemed to stretch ahead in peaceful, prosperous, well-ordered rows.

"Our first point of interest—Thirty-four and Thirty-six West Tenth Street," Henry told him, pointing out two identical rose-brick houses set well back from the street and built in the restrained classical-Federalist style. "Number thirty-six is where Alix was born and lived the first twelve years of her life. Number thirty-four is owned by Percy Lasky, the theatrical producer. When Alix and her parents moved to Sixty-second Street, he bought their house and converted it into a double townhouse. They're giving a party a week from this coming Sunday night," he continued casually, "and the invitation includes you."

Charles felt an arrow of dread hit him. "I . . . I couldn't possibly interfere in your social life."

"Don't be a silly ass, it's all arranged. Alix and I were discussing it this morning—you've arrived in New York at precisely the right time. My ward, Rupert Randall, who lives with our next-door neighbors, is down with a serious attack of influenza. He gave us all a rather bad fright when he collapsed, but the worst is apparently over, even though it looks like a long convalescence, and—"

"I'll be glad to be of whatever help I can be there," Charles put in, eager to be of some sort of service. "I remember how awful it was to have to lie in bed all the time and stare at the ceiling. I can read to Rupert, or we can visit together—"

Much to his discomfiture, Henry began to laugh. "As far as Rupert's concerned, you're the wrong sex to be planning any bedside visits! No, what I was referring to was that you could fill in for him at the parties he won't be able to attend."

Panic welled in him. "Henry, it's been years . . . I'm not sure . . ."

"Oh, you'll get used to it again," came the off-handed reply, "and it's not that many invitations. Rupert's a sophomore at Columbia with a very heavy load of classes, so his social life is rather restricted. At any rate, we're having a small dinner party tonight. It'll be a good opportunity for you to get used to being invited out

121

again," Henry added in a voice, friendly as it was, that allowed no refusal.

Charles tried to relax against the glove-soft leather upholstery. Like it or not, it appeared he was going to be putting both his dinner jacket and dress suit to use. Just as he was wondering what on earth a sophomore was, the automobile reached the corner, and Pearce guided it in a smart left-hand turn.

"This is Fifth Avenue, and if you turn around, you can see the Washington Square Arch," Henry informed him and, obligingly, Charles craned his neck to get a view of Stanford White's Centennial Memorial Arch that graced the southern end of Washington Square Park.

"Do you dance?" Henry asked unexpectedly.

"What—? Yes, all the latest steps, too. I won't disgrace myself if I have to go to a ball."

"It's not a ball, it's Mr. and Mrs. Clifford Seligman's dinner dance two weeks from Saturday. I was at a meeting of the Board of Directors of the New York Historical Society this afternoon. The women's committee was meeting at the same time and, as I was leaving, Julie Seligman cornered me on the stairs," Henry recounted with a smile. "She heard, via her mother-in-law, that you were arriving today, and after asking me several pertinent questions about you, said she'd put an invitation for you in the mail."

"What sort of questions?" Charles asked, suspicions flaring.

"Just the usual things—how tall you are, if you're a good dancer." Henry shot him an amused glance. "Frankly, Julie had me pinned under the portrait of a Colonial governor of New York who had an unfortunate tendency to transvestism, and having a conversation underneath the portrait of a man wearing a ballgown is not my idea of a place to hold a social talk—or any other for that matter."

122

If the thought of once again having social obligations to fulfill made him uncomfortable, at least Fifth Avenue was living up to its reputation as the finest thoroughfare in America, Charles thought. *This* was the New York he'd read about and expected to see, and he began to feel more at ease as the Packard progressed north, with Henry Thorpe pointing out places of interest.

Here there were no dray wagons pulling freight. Only fine carriages, hansom cabs, shiny motor cars, and the best equipment of the city's mass transportation division moving north and south along the avenue.

He had already glimpsed the Episcopalian Church of the Ascension on Tenth Street; the brownstone square-towered First Presbyterian Church of Twelfth Street; and the Fuller Building, better known as the Flatiron Building because of its odd, triangular-shaped architecture that often caused the wind during storms to reach intensities high enough to rattle the plate glass windows and push pedestrians off the sidewalk. "It was designed by a Chicago firm who probably wanted to export some of the discomfort they have to suffer from the winds off Lake Michigan," Henry explained to Charles, who merely nodded in agreement, not quite understanding all the information that was being passed on to him.

For his part, Henry Thorpe was rather enjoying his new role as tour guide. He was well aware that most of the information he was imparting was making no impression whatsoever on Charles—at least for the time being. Still and all, it was the best way to introduce him to the city. Either he would retain some memory of it and learn to get about on his own, or else . . . Well, better not think about *that*.

"Did you have a good crossing?" Henry asked as they moved up through the Twenties, past the Marble Collegiate Church. "I know I should have asked you that on the pier—it seems to be the traditional question—but you looked rather as if you were developing *mal de mer* in reverse."

"Land-sick instead of sea-sick?"

"It's not unusual, after you've had a bad crossing, to be adversely affected by the solidness of land."

"I never thought of it like that—and the crossing *was* rough. There were storms straight through, but the *Transat* lived up to its reputation for cuisine no matter how many passengers disappeared from the dining room during the meal!"

"Did they manage to provide a Lenten service?"

"Oh, yes. Unfortunately, the priest on board—he was enroute to Baltimore—was absolutely no credit to his vocation as far as being able to deliver a sermon," Charles remarked, and then looked questioningly at Henry. "I shouldn't have said that, considering my own position and—"

"Don't, Charles." Henry moved quickly to soothe him. "That's all behind you now. Besides, here in New York, even if anyone knows, they're hardly likely to bring it up," he added, and resumed his role, pointing out the new office building on Thirty-second Street where Alix's friend Thea had her antiques and interior-decorating business; the red-brick and sandstone mass of German Renaissance-type architecture which was the Waldorf-Astoria; and the Carrere and Hastings building under construction from Forty to Forty-second Streets and which, on completion, would be the main building of the New York Public Library.

The uniform-looking brownstone townhouses that marked Fifth Avenue below Thirty-fourth Street had more variety now, and among the sights Henry pointed out were the famous restaurants, Delmonico's and Sherry's; fashionable schools and clubs and shops; the Gothic-spired edifice that was St. Patrick's Cathedral; the two new hotels, the St. Regis and the Gotham, being built on opposite corners of Fifty-fifth Street, due to open within six months; and the famous millionaires' mansions that, in many cases, covered all or part of a block, and were built in the style of the grand chateaux of France.

Charles found himself both repelled by the extravagance and fascinated by the variety of sights. But, as Pearce took them west on Fifty-ninth Street, along the southern rim of Central Park, he grew less and less interested. The afternoon had grown progressively colder and drearier and, by the time they passed the monument to Christopher Columbus, and at long last turned up Central Park West, Charles couldn't feel either his hands or his feet. And, with some alarm, Henry noted the faint blue line appearing around his guest's mouth.

"It won't be too much longer," he promised him. "Ten more blocks and we'll have you home. Alix will be back from her day at the dispensary, and tea will be waiting for us."

"Alix is practicing medicine again?" he asked, stiff with cold, hoping that if he kept talking he wouldn't freeze to death.

"On a very irregular basis. The Henry Street Settlement dispensary can always use extra medical help, and Alix is more than happy to help them one or two days a week."

Charles fell silent again as he attempted to sort out all of the information he'd assimilated. He knew from his mother that Henry Thorpe was some sort of guest lecturer at Columbia University and, in addition, served as a consultant to various museums. He also knew that Alix was a physician, although he'd naturally assumed that with a seven-month-old baby she no longer practiced. For a minute he thought about the Thorpes and the apartment they hadn't yet moved into, as well as

Henry's ward who lived with their neighbors and who'd conveniently fallen ill so that he, Charles, had by default become the extra man. Finally he gave up trying to sort it all out and mentally shrugged, but he couldn't quite get rid of the feeling that in a very few minutes he'd be joining a menagerie in which he'd be very much *depaysé*.

In the past week, whenever he'd thought about the Dakota, he'd always conjured up the image of a building very much like London's Albany—that famous block of flats in Piccadilly where Byron had once lived—except that this American version obviously permitted women and very young children to number among its residents. This mental alliance with someplace familiar had been a comforting thought. But now, as they approached Seventy-second Street, Charles could see all too clearly that no such American counterpart existed.

The only two buildings he could see that *might* qualify were a tall, massive structure on the southwest corner, and a rather squat, yellowish-brown mass of stone and masonry with gabled roofs, cupolas and all shapes of windows. A totally sorry-looking place, utterly without any sort of architectural redemption, Charles decided just as Pearce made another skillful left-hand turn, and continued along Seventy-second Street for a short distance before steering the Packard through a tunnel-like driveway, emerging in the Dakota's courtyard and pulling up before a set of double doors.

Horrified, Charles turned to Henry. "You . . . you and Alix live *here?*" he blurted out.

"In the apartment Alix had before we were married," Henry replied a shade too casually as the chauffeur opened the door and they stepped out.

"But this building looks like . . . like . . ."

"Like a Balkan brewery that failed and was converted to a post office," he suggested as two porters emerged to help Pearce with the luggage.

126

Charles eyed the dreary courtyard with distaste. If it weren't for the huge bronze fountain, its water frozen solid, this might very well be the entranceway to some obscure prison, he decided as he recalled the Albany. Henry Thorpe had lived there in perfect bachelor splendor, he remembered. If he could give all that up to live in this horror, then the poets had to be right after all—love *was* blind! And without thinking, he voiced his thoughts.

"Don't you ever think about what you gave up—all the beauty that surrounded you at the Albany? Don't you ever feel *depaysé* here?"

Henry Thorpe regarded Charles de Renille in frigid silence, giving him an inscrutable look from beneath hooded lids, making Charles wish he'd never opened his mouth.

"Let's get you inside, you're starting to turn blue," he remarked, leaving Charles nonplussed.

"You mean you don't miss England and your home?"

There was another inscrutable glance, and this time he answered directly, with no doubt whatsoever as to his true feelings. "I *am* home."

In a silence almost as awkward as the one they'd shared that summer's day in 1896, the two men entered the elevator lobby with its handsome wainscotted walls and wrought iron staircase that wound its way up through the nine-story building. The Otis lift took a minute to make its way down and, as they waited, Charles gradually felt some feeling begin to return to his hands and feet thanks to the building's excellent central heating.

The glass top, wood bottom door slid open, and Henry gently steered him into the carved wood cage with its highly polished bronze handrail, greeted the woman operator, and introduced Charles to her.

While the car slowly and majestically rose to the

fourth floor, Charles found himself wondering about Alix. From all he'd read about women who embraced professions generally reserved for men, he was sure he'd find very little left of the young woman who was exactly one week his junior. As with Henry, he had always known Alix, and he recalled that she was the only debutante he'd ever known who'd worn face powder and mascara, and not only gotten away with it, but had everyone remarking how beautiful she was. As most of his last meeting with them was an uncomfortable blur, Charles was sure her elegant chic had been replaced by utilitarian clothes, and she would no longer smell of expensive perfume but of strong medical disinfectant; changes wrought by her profession that not even marriage and motherhood could soften, he decided as the operator stopped the car and slid open the door.

As they stepped into the semi-private hallway panelled in a superbly grained mahogany, Charles looked around him, appreciatively noting that a seventeenth-century console table of gilded limewood with a marble top, and a mirror whose frame was carved and painted and gilded wood, filled the generous space between the heavy wood doors with their elaborate brass doorknobs. A crystal vase filled with an arrangement of dark red roses rested on the table top, and a red and gold Portuguese needlepoint rug covered the marble floor.

"We share this hall with William and Adele Seligman," Henry told him, some of his anger fading as he saw Charles' new appreciation. "The furnishings you see are theirs, but on alternate weeks we share the responsibility for the flower arrangements. This is Bill and Adele's week—the roses come from the greenhouse of their Long Island home," he finished, pressing the buzzer lightly.

Almost immediately the door was opened by a reserved-looking middle-aged man wearing striped trousers, a frock coat, and a winged-collar shirt, whose serious face smiled. "Good afternoon, my lord."

"Good afternoon, Hodges. Charles, you remember Hodges, don't you?" he asked as they entered the apartment.

Charles replied that he did, and while Hodges, who was Henry Thorpe's butler and valet, helped them off with their topcoats and hung them away in the roomy cedar-lined closet, he looked around him, trying to absorb this new setting.

The well-proportioned entry hall was decorated with a mahogany bombe chest with a finely framed landscape hanging over it.

"This chest is a superb example of pre-Revolutionary Boston cabinet-making, and the painting is a Thomas Cole view of the Hudson River Valley," Henry informed him.

"It's very handsome."

"Unfortunately, it's a debatable and mostly unappreciated school, but we love it. Is everything in order, Hodges?" he questioned, quickly switching topics.

"Quite so, my lord. Her ladyship is in the drawing room, and I've sent Doris and Carrie in with the tea," he said as the buzzer sounded again.

"That will be the porters with the luggage, Hodges."

"Then if Mr. de Renille will give me his keys, I'll see to everything, my lord."

With his keys handed over, Charles obediently followed Henry out of the entry hall and toward the drawing room, wide-eyed at what he was seeing. The Dakota's unattractive exterior gave no hint of the beauty that lay within, and the Thorpes' excellent taste gave their home an air of uncluttered simplicity with elegant furnishings and paintings, most of which would have gladly been accepted by any museum.

The drawing room, measuring twenty-two by twenty-seven, with an elaborately molded plaster ceiling, carved marble mantel, and large windows overlooking Central Park, was the showplace of the apartment, and Charles, still off balance from the events of the afternoon, stood silently at the open double doors, as much taken aback by the beauty of the room as by the tall, slender woman seated on one of the two large, deep-pillowed white silk damask-covered sofas that flanked the fireplace.

At twenty-nine, Alicia Turner Thorpe was the wife of Lord Henry Thorpe, the mother of Isabel Leslie Thorpe, a physician occasionally practicing at the dispensary of the Henry Street Settlement—and a very apprehensive hostess as she waited for her husband and Charles de Renille to arrive. Alix could recall with startling clarity the last time she'd seen Charles; how he'd wandered into his mother's garden, his face and frame little more than bone structure with parchment-like skin stretched over it, his hair a short black stubble. His walk had been jerky and uncertain, his speech slurred, and his eyes unfocused. She and Henry had talked about that day when Solange's letter had arrived, asking if she could send Charles to them. His condition had undoubtedly progressed, they'd agreed, and if it was as Solange said, that he was at a plateau, then they had to try and help him the rest of the way . . .

Easy to say when you're discussing a letter, Alix told herself as she checked over the tea things. She hated meddling in other peoples' lives as much as she disliked interference in hers. Besides, in the end it's all going to boil down to what Charles is willing to do for himself, she added firmly as she heard footsteps and turned to greet the two men.

"Hello, Charles." She held out both hands to him. "It's so good to see you again!"

"Particularly since I no longer look like a circus freak." He smiled, crossing the exquisite early eighteenth-century Bessarabian rug woven in delicate tones of pale blue, cream, apricot, and gray that covered the inlaid parquet floor. Could he have really been so stupid as to think that Alix Thorpe would *ever* turn herself into a magazine-story stereotype? he asked himself as he grasped her hands and leaned over to kiss her cheek. She was wearing an exquisitely draped white chiffon teagown from Lucile with two crimson satin roses caught under her breast, and the scent of Jicky perfume drifted around her.

"You're absolutely frozen," she said, kissing him in return. "Go stand in front of the fire for a moment, and then we'll get some tea into you."

Obligingly, Charles stood in front of the immense marble fireplace where a small, welcoming fire burned brightly and neatly. It was hardly necessary considering the central heating, but it was a pleasant sight on a merciless winter afternoon. According to all the rules of etiquette, Charles knew he should sit next to Alix on the sofa, but one quick look into the gilt-framed mirror hanging over the fireplace gave him the reflection of Henry and Alix's affectionate greeting to each other, and deftly, tactfully, he moved to the other sofa, seating himself directly opposite them.

Tea was appropriately lavish. The Oriental rosewood coffee table between the sofas was covered in a delicately embroidered white cloth; there were plates of cucumber and chicken salad and *pate* sandwiches; as well as hot, raisin-studded scones with curls of sweet butter and strawberry preserves; and an angel-food cake with pink frosting. Earl Gray tea was poured from a footed Tiffany sterling silver tea service in an unusual zigzag pattern with ebony handles into the green and white Blind Earl-patterned cups.

"The silver service was my mother's, and the china was Henry's mother's," Alix informed him as she poured out his tea and offered him lemon and sugar, both of which he refused.

"They're both very handsome," he agreed, taking the cup and saucer, noticing that the only jewelry Alix wore were her gold wedding ring, and the massive oval-cut canary-diamond that was her engagement ring. "But all for my benefit. . . ."

"Wait until you see all our other silver and china," Alix laughed. "If we're ever robbed, the thief will be able to retire for life!"

"When all our wedding presents were pouring in, Alix swore a silver mine had been depleted," Henry added. "Would you like some brandy to help you along?"

"No, thank you. I think my circulation's been restored by the fire and the tea."

"And don't forget the central heating," she added, passing him a plate of sandwiches. "Did Henry mention that you have two invitations?"

"Yes, to a dinner-dance and a buffet. Is it usual in New York to go or to give parties on Sunday?"

"We like to have friends in on Sunday evening just to sit around and talk and eat Italian food," Alix told him, "but Percy and Charlotte Lasky's party will be much more formal. Percy is a very important theatrical producer and, at this time of year, Sunday is the only night to bring everyone together. You'll have a wonderful time," she assured him.

Over the next half-hour, Charles found himself increasingly grateful to the Thorpes. They didn't pester him with questions about his family or his shipboard life or how he was feeling. That was all taken for granted. Their conversation centered around New York and the life they lived. Their attitude helped, but he was still left with the feeling that he was overwhelmingly out of place and that the couple opposite him had suddenly become strangers.

They sat close together, Henry's arm stretched out

132

along the back of the sofa, not directly touching Alix, but the indirect gesture was more powerful than if he had been. There was an aura surrounding both of them that Charles couldn't quite identify. It was an extension of the air Henry had projected on the dock, only now it had centered, intensified and . . .

"If you're feeling more like yourself, would you like to come and meet Alix's and my joint creation?"

Charles blinked, mystified. "Your joint creation—? Oh, your baby. I have a present for her. It's a doll from Au Nain Bleu," he said, following him out of the drawing room.

The rooms in the apartment opened off a central corridor which Henry and Alix used as a sort of art gallery for their favorite prints and watercolors. As Charles trailed behind them, he caught glimpses of works signed by Fragonard, Constable and Delacroix. The nursery was located near the end of the corridor, past the closed set of double doors that Charles instinctively knew must lead to the master suite.

The perfection in decor that he'd seen so far carried over to the nursery. Besides the large, white, modern-looking crib, there was a ribbon and lace bassinet, a Chippendale highchair, a carved mahogany Chippendale child's chair, and a rocking chair placed near the fireplace. There were Kate Greenaway-framed water-colors on the walls, ruffled curtains at the windows, and dolls and stuffed animals—including the newly created Teddy bear named in honor of President Roosevelt—were arranged around the room.

With obvious pride, Henry bent over the crib and lifted his daughter. "Isabel Leslie Thorpe," he said softly to Charles. "Would you care to hold her?"

"Yes . . . oh, she's perfection," he said as Henry carefully transferred the tranquil bundle to his arms, and he looked down at what appeared to be a sleeping

133

bisque doll.

"How old is she?"

"Just seven months. Look, she's waking up."

Transfixed by the infant in his arms, Charles watched as her long-lashed eyelids fluttered open. A small rosebud mouth gurgled happily at him, one tiny fist waved in the air, incredibly green eyes met his, and Charles felt his heart turn over.

"I think she looks like an angel."

"That's only because you haven't heard her cry," Henry said in a way that told Charles it didn't bother him at all.

"I don't think I could mind anything she did."

They were still discussing Isabel when Alix—who'd disappeared into the adjoining room—returned. "This is Miss Darty, Isabel's nurse," she said, indicating the cheerful woman in the nanny's uniform at her side. "Miss Darty, this is Charles de Renille, our house guest."

"Very pleased to meet you, sir," she smiled. "And if I may say so, you hold Miss Isabel very well for a bachelor gentleman."

"Three nephews," he smiled in return. "Of course, Isabel seems to be very friendly."

"Oh, that she is, sir."

"I know that our daughter is an endlessly fascinating topic for conversation, but I'm afraid we've reached the point where she's my responsibility alone," Alix put in, amused, as she took her daughter back from Charles.

While Alix sat down in the rocking chair, Henry and Charles returned to the corridor.

"Is there a particular reason why you employ a nurse instead of a nanny? I don't mean to pry, but I was wondering—?"

"Alix has a very poor estimation of nannies in general, and it's a feeling I've come to share. In the month before

134

Isabel was born, we had a stream of so-called 'suitable' women coming in to be interviewed. We both wanted our baby so terribly that we saw red every time one of them said we'd never have to know our child was in the nursery."

"I can't see parents hiring such women," Charles said, appalled.

"Unfortunately, too many do. It took us rather a long time to find Miss Darty. She'd been the nurse and nanny to a large family who owned a ranch in Canada, and when they sent the last child off to school, there was no more need of her. She'd been away from England for over twenty years and didn't want to go back, so she came to New York."

"How fortunate for all of you."

"Yes. Particularly since Miss Darty has absolutely no illusions as to whom Isabel's mother is," Henry said as he opened a pair of double doors and ushered Charles into the second bedroom of the master suite. "The furniture belonged to Alix's father," Henry informed him as Charles took in the handsome ebony furnishings, the blue-gray accents, and the Monet painting of the Seine near Giverny that hung opposite the bed. "That was my contribution to the decor. Alix has one of the Japanese footbridge series hung in the next room. Now, shall we see how Hodges is progressing with your luggage?"

They found the valet in the dressing room, calmly hanging Charles' suits in a six-and-a-half-foot tall rosewood clothes cupboard. "All finished, my lord, Mr. de Renille," the valet said pleasantly as he closed the double doors that were carved in a motif of dragons and mountains. "I'll send your dinner clothes to the tailor to be steamed, sir, and my lord, I've laid out your dinner clothes in her ladyship's dressing room. Shall I run your bath now, sir?" he questioned Charles, but his respectful request seemed to be directed as much at his employer as

135

at his guest.

"I think you'll find that a very satisfactory idea," Henry remarked. "It will give you a chance to rest up from all you've been through today."

For the next few minutes, Henry helped him get settled, checking over the room, finding where Hodges had stored the rest of his clothes, and finally standing him at one of the two large windows to see the sweeping view of Central Park for the first time.

"It's too late now, but tomorrow morning—provided it's not snowing—you'll be able to see the lake."

"I think that delay will be a good thing. I've run out of superlatives to describe your home. I feel like a terrible fool for what I said earlier."

"Oh, everyone says that about the Dakota to begin with," Henry shrugged with a smile. "In another week you'll be used to it. Now, before I go, is there anything you need?"

Charles looked around him thoughtfully. This day hadn't been anything like he'd expected, and tonight would probably be no better. Henry and Alix had been tactful, but there was no certainty that their guests would be. A cold curtain of self-doubt fell around him, increasing his feeling of being a stranger in an alien country, taking up residence with people who—despite their wealth—lived in what was to him, raised in spacious *manoirs* and *hotels particuliers*, very small quarters indeed.

"No, I have everything I need," he said as he heard the sound of his bath being run. "*Maman* thought you'd moved already, I hope I won't crowd you and Alix too much."

"Not at all, there's more than enough room here. Incidentally, dinner is at eight, but we have cocktails in the drawing room at half-past seven. If you want to nap, Hodges will wake you in plenty of time, and you can come into the drawing room whenever you're ready."

136

"Still," he insisted, "I'm sorry to be turning you out of your room."

Henry Thorpe, his hand on the door leading to the connecting bedroom, paused, and regarded Charles the same as he had a few hours before in the courtyard, but this time his expression was tinged with amusement and a touch of tolerance.

"Do you really think so?"

Alix Turner Thorpe, having fed her daughter and settled her in her crib, now sat back against the pillows on the bed and watched her husband enter the bedroom they shared and lock the door. .

"What are you thinking, darling?" she asked, seeing his half-amused, half-perplexed expression.

"That we may have problems. I don't want to tell you what he just said."

"Henry, he's bewildered and probably wildly tired. He's going to need *days* to get himself together!"

"Well, as I've said before concerning other things, I'm glad one of us has faith."

For a long minute, Henry Thorpe regarded his wife as she sat on the wide bed with its delicate shell carvings decorating the cane headboard and footboard. His eyes seemed to pick out every detail of the white, blue and gold room with its Louis XV furniture and faintly Rococo touches—a room that was feminine without being frilly and where they'd found such happiness together.

Alix watched as he carefully studied Monet's painting of the Japanese footbridge that hung opposite their bed. "Henry, I can't stand this another second. What exactly did Charles say?"

"To begin with, when we came into the courtyard, he asked in utter horror if we really lived here."

Alix smiled in remembrance. "If I recall correctly, when I told you that I lived in the Dakota, you had several choice things to say."

He smiled in return. "That, at least, is a condition that can be cured with time, but the rest of it is going to depend on how adaptable he is." His hooded lids lowered slightly as he advanced into the room, stopping to lean against the back of the six-foot-long white brocade sofa that was placed in front of the fireplace. "It's rather like learning to swim. Figuratively speaking, we have to toss Charles into the water and let him make his own way from there."

"I agree, but there's more to it than that. First we have to find him some sort of work to do, and then we have to find him a girl!"

Henry shot her an amused look. "In other words, you intend to make his life hell—rather the way you did mine when we met," he finished, and deftly caught the white satin shoe that Alix pulled off and tossed at him in mock anger.

"My dear Lord Thorpe, you do have the nicest way of putting things!"

"And you, my dear doctor, have the oddest way of replying to my compliments!" He sat down on the edge of the bed, returned her shoe to her foot, then thought better of it and took the other one off as well.

"At least it got you over here with me instead of at the other end of the room," Alix said, putting her arms around his shoulders and nestling close to him.

"Are you serious about introducing Charles to a girl?"

"Why not? Oh, nothing serious to begin with. Just someone nice whom he can have an intelligent conversation with while they dance or have dinner."

"Such as your cousin Mallory?"

"Mallory is a fine beginning," Alix replied, referring to her second cousin, Mallory Kirk, an eighteen-year-old Barnard sophomore who lived with her godparents, Newton and Esme Phipps.

138

"She isn't coming to dinner tonight, is she?"

Alix shook her head. "They'll meet at Cliff and Julie's party—that's more than enough time for Charles to make his first adjustment."

"You have this all worked out, don't you?" he said wonderingly. "Rupert might not like the idea of your passing his best girl friend on to our house guest!"

"Rupert isn't going to be leaving his room for the next few weeks, and by the time he's up and about again, Charles will have found his own place." Alix kissed her husband under one ear. "Are you in agreement with me?"

"I don't see why not. It reminds me of a very strange conversation I had with Cliff a few months ago. You know how he's always taking verbal shots at Rupert, so I finally asked Cliff why he disliked Rupert so much. He told me, 'I don't dislike him. If I did, I'd never let him in my home or near my children. But Rupert has a very easy time of it, as far as the rest of my family is concerned, and it's up to me to give him a few difficulties and teach him what life is all about,'" Henry recounted, smiling. "I have an idea that the same might just hold true for Charles. At any rate, it's worth the effort," he finished as his hands curved around Alix's back, came forward to cup her breasts, and then went to the teagown's delicate fastenings, his mouth eagerly meeting hers.

"I've been waiting all day for you to do that," she said a few moments later, moving back enough to unknot his tie. "Did you miss me, darling?"

"Terribly. I've been thinking about you all day," he said, his voice growing thicker. "Lucky thing that it's winter and I was covered by my overcoat!"

To Henry and Alix, their love mattered beyond all else. It was a love that reached out to encompass their friends and business associates; a generosity of spirit and a natural desire to share their abundant happiness with others. Running parallel to that love was the joy of their sexual union, and as their embrace grew more and more demanding, their talk of Charles faded into unimportance.

As they undressed each other, they traded kiss for kiss, their excitement mounting as the removal of each garment revealed more and more. Finally, they were stretched out across the bed together, the world outside the bedroom door fast receding.

Alix held her husband closely, caressing him in the way he liked best, reveling in his touch as his hands moved from her bared breasts down her sides to her hips. One arm encircled her waist while the other continued its downward pattern in long, delicious strokes that ended between her thighs, rousing her to the point that all she wanted, all she cared about, was their mutual lovemaking, the ultimate fulfillment that their bodies could give each other.

His swollen hardness entered her pliant, eager body so quickly that Alix felt her mind shut off in the searing heat of his first thrust, not functioning again until long after the final climax had claimed them simultaneously.

It was nearly an hour before they spoke again as Alix ran her hand lightly along the taut, lean strength of Henry's spine as he lay stretched out alongside her, his face buried in the pillows.

"We're going to have to start getting ready soon."

"Not if you keep doing that," he responded in a muffled voice as her hand made tantalizing contact with the small of his back and he felt the first tuggings of renewed passion. "But I suppose you're right. It would hardly do for us to be making love just before our guests are due to arrive."

"Oh, I don't know," Alix drawled. "It seems to me that a last minute tumble adds a certain private spice to a dinner party."

Henry raised his head. "My dear doctor, we do *not* tumble!"

"Have you got a better expression?" she challenged, smiling.

"Not off hand. But tumbling is something one does in a hayloft and tends to be very messy—not to mention totally undignified," he finished, drawing her into his arms.

"Tory snob," she whispered lovingly in his ear.

"New York Reform Democrat," he responded as their bodies molded naturally together. Their teasing and mock indignation faded as their love rekindled.

"Are you really going to introduce Charles to one of your girlfriends?" he asked some time later.

"Eventually."

"Whom do you have in mind?"

"I've been thinking about Thea—"

"Thea? My darling, if you're going to matchmake, at least look for compatible types! Charles is still caught in the murky depths of the Church, while Thea is completely outspoken, too well-dressed, and totally agnostic."

"Then she's perfect for him!"

"Can't you come up with someone else?"

"You mean a woman who's dignified and neatly dressed and devoted to her religion—High Anglican if not borderline Catholic?"

"That would be more in keeping."

"Except that the women who fit that description don't really like men! That's what Charles is and, sooner or later, he's going to realize it, and if he wants to indulge in a few male proclivities, it would be nice if he had a willing partner!"

"But they'd be such a damn unlikely couple!"

"I can think of one who had even less on their side," Alix laughed. "In the beginning, all their friends said

141

they had nothing whatsoever in common and no possible mutual attraction. A *very* mismatched pair."

Henry raised his head from Alix's full breast. "My dear doctor, whom are you talking about?"

"You and me."

"Dick, you're not only the first to arrive, but you also look like you could do with a nice dry martini."

"Hemlock is more like it, Alix. A nice big glass—and don't bother about the ice," said Richard North, a senior editor at Doubleday, Page, as Hodges showed him into the drawing room.

It was five minutes past seven, but Alix and Henry displayed no undue surprise at Dick North's early arrival. In their eclectic circle of friends, one guest or couple per party generally arrived early, and they made it a point to be in the drawing room a half-hour before the time designated on the invitation.

"Where's Megan? Or are you so distracted that you've forgotten your wife?" Alix teased as he collapsed opposite her in the same spot Charles had occupied a few hours earlier.

"Meggie will be here in a few minutes. She was nearly ready when I left, but I've been so agitated since I got home this afternoon that she told me to take a hansom cab up here and let her get dressed in peace!"

"Words that a wise husband always listens to," Henry remarked, handing him a frosty, long-stemmed glass. "Take a few restorative sips and let us know if there's something we can help you with. Is it something in particular, or just business in general?"

"Henry, publishing gets worse and worse. Six-page outlines for thousand-page books, mystery stories with no bodies, authors who want an advance before they write a single page, not to mention the latest invention of the devil—the literary agent. And now there's the problem with the two French books I can't get translated."

A faint tremor combining surprise and certainty rippled through Alix. "I thought you'd already retained a translator?" Alix forced herself to keep her voice normal as she held out a small *blanc de chine* cachepot filled with spiced pecans. "Isn't he a young professor at New York University?"

"Don't remind me of that pretentious ass," Dick groaned, taking a handful of nuts. "He has the misconception that he's too intellectual to be bothered with a romance and a book of fairy tales for children. If I could find someone who could do a good job of it, I'd give Mr. Intellectual a surprise he won't forget!"

"You're looking for another professor, aren't you?" Henry questioned with deliberate casualness. He'd already guessed Alix's motives, and while he agreed with them, there as no need to take anything for granted.

Dick pushed his wavy, dark-brown hair out of his eyes. "Not necessarily. All I want is someone who can read and understand both languages easily. We want both these books on our next list, and I hate the idea of having to postpone them."

"I don't think you'll have to," Alix smiled as she saw that Charles, looking rested and more at ease than he had when he'd arrived, appeared at the drawing room doors. "Dick, this is our house guest, Charles de Renille, who came in on this afternoon's *La Savoie*. Charles, come in and say hello to a friend of ours, Richard North, who toils for Frank Doubleday and Walter Hines Page," she said, making the introduction. "Now that he's been revived by a martini, and you've thawed out, I think you might be of help to each other!"

Whatever happened to him over the next weeks, Charles knew that the memory of his first dinner in New

York would live forever in his memory.

In the white-walled dining room with the rose-pink satin draperies which were closed against the uninviting view of the Dakota's courtyard, the delicate, oblong Chinese Chippendale table was covered with damask tablecloth and napkins. The china was Ceralene's Nyon pattern with its gold and blue sprays of *barbeaux* and gold edging, the stemware was Baccarat's new Monte Carlo pattern, and the silver was Tiffany's famous Chrysanthemum design. A graceful pair of Lalique candlesticks holding beeswax tapers flanked a silver bowl filled with an arrangement of red and white Rubrum lilies.

Even more soothing and satisfying than the table setting was the food. Dinner began with sections of fresh in- and out-of-season fruits in crystal cups that were set in long-stemmed silver dishes. This was followed by slices of mushroom quiche whose fluffy filling and buttery crust seemed to melt in his mouth, and then by a green salad in an herb dressing, accompanied by a fine, runny Camembert.

Under the watchful eye of Hodges, who kept the champagne glasses filled in a steady golden stream of Mumm's, Doris and Carrie skillfully served the meal, making a pretty picture in their evening uniforms of silver-gray silk with white ruffled aprons, delicate caps with black velvet streamers, and black patent-leather shoes with silver buckles.

It wasn't until the main course of filet of sole *bonne femme*, with rice and baby peas and carrots, was placed in front of him that Charles really looked around him, taking in every detail of the other thirteen people at the table.

Henry and Alix, he realized early on in the evening, did not entertain for prestige, only for people they liked and who liked them. And, he further realized in a sudden flash of perception, any guest who didn't get on with the others wouldn't be invited back—and that included him.

The women at the table were an endless source of intrigue. At one end of the table there was Alix in Lucile's froth of absinthe-colored chiffon with long pointed flounces bound in silver ribbon, a diamond and peridot necklace—his mother's wedding present to her—glittering on her swanlike neck as she laughed and talked with Newton Phipps on her left and William Seligman on her right. His gaze moved to the women at the opposite side of the table; talkative, pretty Esme Phipps in Worth's blue-gray mousseline with a belt of black tulle set off by an aquamarine necklace; delectable, blonde Kezia Leslie—Alix's cousin's wife—seated on Richard North's left, wearing creamy *pointe de Venice* lace over shimmering pale green satin from Doucet, her only jewelry an outstanding pair of emerald and diamond earrings; and, at Henry's left, amusing, chic Adele Seligman in Doucet's yellow crepe de chine with deep insertions of ecru lace, and a double strand of creamy, antique pearls with a canary diamond clasp. At Henry's right and Philip Leslie's left sat elegant grande dame Kathryn Neal, resplendent for her years in Worth's pale gray chiffon with bell sleeves over long fitted ones trimmed with lace-encrusted satin. Charles himself was seated between Emily Stern in Callot Soeurs soft rose silk with fan-shaped insets of lace and rose velvet ribbon, and Megan North in Lucile's mousseline gown that was shaded from palest pink to deepest rose and trimmed with varicolored shirred silk ribbons.

All the bits and pieces of conversation that came his way swirled around him, and he was fascinated by the seemingly endless number of topics they had to discuss.

". . . and we're still giving parties for the sole purpose of showing off our wedding presents . . ."

". . . J. P. Morgan told me: 'Bill, if I'm not careful, you're going to be richer than I am,' and I told him, 'Jack,

145

is there something that makes you think I haven't always been . . . ?'"

". . . I told the women's committee that if they didn't press to see that that absurd rule about a visitor having to be introduced and accompanied by a member abolished, in twenty years no one is ever going to know there was a New York Historical Society . . ."

". . . there's the Stock Exchange, all snug in its brand new building with about as many controls to regulate it as a runaway locomotive . . ."

". . . we all stay in the Social Register for the same reason Bill keeps up his membership at the New York Yacht Club—sheer spite . . . !"

". . . a manuscript that was so awful all I could think was that to print this book we'd be responsible for chopping down an innocent tree . . ."

They were still laughing with Adele and agreeing with Dick when Henry caught Charles' eye. "Is all this too confusing for you?" he asked sympathetically as the rest of the table turned their attention to him.

"A little," he confessed. "I'm still trying to adjust to the Dakota. Is this the only apartment building in New York with a name?"

"No, but it was the first," Alix told him. "When it was built twenty years ago, Seventy-second Street was considered to be so far uptown that taking an apartment here was almost the same thing as moving to the Dakota territory in the West—hence the then-appropriate name," she finished, and their dinner-table conversation turned to all New Yorkers' favorite topic—where they lived.

"Alix, the Dakota may be the first apartment building to be formally named, but kindly remember that Dick and I live in the second," Megan North teased in a voice that still held a faint trace of her South Carolina girl-hood. "Our building is exactly one year younger—name

146

and all!"

"We live at 205 West 57th Street," Dick North elaborated to Charles. "It's called the Osborne—named after the stone contractor who went bankrupt building it!"

"At least your building has one name," dignified, handsome Philip Leslie put in. "Kezia and I live in the only apartment building that's known by three names at the same time."

"The proper name is the Central Park Apartments on West Fifty-ninth Street," his wife went on, "but because the buildings are named after Spanish provinces, it's generally called the Eldorado."

"Or the Spanish Flats. I live there also," Kathryn Neal added. "And, my dear Alix and Megan, you are *both* incorrect—*we* were the first apartment building with a name."

"That was 1883," Esme Phipps continued. "But Newton and I have the distinction of living in one of the most recent buildings—667 Madison Avenue."

"It's of a rather radical design, as apartments go," Newton remarked. "Ten floors, two apartments to a floor, each with fifteen rooms. It'll be interesting to see how well that design stands up."

"I've just realized that John and I are the only ones here who still have a townhouse," Dr. Emily Stern interjected. "Suddenly I feel about as up-to-date as a dinosaur!"

"In Manhattan, it's not only which building you live in, but whom you live next door to," Dr. John Stern told Charles. "We live at 216 East 17th Street—that's the north side of Stuyvesant Square—but we're saved from being thought of as out-of-step since our neighbors at 214 are William Faversham and Julie Opp, the British theatrical couple."

"Charles, you've just received a capsule history of

147

luxury apartments in New York City," William Seligman told him, a smile lightening his reserved features. "And after hearing it, I wouldn't blame you one bit if you decided to return to France immediately!"

The entire table was still laughing as the remains of the main course were cleared away, but when their dessert was carried in on a silver cake stand, their merriment turned into exclamations of appreciation. It was more than a cake, it was a mouth-watering creation frosted in dense, dark chocolate festooned with additional pieces of chocolate, dusted with confectioner's sugar, and when it was cut, three layers of almond meringue and chocolate mousse were revealed.

Helped by a fresh stream of champagne, the cake was quickly consumed amid renewed conversation. When only the crumbs were left, Charles expected that this would be the moment when Alix would suggest that the ladies withdraw and leave the gentlemen to their cigars and brandy. But, like so many of his expectations today, this didn't quite work out the way he expected.

They all rose from the table at the same time and returned to the drawing room. The only guest to excuse himself was John Stern, who announced this was a good time to have a look at his patient, asked Hodges for his medical bag, and went next door.

There was *cafe filtre* served in Ceralene's gold-banded Anneau d'Or pattern accompanied by chocolate-dipped Florentines, and more good conversation as they broke into convivial and interchanging groups.

Charles was promptly cornered by Dick North, who promised to send the books to him by messenger. "Do you think you can get both of them translated and back to me in the next two weeks? I assure you, both my firm and I will be very grateful."

They were standing by one of the large windows that overlooked Central Park and, for a minute, Charles studied the large, thick white snowflakes that were drifting down steadily. He still couldn't quite believe the offer this man had made him. In the world he came from, books were simply *there*. Not once, he realized with a start, had he ever thought as to how they progressed from a manuscript into bound covers.

"I'd be honored to help you any way I can, of course, but—"

"Excellent," Dick said before Charles could continue. "Naturally, I know you're on vacation, and I wouldn't dream of disrupting all that Alix and Henry have set out for you to do, but I might have another book for you to translate."

"Another book?"

"Yes. It's a biography of Napoleon, written by a professor at the Sorbonne. Are you familiar with it? No? Well, I suppose books about Napoleon in France are rather like books about George Washington here—a new one every year or two. At any rate, it's a thick book, and we gave it to one of our finest translators."

"The same man who's refusing the books you want me to translate now?"

"No, this gentleman is quite elderly. He's the retired head of Columbia's French department. His faculties are superior, but his health—" Dick North shook his head. "He may need an operation, and after that a long convalescence. We can't let the book languish about unfinished and—" He broke off abruptly. "I see that Kathryn is very eager for your company, and I've monopolized you long enough. We'll discuss this again very soon."

They separated, and Charles, with more relief than he cared to admit, spent the rest of the evening seated beside Kathryn Neal on an ice-blue antique satin-upholstered Louis XV love seat, having a non-stop conversation.

In the society he came from, men like himself who

were the youngest in their families, and therefore without financial prospects, were most useful at parties when it came to entertaining either very young girls of seventeen or eighteen who were not yet fully fledged in the social world, or dowagers who still knew how to entrance even as their beauty faded.

Kathryn Neal might have been nearing seventy (no one was really sure), but she was still erect and slender and sparkled as much as the priceless jewels she wore and the painted silk on carved ivory spangled fan she used as she emphasized points in their conversation. She had been born in a day when there had still been farms in the section of Manhattan where they were now so comfortably sitting, and living as far north as Fourteenth Street was considered adventurous and just a bit *outre*. She was raised in Paris while her father had been the American Minister to France, returned to New York, married an important young banker, and became a mother, social leader and the important backer of several notable and important charities. Her daughter, Evangeline, was the wife of Admiral Bruce Dalton, her granddaughter Angela was in San Francisco, and her grandson Neal was in his junior year at Yale, she told Charles, who listened in rapt attention.

To him, she was the living history of New York. A woman whose age span had taken her from horse-drawn phaetons and full-masted clipper ships to motor cars, telephones and two-or-three-funnel floating hotels that crossed the Atlantic in one short week. When she'd been born, Thomas Jefferson hadn't been dead ten years, veterans of the Revolutionary War were still alive, and Andrew Jackson had been President, Charles realized in amazement. Slavery had been the order of the day in the south, cities like Chicago were struggling out of their frontier-town beginnings, and gold was yet to be discovered in California. All the American history he'd gleaned from his Baedeker took on a living, breathing glow as he spoke with this woman who'd lived through twenty Presidential administrations and had known the White House's current occupant when he'd been a baby in the nursery.

It was the New World finally made real to him, and he was startled when she touched his arm and said, "I think we're both in danger of wearing out our welcome."

He looked around him in surprise. While they'd talked, the party had begun to wind down, and everyone was about to leave, and he and Kathryn Neal were alone in the drawing room.

"You've made the evening fly for me," he told her truthfully, bending over her right hand to kiss it. "I hope we can talk again soon." Charles meant every word he said, and the last thing he expected Mrs. Neal to do was take her decorative fan, close it, and smack him smartly on his upper arm.

He winced sharply. *"Madame—"*

"Have I hurt you?" She was instantly contrite. "I certainly didn't mean to, only to bring you to your senses. My dear Charles, you are a very good-looking young man. Not *that* handsome," she added critically, putting her fan under his chin to better consider his face, "but it will keep you modest. I find too many young men today are far more sure of themselves than they have any right to be. And the only thing worse than that, are men of your age paying court to old ladies when they should be off enjoying themselves with pretty young ones!"

"But talking with you tonight meant a great deal to me!" he protested, thoroughly puzzled. Where he came from, *grande dames* relished the power they held over younger men.

"And I'm very appreciative of your company. But you can discover much better things to do with your time," she told him firmly, not giving him a chance to reply. "If

151

you don't mind a word of advice, a pretty young woman to kiss in a conservatory will do far more for you than listening to me recall the history of New York City. And, my dear Charles, if you'll forgive me, *do* see about getting a proper dinner jacket. Frankly, I can't see how you were allowed to leave home with the one you have on now!"

Charles came slowly awake in the cocoonlike silence of his room. As always, he couldn't remember the formless, fragmented dreams that haunted him nightly, often causing him to wake up in the middle of the night for a two- or three-hour bout with sleeplessness before returning to their spectrelike grip.

After he'd collapsed, in an effort to keep him from raving, the doctors had filled him with morphine. And now, two years later, he often wondered if he were suffering from some not-as-yet ended side effect of those opiate injections.

More like a champagne drunk, he told himself sternly, rolling onto his back in a warm tangle of quilted silk comforters and large, plump pillows. Last night he'd been so tired he'd actually ached with fatigue, and this morning his mouth was dry, his stomach slightly queasy, and he felt as if two little screws were being turned in his temples. Quite a morning-after. It was obvious he was going to have to get used to eating and drinking all over again—the Thorpes weren't a couple who appreciated guests who picked at their food and wine.

He stretched full-length in the bed, slowly adjusting to the room around him. Except for the sound of snow picking against the window panes, and the faint hiss of steam from the radiators, there was nothing but silence. Curious about the time, Charles craned his neck toward the writing table and the massive crystal and silver Tiffany inkwell resting on it. Mounted on its lid was a clock, its hands reading half-past nine. Henry told him that the combination inkwell-clock had been his birthday present, but Charles couldn't help thinking that it would be much more convenient if it were placed on one of the bedside tables, and he wondered if Henry ever found it a problem when he woke up in the morning . . .

Abruptly, realization dawned, and Charles sank down among the pillows, his face burning with embarrassment. Yesterday it had struck him that his bedroom had seemed oddly untouched, as if it never had a full-time resident, and now it all fell into place. What need could Henry Thorpe possibly have for a bedside clock when he probably rarely, if ever, woke up in this bed? *How* could he have been such an imbecile to say what he had to Henry, let alone miss the unmistakable aura that surrounded the couple? Henry Thorpe had the look of a man who was loved in frequent and satisfying doses, and the only way he, Charles, could displace him from his bed was if he slept with Alix!

Cursing himself for his stupidity, Charles reached for the bellpull. Now was as good a time as any to see if, in spite of his *gaffes*, he was still a welcome guest.

His summons was answered with gratifying promptness as Hodges, carrying a handsomely set breakfast tray, opened the door.

"Good morning, sir," he intoned politely, leaving the tray on the bed to pull the curtains back. "I'm sorry to say it's still snowing, but it has lightened considerably over the past hour, and it should stop soon," he continued as the dim morning light filled the room. "Do you care to breakfast now, sir, or would you prefer I draw your bath first?"

"I wasn't expecting you to come in with my tray, but I'll eat now, and run my own bath afterwards."

"As you wish, sir," the older man replied, settling the tray across his lap. "Lady Thorpe left specific instructions that I was to bring your tray in to you whenever

153

you rang."

"Have both Lord and Lady Thorpe left already?"

"A half-hour ago, sir. Lord Thorpe to the University, and Lady Thorpe for her sitting—her portrait is being painted," he said as Charles investigated the attractively arranged tray with its violet-painted china breakfast set. There were still-warm breakfast rolls wrapped in a large damask napkin, golden pats of butter on cracked ice, honey in a covered crystal pot, an orange that had been peeled and sectioned, and a pot of steaming hot tea. Two cream-colored envelopes addressed to him were propped up against his cup and saucer, two newspapers were folded in one of the side pockets, while the other held magazines.

"It's English Breakfast Tea, sir," Hodges volunteered, "and there's heather honey from Fortnum & Mason. Lady Thorpe felt this would be the best breakfast for you, considering your day yesterday. But, if you'd prefer bacon and eggs—"

Charles, who'd been expecting porridge and stone cold toast on a silver rack, the traditional English breakfast fare he'd always detested, moved to reassure the waiting servant.

"This is just what I want this morning, Hodges. Now, what are my instructions for today?"

"Well, sir, both his lordship and her ladyship feel that a walk around the block before lunch would be your proper introduction to the neighborhood. Also, you'll find a stationer's and a shoe store on Columbus Avenue. There's at least another month of snowstorms, and his lordship suggested that you purchase a pair of rubber overshoes—galoshes as they're known here—and her ladyship thinks you'll be much happier translating the books for Mr. North if you select your own pens, writing paper and copy books." As he spoke, Hodges moved to switch on both bedside lamps, whose bases were blue and white porcelains from the T'ung Chih period. "There now, sir, more than enough light to read the papers by. Her ladyship also said that after lunch you should feel free to explore the library and drawing room, and she'll be back in time for tea. Mrs. Seligman will be joining you." He took a few steps backward. "If there's anything else I can do for you, sir—"

There was nothing else, and Charles settled down to enjoying his breakfast tray. The large, square, cream-colored envelopes he recognized instantly as invitations and, deciding to get the worst over with first, he opened them as he sipped his first cup of tea.

Mr. and Mrs. Percy Lasky
request the pleasure of
Mr. Charles de Renille's
company at a buffet dinner
on Sunday evening, the 6th of March
at eight o'clock
Thirty-Six West Tenth Street

R.s.v.p.

And . . .

Mr. and Mrs. Clifford Seligman
request the pleasure of
Mr. Charles de Renille's
company on Saturday evening, the twelfth of March
at eight o'clock
Nine Twenty-Three Fifth Avenue

Dancing
R.s.v.p.

The two engraved invitations, both so similar in their wording, were the unmistakable milestones that would mark his stay, Charles realized. And, at the same time, he had to acknowledge that he was almost as afraid of being a success at these functions as he was of being a failure.

The thought of becoming a much in demand extra man was repellent to him. It was simply a variation of being a playboy or some other type of useless hanger-on—the typical fate of the penniless younger son, and the one he shrank from more than any other.

Resolutely, Charles put the invitations aside. There was no use in courting trouble ahead of time, or in dredging up painful memories, he decided, and turned to the newspapers, enjoying the precise, well-written *Times*, and the more colorful, iconoclastic *World*.

As he continued eating breakfast, he read the two issues of *Town & Country*, the weekly society journal with its listing of sporting events, theatrical and musical schedules, articles on the lives lived by the best families in the major American cities, with announcements of their marriages and comings and goings. Here and there he saw a familiar name, but most of the magazine's reporting left him as much in the dark as if he were an every day working man who accidentally found a copy of the publication. Only the covers amused and distracted him.

Town & Country was celebrating the New York mother, and the caption under one charming photograph read, *Lady Henry Thorpe with Isabel,* and the other, *Mrs. Clifford Seligman with Paul, Jonathan, and Virginia.*

At least he now had a look at one of his prospective hostesses, Charles observed. No doubt about it, he was about to be plunged into the social swim of New York, and left to either float or sink on his own merits. Still, he felt far more optimistic than he had in a very long time, and it wasn't the false-cheerful face he was used to putting on either. His feelings came from a source deep within him that he thought had been burned out forever. The faint, yet undeniable certainty that life might just be all right.

It was probably the breakfast, he reasoned. He'd been

fed exactly the right thing, and the ill-effects from the day before had vanished. It might all be temporary, but still—

Charles glanced toward the window. The snow had stopped, and a faint sun was beginning to break through. If he was looking for a sign, there it was, he decided, putting aside the tray, pushing back the covers, and swinging his legs to the floor. How well the rest of his stay worked out, or, for that matter, how the remainder of this day went, was still a mystery, but for now he had enough to get started on.

Hodges was busy counting butter knives. On the central table in the butler's pantry was the massive mahogany and walnut chest that was the repository for the Tiffany Chrysanthemum-pattern silver that had been used the night before. Packed in its red-velvet-lined interior was service for twenty-four; the top of the chest holding a rarely used seven-piece coffee and tea service, while the first two drawers contained sixty-eight serving pieces, and the two bottom drawers all the four-hundred-and-thirty-two pieces of flatware.

After this task was completed, Hodges would then proceed downstairs to the Dakota's cellar to check the inventory in the Thorpes' wine bin, and lastly he would return to the apartment and settle down with his pantry book—that loose-leaf notebook that held a record of every dinner party that the Thorpes had given since September 1902, and listed which guests had been invited, the seating plan, the pattern of the china, silver, and crystal, the flower arrangements, and which florist had done them—and enter the details of last evening.

He was well aware that at that moment, in the kitchen, the female staff which was made up of his wife Aileen, the head parlor-maid; Doris and Carrie, the general maids; Mrs. Wiley, their superb cook; Mrs. Land, who did the heavy cleaning, and both of whom worked on a daily basis; and Miss Darty, Isabel's nurse; were in a deep discussion of Charles de Renille as they all enjoyed a mid-morning cup of tea.

It was inevitable, he supposed, for the house guest and the first impressions he created to become a topic of conversation among them but, just for a fleeting moment, Hodges wished that Lord Thorpe, when he married, had wanted a *truly* proper home and staff. But Henry Thorpe disliked having male servants, saying he'd never heard of a footman who didn't make trouble sooner or later, so the staff remained heavy on the distaff side. And since Pearce, the chauffeur, was answerable only to the master himself, Hodges remained the lone male, and in matters of conversation such as the one now going on, he'd learned that the best tactic was to remove himself from the situation.

Unable to keep what he considered to be a proper sense of decorum in the conversation, and more tired than he cared to admit, Hodges allowed himself to relax and let his mind wander. He was thinking about the mahogany roast beef cart with the silver dome that Lord Thorpe had purchased from Christofle, and which was now safely stored in the basement storage area, waiting for the day that they moved up to the larger apartment on the sixth floor. He suddenly became aware of Carrie standing in the doorway, holding a square florist's box covered in glazed white paper in her hands, a perplexed look on her pretty face.

"Is that something I should know about, Carrie?" he asked almost absently, counting out the last of the butter knives and putting them away.

"No, it's only the arrangement of tiger lilies that her ladyship ordered from Wadley, Smythe," she volunteered. "The rest of the flowers from Thorley's and The Fernery have come as well, and so has the wild rice her ladyship ordered from that firm in Minnesota—Mrs. Wiley's going to steam some of it tonight and serve it with the roast duckling—and the expressman is on his way up with a crate from Mr. and Mrs. MacIverson in California—a new shipment of oranges, avocados, dates and figs, I expect. Also, Pearce just rang up. He wants you to know that he's on his way back with the order from Maison Glass. He has the Russian Beluga caviar, those tins of *foie gras* his lordship likes, the Dutch cocoa, Mrs. Wiley's *pain de sucre,* the Linden tree honey, and that cheese, the one they wrap in spruce bark . . ."

"*Vacherin Mont d'Or,*" he pronounced carefully, referring to the difficult-to-obtain cheese that had to be specially ordered from Switzerland. "Thank you for the information, Carrie. Now, you and Doris know where the flowers go, and you should have the arrangements put out by the time Pearce gets back. The groceries from Park and Tilton's should be here by then, too. Lucky thing the Walker Gordon Dairy delivers early, and Pearce drives Mrs. Wiley down to the Washington Market so she can pick the fruits and vegetables personally, or we wouldn't be able to move in the kitchen for all the food that comes in," he said, wondering for the nth time why her ladyship insisted on ordering meat and poultry from *both* Shaffer's and Tingaud's, when either would do admirably . . . He came out of his tangent to notice Carrie still standing in the doorway.

"Is there a problem, Carrie?"

"It's Mr. de Renille. He asked me the oddest question just before, Mr. Hodges, and I'm not sure if I said the right thing," she blurted out.

The butler came out of his inactivity with a snap. "When was this, Carrie?" he inquired gently, motioning for her to come in. Mr. de Renille was a gentleman, but one never knew what ideas even a member of an esteemed family might come up with regarding servant girls.

"Just before, Mr. Hodges. I was dusting in the hallway when Mr. de Renille came out," she told him in her clear voice. "He said he was going for a walk, and then he asked me where the nearest church was. The church I go to," she clarified.

Hodges nodded in comprehension. He knew that Carrie, as the only Catholic on the staff, was proceeding cautiously. "I understand. What did you tell Mr. de Renille, Carrie?"

"That my church was no place for him. It's a parish for servants and tradespeople, not gentlemen. I told him he should ask Lord Thorpe."

"You did exactly the right thing." Hodges' voice was approving. "I'll mention the matter to Lord Thorpe when he returns this afternoon. Just remember Mr. de Renille asked you that question with the best of intentions."

"If you say so, Mr. Hodges," Carrie replied, her voice a bit doubtful. "Still, I can't see why he asked me in the first place. Being French Catholic isn't the same thing at all."

"Just remember Mr. de Renille has a lot to adjust to here in New York. He has been ill a long time, America must seem very strange to him, and he was only reaching out to something familiar," he said seriously. "It does us all well to remember difficult times in our own lives, and how we counted on others to help us through. And now that this matter is resolved," he finished with a smile, "I believe it's time for all of us to get back to work."

For Charles de Renille, his first trip out of the Dakota was any number of things—mainly bitterly cold, wildly strange and totally uncomfortable—but it provided him with the key to getting on in New York—he found its pace.

Not at first, of course, and as he slogged along Central Park West from Seventy-second to Seventy-third Street in an overcoat that was far too thin to keep out the icy blasts of cold wind blowing off the Park, and a pair of borrowed overshoes that didn't quite fit, he almost turned back. Later on—*much* later on—he would bemusedly reflect that the major events of his life always depended on such small things—in this case that the Seventy-third Street entrance to the Dakota was kept permanently locked. If it had been open, and he'd taken the cowards' way out, his new life might have ended then and there, but after fruitlessly rattling the iron gate, he grimaced, turned up his collar, stuck his hands in his pockets, and trudged on toward Columbus Avenue. Even the prospect of walking under the Elevated was preferable to traversing Central Park West again.

Hodges' directions had been precise, and he found both the shoe store and the stationers without difficulty. Laden down with parcels, he returned to the Dakota approximately an hour and a half after he left. The walk along Columbus Avenue to the corner of Seventy-second Street, with the Ninth Avenue Elevated clattering overhead, didn't frighten and disgust him as much as he expected. And, much to his surprise, he found himself moving along with the crowd, easily avoiding the puddles of melted snow and the odd patches of ice.

Lunch was steaming hot cream of mushroom soup, melted cheese sandwiches, and cinnamon-scented applesauce with slices of home-made pound cake. A place had been set for him at the dining-room table and, although he enjoyed the meal, he finished it quickly. Eating alone in the elegantly appointed room disturbed him. It was a room that demanded a dinner party laughing and talking, or else a man and a woman romantically alone together over a candlelit meal, not a lone man in the middle of the day eating a solitary lunch.

Lunch over, he wandered back into the corridor. Since he had several hours before Alix's return, he decided to take her advice and explore the rest of the apartment, beginning with the two-drawer French commode table of oak with black and gold lacquer gilt-work and a marble top. Charles remembered it from Henry's Albany flat when it had been placed opposite his bedroom door. Now it rested between the two doors of the master suite and its marble top, which had previously held a pair of candlesticks, was now adorned with a pair of jade horses from the Ming Dynasty, an assortment of silver boxes from various periods, and a dark green leather writing portfolio placed squarely in the center of the marble surface. Above it, on the wall, hung a small but excellent Renoir watercolor of the Bois.

Yesterday he'd been unable to absorb much of the drawing room's character, but now, with his veil of confusion gone, Charles was able to appreciate the spacious, delicately furnished room with its pale colors and airy, yet warm, feeling. There was no useless clutter here, and every side table had its own theme. The tables that flanked the six-foot sofas held cream-silk shaded lamps with rose, blue and cream bases from the K'ang Hsi Dynasty. There was one table reserved for a selection of Limoges boxes, another for English enamels, a third for priceless presentation boxes, and a fourth for Chinese Export *objets d'art*. Even the flowers fitted in with the decorating scheme, he observed as he moved around the room. A mixture of pink roses and tea roses in a silver pitcher with the presentation boxes, costly Dendrobium orchids filled a Chinese Export punch bowl, two crystal vases filled with an arrangement of blue irises and deep red roses, and tiger lilies in a flowered porcelain dish were placed on the Italian writing table with the Palisander border and criss-cross chestnut burn that was placed against the back of one of the sofas.

The lacquer-work grand piano was mercifully free of photographs of family and friends. It was a fashion

Charles had been raised to dislike—his parents had always held that such personal objects belonged in one's private rooms—and as he wandered around the drawing room, admiring the deceptively simple *luxe*, he recognized that a man never really escapes the way he's raised, and how he sees others is based on that early influence.

And I should know, I certainly tried hard enough to forget it all, he told himself amusedly as he came to the last table. Placed against the farthest wall—and in the most inconspicuous spot—it not only held two signed photographs, but Henry and Alix's small collection of Faberge.

There were no Easter eggs—those gem-studded miracles of art that were the prize of Europe's royalty—but King Edward and Queen Alexandra, in a frame of wood, silver and yellow guilloche enamel, faced President and Mrs. Roosevelt, who resided in a silver-gilt and pale blue guilloche enamel frame. A nephrite and gold shell-shaped dish was flanked by a three-inch jade donkey with rose-diamond eyes mounted on a chased gold-banded base of scarlet enamel, and a silver box embossed with red, blue and gold enamel-work, while a box of translucent blue enamel with tiny diamonds along the edges of the top held Russian cigarettes.

Leaving behind the treasure-filled drawing-room, he went on into the library with its book-filled walls and tables of American and English magazines. The selection of books ranged from expensively bound first editions to the latest publishers' offerings, and it was here Alix found him when she returned at half-past three, comfortably stretched out on one of the two leather chesterfields, happily reading a whodunit.

He immediately put aside his book, of course, and a half-hour later, over richly flavored Yunnan tea, watercress sandwiches and tiny brioche stuffed with *creme de foie gras* and plates of *petit fours*, Alix, along with

163

her neighbor Adele Seligman, provided Charles with a crash course in the history of New York City.

Adele Franks Seligman, like her younger neighbor, counted her ancestors among the city's great pre-Revolutionary War families. She was, in fact, a direct descendant of one of New York's first Jewish families who arrived on Peter Stuyvesant's island in 1654 aboard the *St. Charles*, having fled formerly Dutch-controlled Brazil when that country came under the unfriendly rule of Portugal. Her husband's family arrived from Amsterdam twenty years after that. And some hundred and ten years later, along with other New York families who were followers and contributors to the Cause, they left New York ahead of the invading British Army, pausing only long enough to remove the lead weights from their windowsashes to give to General Washington's army to be melted into bullets.

They entertained and informed him, and then he recounted that morning's adventures to both women.

"Poor Charles," Alix said, laughing. "I *am* sorry, but Henry and I decided that the best way for you to be introduced to New York was just to push you right out the door."

"Don't be *too* apologetic, Alix," Adele teased. "Charles doesn't look like the type of man who goes into shock because he's seen a few tenements, or gotten a few gusts of cold wind."

"I hope I'm not, either," he assured them. "When I read my Baedeker, I thought it was all going to be so easy, but after this morning, I realize I have a lot to learn about New York!"

Part of learning about New York is learning about its traditions, and its favorite tradition by far was the ritual of the Sunday newspapers. They were a law unto themselves, and a surprise to the unsuspecting—which

164

Charles de Renille certainly was.

No one had warned him about them, and on Sunday morning he could only stare in disbelief at the mountain of newspapers that Hodges carried into the bedroom and placed on the straight-back chair that went with the writing table. "Hodges, I know New York has a lot of newspapers and that the Thorpes take every one, but this . . ."

"These are the Sunday editions, sir," Hodges replied, silently offering a prayer that the sleep-rumpled young man sitting up in bed wasn't going to be one of those religious sorts who felt he not only had to mind his own morals, but everyone else's as well. "They're a New York original, as her ladyship puts it, rather like those skyscrapers one sees in the financial district." He moved the newspaper-laden chair closer to the bed. "You have the *Times*, the *World*, the *Herald*, the *Sun*, the *Tribune*, the *Telegram*, the *American* and the *Journal*," he intoned.

"Thank you, Hodges, but I really should leave them until I come back from church."

"If you'll forgive my saying so, sir, I really don't think it's a morning to be going out," he said, and pulled back the curtains to reveal a strong, steady snowfall.

Charles considered the view. "I guess I don't have a choice after all. But how do I make my way through that mountain of newsprint? Wouldn't you like to take a few copies back to the servants' hall with you?"

"Oh, no, sir. We have our own identical set of papers, as do Lord and Lady Thorpe. This is all yours."

"It's going to take me until next Sunday to read it all!"

"There is a trick to it, sir. Her ladyship taught it to us. You take the papers apart by sections—the news, drama, book review, rotogravure, financial, sporting pages—put all the groups together and read them like that. Except for the *Times*, they all have funny pages, and one generally begins with them," Hodges added helpfully.

"Thank you again, Hodges." He ran a hand over his face. "I'm going to shave first before I attempt any of this. I'll be ready for breakfast in about fifteen minutes."

A half-hour later, freshly shaved and bathed, Charles was back in bed, the papers divided up and arranged in front of him, his breakfast tray beside him. As he poured maple syrup over his hot waffles, he reflected that this morning he would have liked to attend mass at one of the churches on the list Henry had given him for parishes in which he would feel at home. But, he had to admit, considering how blameless his life now was, his nonattendance at Sunday mass today was at least going to give him something to confess.

Having to accept that his spiritual life was temporarily in the best order it could be, Charles picked up the funny pages of the *New York Herald* and began to read about the absurdly funny adventures of Buster Brown. It was a great deal later before he put the final section—the drama pages of the *Sun*—down on the floor with the rest of the morning's reading. *All done*, he thought, and reluctantly his gaze slid to the neatly wrapped package on the writing table. Beneath the brown paper were the two books Dick North wanted him to translate. They had been waiting for him when he'd returned from his first morning's excursion, and now, days later, he finally faced the fact that the time had come to fullfill his obligation to the editor.

The untouched books bothered his conscience far more than his nonattendance at church. When he got down to base facts, one activity could be postponed, on the other he'd given his word as a gentleman.

Resolutely, he got out of bed, washed the newsprint off his hands, dressed quickly, put his breakfast tray on the floor outside the door, sat down at the writing table, and unwrapped the books. He opened the book of fairy tales first and found that they were ten short, delightful tales

166

full of fairies waving wands and elves dancing in magical glades. He could almost see the sugar plums and the silver dust. With the other book, Charles found his lip curling in a combination of dismay and dislike. It was, as Dick had told him, a romance, the sort of happily-ever-after tale that Charles couldn't bring himself to believe any *truly* intelligent woman ever read.

You're not being asked to review them, just to translate them into English, he told himself severely as he took out the supplies he'd purchased, lining up the sharpened pencils in a neat row, filling his new fountain pen with ink, and checking over the stacks of thick white pads and the blue-covered, ruled copybooks.

He began with the fairy tales, and did two versions of each story. First a literal translation from French to English, and then a more refined one, substituting words when necessary, rearranging sentences so they flowed smoothly, and always imagining himself reading them aloud to a child.

He worked with the single-minded dedication that made him a first-class scholar and, when he closed the large, illustrated volume with its gold-edged pages, it was well after five in the evening. Charles stretched, easing tight muscles, and looked out the window. It was still snowing, but Alix and Henry were having a few friends over for dinner, and Charles didn't suppose that a little thing like an all-day snowstorm ever kept anyone away from any function in New York. It was all to be very informal, he'd been told. Everyone would just twirl spaghetti, drink red wine and talk.

Enough, he decided, putting away his work. To really do this properly he needed both a dictionary and a thesaurus, as well as the Thorpes' Remington typewriter. That meant if he went into the library to search them out now, he'd still be in his shirtsleeves when the first guests arrived. It was time for him to wash up and put on a tie and his suit jacket.

In the dressing room, he opened the doors of the rosewood cabinet and studied the row of ties from Sulka and Charvet that hung from the specially constructed rack. For a moment, he admired their rich look and feel. They were all new, not like . . . like . . .

Reluctantly, Charles looked at his suits, all hanging neatly, each one an inch apart from the next, and he finally saw his clothes through Louis' eyes—and the eyes of the people he'd met in the past few days. He didn't purposely want to go around New York City looking like a borderline charity case in suits and shirts that no longer fit properly and an overcoat that couldn't keep him warm. The way he looked at home, among people who understood him, he belatedly realized, wasn't going to do while he was in America—not at all.

He examined his dinner clothes and his dress suit. They would have to be replaced, as would all of his shirts. A new suit or two, and possibly an overcoat. Yes, that would suffice. No need to go overboard and recklessly spend his entire letter of credit, he resolved firmly, closing the cabinet's doors. Now, before anyone arrived, was the perfect time to take Henry aside and ask him if there was a decent tailor in New York City.

Since its opening day in 1818, Brooks Brothers has been the premier men's clothing shop in America. Its founder, Henry Sands Brooks, a successful provisioner of solid Connecticut stock, was forty-six when he opened his door in the then-busy location of Catherine and Cherry Streets. It was a year after the New York Stock and Exchange board hammered out its first formal constitution, and its members—no doubt attracted by the quality and quantity of the merchandise they could purchase in their own city without having to send to London's Savile Row—became faithful and steady customers—as did their descendants.

Theodore Roosevelt was a regular customer at Broadway and Twenty-second Street, as were many members of government. They sold to men who came from old-money families, and men who had just made their fortune. There were Army and Navy officers who wouldn't allow their custom-made uniforms to be ordered anywhere else. Hard-working giants of industry and the idle rich alike shopped here. And, in all truth, Brooks Brothers could make the claim that they had outfitted men from childhood to the end of their mortal coil.

A special department functioned solely for the outfitting of male servants. For gentlemen, there were clothes for every hour of the day, and for all sports. And when the doors were unlocked on the last day of the month of February, Leap Year 1904, the first gentlemen to step inside were Henry Thorpe and Charles de Renille.

He knew he was being ridiculous, but as Henry introduced him to Frederick Webb, Brooks Brothers' stellar salesman, who had been waiting to greet them, Charles suddenly felt like the new boy at school meeting the headmaster. Without displaying one outward sign of approval or disapproval, this was the man who would pass judgment on him in all matters sartorial.

Pleasantries were exchanged as Mr. Webb led them upstairs to a large, well-lit, mirrored fitting room and, once coats, hats, gloves, mufflers and galoshes were removed, it was time to get down to the business of selecting clothes.

"I need dinner clothes and a dress suit," Charles told the patient, intelligent man who sold clothes to the king of Wall Street, J. P. Morgan, as well as every man who'd been a guest in the Thorpe home on Wednesday night, including Henry Thorpe himself. "I have one function this coming Sunday, and another the following Saturday, but I'll understand if they can't be finished in time—"

"Of course they can be finished in time, Mr. de Renille." Mr. Webb made a few notes in his little black notebook where he kept the clothing details of his customers. "We'll arrange fittings all this week, and your dinner clothes will be ready by Saturday. Now, while we're discussing formal clothes, will you need a suit of morning clothes?"

"No, I don't think so."

"You will if you go to Kentucky for the Derby." Henry's interjection was gently put. Charles had that skittish look on his face again, and he moved to forestall any unnecessary comments that his friend might make. "Haven't those horse friends of your mother's written you yet?"

"Yes, the Woodwards. But I haven't decided . . ."

Even as he spoke, Charles had the sinking feeling that the entire matter had already been decided, and his going to Louisville was no longer a question, but simply a matter of time.

Before he could say anything else, a fitter arrived, and he was measured from every conceivable angle, followed by a long consultation with Mr. Webb over fabrics and colors. Charles discovered he could wear either single- or double-breasted sack suits, but fancy waistcoats didn't suit him any more than double-breasted ones did, or bow ties, or even the pink shirts that Brooks Brothers alone sold.

"You're a white shirt type of man, Mr. de Renille," Mr. Webb said in a voice that was anything but disapproving.

Charles' firm decision for one or two suits fell quickly by the way-side, and he found himself selecting clothes to get him through the remainder of the winter, as well as lightweight clothes for the spring and summer seasons. He added a dozen carefully selected foulard ties, and cashmere and Shetland sweaters, all with long sleeves and crew necks, to his purchases before turning his attention to white flannels, dark-blue blazers, gray-flannel golf trousers and white ducks for tennis.

It took all morning. And, following lunch at the Café Martin, they returned to the store for the rest of the afternoon. Charles was grateful to Henry for his calm support and judicious advice. But, as he endlessly tried on garments, and was measured and pinned and chalked, he hated every second of it. From the way he'd been raised, men did not buy clothes in such quantity at one time. It smacked of being a useless playboy, or, far worse, effeminate.

Finally it was over—or so he thought.

"You need another coat," Henry remarked unexpectedly. "That black cashmere is much too thin. How long have you had it?"

Charles looked up from the sales slips he was signing, Mr. Webb having opened a charge account for him. "It was my father's," he said painfully.

"I'm sorry. But the fact remains we have at least another month of weather like this."

Charles bowed before the inescapable fact of New York weather, and Mr. Webb was dispatched to bring some proper selections. He'd already chosen a dress overcoat for evening wear, and a raincoat for the spring, but as much as he clung to the wholly inadequate overcoat because it had been his father's, he was also sharply aware of its inadequacy in keeping him warm.

A vicuna overcoat was tried on and rejected, as was a handsome Harris tweed which was woven in Scotland. Neither quite suited him.

"Perhaps this will do, Mr. de Renille," Mr. Webb suggested, helping him into a camel's-hair chesterfield. "Warm and good-looking at the same time."

Cautiously, he regarded his reflection. Charles took no

joy in looking in the mirror. In his mind's eye, he still retained the vision of the skeletal figure he'd once turned into. He stared at himself grimly, uncompromisingly, and after an endless minute, with Henry and Mr. Webb looking on, he slowly began to smile. It wasn't as bad as he'd thought. Not at all bad, he decided. He'd never be asked to pose for a magazine illustration, but he wouldn't frighten anyone either and, best of all, if his valet were here, he would finally have Louis' unqualified approval.

The Dakota was still the center of Charles' universe, and once his shock at his first sight of it wore off, he began to find that it fascinated him. Its architecture would never win a prize, but the building was fireproof, and the sixty-five apartments comprised its own version of a well-fortified city-state.

The smallest apartment was four rooms, the largest had twenty, and all were floored in mahogany, doored in oak, embellished in marble and swathed in carved plaster.

In addition to the regular staff of doormen, porters, janitors and elevator operators, the Dakota had its own painter, plumber, electrician and glazier, as well as a tailors' shop to steam the suits of the gentlemen tenants, and a complete bastion of maids under the direction of Mrs. Crate, the housekeeper, who served to supplement the tenants' own servants.

There was a restaurant which would deliver any or all of that night's dinner menu to the apartments of those who either did not wish to come downstairs, or who did not retain the services of a cook. In the summer there was a private park with a rose garden and tennis and croquet courts. The building's laundry did superb work and, as he approached the completion of his first full week in New York, Charles was becoming used to getting his shirts, socks, underwear and nightshirts back from the laundry wrapped separately in pink tissue paper and placed in a

172

wicker basket.

If the Dakota was very nearly a self-sufficient entity, he often thought, then its tenants, appropriately enough, were of all types in the person of Rupert Randall.

He was, more or less, Henry Thorpe's ward. A nineteen-year-old boy, who, Henry remarked to Charles when explaining him, had once had the morals and outlook of a *roué* of thirty. That had come to an end in September 1902, shortly after Henry and Alix's marriage, when Rupert had been discovered in his rooms at Magdalen College, Oxford, in bed with two very high-priced prostitutes. For that transgression, as well as all the others he'd committed, he was summarily sent off to a monastery in Gloucestershire.

"A year of hard work and contemplation of his sins," Henry wryly informed Charles. "It seemed the only way to teach him a long-lasting lesson. I never thought it would have that much effect on him, but I'm glad to see I was wrong. However, I have to warn you in advance about a few things."

"That he prefers women, and won't be overjoyed at my company?" Charles hazarded.

"That's one thing. The other is that while Rupert's mother, Lady Allison Randall, is Catholic, Rupert is not, and he views every Roman Catholic he comes in contact with as wanting to convert him."

"But that's ridiculous!"

"Obsessions generally are."

"Is that why he lives with the Seligmans?"

"No. At first it was a matter of convenience. Rupert arrived in New York shortly after Isabel was born, and it was easier to have him stay next door. As it turned out, Bill and Adele are able to provide him with the sort of steady, affectionate life he needs."

"So he's totally reformed?"

"I wouldn't go so far as to say that. But he fits in with

173

the Seligmans far better than he ever did anywhere else. Fortunately, he looks a great deal like them, too, although that sleight of nature's hand sends Cliff straight up the wall." Henry regarded him obliquely. "If you were another sort, Charles, I'd hesitate. But you're no proselytizer, and you would have made a worst causist, so I guess it's all right to expose you to Rupert!"

Charles was still bemusedly turning over that conversation in his mind when, exactly one week after his arrival, he was ushered into the Seligmans' apartment by Sackett, their English butler, and shown to Rupert Randall's room. He had arrived before the start of Bill and Adele's dinner party in order to make Rupert's acquaintance. He took Henry's warning seriously, but he was still unprepared for the greeting that was flung at him as he stepped into the bedroom.

"Well, look who has come to call! The erstwhile Jesuit himself. Are you here to gather my soul?"

"No, I just thought I'd say hello and ask how you're feeling," Charles said, forcing himself to speak mildly, and at the same time uttering a silent prayer of thanks to Henry for warning him in advance.

"Oh? And how long before you work the Church into your polite conversation? Tell me, was that one of the rules in your being let go? Did you have to promise to convert all who pass your way?"

Charles regarded the young man in the bed with annoyance tinged with acute sympathy. Rupert Randall looked terrible, he thought. The high fever and severe pain of influenza had left him white, haggard and suspiciously red-rimmed about the eyes.

His bedroom was handsomely proportioned and well-decorated, but it was obviously inhabited by a student: books were jammed to overflowing in the bookcases, a typewriter, notebooks and textbooks were neatly arranged on the writing table. For a long minute, Charles silently considered Rupert before taking the straight-backed chair and sitting across it so he could fold his arms over the back.

"Look," he told him finally, "I don't like being insulted, or having my past referred to as a dirty joke. I came in here because I thought you'd like to visit. If it turns out all you want to do is see how angry you can make me, I'll go into the drawing room for an aperitif and some decent conversation with well-behaved people."

Rupert regarded him out of thick-lashed silver-gray eyes that gave Charles the uncomfortable feeling that this black-haired boy knew every detail of his life, every secret, and he would have no scruples about mocking him if so inclined.

"You ought to be careful how you sit in that suit," he observed abruptly, pushing the pillows up behind him. "It looks like it's seen better days, and I don't think you'd like it if the seat of your trousers split!"

It was an opening, and Charles seized the moment. "I'd feel like the biggest idiot alive. That's why I spent the morning at Brooks Brothers having pins stuck in me."

"For a dinner jacket and trousers?"

"For half the store, I think." The tension eased between them, and Charles ventured gingerly, "I don't ever remember ordering so many clothes at one time before."

"From Mr. Webb?"

"He was incredibly patient. I hadn't worn most of my clothes in a very long time. I'd also convinced myself I had absolutely no use for any new ones, except for riding gear. I feel as if I single-handedly depleted their stock!"

"Well, at least it'll give you something to confess." Rupert's voice was wicked.

Charles was at a momentary loss for words—at least ones he could utter in a sickroom—and the best course open to him seemed to be to remain silent and let the comment pass.

"Have they been keeping you busy?" the younger man finally asked, breaking the awkward silence.

"Very much so. I've been to the Museum of Natural History and the Metropolitan Museum of Art, and tomorrow I'm going to the New York Historical Society," Charles replied, wondering what type of response his answer would elicit this time. "I'm also translating two books from French to English for Dick North."

"My, but you *are* busy. It's Alix's doing of course. Uncle Henry was never one to overly involve himself in anyone's life."

"That's a *very* unfair remark! Henry is a good host and a loyal friend, and you should pay more respect to your guardian."

"Uncle Henry isn't my guardian, except in a very roundabout way. He's the executor of my father's will. Oh—all right. He's a wonderful man." He smiled in remembrance. "When I arrived last August, I asked Alix if I should call her Aunt, and she said only if I were interested in a quick but expensive trip to the dentist!" He began to laugh, but a look of pain crossed his face and he sank back against the pillows.

Charles was instantly concerned. "Are you feeling ill? Shall I get help?"

"No . . . no. I just gave out all of a sudden. How did you bear it, being laid up so long?"

"Most of the time I was too disoriented to care. Does your head still ache?"

"How did you know? No, the headache's nearly all gone, but my throat hurts and I'm tired all the time. It's rotten being sick like this," he went on. "I'm never going to crawl out from under the mountain of work I'll have to make up. It'll be weeks before I visit at Cliff's or Gareth's or Jimmy's because I might infect their children. I won't even be able to go next door and read to Isabel the way I

176

always do. Do you know that she's the first baby I ever really saw or held?" he added.

"You'll be well again before you know it," Charles comforted Rupert, echoing words that had been said to him so many times.

"Are you going to steal my girl?"

"*What?*"

"Mallory Kirk. She's a cousin of Alix's and, as the saying goes, we're rather attached to each other."

Charles felt rather at a loss. "How nice."

"Do you like girls?"

"Of course I do!"

Rupert considered him, amusement dancing in his eyes. "One never knows."

"I was at a matinee this afternoon. *Glittering Gloria*—"

"Good for you. I'm glad to see the Jesuits weren't able to squeeze all the red-blooded impulses out of you. Or do you confess that also?"

"If you don't watch your mouth, I am going to have something to confess, and it won't be looking at chorus girls!" Charles snapped, forgetting all his good intentions about dealing with the invalid. "You have the mind of—"

"Is this brat bothering you?" a cool, well-bred voice asked as the door opened and a black-haired man with intense blue eyes entered the room. "I can't understand why Dad hasn't taken his razor strop to him yet." After a withering glance at Rupert, he held out his hand to Charles. "I'm Clifford Seligman. No—don't bother getting up. Welcome to New York."

"Thank you." They shook hands. "I saw the picture of your wife and children on the cover of *Town & Country*."

"It doesn't do them justice," Clifford said, and flashed a smile that transformed his face, making him seem younger and more carefree. "When you meet Julie in a

177

few minutes, you'll see why."

He leaned back against the wall, and with that casual stance he overwhelmingly reminded Charles of Guy. There was no real physical resemblance, except for the same color hair, but they both had the steely self-assurance that comes naturally to first-born sons of old-rich families, and the fact that Clifford Seligman, Columbia '91, was a few inches under six feet tall, didn't lessen one bit the aura of power Charles immediately sensed surrounding him.

"Has Rupert been applying his version of the Chinese water torture to you?" he inquired.

"Oh, Cliff, come on," Rupert interjected, his face no longer mocking. "I was just curious to see what Goody-Two-Shoes over there was made of!"

"Flesh and blood, just like the rest of us, and don't let me *ever* hear you call a guest in *my* father's house names, or I'll take care of you myself!"

"Boys—boys, no fighting. Not in a sickroom." The door opened again, and a kind-faced, middle-aged woman in a nurse's uniform looked in. "Five minutes more to visit, Mr. Clifford, no more. Then it's time for Mr. Rupert's medication and nourishment."

The nurse closed the door, and Cliff turned to Charles. "I want you to know, Charles, that you have a standing invitation to come out to Cove House for July and August. That's the family's summer place in Woodbury, Long Island."

"Thank you, I'm honored by your invitation. If I'm still here in the summer, I'll take you up on it—that is, if you have room for me."

For the first time, he saw Rupert Randall and Clifford Seligman exchange a look of amused tolerance and, once again, Charles had the nagging feeling he'd made yet another *gaffe*. But, before he could ask for clarification, Cliff remarked that they'd really better be getting into the drawing room.

"But before we leave you to your chicken soup and vanilla custard, I have a story I think you'll find amusing. I had lunch today with that idiot Rob Gilchrist. I truly hope you never see his house, Charles, it'd turn you against America and Americans in a minute."

"Surely not that bad?"

"Worse. His wife has a fixation on grand French furniture. The whole place is *faux maison de plaisir*. It's too bad, really. Thea would have done a superb job but, to get back to lunch . . . I took him to the City Midday Club, and all Rob could talk about was his new membership at the Metropolitan. He had the unmitigated gall to end up by saying he was terribly sorry I couldn't join also, and would I like him to see if the Board might make an exception in my case!"

"No wonder you took him *out* to lunch, you didn't want to be seen with him in the firm's dining room," Rupert put in. "I hope you told him what he could do with his membership!"

"Oh, no, brat. Nothing so crude or direct as that," he said smoothly. "I thanked him nicely, returned the compliment by saying I wished the Sons of the Revolution and the Sons of the American Revolution weren't closed to him because of those ancestors of his with the unfortunate Tory sympathies, and said I would never consider applying to his club for membership under any circumstances." Clifford opened the door and motioned to Charles. "I told Rob it would be a complete impossibility, not to mention an insult to my palate. After all, I said to him, have you ever tasted the *food* in the Metropolitan Club?"

When he'd first heard about the party at the Lasky townhouse, Charles had been somewhat nonplussed at the idea of a lavish—although not full-dress—party being given on a Sunday evening. Fortunately, however, he'd been too overcome by his first experiences in New York to ask questions that would, on top of all his other mistakes, show him up to be a social idiot. Charles reflected as he stood in a corner of Percy and Charlotte Lasky's double drawing room, watching the guests who were a mixture of theatrical luminaries and the so-called "civilians"—men and women who enjoyed socializing with actors.

Percy Lasky—along with his brothers Cyril and Maurice—were the latest in their family to assume the mantle of producer-manager, a family tradition that stretched back to the New York and London of the 1700s, and now made them pre-eminent in American and British theatrical circles.

From his vantage point, Charles could observe his host and hostess as they circulated among their guests. Percy was as impressive a figure as any actor in the room, and Charlotte, elegant in Doucet's black-spangled tulle gown with black velvet shoulder straps and belt, had welcomed him warmly and asked after his family when he'd arrived with Henry and Alix an hour before.

He accepted a fresh glass of champagne from one of the smiling maids who were carrying trays of tulip-shaped glasses around the room that was furnished in fine English antiques. Charles' gaze found Henry and Alix who were in the center of an admiring group that included Louise Homer, the Metropolitan's contralto prima donna, and the popular actress Drina de Wolfe, whose striking portrait had graced the cover of the January issue of *Theatre Magazine*.

It was thanks to Alix—stunning as usual, this time in Lucile's white Japanese crepe evening gown with a draped gold belt and gold ribbon outlining the shoulder straps and decolletage—who had provided him with a year's worth of *Theatre Magazine* for background reading. And he was able to feel relatively comfortable in this atmosphere, as well as recognize some of the celebrities enjoying themselves on the theatre's traditional "dark night"—the only night working actors had off.

Holding court in front of the fireplace was Arthur Hornblow, editor of *Theatre Magazine*, and William Gillette, who had made a tremendous hit three years earlier with his portrayal of Sherlock Holmes, and was now pleasing audiences at the New Lyceum Theatre in *The Admirable Crichton*. Eddie Foy, the comic actor, was surrounded by guests who still wanted to know details of the tragic fire that had swept the Iroquois Theatre in Chicago at the height of the Christmas season. Mr. Foy had been onstage during the matinee of *Mr. Bluebeard* when the horrifying conflagration had started, killing nearly six-hundred men, women, and children before it was extinguished.

On a happier note, Charles recognized Violet Dale, the smoldering-eyed actress of *A Chinese Honeymoon*; Arnold Daly who was Shaw's Marchbanks in *Candida*; and May Robson, who was an admirable Queen Elizabeth in *Dorothy Vernon*, was chatting with Ida Levick, who was scheduled to succeed her. He also spotted Joseph Kilgour who had a good likeness to the George Washington he portrayed in *Captain Barrington*, as well as the very pleasing sight of the insouciant Grace Franklin, whose *Mother Goose* at the New Amsterdam Theatre was *not* for one's children.

To be sure, Charles had been introduced around, but he found that, for the time being, he preferred to be the observer on the scene. He was well aware of the interested glances that many of the room's elegantly dressed women were throwing at him. Brooks Brothers, he reflected, delivered a superb garment; not Savile Row, but still good enough to fit the cliche of the clothes making the man. It was still beyond him that a woman might be interested in him no matter what he was wearing.

Looking around him, he supposed that the enthusiasm of the guests in greeting each other—handshakes that went on a shade too long, embraces easily exchanged, and endearments too freely used—might surprise and offend a guest who was used to more formality at parties. Fortunately, coming from an affectionate family, the open attitudes of the men and women around him didn't cause any difficulties or . . .

"We've been under your scrutiny all evening, Mr. de Renille. Tell me, do we pass inspection? Or can it be you're a writer hoping to overhear a good story?"

The voice that interrupted his thoughts sounded to Charles like melted silver, and the woman to whom it belonged had one of the most arresting presences he had ever come in contact with. "I might be a newspaper reporter," he responded.

"No, then you'd be as busy as a bee, going from group to group, trying to get our names and faces correct for your story."

"It would be a pretty poor one. I don't think I could ever capture a party like this one on paper. The conversations—"

"Seem very glamorous to you now because we're all talking about the play we're currently in, or just closed in, or are auditioning for, or are rehearsing for. In a little while, probably after dinner, we'll talk about our families, or the stock market, or Ida Tarbell's latest exposé, and you'll think what a dull lot we are!"

"That's very unfair," he protested to the very attractive chestnut-haired woman in the expensive Lucile *princesse* gown of lace over very pale blue silk. They had met earlier in the evening, but he hadn't heard her name over the din of conversation swirling around him. "The real reason I'm standing here is that I don't want any of the other guests to know how ignorant I am about the American theatre. I've read through *Theatre Magazine* for the past year, and I thought I was well prepared, but recognizing faces and discussing the theatre itself are two entirely different things!"

"Alix told me you haven't been here very long." Her voice was enthralling. "Have you been to the theatre yet?"

"This past Wednesday afternoon at Daly's Theatre. *Glittering Gloria*. It's not Shakespeare, but still . . ."

"Go on, please. Tell me what you thought of it," she urged and, at her prompting, Charles told her about the matinee.

Glittering Gloria—a puff piece imported from London—had a basic plot that was so old it creaked. The married man and his engaged friend, both enamored of the same chorus girl nicknamed "Glittering Gloria"; the husband purchasing a diamond necklace for the chorine while his wife is in another room of the jeweler's establishment. There were the usual hapless attempts for the husband to dispose of the jewels by pressing them on his friend, followed by the second act where both men are forced to take refuge in trunks in Gloria's flat to avoid the outraged wife and fiancée.

The bull-dog who ran amuck on stage when sighting a red scarf turned out to be the best entertainment. "Cordelia," sung by Eugene O'Rourke as the baggage master, was warmly applauded by the audience. Adelaide Prince and Phyllis Rankin as the wife and fiancée were attractive figures, the Hengler Sisters' dance routine was graceful, and there were the usual number of pretty chorus girls. But as for Adele Ritchie, the "Glittering Gloria" of the play . . .

"I thought the critics were most unfair to poor Adele," his companion said firmly. "All that business about a

183

'lackluster performance' was nonsense. You're right, of course, Mr. de Renille, the play is hardly *Hamlet*, or even *All's Well That Ends Well*, and her singing voice is barely passable, but—"

"I haven't been to the theatre in such a long time that if Miss Ritchie had croaked like a frog, I probably wouldn't have cared."

He was still telling the actress whose name he could *not* remember about his afternoon at the theatre when a young man detached himself from a nearby group and joined them.

"Hello, Ethel darling," he said, kissing her cheek. "Has Charles Frohman been cracking the whip over you? You can always come over to my father and uncle's if it gets too terrible."

"Now, Davey—" she warned with a laugh that sounded like a graceful waterfall. "Have you met Charles de Renille yet?"

"No, we missed each other on the first go-around. How are you getting on?" he asked as they shook hands. "Are all of us too much for you?"

"I'm having a wonderful time," he replied, and this time, instead of a mocking gaze, there was a genuine smile in return.

"Good, then you can both fill me in on everything. Ethel, what's next for you?"

"A new play by Thomas Racewood. I'm reading the script now."

"What's he calling it?"

"*Sunday.* It has all the elements that theatre-goers love. Lots of adventure and romance, and the setting shifts from the Far West to England and then back again. Now don't try to get any more information out of me, David Lasky, because I won't tell," she added archly. "I see that Arthur Hornblow wants a word with me. Please excuse me, gentlemen."

184

"She's enchanting," Charles said when they were alone.

"Oh, definitely," David agreed, then looked at him intently. "I heard you rambling on about Adele Ritchie, and I decided to come over before you began telling tales about your adventures at the stage door."

"I never went to the stage door," Charles snapped.

"Don't get upset, I didn't mean anything by it," David said in a conciliatory voice. "Did you know to whom you were talking just now?"

"I didn't catch her name, and as far as I know, that's not a crime."

"No," David sighed, "it's not. Look, it'll be time for dinner soon, so stick with me. We have some touchy people here, and Dad permits only one faux pas per night."

"If you say so."

With that much settled, David skillfully moved the conversation back to Charles' New York visit. "How long do you plan to stay? Easter week isn't long enough. Oh, don't look so surprised." He smiled knowingly. "This trip to New York is your Lenten sacrifice, and if you keep treating it like that, you're going to have one heck of a rotten time!"

"The day I got here—it'll be two weeks this coming Wednesday—and I saw the docks and the Elevated for the first time, I couldn't believe that this was the greatest city in America," he told David. "I hadn't wanted to leave my family's home in France—my home. I'd been . . . ill for a rather long time, and when I recovered, I'd lost interest in a lot of things," Charles went on, amending and altering the truth slightly. "Finally, my mother and brothers couldn't stand it any longer and they packed me off to visit Henry and Alix—"

"With the proviso they don't see your face for the next six weeks," David humorously finished for him.

"Those aren't the sort of instructions that make a good tourist. Have you been any further than a ten-block radius of the Dakota before tonight?"

"Except for Brooks Brothers and Daly's Theatre, not really," Charles admitted. "Do you have any suggestions?"

"Walk. Walk until you think your feet are going to fall off. It's the only way to see this city and learn what it's all about. Forget about maps and guidebooks, just point yourself in a new direction every day and take it from there," he concluded, and then grinned. "And once you're used to that, get on a train and come up to Boston for a weekend and I'll show you around. I'm a sophomore at Harvard."

"Thank you. But if I'd be interrupting your studies—"

"If you were, I never would have invited you," he retorted. "I think you'll like Boston, but if you go up there on your own, you won't find it a very pleasant place. As far as those Beacon Hill snobs are concerned, you'll just be one more Papist."

Charles flinched. "Surely not."

"Oh, yes. Look, forget about that. Why don't you plan to come up some time in April? The weather's generally pretty good. Also, Anthony Kendall—he's a new actor under contract to Dad—is touring in a show that'll be in Boston then, and the three of us, along with some chorus girls, can have a night on the town."

Less than two weeks earlier, such a suggestion would have filled him with panic, but tonight he agreed with David's suggestion, his only trepidation caused by the mistakes he kept making.

"So I've noticed," David commiserated with him. "Some day you'll find it all very funny."

"I hope so," Charles replied doubtfully. "So far, I always seem to put my foot in it somehow. What did I do tonight with the actress I was talking to? I may as well get

186

the worst over with."

"Nothing all *that* bad," David told him as they joined the flow of guests going toward the dining room. "My kid brother would call you a dope," he went on as Charles blanched, "but there's no real harm done, so don't look like that. But, Charles, if I were you, the next time I decided to go head over heels for music-hall fluff like Adele Ritchie, I'd make sure I didn't confide how wonderful I thought she was to Ethel Barrymore!"

Charles went reluctantly to New York, but as the weeks wore on, contrary to every expectation, he began to love it. There was something about its shifting, pulsating, ever-moving populace that stirred him and, after the first two weeks of astonishment and adjustment, where every street sound seemed to grate on his nerves, he found himself moving along with its pace.

It was an ideal time to be in New York. Only a few years earlier, Manhattan made its final move uptown, forever erasing the final remnants of its rural past, and now, in the late winter months of 1904, New York City was a complete kingdom. From the tip of the Battery to the furthest reaches of Morningside Heights, from the East River to the Hudson, there wasn't a square block that was free from some sort of change. Old buildings came down, new ones were put up, grand old residential communities slowly turned commercial, and a neighborhood where no one would have dreamed of living five years earlier could seemingly overnight transform itself into the newest and most fashionable place to live. Buildings grew taller, luxury apartment houses more prevalent, mansions and town houses grander, and three new luxury hotels would make their debuts by the end of the year.

Was he really here? Charles would often ask himself as he craned his neck upward to look at yet another twenty-story building. Was he actually moving deftly through crowds? And, most important and yet most unanswerable of all, had he really thought that he'd been sent across an ocean to a meaningless exile?

He still didn't feel truly at home in the Thorpe household. How could he when he felt he was trespassing on their privacy? That would change when they made the move upstairs to the twenty-room apartment, but in the meantime his days, for the first time in years, had both variety and structure, beginning nearly every morning with a ride along Central Park's bridal paths.

Charles visited every museum, art gallery, department store, and book shop he could find, and in the process, he became adept at the public transportation system. If, on his first day in New York, when he'd seen the Sixth Avenue Elevated, Henry Thorpe had told him that in less than three weeks he'd be riding it, Charles would probably have laughed in his friend's face. But now that mode of transportation, along with electric street-cars and horse-drawn omnibuses and hansom cabs were his accepted conveyances for getting around the city.

Henry Thorpe introduced him at the Automobile Club of America, Clifford Seligman invited him to lunch at the Columbia University Club, Newton Phipps invited him to both the Metropolitan Club and the Union League Club, he went with Philip Leslie to the Century Association, and accompanied William Seligman, his youngest son James, and Rupert Randall, when Bill made his semi-annual visit to the confines of the New York Yacht Club.

But as much as the sightseeing filled his days, and invitations to dinners and theatre parties and opera events filled his nights, it was not enough. Something was missing, and he felt the lack keenly, even though he couldn't center on the free-floating need that he had to *do* something.

The party at the Laskys' had been his turning point.

The moment when he left one familiar path and started on a new and untried one. Until that night he'd thought he had the rest of his life planned out—the six weeks in America, and then home to Normandy, followed by the secluded house he would purchase. For health reasons, it would have to be in the south of France, probably the Juan-les-Pins side of Cannes. A hidden spot for the reclusive bachelor—the only life now open to him. Or so he thought. He still brought up the plan and reviewed it in his mind, but more and more it seemed to him to be the device of a wretched, stunted man.

And that is what you no longer are, he told himself brutally. Any more than you're in precarious health. It's not because of all the invitations either—those things don't matter to you, they never have. It all comes down to the fact that here in New York no one cares.

It wasn't really true, he amended instantly. Everyone he met *did* care. They cared if he was happy and having a good time and seeing all the sights and enjoying the company he was keeping. What they didn't care about was his past. In New York he wasn't the youngest son with no place in the world. In New York no one knew—or didn't care—that he'd spent five years with the Jesuits. And, most important, in New York he had never been *non compos mentis*. When he left a party, or after Sunday mass at St. Jean Baptiste, there were no whispers or speculation behind his back. His mental condition, both past and present, was of interest to no one.

Slowly, bit by bit, he began to release the fantasy of the reclusive life. He couldn't live like that now, not after the weeks of exposure to a way of life where what mattered was what he offered of himself.

He was alive again, he realized, and New York was his Lourdes. But now, like the suppliants in search of a miracle, he had been cured, and what *he* had to do was put

189

his life back together.

Long ago Charles learned that the true power of having prayers answered was in offering them up and letting them go. It was sound advice and he followed it. He knew what he had to do. His first priority was to be of service to someone, to help out. And, if he were truly to find a new life in this city, the way would eventually be shown to him.

It didn't take very long, and once again it was Dick North who came to his aid.

Charles had translated both books and returned them to Doubleday, Page, ten days after he'd begun work on them, receiving in return a note of thanks from Frank Doubleday, informing him that he would receive a credit line listing him as the translator when the books were published. But there was no mention of the Napoleon biography.

It's probably being handled by someone else, Charles told himself. After all, why would a prominent American publisher want to hand over an important book to an unknown Frenchman solely because he had a British education?

In his own mind, Charles closed off any further speculation on the matter and lost himself in the exploration of New York. When he got right down to it, there was much more fun in eating butter cakes drenched in maple syrup at Child's following a visit to the Stock Exchange, or enjoying jelly-filled doughnuts and hot chocolate at Mary Elizabeth's after a behind-the-scenes tour of the Metropolitan Opera House, or savoring frogs' legs provencale, partridge Venitienne, and peaches *flambée* at the Cafe des Beaux Arts following an opening night on Broadway than there was in brooding about a book he would never see except in a bookstore and translated by someone far more qualified than he could ever be. With that much settled and put aside, he found himself utterly speechless when, some weeks later, Richard North asked him if he remembered the book.

"It's been a month now, and I thought you might have forgotten," Dick told him. "You've never mentioned the matter to me since Alix's party."

"I didn't want to press," Charles admitted, still somewhat stunned. He saw Dick and Megan on a frequent social basis, but the idea of asking him what was being done about the Napoleon biography was a question one simply didn't ask. "I assumed it was either being translated by the professor you told me about, or it had been passed on to a more suitable scholar."

"I understand from Alix that you're a scholar. But whether you are or not, do you want to do the book?"

They were standing in one of the reception rooms of the Whist Club and, as Charles looked at Dick, calm and complacent after an evening of excellent bridge, lighting a fresh Turkish cigarette to replace the one he had just finished, he couldn't resist thinking that if this were indeed the answer to his prayers, it was happening in a very unlikely place.

Charles was an excellent bridge player—he knew the latest techniques, always made the proper bids, and never forgot his partners' signals. Had he used these skills in Paris, he would have been hard put to find a welcome at any table—no gentleman was supposed to play *that* well. But in New York his ability at auction bridge was taken as a sign of being a good sport.

His talent had come to light at William and Adele Seligman's dinner party. There had been bridge after dinner, and Charles was partnered with Julie Seligman, herself a more than competent player and, at the end of the evening, when all the scores were totalled and compared, they were the clear winners.

"My wife plays like a Philadelphia lawyer," Clifford

told him as they were being congratulated. "Julie generally chews up her partner along with the other team," he said of his tall, beautiful, auburn-haired wife. "If you can do that well, you have to meet my brother. Gareth's a demon player just like you. I think you'll both get on."

And they did. Naturally, Gareth Seligman, who was not quite as flinty as his elder brother, would have been amiable to him in any case—once Charles had been received and accepted by his parents he could hardly do less—but with his obvious skill at an informal after-dinner just-for-fun game, Charles had proven himself to be invited to play at the Whist Club, an honor not extended lightly by any member of that august group.

Since he was Gareth's guest, he played only with Gareth, with Dick North and Philip Leslie generally completing the foursome and, as usual, the game had been easy and enjoyable for all concerned but, when he heard Dick's casually put question, Charles felt rather as if a pitcher of ice water had been poured over his head.

"Yes . . . yes, I want to translate the book very much," he said at last, the shock wearing off. "How much is left to be done, and how much time do I have to complete it?"

"There are twelve chapters plus footnotes, but only three have been done so far. I'll send it all over to you first thing in the morning," Dick informed him, a serio-comic look coming into his warm brown eyes. "In publishing, the general order of the day is cool your heels but, right now—fortunately or unfortunately as the case may be—the orders I received were to get cracking. Finish this in the next month and we'll be properly grateful."

It was his first step, albeit a very small one, he decided as they left the club on Thirty-sixth Street to return to their respective homes. But the next morning he reached the grim conclusion that if God were indeed finding work for him, the way certainly wasn't going to be easy.

The notes accompanying the book were a mess—a useless jumble.

Charles had gone out for his usual early-morning ride in Central Park—a long, healthy gallop through bridle paths shielded by still-bare trees through which, no matter how far he rode, he could still see the Dakota. When he returned, Hodges told him that a package from Mr. North had arrived and was in his room. Two minutes later he was unwrapping the bulky, brown-paper wrapped parcel with a feeling of expectation that faded when he saw the contents.

What a horror, he thought, checking over the sheaf of unlined white pages covered with thin, spidery writing. He tried, unsuccessfully, to read the first translator's work. But after a few pages of trying to decipher the handwriting that looked more like useless scribblings, he gave up and turned to the book itself. Well over two hundred pages, it carried the imprint of a highly regarded Paris publishing house and, as he flipped through the pages of closely packed type, Charles was caught by the author's feel for his subject. It was a superb book, its American edition had to live up to the original, and it was up to him, Charles de Renille, to do it.

For a long time he looked out the window, studying the skaters on the park's frozen lake as he planned out his strategy. The old professor's work would have to come first, of course. He was a *savant*, a highly regarded academician, but his handwriting was all but illegible. Charles knew that the time he'd spend redoing the other man's work would take its toll when he started on his own. The only reasonable thing for him to do was to disregard the previous work and start fresh. Instinctively he rebelled against the idea—all his background and education, reinforced by five years of absolute and unquestioning discipline, had made his deference to age and authority almost automatic—but it was a short war. Publishing was big business in America, and spiritual qualities and intangible instincts weren't acceptable or explainable to people facing a deadline and, besides, he'd given his word to do the job as quickly as possible.

Forgive me, *Monsieur le Professeur*, he murmured, putting the pages aside. I know what this must have cost you in terms of your health and energy. And, if there had been time, I would have made use of your efforts, but as time is of the essence . . .

First things first, he decided, and crossed the room to knock on the connecting door. Through the panel, he could faintly hear the Thorpes. This morning Henry wasn't holding forth on the subject of museum acquisitions to a dozen rapt Columbia and Barnard seniors. Instead he was quite happily engaged in passing the time in the company of his wife and daughter. He was in a superbly good mood, and when he opened the door to Charles and took one look at him, he burst out laughing.

"Are you coming or going?" he asked and, belatedly, Charles realized he hadn't changed out of his riding clothes.

"I forgot all about this," he admitted, joining the laughter. "Can you spare a few minutes for me?"

"Of course," he said instantly. "And if you have no objection to sitting on the floor, we can discuss your problem while we observe Isabel. I take it you want to talk about the Napoleon biography? Have you just been handed someone else's mess?"

"Yes to both questions. But how did you—?"

"Oh, I'm rather an old hand at that. At one time, being given the messes other people made of projects was practically my lot in life."

Charles hadn't been in this bedroom before, not even to see the Monet footbridge. Living in such close

194

proximity with Henry and Alix, he felt any such visit would be the final infringement on their privacy. And, as he entered the room behind Henry, he had only a moment for a quick look around before sitting down on the edge of the patchwork quilt that had been spread out over the delicate carpet. Alix, wearing a morning dress of heavy white crepe, was holding her daughter in her arms, and Isabel looked up from the rope of pearls around her mother's neck that she was intent on putting in her rosebud mouth.

"Alix, Isabel is trying to chew on your pearls," Charles said, trying to suppress the envy he felt at this perfect family scene—one which he would never have for himself.

"She's teething," Alix explained. "And these are the Leslie family teething pearls. My mother cut her first tooth on them, then me, and now Isabel!"

Feeling somewhat baffled, Charles launched into the problems he was facing. "I'll need the use of your typewriter again, but first I want to do some further reference work. I know I don't have to, but I hate the idea of just changing the words from French into English. What books do you have on Napoleon and France?"

"None . . . only the works of great literature, history and risqué novels," Alix smiled, setting Isabel down on the quilt.

"Since it's obvious we can't help you from our own library, what do you say to using the library at Columbia?"

"The University—can such a thing be arranged?"

"Of course," Henry shrugged. "I'll speak with Nicholas Murray Butler this morning and arrange all the details. Better yet, why don't you come up with me tomorrow morning to get the feel of the place? You can have a tour of the buildings, we'll have lunch at the Faculty Club and, if you like, you can sit in on my seminar."

Charles honestly didn't know what to say. At Oxford, the libraries had been closed to all but residents of the colleges, and visitors were severely restricted in what they could do and see. In his month in New York, Henry had made no offer for Charles to see Columbia University, and he'd assumed that their rules were more or less the same. The concept that it might be quite different hadn't occurred to him and, at a loss for words, he was grateful to Isabel who had crawled over to him and was now investigating his highly polished Hermes riding boots.

"I thought you had quite enough to get accustomed to as it was, without having Columbia shoved at you," Henry explained, immediately understanding Charles' silence. "It's certainly not off limits to visitors—at least not within reason. And since you were so involved with your sightseeing . . ."

Just a few short weeks ago, he would have been utterly disconcerted, Charles reflected with some surprise. Every faux pas was worse than the one before, leaving him feeling like the Dakota's village idiot, but all that was beginning to change, and he was finally learning to smile over his mistakes.

"That's just what I'd like to do," he assured him. "Baedeker doesn't pay very much attention to Columbia. Will I need an academic gown?"

"Not unless you want everyone on campus to think you're two months early for graduation," Alix laughed.

Henry stood up, swinging his daughter into his arms. "Come with me, Charles, and I'll ring up Columbia. It's time I went into the library anyway. I have several hundred bills to pay."

"I thought the object of marriage was that a husband and wife could live as cheaply together as an unmarried person does alone," Charles said, feeling secure enough

196

to tease them for the first time.

"Charles, you're a first-class scholar," Henry replied with a smile, "but like most scholars, you haven't the slightest idea of the practical side of life. If you believe that old cliche, you deserve to have someone sell you the Brooklyn Bridge!"

With one fifteen-minute telephone call to Nicholas Murray Butler, the highly regarded president of Columbia University, Henry Thorpe arranged not only for Charles to have full use of the library, but saw to it that he would have access to all of the buildings as well as a pass to the gymnasium.

"You might want to sit in on a class or swim in the pool," Henry told him when he hung up the phone. "Columbia's quite an active and open academic community, and there's no reason you should feel restricted to the library. There's a lot to be learned there," he added with a knowing smile as Charles tried to thank him, "and I think you'll find that most of it isn't between the covers of books."

Although Harvard preceded it by nearly a hundred and twenty years, Columbia University, the oldest and most important institution of higher learning in New York, had undergone as much change and expansion as the city that was its home.

Founded in 1754 under a royal charter, the activities of King's College were suspended during the Revolutionary War. It was reorganized as Columbia College in 1784, and became Columbia University in 1890. From 1857 until 1897, it was located at Madison Avenue and Forty-ninth Street, but when Charles de Renille arrived in New York, it was seven years into its new home in Morningside Heights, high over the Hudson River.

St. Paul's Chapel, some of the dormitories, and the building that would house the new School of Journalism,

197

were in various stages of construction, but Schermerhorn Hall for natural sciences, Havemeyer Hall for chemistry and architecture, Fayerweather Hall for physics and astronomy, and the Engineering Building, as well as Earl Hall, which was the students' building, and East Hall which housed the administrative offices, were active and functioning. The Bursar, Registrar, Dean of Graduate Studies and the Provost had their offices here, as did the offices of the Columbia University Press. It was here that Henry Thorpe held his museum seminars, and it was in his spacious office that Charles, perched on the window seat and listening to the flow of discussion going on around him, had his first initiation into the give and take of American university life.

As Henry had advised, the first time on campus was simply to orient himself to its location, to pick up the passes that were waiting for him in the Registrar's office, and generally get the feel of the place.

Most of the time, Henry Thorpe wasn't quite sure what to make of Charles de Renille. At various times he found himself amused, annoyed, or baffled at his house guest. Having at one time in his life been frequently ill himself, he felt keenly for Charles for both the emotional and physical aspects of his illness, and the havoc it had wrought in him. Breakdowns took a long time to recover from, a body rebuilt itself at its own pace, but some effects were irreversible. At first he'd wondered if Charles were permanently *embetant*—a total, uncompromising bore—but, fortunately, Alix had been right, it was just a long-lasting sense of shock. When you thought about Charles, it was almost funny, Alix had told him a few days earlier. There were hundreds of book and magazine articles about the mistakes innocent Americans make on their first trip abroad, and how they always stumbled over their own feet when it came to local customs. It was pure joy to find that the situation was reversible.

Yes, it *was* rather, Henry thought as they ate lunch in the handsome dining room of the Faculty Club, Charles full of questions. He purposely hadn't taken him on any sightseeing expeditions (the trip to Brooks Brothers, the visits to the Automobile Club and the National Arts Club, and the parties they'd all attended together didn't count), preferring to wait and see if Charles' shock was a temporary thing or not. Solange's letter, asking them if she could send Charles over for a visit, had clearly outlined his condition. And, in his first week, his obvious surprise at everything and everyone in New York was only to be expected. There were only two routes open to their guest, he and Alix had agreed, either expansion into a normal human being, or withdrawal into a hopelessly locked shell. Solange said it in her letter, Henry thought as they finished lunch and he showed Charles the rest of the club, it was kill or cure—and fortunately for all concerned, it seems to be the latter.

In fact, Henry decided during the walk back to the campus, he wouldn't be at all surprised if Charles never went back to France—at least not permanently. Of course that obstinate de Renille pride of his might get in the way of his deciding to remain in New York. Henry knew all about obstinate pride. His own had come close to destroying all he and Alix had found; fortunately for him, however, Alix wasn't the sort of woman to be put off by his tactics. Possibly Alix had been right after all when, on Charles' first day in New York, she'd stated her intentions of seeing he eventually had some sort of romantic involvement. *No*, he thought as they braved the windy College Walk, *not yet*. Right now, it was just enough that he was getting on so well with all their friends. Henry strongly approved of Charles' translating the books for Dick North, was pleased to see that he was a regular guest at the Whist Club, and was relieved

199

that he no longer looked like a badly dressed sleepwalker.

The next few weeks would tell the tale. Provided Charles wanted to make a new life for himself in New York, *then* they'd see to Alix's idea, although, he had to admit, for the life of him, he could *never* imagine a more unlikely couple than Charles de Renille and Thea Harper.

To be sure, Charles had no idea whatsoever as to how Henry's innermost thoughts ran. Whereas, in social situations, Henry Thorpe was a strongly funny, totally open man, when he was deep in thought his face was totally unreadable. And, although Charles was well aware that he was under his scrutiny, there was no way he could guess what was going on in his friend's mind.

Not that he wanted to. The deep self-consciousness that had enveloped him for so long was gone, naturally dissipated as he became further and further involved with the Thorpes, their friends and the life they lived, as well as the rebirth of his own dormant interests. It was almost as if he were being taken step by step down a path, each event linking on to the one before, and the latest one had delivered him to the intellectual treasure trove that was Columbia University.

Most important to Charles was the McKim, Mead and White-designed library that dominated the Quadrangle. It was to this classical-style building of Indiana Limestone that he came every morning, checking his coat in the basement cloakroom before proceeding upstairs to the card files for the library's 350,000 volumes, and then to one of the long tables in the domed general reading room where he worked from nine until noon, translating the biography of Napoleon from French into English, carefully checking and rechecking his facts before transcribing his version into the notebooks he carried with him. He ate an early lunch in the cafeteria at Earl Hall, returned to the library for a few more hours of work, and then availed himself of the gymnasium's facilities. If the swim team wasn't practicing, he swam endless laps in the pool. Otherwise, there were always some students or faculty members eager for a handball game, or he made use of the running track that was suspended above the gym like a gallery. Nine laps made a mile, and Charles grimly conditioned himself to run, wondering how the members of the track and field team rushing past him ever attained such speed.

The Morningside Heights area was its own self-enclosed center for education, medicine, religion, and history. If Columbia University was the main jewel in the diadem, the affiliated, yet independent, adjacent Barnard College, with its 450 women students, and the Teachers' College, 3,000 students strong, gleamed no less brightly. That they were independent organizations made them no less integral to the university system, and let no one forget it. Also in the area was the highly competitive Horace Mann School, and Wadleigh High School, one of the stellar schools of the city's public education system.

Nearby was the Hebrew Home for the Aged, and the white marble and brick edifice of St. Luke's Hospital, as well as the Cathedral of St. John the Divine. Under construction for twelve years, with most of the work uncompleted, it nonetheless dominated 112th Street.

As March stretched toward April, and Charles made more progress on the translation, he allowed himself time off to explore those places, as well as venturing even further uptown to the Soldiers and Sailors Monument, erected to honor those who'd served in the Union Army in the Civil War, and to Grant's Tomb, its white granite structure reminded Charles of Napoleon's Tomb at Paris' *Hotel des Invalides*, and gave him an unexpected pang of homesickness.

Further north, Morningside Heights became Manhattanville, the last secluded section of New York City.

The Convent of the Sacred Heart and the popular Claremont Inn were here, as was "Oak Lawn," the home of the Hoguets, who, along with the Noels and Couderts, were the leading French-American families of New York—families Alix and Henry had made sure Charles didn't meet.

He'd speculated about that at first. But now, as he wandered through the far reaches of northern Manhattan, the reason behind their action became clear. If he had been introduced and displayed in front of that conservative, old-guard elite, he would never be as he was now, Charles realized as he rode the Ninth Avenue Elevated down to 72nd Street. One way or another, after receiving him, he would have been invited to leave the Dakota and make his headquarters with them. And if that had happened, he would have been lost.

To be sure, he would have been cosseted and protected, but as for an unqualified welcome— Instinctively Charles shuddered and glanced out the window as the train pulled out of the 116th Street station. In a way, it would have been as if he'd gone on holiday to Paris or London: the people he'd meet through that set of hosts would know everything about him, and once his back was turned, the whispers would begin. And, he now realized, far worse than the secret talk would have been the cocoon of propriety around him.

There wouldn't have been any informal Sunday night dinners where the guests, Social Register or not, had no compunction about spending the evening eating vast quantities of Italian food and engaging in long discussions. Certainly he wouldn't have had to learn to hold his own in discussions about Reform Democratic politics, women's suffrage, the Henry Street Settlement, the Fresh Air Fund, Carnegie Hall, the Broadway theatre, and the latest *New York Times* editorials, because those topics wouldn't have been raised. He would not have been brought into association with theatrical personalities or asked to translate three books or even be expected to find his way on public transportation. Even plans to go to Washington Heights' Polo Grounds next month to see the New York Giants play baseball would have been off-limits as unbefitting someone of his rank. His entire stay would have been geared to what others considered proper for him. He would have been kept inviolate of any sort of enriching experiences, and eventually he would have withered emotionally.

In the remainder of the five stops that the Elevated made from Columbia University to the Dakota, Charles gave a silent and fervent prayer of thanks to his family and to the Thorpes. The former for knowing where he best belonged, and the latter for providing him an environment in which he could not only expand his horizons, but where he could safely make all the mistakes that were part of being in a strange country.

The guidebooks never mention any of that, he told himself as the train gathered speed out of the 84th Street station; the next stop was his. They tell you to forget about formalities, but they never say you have to replace it with laughter. Thank you, everyone, for letting me learn all over again how to laugh at myself!

Within the next ten days the book was finished; translated, typed, and ready to be turned over to Dick North, who reacted to the news by inviting him to lunch at Luchow's.

"This restaurant is rather . . . unexpected," Charles said as the maitre d' showed them to their table. He looked around him, taking in the heavy-beamed room with its potted-palm decor and the multilingual conversations accompanied by substantial platters of food.

"Oh, no." Dick North, following Charles' glance around the restaurant, looked stricken. "Charles, I *am* sorry. Please forgive me, but I honestly forgot that as a Frenchman, this restaurant is detestable to you on principle alone."

"I wasn't being critical," Charles reassured him quickly. "I really *was* remarking on the decor. I only hope," he couldn't resist adding, "that there's something on the menu besides beer, bratwurst, and weiner schnitzel!"

Fortunately, Luchow's, as much a New York restaurant tradition as Sherry's and Delmonico's, had quite an extensive menu, and it wasn't too long before the chicken in casserole as placed in front of Charles, and the stuffed quail braised in Weinkraut presented to Dick.

"Did you do any writing while you were at Oxford, or when you were with the Jesuits?" Dick inquired as they ate. "I understand both places encourage that—within bounds, of course."

"Not at Oxford," Charles replied, somehow not surprised that Dick, through one means or another, had gleaned his background. But since he acted as though it was nothing out of the ordinary, Charles decided to treat the subject in the same manner. "In the year before I . . . in the year before I left, I was working on a study of Saint Vincent de Paul."

"He wasn't a Jesuit."

"No, but he was a fascinating figure. I think that when a writer attempts a biography he shouldn't be too involved—either in love or hate—with his subject."

"I agree totally. Unfortunately, there's no market for a book like that right now."

Charles felt stunned. "You want me to write a book for you?"

"I don't see why not." Dick looked nonchalant. "Most people have a book in them, and you're more intelligent than most."

"Then why not the Saint Vincent de Paul?" Charles

questioned, remembering his long, cold hours of research in the Bollandist's library in Brussels. All that work for nothing; he wanted a chance to salvage it. "I assure you, it's very accurate."

"I'm sure it is. But so is the one Longstreet translated and published a few years ago. It's still selling, so—" He gave an expressive shrug. "But if you had one good idea, and even if it's not for us, you might be able to work it into an article if you angle it properly. Nonetheless, I have a feeling you're going to come up with something eventually—either another translation or a book of your own—and I don't want to lose you to another publisher."

"You have great faith in my literary abilities, Dick. Right now, I'm not sure I'll ever write again, except for letters."

"That would be a great loss." Dick reached for his billfold, extracted a calling card, and placed it in front of Charles. "David Belasco always says, 'if you can't write your idea on the back of my calling card, you don't have a clear idea,' and I happen to agree with him. Someday I expect you to give this back to me with your idea on the back."

They had coffee and Black Forest cake for dessert, and their conversation turned from books and publishing to bridge and the Whist Club, a topic that kept them occupied as they walked back to the Union Square office of Doubleday, Page.

"I'm sorry Frank Doubleday and Walter Hines Page are out of town today," Dick said as he finished giving Charles a tour of the publishing house and showed him into his office. "They both want to meet you at a later date. But, in the meantime, this is our *very* grateful thank you," he finished, handing him an envelope.

Charles pocketed the envelope without comment, and they spent the next hour chatting about tennis, horses and newspapers, until Dick apologized, said he had a meeting to attend, and Charles found himself down the elevator and out on the street.

Feeling somewhat adrift, he went into Brentano's and spent twenty minutes wandering around, but left without buying a single book, and eventually drifted into Tiffany's.

Here's a place to catch the imagination, he thought, checking out the glass display counters filled with the finest of jewelry, stationery, and accessories. Charles spent several minutes studying a selection of ladies' umbrella handles. They came in all shapes and sizes, in silver and in gold, many decorated with precious or semi-precious stones. Each was a marvel of exquisite taste and craftsmanship, and he would have loved to send the swan-shaped one to his mother for her birthday, but he was afraid its price might bankrupt him.

The eternal peril of the youngest son, Charles thought bitterly as he turned and left the establishment. To be ever uncertain about money. It's my cross—never to be quite sure how much I have at any given time. And if I *do* stay on, he added grimly, his eyes searching out a cab stand, there's no telling how long I'll have to make that letter of credit last. Lucky for me, I'm still living off the money Andre put in the billfold . . .

Feeling depressed, he hailed a hansom, gave the driver the address, and settled back against the cracked leather seat. Almost without realizing it, he reached for the envelope Dick had given him.

Funny, it feels too thick for a thank-you letter, and too big, he thought, studying the imprint on the legal-size envelope. Cautiously, he felt its thickness again, and a strange feeling coursed through him. No, of course not. It couldn't be. What an idiotic idea—

Quickly Charles broke the seal, withdrew a folded sheet of stationery and, as the cab made its way up Madison Avenue, stared dumbstruck at its contents.

206

He read the note slowly, counted the bills twice, and smiled in sheer disbelief. Five ten-dollar bank notes. Fifty dollars. Payment for translation of the three books.

The thought crossed Charles' mind that he'd done it as a favor, not for monetary remuneration, and that a gentleman would never look for such a reward. But he dismissed those ideas that had ruled and stifled him all his life, sending him down a path he might never have wandered in the first place. France's rigid caste system, and the unwritten yet always obeyed rules of the *haute noblesse* were 3,000 miles away, and Charles de Renille added the fifty dollars to his billfold. The very first money he'd earned in America. The very first money he'd earned in his life.

Like the Sunday newspapers, the department stores, the Elevated and the New York Giants, moving was part and parcel of life in Manhattan. *Everyone* moved, but Charles had never known anyone who did. Oh, his parents and their friends moved from city mansion to country house to shooting box to winter villa on the Riviera. But those abodes never changed locations unless the roof fell in or there was a fire—and sometimes not even then. The concept that in New York—and the rest of America as well—people simply packed up their belongings and moved for any reason—including boredom—was unknown to him. But, on the day following his lunch with Dick North, he took part in the Thorpes' move to the Dakota's sixth floor.

Alix and Henry had had their eye on the twenty-room apartment since December, 1902. It had become available a year later, and since Christmas 1903, when Henry Thorpe signed the lease, he had been paying rent on two apartments while the larger one underwent extensive renovations.

Early on in his stay, Charles had been given a tour of

the new apartment. Henry and Alix guided him around the plasterers from William A. Burr, the floor refinishers from Erbe and Beers, and the painters who worked under the direction of William Eichhammer, the Dakota's head painter, so that he could see the splendor that was emerging after years of disuse by the previous tenants, and so that he could select a bedroom.

The huge kitchen had to be totally modernized, as did the servants' quarters, and the bathrooms completely renovated. There were fireplaces in every room, a formal drawing room measuring twenty by forty, a ballroom twenty-four feet wide and forty-nine feet long, and the bedroom of the master suite measured twenty by twenty. The library had twice the space of the one on the fourth floor, and Alix and Henry were planning a smaller, more cozy second drawing room.

Bit by bit, over the month of March, the household began to move upstairs. As the workmen finished in one room and moved on to the next, the Thorpes started decorating. Paintings were hung, books filled the shelves, clothes made their appearance in the cavernous closets, and a brand new square, stout, huge black Garland stove with two ovens and six burners, broiler and warming shelf and hood, was installed in the kitchen.

Charles was admittedly curious about what would go on during the actual process of moving, but Alix's request the evening before the actual day, took him by surprise.

"Tomorrow has to be a group effort, or else it'll be a disaster," she told him during dinner in the Dakota's restaurant, their own dining room having been dismantled. "That's the only way we can count on it to work. Rupert's offered to help us out, and we'd like the two of you to work together."

"You mean to supervise the moving men?"

The Thorpes exchanged amused glances.

"No, Henry and I will do that," Alix said after a moment's pause. "I mean I want the both of you in work clothes, lifting and carrying some of the things I don't want to trust to the movers. We've had dozens of workers in and out over the past months, and most of them have left extra clothes behind, so that's no problem," Alix explained. "Now—will you help us out?"

He couldn't very well refuse, and the next evening at six o'clock he was stretched out across his bed in the new bedroom, too exhausted to remove his clothes and take a much-needed shower. The move had gone splendidly—nothing was lost or broken or missing—but Charles felt as if he'd been beaten with a cricket bat.

Baseball bat, he reminded himself wearily. If my family could see me now. Blue jeans and work-shirt and work-shoes. Well, if nothing else, today proved that I'm employable as a day laborer!

Charles had imagined that he and Rupert would bring the more fragile things—the Faberge *bibelots,* the Baccarat crystal, the Chinese lamps, Alix's veneered-wood dressing table—that the Thorpes didn't want to trust in the hands of the moving men. They *did* move those things—as well as cartons of books, several paintings and the various chests containing their assortment of Tiffany silver.

"The last chest did it," Rupert groaned, leaning against the dining room doors. It was shortly after noon, and Mrs. Wiley and the rest of the staff were setting up for lunch. "My back is destroyed. Which pattern was it?"

"The one with the eight-piece coffee and tea service," Charles said, rubbing his aching arms. "What do we do next?"

"Eat!"

"And that, Alix claims, is the one sure way to tell if an influenza patient is well again—when they're hungry," Henry remarked, joining them. "After you two wash up, go into the ballroom and make yourselves comfortable. Hodges will bring your food to you."

During the morning's move, the ballroom had become the repository for barrels, boxes and cartons that no one was quite sure what to do with. According to Alix, the most important thing was that they all had comfortable rooms to sleep in that night, and an operational kitchen—everything else could wait.

"I think what we've been doing this morning is slave labor," Rupert remarked as they sprawled on the hardwood floor. "I'd complain to Uncle Henry, only he'd say that a little exertion is good for my soul and will keep me out of trouble—as if I had any time to find any."

"Rupert, if there weren't a way to stray, you'd invent one," Charles replied without thinking. "Haven't you made enough trouble already?"

"Oh, but that was the old, unrepentant me. Now I'm absolutely cowed into submission, and a grind besides."

"What's a grind?"

"That's American university slang for what we used to call a trog at Oxford. You know, someone who never stops studying."

"It has its advantages."

Before Rupert could reply, the ballroom doors opened and Hodges, looking proper and correct, entered wheeling a tea cart with their lunch. And, as if it were some sort of very informal picnic, he set out the meal on top of a low packing crate.

There were huge sandwiches of rare roast beef on seeded rye bread, as well as a combination of sausage, tomato and pepper, still hot, between halves of crusty Italian bread. This was accompanied by whole pickles and icy bottles of Dutch and Danish beer, huge slices of devil's food cake, a pot of coffee and a bowl of apples.

Charles forgot that he didn't eat red meat any longer, forgot that he hadn't had a glass of beer in years, and almost forgot his manners as he and Rupert tore hungrily into the meal.

"You know, in a way, we're rather alike," Rupert said some time later as they relaxed over a second glass of beer. "I was thinking about it the other day." His face took on a mock angelic expression. "Whether or not we like it, we both live according to vows. Not poverty, of course," he remarked, looking around him. "But I'm very obedient to Bill Seligman and, much to my own amazement, I'm remarkably chaste. I've discovered influenza tends to take the starch out of one. Tell me, Charles, how do you manage? Without sex, that is."

"Try having a nervous and physical breakdown at the same time," Charles snapped. "That'll take your mind off it for a good long time."

"Well, what about before that? And now?"

Part of Charles had been expecting this question from the day he'd entered the Thorpes' social sphere. But, among the men he'd met, it had never been broached. And, gradually, he'd ceased worrying about having to answer—until now. A sort of uneasy truce existed between him and Rupert since the night they'd met. They saw each other frequently, both socially and on the Columbia University campus, but Charles remained wary, instinctively knowing that a troubled thread still ran through the younger man's life. He was sure Rupert was outrageous only for effect, but his first shock at the question quickly wore off, leaving Charles regarding Rupert, dumbfounded at his presumption.

"That is not your business," he exploded. "None of it. And I warn you, don't try your voyeuristic tendencies out on *me*. Henry thinks that Bill is doing a fine job of keeping you in line," he went on scathingly, "but if you go around asking questions like that, maybe you need the razor strop that Cliff mentioned after all!"

For a long time there was no reply as Rupert looked

211

fixedly at the contents of his glass. "I think that you should know that William Seligman has been more of a father to me in seven months than my own was in seventeen years!" he burst out passionately. "My own father didn't care about anything except liquor and women—the more of each the better—and never thought about me except as the continuation of the Randall name. And my dear mother's no better. She thinks my conception and birth was her personal punishment from God and, since she hates men like crazy—"

"You shouldn't say things like that," Charles interrupted, wishing he'd never heard any of this. Why hadn't he simply said that there was an aspect of his life he wasn't quite ready to consider resuming yet? No—he always had to take offense, and now look at the can of worms he'd opened up. "They're your mother and father, you owe them that much respect—"

"Why? Because you had decent parents you think everyone else did too? For most of my life, no one ever really cared about me, and I made no secret of how I felt about them. But it's all different now, and I'm never going to let anyone tell me anything else. When I was at Oxford," Rupert went on after a short pause, his face and voice calmer, "some idiot told me American universities were a snap. Would I love to get my hands on him now! Between classes, seminars, library work, home assignments, term papers, quizzes and finals, I never thought I'd last the first month. *That's* how I became a grind. It was the only way to survive. But if I keep on going like this," he added, brightening, "I might make Phi Betta Kappa as a junior."

"That should make the Seligmans very proud of you."

"Why else do you think I work the way I do?" Rupert questioned, and both men fell silent. They drank the hot coffee and ate the fudge-frosted cake with nothing more than automatic remarks passing between them.

When their lunch was over, Charles went almost gratefully back to work. The conversation with Rupert disturbed him, and he wanted to take his mind off it. For the first time in his twenty-nine years, Charles de Renille had learned that there were sons who did not love their fathers.

With a deep sigh, Charles hauled himself off the bed, and stood in the center of the room, his hands in the pockets of his sweater, recalling how, only an hour before, the movers had left. Each man politely accepted an envelope from Henry containing a very generous tip for the day's work.

The idea of money—or rather, his lack of it—was never very far from being paramount in his thoughts. And, since yesterday afternoon, the envelope with the fifty dollars had been haunting him. Particularly since his Brooks Brothers bill had come in the afternoon mail. Reluctantly, Charles opened the center drawer of the writing table. There it was—his billfold, his letter of credit, an envelope containing the as yet untouched supply of money given him by Guy, and the clothing bill he hadn't quite worked up the courage to open.

"Suppose I don't have enough money to pay?" Charles thought, wincing at the idea of having to cable home for additional funds. I'll dig ditches or lay railroad track before I'll ever do that, he swore to himself as he counted the bills and took his letter of credit out of its leather case.

To Our Correspondents:
    Gentlemen:
        We beg to introduce to you and to commend to your courtesies *Charles de Renille* to whom kindly furnish in sums as desired up to an aggregate amount of . . .

It's useless, he decided, tossing the form back onto the writing table. Weeks in New York, and I *still* don't understand American money. I don't have very many expenses except for lunches, fares and the occasional book and flowers to a hostess after a party. My galoshes and writing supplies represented my only real outlay of cash. Well, what can I expect? Nearly seven years without touching a *sou*, no wonder all of this is a meaningless muddle!

"Charles, Alix and I decided you could do with a cold, dry martini." Henry spoke from the doorway, taking in Charles' perplexed face. "Is something the matter?"

"No—nothing at all," he said too quickly, taking the proffered drink.

But Henry knew better than that. "What's wrong?" he persisted. "Money troubles?"

Charles breathed a sigh of relief. "Yes. My bill from Brooks Brothers is here, and I'm not sure I have enough money in my letter of credit to pay it. I don't understand American money very well," he admitted reluctantly.

"Dollars and cents aren't all *that* difficult." Henry looked nonplussed. "Have you run through your letter of credit already?"

"No—I haven't even used it," Charles protested, and then knew the moment had come for him to discard any pride. "Henry, I don't understand money—any country's money—at all!"

Henry looked at the writing table, surveying the neat piles of greenbacks. "Is it all there?"

"What—? Yes," he said as horrible reality dawned. "Henry, you're not thinking that the movers would have . . ."

"If you're naive enough to leave all your money lying around in the writing desk, then by their standards, you're asking to have it taken," Henry told him shortly. "There's more cash on the writing table than most of those men earn in a year. Do you care to give me an accounting?"

"Andre gave me two thousand, and I've used about a hundred of that," Charles explained, feeling like a schoolboy caught at a prank. "Guy gave me another thousand—he called it walking-around money—but I haven't touched that yet."

"I'd hardly think so," Henry murmured. "Is this all of it? Where's your ticket home?"

Charles felt his face grow red. This wasn't the time or place to discuss *that* matter, but he was left with no choice. "I don't have it any longer."

"You *lost* it?"

"I cashed it in. I—I don't think I'm going back. Please, don't think that I'm going to be a permanent house guest—"

"We can discuss that at another time." For the first time since their conversation began, Henry smiled. "But, to get back to our topic at hand— Did you give the money to charity? With Good Friday coming up, I'm sure the poor box at St. Jean Baptiste appreciated the contribution."

"I thought about that, but I gave the money to the Fresh Air Fund. It seemed the right thing to do—to give a child a summer in the country."

Even the fact that the Fresh Air Fund was one of the Thorpes' favorite charities didn't deter Henry from wanting to get the matter of Charles and his money settled. The younger man wasn't stupid, merely confused and, as it turned out, rather careless. The sooner this matter was settled, he decided, the better.

"May I see your letter of credit?" Henry asked, and Charles handed it to him.

While Henry studied the letter of credit, Charles sipped the drink he'd been holding. Like any true Frenchman, he disliked cocktails, but tonight he needed the subtle blending of fine gin and vermouth, and he enjoyed every icy drop as it burned through his tired, aching body.

"Is there any more money I should know about?" Henry Thorpe's voice was cold.

"Fifty dollars from Doubleday, Page, for translating the books." The warmth given him by the martini disappeared at the bare anger on Henry's face. *The letter of credit's worthless*, he thought with a surge of fear.

Like most people in New York, Charles de Renille had little idea that Henry Thorpe had a bad temper. Alix could have told him, having come up against it twice during their courtship, the second time almost destroying them both. But Henry's formerly black moods were all but vanished now. Passionately in love with Alix, a devoted father with the prospect of more children to come, he was far too wrapped up in a life that gave him the first sexual fulfillment he'd ever known, and a longed-for home and family to find too much fault with events that only two years earlier might have set his temper off. Until now.

Charles felt as if his heart had stopped beating. All he could feel was Henry's carefully controlled anger as he watched him turn the letter of credit over and over, as if each new reading might provide new information. Charles wasn't sure which he was dreading more, Henry's seething silence or his eventual comments.

"I'm going to ring Bill up right now," he said at last, his voice oddly calm, "and then, first thing tomorrow, you're going downtown with him and he'll dispose of this properly for you."

"Dispose—?"

"Investment advice. Bill is the best. You don't have to take it, of course, but you *do* need a checking account, and several savings accounts."

"A checking account?" he repeated, nonplussed. "But

all I want to know is if I have enough money to pay my Brooks Brothers bill—"

"You really *don't* comprehend money," Henry interrupted, his voice full of wonderment. "Oh, well, Bill will take care of that tomorrow. I don't envy him his task, but by this time tomorrow evening you should have some idea of what to do with a letter of credit when it's worth seventy-five thousand dollars!"

"I suppose Henry told you that I was the greatest idiot in the world," Charles said to William Seligman as they sat in the latter's book-lined, antique-filled office the next afternoon.

The Seligman investment firm had existed since the early days of the New York Stock Exchange. William Seligman, Columbia '68, was the latest of his line to be Director and President. It was a firm run under strict family control, and since the turn of the century it occupied two floors of luxurious quarters in one of Wall Street's latest skyscraper office buildings. He'd given Charles the grand tour when they'd arrived at nine in the morning and introduced him to everyone before they settled down to work on his finances. They'd stopped for lunch in the firm's private dining room whose chef was the envy of every other financier. Naturally, Bill had shown Charles every visitor's favorite sight—the ticker-tape machine with its steady stream of stock quotations.

It was shortly after three in the afternoon and, looking back on the day, Bill felt he'd done his best for Charles. Henry might have been shocked and angered at Charles' carelessness, but Bill had seen it all, from millionaire miser Hetty Green (who always stole the cloverleaf rolls when she came to lunch) to men who lit their cigars with hundred-dollar bills. One young man unable to make sense of a seventy-five thousand dollar letter of credit didn't even cause him to blink.

217

"All Henry said was that you wanted to remain in New York indefinitely and needed some help in getting settled financially," Bill said at last, bending the truth a bit as he recalled Henry's biting comments. "Now, you have both a checking and savings account at Morgan Guaranty, two other savings accounts at other banks that I think will withstand any problems that the American system of banking can come up with, and a nice-sized stock portfolio which should bring you a fine return."

"But is it all safe?" Charles questioned. Even in the short time he'd been in New York, he was aware of the financial panics that periodically gripped America.

"There's no sure answer to that, but this country has over 193,000 miles of railroad, and we produce over ten million tons of steel a year, so something *always* works."

"But will the stock you've advised me to purchase?"

William Seligman regarded him out of world-weary eyes. "It's safe as long as people continue to use the telephone, buy camera film and boxed cereal, turn on electric lights, need new tires for their motor cars and glass for their windows. There are no guarantees, Charles, not on anything, but if you really want to make an investment in what may become your new country, and help it grow, this is it."

Charles remained in New York for another ten days, through the end of the Lenten season which concluded in the brilliant burst of Easter Sunday when, following the conclusion of all church services, Fifth Avenue turned into the ultimate promenade, men and women in their newest finery went to see and be seen on one of the greatest avenues in the world in the rite of the Easter Parade and the beginning of spring.

But once the obligations of Holy Week were concluded, on the very day he'd sworn he'd return to France, Charles began the first of his travels, journeying to

218

Ottawa, Canada, where his cousin, Maurice de Hautraviant, was an attaché at the French Embassy. Maurice and his Canadian bride, Emily, were favorites of the Governor-General of Canada and his wife, the Earl and Countess of Minto, and were much in demand at official functions at Rideau Hall. They were also among the leaders of the capital's "young married set," and when Charles arrived, they took him with them on their social rounds, proud to show him off. He spent a pleasant ten days in the still-snowy city before recrossing the border and proceeding to Boston.

He'd looked forward to seeing Boston—the Athens of America—with its strong intellectual and cultural atmosphere, and in that he was not disappointed. But sharing that long weekend with David Lasky and Anthony Kendall had placed him in a situation it took him months to come to terms with. Even in a city as strait-laced as Boston, life wasn't all Harvard Yard, the Public Garden, the Museum of Fine Arts and the Handel and Hadyn Society, and young men could always find their pleasures.

Charles returned to a New York blooming in the first delights of spring. Alix and Henry were preparing to leave for San Francisco to attend the wedding of Angela Dalton and Morgan Browne, but they took time out to sit down with Charles and discuss his future plans.

He wasn't going back to France. His foray out of New York City had reinforced what he'd learned over the first six weeks—he had his health and his freedom, and if he wanted to live in an atmosphere where he was accepted on his own merits, he had to stay in New York.

"Are you thinking about going for your doctorate?" Alix asked him as they sat in the small drawing room. "Columbia may be a good temporary haven."

"Oh, it's that," Charles agreed, smiling. "But I have this horror of becoming some sort of perpetual student.

Dick wants me to do a book for Doubleday, Page. Either my own or a translation. The problem is, I'm rather dry on ideas."

"If you relax and don't worry too much over it, it will all fall into place," Henry reassured him. "Have you considered your other options? Teaching, for instance."

"In the public school system?"

"Hardly," Henry said, and Alix quickly added, "Private schools like Horace Mann and Dwight are always short a French or Latin teacher when the term starts. Wait and see."

"I think Alix has the right idea," Henry put in. "You've gone through too many changes too quickly to make this kind of decision now. Go to Kentucky and Virginia," he advised. "Make a long trip out of it, and then come up to Cove House for the rest of the summer. If you don't try too hard, Charles, you'll find life has a funny trick of working out."

Charles went South, Henry Thorpe's advice still ringing in his ears. His need to be of service, to finally do something that would count, was as strong as ever, and he knew his answer would come in its own good time.

Armed with invitations extended to him by horse people his mother had come to know, he travelled through Kentucky's beloved blue-grass country, arriving in the last week of April in plenty of time to enjoy the round of parties that marked Louisville's Festival Week, listening to old-timers tell tales of previous winners like Aristedes, Ben Ali, Spokane and Montrose. The annual event at Churchill Downs was America's Gold Cup Day, its Prix du Jockey Club, and it was impossible to find anyone, whether they viewed the race from the grandstand or the crowded infield, who did not have a good time. And, by the time the thirtieth running of the Kentucky Derby was completed, Charles had more than proven his worth to his hosts.

Adrian de Renille had taught his sons that, when attending a major racing event at a track where they'd never been before and might not come again, they must not bet the favorite. Instead, he'd impressed on them, it was their place to remember that they were strangers and to bet the long-shot. Even though he'd never followed that advice before, Charles always remembered it and, when it came time to place his bet, well-aware of the open-handed company he was keeping and now knowing that he would never miss the money, he didn't select the favorite Proceeds, or Ed. Tierney, or Brancas, but placed his hundred dollars on Elwood, a fifteen-to-one shot who compounded his status of dark horse by having the unheard combination of woman owner and woman breeder. The horse was just like him, Charles felt, an outsider with one chance to belong unquestioningly.

It had no business working out the way it did, but in the heart-stopping race that was over far too quickly, the three-year-old bay colt broke away from the other four horses that started with him, and with F. Pryor on board as jockey, crossed the finish gate with a half-length lead, while in the grandstand an almost unbelieving Charles de Renille was being pounded on the back and congratulated on his lucky pick and his fifteen-hundred dollar win. In their eyes, that one lucky bet had instantly transformed him from just a polite visitor to a man who knew horses and was willing to take a chance—a dual compliment that was very hard to come by.

During the month of May he went through the state, visiting the horse farms of the men and women he'd met at the Derby, seeing some of the finest horses since he'd left his family's *haras*. The same held true in Virginia's historic Clark and Fairfax counties, and everywhere Charles went he was greeted with great warmth and shown the greatest hospitality. By the time he arrived at the French Embassy in Washington at the end of June, it was with an acquired taste for mint juleps, bonded bourbon, hot beaten biscuits and pecan pie.

Washington, D.C., despite its location, is not a city famous for open-door hospitality and charm, and it tends to become even less attractive once the warm weather arrives. The British Foreign Office considers it one of their "hazard" spots, giving all diplomats assigned there double pay. Native Americans are, at best, noncommittal about their nation's capital, foreign visitors are even less complimentary, and Charles de Renille, who, at this juncture of his life, might have placed himself between both groups, was no exception to the rule. After a day-long tour of Pierre L'Enfant's city sweltering under the early summer sun, he retreated to the Embassy library and, if it hadn't been for the ambassador, he might have stayed there.

At forty, Jules Jusserand was the youngest ambassador France had ever sent to the United States—and the most popular. Since his arrival in January of 1903 aboard the *Lorraine*, he had undertaken a wide range of activities in his attempt to strengthen French-American relations. He was a popular speech-maker with a wide range of topics, and he was wonderfully received wherever he went. So far, Jusserand had received an honorary Doctor's Degree from Columbia University, been made an honorary American architect, and an honorary member of the New York State Bar Association. He had presented the White House with a pair of Sevres vases to compliment the Houdon busts of Washington, Franklin, Jefferson, and the Volk bust of Lincoln that decorated the mantelpieces of the East Room. In April he had attended the opening of the Louisiana Purchase Exposition to inaugurate the French Pavillion.

Jules Jusserand and his wife, the former Elise Richards, the daughter of an expatriate New England family, who had been born in Paris, had met Charles de Renille during a weekend party at a historic Fairfax county horse farm and invited him to be their guest in Washington.

By the end of June, the nation's capital has no social life to speak of. The weather is far too warm for the multi-course dinners and musicales and Embassy balls that mark the winter social season, but there are always garden parties, and it was out of the friendship he felt for his hosts, rather than for the social aspects, that Charles abandoned the library's cool darkness for the midday heat of the garden. But the champagne was plentiful and the buffet extravagant and Charles didn't even mind the hawk-faced man who suddenly appeared at his side and, after the usual pleasantries, began questioning him closely about France and America, questions he answered truthfully but which, when the older man excused himself saying he had to rejoin his wife, left him with the same feeling of deep confusion that had marked his first week in New York.

"Charles . . . I hope our charming Washington rite of the garden party hasn't worn you out," Ambassador Jusserand remarked a few hours later when the last of the guests had left and they were relaxing in his office. "Elise tells me this is our practice party for our Bastille Day reception!"

"Then it should be an even greater success than today," Charles replied, wondering why the Ambassador, who had spoken to him only in French, had suddenly switched to English.

"I'm glad that you enjoyed our afternoon's entertainment, and I'm equally glad that it hasn't tired you out," he went on softly, his gaze shifting momentarily to the clock on his desk. "We've been invited out to dinner."

Without meaning to, Charles felt an expression of distaste form on his face. On his first evening in

Washington, Jules Jusserand had taken him to a stag dinner party at Henry Adams' Lafayette Square residence across the street from the White House. Charles had looked forward to meeting this eminent American man of letters, but on that particular night, this personage, who was the direct descendent of two American Presidents, was in a vitriolic and bigoted mood. By the time the evening was over, Charles was left with several shattered illusions and a bad taste in his mouth. The last thing he wanted was to endure another such party.

"Jules, can't you make my excuses? The dinner at Mr. Adams—"

"I quite understand, Charles. But tonight's request cannot be declined."

For a second, Charles was nonplussed. Almost all invitations could be declined. The only mandatory invitations came from royalty—and heads of state. With new comprehension, he gazed at the tall man with his full beard and moustache which offset his thinning hair. His expression was effectively bland, but the light in his eyes was unmistakable.

"Do you mean to say we're dining at the Wh . . ."

"I always thank *le bon Dièu* for perceptive guests," Jusserand interposed skillfully, smiling. "I've asked Jacques to lay out your dinner clothes. We leave in one hour."

Beneath his excitement at the idea of meeting and dining with the President of the United States, a faint sense of unease was forming. It didn't seem likely that a busy man like Theodore Roosevelt would suddenly find himself free for dinner, ring up the French Ambassador at the spur of the moment, and not only invite him to dinner, but insist he bring his house guest as well. He knew that Roosevelt and Jusserand had formed a close friendship but, as he dressed, Charles couldn't shake the

224

feeling that something wasn't right. It was the same feeling that he had about the man who had engaged him in conversation earlier, and who didn't appear to be the sort who had nothing better to do than attend garden parties.

Charles was still turning over all the mysteries in his mind when the Embassy carriage turned into the White House driveway and pulled up in front of the South Entrance. Ike Hoover, the head usher, was waiting to greet them, and he waited patiently while Jusserand gave Charles a tour of the entry corridor which, following the renovations of the Executive Mansion, had been transformed into a gallery for the portraits of the First Ladies—the most recent being the Theobald Chartran rendering of the handsome and dignified Edith Roosevelt.

"So this is the President's house," Charles murmured after his brief tour which included glimpses of the newly redecorated Red Room, Blue Room, and state dining room.

"No," Jules Jusserand corrected gently as the elevator took them noiselessly up to the second floor, "this is the house of the American nation where the President lives. And its present occupant honors it indeed," he added as they entered the First Family's living quarters. Charles, who had seen most of the sights downstairs through a blur of nerves, felt his confusion lift when he sighted the most well-known man in America waiting for them.

"Jules . . . good evening. I hope tonight's dinner isn't going to cause any problems for you."

"None at all, Mr. President," Jusserand responded warmly. "Privately, I think Elise is quite relieved that I'm dining with you tonight. There's nothing quite so annoying as to have a husband around after a successful garden party!"

The President chuckled as they shook hands. "I know

that feeling myself," he said as he wheeled around to regard Charles out of large, pale-blue eyes shielded by pince-nez spectacles.

"Mr. President, I'd like to present Mr. Charles de Renille. Charles, I'm honored to introduce you to Theodore Roosevelt."

The President was a good three inches shorter than Charles, and had rather small hands, but his grip was like being caught in a vise. For some unknown reason, Charles knew he was being both observed and tested by this man who held the greatest office in the country, and whose very demeanor radiated supreme self-confidence and power.

"I'm very honored to meet you, Mr. President," he said, and a long-buried memory came to the surface, "and if you won't mind my compliment at this late date, I want you to know how much I enjoyed your book, *Hunting Trips of a Ranchman.*"

For the first time, Theodore Roosevelt flashed his famous smile. "That was published nearly twenty years ago! How did you come across a copy?"

"When it was published, an American friend of our family sent it to my father as a Christmas present. Every night he would read it aloud to my brothers and me—we never wanted it to end."

"I wish that book had had the same effect on *my* sons," he said, smiling again. "But if my tales of life in the Dakotas could thrill young boys in France, then I'm doubly proud to have written it." The President led them into the family drawing room. "Hugh's been delayed at Sheridan Circle, but he'll be here shortly. Now, Charles, I'm anxious to hear all about your family. How is your dear mother? The *comtesse* most graciously called on us two years ago at Sagamore Hill—"

Theodore Roosevelt was the consummate host—a perfect blending of the old New York society he was born to, the political savvy that was second nature to him, and the machinations of his superior mind. He drew Charles out of his natural reserve with questions about the books he'd translated. Both he and Mrs. Roosevelt had read the Napoleon biography. His daughters, Alice and Ethel, were fond of the romance, and the fairytales were the favorite bedtime tales of his youngest sons.

"Now all you have to do is find a fine boys' book to translate and you'll have provided my whole family with reading material," Roosevelt told him smilingly when Charles had concluded his adventures in publishing. "I think you've done a superb job, a true accomplishment, and—" He broke off as a steward showed another man into the room. "Hello, Hugh, we'd almost given up on seeing you tonight."

"Good evening, Mr. President, and please forgive my being late. Ambassador Jusserand, it's a pleasure to see you again, sir. Mr. de Renille—"

Charles felt a sharp jerk of surprise. The tall, middle-aged man standing in front of him was his new acquaintance with the cryptic questions at the garden party.

"Mr. de Renille, I'm sorry I didn't introduce myself this afternoon but I hope that, before the evening is over, you'll understand why. I'm Colonel Hugh Miles of Military Intelligence."

Just as he would never forget his first dinner party in New York, Charles knew that the night he dined at the White House with the President of the United States as his host, was forever burned in his memory. Without a word being mentioned, certain facts began to fall into place, and an odd sort of calm settled over him—which was just as well since there was no immediate discussion of the Colonel's motives.

Dinner was a simple, leisurely meal of jellied consomme, cold trout with mustard sauce, a green salad, and vanilla ice cream for dessert. But, as the meal was served to them by white-jacketed White House stewards, their conversation stayed on general topics with the President, in Charles' eyes, more than proving his reputation as a master raconteur.

"Before I turn the floor over to Ambassador Jusserand, Charles, there is one thing I want you to know," Theodore Roosevelt told him as they sat in his study, snifters of brandy in hand. "After we've concluded our conversation, I don't want you to think that was the only reason you were invited to the White House. Even if we didn't hope that you could be of service to us, I'd be delighted to receive you—and which I hope I'll do many times in the future," he concluded. "Now, Jules—"

"Thank you, Mr. President." Jusserand sat forward in his chair, ignoring the others and concentrating solely on Charles as he began his story. "Like President Roosevelt, Charles, I want to reassure you that you were not invited to the French Embassy for any reason other than the pleasure of your company. We had no ulterior motive in mind. At least not at first," he added truthfully after a second's hesitation.

"But you—all of you—have reached the conclusion that I may be able to fill some need," Charles prompted, not wanting to see the Ambassador in any way discomforted. "I thought as much," he added, half to himself, feeling as if a weight he hadn't even known was there had been lifted from his back, as he waited for Jusserand to resume speaking.

"A little over a year ago, Charles, I attended the celebration of the Louisiana Purchase in St. Louis. This was also the occasion of the ground-breaking ceremonies for the Exposition that's going on now. President Roosevelt was there, of course, as was former President Cleveland, and Secretary of War Root, and Cardinal Gibbons of Baltimore, and my fellow ambassadors from

Mexico and Italy. There was a banquet that night, but for reasons I need not go into, only President Roosevelt, former President Cleveland, the other two ambassadors, and myself attended. After the banquet and the speeches were over, the Italian Ambassador became ill and left, and President Cleveland retired early. It was then the Mexican Ambassador, Secretary Root, and myself retired to President Roosevelt's suite to discuss a problem that had recently come to all our attentions—the German infiltration of Mexico."

For the next half-hour, Charles listened intently as Jules Jusserand, Theodore Roosevelt, and Hugh Miles, each in turn, told him about the influx of German citizens into Mexico, and the complexities of determining whether or not they were agents of the Kaiser.

"Germany is far more clever about sending its citizens about and abroad than we are," Theodore Roosevelt pointed out. "When a German citizen leaves his country, whether it's entirely on his own business or on assignment from his government, he knows in advance he may never return to his homeland. Even their diplomats remain at their posts two and three times longer than their opposite numbers at other embassies. It's quite easy to assimilate into another country when you know you're not likely to return to your own."

"I can understand the problems that creates for your intelligence system, but I don't quite see where I can be of help," Charles replied. "I'm not a spy."

"And we don't want one," Colonel Miles put in emphatically. "We're not looking for military secrets, mainly because we don't think there are any down there. And, if by some chance, there are, we have other means of obtaining them."

"We've been looking for someone who would be free to travel to Mexico with no ties to call him back at an inopportune moment. A free agent, as it were," Jules

Jusserand smiled at him. "And, most important of all, a gentleman above reproach. Would you care to be of help to us, Charles? It will be of aid to both France and America, and it will prevent Mexico from being used as a pawn."

So here it is, Charles thought. *My chance to be of service. To do one thing from beginning to end. I've asked and been answered and there's no looking back.*

"I'd be proud to be of aid in any way I can," Charles said quietly. "I'll try to serve the best way I can. Do you wish me to leave immediately?"

At his answer, everyone visably relaxed.

"We still have quite a few loose ends to tie off," Hugh Miles replied. "We won't need you before the end of August, at least. Just let me have your address for the rest of the summer."

"You can reach me in care of William Seligman at Cove House, Woodbury, Long Island. If an extra person isn't going to be too much of a strain on their household, I may stay there for the remainder of the summer—or until you need me."

Theodore Roosevelt hid a smile. He could put the entire First U.S. Volunteer Cavalry inside Cove House without creating a strain. But he liked Charles de Renille's naiveté. It was refreshing, and blended well with his intellect and perception—both of which Jules Jusserand and Hugh Miles praised to the skies. Yes, it might all work out splendidly. There was just one more matter . . .

"I'm not sure how much one person can do," Charles was saying regretfully, and Theodore Roosevelt knew the moment had come.

"My dear Charles," he said with a warning glance that clearly told the other two men they were to leave *this* explanation entirely to him. "We appreciate your sacrifice more than we can ever say, but before you leave.

there is one more matter. Your expedition, as important as it is, cannot be a solo venture. . . ."

An hour later, Charles closed the door to his bedroom at the French Embassy, his mind still reeling from the last part of the conversation. Without turning on the light, he placed the autographed copy of Theodore Roosevelt's first book, *The Naval War of 1812*, which the President had presented him with, on the nearest available surface and began to get ready for bed.

What have I agreed to? he wondered as he undressed, draping his clothes over the nearest chair. To go to Mexico with a young woman whose name they won't tell me to see if the German Embassy is planning anything special. Well, idiot, you wanted to serve for the greater good, only the next time I pray, I should remember to be more specific!

I wonder who thought up this idea? Charles speculated as he grew calmer. He pulled his nightshirt over his head and sank into the bed's cool softness.

If I think about it long enough, he told himself, I may actually find it funny. Of course, first thing tomorrow, I'll have to apologize to Jules. I didn't say a word to him on the ride back here and, by now, he either thinks I'm furious, or in shock . . . and I can't figure out why I'm not one or the other.

Everyday run-of-the-mill curiosity had never been Charles' long suit. He was deeply introspective when it came to intellectual matters, but until the last few months when there had been so much to hold his interest, he had always taken the working world around him pretty much for granted. He knew espionage—or whatever it was they wanted him to take part in— flourished in every nation of the civilized world, but it was an activity he thought was carried on by persons more at home in the underworld than in the drawing rooms and libraries of power.

Charles, you still have an awful lot to learn, he told himself severely, punching his pillow. And whether or not you like it, there's no turning back. You've given your word as a gentleman—that's why Ambassador Jusserand and Colonel Miles proposed you, and why President Roosevelt accepted you.

Gradually, Charles began to relax, his mind planning out his next moves. In another month, he might well find himself in Mexico. But now, as he lay in bed, he knew what he wanted to do more than anything else. Before he carried out whatever plan Colonel Miles had in mind, before he found out the name of the unknown woman whose . . . *companion* he'd be, before he passed the next weeks on Long Island, he wanted to go back to New York City, to go to the ninth floor of the Dakota and out onto the roof. He wanted to stand there as the late afternoon turned to twilight and watch all of Manhattan spread out before him change color in the approaching evening. He wanted to go home.

Standing in the Archbishop's library, looking out of the window at the Cathedral's garden, Charles shook his head slowly. Every experience he'd been through over the past seven months paled before the turn of events that had been awaiting him in San Antonio.

When Major Donovan had put forth the final details of the plan that, until that moment, Charles had only the barest outline of, the Archbishop's fury could have bounced off the walls. For his own part, Charles had been more surprised than shocked. Surprised because Alix and Henry had always said that the President was the most moral of men. Not a prude, but a man who believed in the sanctity of marriage vows. Charles had been amazed that Theodore Roosevelt, a faithful and devoted husband, would approve of the idea that two totally respectable people were to *pose* as husband and wife. It was only now, with the Archbishop's outspoken opinion changing everything, that Charles belatedly realized that *this*—a real and legal marriage—might have been part of the plan all along. And Roosevelt, canny politician that he was, had preferred the Archbishop of San Antonio, an authority figure Charles would dare not refuse, insist on a marriage of convenience before he and Theodosia Harper put one foot outside of San Antonio.

There was a soft rapping on the door, and one of the Archbishop's servants entered. "Pardon, *señor*, but the guests are arriving, and His Grace would like you to meet them in his study."

"Thank you, Miguel," Charles said. His hand went to his tie in a self-conscious gesture of vanity. "You may lead the way. This particular Christian is ready to face the lions."

Chapter Six

Despite her confusion and apprehension, Thea's exhaustion was so overpowering that she slept straight through the night, waking up only when Nela knocked on the door.

"I'm sorry, honey, but the Archbishop wants to see us this morning about the last-minute arrangements," Nela said as she flung the curtains open and sunlight flooded the room. "I think our Major Donovan was rather surprised that you agreed so easily."

"I couldn't care less *what* Major Donovan thinks, and if I've confused him, so much the better," Thea responded definitely, sitting up in bed and pushing the pillows up behind her. "Besides, Charles isn't that much of a stranger, even if we've never met."

"No, he isn't," Nela agreed, coming over to sit down on the side of the bed. "But did you know that he's been living with Alix and Henry in New York for the past seven months? I'm surprised you haven't met already."

"Oh, my," Thea said, taking her hair out of her eyes. "Well, when you get right down to it, I guess he had to be somewhere. They certainly didn't send all the way to France for him."

Nela looked perplexed. "Are you *sure* Alix didn't tell you about him?"

"How? I wasn't in New York very much this winter. First I was in New Orleans with that house in the Garden District, then I was in Philadelphia, then San Francisco for your wedding, and finally the whole summer in Europe." Thea thought for a moment and then burst out laughing. "What would you like to bet that Alix was hiding Charles and planning to spring him on me at a later date? If all of this hadn't happened, I think one night soon I'd walk into that glorious new drawing room of theirs and find Charles de Renille waiting for me!"

"I wouldn't be at all surprised," Nela agreed. "If Alix weren't saving him for you, waiting for the proper moment, she would have written you with all the details she gave me. And, speaking of details—" Nela hesitated, uncertain of Thea's reaction.

"Nel-a," Thea drawled, "do you have some plan of your own?"

"You might say that. What would you say to a real wedding reception for you and Charles? Here, of course, with champagne and a cake and guests."

"Oh, Nela." Thea looked delighted. "I'd love it. One never knows," she went on, hugging her friend, "this marriage of convenience might be the closest I come to the real thing."

"Oh . . . you know that's not true!"

"What do you suppose Charles looks like?" Thea speculated, switching topics. "Do you think he looks anything like his brothers or the comtesse?"

"Well, the whole family is very good-looking, so I don't see why he should be the exception." Nela stood up. "As soon as we've finished with the Archbishop, we'll run over to the store and pick out your wedding dress. Some of our Paris purchases have arrived, and there'll be a ton of things you'll want to add to everything you've brought with you."

Nela was terribly tactful, Thea thought an hour and a half later as Morgan pulled his new four-passenger Cadillac Model B up in front of the Archepiscopal residence. She didn't mention the word trousseau or

235

honeymoon or any of the usual things one discusses with prospective brides. But then, my upcoming . . . marriage is hardly run-of-the-mill. And while I'm counting my blessings, be grateful Charles is a Frenchman. Former religious or not, he'll be able to create the illusion of devotion, if not actual romance.

Thea had dressed carefully for this first meeting, selecting a Lucile dress of pale turquoise Swiss muslin embroidered in white with a turquoise taffeta belt. She'd chosen the dress for courage, somehow remembering that the ancient Egyptians viewed turquoise as the favorite color of the gods, and therefore likely to bring good fortune to those who wore it.

And if there's one thing I need as much as courage this morning, Thea thought as they left the automobile, it's for someone to send a little luck my way.

They were shown into the Archbishop's study by a rather disapproving priest who looked as if allowing Protestants into the sacred confines of the residence was definitely lowering standards.

The room, except for a large desk with several straight-back chairs drawn up in front of it, was rather bare-looking. The Archbishop hadn't arrived yet, and the only occupant of the room was Charles de Renille.

He came forward quickly to greet them, shaking hands with Morgan, whom he already knew, and then gracefully kissing Nela's hand.

While he was doing this, Thea had her first opportunity to observe Charles at close quarters. *Not bad at all,* she thought with relief, noting that he was tall, just over six feet, with thick, straight black hair, and eyes that were the color of rich topaz.

He turned to her, and they faced each other hesitantly before gravely shaking hands.

"I hope this—what we have to do—won't be too difficult for you. I couldn't stand it if you felt like some

236

sort of useless appendage." Thea, her heart racing, forced herself to look directly into his eyes. "I would like us to be able to trust and depend on each other. That is, if you're agreeable."

His long-fingered, well-made hand was cool to her touch, but there was no mistaking the sincerity in either his eyes or his voice. "Of course I'm agreeable to your suggestion. That's how it should be between us. We have to be partners from now on."

His voice, Thea realized with some surprise, was free of any French accent and, instead, was overlaid with faint British inflections and had a clear, well-balanced tone—in short, the sort of upper-class New York accent she almost took for granted.

Before any real conversation could begin, the Archbishop entered the room through a side door. He greeted them, and they spent the next two hours with the rather severe-looking man who turned out to be more than fair, considering the circumstances which were causing him to perform a marriage of convenience.

Thea had honestly expected him to be in Charles' corner rather than hers. Instead, he made it quite clear that it was her reputation and future he held dear. A man could—and generally did—surmount any scandal, while a woman was usually destroyed by it. The fact that this was to be a marriage in name only made no difference to him.

"You are both human," he said, fixing Charles under such a severe eye that he actually flinched like a schoolboy. "Far better that, if you wish to realize your marriage vows, you are already bound to each other. But, in the event you return from Mexico and do not wish to remain together, an annulment will be arranged with a minimum of fuss and scandal."

The Archbishop, having successfully made his point, moved on to the more practical considerations regarding the ceremony itself. It was fixed for three days later at noon with the prelate himself officiating. He approved of the reception Nela and Morgan would give, while graciously declining their invitation to attend. It was determined that afterwards, Thea and Charles would go to the Menger Hotel, and the following day would take the morning train to El Paso. They would then continue across the border to the city of Chihuahua where they would be met by the de Veigas and taken to their estate for an ostensible honeymoon while they waited for word to proceed to Mexico City.

It was fixed, and there was nothing for either of them to do but move with the flow of events. They bid the Archbishop good day and left the residence.

"Nela and I are taking Thea over to the store," Morgan told Charles as they stood in front of his automobile. "Will you have any trouble finding the County Clerk's office?"

"I have good directions," he smiled. "Morgan, do you have a jewelry department in your store?"

"No one in San Antonio buys jewelry anywhere but at Harry Hertzberg's," he replied, giving him the address which Charles noted in his appointment book. "We'll see you later at dinner—don't dress."

"I'm honored to be invited to your home and, Thea, tomorrow, if you're interested, would you care to visit the Alamo and the Missions with me? I've been here for two weeks, and I've found this city has a great deal of history to it."

Thea felt her racing heart calm. "I'd love to visit the Missions with you, Charles. We can take a picnic lunch."

"Consuelo will pack a beauty for you," Nela said, "but why don't you save the Missions for Friday? Tomorrow, after you finish at Hertzberg's, you can visit the Alamo and Fort Sam Houston. If you only knew how to drive a motor car, I'd lend you mine. It's only a two-passenger runabout, but—"

"I do know how to drive," Charles said with one of his rare, brilliant smiles. "Does the offer still stand?"

Nela blinked, and then gave him a brilliant smile of her own. "God, but you're Americanized."

"After living in New York, was anything else supposed to happen?"

"Considering whom you were living with, no," Thea put in.

The final tension around them dissolved under their exchange of light-hearted banter, and they parted, Charles promising to meet Morgan at the store at half-past five.

"Thea, one thing," Charles ventured. "I know in America many people have the same names and are not at all related. Would you be insulted if I asked if you are related to someone with your last name? He is a rather well-known man in his field, and his books were a great source of enjoyment to me during my convalescence. His subjects are specialized, so I'm not sure if you've ever heard of Elston Harper."

Thea looked into Charles' grave, proud face, and suppressed a smile. "I've read all of his books," she told him, "and every once in a while Elston Harper comes home and reminds me that he's my father."

Covering just over 40,000 square feet of space spread over three floors and a basement, Browne's of San Antonio was a women's and children's specialty store selling some of the finest merchandise available in the Southwest—all in a building whose exterior bore a distinct resemblance to a warehouse.

At first, when Morgan had turned the Cadillac off Commerce Street and driven past Joske's department store and the Menger Hotel to pull up in front of the dull-brown building, Thea had experienced a moment of shock. But then she saw the canopy that extended from the main entrance to the edge of the sidewalk, the doorman to tend to the customers who arrived in carriages and automobiles, and the two large plate-glass windows flanking the entrance, one displaying a variety of accessories, the other several elegant silk gowns, and both showing cards that said *From Our Latest Paris Imports*, Thea instantly relaxed. This place was real and right, her instinct said, and she eagerly followed Morgan and Nela through the door.

This store was Morgan's laboratory, his ongoing experiment and, if finding out San Antonio was not a dusty Wild West town but a bustling and up-to-date city, then seeing Browne's for the first time was to know for certain that Texas truly *did* have citizens of wealth, taste and discernment—and if they didn't, they could be taught here.

"Are you just being polite, Thea, or have we really surprised you?" Morgan teased her as they stood by the display case nearest the entrance.

"I should hate the both of you for not warning me in advance," she told them. "Why didn't you at least *hint* at how glorious this store is?"

"This is all Morgan's brainchild," Nela said, looking at her husband with adoring eyes. "From now on, we decide everything together, but the original concept was all his."

"Well, I want the grand tour, and a chance to sample some of your more exclusive merchandise. Remember, you have a bride to outfit."

Well aware of what he had to put up with when it came to the building's unappealing exterior, Morgan had striven mightily to make sure the interior was an oasis of calm and beauty. The overall effect was to make the women who frequented his store feel as if they were shopping in a private home where every consideration

240

would be offered. The aisles were wide, the wood and glass cabinets were the best available, and the carpets underfoot were of thick pile. The stationery and gift department was placed just inside the front door; the millinery salon was off in its own alcove, fitted with decorative tables, flattering mirrors, and velvet-padded benches; departments for gloves and all other accessories, and vitrines offering the finest French perfumes took care of the rest of the main floor front; and the rear was divided between the cheerful children's department and the white-walled shoe salon with pale gray carpeting, chairs and loveseats upholstered in dark gray velvet, and small round ottomans of charcoal-gray velvet for the salesmen to sit on.

If Morgan capitalized on his strengths, he was also well aware of his weaknesses as far as the merchandise he could successfully sell. He did not offer clothing for men (everything he wore came from either Brooks Brothers, Tripler's or Sulka); no jewelry, since, as he'd told Charles, it was useless to try and compete with Harry Hertzberg; and no furs, since Joske's had the best fur salon in the city.

"There can't be another store like this in all of Texas," Thea announced as they climbed the large, wide Louis XVI-style staircase to the second floor. "You've created a masterpiece, Morgan," she said, and couldn't resist adding, "I couldn't have done better myself!"

"On behalf of my decor, I thank you with all my heart," Morgan said with a devastating smile, "and I accept your second compliment gratefully, but I don't think my store—or rather, the quality and selection I'm providing—can be duplicated by another merchant. There are already good stores in Texas—Joske's is only one of them—and I'm sure there will be more to follow. A real nice fellow named Herbert Marcus has my old job at Sanger's in Dallas. He's as knowledgeable as they come, and I wouldn't be at all surprised if he opened his own store one of these days."

"And that is Morgan's one problem," Nela teased lovingly. "He's not only fond of his competition, he's eager to encourage more."

"And if I don't go up to my office right now, I may have another problem—in the form of a sheriff's sale. My desk is covered with paper!"

They reached the top of the stairs and Morgan kissed both women before continuing on to the third floor where his office, the accounting department, a small infirmary, the employees' dining room, and the work-rooms were located.

"I'll show you all the behind-the-scenes departments before we leave," Nela said, marveling at Thea's calm attitude. "But now it's time for our *creme de la creme*—the second floor."

Thea wasn't as calm as she was resigned to her fate. On Saturday at noon, she was going to be married to a man she'd just met and exchanged approximately a dozen words with. On Charles' plus side, Thea reflected as Nela showed her around the white wicker and pink chintz-decorated lingerie department, were his looks—made all the better since he seemed to be unaware of them—his intelligence, and the fact that he was Americanized without having given up his French individuality. On the minus side was the fact he'd been a Jesuit seminarian, had suffered a severe nervous breakdown, and was intensely proud. How all that would blend together in relation to her, and how it would ultimately affect them troubled Thea in ways she couldn't even begin to formulate. One thing was sure, the next days were crucial, and she'd have to call on all her reserves of tact and charm and . . .

"Have you been paying attention to me at all?" Nela's teasing voice broke into her thoughts. "Since you're behaving like a typical forgetful bride, shall we discuss your wedding dress?"

"I was thinking about Poiret," said Thea, recovering quickly.

"So was I. Something on the line of a garden party dress, and with it you can wear—"

"Oo-ee, Nela! Wait up a minute, girl. I'm just dyin' to talk with you all . . ."

"Now I know just what a cattle auction sounds like," Thea muttered to Nela as the piercing Texas tones halted them and they turned to find an extremely tall young woman swooping down on them. Both women were well above average height, but the approaching figure had them beat by at least three inches.

"Why, Coralee, I didn't know you were back in town," Nela said, turning on her charm. "Is your mother better?"

"Fit as a fiddle, so I came right on back to San Antonio. And who do you think met me at the station but Dax, and what did he have to surprise me with but a brand new auto-mo-bile. Not as grand as your Cadillacs, but it's as cute as a bug anyway."

Thea, who thought of bugs as anything but cute, was trying to keep a straight face. Here she was in a store worthy of anything New York could offer, and at least one of its customers sounded as if she were breaking in her very first pair of shoes!

"Coralee, this is my friend, Thea Harper. Thea, this is Coralee Wilder."

"Mrs. Dax Wilder," she acknowledged, smoothing a fold of her flat white crepe summer dress and touching the opera-length necklace of oversized pearls around her long neck before holding out a hand to Thea. At an inch over six-feet tall, Coralee Wilder had spent nearly all her life in over-ruffled, fussy dresses. But, in the three years since she'd married wealthy rancher Dax Wilder, and had become a customer at Browne's, her taste had been re-educated to simple clothes in pure colors to accent her height, wavy dark hair and sky-blue eyes. "I understand from my husband that you all are here in San Antonio to get married. Dax met Morgan and your intended at the Menger yesterday and Morgan let drop the good news. I wish you all the best."

"Thank you for your good wishes," Thea replied warmly.

"I hear he's a Frenchman—and real good lookin'!"

Thea flashed a bright smile. "Right on both counts. He's a very special person."

"Well, honey, you should know."

But do I? she thought with a sudden lurch of apprehension as Nela skillfully turned the topic of conversation to her newly hatched plan.

"Thea and Charles are getting married at noon on Saturday, Coralee. Morgan and I are giving a little reception for them at home afterwards. I was going to ring you up this afternoon. We'd be honored if you and Dax—"

"Shucks, Nela. When was the last time you heard of a Texan turning down an invite to a wing-ding? I'll wear that new pink Worth garden-party dress," she decided, and flashing a wide, toothy smile, and a little wave, disappeared quickly down the stairs.

"*Shucks?*" Thea questioned, as soon as Coralee was out of sight, choking on her laughter. "I think she also invented a new pronunciation for the word automobile."

"Oh, Coralee's an original. Mrs. Henderson, the head saleswoman, said she never saw someone who wore so many ruffles, bows and ribbons at one time. This store taught her how to dress, but Morgan says diction lessons are not one of the offered services."

"I think if she ever had those, she'd only be another exquisitely dressed Amazon," Thea warned, tucking her

244

arm through her friend's. "Now, if you can do that for Mrs. Wilder, how are you going to dress me, Mrs. Browne?"

"With great care, Miss Harper. With great care."

Precisely at five-thirty, Charles de Renille walked through the doors of Browne's for the first time. And had much the same reaction as Thea had some five hours earlier. He looked around him in pleased astonishment. As with most Frenchmen of his class, he'd been raised to appreciate beauty in all matters, particularly when it was in that most elusive of forms—good taste.

When he'd first arrived in San Antonio, Charles had secluded himself in the Archepiscopal Residence, alternately walking in the garden, reading in the library, and praying in the Cathedral, using those first days to prepare himself both emotionally and spiritually for the task he had agreed to. Gradually, however, he'd begun to explore this most historic of Texas cities much the same as he had New York, a small section at a time. San Antonio was, he discovered, a city where Sunday afternoon cockfights in the Mexican district were considered an acceptable diversion, where the bars were too numerous to count, where the gambling dens were honestly run, and where the law generally turned an unseeing eye to houses of prostitution. But it was also a city of deep historical roots, having in its history lived and grown under the flags of Spain, Mexico, the Republic of Texas, the Confederacy and the Stars and Stripes.

Charles had visited the Alamo, discovering that the low adobe building was the most revered spot in the entire state, and the International Fair Grounds where Theodore Roosevelt had drilled his Rough Riders in the spring of 1898. He took long walks through the adjacent Riverside Park with its groves of pecan trees, and visited the zoo and the natural springs at San Pedro Park. He was

245

given guided tours of the City Hall, the Federal Building, the Grand Opera House, and in turn visited each of the four Spanish missions, finding that their now limited use in no way diminished their air of sustained holiness.

All of these visits had been a pleasant diversion while the plans were being completed. It took his mind off the fact that, like it or not, he was about to become a bridegroom. But his pleasant, interim state, had come to an end just after noon on Tuesday when he'd entered the Menger Hotel and, following the instructions of Major Donovan, gone to the far end of the bar to await the arrival of Morgan Browne.

He liked Morgan instantly, particularly when, after introducing himself and shaking hands, he'd eyed Charles' mint julep and announced, "You actually *drink* those things?"

"Worse, I like them," he shot back with a smile.

"God—where'd you pick up the habit?"

"In Kentucky and Virginia, along with bonded bourbon and pecan pie and—"

"Spare me your conversion to American food," he joked, and then told the bartender to fix him a julep, but to forget the sprig of mint. "Shall we go into the restaurant, Charles?" Morgan suggested. "I don't care to stand too long at the bar. The last time I did, T.R. recruited me to be his supply officer."

Over lunch, they forged their friendship.

Morgan Browne was the closest thing to an aristocrat that Texas was ever likely to produce. His family had originally come to Albemarle County, Virginia, on a land grant from Charles I and, he told Charles, at one time there'd been a saying that whatever the Carters and Maurys—two of the most prominent San Antonio families—hadn't owned in Albemarle County, the Brownes did. But seventy years before they'd pulled up stakes and pushed into the new American frontier, settling in Texas in 1835. Morgan's father had been a United States Senator who'd moved his family to Washington while he served his country with the long tenure with which Texas generally rewards its politicians.

"My father thought that the best available education in America was in a New England boarding school. So when we came East, I was duly sent off to Philips Exeter, and when I graduated there, Amherst College."

"When did you decide to open your own store?"

"I got the idea during my senior year—about a month before graduation, in fact. I came across a copy of Emil Zola's *Au Bonheure des Dames*, and decided that eventually owning a specialty store for women sounded like much more fun than law school at the University of Virginia. I worked for Filene's in Boston, and Sanger's in Dallas. About nine years ago, I came into several inheritances, one right after the other, and now I have my store. Have you been there yet?"

"No, but I will," Charles promised, regarding Morgan with a faint sense of curiosity. They had never met before today, and yet— "Morgan, forgive my asking, but were you married in San Francisco this past April?"

Morgan looked amused. "Did Angela and I make the Paris edition of the *New York Herald?*"

"I wouldn't know about that, but I *did* hear all the details from Henry and Alix Thorpe. I came to New York last February, and they were good enough to open their hearts and their home to a very confused Frenchman."

"I think I'm going to strangle Major Donovan," Morgan remarked conversationally. "All he told me was your name, that you were from a fine old French family, and that you had been visiting Ambassador Jusserand in Washington. That underhanded, thick-brained . . ."

"It's the truth," Charles pointed out, but he was secretly relieved that Morgan shared his view of Major Donovan, who, from the moment they'd met in the

Archbishop's study, had set his teeth on edge.

"Still, he held out on you, too. Did you know that my wife, Alix Thorpe and Thea Harper are best friends? Not only that, but— Oh, hello, Dax," he said, as a widely smiling man in his middle forties with a head of thick, wavy, silver-touched brown hair, approached their table. "You look mighty happy."

"I sure am," he informed them brightly, pulling up a chair so he could join them. "My new automobile came today. A Rambler Surrey, Type One, Model Two, with sixteen horsepower, and worth every penny of the $1,350 I paid for it," he explained enthusiastically. "Coralee's due back tomorrow from visiting her mama in Brownsville, and I can't wait to see her face when I meet her at the station in it!"

"She's going to love it—as you well know," Morgan said, wondering if he could carry off what he was about to say, and hoping he wasn't about to insult his new friend. So far, Charles appeared to be remarkably eventempered, but one never knew with the French . . . "Charles, I'd like you to meet Mr. Dax Wilder, one of San Antonio's leading citizens, and owner of a fine cattle ranch about fifty miles from here. His wife is one of my favorite customers. Dax, this is Charles de Renille, who has been in our city for the past two weeks."

"We're getting to be quite an international town. You're here on business, Mr. de Renille?" he asked after a friendly handshake.

"No . . . Charles is here to be married," Morgan interjected.

"Well, you don't say! A San Antonio girl?"

"No, she's from New York," Charles replied, totally mystified at Morgan's disclosure, but nonetheless playing along. "I'm waiting for her to arrive."

"Got a little bit of bridegroom's nerves?" Dax gave him a knowing grin. "Buck up, son, you won't be left at the altar."

When Theodosia Harper finds out who she's expected to marry, I wouldn't blame her if she did, he said to himself, but aloud he told Dax, "I'm sure I won't be."

"Well, in that case, we have to see about doin' you up with a proper send-off. A bachelor party at the San Antonio Club."

Charles felt he was choking. "No . . . I mean, I'm deeply honored, but—but I don't think the Archbishop would approve," he said, grasping at that one last straw. "I'm his guest, and I'm not sure if he would consider a bachelor party to be suitable entertainment . . ."

"Why, the Archbishop's a grand fellow—if you'll permit an old Baptist like me to say so—and he wouldn't object to your having a proper send-off with the boys. Heck, it's only a little bit of Texas hospitality, and the San Antonio Club's no cat house. Morgan would do the same for you if he were a member—"

There was nothing else for Charles to do except agree to the bachelor party, the date to be arranged when his "fiancée" arrived, and their "wedding" plans finalized. With another round of handshakes, Dax Wilder departed, and when he disappeared out of the restaurant, Charles and Morgan regarded each other.

"Before you get upset, Charles, I'll explain with the old saying about going naked being the best disguise, and the open truth covering all lies."

"I'm not angry," he reassured Morgan quickly. "I understand you must uphold your position in the community. But will I really have to go through with the bachelor party?"

"Probably." Morgan looked amused. "Don't worry, it'll be all dull and respectable. The San Antonio Club's very conservative."

"Is that why you're not a member?"

"No, I lost interest in clubs at a very early age,"

Morgan said, signaling the waiter for their pecan pie and coffee. "My father was a member of the most exclusive club in the United States, the Senate, and after that nothing can quite measure up."

Charles was more grateful to Morgan than he could ever say, and now, a day later, he leaned across the counter, putting the final pieces together.

From the first moment he'd heard the name Theodosia Harper, Charles had been trying to place her without success, and when they'd finally met, her face, as attractive as he found it, provided no immediate clue. It was only when she'd informed him of her relationship to the naturalist-explorer-writer whom he admired so much that the pieces gradually began to fall into place. He now wondered if, in all his months in New York, a day had passed when Thea Harper's name hadn't been mentioned. With sudden clarity, Charles recalled Henry pointing out the building where Thea had her office, and Clifford remarking how a certain hostess would have had a much nicer home if only Thea had been the decorator. Bits and pieces were floating back to him now and, all in all, it was probably very fitting that after having more or less lived with Theodosia Harper for the past seven months, he should now be about to marry her.

"May I be of help to you, sir?"

The clerk's quiet, Texas drawl jerked Charles back to the present and, to cover his uncertainty, he gazed into the cabinet on the pretext of looking for something, and found it contained boxed writing paper, Mont Blanc fountain pens and other desk accessories.

"I was on my way upstairs to meet Mr. Browne, but I think I'd like to make a purchase first. It's for my fiancée," he said at last. It was his only way to gracefully get out of this predicament. The very last thing he needed was for Morgan to find out that he'd come into the store, leaned against a counter to get his bearings, and then slipped into a trancelike state.

"I'm Mr. Bates, the stationery buyer and head salesman," the young man informed him politely. "I'll be happy to help you with your purchase. Did you have something specific in mind?"

"A paperweight." He spoke without thinking, and Charles heard his request with a mixture of amazement and horror. He had not come here with the idea of buying a gift for Thea (instinct told him she was not the sort of woman one bought trinkets for), and certainly not a paperweight—a gift that was almost sacred in his family circle.

Dazedly, Charles watched as Mr. Bates showed him paperweights from the firms of Clichy and Val St. Lambert and the New England Glass Company. Paperweights were the present every male de Renille bestowed on the young woman to whom he had just become engaged. It was a selection he'd never expected to have to make and yet, in a way he couldn't quite comprehend, an unconscious part of his mind had taken over and urged him on.

He was regarding two Clichy weights, one of swirling green, white and purple spokes, and the other of interlaced trefoils on a moss-green ground, when Mr. Bates placed a third selection in front of him. Charles knew his decision was made as soon as he saw the clear crystal with a quatrefoil garland of red and white florets with an additional circle encompassing a multi-colored complex cane.

"Baccarat?" he asked, already knowing the answer. His ancestors had been among the company's first titled patrons, and he could recognize their work on sight.

"Absolutely correct, sir. And it arrived only the other day. It's the only one we have from the firm."

Somehow he knew it would be, Charles decided as he paid for the paperweight and waited for it to be gift-wrapped. When a de Renille paperweight was ordered for

251

a fiancée, it was the only one of its kind. Obviously, this weight was not exclusive, but it was equally clear that there was not only not another one like it in the store, but also possibly in the entire state.

Charles was still pondering this latest turn in his life when he and Morgan arrived at Johnson Street less than an hour later. Charles had had a tour of the King William District, so the well-to-do neighborhood was no surprise to him, and he viewed the Brownes' house with frank admiration.

"I was hoping this was your home," he said as they went up the path to the front door. "It's one of the most *American* houses in the area."

"I deliberately had it built like that. It's not too large, but we have plenty of room," Morgan said as he opened the front door and held out his arms to a little girl who sat at the bottom of the stairs. "Hello, sweetheart."

"Daddy!" The child flung herself into Morgan's arms. "Aunt Thea wants me to be her flower girl. What do you think?"

"I think that's wonderful. Now, Christy, say hello to the man your Aunt Thea is going to marry. Charles, this is my daughter, Christine," Morgan said, transferring the girl to his arms. "We call her Christy."

"Hello, Christy," he said softly, kissing the child's soft brown curls. He knew Morgan's present marriage was his second, and that he was a widower with a young daughter. "You're very pretty, *cherie*. How old are you?"

"Eight, almost nine." She regarded him through deeply fringed hazel eyes. "Do I call you Uncle Charles now?"

"I'd be very honored if you would." After a few more questions, he set her down on the floor as Nela, glowing in Lucile's pink silk muslin gown with insertions of Cluny lace, a black taffeta belt and a single strand of perfect black pearls with a ruby and sapphire clasp, came down the stairs to join their group.

"Welcome to our home," she said warmly, kissing his cheek. "Would you like me to show you around, or do you just want to sit in a corner with a cold drink?"

"Take the drink and the tour," Morgan advised. "That way I'll know you're being suitably occupied and are receiving Texas hospitality at the same time!"

"I've already had more unexpected hospitality than I could have wished for," Charles said frankly. "I think it's safe to tell you this now. I pictured San Antonio as a dusty town in a Karl May penny, dreadful!"

"Well, in case you have any lingering doubts that we're really a bunch of trail-stained cowboys, I have the final cure," Morgan laughed as he ushered them, Christy included, into the butler's pantry where two bottles of wine were open and breathing on the counter. "Mazy Chambertin, 1897," he told Charles, pouring a small amount from one bottle into a wine glass. "Does it meet with your approval?"

Charles sampled the excellent burgundy. "It's superb."

"I also have a good supply of Romanee Conti '93 and '94, but it needs a bit more time to settle. The Mazy Chambertin is better when it's younger."

"Absolutely—I'm looking forward to enjoying it at dinner," he said, no longer bothering to wonder about finding fine French wine in the Far West.

"If we're going to have dinner on time, I'd better get ready. Nela and Christy will finish showing you around."

The kitchen was a spacious, up-to-date room where Consuelo was busy putting the finishing touches on the dinner, and she proudly showed off her efforts, opening the icebox to display the cream of mushroom soup chilling there. Charles made the appropriate comments about the soup, the large bowl of just-made potato salad, the rolls about to go into the oven, sampled the perfectly ripe brie and camembert that Nela told him was ordered from Rouge et Noir in California, and which would accompany their salad whose dressing was made from a Dalton family recipe. On the central work table, a large bowl of fresh strawberries nestled alongside the four-quart White Mountain ice cream freezer made of New England pine. Charles loved ice cream, but he didn't love what he saw at the opposite end of the table. Resting in a copper pan filled with cracked ice were four of the largest steaks he'd ever seen.

"Juan is firing up the barbeque now, and in a little while he'll grill them over charcoal. Come on, Charles, you look like you're ready for a drink."

As they went toward the library where an icy pitcher of daiquiris were waiting, all Charles could think about were the slabs of meat that were going to be their main course. Even after all these months, he still had problems looking at—let alone consuming—red meat, but he would never plead this last after-effect of his illness to Nela and Morgan.

No, he decided grimly, glancing around the library that would have normally enthralled him. I'll just have to choke it down. In seven months I haven't had to sacrifice my pride for my health, and I won't start now!

"I see you've been shopping at the store."

Charles glanced at the present he was holding. "This is for Thea."

"How sweet of you to buy a gift for her," Nela exclaimed, handing him a daiquiri. "Why don't you give it to her now? She's out in the garden. Let me give you a quick tour of our drawing room, and then you can go outside and visit together until dinner is ready."

Even as she spoke, Angela Dalton Browne couldn't entirely suppress the thrill of certainty that ran through her. Contrary to Morgan's protestations, the Archbishop hadn't objected to their plan for the wedding reception,

Charles had turned out to be more than presentable, and as for Thea and Charles themselves— Well, you can't make people fall in love, any more than you can make them buy something they don't want, Nela told herself.

But the present in his hand is a step in the right direction, her thoughts ran on as Charles went out to the garden and she sat down on the drawing room sofa, cuddling her stepdaughter, her mind touching on the traditions of Charles' family. I'll have to tell Morgan how right he was to promote Mr. Bates to running the stationery department. How very conscientious of him to ring me up and let me know that he'd just sold our only Baccarat paperweight to Charles de Renille!

From her perch on the steps of the gazebo, Thea watched Charles come through the open French doors, pause for a moment beside the two large blue and white Chinese porcelain vases that flanked the terrace entrance, and step out onto the lawn, going past bushes of yellow tea roses and the white Blanc Double de Coubert, whose hips made excellent jelly. He passed the free-standing Frau Karl Druschki rose bush that a neighbor had planted as a memorial to Ellen Browne, as he came toward her.

Now that their first meeting was over, Thea actually found herself happier and more relaxed than she'd been in weeks. Her annoyances in the form of Jane Miles and Paul Merrill were behind her, and now she knew what she'd be facing—and the man whom she'd be facing it with. Donovan, she knew instinctively, was going to be a problem, but she'd surmounted their first encounter successfully, and there was no reason they couldn't settle whatever else would come up between them later on.

Mostly it was Morgan and Nela's attitudes that helped soothe and reassure her, Thea acknowledged. She secretly suspected that Morgan might have had a few choice words when Nela first suggested a wedding reception, but his friendship and steadfastness couldn't be bought at any price. And as for Nela—

Thea smiled, recalling her afternoon. There was nothing like a few hours devoted to trying on the finest of dresses, lingerie and accessories to bring a woman back to life. Despite the heat of the day, the endless trying on and fitting of garments in the spacious fitting room had been a joy. Briefly, Thea's thoughts dwelled on the lingerie she'd chosen to supplement her extensive collection of delicate, lace-encrusted Lucile night-wear and undergarments. Now there was more silk, satin and crepe de chine, all richly embellished with lace. There was even what Mrs. Sanders, the head saleswoman for lingerie, called a wedding ensemble; a delectable nightgown and negligee of ivory satin and ecru lace. There had been no way to tell the older woman that she had no need for that set. She hadn't even been able to look at Nela for fear of either laughing or crying and, without further ado, she'd added it to her growing list of purchases. It was beautiful, the ultimate in nightwear *luxe*, and it was likely that the man she was ostensibly going to impress would never see her in it, or in any of her other wildly luxurious, totally feminine lingerie . . .

"Hello, did you have any difficulty at the County Clerk's office?" Thea spoke a shade too breathlessly as she tore her thoughts away from what their eventual sleeping arrangements would be.

"None at all, everyone was very helpful," Charles informed her as he placed his glass and the box on the ledge and leaned against the side of the white-painted wood structure, taking in Thea who sat on the top step in a tucked and shirred white mull Poiret dress with lace insets. The neckline was cut low enough to give him an excellent view of Thea's full bosom, and the short sleeves of the dress showed off her only piece of jewelry, a four-coil gold serpent bracelet studded with diamonds and emeralds, to perfection. She looked so cool and collected that Charles suddenly felt awkward and unworthy of her. "I've also been to Hertzberg's," he went on. "They've set aside some rings I think you'll like, and you can pick one out tomorrow."

All she needed was one look at his face to know what this was costing him in terms of pride, and Thea moved quickly to smooth over the situation. "That sounds fine. Shall we say around eleven?"

Charles relaxed instantly. "After we choose the . . . the ring, we'll have lunch at the Menger, and then go out to Fort Sam Houston."

"So far, I have no objections."

"Does that include having a meeting with Major Donovan?" Charles' voice was cautious.

"Oh, *God*. I thought we were through with him until Mexico City." Thea made no attempt to hide her annoyance. "I can't stand that man."

"Neither can I," he responded briefly, and a look of immediate understanding passed between them. "That man is a fount of information—most of which he chooses not to pass on."

"I agree completely," Thea said, and couldn't resist adding, "What did he tell you about me?"

"Only that I shouldn't worry about whom I'd be with; that you were a lady."

Thea raised her eyebrows. "I guess I should take that as a compliment."

"And Morgan told me you were both *la decoratrice* and *l'antiquaire*."

"Oh, interior decorator and antique dealer sound so much nicer in French!"

"Rather like these roses." Charles looked at the flowering bushes that surrounded the gazebo. "In French they're *cuisse de nymph*. They're my mother's

257

favorite, and I've lost count of the number of bushes there are in our garden."

"Maiden's Blush." Thea supplied the translation, tactfully passing over the rest of his comment. "You're right, Charles, once again I prefer the French." For a moment, Thea looked down at her white silk shoes with their tiny, bow-shaped diamond buckles. "One more thing, didn't Alix *ever* mention me to you?"

"Your name came up almost every day, even in my first hour in New York. We were going from the dock to the Dakota, and Henry pointed out your office to me. Unfortunately, I was still in shock from my first sight of the city, and was also in the process of turning blue from the cold, so most of the information I was given that day went clear over my head!"

"How terrible those first days must have been for you!"

"I think I came close to qualifying for the position of village idiot. I'm glad we didn't meet then, or when the President suggested his plan, you would have refused outright!"

Thoughtfully, Thea studied Charles' face, really seeing him for the first time—the aquiline wedge of his nose, the good tan, and the faint trace of black beard that remained no matter how close he shaved, and gave him a raffish look of which he seemed to be totally unaware.

"No," she told him quietly. "I don't think I would have ever done that."

They looked transfixedly at one another, both of them aware that at that moment a bond had been created between them. It was a silence neither quite knew how to break. Out of the corner of his eye, Charles could see Juan in the kitchen garden, setting the grill on the brick barbeque. There wasn't much time, and he handed her the box.

"This is for you," he said rather needlessly, but ready

258

to say anything to keep things flowing smoothly. "It isn't very much, but I don't want you to think you're marrying a stingy Frenchman."

Thea was touched beyond words. "Oh, Charles, you may be a lot of things, but something tells me stingy is *not* one of your faults." She set the box on her lap and carefully began to unwrap it. "Don't you hate opening boxes that are as pretty as this? I'm sure it's perfect, and . . . oh . . ."

Thea had removed the silk ribbon, broken the gold seals, turned back the paper, opened the white glazed gift box, and lifted the lid of the black velvet presentation case. The bright Texas sunlight glinted off the flawless crystal, and Thea felt her eyes fill with tears.

"Charles, thank you." She blinked furiously, well aware of the effect of tears on her Rimmel mascara. "I can't believe—"

"Thea, please." Charles was alarmed, he hadn't expected this reaction at all. "It isn't worth crying over."

"I'm very honored," she said. And suddenly Charles understood the reason behind the depth of her feelings.

"Thea, how well do you know my family?" His voice was gentle.

"Not as well as Alix or Nela does, but it's more than just a passing acquaintance. And I know that, in your family, when a man becomes engaged, he presents his fiancée with a paperweight. This," she added, running her fingers over the crystal surface, "is a very unexpected gesture."

For a moment, Charles felt himself choke. "And if I hadn't—?"

Thea looked at him through her lashes. "Do you really think I'm the sort of woman who would have made a fuss?"

A tide of self-reproach swept over him. How close he'd come to hurting her. The fact that it would have been

259

unintentional was no excuse, and there was only one way to set things right.

"You mustn't think that I don't hold you in high regard, or that I won't honor you. Thea—" Charles' voice was filled with emotion. "Will you marry me?"

From any other man who might have agreed to their undertaking, it would have been a useless question. But coming from Charles, Thea realized, it represented the one opportunity they would have to settle affairs between the two of them, to operate as two independent people, not as pawns on a chess board, and a new feeling of warmth enveloped her.

"Yes, Charles," she said in a voice whose tone matched his. "I'd like very much to marry you."

Chapter Seven

In the next three days, Thea had ample opportunity to observe Charles de Renille. In Texas, his height went almost unnoticed, and his restrained, almost formal manner wasn't shyness—no de Renille was *ever* shy—but was a product of his education and, she realized almost at once, his illness.

His speech pattern was an endless source of curiosity. Stonyhurst, he told her when she asked, followed by All Souls College, Oxford. "My father was a firm believer in the British system of education. My brothers and I had a proper nanny, and I think we spoke English before we did French," he told her the following afternoon as they stood by the lake at Fort Sam Houston, feeding the ducks that glided across its surface, waiting for Major Donovan to join them.

The M K & T route ran through part of the post, so both Thea and Charles had a glimpse of it as the Katy completed its journey, but it was a poor preparation for the sweep of the fort. Charles had skillfully navigated Nela's Cadillac two-seater out of downtown San Antonio and onto New Braunfels Avenue. When they'd been cleared at the main gate and told where to park, both were unprepared for the sights that awaited them.

Fort Sam Houston had come a long way since the land's purchase by the War Department in 1870, and its first occupation by the Third Cavalry Regiment in 1875. Back then it had been little more than a grouping of log barracks, but now, nearly thirty years later, there were perfectly tended green lawns, ivy-covered white stucco buildings with wide verandas shaded by large leafy trees, and a stone clock tower that held the dominant position in the center of the quadrangle. Except for the Presidio, *this* was the showplace western fort of the United States Army, and its perfectly landscaped acres often caused British visitors to compare the post with the finest of their own army's garrisons in India.

They recovered quickly enough, however, going to the top of the eighty-eight foot tower so they could marvel at all of the fort and San Antonio spread out beneath them. Charles brought his Kodak along, and they took snapshots of each other. All of Fort Sam Houston, they agreed, made a perfect backdrop.

Nearly the same height, together they made an arresting-looking couple as they strolled the lush grounds, Charles in one of his immaculate Brooks Brothers Palm Beach suits, and Thea in a Lucile summer gown of cream-colored tucked lawn with English embroidery and Valenciennes lace, and many of the people they passed turned back to look at them. They had been creating that reaction since they arrived at Harry Hertzberg's jewelry store earlier in the day.

Mr. Hertzberg had attended them himself, greeting them warmly as they walked in, settling them in a private alcove, and bringing out the black-velvet-lined tray that held the gold wedding rings Charles had asked him to put aside.

Thea made her selection easily, and Harry Hertzberg promised to deliver it to the Archbishop's residence in plenty of time for the ceremony. In less than an hour their business was completed, and as he watched them leave, the jeweler felt puzzled. He had seen at once that Miss Harper wore no engagement ring, and he'd fully expected Mr. de Renille to purchase one for her. True, he probably had some family heirloom he would present her with at a later date, but nowadays it wasn't at all uncommon for a man to purchase a diamond solitaire to supplement the ancestral engagement ring. Even the inscription to be engraved on the inside of the ring struck him as a little *too* proper. *C de R to T H - 24.9.04.* Ah, well, Mr. de Renille was wealthy, French, a guest of the Archbishop of San Antonio and in the process of an elopement. In Harry Hertzberg's book, that explained a lot. But still . . .

"Are you going to mind having to tell everyone we eloped?" Thea asked as they tossed their final handful of breadcrumbs to the waiting ducks.

"It seems to be the best possible story," Charles replied. At dinner the previous night, it had been decided that from now on, when anyone asked, they would say that they'd met in New York, fallen in love, and decided to get married. But, with his family in France and her father on an expedition in Egypt, the best solution seemed to be to take matters into their own hands. "All of the magazines are touting Mexico as the latest tourist discovery, so that makes San Antonio a logical stop-over."

"Particularly since one of my closest friends is the new bride of a very popular citizen," Thea continued. "It's also the most natural thing in the world that they should want to give us a wedding reception. And it's entirely proper that we spend the first part of our honeymoon in Chihuahua at the de Veiga estate, since they did invite me to visit them when we met in Budapest two years ago."

Gradually, they began to smile at each other, dissolving still more of the tenseness and uncertainty that was only natural considering their situation.

"When you think about it," Charles ventured in a teasing voice, "the only thing we may have to worry about is what to do with any wedding presents we may get!"

"Unfortunately, I think there *are* a few more important considerations," a voice said coldly behind them, and they turned to find Major Donovan standing close by, a sour look playing across his blunt-featured face.

A tremor of dislike passed through Thea, but she kept her voice calm. "Have you been observing us long?"

"Long enough." He studied them intently. "I hear via the grapevine that you're both the latest rage in engaged couples."

"We were never told we couldn't be." Charles' reply was icy.

"Oh, don't get me wrong, Mr. de Renille. I'm not here to object. In fact, a little flurry of wedding activity is probably a good idea. People get suspicious when your sort *don't* make a fuss."

Charles felt a flash flood of rage boil in him. No one had ever spoken to him in that drawling, insolent tone of voice. He didn't care about himself. If an endless number of Jesuit instructor-priests had been unable to destroy his de Renille pride, a lone Army major wasn't likely to do so in the space of a few minutes. What he cared about was that his words reflected equally on Thea, disparaging her as if she were a mindless woman interested only in frivolities.

"We feel we're being very honored by our friends," Charles said coldly. "Whatever they've offered to do, it's for love, not for show, as you seem to think. Now, if that's all you have to say to us, good day, Major. Thea and I are due at the Forrests' in twenty minutes for tea."

Donovan held up a calm hand. Today he was in uniform, a mode of dress that became him more than any business suit ever could. "I won't keep you long. I have one or two questions—points we need clarified. How's your Spanish?"

Of all the questions he might have asked, this was the most ridiculous of all, and Thea and Charles felt their anger fade into amusement as they answered deadpan.

"Not as good as my French."

"Not as good as my English."

Donovan flushed uncomfortably as he saw their faces. *Damn society know-it-alls,* he thought. Abruptly, he pulled out a white envelope and held it out to Charles. "Your expense money."

"My *what?*"

"Expense money. Fifteen hundred dollars. You'd be surprised how far that'll go in Mexico. You'll have a suite at the Sanz Hotel—it's the best—and its daily rate wouldn't get you a sliver of a room at the new Astor in New York." Another envelope came out of his pocket. "This is yours, Miss Harper, the same amount."

They looked at the envelopes as if they were crawling with maggots. Finally, Thea broke their silence in a voice that surrounded her words with ice.

"I *never* take *any* sort of monetary payment."

Donovan seemed momentarily nonplussed. "Well, then . . . I guess it's all yours, Mr. de Renille."

"Major Donovan, with all due respect, I strongly suggest you remove those envelopes from our sight, or I will throw them in the lake." His voice, like Thea's, was totally cold and uncompromising. "I agreed to go to Mexico as a *favor.*"

"A gentleman's agreement may be what you entered into, Mr. de Renille, but it won't pay your bills!"

"I have no trouble whatsoever in meeting my expenses; and Miss Harper's as well when we're married," Charles shot back, barely holding his temper. "I came to San Antonio with a letter of credit for ten thousand dollars, five thousand dollars in my checking account, and a substantial amount of cash. I think that's quite enough for both of us to live on."

"I guess it is," he agreed somewhat reluctantly, pocketing the offending envelopes. He bid them good afternoon and sauntered off, leaving the same bad feeling in the air that Thea had felt two nights earlier.

"Charles, there's something you have to know," Thea said seriously as they took another path to the quarters of Colonel and Mrs. Randolph Forrest. The Colonel held senior rank at Fort Sam Houston, his wife was a favored customer at Browne's, and when Nela had invited them to the reception, the officer's lady had not only accepted with pleasure, but had invited the engaged couple to tea. "When we get to Mexico City, I expect to conduct some business. That means buying antiques, and I won't have you paying for them."

Charles looked at her in understanding. "Oh, Thea, my masculine pride isn't *that* fragile! Any antiques you purchase you pay for with your own money, as well as your own clothes, but I take care of all other expenses."

"Agreed." Thea smiled, tucking her arm through his. "With my clothing bills, I don't think your letter of credit would last too long!"

"Is that why you don't accept payment?" Charles teased her gently. "Are you afraid you'll create too much of a strain on the Treasury?"

"I wish I could say yes. But the truth is I'm a true New Yorker, and that means being very, very cautious. You'd be surprised at some of the favors I've done for T.R. Some of my fellow citizens aren't terribly bright when they go abroad," she told him, her voice growing serious, "and sometimes problems they create have to be straightened out. If I don't accept payment for my services, then no one can tell me how to go about my business. You see, once you take money from the government, everything you undertake becomes their business."

*   *   *

266

"Do you know, I still can't get over the gall of that man," Thea announced the next day as she and Charles set out a picnic under a shade tree at the Mission San Jose de Aguayo, the second of San Antonio's four Spanish Missions.

"He thinks that you're a useless society girl, and that I'm a no account remittance man."

"My dear Mr. de Renille, you make us sound utterly delightful!" Thea replied, and began to laugh, the last of her annoyance fading.

They had spent the morning exploring the Mission Concepcion, the first mission which dated from 1731, and was noted for its church with thick adobe walls, twin towers and massive dome, all of which seemed to dwarf the trees and bushes it towered over. It was the best preserved of the missions, not like the isolated community of San Francisco de la Espanda, Charles told her as they'd explored the grounds. He'd been out there to meet the missionary Father Francis Boucher who was working almost single-handedly to restore the mission as it had been in the days when the Indians had come to carve statues to honor their new church.

"I think I was the most affected by San Juan Capistrano. It's practically nothing but ruins now," Charles told her as he opened the wicker picnic basket from Fortnum and Mason and took out the Lenox plates, Waterford crystal and Reed and Barton cutlery. "That was the one mission destined to remain spartan, even while the others flourished."

"Strange to think that it's only nine miles out of San Antonio," Thea remarked. "In those days, it must have seemed very remote. Imagine if they had motor cars then."

Charles shook his head. "I can't imagine a motorized Spanish army—even the one today."

"Whether you can or not, some military friends of

mine tell me it's the next step. Have you read *Progress In Flying Machines—?*"

The possibilities of what might come from the Wright Brothers' noble experiment the previous December at Kitty Hawk, North Carolina, took up the next few minutes as they unpacked their picnic lunch.

Consuelo had provided them with a feast, they agreed. There were two kinds of sandwiches: delicate cucumber, almost thin enough to see through, and wafer-light slices of Smithfield ham enhanced by herb mustard, both on crustless slices of fresh-baked white bread. In addition, there was a quiche prepared with spinach, generous wedges of brie and camembert, an assortment of crudités, a bowl of large strawberries dusted with confectioners' sugar, a small loaf of sourdough bread, four large, perfectly ripe peaches, thin butter cookies, puffy chocolate meringue cookies, a bottle of White Rock mineral water, and a bottle of dry white wine from a California vineyard Morgan was fond of.

"When Nela was employed by Mary Anne Magnin, there was a saleswoman there who didn't like her very much," Thea related to Charles as he worked at extracting the cork from the bottle of wine. "Nela says that Miss Gertrude used to remark that Angela Dalton was part of a dangerous new trend—a society girl who worked. It was just like those other new inventions: the nickelodeon, the motor car and that queer new flying machine, inconvenient, interfering in the old way of life—and not likely to go away!"

Charles was laughing as he poured wine into their glasses. "Thea, may I ask you a question?"

"Only if I can ask you one back."

"*A votre santé.*" They touched glasses. "Of course." For a moment his topaz-colored eyes regarded her gravely, taking in her cool cream and mauve batiste summer dress. "I know that your father and President

268

Roosevelt are good friends. Is it for that reason that you won't accept payment, and not that you don't want a government official looking over your shoulder?"

"Poor Charles, I'm going to disillusion you terribly," Thea laughed. "I'm not *that* altruistic. True, I've never taken a penny for any of the favors I've done for T.R., but I've been paid just the same—in clients."

"I'm sorry, I don't quite see how—"

"Don't worry, T.R. doesn't strong arm anyone. When the President asked me to do a favor for him two and a half years ago, I agreed on the condition that I be hired to redecorate the ladies' retiring room at the White House. I was seriously thinking about opening my own firm, but clients are hard to come by. I couldn't think of a better advertisement than having done one small room in the newly redecorated White House!"

Charles' look of puzzlement faded, and was replaced by a smile Thea discovered she liked to see; a smile that began in his eyes and gradually transformed his whole face, changing him from a preternaturally proud and serious man to one who knew how to take a joke.

"You must have had clients lined up at your door."

"Hardly. At least, not at first. You'd be surprised at the number of women who wouldn't dream of hiring a decorator who wasn't a nice, nebulous young man devoted to billing and cooing over his clients!"

Charles' face was a combination of amusement and distaste. "Surely not."

"Oh, you'd be surprised." Unexpectedly, Thea began to smile as she recalled events and clients that had marked the start of her career. "Remind me to tell you about the woman who wanted to be my first client. Claimed she'd make my business."

"Something I think you managed to do very well on your own."

Thea smiled at his compliment and said, "It's my turn

now, but you might not like my question, or want to answer it."

"No shirking, I promise. Besides, what sort of an awful question could you come up with?" he said, all too aware of what questions his emotional condition could raise.

"Then you won't be offended or insulted if I ask you a question about the seminary?"

Charles felt his mouth go dry. *Dear God,* he thought with a sickening lurch. *She's going to ask me about sex.* He'd known all along that a woman like Thea—a friend of Alix's—would have no compunction whatsoever about either speaking her mind or asking a direct question. Well, the sooner faced the better. "What did you want to know?" he managed to get out.

"How you shaved."

For a second, he wasn't sure if he'd heard her right. "With shaving soap and a razor." He looked at her, thoroughly mystified.

Thea felt his perplexity immediately, and in turn felt her face grow warm. *Blast,* she thought, angry at herself. You sure know how to fix things, Thea. In twenty-four hours you're going to be married to this man. Couldn't you wait until *after* the ceremony to ask offensive questions?

Finally, aware she owed Charles an explanation, Thea said, "When I was at Barnard, one of my classmates had spent six months in a convent, and Peggy said there weren't any mirrors. I was just curious if . . ."

As Thea's voice trailed off, the fog surrounding Charles lifted, and he began to see the humor in her question. "Of course there were mirrors. There had to be unless they were interested in a great many slit throats!"

Thea relaxed. "Then I haven't offended you?"

"Oh, Thea, you have no idea the strange questions people ask about seminaries—and most of them come from good Catholics. My father had his own series of

270

misconceptions." Charles' amused expression faded. "When I told him I was going to the Jesuits, he informed me that I'd be starved, scourged, and beaten—among other things."

"Were you?" The question slipped out before she could stop herself. Thea could clearly see the pain on his face and, in response, she found herself close to tears.

"No." He looked as if he were seeing past her, into a world long gone. "The mood there was disciplined and intense, but it was no torture chamber. If only I could have convinced my father . . . He hated what I'd done."

"I'm sorry you couldn't, Charles. Truly I am. I never knew. I'd always been told that in families like yours, the Church was not only an honorable choice, but a pre-chosen destiny."

"In most families, yes. But not mine. There has never been a de Renille who dedicated himself to the service of God. My father was no remote aristocrat, and he always said exactly what he thought."

"Your father was a great and kind gentleman."

He looked at her in amazement. "When—when did you meet him?"

"I met your father and mother in the summer of 1895," she remembered for him. "I was sixteen going on seventeen, and halfway between Brearley and Barnard. My mother had died in March, and Daddy took me to Europe for the summer to make it easier to adjust. It was awful and a thrill at the same time. I had graduated preparatory school and was going to college and was wearing grown-up clothes, but my mother wasn't there, and Daddy and I missed her so much."

She paused to blink back tears, and Charles waited patiently for her to continue.

"I wasn't wearing mourning, but we weren't accepting invitations to large parties either. Anyway, when we were in Paris, your parents invited us to tea. Your father was

271

very fond of two of Daddy's books, *The Unknown Caribbean*, and *A Season in the Dakotas*, and he also wanted to discuss the Boone and Crockett Club with him. While Daddy and your father were having their talk, your mother showed me around your Paris house, and while we were in the Louis XV salon, she mentioned that she was sorry her youngest son was off mountain-climbing in Switzerland, because she would have liked us to meet."

Charles turned pale under his tan. "Then . . . then I could have met you nine years ago?"

Thea saw his look. "Would that have been so awful?"

"No . . . *no!*"

"And we might have met this winter," she added. "It was only because I was out of town so much that we didn't."

"And in between? What did you hear about me?"

"Nothing. Or almost nothing. When I was in Paris again three years later, everyone said not to mention your name to your family. I thought you'd done something disgraceful—or were dead."

"To my family, for almost five years, I was," he got out painfully. "The day I walked out of my father's house, he said I was dead to him, that he didn't have a third son, and from August of 1897, to December of 1901, I never heard a word from my parents, my brothers, or my four cousins."

Thea felt her heart fill with pain. "Oh, Charles. How horrible for you. How did you ever bear it?"

"One adjusts, but it's never the same," he admitted at long last. "Fortunately, that December there was a *rapprochement* between my father and myself. But by the time I . . . I collapsed and was brought home, he had died."

For several minutes neither of them spoke. They sipped their wine, ate the strawberries and nibbled on the

272

cookies. In spite of the serious turn their conversation had taken, they'd done justice to their picnic lunch.

"And here we are," Thea said at last. "In nine years, we've missed each other at least twice, and it took Theodore Roosevelt to bring us together." Even as she spoke, Thea wasn't sure if she were starting a philosophical discussion with Charles, or attempting to flirt with him. "It's all been very suitably arranged, but it remains to be seen as to what we're going to do on our own."

For a long time, Charles studied the bottom of his wineglass. "Only one thing, Thea," he said at last, in a quiet voice. "We're going to get married."

It was ten hours later, and Thea was still turning over Charles' remark in her mind. She was desperately trying to place the tone of his voice. Had he spoken out of resignation, annoyance, or out of the possibility that there was something out there for both of them that neither could foresee?

She turned over in bed, trying to find a comfortable spot, wishing she could slow her racing heart. It was no use trying to convince herself that everything was going to be fine. In the end, it might well be but, nonetheless, Thea had a full-fledged case of pre-bridal nerves.

If Charles de Renille had a first-class intellect and was one of the finest men she'd ever met, it was also obvious to her that he'd suffered greatly, was still—in a much more quiet way—continuing to suffer, had taken a great chance in confiding in her, and was secretive out of sheer self-defense.

And so are you, she told herself. But with one great difference. Underneath it all, you *like* being secretive. You think it adds to your personality. You love the idea that no one—well, almost no one—knows that you're an operative for the President. How much fun it sounded like back then, she thought, her mind propelling itself backwards. It was an absolute lark, and look where it's brought you. . . .

Mrs. Theodore Roosevelt
invites you
to
the debut
of
her daughter
Alice
at
The White House on January 3, 1902

Short of the coronation of Edward VII, which was scheduled to take place five months hence in London, and one or two highly regarded society weddings, *this* was the most coveted invitation of the year. Six-hundred engraved cards had been sent out weeks before, and not even the numbing fifteen-degree night was dimming the excitement as the guests arrived at the White House.

Her firm didn't exist then. Instead, Thea worked as a sort of glorified assistant to Benjamin Altman, the department store owner and art collector, who taught her about Chinese porcelains while she handled the paperwork involved with those purchases. She had come to him with the highest recommendations from Philip Lehman and Gertrude Vanderbilt Whitney, both of whom she'd worked for in the past year. Prior to that, she'd toiled for various curators in the Metropolitan Museum of Art in the year following her graduation from Barnard.

Thea had enjoyed the museum for what it was—a perfect training ground—and had held no illusions that there might be a future for her there. Indeed, her male superiors had let her know very clearly that they considered her position—obtained through the influence of board chairman, Philip Leslie—to be a very temporary one. After all, wasn't she going to turn up one morning sporting a diamond solitaire on the third finger of her left hand, and permanently depart soon after? Well, she departed all right, not to matrimony, but to the discreet, well-ordered world of the wealthy private collector. It was far nicer in the elegant Fifth Avenue mansions where she worked during the day and dined and danced at night—the heat and hot water worked, and there was no flooding when it rained—but the pleasant, neutral young men who also worked there lost no time in letting Thea know *exactly* where she stood in their miniature hierarchy. They liked her well enough—with her Paris clothes and carefully made up face she was far more acceptable than a run-of-the-mill female office worker would have been, and her social credentials were, in some cases, better than theirs—but it was clear from the outset that they were the favored ones.

Still, Thea told herself, it wasn't worth fussing over, particularly tonight, when every fireplace in the White House reception rooms were blazing a welcome, and the Marine Band, from their position close to the entrance of the Rose Room, was playing the most popular of John Philip Sousa's marches. There would be plenty of time in which to indulge in introspection about her future, but definitely not while she was on the receiving line, waiting to greet the stately, correct First Lady, her tall, amber-haired, white-organdy gowned stepdaughter (*that* very well couldn't be put on the invitations!), and the President himself, who was smiling from ear to ear.

"T.R. is in his glory tonight," Admiral Bruce Dalton remarked, as they waited their turn, and Evangeline Dalton added, "I'm sure he had a hand in every preparation that went into this party."

"And why shouldn't he?" Thea replied, smiling. "What's the good of going to a party where the host doesn't quite know what's going on?"

"True enough. But, from where I stand, there seems to be a look in the President's eyes tonight that makes me think that something is—as Arthur Conan Doyle says—afoot."

Alice Roosevelt's coming-out ball was a young people's party filled with Army, Navy and Marine officers, the younger and less-staid members of the Diplomatic Corps, influential Washingtonians, old New York friends, and token representatives from Boston and Philadelphia society.

Thea had come down from New York on New Year's Day, travelling on the Congressional Limited with Bruce and Evangeline Dalton, their daughter, Angela, and Alix Turner and Regina Bolt. It had been a pleasant, uneventful trip and, once they'd arrived at the Daltons' N Street house, the four best friends plotted their strategy for the ball, deciding to spend it mowing down the military.

"The easiest thing in the world," Nela announced. "Those poor things are so thrilled to have a partner who isn't either straight from the schoolroom, or a superannuated dowager, that we can get away with *anything!*"

Nela, as usual, had been right, and Thea was so busy with her partners that, as the evening wore on, the admiral's comment was quickly forgotten. It was only later—much, much later—that she wondered if Bruce Dalton, no stranger himself to the complex world of secret intelligence, had been trying to give her advance warning of what was to come.

There were twenty dances scheduled for that night, all the way from lively polkas and lancers to proper Strauss waltzes to the latest two-steps, to be followed by a midnight buffet in the State Dining Room, after which they would bid the First Family good-night and leave. On paper, it was a perfect White House debut, but America's self-proclaimed "princess" had her own ideas of what this night should be and, even though she'd been overruled on most of them, she still had one last card.

"More dancing?" Thea inquired as the Marine Band, resplendent in their full-dress uniforms, struck up "There'll Be A Hot Time In The Old Town Tonight," the Rough Riders' own anthem. "T.R. is going to be *furious!*"

"He is already," Alix laughed. "But Alice is his pet and, by the third dance, he'll be ready to say it was his idea. After all, with no cotillions and expensive favors and only that ghastly New York State cider instead of champagne, T.R. will start figuring he owes it to her."

"Did you see the crowd from the French Embassy trying to drink the cider without choking?" Regina said as her eyes swept over the East Room, making mental notes for the story she'd write for the *World*. "I wonder if I should include that in my piece?"

"If you do, Ralph Pulitzer will only cut it out," Nela warned. "I suggest you save your typewriter ribbon."

With the older and more sedate guests gone, the younger and more lively guests returned from the State Dining Room to the East Room for more merriment. Thea was approaching the waxed linen dance floor (Congress had carried on such a debate over the appropriation money for a hardwood floor that, when the bill was finally approved, it was too late for installation in time for the ball) with a Marine officer who'd been her partner earlier in the evening, when the President stopped them.

"Would it be possible for the Marines to yield?" he inquired with a flash of his famous smile. "This young lady's father is one of my oldest friends."

The young officer had no other recourse but to defer to his Commander-in-Chief, and Theodore Roosevelt led her out to the dance floor.

"Are you having a good time, my dear?" he questioned

as they joined the swirling couples.

"Oh, *yes*. It would be impossible not to when the host is enjoying himself so much!"

He chuckled happily. "Well, I'm only living up to my reputation of wanting to be the baby at every christening, the bride at every wedding, and the debutante at every coming-out. I wish some of my critics would realize that all of those are far better than being the corpse at every funeral. Now . . . how is your father? Still in Hawaii?"

"Daddy's fine, and just about now he should be leaving Honolulu aboard the Pacific Mail Line's *Mongolia*. He'll be home in about two weeks, drop his manuscript off at Doubleday, Page, and get busy on his next exploration."

"Hmm. Something about going down the Amazon, if I remember correctly."

"Yes. He'll be pushing off at the end of May, but I'm sure he'll make time to come down here so the two of you can have a long talk."

"I'm looking forward to it but, until then, I'd like to be sure his daughter is happy. Is Benjamin Altman keeping you busy?"

Thea gave him a brief synopsis of her work. "It's been a marvelous experience, but I don't think I'll stay on past April or May."

"Another collector demanding your talents?"

"Hardly, Mr. President."

"Then you have some special plans? You're a very talented young woman, Thea, and I can hardly believe you plan to do nothing. I'm sure you have a special dream."

For a second, Thea hesitated. This was *her* secret dream, something that she pulled out on bad days, not to discuss with the first person who asked—not even if he *were* the President of the United States.

"I'd love to have my own decorating firm," she heard

herself say. And, to her surprise, the President nodded approvingly.

"An admirable ambition," he said. "When do you plan to begin?"

"I've been looking at a few of the new office buildings near the Waldorf, but the rental agents won't take my name alone on the lease, and Daddy won't co-sign."

"I take it your father doesn't approve."

"Oh, no. Daddy's all for my trying, but he'd rather I worked out of the apartment until I acquire enough clients to be sure I'll make a go of it—*then* he'll co-sign the lease."

"Don't fault him for that, Thea," Theodore Roosevelt said gravely. "He's a cautious man. That's how he stayed alive on some of those expeditions of his."

"I know. But 34 Gramercy Park is my home, and I don't want to live with the store, so to speak. It isn't the White House."

"No, it's better decorated," the President said with a smile, referring to the White House's decor which specialized in hideous furniture in both the public and private rooms, potted palms in nearly every corner, and overpowering stained-glass windows. "Don't give up your dream, my dear. I'm sure you'll have it in the end."

"If I only had one client," she began, but the music stopped, and the President offered her his arm.

"Would you care for a glass of cider?"

"I'd prefer champagne," she said archly.

"So would Alice. She claims we've been permanently disgraced because her ball is teetotal. I daresay we'll survive, though," he added dryly.

"I daresay," she murmured, accepting a glass of the hotly contested cider, and feeling very foolish for saying everything she had. What *had* she been thinking of?

"—and the renovations will be starting in June," the

279

President was saying, and Thea brought herself back to reality. "Charles McKim and Stanford White are going to renovate the front of the mansion and move the guest entrance around to the east end."

"It sounds like a tremendous amount of work and worry."

"Yes, it is," he agreed, "but there is something else which worries me more, and you're the only person who can help me resolve this problem, my dear."

Thea was momentarily nonplussed. "Me?"

He nodded, offered her his arm, and together they walked in the direction of the alcove where the Marine Band was playing. "The daughter of a rather important, although not political, man in our country was in Europe last summer with her family," Theodore Roosevelt said when they reached a spot where the music would cover their speech. "At some watering hole or other, she met a young man who turned out to be a member of one of the Continental Royal Families travelling incognito. For reasons I won't go into, there could never be any question of marriage but, before they parted, our Prince gave this young lady a present."

While he'd been talking, Thea's brain had been absorbing his words and, as he finished, comprehension dawned. "Couldn't that cheapskate haul himself over to Cartier's instead of dipping into the crown jewels?" she asked bluntly.

"Not quite the crown jewels," Roosevelt corrected, an expression of relief at her quick grasp of the situation coming into his eyes. "It was a tiara which belonged to the Empress Josephine, and can never be worn without being instantly recognized. If it were, or if it were discovered to be missing, the scandal would be monumental, and both the girl's father and I are determined to avoid *that*. The tiara is to be returned, and I would greatly appreciate it, Thea, if you would function as our go-between. This summer would be the best time, and it will have to take place on the Continent, but all the details can be worked out later. Naturally, if you agree, you'll be reimbursed for all expenses—"

The music seemed to swirl around Thea in a calliope of sound, and suddenly it was as clear as crystal. It was the opportunity she'd looked for, the chance she needed—all thanks to a doll of a dollar princess who should have known better than to take the tiara in the first place.

"I can make a dozen trips to Europe, Mr. President, and never miss the money," she said, trying to keep the excitement out of her voice. "I'll be more than happy to return the tiara, provided you hire me to redecorate the ladies' retiring room. All I need is one client, and I can't think of a better one to begin with than the White House. And," she added as Roosevelt's eyes began to twinkle, "considering the way I like to travel, when you add up the cost of *cabin de luxe* passage to Europe, and all the other additional expenses I'll probably incur, you'll find my bill for pink chintz and silk-lined lampshades a whole lot easier to take!"

Thea stirred in her sleep. Dreams and memories . . . I don't know which is worse. I care so much about doing it right . . . too much . . . I can't be obective . . . only pretend to be . . . not calm and accepting and knowing . . . not like Charles . . .

Charles de Renille came awake with a start that seemed to jerk his body several inches off the mattress, and he lay in his bed in the Archbishop's Residence feeling as though a rubber ball were being bounced off the walls of his stomach.

The sickening spasms continued, and with one motion he flung back the covers, swung his legs over the side of the bed, and bent over until his head was between his knees. Dear God, he wondered, did I really eat that tremendous steak?

And not only the steak at his bachelor party, but the one two nights before at the Brownes'. Somehow he'd managed to eat them both. But now the idea that he'd eaten two slabs of charcoal-grilled red meat in three days when it had been years since he could even *think* about food like that without suffering a bout of nausea was almost incomprehensible.

Cautiously, Charles lifted his head, and as his queasiness receded he stood up and crossed the highly polished bare wood floor to the bathroom. Shielding his eyes, he switched on the light and then braced himself against the washing stand as he turned on the cold water faucet.

His bachelor party, as Morgan had promised, was the pinnacle of good taste—good *Texas* taste. There had been turtle soup, steak, cole slaw and German-fried potatoes. "Your last dinner as a free man," Dax Wilder had chuckled as he directed the club's steward to open one of the bottles of Schramsberg champagne. "Good thing the Archbishop said you could make an exception and eat meat tonight—it ain't a proper bachelor wing-ding without a fat, juicy steak!"

Or without several toasts to the bride, Charles recalled, watching the water flow from the faucet into the sink.

He had never had any doubts about his liking Thea Harper, but he had never expected there to be such an immediate sense of trust between them. He had spoken to Thea more intimately than he had to members of his own family on a subject he belatedly realized he'd been silent on for far too long. He respected her intelligence, was appreciative of her chic, and recognized her as a *femme savante*, but there was one conflict on which he had never counted.

282

When he'd heard the final details of the plan, he decided right then and there to treat Thea with the greatest of respect and deference, but at the same time maintain a correct distance from her. After all, none of this was *her* idea. But now, after three days of talking to Thea, of being with her, of sharing his thoughts and observations with her, Charles was becoming acutely aware that his planned air of detachment was not going to be as easy to maintain as he'd assumed.

If only he hadn't gone to Boston. Or if he'd gone one week earlier, or one week later, the events that transpired over that Saturday night might not be coming back and threatening his equilibrium now.

As he lowered his face to the cold water, Charles found his thoughts relentlessly turning back to the weekend nearly five months before when he'd arrived in Boston from Ottawa. As he'd promised, David Lasky was waiting for him in the sumptuously appointed lobby of the Touraine Hotel.

"Have you thawed out from your Canadian adventure yet?" David inquired jokingly as they went upstairs to the luxuriously appointed suite of rooms overlooking Boston Common which Percy Lasky maintained in the hotel on a year-round basis.

"Just about. My welcome from my cousin and his wife was quite warm, but I have an idea Ottawa has winter about ten months of the year," he said, looking around his bedroom while David lounged in an armchair. "What French chateau am I supposed to be in?" he asked, amused.

"What, you don't recognize the Touraine's remarkable likeness to the Chateau of Blois?" David leered in mock horror. "Seriously though, this *is* one of the finest hotels in America, with a telephone in every room, a darned good restaurant, and a four-thousand volume library for the guests."

"I'm suitably impressed. But speaking of libraries, when do I get to see Harvard's?"

"Monday morning. I don't have another class until Monday afternoon, so I'll have the whole morning to show you around, and you can have lunch with me at Adams House. That's my dormitory, and the food's quite good but, for now—" David unwound himself from the chair. "There are three bedrooms opening off the sitting room," he explained. "I have the one next door, and Anthony Kendall the one after that. Right now, he's in rehearsal at the Colonial Theatre—the show opens next week—and he'll probably be there until late tonight, but we'll all get together tomorrow evening. Anyway," David went on with a grin, "why don't you ring for a valet to unpack you, and then wash up and meet me in the sitting room in about twenty minutes? I'll give you a tour of the State House and City Hall but, first, lunch at Durgin-Park. I think you're about ready to be introduced to Boston baked beans and Indian Pudding!"

When he recalled the strict rules that had governed his student days at Oxford, Charles found it a bit incredible that an undergraduate at the most prestigious university in America could simply, once his Friday classes were finished, sign himself out and cross the Charles River into Boston. From the world Charles came from, it wasn't done. But, like so many other beliefs, traditions and unwritten laws he'd lived by, this latest revelation also fell by the wayside. Even proper Boston had its happy-go-lucky side, it appeared, and there was no better way for three well-off young men to spend a Saturday night than in the company of three beautiful actresses.

Grace Danson, Anita Walker and Tildy Barnett were all featured players in the new Clyde Fitch musical in rehearsal at Boston's Majestic Theatre. When Charles inquired why the young women they were taking to dinner at Locke-Ober's, followed by the new Charles Frohman production at the Tremont Street Theatre, and ending up back at the Touraine's restaurant for late supper and dancing to the hotel's orchestra, were not involved in one of his father's productions, David had given him a considering look before replying succinctly, "When you're looking forward to a pleasurable evening, *never* bring business of any sort with you!"

At any rate, as the evening wore on, he had to admit that the three girls were suitable adornments to any occasion. All were in their early twenties, having gotten their starts in the chorus before any of them saw seventeen. Their talents and looks had allowed them to move up to better roles in the better musical comedy productions and, contrary to the commonly held opinion that off the stage actresses dressed either like floozies or drabs, tonight's trio was superbly turned out in the latest fashions. A bit much for conservative Boston, perhaps, but there was nothing to object to, either.

"Charles, would you think I was the most awful wet blanket if I said I didn't want to dance any more?" Tildy asked him appealingly as they waltzed sedately.

"Are you feeling ill?" he questioned, concerned, leading her from the floor and out of the restaurant into the hotel lobby.

"Oh, no," she assured him. "Just rather tired. We rehearsed until two this morning, and then had our final costume fittings this afternoon. Oh, you're so kind to see me upstairs. I don't know how Grace and Anita can keep going . . . don't worry . . . the others won't miss us . . ."

They collected their keys from a disinterested desk clerk and were taken upstairs by a bored elevator operator. "Isn't it nice that our rooms are on the same floor?" Tildy inquired, linking her arm through his, and gazing wide-eyed at him. "It makes it so much more convenient."

Tildy Barnett had the sort of half-teasing, half-serious, well-modulated voice that drew attention. It was an asset in her career, as was her honey-blonde hair and deep-lashed china-blue eyes. Her face, with its well-defined cheekbones, was deftly made up and, for this evening's festivities, she had chosen a deceptively simple gown of Nile-green chiffon edged in darker green satin.

Charles led her down the deserted corridor, suddenly certain that something in his life had quite definitely gone out of kilter. David's words flashed through his mind, and that self-evident sentence took on a new meaning.

"Here we are."

It was the door to the suite he was sharing.

Charles drew a short breath. "I don't think—"

"Oh, a gentleman," Tildy said without malice. "That's so nice, but I've been waiting for you all evening—"

While Charles' life could in no way be considered blameless, there were any number of things he hadn't done, and one of them was being intimately kissed by an actress in a hotel corridor. But, in the length of their embrace, he went swiftly from surprise to enjoyment, mixed with the certainty that certain basic skills aren't lost with temporary disuse.

"This is Boston!" was all he could think of to say when she took a step back and regarded him out of half-closed lids.

"Charles . . . Charles, forget what you've heard. Boston can be as understanding as, well, Paris when it comes to a grown man and woman. We're absolutely respectable."

"I wasn't suggesting anything to the contrary, but someone, even if it isn't the house detective, is going to come along in a minute . . ."

"Then why don't you unlock your door and we can talk as long as you like, until we're both comfortable."

286

"Tildy, I don't think you understand." To his increased discomfort, Charles felt his color mount. "I wasn't planning to—"

"Are you a fairy?"

With a question like that, there was no other course left open to him. Charles unlocked the door and ushered Tildy into the dark sitting room.

"I've been ill," he explained, closing the door.

"Oh?" Her voice was mistrustful. "Just what kind of illness are we talking about?"

Charles felt a sense of panic close in around him. In an attempt to sidestep the situation he'd landed himself in a hole and, in an attempt to remove himself from *that* spot, he'd only dug himself deeper. He groaned silently. The truth might not be pleasant, but it was the only way open to him.

"I had a nervous breakdown, and a physical one as well. I'm not a homosexual or a syphilitic, and I'm very fond of women, but it's been years—"

He got no further because Tildy was in his arms, kissing him gently while her fingers fluttered lightly over his shoulders and upper arms.

"My poor darling . . . I understand . . . I never really thought any of those vile . . . there . . . let me kiss you again . . ."

Her mouth was rich, warm and knowing, and the last rim of ice around his heart, the last secret fear that because of his illness no woman—unless he were paying her—would ever want him in an intimate way again, began to dissipate, finally setting him free.

He could never remember exactly how they reached the bedroom, only that they were there, Tildy teasing him that unless a man was trying to remove a full-dress suit in a hurry, he could never understand the complications women had to endure every day with their clothes, and then they were across the bed.

287

"This is for you, Charles . . . all for you . . . I want to make you happy . . . you need a woman to make you happy again . . . to make you feel all the things you had to give up . . . I knew you'd be beautiful . . . ever since I saw you—right there in the lobby—I knew . . . I've wanted you inside me all night . . ."

Her soft voice, combined with gentle hands caressing him, seeking out his most sensitive spots, did their work and he forgot that he hadn't expected her approach, hadn't expected to make one himself, didn't have any plans to see her after tonight, as well as any of a dozen other plausible reasons that they shouldn't be together, only that he was hot, hard, full of desire and that there was no going back to what had been, not ever.

Moving swiftly, Tildy straddled his body, slowly lowering herself onto his swollen stem, moaning softly as she sheathed him in a wall of mutual heat and rode him gently, expertly, to their mutual completion.

"I *am* an actress," she assured him an endless time later as he held her while she lay across his joyfully depleted body, her fingers gently tracing circles across his chest. "Stay around for another week, and I'll prove it to you."

"I'm not a suspicious man," he replied, well aware that a small part of him had well suspected that David and Anthony might have hired their companions and introduced them as actresses for delicacy's sake. But he'd been wrong, and now he wanted to set the situation straight. "You're my first actress."

"You're joking! Why, all the time you were telling us about Oxford, the only thing I could think of was the hundreds of Gaiety Girls you must have had." She raised her head to peer at him in the dark. "Come on, tell! You might have been out of it for a while, but I'll bet you've never paid for it!"

"A gentleman never pays a grand lady—at least not in

a monetary way," he said, thinking of secret meetings, stolen hours and the inevitable pleadings and demands. Was it any wonder that after those love affairs, which took more than they ever gave, that the unyielding Jesuit discipline had seemed a steady beacon in comparison?

"I was sixteen when I started in the chorus," Tildy told him. "But I'm twenty-two now, and I want more out of the rest of my life than a new show every year or two. I'm not Ethel Barrymore, who'll probably go on forever. I'm looking for a husband, and not an actor, either. And in case you're wondering, I don't go to bed with every gentleman who buys me dinner," she finished fiercely.

"I'm sure you don't, and I'm very honored you thought I was worth your time," Charles said honestly, pulling her closer for a kiss.

"I knew you were the right sort. David and Toby don't pal around with trash." Suddenly she flashed him a wicked smile and kissed him expertly on the mouth. "You were fine, real fine. I'll never figure out how you haven't let a woman get close to you since you got well. You must have been holding them off with a baseball bat!"

"Why?" He was genuinely puzzled by her remarks.

Tildy brushed his hair back from his forehead. "What's the matter with you, Charlie? Don't you ever look in a mirror?"

As little as possible, he said to himself, turning off the faucet with one hand and reaching for a towel with the other.

Charles played a dangerous game with himself. Not only by never looking directly into a mirror, but by adding an additional gloss to it—pretending that whenever he looked at his reflection there was an invisible person at his shoulder, seeing him for the first time. Since early 1902, he'd played the mirror charade, but tonight, in the small bathroom that opened off the spartan guest room, he removed the towel from his face and looked unflinchingly into the mirror above the washstand.

Charles had once seen himself in a condition so terrible that it would frighten the least shockable person. And, since that day, a mirror was something to be avoided as much as possible. But now he looked—really looked.

If indeed there were someone looking over his shoulder, Charles realized, all that invisible person would see was a sleepy-looking man in a rumpled nightshirt whose thick, black hair was uncombed, and who would need a shave very badly in a few hours. Without a doubt, he was a somewhat ridiculous-looking figure, but he was not a frightening one.

Sighing, Charles switched off the light and returned to bed. At this moment, he knew he owed far more to Tildy Barnett than the two dozen Madame Gabriel Luizet roses and the five-pound box of hand-dipped chocolates from Bailey's that he'd ordered sent to her dressing room at the Majestic Theatre. It was not that he ever feared he would not be physically able to make love again, he simply didn't want to. And, if and when he did, it would all fall into place. Charles hadn't counted on ever meeting Tildy, but now, months later, he was finally grateful that he had. She had pushed him over his self-created emotional barrier and reintroduced him to the joy of sensual fulfillment. But, at the same time, their brief time together had forever shattered his illness-induced perception of women as individuals who would have no special interest in him as a man.

Deep down, Charles knew, he really hadn't believed that absurd theory. If he had, it wouldn't have been so easily and pleasantly ended by Tildy's frank advance on his person. But even as he accepted this, Charles de Renille now had to face the unalterable fact that, since

Wednesday evening, he had begun to regard Thea Harper in a very special way indeed.

Thea opened her eyes slowly, savoring those last moments when sleep has ended but true wakefulness hasn't returned.

It had all started that night at the White House, both the ending of her old life and the beginning of the new. And, even though subsequent events in her life had moved so slowly at times as to be nonexistent, the machinery was nonetheless in motion.

The tiara had been successfully returned, with no one the wiser, and Budapest had been beautiful. Following that, over the next two years, there had been other "favors," mostly concerning Americans who had, either through greed or innocence, purchased stolen works of art. Somehow, in the back of her mind, Thea had always known that one day the President—or someone in his circle of advisors—would come up with the idea that she would make a perfect agent. After all, who would suspect her?

But as she lay in the bed, looking up at the drifty material that formed the canopy, Thea made one promise to herself. Whatever debt, real or imagined, she felt she owed was now paid in full. And this assignment, no matter how it ended, was going to be her last.

Chapter Eight

"Are you sure, Thea? About not wearing your pearls, I mean," Nela added hastily, well aware of the double entendre she had just uttered. "Since they were your mother's, I thought—"

"No, as long as I still have a choice, I think this dress is better off without them. The Archbishop isn't going to be thrilled about this neckline, and there's no need to compound it by standing in front of him draped in jewelry."

It was well after eleven on Saturday morning, September 24, a perfect, sunny, late summer day, and Thea was nearly ready for her wedding. As long as she did not think too much about what was going to—or rather, *not* going to—happen after the ceremony and reception were over, she might actually be able to enjoy the day, her reasoning ran, and so far there had been no difficulties.

The whole household had been running at full speed since the first light of dawn. In the kitchen, Consuelo was expertly frosting the wedding cake; in the drawing room and library, Lupe and Maria were setting out the flower arrangements; and in the butler's pantry, Juan was putting supplementary bottles of champagne on ice. Nearly everyone on the list had accepted, and Morgan and Nela believed that at a wedding reception there was no such thing as too much champagne.

Morgan, resplendent in his morning clothes, had left

for the Cathedral at half-past ten. Later in the day, he would host the reception, but this morning his main duty lay in being best man. And, until Charles and Thea were safely married, his main objective was to support the prospective groom. Not that Morgan expected Charles to flee, but weddings could have the oddest effect on even the best and strongest-willed of men. He stopped at Thea's room just before he left to tell her and Nela that he was off to be both a pillar of strength and an offerer of moral support to Charles. The prerequisite demanded of all best men, he'd joked, kissing both women.

Recalling Morgan's parting words, Thea finally smiled. The idea of Charles being nervous, or even having second thoughts for having agreed to this marriage was ridiculous. No doubt, at this very moment, he was cool, collected and probably more than a little bored at all the fuss. Her smile deepened when she thought of his reaction to her dress. It might evoke any number of comments from him, but she could bet none of them would be *blasé*.

In keeping with the tone of the wedding—simple but elegant—Thea had selected a gown created by the near-genius talent of Paul Poiret. It was not a traditional wedding gown, a garment Thea recognized as being totally wrong for the circumstances surrounding them, but a garden party dress—a confection for a very sophisticated, very exclusive garden party. Made of layers of white chiffon inset with handmade lace and decorated with satin ribbon, it flowed over the soft, full curve of her bosom and hips, leaving no doubt whatsoever that her feminine attributes were natural and not the result of strategically placed ruffles and pads, and yet revealing nothing that could be termed unseemly for a ceremony in the cathedral.

The combination of lace, chiffon and satin turned Thea's skin to porcelain and made her eyes a more intense green-gold, and while the square decolletage was lower than any wedding dress had a right to be, only an Archbishop might blink disapproval.

"How are you feeling?" Nela questioned her gently as she crossed the room, looking totally unpregnant in her Paquin *princesse* gown of India mull over pale lavender silk with medallions of handmade lace. A remarkable necklace of lavender jade and diamonds was clasped around her throat.

"My heart is pounding, I have butterflies in my stomach, I'm terrified whenever I think about Mexico—and I can't wait for Charles to see me in this gown!"

"You sound perfectly normal to me. That's just how I felt; and so did Alix, and so did Regina."

Thea's smile faded. "That was very different. You were all marrying for love."

"Maybe you are, too."

"Don't, Nela, please." Thea felt her panic spread. "It's too soon."

"There's no such thing as too soon. A relationship doesn't begin full-blown, but I know that when it's right, you know straight off."

"But it has to be a two-way street. What good is caring if it can't—or won't—be returned? I can have all the fantasies I want about Charles, but if I start believing something can come out of it, then I'll be terribly hurt. I probably will be anyway," she added regretfully. "But I don't have to compound the situation, and—"

Thea's speech was cut off by a polite knock on the door, and Nela opened it to reveal her stepdaughter, looking enchanting in a Fairyland party dress of fine white lawn with delicate tucks, English embroidery and a wide pink satin sash.

"Hello, sweetheart." Thea forced herself to speak cheerfully. "Are you all ready to be my flower girl?"

"All ready, Aunt Thea," Christy said, holding out a

beribboned basket filled with pink and white rose petals. "Are we leaving now?"

"Just one more thing. Nela—"

Ever since she'd picked out the dress, Thea had been uncertain as to what to wear instead of the traditional wedding veil. A wide-brimmed picture hat would have been the logical substitution, but it seemed to be as out of place as yards of flowing rose-point lace. Neither would have been right and, while she and Nela had been casting around for an alternative, the solution had arrived from Mexico.

"Christy, darling, look what Aunt Thea's friend, Señora de Veiga, sent for her to wear," Nela said gaily, opening a brocade-covered box. "It came last night by special messenger."

It was a mantilla of antique lace, and Thea held her breath while Nela adjusted the creamy length over a small silver and diamond-studded Spanish-style comb that Dona Imelda de Veiga had also included.

Christy regarded her for a moment. "Now you look like a *real* bride, Aunt Thea."

"Didn't I before?" Thea couldn't resist asking. Really, this child was adorable, and in just about ten years, Morgan would be holding off potential suitors with a baseball bat.

"You have to look very special if you're a bride. It's the lace," she explained solemnly.

There wasn't that much lace, not really, Thea decided silently, checking her reflection one more time. But the way it covered her hair and draped over the comb to come down to her shoulders transformed her from just another expensively dressed woman into a bride. Before any more disquieting thoughts could surface, she turned away from the mirror.

"I think I've done everything I can here," she said with a smile that she hoped looked natural. "Shall we get the bouquets out of the icebox and see about getting me married?"

While Thea was preparing to leave the Johnson Street house, Charles, waiting in his room at the Residence, was reduced to the worst case of nerves he had ever known.

If, over the past weeks, he'd sometimes felt like a pawn in the events he was swept up in, this morning he was little better than a prisoner, with Miguel functioning as a very benevolent guard.

The servant had woken him promptly at nine, led him to the bath he'd already run for him, and had been waiting to wrap him in a large towel when he finished; ministrations Charles connected all too painfully with the long months when those tasks had been performed by Louis. From the day he'd finally recovered, Charles never allowed a servant to tend him in that manner, but he only wasted his breath trying to explain his aversion to Miguel.

"It's the Archbishop's orders, *señor*," he said placidly, holding out Charles' dressing gown.

Charles stopped towel-drying his hair. "Does the Archbishop think I'm going to run away?"

The servant helped him into the robe. "Apprehensive bridegrooms have been known to desert their brides at the altar, *señor*."

"What have I done to make His Grace think I've turned into a disreputable cad?" he inquired hotly. "The idea that I would desert Miss Harper—not live up to my responsibility—"

"I'm sure that was the last thing on His Grace's mind," Miguel interposed smoothly, deftly wringing out a towel that had been soaking in hot water in the bathroom sink. "Now, *señor*, if you will be so good as to return to the bedroom so I can shave you—"

Miguel settled Charles in a chair, tilted his head back,

and wrapped his face in the hot towel, cutting off any further conversation, and left him until the towel cooled. Then he deftly unwound the towel, covered the lower half of his face with a thick layer of shaving soap, and proceeded to remove a night's growth of beard with a straight razor that, Charles realized as the blade swept along one cheek, was probably sharp enough to remove his head with a single swipe.

While he ate breakfast, Miguel laid out his wedding clothes. And, by the time Morgan Browne arrived, Charles was reduced to the same stomach-lurching condition with which he'd woken up in the middle of the night.

"I thought you were never going to get here," he told Morgan thankfully. "This has been the longest morning of my life!"

"All bridegrooms feel like that—it's the last hour," Morgan reassured him as Miguel quietly withdrew. "You'll be fine as soon as the ceremony starts."

"The Archbishop has had Miguel guarding me all morning. He did everything except lock me in," Charles remarked.

"Well, it wouldn't reflect too well on the Archbishop if you bolted," Morgan replied, amused by Charles' indignation.

"But I wouldn't do such a thing!" Charles' exclamation was full of surprise and hurt. "The President himself asked me to be of help, and if I can't live up to my word, to my responsibilities, then I really haven't any honor left."

For a moment, Morgan regarded Charles. "Shall I help you with your cravat?" he asked with a glance at the clock. Except for his coat, vest and four-in-hand tie, Charles was fully dressed. "After we've completed your wedding costume, you can give me the ring. In case you've forgotten, that's my main duty as your best man."

Morgan expertly knotted the silk tie and, while Charles

added the last pieces, both men discussed Mr. Webb, Brooks Brothers and the strange demands that social events made on their wardrobes.

"I find that I either have my morning clothes in moth balls for months on end, or they get rather regular wear. I wore this for my wedding, to several receptions in London, Gold Cup Day at Ascot, and to the races at Longchamps. What about you?"

"Only to the Kentucky Derby—and today, of course," he added, a sudden chill running through him as Miguel knocked on the door and then entered.

"Your bride has arrived, *señor*," he said with a broad smile, "and the Archbishop is waiting."

"And this is it," Charles said more to himself than to Morgan. "I thought this would never happen to me."

"It happens to the best of us," Morgan said in a cheery voice he didn't quite recognize as his own. His glance travelled over Charles, making sure his tie was straight, and that the white carnation was secure in his lapel. "Try and be *hombre valiente* about it, and don't worry, it'll be over before you know it."

"I'm a de Renille, Morgan. My duty has been set out for me, and I'll follow it."

"I'm sure you will," he responded, noting that Charles had gone quite pale under his tan. "But right now, would you mind a bit of advice from your best man?"

"Not at all," he said as they left the room and started down the stairs. "I think it's part of your chores—just like getting me to the altar is," he went on with a smile.

"All I have is one suggestion. Over the next few weeks, if you're really interested in making a proper impression on Thea, forget about pontificating. Remember, Charlie, nobody loves a prig!"

This wedding, Thea decided as she stood at the back of the Cathedral waiting for the music to begin, was, in some obscure way, her punishment for not being one of those girls who had her wedding fully planned out in her mind long before a potential husband ever appeared.

When Nela had put her plan before the Archbishop three days earlier, she'd pointed out that there was no reason why Thea should be cheated out of all the frills that normally accompany a wedding ceremony, and the prelate agreed. The fact that there were no guests shouldn't prevent Miss Harper from the joy of walking down the aisle to meet her bridegroom, he'd said. In fact, all things considered, the more it appeared like a normal wedding, the better. There should be no room for suspicion later on.

That was the main thing, Thea told herself, that for however long she and Charles shared this marriage, no one would *ever* be able to guess the reason for their coming together. Her mind slid back to her conversation with Nela. Thea was normally an introspective person, but the ideas Nela had stirred in her were better left unspeculated on. To dwell on them was asking for long-lasting pain and unending heartache, neither of which would be of any help to her in the coming weeks. Charles was to be her partner, not her lover, and if she ever forgot that . . .

The opening strains of *A Midsummer Night's Dream* sounded from the organ and, instinctively, Thea tightened her grasp on her bridal bouquet of gardenias, white Orleans roses and bell-shaped Madonna lilies tied with silver ribbon. There had been a bit of discussion about the proper music for the processional. The Archbishop suggested Meyerbeer's *Le Prophete*, which was very much in vogue, but Morgan gently pointed out that, as impressive as the music was, it was far more suited to a large-scale wedding. There had been a moment of silence, and then Thea spoke up. She knew the music she wanted all along, and now she followed Christy, who

299

was scattering rose petals, and Nela, who was her matron of honor, down the left aisle to the side altar where the rest of the wedding party awaited her.

Who would have dreamed that the morning Colonel Miles walked into my office it would end—or is it begin?—like this, she thought. Oh, I wonder what Mrs. Miles would say if she could see me now! Why is it that people say Westerners can't wear formal clothes? Morgan looks wonderful . . . lucky, lucky Nela . . . I'm sorry for the cleaning woman who'll have to sweep up all these rose petals . . . Oh, God, Charles looks as pale as I feel . . .

She reached Charles' side on the last chords of the music that had carried her down the aisle, and her disjointed thoughts came to an end as she met Charles' topaz gaze.

Their eye contact didn't last long, but it was enough for Thea's butterflies to fold their wings, and for Charles' face to regain most of its lost color. Thea turned slightly to hand her bouquet to Nela, and when she faced Charles again, he smiled and held out his hand.

Without a second's hesitation, as though it were the most natural thing in the world, she put her hand in his and, together, they faced the altar, banked in pink and white tea roses from the Brownes' garden.

The Archbishop, impressive in his white vestments, stood in front of them, and for one long, solemn, silent moment he projected the uncanny image of both studying the couple he was about to marry as well as offering a personal prayer for them. When he spoke, his voice was low and resonant.

"Charles, wilt thou take Theodosia, here present, for thy lawful wife, according to the Rite of our Holy Mother the Church . . . ?"

Chapter Nine

Forty-eight hours later, Theodosia de Renille, looking cool and elegant in a Lucile dress of flowered muslin with a V-neck and a scalloped skirt outlined in black velvet and a strand of pearls around her throat, sat on a silk-covered sofa in the sitting room of Don Renaldo de Veiga's private railroad car trying very hard not to look too often at her new husband. Charles sat across from her in a comfortable-looking armchair, apparently completely involved in the first volume of Alexander Griswold Allen's *Life And Letters of Phillips Brooks,* which he'd purchased at Clarke's Bookstore in Boston. Reluctantly, Thea fixed her own attention on Edith Wharton's *Italian Villas And Their Gardens,* but the thick, well-written, green-bound, gold-stamped volume, illustrated in color by Maxfield Parrish, failed to hold her attention. Thea was an admirer of Mrs. Wharton's works, particularly *The Decoration of Houses,* insisting that all her potential clients read it but, on this sunny Monday morning, her mind was off on its own tangent, and the book in her lap was only a pretext.

So far, everything was going so smoothly that Thea could scarcely believe it. Mentally she'd prepared herself for any number of problems and mishaps, but none had occurred, and the easy companionship she'd found with Charles in their first three days together had taken firm root. They shared good conversation and laughter, and she was sure that anyone who saw them together on the train to El Paso, or in the restaurant of the Sheldon Hotel, remarked to each other on what a happy couple they looked.

Looked was the key word, Thea realized as she considered the illustration of the Villa Gamberaia outside of Florence. To the casual observer, she and Charles *looked* like any other newly married couple. It wasn't a difficult performance at all, and they'd been playing their parts from the moment the Archbishop pronounced them man and wife.

The much-shortened Roman Catholic marriage service used to unite the practicing Catholic groom and the agnostic bride went smoothly, only the Archbishop's voice, and their clear, quiet responses, breaking the quietude surrounding them. The scent of the roses on the altar, the fragrance of the bouquets, and the perfume she and Nela wore, all seemed to blend together in the sacred stillness. That, and the votive candles flickering nearby, seemed to intensify the atmosphere and, for the first time, Thea understood the meaning of the expression *cathedral quiet.*

Thea knew that at the end of the ceremony there was no provision for the groom to kiss the bride. The Archbishop merely said the final words over them and they were married; the unseen organist played the recessional, and Mendelssohn's exquisite music led them back up the aisle and out into the bright sunlight where a small curious crowd had gathered around the motor cars.

They returned to the Brownes' house, and there was just enough time for San Antonio's best photographer to pose the wedding party in an assortment of groupings before the first of the invited guests made their way up the flagstone walk, through the front door, and into the entrance hall to greet their hosts and the newly married couple before moving on to the generous buffet.

In the dining room, the table, with all its additional leaves extending it, was covered with a pale pink damask cloth, and Nela had pulled out all her wedding silver, plus a few pieces that had belonged to Morgan's mother. Silver trays held offerings of *paté de campagne*, chicken mousse with green mayonnaise, cold tongue in aspic jelly, and a variety of fancy tea sandwiches; a silver cake stand held the three-tier wedding cake, garlanded with sugar roses and topped by the bride and groom figures that had graced Nela and Morgan's cake five months earlier; and long-stemmed silver dishes resting in shallow pans filled with ice held raspberry sherbert. Moet et Chandon '95 was offered, and shell-shaped silver dishes held pink and white sugar-covered Jordan almonds—the *dragees* that no wedding in France was complete without.

There was no dancing, but a group of musically inclined ladies seated in the gazebo played selections from Purcell on recorders while the guests wandered through the downstairs rooms and fanned out onto the back lawn and the garden.

There had been only one bad moment for Thea, and that was when Major Donovan walked through the front door. He arrived with the Forrest family, shook hands with Thea and Charles as though they were perfect strangers, wished them well, and disappeared among the other guests.

Before either of them could say anything about his unexpected appearance, Nela said it was time to cut the cake and, almost before she knew it, Thea was back upstairs, changing into her going-away dress, a Paquin model of cream-colored French batiste with batiste embroidery and a wide belt of ombre blue Liberty satin. And then she was standing at the top of the stairs, looking down at the assembled guests. As if she'd been waiting for this moment all her life, Thea pitched her bouquet into the smiling crowd, taking careful aim to direct it at

Colonel Forrest's eighteen-year-old daughter, Catherine, who caught it with an exclamation of pure joy. Then she was running lightly down the stairs to join Charles, and together they passed through the throng of well-wishers and out to the sidewalk where Juan was behind the wheel of the Cadillac, waiting to drive them to the Menger Hotel.

"I think it was very good of you, Thea, to make sure the Colonel's daughter caught your bouquet," Charles remarked warmly as they arrived in the handsomely furnished bridal suite of the Menger Hotel. Their luggage had gone on ahead, and all Charles had to do was sign the register. The assistant manager showed them upstairs.

"Well, I thought Christy was a little young, and nearly everyone else seemed to be married. Besides, Nela mentioned that Cathy is very fond of one of her father's junior aides, and maybe my bouquet will help things along," Thea said as she explored the suite. "But, Charles, are you going to still think so highly of me when I tell you that I loved the bouquet so much that I almost *didn't* want to toss it?"

"And I was worried that you wouldn't like the flowers I chose. Until the Archbishop reminded me," he admitted with a smile, "I'd forgotten that I had to supply the bouquets for you and Angela. Isn't it ridiculous, the things we worry about in advance?" he asked as the nervousness they'd both felt upon entering the suite vanished.

Like its counterparts, the Menger Hotel ranked as one of the luxury hotels of the American West. Almost every notable person to pass through San Antonio had signed its register, and Theodore Roosevelt had recruited some of his Rough Riders in the bar. The bridal suite was the last word in luxury but, as Thea and Charles adjusted to their new surroundings, both became aware that there was one bedroom—and one bed.

304

"I'll sleep on the sofa, if you like," Thea offered as she unpacked her dressing case.

"No, I will," he countered, aghast that he hadn't offered it first. Somehow he'd overlooked the reality of their sleeping arrangements, and as long as Donovan—or whoever else was in charge of these things—hadn't (or wouldn't) seen to separate bedrooms, it was up to him to make the sacrifice. "Remember," he went on, adopting a lighter tone of voice, "I was educated in England, and spent several years at two Jesuit seminaries, as well as teaching for several months at le College Saint Michel in Brussels. Compared to some of the beds I've slept in, that sofa will be a luxury!"

Thea looked from the bed, already turned down by the maid in anticipation of the newlyweds' arrival, to Charles' quiet face. "I don't think that's necessary. I have an idea. The bed is huge, and unless you can't stand sleeping with another person, we both should have plenty of room. Is that agreeable to you?"

"I don't see any reason why we both shouldn't be comfortable," Charles concurred. Thea's suggestion struck him as not quite *proper*, but all things considered— "But if one of us finds it doesn't work, *I'll* go to the sofa."

"Agreed." Thea flashed him a bright smile. "Why don't you order our dinner from room service? And while you're doing that, I'll slip into something more comfortable."

Must you sound like a real bride? Thea asked herself, annoyed, as she changed into a Lucile teagown of rose chiffon and shaded satin ribbon. Do that again, and Charles may just tell you off. He certainly knows how to behave, even if you don't!

It was sound advice, but all the same, Thea couldn't help recognizing the fact that right now, if she were married to Charles out of love, not necessity, she wouldn't care about changing into a teagown. All she'd want—all she'd care about—was to be in her new husband's arms, and on the bed, going step by step together into a world of discovery, renewal and passion . . .

Somehow, they made it through dinner.

Charles, in an uncharacteristic fit of indecision, had ordered all the hotel's specialties but, when they sat down at the laden table, they discovered they were both starving.

"I think it was all those little sandwiches and the wedding cake," Thea said as they ate the delicately prepared pompano.

"Don't forget all the champagne. I'm sure all the guests ate well, but I can't remember anything except a few mouthfuls of wedding cake," Charles admitted. "Still, I think we pulled it off rather well."

A sliver of ice entered Thea's heart. "You make it sound like we robbed a bank," she said, looking down at her wedding ring. And that's all it really is to him, she thought. A hoax successfully pulled off. The fact he likes you is an unexpected dividend, but it'll be no impediment when it comes to an annulment . . .

Their conversation moved on to more neutral topics and, an hour later, they were at the point of no return.

"We have a very early train to make tomorrow morning," Thea said needlessly, standing up. "Shall I get ready first?"

"Of course." A strange look appeared in Charles' eyes, and he looked away from her. "Let me know when you're . . . ready."

In an effort to be fair, Thea didn't waste any time getting ready for bed. Since they were only spending the night, she didn't bother setting out all of her personal belongings, and the only addition she made to the decor was to take her ivory-handled French-gilt travelling clock out of its velvet, leather-lined case, set the alarm, and place it on the night table on her side of the bed.

Thea undressed quickly, washed off her makeup, brushed out her hair, and changed into a nightgown of white silk-satin crepe with a top and narrow shoulder straps of St. Galles embroidery. Even as she called for Charles to come in, Thea couldn't help speculating if Charles expected her to wear a nightgown with a high neck and long sleeves.

She slipped under the covers as the door opened, and Thea tactfully turned her back to him. She stayed like that until Charles came out of the bathroom some minutes later. "I set the alarm for six, that should give us enough time to make the train at half-past eight," she said, and turned over to face Charles.

He stood by the side of the bed, looking rather uncomfortable which, instinct told Thea, was not caused by her presence, but by what he was wearing. Underneath his dressing-gown of heavy figured silk, he wore a pair of pajamas that looked brand new. Charles, at not quite thirty, was part of the last generation of men raised to sleep in nightshirts, and the newly popular pajamas were really not his sort of sleepwear.

"That sounds like an excellent idea." Charles switched off the bedside lamp and, in the darkness, Thea could hear the rustle of his robe as he removed it, and the next moment the bed took his weight.

"Are you comfortable?" Thea asked a few seconds later as they lay as far away from each other as possible.

"Very much so. Thank you for insisting on the bed."

"I'm glad." Thea sighed with relief. "Charles—"

"Good night, Thea." His voice in the darkness was pleasant but firm. "We'll talk again in the morning."

Unlike a great many of her contemporaries, Thea's imagination didn't end with her wedding reception. She knew full well—at least in theory—about lovemaking between a man and a woman. That was why she never indulged in endless fantasies about her wedding day, reasoning that when she fell in love the most important part of that special day would be when she and her husband were alone together. She looked forward to *that*—not the idea of preening in front of hundreds of guests at a "proper" society wedding.

But she had never expected this. Charles was already in a deep, peaceful sleep and, as she listened to his even breathing, Thea found herself slipping into a state of dangerous emotional speculation. She was sure beyond a doubt that Charles was celibate now, but the same instinct she'd always depended on told her that he hadn't always been so. Could his breakdown have left him permanently impaired, or was it that, deep down, he had never really cared for women and had used the Church for the welcome protection it gave only to have it turn on him in the end? No, she decided. The former was a very faint possibility, but somehow the latter didn't ring true.

She fell asleep, still working out possible variations and solutions. And, when Thea opened her eyes to the alarm's trill, bright sunlight was pouring in and Charles was coming out of the bathroom, dressed and ready. It was Sunday morning, and time to begin their journey.

The day-long train ride to El Paso was uneventful. They had a Pullman compartment to themselves, and passed the hours alternately reading and looking out the window at the passing scenery. Over a surprisingly good lunch in the dining car, they discussed music, books and mutual friends, but as the day wore on, both grew increasingly hot and tired and, when they finally reached El Paso and the Sheldon Hotel, the question of sharing the same bed didn't even arise. It was simply a matter of giving each other enough privacy to wash, change and then sink gratefully into the cool, fresh bed.

It was only the next morning when they returned to

Union Station to board the de Veigas' private railroad car that would take them to Chihuahua that Thea, feeling rested and refreshed again, once more began to plunder the depths of her emotions.

It was impossible to believe that anything could come out of two nights of having shared the same bed, and yet— But even as she toyed with the idea, Thea's mind went further back—back to the reason why she'd accepted this assignment in the first place. She had wanted the intrigue of working with a man. Well, here she was and, as the train covered the miles between El Paso, Texas, and Chihuahua, Republic of Mexico, Thea began to wonder if, having made her bed with that impulsive decision, she was now going to have to endure the bitter pill of having to lie in it.

"I'd forgotten how wonderful it can be to travel in a private car," Thea said at last, closing her book and putting it on the nearest table. "I don't think I'll ever be able to thank the de Veigas for sending it for us."

"It does eliminate a lot of potential problems," Charles agreed, putting aside his own book to join her on the sofa. "You said you travelled to St. Louis on the Presidential train. Was it anything like this?"

"Hardly." Thea's glance travelled over the sitting room, rich with Honduran mahogany panelling with gold accents and impressive furniture covered in silk brocade. In addition to the sitting room, there were four bedrooms, a baggage room, a galley, and quarters for the servants, Diego and Carmen, who had come from the de Veiga estate to attend to them on the 225 mile return trip. "It was all purple plush and dark window shades, and when I got on board in Washington and saw how dreary it was, I couldn't believe it. I wasn't allowed to get off in case someone saw me, so I sent a Secret Service man off to the Union Station florist shop to buy carnations and tea roses so I could liven the place up!"

"I'm sure the President was appreciative."

"Oh, he was, but the Secret Service man wasn't particularly thrilled with me."

"Then that was *his* loss," Charles assured her. "You seem to charm everyone else. The customs inspector at Ciudad Juarez was so taken by you that he barely bothered to look inside our luggage."

"I think *that* had more to do with the amount of trunks and suitcases we have with us, rather than my alleged charm."

"What a beautiful book," Charles said, looking at *Italian Villas And Their Gardens.* "Are you enjoying it?"

"Oh, yes," Thea lied. "When I'm finished, shall we trade books?"

"Agreed." Charles leaned toward the window. "Look, we're passing Laguna."

"The duck hunters' spot? Did Cliff and Julie ever tell you that the winter before last they hosted a duck-hunting party down here? There were eight couples and two private railroad cars put off on a siding and—"

"And all the men were Wall Street magnates and members of the Sons of Revolution, and it was the wives who got the best bags!" Charles finished, and they began to laugh.

They spent the remainder of the train ride gazing out the window and, after they passed Cuilty with its cattle-grazing prairies and herds of untamed mustangs, Thea finally began to realize that she had indeed left her country behind her. She was on foreign territory now, in a nation which she knew precious little about, and the only reassurance and support she had was sitting beside her.

"Charles . . . are you sure?" she asked softly, turning to look into his face as the train hurtled over the high bridge spanning the Rio Chubisear. "If you were coaxed or coerced, I'll never forgive myself—"

"It was all my choice—the same as it was yours. *Je regret rien du tout.* I may end up having quite a few regrets about Major Donovan," he ammended, "but as for you . . ."

For a second, as she looked into his topaz-colored eyes, Thea had the oddest feeling that Charles was about to kiss her. Something was between them that hadn't been there even five minutes earlier. Or possibly it had been, her mind warned, and was only waiting for the right circumstances, the right moment, the right words.

For a suspended minute, she studied Charles' mouth, sensual in an ascetic face—wondering what his kisses would be like. All she had to do was make some small sign—

And then the moment was gone, lost in a screech of brakes and the jerk of the train as it came to a halt.

"Chihuahua," Charles said neutrally as he stood up, all the amazed expectation gone from his face. "It looks as if we've arrived."

Thea and Charles alighted from the private Pullman car. Although this part of the trip had been far easier on them than the train ride to El Paso, both were affected by the unrelenting heat and the higher altitude.

Swiftly, the station master, accompanied by the de Veigas' coachman, detached themselves from the crowd and, after polite introductions, the de Renilles were taken through the station to the open landau that was waiting for them. Their luggage was loaded onto the waiting brake and, with a final farewell from the station master, they were off, moving away from the city and into the open countryside.

For the first few minutes, they exchanged comments about the surprisingly rich, green area but, gradually, they lapsed into silence, and Thea found her thoughts straying back to Charles.

What would have happened if I'd spoken sooner? she agonized. Would Charles have kissed me, or am I just making up a romantic fantasy? Let it go, Thea, she advised herself firmly. Charles thinks highly of you and, as far as you're concerned, *that's* the only thing that matters. And, as long as you don't count the one lack in your relationship, you have nothing to complain about.

Intellectually, her reasoning was correct. They were comfortable in each other's presence, and that made them believable. Arranged marriages and brides and grooms suffering in each other's company were far from unknown in Mexico, but with the story they had invented for themselves, the usual awkwardness wouldn't have done at all.

There were no problems—except that Thea was beginning to realize that she wanted more. It was impossible for her, knowing in theory the possibilities that existed within a relationship for a man and a woman, and having shared a bed with Charles for two nights, not to have her active imagination dwell on what could be between them.

In both those nights he had made no move toward her, or even hinted that the thought of doing so ever crossed his mind. Now Thea was wondering about making the first move, but the only thing worse than his rejecting her would be his making love to her and then blaming her afterwards.

He's really doing more than his share, Thea said to herself as she sat beside him in the carriage. No one who looks at the two of you would ever guess there was no physical relationship. Publicly, you're going to be everything the government wants to pass you off as. And then, in a few months, when this assignment is over, it can be arranged to look as if the ceremony never took place. The records will be destroyed, and you'll never

312

have to lay eyes on each other again. Inadvertently, Thea shuddered. More and more, as each day passed, she was growing more and more sure that she would never want Charles de Renille out of her life.

"Are you feeling well?" Thea came out of her thoughts as Charles took her hand. "You look rather pale and tired."

"So do you." She smiled, at the same time wondering if Charles, instead of an annulment, would agree to their remaining married. That way, even after he went back to France, she would have an excuse to see him again, if only for a few months of the year. They could spend the summer season together in Paris; there wouldn't even have to be a deeper relationship between them, if he didn't want it. But even as this last chance idea formed, Thea knew that she didn't want a long-distance, quasi-separated marriage any more than she wanted one without love . . .

For the rest of the trip, they confined their conversation to wondering what the hacienda would be like. And when the carriage turned off the main road, went through the open gate of the stone wall that was covered in scarlet bougainvillaea and continued along the tree-lined road, Thea and Charles were still holding hands, inadvertently presenting themselves as the perfect bridal couple as they approached a house that, the closer the carriage came, assumed greater and greater palatial proportions.

"Hacienda de Veiga," the coachman offered helpfully over his shoulder. Thea and Charles, neither of whom were unused to grandeur, were dumbstruck by the sight.

Appearing before their eyes for the first time, Hacienda de Veiga, in its own way, was as impressive as any of the great houses in Europe and the United States that they knew. Built in the early 1700s, the immense, Spanish-style house with the red tile roof and wrought iron balconies was shaded by palm trees, and a spouting fountain was placed in the center of the circular driveway.

A long gallery ran the length of the house and, as the landau pulled up in front of the central arch where the de Veiga family was waiting to greet them, Don Renaldo, a tall, aristocratic-looking man in his late forties, came through the carved archway flanked by over-sized pottery urns filled with colorful geranium plants, and opened the carriage door to take Thea's hand and raise it to his lips—a gesture made only to a married woman.

"*Mi casa es su casa*," Don Renaldo de Veiga said warmly, saluting them with Mexico's traditional greeting of welcome. "My house is your house."

"*Muchas gracias*, Señor de Veiga," Thea replied. "My husband and I are honored by your hospitality."

"*No hay de que*, Theodosia, and to you, Charles, as well. We are pleased that you are spending the first part of your honeymoon with us."

Recalling all too clearly that, while the de Veigas knew why they were going on to Mexico City, they did not know that their marriage was for the sake of convenience only, Thea and Charles followed Don Renaldo to the gallery where they were instantly surrounded by the rest of the family.

Dona Imelda, a slender, elegant woman, embraced them both warmly. Like her husband, she was a descendant of one of the first Spanish families to arrive in Mexico in the 1500s on land grants. Of better than average height, and wearing a white silk and lace afternoon dress from Worth, she nonetheless projected a faint aura that, despite her modern costume, hinted at her ancient lineage. She had a creamy complexion, and her satiny black hair was done in an elaborate style set off by an antique comb over which was draped a mantilla of heirloom lace, much like the one Thea had worn forty-

314

eight hours before.

"We are so pleased to welcome you. Let me look at you, Thea. Ah, success as a decorator agrees with you—as I'm certain marriage will," she added with a woman-to-woman smile as her husband brought forth their three youngest sons to be introduced.

The de Veigas were the proud parents of six sons, but only thirteen-year-old Jorge, eleven-year-old Enrique, and nine-year-old Gerardo were still being educated by tutors at the hacienda, while fifteen-year-old Sebastian, and seventeen-year-old Ricardo were both students at The Thatcher School in Santa Barbara's Ojai Valley, and nineteen-year-old Roberto was a sophomore at Stanford.

"They have been given the afternoon off from their studies in order to be on hand to welcome you," Don Renaldo said indulgently as each boy in turn offered them their good wishes. "Your arrival has been eagerly anticipated all week—not only by my sons, but by their tutors," he added wryly, and ushered them into the hacienda.

Judging by the exterior, Thea and Charles had been expecting interior grandeur, but not on the scale they saw as they passed through some of the downstairs rooms leading to one of the two patios which flanked the large courtyard that led to the formal garden.

"All three patios interconnect," Don Renaldo told them as they crossed the red-tiled floor of the wood-beamed entrance hall. "No—don't worry about what you're not seeing. There will be more than enough time for your explorations later."

"We could stay here for the next three months and still not see it all," Charles whispered quickly to Thea as they passed a series of drawing rooms, each decorated in Spanish, French or Italian antiques, and she nodded in agreement. The beamed ceilings, elaborate moldings, and priceless furniture and paintings were melting into one solid, jeweled ball of heritage, wealth and privilege.

With its floor of handpainted brick tiles, arched doorways, and vine-covered walls, the patio where they enjoyed iced fruit drinks could have been lifted from an El Greco canvas, but their conversation was totally up-to-date, centering around Charles and Thea's wedding reception, and the de Veigas' twentieth anniversary celebration which would take place a week from that coming Saturday.

"By then you will have adjusted to our climate," Dona Imelda told them. "Right now, the important thing is that you rest. You are not used to our altitude, and sleep will help you over the first hours. We do not dine until half-past eight, and the dressing bell will ring in plenty of time."

They were taken back through the ground floor, up an impressive staircase, and down a long hallway with Moorish arches and walls hung with family portraits.

Don Renaldo and Dona Imelda apologized to them because they had been given one of the smaller suites, since the largest of those that comprised the guest quarters had to be reserved for the de la Garzas, Dona Imelda's family, who were coming *en masse* to the anniversary fiesta. Charles and Thea accepted the "apology" in the manner in which it had been offered, assuring their hosts that size was of no importance. But, once the de Renilles were alone together, they regarded each other and their quarters in wide-eyed amazement.

"I know that to Mexicans the concept of saving face is as important as it is to the Orientals, but I think just this once it has been carried a bit too far," Charles remarked slowly, his gaze travelling over the molded ceiling.

"If this is supposed to be one of the lesser suites, I'd be afraid to find out what our rooms would have looked like if we'd had the main guest suite," Thea added humorously as they left behind the elaborate little

316

drawing room and went into the bedroom.

Their suite, Thea thought a moment later, would more than make up for their exhausting trip. Once again, they were faced with only one bed—a huge, carved one—not at all out of place for a newly married, passionately in love young couple—if only they *were* that. Thea forced her thoughts onto other topics. At least they'd have a bit more privacy, she noted approvingly. Two modern dressing room-bathroom combinations opened off opposite sides of the bedroom.

Thea stepped carefully around the small mountain that their luggage made, opened the French doors, and stepped out on the long gallery that ran the length of the side of the house and had a stairway that led down to the landscaped garden.

"Doesn't it look like it stretches on forever?" Thea said over her shoulder to Charles who stood in the doorway. "All those incredible flowers—"

"We can admire it better tomorrow."

"Do you always have to be so serious?" Thea teased, returning to the bedroom. "This is heaven after all that dust and dirt and heat."

Charles looked hurt. "Do you mind my being serious?"

"No," she said, wishing she could put her arms around him. "I don't mind at all. But," Thea couldn't resist adding, "serious and stuffy *are* two different things!"

Charles' face relaxed into a smile. "Morgan warned me not to be a prig around you. I won't ever be—if you'll remember that I can't accept this . . . assignment in the same manner that you do. Everything in the life I come from demands that I treat this—and all that we have to do—in the most solemn way possible."

"Charles, may I say something to you?" Thea said as his words sank in. "I should have told you this before we left San Antonio, but there was never a right moment."

"I'm not crazy, Thea, no matter what you may have heard."

"I never thought you were. But you are a very sensitive man, and you probably never gave too much thought to marriage. And yet, here we are."

"You told me that we should be friends, and be able to depend on each other. I think we've achieved both those goals very easily."

"We have, but I also want you to know how proud I am to have your name. Not because of your family, but because you're you and, for however long I'm your wife, I promise never to behave in a way that will make you regret having agreed to become a part of this assignment."

Long after Thea had fallen asleep that night, Charles remained awake, the words she had spoken so passionately hours before, as well as other, far more distant events, continued to haunt him.

Servants had arrived to tend to their luggage almost as soon as Thea finished speaking, and there had been no opportune moment for him to reply since then.

He would have been a total fool not to have felt intense pride at her words. Thea was steadfast, loyal and beautiful, not only in face, but in character, and she would no more disgrace them than she would commit murder.

Now, for the first time, Charles began to admit to himself that, if he had found those qualities in any of the sophisticated, titled, married ladies who had introduced him to physical love at nineteen, or if he had found the same degree of immediate mental and spiritual companionship with any of the well-bred young girls he was steered to, he might never have undertaken the five-year exercise that had ended, for him, in the dark pit of emotional and physical collapse.

The de Renilles, in spite of their long history, were not an ecclesiastical family. His parents' reaction to his entering the Jesuit order at twenty-two had been strenuous to the point of violence. But he had not been cut out for the life of a diplomat, a gentleman officer or a playboy. He was a scholar, and the Church was the only place he could respectably practice it. For the nth time, he repeated the familiar history to himself, but it changed nothing.

The years of study and sacrifice had slowly but inexorably eaten away at him. But, in the end, they had only been the contributing factors to his breakdown. The final element, the one he still kept secret from everyone, was the overwhelming certainty that he had, through his own foolish pride, contributed to his father's death.

At the other side of the bed, Thea stirred and Charles, anxious to put aside the one secret he could never share, fixed the silken comforters over her and smoothed back a few strands of her hair. None of the other women he had ever made love to had stirred him deeply or roused his deep, untapped reserves of affection and loyalty. And, lying next to Thea, he wondered how long their consummated companionship would transcend the needs of the flesh.

Chapter Ten

Over the days that followed, Thea and Charles began to realize that when they'd passed through the gates of Hacienda de Veiga they had entered a world of wealth, privilege, luxury and convenience.

De Veigas had lived on this land in an unbroken line for nearly three-hundred years, and they were established leaders in Mexico's ruling class. The estate, which covered more acres than most American counties was, primarily, a cattle ranch, but also produced over a million bushels of wheat a year, and had three thousand peons whose sole purpose in life was to till and harvest the land.

In addition to the palatial hacienda, the gardens, and the well-stocked stables, there were two substantial guest houses and, tucked away from the others, in a grove of avocado trees, was a good-sized house of adobe brick where the three youngest de Veiga boys had their lessons, and where their beleaguered tutors lived.

It was, Charles and Thea agreed, as near to a private principality—or a Balkan state—as one was likely to find in North America.

Don Renaldo de Veiga's fortune went far beyond the boundaries of his estate. He owned silver mines in Santa Eulalia, a factory for bottling mineral water in Tehuacan, a clothing factory in San Luis Potosi, and a chocolate factory in Guadalajara. Closer to home, in the city of Chihuahua, there was a soap factory, an iron foundry and a share in a newly established experimental sheep farm located in another part of the state.

All in all, it made a steady, substantial supplement to his inherited fortune—a fortune that would withstand whatever political winds might blow through Mexico over the coming years.

Don Renaldo was prepared for all eventualities—even that of exile for himself and his family. It was rumored that at Brown Brothers Bank in New York, he kept several safety deposit boxes filled with cash and high-yield securities, and had purchased a townhouse in the newly fashionable East Sixties off Fifth Avenue.

But the events that these protections had been formulated against were still six years in the future, and what Thea and Charles saw in September of 1904 was the *hacendados* system in its final blaze of glory. Rather, Thea frequently mused as she and Charles went from one day to the next in their charade, like the life she was now leading. Calm and beautiful and making no great emotional demands—and destined not to be allowed to last.

Thea, who had erroneously thought of Mexico as a country of arid land with banditos making border raids, was thrilled at the richness, beauty and prosperity of this northeast state.

On the estate, the formal gardens extended for over half a mile. Roses grew in abundance, as did carnations, hydrangeas and incredible purple orchids. There were great bushes of peonies in all colors and variations, and rich gardenia trees.

All the lemons, limes, oranges, avocados and olives came from the de Veigas' own trees, as did the mangos, papayas and coconuts that appeared with every meal. The family chef had been trained in France, and the food was a delicious blending of the two cuisines.

321

Don Renaldo and Dona Imelda were generous hosts, and Thea and Charles played tennis on their court, rode the excellent saddle horses from the stables, and were included in invitations to the equally impressive homes of their nearest neighbors where they danced at parties as formal as those they were used to on the other side of the Rio Grande.

All in all, over the next week Thea and Charles wanted for no material thing. There was no word from the Embassy in Mexico City, and Thea began to wonder if they'd been forgotten. The way the government worked, she told Charles, she wouldn't be at all surprised. On the surface there were certainly no complaints. Yet, as each day passed, she was increasingly aware that the longer they stayed in this voluptuous setting, the harder it would be to conceal her growing love and desire for Charles. It was clearly a situation destined never to resolve itself, Thea told herself with increasing frequency. This was her secret, her burden, and she would have to make sure that no one ever, ever found out what lay beneath the facade of her supposedly happy marriage.

"I think that there is something very wrong," Dona Imelda de Veiga remarked unexpectedly. It had been ten days since the arrival of Thea and Charles, and their perceptive, intuitive hostess had been carefully observing her guests. Better educated than most women of her age and class, she knew one did not reach a decision overnight, much less voice one's suspicions, but she was certain now. As she and her husband were in the library checking over the final arrangements for their twentieth anniversary ball, she broached the subject. Unfortunately Don Renaldo, momentarily distracted by the complexities of the guest list and seating plan for the formal dinner, misconstrued the meaning of his wife's comment.

"No, Imelda, all is in order. Someone will complain about their room, or their place at the table, but that's to be expected—"

"I wasn't referring to our prospective guests, as I'm sure you're well aware," she retorted indignantly, sitting bolt upright against the soft rose silk decorative pillows on the moss green velvet sofa. "I was talking about Thea and Charles. They're deeply in love—and wretchedly unhappy."

"Aren't those two experiences supposed to be mutually exclusive?" Don Renaldo questioned mildly. He had been educated at Trinity College, Cambridge, and that was not an institution that encouraged wild reactions. "I thought they were just like any other newly married couple."

"Who never touch each other, except when dancing? Who don't kiss when they walk in the garden? Who don't make elaborate excuses so they can retire early? Who, on a warm day like today, prefer to go into Chihuahua rather than take a picnic basket and spend the afternoon swimming?"

Don Renaldo listened to his wife's arguments, but remained unconvinced. "Possibly they thought we were shocked enough at what they will be doing in Mexico City and, at least publicly, decided to be on their best behavior."

"You do not see—not at all." The de Veigas rarely disagreed or argued, but Dona Imelda was concerned enough about the happiness of their guests to stir up their placid, contented life—for a few minutes at least. "Haven't you seen how they look at each other? Not like lovers, but like two people who have just discovered their love, but haven't told each other, and don't know how!"

"Imelda . . . please." Don Renaldo's voice was conciliatory. "Please remember that Charles and Thea are giving up part of their honeymoon—the most important period of time a couple can share—to aid President Roosevelt. What they do now may help all of us at some future time." He was as aware as his wife that beneath the guise of a happy, newly married couple, the de Renilles were projecting another aura entirely but, unlike his wife, he did not think what might or might not be going on between the couple was any of their concern. It was not out of meanness that he held this view, but of practicality. Nothing was ever gained by meddling in other people's lives, and he told this to his wife. "Charles and Thea have taken on a grave responsibility, and any interfering on our part will make matters worse, not better. If they ask our help—well, that is different. But, until they do, it is in everyone's best interest if we remain on the sidelines."

The fiesta being given by Don Renaldo and Dona Imelda de Veiga on Saturday, October 8, 1904, to celebrate their twentieth wedding anniversary, was rightly regarded as one of *the* social events of the year by Mexico's elite. There was no way to beg an invitation. One either belonged on the guest list or they didn't and, even though Thea and Charles ranked rather low on that coveted roster (due to matters of protocol, not personal preference), they were included in all the plans.

They were shown the menu for the multi-course dinner, and the vintage champagne that would accompany it; knew that the musicians had been hired from Chicago; and that all the favors had been ordered from Tiffany's in New York.

"Did Dona Imelda mention to you that Japanese lanterns are going to be strung along both patios, the courtyard and—"

"—and on into the gardens," Charles finished, and they both began to laugh. "Every so often, when I hear more of the plans, I have to remind myself we're in Mexico."

"So do I. Every time I look at the hacienda, I think of something Longfellow wrote," Thea said. "'As ancient is this hostelry, as any in the land may be; built in the old colonial day, when men lived in a grander way, with ampler hospitality.'"

"That's better than all the superlatives we've been using to describe this house," Charles said honestly as he stood in the doorway of Thea's dressing room, watching as she put the finishing touches on her *maquillage*. "Will you be ready soon? Don Renaldo wants to show us some pictures he received from his dealer in Mexico City."

It was Friday, the day before the anniversary ball, and Thea and Charles had spent the warm, sunny morning quietly reading on the gallery outside their suite. They had spent Thursday in Chihuahua, a city which, like El Paso, was growing thanks to its new industrial importance. There was the Cathedral to visit, fine shops of the Calles de la Libertad and La Victoria to browse in, the Foreign Club on the Calla de Aldama to have lunch in, and the Palace Hotel for a refreshing afternoon tea of lemon ice and French pastries.

It had been a fine way to spend the day. Charles had tipped the sacristan so they could climb to the top of one of the two 146-foot-tall towers that graced the Cathedral. From that perch they were able to view the distant mountains and plains, and the great aqueduct, first erected in 1790, which stretched over three miles of valley into the hills. Once they made their way down, they explored the Cathedral's Doric interior where sixteen Corinthian columns in groups of four with a statue of San Francisco de Asis supported the Altar Mayor. The same sacristan who had allowed them access to the tower explained that many of the church's fine silver ornaments had been removed in the 1860s following the first of the Reform Laws to separate church and state, and that while the art work in the various chapels was not really worth viewing from an artistic standpoint, visitors always found it worth their while in a spiritual sense to pause at the black marble slab at the foot of one of the *Capilla de San Antonio*, where Don Miguel Hidalgo y Costilla, the priest who had endeavored to lead Mexico to independence, had originally been interred following his assassination by Spanish troops in 1811.

Thea knew instinctively what such places of sustained faith and holiness meant to Charles, and she shared as much of the experience with him as her basically agnostic beliefs allowed. In turn, when they left the Cathedral, he escorted her in and out of the antique and curio shops, waiting by her side as she scanned the available merchandise with a professional eye, and in the end bought nothing, telling him that the *real* antiques she was looking for were in Mexico City.

And that was their relationship, Thea acknowledged twenty-four hours later as she added a last touch of powder to her face and left her dressing table. A blending of mutual deference to each other's needs, but never going beneath the surface, and never, ever, expressing the slightest physical desire.

At least it is for Charles, she thought despairingly. If he doesn't want me by now, he never will, and I can't say I love him because I don't know which result would be the worse—his rejection, or his making love to me, and staying married to me, out of a sense of responsibility.

Thea honestly didn't know what to do. There was no going back to a time when they didn't know each other, and yet there didn't seem to be a way to go on together. She felt like a rock buffeted by waves. She saw Charles in a dozen different ways and moods, knew almost every motion and expression he made by heart, slept in the same bed with him every night, and was his wife in every way except the one which was most important . . .

"You simply *cannot* go down to lunch looking the way you do!"

Thea spoke without thinking, and Charles, his hand on the doorknob, gazed at her, thoroughly nonplussed.

"What's wrong with the way I look?"

"You need a haircut. You've needed one for days," Thea said firmly as Charles' hand went self-consciously to the black hair that was now growing thickly over his collar. "If you don't get a trim, Don Renaldo is going to start thinking he has made some terrible mistake about you, and you're not a French aristocrat, but some sort of dreadful bohemian!"

Charles slowly began to smile. "I can see where that might have repercussions for you. After all, the de Veigas regard *you* as their friend, not me!"

"What an awful thing to say!" Thea exclaimed, not sure if Charles were being funny or deadly accurate. "You know how highly they regard you!"

"But I had to earn that regard," he pointed out. "I recognized that at dinner on our first night here. I sat there listening as you and Don Renaldo and Dona Imelda reminisced about Budapest, and suddenly it struck me that, despite the fact that I shared a religion and an aristocratic heritage with them, you were their honored friend, and I was right back where I'd been in New York this past February—the only outsider at the dinner party!"

He was speaking humorously, but his words still stung Thea, and she wanted to make it up to him.

"It's odd . . . on our first days here, I used to think how much more you fitted in than me—for precisely the same reasons you gave. I thought I'd become more acceptable to the de Veigas because I'd married a Catholic from France's *ancien regime* and *haute noblesse*." She favored him with a challenging look. "Lucky for you, I'm not one of *those* girls."

"So you told me," he acknowledged, visibly relaxing. "And I promise that, immediately after lunch, I'll have Don Renaldo's valet barber me."

"Oh, no you won't," Thea retorted, and she swung around on her heel, and disappeared back into her dressing room. She reemerged a minute later holding a lethal-looking gold scissor in her hand. "I'm going to put the shears to you myself!"

Charles' eyes travelled from his wife's determined, amused face, to the instrument she held. "You couldn't possibly."

"Why not? I cut my own hair all the time. Yours can't be *that* different."

That much was true, Charles allowed. In the beginning, he had assumed that once the pins were out, Thea's hair would hang to her waist, but that illusion had been shattered the first night when he saw that her glossy brown hair hung only an inch or two below her shoulders. Eventually he'd learned from Thea that she'd cut it this length years earlier as a matter of convenience. But, however adept Thea was at trimming her own hair, his was another matter entirely.

"*Pas miche,*" he told her briefly, but Thea merely smiled and motioned at her husband with the shears.

"We're losing time. Besides, if you wait until *after* lunch for a haircut, the first of the guests will be arriving. And if Don Renaldo and Dona Imelda are beginning to think of you as a bohemian, their family and friends, who are quite conservative, will have even *more* interesting comments to make!"

With that, Thea delivered one significant glance over her shoulder as she walked past him and stepped into his dressing room.

"Now, you sit right down here," she instructed genially, pulling a straight-backed chair to the center of

328

the room. "This won't take long at all." Thea went quickly into the marble-heavy bathroom, took several towels from a pile by the tub, and returned to the dressing room to find Charles, his suit jacket off, his tie loosened and collar open, sitting patiently in the chair, rather like a prisoner awaiting sentence from the judge.

"Did I ever tell you that when I was in Budapest two years ago, I went to a hairdressing salon and had my hair marcelled?" Thea began as she expertly tucked the large towels under his collar so that they covered his shoulders. "It turned out very successfully, but once the initial novelty wore off, I *hated* it." She took his gold-mounted tortoise-shell comb from the top of the dresser and ran it through black hair that felt and flowed like silk. "Men have it so much easier," she continued, more to get her mind off wanting to bend over and kiss him than anything else.

"Do you really think so?" Charles' voice was tight.

"Of course you do." Thea strove to sound teasing. "Just look at your tan. Not that I'd ever want one, though. Where were you this summer? Newport?"

"Cove House," he said as the shears made their first, careful snip. "After I met with the President, I spent the rest of the summer on Long Island."

Thea stopped her ministrations long enough to laugh. "Now there's another place where we might have met, except that I was delayed in Europe. Did you have fun? Tell me about Adele's birthday party? Was everyone there?"

As the shears, guided by Thea's steady hand, did their work, Charles recounted to her his stay at the Long Island estate of William Seligman. Cove House had been the last of the great surprises Charles had found in America. Not even San Antonio and the Hacienda de Veiga had given him the same astonishment that had enveloped him as the carriage that had met him at Long

Island's Woodbury Station passed through a pair of massive wrought iron gates and gone down an almost mile-long avenue of beech trees that finally cleared to show wide sweeping lawns and an all-dominating, four-story, rose-brick, Georgian-style house.

Built in 1895, Cove House, at eighty-five rooms, was not only one of the largest mansions gracing Long Island's North Shore, but one of the largest private homes in America. The seventy-eight acre property included their own dairy, a greenhouse, a tennis court, stables, a brick carriage house ornamented by circular turrets, and a wood-framed bath house at the edge of the beach.

The number of guests at Cove House rose and fell with almost weekly regularity during that July and August. In addition to Bill and Adele, their sons, wives and six grandchildren, the rest of the core group was made up of Alix and Henry Thorpe, just returned from five weeks in London and Paris, Regina and Ian MacIverson, who had come east from California, Kezia and Philip Leslie, Megan and Richard North, Rupert Randall, and Charles de Renille. The guests came not only from New York, but from as far afield as Philadelphia, Washington, Baltimore, Boston, and Chicago.

If the weather was good, which it almost always was during the weeks Charles was there, they swam and sailed on Long Island Sound, rode the excellent horses on bridle paths bordered by cherry and linden trees, and took afternoon tea on the loggia that was filled with white wicker furniture and chintz-covered cushions while they enjoyed the view that looked out over the rose garden. On rainy days they made good use of the mosaic-tiled indoor swimming pool, or the billiard room, or the oak-panelled library, or the Turkish Bath that Bill had installed for the convenience of his male guests.

Now, nearly two months later, as he forced himself to

sit through Thea's tonsorial experimentations, Charles could see the rooms clearly in his mind's eye. Not only his room with its restrained Adam furnishings and incomparable view of the Sound, but the sun-filled breakfast room, the marble entry hall and sweeping staircase, the crystal and gold ballroom, the main drawing room of yellow and cream with an impressive rock-crystal chandelier and, most of all, the dining room with the beige silk chinoiserie wallpaper and the endless length of table around which fifty guests had gathered on a Friday night at the end of July for Adele's birthday party.

"I wanted to come home in time *so* badly." Thea made a few more snips. "Was there duck for dinner?"

"Canard aux framboises." He smiled in remembrance. "A wonderful meal. It gave me something to confess, to admit I have the secret soul of a glutton."

The kitchen staff at Cove House produced prodigious amounts of food and, thanks to the fresh air and athletic endeavors of nearly everyone, only empty plates were returned from whence they came. Visions of whole wheat pancakes and Vermont maple syrup to begin the day floated through his mind, and were joined by strawberries floating in thick, fresh cream, peach, cherry and blackberry cobblers which were made from fruit grown on the estate's garden and eaten while still warm from the oven. He dwelled on clams steamed on the beach and crayfish eaten out of their shells, as well as soft-shelled crabs swimming in sweet butter, and cold poached salmon accompanied by herbed mayonnaise. Ice cream had been churned out endlessly—rich chocolate, vanilla studded with fruit, and plain vanilla topped by fruits from the summer before that had been bottled in brandy. He could still taste the perfectly brewed coffee, the iced tea, the bottles of incomparable champagne . . .

"Finished!" Thea's voice was triumphant as she put

the shears and comb aside and carefully removed the towels. "Take a look in the mirror and let me know what you think."

Stiffly, Charles stood up and surveyed the results in the large, mahogany-framed mirror. Thinking about his weeks at Cove House had served a purpose—and it wasn't to relive a very pleasant time. It was the only way to keep his mind off of Thea standing behind him, cutting his hair, talking to him, teasing him gently. In other words, behaving like the true wife and lover she wasn't.

The longer he remained around Thea, the more Charles felt himself turning into dry straw just waiting for the moment the careless toss of a match would send him up in smoke. As she'd stood over him, it had taken every ounce of self-control that Charles had not to stand up and take Thea in his arms and not let her go until he told her all that was in his heart. There was so much he wanted to tell her, to share with her. He wanted to begin all over again with Thea, but the impediments in the way required careful surmounting.

"Well?" Thea drawled. "You've been studying the results from every angle. How did I do in my first attempt as a barber?"

"Very well." Charles fixed his tie and put on his suit jacket. "My compliments," he said with a courtly bow in her direction.

Thea laughed. "Well, it's good to know that, if the supply of women who need interior decorators dries up, or if all the antiques in the world suddenly disappear, I have another option open to me!"

"I don't think you'll ever have to worry about either of those eventualities," Charles assured her. "Your place as *la decoratrice* is quite safe."

Undoubtedly, he was an imbecile, Charles chided himself as they went down the long gallery lined with paintings by the great artists of Spain and Mexico. He had

had his opportunity—one of several in the past days—and he had let it go again. He couldn't believe that Thea didn't care for him—if not deeply and passionately, at least to some extent. He had to make her understand that he would wait until she could come to love him as he loved her. And that this love, as unexpected as it was, was real and lasting. The words were simple and direct and he couldn't say them. Instead, once again, he had chosen silence, and now, in place of opening his heart to the woman he loved, he was walking silently beside her down the stairs—a perfect fool with the best haircut of his life.

Every painting in Hacienda de Veiga was worthy of being in a museum. But it wasn't the variety of art work that occupied Thea's mind as she stood in Don Renaldo's library, having been greeted by their host and hostess as if their being a few minutes late was of no importance whatsoever.

They probably think we were making love, Thea thought. After all, isn't that what two honeymooners are supposed to do whenever they're alone together? A sharp pang of longing went through her, she tightened her grasp on the slender-stemmed glass she was holding and looked down into the fine Spanish sherry it held, but there were no answers there. It's no good, she told herself dully. You gave it your best try, and if Charles didn't respond then, he never will.

In Thea's mind, the scenario had been all worked out. Charles *did* need a haircut and, after she performed that service, which could be either as impersonal or as intimate as one wished to make it, he would turn to her and she would be in his arms. Finally, she would be able to hold Charles, and touch him, and say all the things . . .

Fantasies, she told herself harshly. Stupid, idiotic fantasies that a schoolgirl would be ashamed to have. Grow up, Thea! This isn't going to work. You can't infuse

333

Charles with your feelings any more than you could stop those feelings from developing in the first place. It's life, and this time it isn't going to work out very well . . .

While she'd been delivering her silent lecture, Don Renaldo and Dona Imelda had been telling them about their paintings, which ranged from Murillos and Goyas to canvasses done by every major artist of Mexico in the past three hundred years to a delicate Renoir oil in Dona Imelda's dressing room and the Constable landscape Don Renaldo kept in his office.

"It's my British university education coming out," he told them with mock resignation. "I have a secret weakness for the serenity of the English countryside. Now . . . shall we see what my dealer has sent for my approval?"

The framed canvasses were propped up against the desk and Don Renaldo began to show them off, explaining each one in detail. But Thea was lost in her own thoughts, giving only perfunctory attention to the various paintings, but one *did* capture her eye, and she shuddered looking at it.

Thea had ambivalent feelings about religious paintings in general. She had seen pictures of such deep spirituality that it was difficult to believe they had been painted by human hands, and then there were those paintings which, despite their obvious talent, had left her cold. But the work she was now seeing made her skin crawl.

It was a painting of a contemplative brother holding a crown made of rich flowers, and the four of them gazed silently at it.

"The provenance on this is a bit confused," Don Renaldo said at last. "My dealer was able to ascertain that it was probably done in the latter part of the 1700s, painted at the time of his final vow-taking. That's what the decorative crown of flowers indicates," he pointed out, more for Thea's information than anyone else's. "This painting in itself is rather unusual. Although nuns were frequently painted at the time of their final vows, monks, particularly those in the stricter orders, were rarely done. Look how the artist captured the newly made brother. One can almost feel the tonsure—"

Thea looked at the portrait with the same horrid fascination that people generally display toward street accidents. The artist had clearly caught the aura of spirituality surrounding the young man, but the large, dark eyes seemed to burn out of the canvas. But, whether it was with religious fervor or another emotion entirely . . .

"Charles, is something wrong? Sit down at once—"

Don Renaldo's concerned voice drew Thea away from the painting to her husband and, as she saw Charles, a sick feeling began in the pit of her stomach. Under his tan, his face was chalk white, and beads of perspiration were forming on his temples.

Thea reached out to him. "Charles—"

They all moved toward him, but he shook them off. And, without a word, spun around and rushed from the library, leaving the others dumbfounded.

"That poor boy!" Dona Imelda exclaimed. "Whatever happened to make him behave like that?"

"I—I don't know," Thea hedged, moving backwards, having a perfectly good idea as to Charles' sudden attack. "Don Renaldo, Dona Imelda, please excuse me, my husband needs me."

With her heart in her mouth, Thea fled into the corridor to begin her search for Charles. The de Veigas had countless servants but, as so often happens in times of crisis, none appeared to tell her where her husband had gone.

For a moment she paused at the foot of the stairs, forcing herself to think like Charles. Where would she go if she were in need of immediate refuge? Not upstairs to

335

their suite, not to the patios, or the courtyard, or into the garden, she decided. But where—? And then she knew.

Unlike some of the hacendados families, the de Veigas did not have a chapel on the grounds, preferring to attend church in Chihuahua, but they *did* have a small room tucked away near the courtyard for the purpose of quiet contemplation. Decorated with a small *prie-dieu*, as well as carved wood Baroque-style painted and gilded statues of the hermit St. Rosalie and the Archangel St. Raphael, it provided a restful harbor.

It was here she found Charles. He sat on one of the benches that lined the wall, and when Thea saw his white, strained face and trembling body, her heart broke for him. Without stopping to think, she dashed across the floor, sat down beside Charles, and put her arms around him.

Immediately, he rested his head on her shoulder and, at this instinctive gesture, Thea felt another emotion begin underneath her worried concern; one of unrequited tenderness and longing. As far as she knew, this was the closest she'd ever come to embracing the man she loved, and she held him wordlessly, marvelling at the wonderful feel of his lean, muscular frame, running her hands lightly over the thick dark hair she'd just cut, wanting to weave her fingers in it. Finally, she put her arms around his strong shoulders and held him close. They were alone in almost utter silence and, even if they were in a holy room, there was nothing wrong in what she was doing, Thea decided. She only wanted to help Charles.

Gradually, his body stopped trembling, and he lifted his face to hers. "I'm sorry you had to see me like this," he said painfully.

"Then it was the painting," Thea replied, deciding that being direct was the best route to take. "It was so beautiful, it was horrible. It must have brought back all

336

sorts of memories for you."

"It did," he admitted. "But not the sort of memories you may be thinking about. All I could see in that picture was what happened to me when I collapsed."

"I'd heard . . . how awful it must have been for you to have all your years of study and sacrifice wiped out by . . . by . . ."

"By going crazy." His voice was cold. "And don't protest, because that *is* what happened to me. For a few days, I went mad. And the way patients afflicted with a *grand nerveuse* are treated isn't very pleasant."

His topaz-colored eyes were filled with a stark pain that frightened Thea—not for herself, but for Charles. Her heart cried out for her to put her hand over his mouth and tell him none of it mattered any longer; only that he was well again and she loved him and what was past could never come back, but her brain spoke differently. He'd suffered unspeakable torture, still carried the scars, and his carefully hidden pain was threatening to eat him alive.

She met his gaze steadily, tenderly, ready to hear whatever he had to tell her.

"I'd been ill for weeks before I snapped. I won't tell you all the details—most of them are too gory—except that first I lost my appetite, then the migraines started, followed by dizzy spells. Finally my hair began falling out in patches. One symptom piled itself on top of another," he related to her in a detached, dispassionate voice, his words more clipped than usual.

"The end was inevitable—nothing I could have done would have changed it. My mind and body had taken all it could, and when it received the final blow, I went off on a mental tangent some never return from, and for which the treatment is worse than the illness."

As she heard his words, it was all Thea could do not to take him back in her arms, comfort him and wipe the

337

look of pain from his face, but she restrained herself. His tale of travail had to come out all at once, and with no other emotions diverting it.

"There's a standard treatment for cases like mine, and I underwent every brutality," he went on grimly. "It's so strange, by the time I was carried into the infirmary, I was totally out of my mind, and yet I can remember every detail from the moment they put me down on the bed. I was nothing to my superiors any longer, just a dead weight to be turned over to an incompetent doctor and infirmarians, to be stripped, to have restraints put on my arms and legs, to have my body packed in ice, to be entubed, to be injected with morphine, to have . . ."

"Charles . . ."

"To have my head shaved," he went on tonelessly, "shaved against the grain so it wouldn't grow back evenly or too quickly."

Thea would have given anything if only the story Charles were relating to her weren't true. "But what about your family?" she heard herself asking. "Couldn't they have done something?"

"There were four days between the time I collapsed and when my family arrived. I was almost lucid again, and my fever had gone down somewhat, but the damage had been done. I was finished as far as the Jesuits were concerned, and they wanted me gone as quickly as possible. It was suggested that my mother might want to commit me to Chateau Suresnes . . ."

"That's an insane asylum!" Thea interrupted, horrified. "It's outrageous—"

"Was it, Thea? I *was* crazy for those few days, and when it was over, I was nothing more than a shell."

"My poor darling." Thea reached out to brush back a lock of hair that had fallen over his forehead. "My poor punished darling—"

338

He jerked his head away as if she held a rattlesnake in her hand. "I don't need your pity!" he snapped.

Tears welled in Thea's eyes. "I don't pity you!"

"Of course you do—everyone does as soon as they find out. Why should you be any different?" he blazed at her. "Wondering about me behind my back . . . Well, I don't need them, and I don't need you. I'm sorry I ever told you anything. The only favor I want from you is to stay out of my life!"

Thea had realized early on in her relationship with Charles that she must not, as Desdemona had Othello, "loved him for the dangers he had passed." That was the worst route to attempt with a man of his pride and, as she now knew, temper.

It was thirty-six hours later, with the de Veigas' wedding anniversary fiesta in full swing, and Thea was still castigating herself for how she'd handled the incident with Charles. But no matter how many times she replayed it in her mind, the answer came out the same—loving Charles, she had wanted to comfort him, but he had mistaken her concern for pity and had turned on her with all his fury.

All for nothing, she thought, automatically smiling at the guests she passed. It's a terrible choice, but I'd do the same thing all over again. The only question is, am I a woman in love, or the prize fool of all time?

Thea was determined to put a good face on tonight if it took every ounce of strength and every bit of acting ability she possessed. Since he'd stormed out of the alcove, Charles had barely spoken to her. In front of the de Veigas he was polite, if somewhat distant. In private, for the most part, he ignored her as much as possible. Even as they were about to leave their suite a few hours before, the only reaction he'd had to her Poiret ball gown of white Liberty satin with white lace

339

and silver embroidery and blue satin shoulder straps was a sweeping glance and a slight nod—very different from his usual compliments.

As she left the ballroom where couples were waltzing to the strains of a Strauss melody, the music followed her through the corridors, passing smiling, elegantly dressed couples, and *lacayos* holding ornate silver trays on which champagne was offered. The hacienda was ablaze with light and, in the garden, colorful Japanese lanterns were hung as far as the eye could see.

In addition to an endless array of de Veiga and de la Garza relatives, each more impressive than the other, everyone who mattered in Mexico's social world had been invited. That included not only the other great land-owning families, but participants in Mexico City's foreign and diplomatic contingents, as well as important and influential members of the government. The de Renilles had been introduced to Señor Fernandez, the Minister of Justice, whom, Dona Imelda warned them, liked to cultivate his slight resemblance to the British playwright George Bernard Shaw; Señor Limantour, the courtly and cultivated Minister of Finance; and Señor Landa y Escandon, the British-educated governor of the Federal District and Mayor of Mexico City, and the principal representative of the aristocratic Escandon family. The last time Thea had seen Charles, he had been in the library, deep in conversation with Señor Mariscal, who was not only the Minister of Foreign Affairs, but a well-known writer and translator of the better known American authors.

He wasn't in the library any longer and, a moment later, she found him in the main drawing room. Thea paused in the doorway, taking in his tall, slender frame in his perfectly cut dress suit. He stood with his back to her, talking to Dona Jeronyma and Don Francisco de la Garza, Dona Imelda's mother and father, who were

340

seated on the room's largest sofa, over which hung their prize Murillo.

Charles stood in front of the couple, talking respectfully with them in French, a language Mexico's aristocracy preferred to speak. In fact, Thea noted, more conversations in the ballroom were being carried on in French or English than in Spanish.

If she and Charles were on speaking terms, that observation would have been something to discuss when they were alone, just as they had, in days past, traded views of the society they were living in. But now Thea was literally afraid to open her mouth to him. Just what this new turn held for their future didn't look good and . . .

"Ah, Theodosia." Dona Jeronyma, resplendent in a conservatively cut elegant bronze satin gown from Worth, set off by her perfectly faceted diamond necklace, motioned to Thea with a warm smile. "Charles, here is your charming and beautiful bride. Come and join us, my dear."

"I think, Charles, that if I were newly married, I would want to spend every possible moment of this fiesta at my bride's side," Don Francisco, a handsome gentleman who looked as if he'd stepped out of a Velasquez portrait, stopping only long enough to change into a modern full-dress suit, chided with a smile as Thea joined them.

"I'm sure Thea understands and forgives my temporary dereliction," Charles said, turning slightly to her. His voice was a good approximation of how he'd always addressed her, but his eyes were cold.

"I consider Theodosia to be very brace," Dona Jeronyma put in, her black eyes twinkling with fun. Like many other conservative women of her age and rank, she was secure enough to tease a younger couple. "I agree, Francisco, she should be at Charles' side—

keeping the legions of other women away from him! In Spanish we call Charles *zipote de partido*," she informed Thea. "The kind of man every woman, even elderly ladies like me, want to be around. A fine catch, indeed."

"You're absolutely right, Dona Jeronyma," Thea said, forcing herself to behave as if nothing were wrong. "But I trust my husband to always come back to me."

At least Charles cares enough to keep up his end, she thought with relief as she looked into Charles' eyes again and saw that the anger and hostility she'd seen there had faded and were now replaced by something much warmer and questioning . . .

"Ah, so my daughter has decided to join us." Don Francisco's voice pierced Thea's thoughts. "Another guest—? Jeronyma, do you recognize the gentleman?"

At his question, both Thea and Charles turned to see Dona Imelda, exquisite in a Doucet gown of delicate blue *eolienne* with mother-of-pearl spangles, ushering in yet another guest. And when she saw him, Thea felt her heart stop and then start again at a sickening pace. It was impossible to believe what she was seeing, yet underneath her shock she wasn't really *that* surprised. After all, with everything else going wrong, it was hardly unexpected that the man in the dress suit crossing the room, deep in conversation with Dona Imelda, was Paul Merrill.

"Mama, Papa, I would like to present Captain Paul Merrill to you, the assistant military attaché at the American Embassy," Dona Imelda said as they joined them. "Captain Merrill, my mother and father, Don Francisco and Dona Jeronyma de la Garza."

Paul Merrill's demeanor, like Charles de Renille's, was faultless. He bowed solemnly before the de la Garzas, addressed them in flawless Spanish before switching to equally fluent French, and he waited patiently for Dona Imelda to complete the introductions.

"Captain Merrill, I am pleased to have you meet Mr. and Mrs. Charles de Renille, who are passing the first part of their honeymoon with us."

"Thank you very much, Señora de Veiga," Paul said as he and Charles shook hands, displaying the sort of congenial wariness that two men of similar age and background usually display when they know they have to be polite, but haven't yet decided if friendship is in order. "I'm happy to say that Mrs. de Renille and I have already met."

"Then you are old friends?"

"I wish I could claim that distinction," Paul told her easily while Thea waited with growing dread as to what he would say next. "We met several weeks ago in St. Louis while I was on leave and Thea was the guest of Colonel and Mrs. Miles. Now, Thea," he chided with a brilliant smile as he took her hand. "Was it nice of you to let me squire you around the Exposition without your dropping so much as a hint that the real reason for your hurry to get to San Antonio was because you were getting married?"

Since their arrival at Hacienda de Veiga, Thea and Charles had more than enjoyed the food offered them. Breakfast always began with platters of exotic fruit, and moved on to scrambled eggs on wheat tortillas, an assortment of breads hot from the oven, and *chocolate con leche*—the delicious Mexican hot chocolate that replaced coffee at the end of most meals. Lunch was always a family affair with the three youngest de Veiga boys joining them in the dining room for the meal, while dinner was a sophisticated affair, the repast more representative of Paris than Latin America.

But none of those meals had been true preparation for the gala dinner of the anniversary fiesta. Extensions had been put in the already immense dining room table so that it was now in the shape of a double L, and was covered in a pure-gold embroidered tablecloth from Noel. The china service was Ceralene's rich, gold-encrusted Imperial pattern, the Baccarat crystal was a pattern that the firm kept for the exclusive order of only its wealthiest patrons, as was the heavy Christofle silver.

As their meal progressed from tiny Vera Cruz oysters to squash flower soup to pompano flamed with shrimps and mushrooms, and duckling roasted with blackberries, Thea was able to observe both Charles and Paul. As she ate and made conversation with her dinner companions, she noted how very much alike they were. Somehow, in light of all the events that had transpired, this discovery didn't surprise her. There was no facial resemblance, of course, but there was the same combination of grace, hidden steel, height and good manners that made them popular among the conservative people they were with.

There was a superb cold mango mousse for dessert, followed by a recreation of the de Veigas' wedding cake and, finally, when the last crumb had been consumed, all the guests filed into the main hall for the ceremony of the *piñata*, the highlight of all Mexican parties.

Made of colorful clay and festooned with silk ribbons, the donkey had a large jar inside which held all the presents. At children's parties it was candy and trinkets, but tonight, suspended from the ceiling were two *piñatas*, one holding favors for the gentlemen, the other for the ladies. Dona Imelda had explained to them that since the gifts came from Tiffany's, she did not wish to disturb the store's wrapping, and therefore had decided to use two clay donkeys.

According to tradition, the youngest guest was given the first chance to break the clay, and the honor went to Dona Imelda's seventeen-year-old niece, Victoria de la Garza, a delicate-looking, sweet, utterly delightful girl in a Worth debutante gown of white lumineuse with a silvery sheen and a full gathered skirt trimmed in deep white Chantilly lace and silver gauze ribbon. Amid much laughter and teasing, she was blindfolded, a cricket bat—a survivor of Don Renaldo's University days—placed in her hands, and with the guests cheering her on, she attempted to free the gifts from their resting place.

On her second try, the bat made contact with the donkey and, with a sharp crack, the clay parted and the familiar blue boxes tied with white ribbons fell onto the colorful, woven carpet.

There was much jostling and joking as the men each selected a box and Thea, standing across from Charles and Paul, noted with pride that both men waited until all the others had selected a box, and then took the two that remained on the floor.

The same procedure was repeated on the other *piñata* for the ladies, and Thea, like both the men in her life, waited until the other women had chosen among the robin's-egg blue boxes before she claimed the final box as her favor.

Every elegant accessory that Tiffany made, all in gold or silver, many of them gem-studded, had been purchased by the de Veigas for favors for their guests. There were repeated exclamations of delight as the men and women undid the ribbons and opened the boxes.

Both Charles and Paul made their way to Thea, and they unwrapped their favors together. Almost as if we're all great pals, Thea thought, all too aware that for her this evening had suddenly become tinged with an overtone of *menage a trois*.

345

Paul had a silver fountain pen, Charles a gold one, and Thea a small gold *poudrier*. They admired each other's favors and, as casually as possible, Thea asked, "Are you in Chihuahua on Embassy business, Paul?"

"As I said in St. Louis, an attaché's job is *very* routine. No, I'm deputizing for the Ambassador tonight. He was invited, but President Diaz requested his presence at a meeting this afternoon, and—"

"And you're the only ranking member of the staff he could trust to make the proper impression," Thea finished for him.

"Can you imagine Major Donovan here tonight?" Charles put in dryly.

"He'd start another Mexican-American war," Paul replied briefly.

"I'm sure the Ambassador will receive nothing but praise for your visit. Are you staying at the hacienda?"

"At the Palace Hotel in Chihuahua. I go back to the capital tomorrow," he responded as the last of the guests surged past them on their way back to the ballroom. "Mr. de Renille, would you object greatly if I had the next dance with Thea?"

Please say no, Thea begged silently. I don't want to dance with Paul. He's going to make some sort of trouble. I'm sure of it . . .

"Of course," Charles was saying politely. "I should have suggested it myself. I know you both must have a lot of catching up to do from the last time you saw each other in St. Louis."

"Did you enjoy your trip through Vera Cruz?"

"It's a very informative city," Paul said obliquely. "For instance, did you know, Thea, that in Vera Cruz, there's a five-dollar fine for killing *zopilotes?*"

"How remarkable. And what are *zopilotes?*"

"They're turkey buzzards. The city's full of them,

346

and they're used as scavengers to pick up after the street cleaners. Very inventive."

"Very repulsive. Please, Paul, I've just eaten!" Thea protested, but she was laughing.

"Well, in that case, you can't object to a little fresh air!"

The musicians were playing Scott Joplin's "Cascades," and Paul skillfully two-stepped with Thea to the edge of the ballroom, and led her out to the courtyard.

"It's good to see you laugh again, Thea," he said, his voice quiet, as they stopped beside the fountain.

"I laugh all the time. Remember St. Louis?"

"As if I could ever forget." He took her hand. "Are you very unhappy?"

"Yes," she told him without thinking, and then stared horror-struck at him, well aware that there was no way she could take her unconscious, impulsive, response back. "You wouldn't understand," she said at last.

"But I do."

"Let go of my hand, Paul. We might be seen and, as it is, I may have to do some explaining about that cute little comment you made to me earlier."

"From what I've heard, the de Veigas are thoroughly up-to-date."

"*That* expression can mean a lot of things!" she snapped back. "And even if Don Renaldo and Dona Imelda pass it off, the de la Garzas might not. They're conservatives of the oldest order and—"

"And you don't want them for one moment to assume you're anything but a radiant bride."

"Exactly!"

In the faint light provided by the Japanese lanterns, Thea could see a smile begin on Paul's face.

"It's all right, Thea. I know."

347

"Know what?" she began, and caught her breath, waiting for him to continue.

"All about your marriage, the reasons for it, and that in a few months—"

"Shut up!" she told him fiercely. "Don't you dare say another word."

"My dear Thea. My dear, sweet, honorable Thea." His voice was soft and his hands reached out to gently grasp her shoulders. "Be brave, my darling. In a few months you'll be a free woman again, and then we can be married. I love you, Thea."

As he spoke, his grasp on her tightened, and then Paul was kissing her. For a split second, Thea was too shocked to move. His embrace was inflexible, his mouth insistent, and he'd said the words she'd longed to hear. Only it wasn't Charles making love to her in the warm semi-darkness of the patio, it was Paul, and she didn't, couldn't, love him.

The reality unnumbed her brain, and Thea began to struggle to get free of his embrace. It was impossible, she was caught in a viselike grip, and finally, in one desperate move, Thea brought her right foot down and smashed in on his instep.

He gave a smothered exclamation of pain. "Darling—"

"From this moment on, I'm Mrs. de Renille to you, and don't ever forget it!" she blazed at him, her eyes shooting off sparks. "Whatever the reasons for this marriage, they're my business, not yours, and if you *ever* betray this secret again, I'll go straight to Colonel Miles, and he'll make sure you'll think about tonight an awful lot—while you spend your next assignment at some fort in Arizona eating dust!"

It was well after two in the morning before the musicians played "After The Ball," and the guests bid each other and their hosts good-night, and either left in their carriages, or retired to their rooms.

"Aren't you coming to bed?" Thea asked as she and Charles entered their suite and he flopped into his favorite wing chair and picked up a book from the table. "It's very late, and there's the celebratory mass at the Cathedral at ten—"

"I'm well aware of the time." Charles' eyes and voice were icy, and he undid his perfect white tie with one sharp tug. "When I feel ready to sleep, I'll come. Good-night, Thea."

Thea took a step toward him. "Please, Charles. I want to help you. I want to tell you—"

"And what makes you think I want to hear what you have to say?" he inquired harshly. "And the only help you can give me is by getting out of my sight!"

For a long minute, Thea met his gaze unblinkingly, her confusion and anger from her encounter with Paul compounding with her sudden fury at Charles.

"You bastard! You total, miserable bastard!" Even as she spoke, Thea couldn't believe her own rage. "When was the last time you cared about anyone but yourself?" she shouted at him, her eyes burning with tears, slamming the bedroom door closed and not caring if the entire hacienda heard what she thought of her husband.

"'I fell abruptly, then, into the love in which I longed to be ensnared . . . I secretly arrived at the bond of enjoying; and was joyfully bound . . . that I might be scourged with the burning rods of jealousy, suspicion, fear, anger, and strife.'"

Charles closed the biography of Saint Augustine that he was attempting to read and wearily closed his eyes. For the first time in his life he had been deliberately cruel to a woman, and he felt like a pig.

He'd regretted his first outburst at Thea the moment the words were out of his mouth, but his indomitable, unbending pride had kept him silent long after he should have begged her forgiveness and told her he loved her. Only hours earlier, when he'd seen Thea crossing the drawing room to stand beside him, the last of his pride had crumbled, and he'd decided his moment of truth had come. As soon as he could take Thea aside, this charade of anger and indifference would come to an end, and finally he could face the woman he loved honestly.

His plan had been perfect—only there had been no place in it for Captain Paul Merrill. He and Thea had talked about their respective visits to the Exposition, but she had never mentioned another man, only Colonel and Mrs. Miles.

And why should you be surprised? he questioned himself. Do you think Thea has spent her life sitting in a corner, waiting for you to make up your mind that you wanted to be married after all?"

Painfully, he remembered the comment his mother had made a year earlier when, once again, he had been telling her that he was not the marrying sort. His mother had only smiled and said, "Charles, you will continue to complain that you are not the marrying sort until the morning after your wedding night!"

Well, all his pretense was over, but it was for nothing. He'd suspected it the moment the young captain had appeared on the scene. And if he harbored any remaining doubts, they had vanished the moment he entered the courtyard. He'd come outside for a few moments of fresh air and privacy and, hidden behind one of the Moorish arches, he had become privy to a scene that froze his blood as it destroyed his dreams.

Charles knew that he either should have left immediately, or made his presence known, but their first words had cemented his feet to the tile and turned him into an inadvertent Peeping Tom.

He heard the words. Paul Merrill's avowals of love, and Thea's response, not returning his affection outright, always conscious of her responsibility, but never refusing his declarations. It was only when the captain moved to take Thea in his arms that he'd turned and gone swiftly back to the hacienda. He knew what the scene foretold, and he didn't have to see any more.

Now, as he sat in the armchair, burning with unspoken love and unfulfilled desire, he knew that Thea was in the bedroom crying from his attitude toward her, and it took every bit of iron self-control that he had not to go and comfort her. But to what end?

Somehow, Charles felt he was being punished. For what specific sin, he wasn't quite certain; possibly a combination of all transgressions, large and small, that he'd committed, beginning with the pride he was so tangled in. Instead of protecting and strengthening him, it had all worked against him. And now that he had found the one woman in the world he wanted to make a life with, she was in love with another man, and it didn't matter if he were going to have a new life or not, because Thea would never be at his side, sharing it with him.

It was late Saturday night and Thea was in bed, her face buried in the pillows to muffle her sobs. This was the second night in a row she'd cried herself into a state of exhaustion, and she reached under her pillows for a handkerchief.

You can't spend the rest of your life crying, Thea told herself as she blotted her streaming eyes. And if you thought crying was going to have any effect on Charles, were you ever wrong!

That wasn't the reason behind her crying fits. If she couldn't make Charles care for her by acting normally, her unhappiness certainly wouldn't rouse any hidden feelings he might have.

It's all downhill now, she thought, and her mind wandered back to earlier in the day when she and Charles had been among those who had attended the special mass that had commemorated the de Veigas' wedding anniversary. Sitting in the Cathedral, listening to the Archbishop of Chihuahua, the resonance of the prelate's voice, the smell of incense, and the flickering candles, brought back their wedding service so sharply that Thea's eyes had filled, and it was only Charles' unyielding profile and crystal-sharp responses to the mass, that kept her from breaking down. If he were merely cold and distant to her now, he would probably choke her if she cried publicly and drew attention to them.

To everyone that morning she was merely the charming and devoted Mrs. Charles de Renille, who was so *soignee* in a Lucile dress of soft white mousseline with medallions of Valenciennes lace set off by a twelve-strand choker of red coral with a cabochon coral clasp and a wide-brimmed white satin hat with a bow at the side of the crown. How many of those same people would imagine that, at this moment, instead of lying ecstatically in her husband's arms, holding each other close and exchanging words of love, she was alone in this huge bed, ready to cry again?

I must have fallen asleep, Thea thought, opening her eyes again, wondering what time it was, and what the noise filling the room could possibly be.

It's running water, stupid, she told herself harshly. Charles must be taking a bath before he comes to bed and—

Thea's thoughts froze as she turned her head toward

Charles' dressing room—and a clear view of her husband as he prepared for his bath.

A strange sort of thrill began to spread through Thea as she forced herself to lie still as she watched Charles undress. *He thinks I'm asleep.* The transparent thought flew through her mind, along with the realization that what she was doing was voyeurism, pure and simple.

Charles would never do that to you, she thought severely, and then she remembered all the times early in their stay, right up until that fateful Friday morning, that he had stood at the door to *her* dressing room, watching as she sat—albeit fully dressed—at her dressing table, making up her face.

Turn around is fair play, even if it isn't very equal, her mind rationalized as she watched Charles, in his shirtsleeves, remove his cufflinks.

Thea had been mentally speculating about Charles' unclad body almost from the beginning of their relationship. She supposed that, in a way, it was all perfectly normal. After all, she was a healthy young woman with straightforward instincts. Charles was more than slightly good-looking and, when it got down to basics, she wasn't going to be too terribly shocked.

As he stripped down, revealing more and more of his perfectly made body, Thea's mind became a jumble of thoughts that mixed desire with curiosity, and practicality with a touch of humor.

Oh, he is careful . . . doesn't throw his clothes around . . . not the sort who needs a valet standing at his elbow and picking up after him . . . what absolutely awful-looking underwear men have to wear . . . I shouldn't look any more . . . his privacy . . . oh, damn his privacy . . . he's my husband and I've earned this . . .

Thea, in theory, had never cared for the sort of man whose body hair made him resemble a furry animal, and had also never understood why some women thought that a man's masculinity ran in direct proportion with the amount of hair on his chest. She had always been well aware of the fact that when she fell in love, there wouldn't be any choice as to her lover's hirsute attributes. And now, as she watched Charles slowly remove his last garments, Thea felt fate was taking its final revenge on her—he was just how she dreamed.

He's beautiful, she thought, seeing him unclothed for the first time, her eyes travelling up and down his tall, slender body with the muscular arms and legs of a natural horseman. He's a statue come to life—and living proof that the human body is a wondrous, restorative machine. Charles came back from the brink, he's made to be loved, but he's never going to be mine . . .

She was just used to seeing Charles in his natural state when he switched off the light in the dressing room and went into the bathroom, out of her view. The running water was turned off and, in the silence, Thea buried her face in the pillows, desolation mixing with desire. She had waited years to feel this way about one special man, only she had expected that those feelings of love, passion and companionship would be returned. It was just her luck, of course, just the way her life had to run, that the polite mask Charles had worn in the beginning was a false front that concealed his loathing of having to take part in this assignment—and of her.

By late Monday morning, it was as if the anniversary fiesta had never taken place.

"This is not like the old days," Dona Imelda told Thea as they cut flowers in the garden. "When I was a girl, guests would arrive the week before a fiesta and stay for the week following, but now—" Dona Imelda cut several white perfumer's roses. "It's the modern life, I'm afraid. No one has as much time as they used to. Now it's all business, business, business."

Although she agreed with her hostess, this morning Thea was too wretched to pay attention to Dona Imelda. Hacienda de Veiga was the perfect honeymoon spot, if only . . .

"Are you happy, Theodosia?" Dona Imelda inquired, and her soft, concerned voice broke through Thea's thoughts like a gun shot, and to her own horror, she burst into tears.

Dona Imelda, who had been watching Thea carefully for her reaction, put her arms around the younger woman and comforted her. She let her cry it all out, and when Thea was calm again, she told the older woman everything, not sparing any detail.

"I've shocked you terribly, haven't I? You and Don Renaldo open your home to us and give us your hospitality, thinking Charles and I are a honeymoon couple, passionately in love, who just happen to be doing something for Washington on the side. Somehow I'll face whatever happens between Charles and me, but I don't think I'll ever get over the fact we disgraced you and Don Renaldo."

"Disgraced us?" Dona Imelda looked thoroughly puzzled. "How could you and Charles possibly bring shame on us?"

"By my government's machinations. Everything looked so easy on paper."

"It generally does. I think Renaldo may know more than he says, but that isn't important. Only you and Charles matter, and your future together."

"Future? We have no future together, Dona Imelda. I've told you all that. Charles—"

"How could Charles fail to care for you?" She

handed Thea a lace-edged handkerchief. "Now, stay here and rest and try not to distress yourself. There are things I must see to—"

She was gone in a swirl of white, and Thea continued to sit on the bench, her heart turned to a lead weight, pulling apart a perfect white rose, petal by petal, until a familiar voice, sounding very grave, broke into her misery.

"Imelda tells me you're very unhappy and I'm to blame," Charles said, sitting down beside her. "I think your government made a mistake sending us here in order to establish a proper cover. If we had gone directly to the capital, we would have been done that much sooner, and you would not have to endure my company much longer. Please try to bear with me," he went on in a stifled voice. "As soon as we get back to San Antonio there will be an annulment, and you'll be free—"

She listened dully to his words, noting the expression on his face. In his eyes wasn't anger but sadness. "You big idiot," Thea told him miserably, not caring about keeping her secret. "Don't you see anything at all? I don't want an annulment! I love you! I have from the beginning, and I wanted you to love me, but—"

Thea was prepared for any number of reactions from Charles, but not the disbelief that spread over his face and, as her voice trailed off, he stood up and pulled her to her feet with him. "Do you mean that, Thea?" The combination of expectation and delight that she'd first seen on their train ride into Mexico, along with a hesitant joy, was transfiguring his face. "I love you, too . . ."

It was the warm spring after the frozen winter, it was sunlight and green grass and newly opened flowers. It was the end of all the darkness, doubt and pain, all lost in the first kiss that neither of them would ever forget.

His mouth parted slowly, reluctantly from hers, and Thea began to cover his face with her kisses. His arms were securely around her, holding her close, and she moved her hands along his shoulders and clasped them behind his neck, pulling back slightly so she could look at him.

"All this time . . . it's been awful . . . I've been so afraid that all you wanted to do was get away from me and disappear back to France in a cloud of dust," she said joyfully, still not quite believing, and kissed him again, experiencing once more the beautiful feel of his mouth against hers.

"No, dearest, no!" He kissed her back, all his pain and uncertainty fading, replaced by far more pleasant—and demanding—emotions. "I thought you and Captain Merrill—I couldn't stand it any longer Saturday night . . . I was going to tell you how I felt . . . that I never meant the things I said . . . but when I saw you together in the courtyard—I thought you loved him—"

"Whatever gave you a stupid idea like that?"

"What he said— What you said— What I saw—"

Thea felt the laughter bubbling inside her. "And what exactly *did* you see?"

"You and Captain Merrill by the fountain . . . he said he loved you . . . and once the annulment was granted . . ." A dark look passed over his face. "He kissed you, and I left. I couldn't stand it another moment."

"It's too bad you didn't," Thea couldn't resist telling him. "Another minute more and you would have seen me stamp on Paul Merrill's foot and tell him what I thought of his marriage proposal! Is that why you've been so awful to me over the past two days?"

"Yes," he admitted shamefacedly. "I thought you were sorry for me. And then, when I realized my love

357

for you was greater than my pride, I saw you and Merrill." His arms tightened around her waist. "I thought it was my punishment. That I'd have to give you up."

In response, Thea molded herself against him, dissolving in delight at the feel of his supple body so close to hers. "Were you really going to be that much of a coward and give me up without a fight? The only man I want is you. I was never going to agree to the annulment. I want us to belong to each other, but I was so afraid that if I tried you'd reject me."

"I couldn't do that, not ever," Charles murmured as their lips touched. "Thea, I don't care— It isn't important— But have you— I mean—"

"Considering the grounds for annulment, I'd have to be," she said, and began to laugh. "That's another reason I wouldn't have agreed to the annulment. No man like you should ever have to be charged with non-consummation—it's not fair. But to get back to your discreet inquiry—I'm not particularly ignorant about anything, in case you haven't guessed already. And you?"

"It's been seven years—except for a . . . a one night . . ." Charles let his voice trail off, feeling his face grow warm.

Thea laughed delightedly at his reaction. "Are you trying to confess to a one night fling with a chorus girl at the New Amsterdam Theatre?"

"She wasn't a chorus girl, she was a featured player in a Clyde Fitch musical. And it was in Boston, at the Touraine Hotel."

"My poor darling. For that confession, later on, you're going to do everything to me that you did to her!"

Charles colored again. "I'm very much afraid it was the other way around."

"Then so much the better for me!" Thea gave him a considering look. "Charles, you're *not* planning to be one of those husbands who gets so sticky about his male prerogatives, are you?"

He denied her question in the only way possible and, when their kiss ended, Charles lifted Thea into his arms and carried her across the garden, up the stairs to the gallery, and into their bedroom.

"We have such a beautiful bed, and I'm so tired of sleeping on the edge of it," Thea said as Charles set her down on her feet. "What do you say to that?"

"That I love you with all my heart and soul. I adore you, and I'm going to make love to you," he said softly, and his hands went to the fastenings of her handkerchief linen dress, carefully separating the tiny hooks and eyes, his hands moving with tantalizing slowness down her back, a motion that left Thea gasping and pressing closer to Charles, triumph mixing with desire as she felt his body harden.

Her dress fell into a circle at her feet, and Thea kicked off her shoes, pushing the dress aside and putting her hands on Charles' shoulders as he skillfully unhooked her stays.

Free of the short length of satin and whalebone, constricting even though she didn't really lace, Thea pushed Charles' suit jacket off his shoulders and unknotted his tie.

"We should be a little more even," she murmured, her heart racing, filled with more emotions than she could name.

"But not equal," he replied thickly, his fingers moving lightly along her collarbone. "You're too beautiful."

As his fingers untied the satin ribbons of her camisole, Thea felt herself dissolve in a long wave of sensation that crested as his mouth closed tenderly over one breast and then the other, his tongue teasing and circling each nipple until it peaked.

He removed the last of her clothes but, with his hands at his belt, Charles hesitated.

"You should have closed your dressing room door last night," Thea said, immediately divining the reason behind his sudden fit of modesty. "I wasn't asleep, I was awake, and I saw you—every beautiful inch. I almost got out of bed then and there."

"I wish you had."

"I thought you'd hate me even more."

"I never hated you. The only thing I despise is my pride and all the wrong assumptions I made because of it," he told her honestly and, a moment later he was free of his clothes, his hands at her waist. "Are you frightened?"

"It's only you." Thea put her arms around his neck. With no clothes encumbering them, she reveled in her first real contact with him, pressing herself against the hard, cool expanse of his chest and the muscular tautness of his thighs. "Much better than oil on canvas or carved marble or cold bronze. I've been around too many museums too long. You're much nicer."

"So are you."

"Then kiss me and prove it," she said, and they merged into an embrace that blotted out everything else. They reached the bed, their bodies fused tightly together in the first rush of passion, their need creating a new world that was theirs alone.

It had been worth all the waiting, Thea thought, moving easily into an endless sea of delight as Charles' mouth explored hers, and his hands caressed each new portion of her, moving lower in their intimate exploration of her body.

360

There was one last barrier between them, and Charles broke through it so swiftly that brief pain came, went and quickly gave way to the give-and-take pleasure of their lovemaking.

Her hands moved down his spine to the small of his back, and she moved with him, each thrust, each movement of his hips turning her blood to liquid mercury. His supple body wooed hers, and together they made their own world of delight and exhilaration where the ultimate explosion from the depths of their beings exploded in a final burst of joy that ended their old lives forever.

"I think your Major Donovan would have preferred us to remain celibate," Charles said hours later as they lay together in the center of the bed.

Nestled in the love and security of his arms, Thea laughed. "He should have thought of that beforehand. Donovan has no imagination," she told him, running her fingers along his side. "He probably thinks I don't have any knowledge of sex, and you aren't interested in it. Ergo, we were safe."

"He's going to know the moment he looks at us, and will probably throw a fit. Will you mind?" Charles asked. He felt his desire rise and his arms tightened demandingly.

"To hell with Donovan," Thea told him joyfully a second before his mouth came down on hers.

Ever since their first night together, Charles had slept with the precision of an effigy of a young knight on his tomb. Stretched out on his back, he'd slept rigidly, his chest barely moving as he breathed. He was still on his back, but his hair was over his forehead, one arm flung over his head, and Thea, observing this

361

transformation, was torn between kissing him awake and continuing to watch him while he slumbered on, peaceful and as free of strain as a young child.

She was still getting used to the fact that they'd found each other at last. Through all of the obstacles and stumbling blocks, their love had finally pushed aside all barriers, and their passionate need had been mutual.

Thea smiled, mentally reliving their first passion. She had been willing to go through any adjustment, from discomfort to outright pain, just to have Charles, to feel him inside her, to have his love in the most intimate way possible, whatever the resulting consequences.

Thea suppressed a smile as she recalled a conversation she'd had with Alix only a little more than a year earlier. Alix had been in the last weeks of her pregnancy, marking time until the baby came, and Thea had been spending the afternoon with her. It seemed only natural, as their conversation moved from one topic to another, that it should inevitably touch on love and sex, pleasure and men.

"What's it like, Alix?"

"Eventually—this." Alix smiled, indicating her condition.

"Be serious!"

"I am, believe me. It's strictly subjective," she went on. "Thea, do you have someone special, or have you—?"

"Oh, I'm still as pure as the driven snow—technically speaking. Let's just say I'm interested in some . . . future research. What do men like? I'm so afraid that when it happens, no matter how much in love I am, I'll be awful . . ."

Alix had understood, and their conversation from

then on, if overheard by a devotee of Anthony Comstock, could have gotten them both arrested, but it served to fill in gaps in Thea's knowledge, providing her with insights into a man's chemical make-up and a woman's responsibility in love.

Now, fifteen months later, just for fun, Thea began to count off the days and, a moment later, a feeling of stupefaction fell over her. No, it was impossible. It couldn't be. She'd made a mistake. With deliberate slowness, she counted on her fingers a second time, then a third, with the same configuration coming up.

Alix had told her that it was one of nature's little quirks that the time of month when a woman found her greatest pleasure and satisfaction in the act of love, was also the period in which she was most likely to conceive. It was a truth tempered by a good many things, such as love for one's partner, and physical well-being. But as Thea lay beside Charles, she realized that if she were likely to have a baby nine months hence, today, October 10th, was the best day for it to begin.

And what a beginning we've made, she thought, laughter bubbling inside her. Of course, I might not be, there are no guarantees, and I'll know soon enough but, in the meantime . . .

She leaned over Charles, her lips brushing against his forehead, his eyelids, the bridge of his nose, and lastly his mouth, kissing him awake.

"For a moment, I thought I was dreaming."

"Resign yourself, my love, your days of carefree bachelorhood are over. And, as of a few hours ago, you made very certain that an annulment is quite out of the question!" she teased between kisses.

"I've burnt all my bridges, and I can't remember the last time I was so happy." Charles' hands went to her hair. "I forgot all about taking down your hair. I couldn't last another minute . . ."

"Neither could I," she murmured as her hair fell around her shoulders and Charles drew her down, their arms and legs entwining in a perfect tangle. "And I can't now. After all, third time lucky . . ."

Part Two

Mexico City—Laredo—New York
October-December, 1904

One sometimes finds what one is not looking for.
Sir Alexander Fleming

In great affairs, the head signifies nothing without
the heart.

Anon.

The best way to hold a man is in your arms.
Mae West

Military intelligence is a contradiction in terms.
Groucho Marx

Chapter Eleven

October 15, 1904

"'The queen o' fairies, she caught me, in this green hill to dwell.'"

Thea opened her eyes to find Charles, wearing a soft white shirt open at the neck, the sleeves rolled up above his elbows, a pair of white duck tennis trousers and tennis shoes, stretched out full length alongside her, his topaz-colored eyes full of love.

"That sounds so beautiful," Thea said, clasping her arms around his neck and drawing him down to her. "Have I really captured you?"

"Forever . . . and you're the best thing that ever happened to me!"

It was five days later, five days spent in near-total privacy as they loved and learned about each other. Charles told her about his first days in New York, about Brooks Brothers and the Laskys where he'd made an idiot of himself in front of Ethel Barrymore. He wanted her to know about the books he'd translated and his win at the Kentucky Derby and how the dinner at the White House had ended in a way he had never expected. In return, Thea told him all about her own life-changing night at the White House, her first assignment in Budapest, her first real client and the ones that had come after. They were besotted with each other, and the only time they left their

367

suite was to join the de Veigas for dinner. Their breakfast and lunch were brought up to them. But, except for that first night together when nothing short of the hacienda burning down could have gotten them out of the bedroom, they always dressed properly and joined their hosts for a few hours every evening.

But now they were expanding their horizons again. And on this unusually warm Saturday in October, they'd taken a picnic basket and gone out to the turquoise-tiled swimming pool at the end of the garden.

Surrounded by a high brick wall, this section of the garden was completely secluded, and beautifully landscaped with rich shrubbery, fragrant gardenia trees and ancient shade trees just made to picnic under.

Despite the extensive wardrobe she travelled with, Thea hadn't packed a bathing costume and, even if she had, she told Charles when they decided to go swimming, she wouldn't let him see her in the ghastly looking thing. Fortunately, Charles had two suits with him, one of which he'd never worn; made of knit jersey, they were the basic tank suits that swimmers in competitions wore, and the style was far more flattering to her than the cumbersome costumes that women were consigned to wear.

Both were strong, enthusiastic swimmers, and for a few hours they were more interested in athletics than romance, but that didn't last for more than a few minutes once they were out of the pool and back at the shade tree where they'd left their picnic things and clothes. Charles had already stripped off his suit and was toweling himself dry when he looked at Thea who stood provocatively in front of him, her smile both an invitation and a challenge. The wet, bright blue jersey clung to every curve, and her breasts were clearly outlined by the clinging material.

Thea watched the expression she'd come to know so

well over the past days form on his face, the expression she wanted to see. Tiny beads of perspiration formed on his upper lip and on his temples, and his towel fell at his feet as he reached out to Thea, hooking his thumbs around the straps of the suit, pulling it off her in one swift motion.

Their mouths met hungrily, and their hands moved over each other as Charles lowered them to the blanket. It was not a moment for words, only for mutual desire. They made love simply, directly, and when it was over they held each other closely. They were still too new to their passion to take for granted the ecstatic heights their bodies achieved.

There had been one more dip in the pool, and then they helped each other to dress. Now Thea pulled him close for another kiss.

"Are you in the mood to discuss a few things?" he asked, sitting up so he could have a better view of Thea, looking like a hybrid tea rose in a pale pink handkerchief linen dress. "I've been going over my finances."

"I can practically hear your mind working, rather like a ticker tape, reading out all your income and expenses," Thea laughed.

"It's at moments like this that I'm very glad you didn't meet me when I first got to New York," Charles told her, and recounted his financial misadventures, finding them funny for the first time. "After I finally found out what my seventy-five thousand dollar letter-of-credit meant, and Bill gave me an investment portfolio, I wrote my family to find out exactly how they reached that particular amount in the first place. It turns out I'm not quite the impoverished youngest son after all."

"It wouldn't matter to me if you were. I think you're smart enough to make your own fortune."

"Which is much better than your saying you'd be happy to live with me in a tenement," Charles responded cheerfully, opening the bottle of champagne that was in the picnic basket. "But, nonetheless, I can't afford a house."

"Good," Thea said, holding out the glasses. "I don't want one, and we really don't need all that waste space."

"I do have a house," Charles informed her, "but it's in Paris, on the Avenue Montaigne. We can decide what we want to do with it later. My mother's uncle, Pierre de Hautraviant, left it to me, along with most of the furnishings." He sipped his champagne. "I didn't even know about it until recently. There's also an income—about three thousand a year."

"Pounds, dollars or francs?"

"Pounds."

Thea calculated quickly. "That's very nice."

"It also turns out that I have a rather sizable inheritance from my father. I'll show you Guy's letter later. He explains all the details in it."

"When you found out how much money you'd brought with you . . . were you afraid that you'd been . . . paid off?" Thea ventured cautiously.

"It crossed my mind," Charles smiled. "It's funny what a difference a few months made in my life. If I'd known how much money I had when I got to New York, I would have felt like a remittance man. Instead, because I'd found some sort of balance in my life, all that mattered was to make some sense of my sudden windfall."

"Charles, are you sure that you don't mind staying on in New York?"

"No, not as long as we're together. But right now I think we should decide where in New York we'd like to live. Are you interested in the Dakota?"

"Not particularly," Thea told him truthfully. "Do you have any idea how much money Henry and Alix spent in modernizing their new apartment? I'd rather we began

370

with something more modern." For a moment, Thea paused, mentally reviewing all of the city's better new apartment buildings. "What about 667 Madison Avenue? It's well-located, and just what I'd like us to start out with."

"So would I," Charles said, thinking pleasantly of the ten-story limestone-faced apartment building, just two years old, that graced the corner of Madison Avenue and 61st Street. Newton and Esme Phipps lived there, as did Jimmy and Kate Seligman, and Charles was familiar with their apartments. "I'd like to move into a building where we have friends."

"That's the best way," Thea agreed, and added, "just imagine the fun I'm going to have decorating it."

"A living advertisement," Charles said, putting his arms around her. "Do you think we'll be able to move in by summer?"

"Summer?" Thea echoed indignantly. "What kind of a decorator do you think I am? With any luck, providing there's an apartment available, and providing we're out of Mexico by Thanksgiving, we should be moved in by Christmas." Thea smiled at Charles' expression. "I can see you don't know much about decorating."

"Until Henry and Alix, I never even knew anyone who moved!" Charles exclaimed, a faint sense of panic passing over him.

"The trick is to treat an apartment—or a house, for that matter—as a shell," Thea explained gently, sensing Charles' temporary confusion. "First of all, it has to be painted, and then the floors polished. Esme, Kezia or Kate will see to it for us and, once that's taken care of, and we're back in town, we can see to the furniture and rugs," Thea said, and began to laugh. "I sound just like I do with one of my clients!"

"No wonder they're devoted to you. I'm enthralled. But," he added, drawing her close, "have any of your clients ever expressed their appreciation for your talent like this?"

"I certainly hope not," Thea murmured as their kiss ended and she put her head on his shoulder. "Charles, would you mind a suggestion?"

"Anything at all," he whispered, his mouth moving along the side of her neck.

"Let's go away."

"We *are* away."

"No, I mean out of Mexico."

Charles slowly raised his head. "You mean this?"

"Of course I do. I've been thinking about it for the past few days. All we have to do is cable Major Donovan in Mexico City and Colonel Miles in Washington that we've changed our minds; they have no hold over us. We can go back to San Antonio, visit with Nela and Morgan, and pay a call on the Archbishop."

Charles gave a low laugh. "I have an idea that when he learns we decided to, as he said, 'realize our vows,' His Grace won't be too surprised."

"Somehow I don't think so either. And then," she went on, "after San Antonio, we can go to California—first to Santa Barbara to stay with Regina and Ian, and then up to San Francisco. We won't have to go back to New York until we're ready." Thea hesitated for a moment before continuing. "Of course, if you don't care for that, I have an alternative. We can go to New Orleans."

"Is there something special there?"

"Yes . . . the French Line." She looked unblinkingly at him. "You could take me to France—to your family."

Thea's words swirled around him, and Charles found himself thinking about what it would be like to return to Normandy with Thea. It would be the end of October by the time they got there, and the hunting season would be under way. Thoughts of day-long hunts with packs of white and brown hounds, the riders mounted on the finest horses, filled his mind. Guests from France and England would be filling the *manoir*, and days in the fields would be followed by dinners and hunt balls. For a minute, he thought about being there with Thea, of their being in his room, making love in the bed where he had recovered from his breakdown. He dwelled on all the possibilities—the problems, the pleasures, and the responsibilities.

"No," he said at last, and watched with surprise as Thea's eyes filled with tears.

"You don't want to take me to your family," she said flatly, accusingly. "Are you worried that, even though your mother was nice to me when I was sixteen, having me turn up nine years later as an unexpected daughter-in-law is quite another matter entirely? Is that why you're so happy to stay in New York? So you don't have to explain your agnostic American bride?"

"Never—don't even *think* such a thing!" he exclaimed, horrified. "My brothers are going to ask me how I ever got so lucky and, as for my mother—she's going to adore you. She'll give you jewelry, and all sorts of advice on how to put up with me!"

Thea finally gave him a faint smile. "What an awful outburst. I'm sorry, Charles, truly."

"No, it's my fault. I should have explained." Charles took her hands in his. "I love both of your ideas, and there's nothing I'd like better than for us to either go to California, or to France, but—" He took a deep breath. "I've always felt so useless, Thea. There was nothing for me when I was younger, and even the Church, the haven for men like me, was of no use."

"If it had been, I don't think I would have liked the results very much."

"We never would have met, then," he hedged, wondering when—or if—the time would come when he could tell Thea that that eventuality, with or without his breakdown, would never have happened. "I've been through fire and water, but if I had to do it because you were there at the end for me, that's the way it had to be. I've finally begun to make some sense out of the life I nearly destroyed but, if we don't go on to Mexico City, nothing will ever really be right. There'll be that loose thread hanging over us for all our lives. I want to do one thing right from beginning to end. I want us to have a new life together, and this is our last payment, our finishing with the past."

Thea accepted his statement quietly. "I *do* understand, and you're right. If we went away now, first I'd feel relieved, but eventually I'd feel the same way you do," she said, reaching up to smooth back his hair. "'I know thou art religious, and hast a thing within thee called conscience. With twenty popish tricks and ceremonies, which I have seen thee careful to observe.'"

To her surprise, Charles began to laugh so hard that he had to abandon his attempt to kiss her.

"You're perfect, Thea, absolutely perfect. And if I ever forget why I fell in love with you, just remind me that there was no way I could resist a woman who quotes *Titus Andronicus* at me!"

"I don't think I ever heard the name Theodosia before. Is it kept within your family?" Charles asked an hour later as they ate their lunch.

"No, I admit it's a little unusual, but I've come across my name a few times. But I don't think I'll ever forget the first time, though," Thea told him. "I was fourteen, and Daddy was writing *In The Footsteps of Lewis and Clark*. Charles, how good is your American history?"

"Not too good," he admitted with a grin. "But I know about Lewis and Clark and the Northwest Passage and Sacajawea, who was the wife of the half-breed

374

voyager Charbonneau."

"That's better than a lot of people can do," she said admiringly. "But to get back to my story—I read all of the research books, papers and letters that Daddy had collected, and I found out a lot of details that weren't taught in history class at Brearley. Did you ever hear of Aaron Burr?"

"The man who shot Alexander Hamilton in a duel?"

"The very same. At any rate, Burr had a daughter named Theodosia, and she fell in love with Meriwether Lewis. He was Thomas Jefferson's secretary and, according to all reports, was handsome and pernickety and—"

"Per—what?"

"Pernickety. It's an old word. Generally it means careful and prickly and a little bit fussy. Lewis' life was lived in a rather masculine context—rather like yours. He fell in love with Theodosia Burr, but her father, who would have liked to be king of America—or at least President—had a better match in mind for his beloved daughter in the person of John Alston, a Carolina rice planter."

"So their love affair ended?"

"More or less. They managed to see each other intermittently, that much is certain, but they both came to terrible ends. Theodosia, along with her young son, was lost in an accident at sea, and Lewis—" Thea shuddered. "In 1807, he was appointed governor of Louisiana, and two years later, in a log cabin on the Old Natchez Trace, he either committed suicide, or was murdered by John Griner, the man who owned the local tavern, for reasons unknown, or best left undiscovered."

"How tragic."

"I cried for days when I read all of this, and when I fell in love with you, and it seemed so hopeless, I thought that through some quirk of history, their story was going to be ours. Not the gory end but that, no matter how much we loved each other, we were going to be separated. I always felt a special bond with Theodosia Burr, and every time I looked at you I'd think this is how she felt about Meriwether Lewis, and even though I don't have a conniving father, my life isn't going to be any happier than hers was."

"Almost a hundred years since they came to their ends," Charles mused, taking Thea into his arms. "Don't cry, please. I don't think either of them would want you to take on their pain."

Thea clung to Charles. "I heard this story at a very impressionable age and carried it around far too long, but I honestly thought it might end up being our story also. It isn't now. We've changed the ending."

"They're not us," Charles agreed. "Not at all. We're going to be a grand and happy story, Thea."

Tired, happy and just a little bit wiser about each other, they didn't return to the hacienda until the late afternoon. Turning over their picnic paraphernalia and damp bathing suits to the waiting servants, Thea and Charles returned to their suite, arms around each other's waists.

"Do we have time to rest before dinner?"

"Of course we do—as long as we don't sleep," Thea told him with an arch look as they opened the door.

The first thing to come into their line of vision was the unmistakable yellow telegraph envelope propped up against a flower-filled silver vase on the sitting room's central table.

They looked at each other, the warm golden aura surrounding them slowly fading, replaced by a chill feeling.

"It *would* come today." Thea's voice was tight. "I'd almost convinced myself it wasn't going to turn up at all."

"Do you want to open it?"

Thea handed Charles the envelope. "The government's terribly proper about this. It's addressed to you."

Charles held the telegram for a brief moment, said a silent prayer and opened the envelope, allowing himself, for one small second, to think like Thea, to hope it would say anything but what it did.

LOOKING FORWARD TO RECEIVING YOU BOTH UPON ARRIVAL IN MEXICO STOP HOPE COMING PART OF HONEYMOON AS PLEASANT AND PROFITABLE AS FIRST STOP READY TO ROLL OUT RED CARPET
                         CLAYTON, AMBASSADOR

Chapter Twelve

October 17, 1904

Mr. Elston Harper
In Care Of American Legation
Mr. Iddings—Consul-General
Sharia Shawarbi Basha 5
Cairo, Egypt

Married Charles de Renille September 24 STOP We
are ecstatically happy STOP For time being we can
be reached care of Sanz Hotel Mexico City STOP
Letter to follow STOP Love

Thea

Comtesse Adrian de Renille
Haras de L'Soigneuse
Lisieux, France

J'ai epouser Mademoiselle Theodosia Harper sur 24
September dans la plus stricte intimite pres
L'Archeveque de San Antonio Texas ARRET
Procede a Mexico City pour lune de miel a Sanz
Hotel ARRET Lettre volonte suivre ARRET Laissez

battre votre coeur—laissez vous aimer—laissez
faire le destin—la vie n'est pas aussi triste qu'on
l'avait jugee ARRET Avec mes affectueuses pen-
sees Maman

Charles

Lord and Lady Henry Thorpe
The Dakota
1 West 72nd Street
New York, New York
USA

We were married September 24 at the Cathedral
San Fernando in San Antonio STOP Nela and
Morgan did the necessary STOP Please place
announcement in Town and Country STOP If
asked please say you introduced us STOP Any
plausible story will do STOP Ask Newton Phipps
about availability of apartment at 667 Madison
STOP Please address all replies to us at Sanz Hotel
Mexico City STOP Expect to return approximately
15 December STOP We have never been so happy
STOP All our love

Thea and Charles

Mr. and Mrs. Morgan Browne
111 Johnson Street
San Antonio, Texas
USA

Wonderful things do happen STOP Thank you with

both our hearts for starting us off right STOP Eager to see wedding pictures STOP Please forward to Sanz Hotel STOP Will write all the news from Mexico City STOP We love you both

Thea and Charles

Miss Amy Collier
In Care Of Theodosia Harper
Antiques and Interiors
317 Fifth Avenue
New York, New York
USA

On September 24 in San Antonio I married the most wonderful man in the world STOP If you feel any mail needs my personal attention please forward to me care of Sanz Hotel Mexico City STOP Otherwise continue to do your usual wonderful job STOP We expect to be home for Christmas STOP Will cable in advance

Mrs. Charles de Renille

"There's one telegram I wish we could send," Thea told Charles as they left Chihuahua's Western Union man with a stack of yellow cable sheets to send off, and moved off toward the Mexico City train that was waiting on the track, nervously expelling blasts of steam as they walked along the platform toward the de Veigas' private car. "But there's no way to send it privately, and on an open wire it'll be seen by too many pairs of eyes."

380

"The President will find out sooner or later," Charles assured her. "But if you could have sent it, what would you have said?"

"Oh, something like 'I don't know how much help we'll be to you, Mr. President, but you're certainly one terrific matchmaker!' "

Chapter Thirteen

October 17-20, 1904

The thirty-six hour journey from Chihuahua to Mexico City was everything that their trip from El Paso wasn't. This time there were no stolen looks while they pretended to read books that couldn't hold their attentions. This passage was spent in the brass bed of the master stateroom, loving each other while the primitive, untamed beauty of Mexico's countryside flashed by them.

Inevitably, their parting from the de Veigas had been hard on all of them, and at their final breakfast together Don Renaldo, always the perfect host, kept things on an even keel, informing them of the letters of introduction he had written on their behalf to relatives, family friends and to his clubs.

"I'm sure the Jockey Club, the Reforma Athletic Club and the University Club will be more than happy to welcome you as a temporary member, and all the national clubs have reciprocal memberships," he informed them.

"Señor Mariscal assured me that the library of the British Club is a fine place to work," Charles replied, silently wondering if he would ever use the as-yet-unseen library for any real work. "I only wish that for Thea's sake the University Club had a women's division."

"At least the American Club is enlightened enough to

382

have some rooms set aside for their female members," Thea pointed out. "As long as we don't have to attend any bull fights—"

"Absolutely not," Dona Imelda reassured them quickly. "Among our set, it's quite declasse, and President Diaz is trying to have them abolished— although without success, I fear."

Their breakfast concluded, Thea and Charles checked over their belongings one last time, and then it was time to leave.

"Hopefully, we shall see you again in a few weeks," Dona Imelda said as she embraced them in farewell.

"I have some business matters that need looking into," Don Renaldo said, "and it's been a long time since we spent All Saints and All Souls Day in the capital."

"Besides which, the French Embassy's first gala of the winter season takes place the following week, and I've informed Renaldo that this year we are going to attend," Dona Imelda put in firmly but humorously as they saw them into the waiting landau. Their final conversation ended on a decidedly cheerful note, and their last view of Hacienda de Veiga was of the sun gleaming off the red tile roof and of Don Renaldo and Dona Imelda standing in front of the stone fountain, waving until the carriage turned out of sight.

The actual writing of their respective telegrams took very little time and, once again, they were in the de Veigas' luxurious private railroad car—with one important difference.

"The moment has come for me to do everything to you that your actress in Boston did," Thea announced meaningfully closing the door to the stateroom dominated by the brass bed, thoughtfully turned down and waiting for them.

They were free of their clothes and between the lace-edged linen sheets before the train was properly out of

383

the station.

Thea knelt beside Charles on the mattress, placing small kisses over his face, brushing his hair back from his forehead. "Was it like this . . . ? And this . . . ? And this . . . ?"

"Just like that . . . only better," he got out after she kissed him fully. Her mouth moved lower, and lower still, apparently intent on kissing every inch of him. Her tongue moved around his navel, tracing a circle of darting fire. Charles groaned and reached blindly backwards to weave the fingers of one hand around the headboard's brass design while he threw another hand over his eyes.

Thea took her time, waiting until he was burning hard outside and melting inside, her exploring fingers and adoring mouth turning the sensual tables on him. *A good rule works both ways.* The old cliche flashed through his mind. He'd never thought of it in terms of physical pleasure before. And then, as Thea lowered herself onto his throbbing maleness, he didn't think again until long after the final whirlwind of pleasure had overtaken them both.

"*Where* did you learn to do *that?*" Charles questioned thickly, amused, pulling Thea closely against his damp, depleted body.

She threw one leg over his hip. "*The New England Journal of Medicine,*" she quipped, still lightheaded from that final climax. "Alix gives me all her back copies—as well as additional pieces of information which I didn't have much use for until recently." She cuddled closer to him. "I've been waiting an awful long time to try it all out on you. Oh, Charles, what the hell took you so long to say you love me?"

"Because, like most alleged scholars, I had any number of blind spots to overcome. The first being that *you* love *me*, not my name, or my family, or even because

384

I'd been so ill and was therefore more vulnerable than other men."

"Suppose we'd met nine years ago?"

"The circumstances would have been different, but the result would have been the same. I would have fallen in love with you no matter where or when we met. We were inevitable—only that wait would have been much longer than the one we just went through," he said, laughing softly. "Our families would never have allowed us—a boy of twenty-one just down from Oxford, and a girl of not quite seventeen—to be married at once. We'd have had to be engaged for a year—"

"Possibly even two or three while—"

"While everyone worked out your *dot* and my allowance—"

"And decided what the wedding would be like, and where we'd live afterwards—"

"Where we would travel—"

"Whom we'd see—"

"You can't leave decisions like that to *jeunes maris*—"

"Who are only children—"

Thea's voice trailed off, and Charles propped himself up on an elbow, their eyes meeting.

The thought occurred to them both at the same time.

"I like this way—*our* way—better," she informed him, smiling. "Just the two of us. All grown up and in charge of our own lives."

"It had to be this way. We had to grow and endure separately before we could come together. For us, the intellectual had to come before the physical—"

"Speak for yourself, lover. I was thinking about you all the time—how you kissed, what you looked like under your clothes, what it would be like to have you make love to me."

Charles was incredulous. "Just how long were you

385

speculating along those lines?"

"Right from the minute you asked me to marry you, and now that I know all your secret, sensitive spots, you have to answer my question. When did you stop seeing me as only an expensively dressed bluestocking?"

"I never— I wanted you as much as you wanted me— I thought I'd never be able to take you in my arms and hold you and kiss you and make love to you in a way that would make you want no other man but me—"

With one deft movement, Charles changed the balance of power between them, shifting so that he was pressing Thea's soft body into the mattress. "There's no other woman for me but you. You're the missing half of myself—"

These were the words Thea longed to hear—the deepest avowal of love he could make to her. She clasped her arms around Charles, drawing herself as close to him as possible, her body moving into a sea of delight with each caress. He was inside her, and they were one, wrapped in a boneless ecstasy that conquered all their past problems and soothed away the unnamed conflicts they knew were awaiting them in Mexico City.

While they remained in the total privacy of the stateroom, the steady motion of the train providing an added aspect to their lovemaking, the countryside they were passing through changed from a rich agricultural region to more arid plains as the altitude climbed closer and closer to the mile-high mark. As the deepening twilight closed around them, Thea and Charles observed the bleak landscape—desert plants whose names they didn't know, gargantuan cactus that looked seven feet tall, and prehistoric-looking mountains whose distance made them no less frightening.

"Do you realize the sights we missed until now?" Thea teased.

"We can always catch them on the way back."

"Definitely?" Thea's voice was provocative.

"I make no promises at all."

"That suits me fine." She nestled closer in his arms. "Charles, do you suppose that, if we'd met in New York, and by now we were engaged to be married, we'd want to wait until our wedding night?"

"I'd like to think that we wouldn't have marred that joy by anticipating it," Charles replied after a minute's thought.

"I like to think I would have felt that way too. But on the other hand, we're hardly Daphnis and Chloe. Our wait wouldn't have been easy."

Charles began to laugh. "Then I'm glad this is only a hypothetical discussion. Our two week wait for me to come to my senses was quite long enough. But seriously, Thea, wouldn't you have wanted a Christmas wedding at St. Jean Baptiste? Your father would have given you away, and my family would have come over from France, and we would have had music for organ and trumpets—"

"I prefer Mendelssohn. And, as nice as all that ceremony would have been, I'd much rather be here with you right now than in New York, having to keep my mind on invitations, fittings and thank-you notes for the wedding presents while the only thing I really wanted to think about was our wedding night at the St. Regis. Now *that*," she added, "I do regret a little. It would have been nice to spend our first night together in New York's newest and best hotel!"

"When we get back to New York, we'll take a suite there until our apartment is ready," Charles promised. "And, in the meantime, when we get to Mexico City, we're going to do all the things that tourists always do, and that includes gaping at all the sights, buying silly souvenirs and taking endless snapshots. We'll go to the parties we're supposed to, but they won't interfere in our lives any more than necessary. I've already cheated you out of a proper courtship and wedding night, and now it's up to me to see that we have a *very* happy honeymoon!"

Since they wouldn't reach Mexico City until rather late on Tuesday evening, Diego and Carmen, who were once again making the trip with them, prepared and served dinner to the de Renilles in the car's sitting room. Monday night's meal had been eaten in the privacy of the stateroom. But now, twenty-four hours later, the servants set forth a proper meal of turtle soup and stuffed roast quail accompanied by asparagus and tiny whole potatoes, finishing up with lemon ice and washed down by a bottle of Mumm's extra dry.

With Thea clad in a Lucile dress of soft beige pongee with elaborate Oriental embroidery around the throat, cuffs, and hem, and Charles wearing what he termed one of his Brooks Brothers Wall Street broker's suits, they seemed very far removed from the passionate lovers of the past thirty-odd hours, except that underneath the table, discreetly hidden by the oversized white damask tablecloth, Charles had firmly captured Thea's knees between his. They were still more interested in each other than in the scenery flashing past them, but, unwillingly, their eyes were drawn to the window.

"It can't be," Thea said, unbelieving. "I didn't expect this."

Charles looked at his watch. "It has to be. We're right on time."

No one had warned them about the extreme change of scenery that occurs in the final portion of the rail journey. Within the space of a few minutes, they left behind the stark, open plains dotted with tall cactus. Gone were the ominous-looking mountains and tiny, mean, sparsely populated adobe villages. Suddenly, they were passing a well-kept, obviously well-to-do suburb with attractive Spanish-style houses set on carefully

388

tended lawns. Further on, the train rattled past American-looking buildings, their roofs sporting billboards with English and Spanish advertisements surrounded by blinking electric lights.

The train was going full-speed as it tore through a dank-looking slum and, suddenly, as all the other sights had passed by, they were gone, blanked out by a long, covered shed. The sound of screeching brakes assaulted their ears and, with a final triumphant jerk of the gears, the El Paso to Mexico City train with its baggage cars, day coaches, Pullman sections and one private, exclusive car, reached its final destination.

Any comments Thea and Charles wanted to exchange were forestalled by Diego and Carmen's presence in the sitting room and by the swift, and not totally unexpected arrival of the station manager, a small, portly, middle-aged man with an understandably harried air, and a hospitable speech of welcome.

"Señor and Señora de Renille, it is with great pleasure that I am the first to greet you upon your arrival in our great capital of Mexico," he announced formally as soon as Diego ushered him in. "I shall offer many prayers that the time you spend among us will help to increase the feelings of friendship between our great republics. Long live President Roosevelt!"

"Long live President Diaz," they responded quickly.

The station-manager shook Charles' hand, bowed low over Thea's and, after the usual exchange of run-of-the-mill pleasantries, he motioned toward the door.

"Now, *con permiso*, with your permission, we will see to starting you on your way . . ."

Now there was only time for Thea and Charles to thank the servants for their good care of them, and to insist they take the generous tips they offered. Without wasting a moment, Thea pinned on her hat, and they followed the waiting station-manager out onto the platform to begin their first hour in Mexico City.

Grouped outside the unimpressive National Railways of Mexico Station, and bearing a great resemblance to the horse-drawn fiacres that crowded around Paris' railway stations, were Mexico City's cabs for hire. Blue flags designated first-class, red flags marked second class, all with drivers distinguished by their high-crowned felt sombreros, they provided an excellent source of transportation, but they were not for Thea and Charles. Set somewhat apart from the other vehicles around the station's main entrance, a correctly uniformed chauffeur standing beside it and a luggage brake behind, was the latest model Columbia 30-35 H.P. touring car with a limousine body belonging to Don Renaldo, which he had placed at their convenience.

As soon as they stepped out onto the street, the uniformed chauffeur came quickly forward and introduced himself as Hernando. "Is all your luggage here?" he respectfully inquired, eyeing the porters who were bringing out their trunks and suitcases. "A few minutes, señor and señora, and all will be ready," he assured them and, with a correct bow, he went off to oversee the transfer of their luggage to the brake.

With seemingly no effort at all, their baggage was arranged. And, once Hernando had settled them in the motor car's tonneau and the station-manager had offered a final personal wish for their visit, they moved off, the chauffeur turning the automobile around the Plaza de Buena Vista.

Shivering slightly in the cool night air, Thea moved closer to Charles. Her first surge of apprehension had been eased by the station-manager's welcome, but now that feeling of free-floating strangeness returned. The long avenue they were driving along was smoothly paved with asphalt and brightly lit by electric street lights—and almost totally deserted.

"Do you have the feeling we're the only people out-of-doors tonight?" Thea said at last as they passed flat-roofed, Spanish-style houses, made all the more withdrawn-looking by their barred windows.

"Don Renaldo warned me that there's very little street activity after nine in the evening, but I'm afraid I didn't take him seriously."

"Well, now we know." Thea felt some of her anxiety lessen. "Funny, I had a mental picture of Mexico City as having an endless night-life, all full of color, music and people in the street."

"So did I," Charles admitted. "But now I have the feeling that nothing is going to be as we expected it to be."

It was only a short distance further to the fashionable Sanz Hotel on the Calle de Mariscala and that, they agreed, at least seemed to be normal. The auto pulled up in front of the well-lighted entrance and, while the doorman helped them out, half a dozen *mozos*, the Mexican men of all work, rushed to tend to their luggage. It was the familiar routine of all superior hotels, one they both knew, and tonight all the usual bustle of arrival was very comforting indeed.

Run under American management, the Sanz Hotel turned out to be a large, square, re-built mansion and, as Thea and Charles walked through the entrance, the Managing-Director came forward to welcome them.

"We've been looking forward to your arrival," Mr. Colton informed them as he ushered them through the marble-columned lobby toward Reception. With a professional eye, Thea noted the thick, well-cared for carpets covering the marble floor, the excellent condition of the furniture arranged in conversational groupings around the lobby and in various small alcoves, and the sparkling crystal chandeliers hanging overhead. The bar was dark mahogany, polished brass, and as they passed the restaurant they could hear musicians playing selections from Victor Herbert's *Babes In Toyland*.

The Managing-Director, a compact-looking middle-aged man long experienced in running hotels, noted the de Renilles' surprise at their new surroundings. "This isn't quite what you were expecting, I see." He smiled at them.

"So far, Mexico has been a place of endless astonishments, and any preconceived notions we had didn't last too long."

"We learned a lot while we were up in Chihuahua," Thea added, unable to resist giving Charles a significant look. "But I have to admit that my interest in your lobby is somewhat professional. Back in New York, I have an interior decorating and antiques firm."

"Then I'm sure you'll find the capital an excellent source—particularly anything French," Mr. Colton said as they reached his office. "In fact, I'll prepare a list of reputable dealers for you to visit."

The registration forms were duly filled out, and once again Mr. Colton escorted them back into the lobby, toward the newly installed elevator, and up to the second floor.

"We've set aside a fine suite for you," he said informatively. "It faces on the patio, so no view of course, but it is quieter than if you were facing the Alameda."

A handsome door of carved mahogany was unlocked, electric lights switched on, and they stepped into a finely proportioned, not overly large, sitting room with walls of striped blue silk, a carved plaster ceiling, and a small crystal chandelier, while underfoot was what appeared to be a Savonnerie carpet of cream and dark blue and gold. Thea ran a quick eye over the furniture. So far so good, but she had to get one thing straightened out.

"Mr. Colton, will I be allowed to make some changes

if I wish to do so?" She gave him a charming smile. "Everything here looks fine, but we will be here a while, and this *is* our honeymoon, and, truthfully, as a decorator, I see every room as a possible laboratory for me."

"As long as it's kept within reason, Mrs. de Renille, there are no objections," he assured her. "Now, as to the rest of the suite—"

The bedroom walls were covered with the same blue silk as the sitting room, and two maids were taking a dark blue silk damask bedspread off the large double bed. The carpet of blue and cream and rose was almost invisible under the mass of their baggage, the overflow of which had been deposited in the adjoining dressing room.

While Charles and Mr. Colton returned to the sitting room, Thea left her hat and gloves and purse on top of one of her standing dress trunks and proceeded to check over the dressing room and the modern bathroom that lay beyond it. Finding both to be satisfactory, she rejoined her husband.

"Is everything in order, darling?" he asked.

"I think we're going to be very comfortable here."

"In that case, I'll leave you two to get settled in," Mr. Colton said. "Have a good evening, and please let me know if there's anything I can do."

The Managing-Director left, followed quickly by the maids, and when the door closed behind them, Thea flung her arms around Charles.

"Alone at last! I thought Mr. Colton, as nice as he is, was *never* going to leave!"

"The curse of hotel managers—they love to talk."

"Did you see the mess in the bedroom and dressing room? Until we get everything put away, we're going to have to pick our way around our luggage."

Charles kissed her. "The first peril of our married life—walking into unopened trunks."

"You're so romantic."

"Speaking of which—" Charles gestured at a side table. "Aren't you curious about who sent those flowers?"

"They're not a gift of the management?"

"Not according to Mr. Colton. He said they arrived late this afternoon, addressed to you."

Her curiosity piqued, Thea crossed the room to one of the marble-topped tables that flanked the fireplace and opened the envelope that was propped up against a porcelain vase filled with apricot tea roses.

YOU'RE HERE AT LAST
PAUL

"Something tells me he isn't going to take the fact I don't—and never did—love him very well," she said, reading the note aloud to Charles.

"Oh, Thea, where's your feminine sense of charity," he teased her. "Look at those roses. There have to be two dozen of them. Think of what all those long stems cost."

"I really couldn't care less." With deliberate slowness, Thea took a rose out of the bouquet to smell its delicate fragrance. For a long minute she regarded him over the soft, barely open petals. "There's only one long stem I have any interest in, and it isn't attached to these roses."

It took a moment for her subtly veiled comment to register, and as it did, Thea watched with joy as an expression of incredulous delight appeared on his face.

"Are you referring to me?"

"There's no one else," Thea said, holding out her arms as Charles came over to her. "I have the man I want."

"Then if you're certain—"

"Without a doubt—"

"In that case—" Charles lifted her into his arms and carried her back into the bedroom. "I think it's time we continued our course in advanced flower arranging."

It was well after nine the next morning when Thea awoke, and for a few minutes she lay quietly in bed, adjusting to her new surroundings, careful not to disturb Charles who slept on, finally peaceful again.

He'd gone through another nightmare, another episode of struggling and sweating in his dreams in a fruitless effort to break free. This was the third time in their time together that he had, to her knowledge, dreamed like that, but this time Thea took action. She woke Charles, freeing him from his sleep-induced horrors, but in no way solving his problem.

He could never remember his nightmares, Charles had told her as she comforted him. They were formless fragments that left him alone for weeks at a time and then returned again to haunt him.

Thea already knew about the morphine the doctors had once filled his veins with, but as she lay beside his now-sleeping form, she doubted if they could still be causing this disturbance. No, there had to be another cause, but Charles kept his secrets well and shared them slowly . . .

Still musing over this problem, Thea slipped quietly out of bed, stepped carefully around their luggage and scattered clothes, and went into the dressing room, closing the door behind her.

While she took bath salts and soap and dusting powder from her dressing case, she cast a considering eye over the dressing room with its blue-gray and white *toile* wallpaper, excellent full-length mirror, and comfortable-looking wing chair placed near a small fireplace—as well as its very generous closet space—deciding that this room at least would need very little work.

She bathed, luxuriating in the hot water and perfumed bubbles, and wrapped in a fluffy towel—large, but definitely not enough of them—she retrieved a night-gown and negligee from one of the suitcases. A few minutes later, with her business portfolio tucked under one arm, Thea returned to the bedroom, fixed the blankets more securely over Charles, and then went into the sitting room.

There she moved quickly, pulling back the heavy blue velvet curtains so that the bright morning sunlight filled the room, showing off both the advantages and disadvantages of their first home together.

This room has possibilities, she thought, sitting down behind the Regence *bureau plat*—a reproduction of the most elaborate of writing tables, not an original, but a good one—and surveyed the room, letting it all register slowly on her mind.

Good—it's definitely good. I wouldn't want to live here permanently, but for the time we'll be here, I think I can do a lot with it. The whole suite is so staid, it needs to be livened up. That hideous damask bedspread has to go. No—the bedroom will have to wait until all our things are put away and the luggage stored. The sitting room first. Now . . .

For a luxury hotel suite, it was more than adequate, but some of its omissions were glaring as far as Thea was concerned. There was a handsome marble fireplace with no firescreen in front of it, and although there was a superb mirror framed in Spanish tortoise-shell hanging above it, the mantel itself was sadly bare. There were more than enough tables: marble-topped tables flanking the fireplace; small, decorative tables, barely large enough to hold a teacup placed at the arms of the twin sofas covered in teal blue silk that were set on either side of the fireplace; a round, thoroughly undistinguished table had four fauteuils, all upholstered in blue and white silk, grouped around it; and an impressive table of veneered wood with lapis lazuli legs was backed against the wall behind one of the sofas.

Thea quickly reached several conclusions. There were no small, personal touches, so important in making a room homelike; all the lamps were ghastly looking; and worst of all, there was no table between the sofas.

And how am I supposed to serve afternoon tea without one? she thought, ringing for the maid. Now that she had some idea of the room's faults, she could have breakfast while she worked on the solutions.

The maid who answered her summons was one of the girls from the night before. Dressed in the hotel uniform of a loose blue skirt, a blue and white blouse, and a soft blue rebosa wound around her shoulders, she was a pretty, dark-haired girl with a flawless olive complexion.

"I am Angelita, Señora de Renille," she introduced herself in very credible English, "and I am your maid. Not only for the suite, but if you wish, as a lady's maid."

"Thank you, Angelita. Since I didn't bring a maid with me, I may need your services every now and then," Thea smiled. "But right now, I want to order breakfast."

There was a brief discussion as to the morning's offerings, and then Angelita departed, promising to return shortly with sliced fresh pineapple, sweet rolls, raisin and cinnamon toast, and hot chocolate, along with all the newspapers and the mail. With everything apparently falling into some sort of order, Thea opened her portfolio, found hotel stationery in the writing table's central drawer, and was deeply involved in making her lists when Angelita returned, wheeling a two-tiered cart weighed down with silver serving dishes, hotel china, an arrangement of white roses that were the gift of the management, several newspapers, and a basket filled with square, cream-colored envelopes that Thea instantly recognized as invitations.

"Thank you, Angelita, it all looks lovely," she said, moving aside her papers. "Right here will be fine. Can you stay and talk for a moment?"

"Certainly, señora. Is there some way I can be of service?"

"Well . . ." Thea hesitated for a moment, not wanting to pressure a hotel employee into gossiping. "I was just curious about the other guests in the hotel that my husband and I will be running into."

"I do not think, señora, that there are too many guests that you and the señor will care to associate yourselves with."

Thea couldn't resist a smile. "Thank you, Angelita. But my husband and I aren't snobs—or all that grand."

The young maid flushed. "I beg your pardon, señora. I am not speaking in a disrespectful manner of the other guests. After all, the Sanz is not the Iturbide where they take in all those who come to Mexico in groups with tour guides. Those who stay with us are . . . much finer. Often they are diplomats or work for some important business. Either they stay here until they conclude their missions, or else they move to a house or apartment in the Colonia Juarez."

"You make very acute observations, Angelita. Would you mind telling me where you learned your English?"

"My mother is the housekeeper for Mr. and Mrs. Frederick Guernsey. He is the publisher of the *Mexican Herald* and the *Evening Post*," she explained, referring to Mexico City's major English-language newspapers. "They come from Boston."

Thea choked back her laughter. Like most servants, Angelita had picked up the mannerisms, outlooks, and perceptions of her employers. It appeared that the long hand of Back Bay propriety as to who belonged and who didn't had reached into the Republic of Mexico.

"Pardon, Señora de Renille, you are a North American, are you not? But Señor de Renille—is he French?"

"Yes, but he's a New Yorker now—just like me."

"There is one guest here that you will probably meet. A Frenchwoman."

Thea picked up on the undertone in the maid's voice. "Is there something you want to warn me about?"

Angelita looked around her as if she were afraid of being overheard. "She is a *traidora*, that one," she said quickly. "A *falsa*. Her husband is in another part of the Republic, and she stays here. A very grand lady—or so she says—who has very particular amusements. Please watch out for her, señora."

Both amused and perplexed by the maid's cryptic warning, Thea agreed, and when Angelita left, she returned to her lists, eating as she worked. She was still writing several minutes later when she heard the bedroom door open, and she turned to see Charles, his hair uncombed, his face unshaven, and wrapped in his dressing gown, standing in the doorway.

"Good morning," she said, putting aside her pen. "Are you feeling better now?"

"Very much so." He pushed his hair out of his eyes. "I'm sorry I gave you a bad scare last night."

"I don't care about that. The only thing I care about is that you were able to sleep again. Charles, are you *sure* you don't recall your nightmare?"

"No—only that it's the same one over and over. That much I am sure of." He leaned back against the wall. "Is the chocolate still warm? I know I look like a denizen of the Bowery, but—"

Before he finished speaking, Thea was on her feet, reloading the tea cart and moving everything over to the conversational grouping of chairs. "Shall we sit down over here? I'll put the food out on the table, and while we eat I can show you the lists I've been working on," she said, pouring him a cup of *chocolate con leche*. "I want to know what you think of my ideas. First of all, we have to find out if Mexico City has a good department store. I hate the idea of having to run around to a dozen different shops for the things we'll need."

Charles sank into a Louis XV-style fauteuil covered in a blue and white silk damask and eyed Thea's ecru-lace lavished ivory satin charmeuse nightgown and negligee. "Are those your work clothes?" he teased as she handed him the hot chocolate. "Looking at you, I can't promise to pay attention to all your lists."

"That's the general idea of this outfit." Thea draped herself over the arm of his chair. "This is what's known as a wedding set. Mrs. Sanders at Browne's sold it to me. I couldn't think of a plausible explanation as to why I *wouldn't* need it. Anyway," she went on, smoothing back his hair, "even back then I think I was hoping our situation might work itself out in a *very* different way than planned."

"If you'd worn this that first night at the Menger, it might have been sooner."

She tugged playfully at his hair. "You certainly took your time in admiring my lingerie. Of course, I'm very happy that lately you haven't been very interested in letting me keep any of my clothes on!" Thea reminded him, deftly moving aside just as Charles reached for her, and thrust a sheaf of papers into his hands. "Look over these notes and tell me what you think," she instructed.

He nibbled on a sweet roll and studied the top page with a growing sense of perplexity. "Scotch, Benedictine, Remy Martin . . . Are we planning to open a bar?"

"No, but we do have that huge, bare table against the wall, and I was thinking that if we wanted to do some

400

entertaining—a few new friends in for drinks before dinner or after the opera—it would be nice to have our own supply of liquor."

"I like that idea." Charles flipped through the other pages. "In fact, I think all your ideas are splendid."

"But is there anything you particularly *don't* like? In a way, this is our first home. A good place to try out ideas and find out what we want in our own apartment. And, since we're going to live in it together, your views are going to be greatly appreciated!"

Charles looked around him. "I never lived anywhere where I had any say in the decor," he told her honestly. "All the furniture was already there, and very little was ever changed. Even at Oxford, I had no say in what I put in my rooms. My mother pulled a lot of odds and ends out of the storage rooms, just the way she did for my brothers, and arranged them for me."

Thea thought carefully before she spoke. "Those days are over, Charles," she said, her voice gentle, understanding both his flood of memories and his apprehension. "I'm not the sort of decorator who forces her taste down her clients' throats, and I'm certainly not going to be that kind of wife. Wherever we live, whether it's here or 667 Madison Avenue, it's *our* home, and I don't care if you've never selected as much as a bud vase, I want your opinions!"

"I hate photographs on display," he told her, slowly beginning to smile. "I can't stand going into a drawing room where every surface is covered with inscribed pictures in silver frames. I don't mind a few here and there, but—" He paused, caught Thea's encouraging smile, and went on. "I also hate overstuffed furniture and lamp shades sporting yards of fringe and second-rate paintings and too-bright rugs."

"Anything else?" Thea's smile deepened.

"That's it—for now."

"It's a good start," she assured him and, as they ate breakfast, each page of Thea's notes and suggestions were discussed. When that was finished, they moved on to the stack of invitations, opening each one and keeping a calendar so they could see how their social life would take shape over the next weeks. Twenty-seven nations had accredited representatives in Mexico City, and their entertainments were accordingly large, with balls, musicales and dinners being the favorite forms of diversion. The first engraved cards requested their presence for an evening of Vivaldi at the Italian Embassy, a chamber music recital at the Austrian Embassy, and a ball to honor some obscure Romanov prince at the Russian Embassy.

"Let's hope the favors are from Faberge," was Thea's comment.

"What an acquisitive witch I'm married to!"

"At least you're laughing. I don't know how much gossip or information or speculation we'll pick up, but we'll probably acquire so many of these little gifts that we won't have to purchase a single *bibelot* for the next five years." Thea broke open another sealed envelope. "Did you know that there's not only a Chinese Legation here, but a Chinese Club as well? We're invited there tomorrow evening for a dinner of Peking duck."

Charles looked at the invitation with a growing sense of the ridiculous. "I think our stay here is about to take on overtones of *Alice in Wonderland.*"

"I wouldn't be at all surprised, but I don't think we're going to be allowed to forget the reason why we came here," Thea replied, her face suddenly serious as she handed him another cream-colored card. "This is from the American Embassy."

"The honor of our presence is requested at a luncheon

402

party tomorrow afternoon at one," Charles read from the invitation. "All very proper and correct."

"Except that we'll probably be the only guests."

For a long minute they considered each other, and the implications the engraved summons held for them.

"I don't care about any of this, not for any reason—social or political—as long as I have you," Thea said at last, rising from her chair to sit in Charles' lap and put her arms around him.

He held her close, and all their apprehensions eased at this contact as they drew security and comfort from each other. There were more invitations to attend to, as well as newspapers to read and unpacking to do, but suddenly none of those tasks seemed very important. Thea's fingers wove their way naturally into Charles' thick hair as his hands moved gently but insistently along her back. Their mutual comforting was quickly becoming something much more intimate.

"Thea . . . after you've made your purchases . . . when we're ready to go back to New York . . . what will we do with them?"

Thea stopped kissing the hollow at the base of Charles's throat. "If we really get attached to what I—we—buy, we'll crate it and send it all to New York," she replied, and then began to laugh, her fingers running from his hair to slip under the collar of his dressing gown. "I've just had a wonderful idea. I'll make all the changes I want and then offer it to the management with the provision that they rename this suite the Charles and Theodosia de Renille bridal suite and offer it to all their newly married guests as the perfect place to start their marriages in!"

Between themselves, Thea and Charles had joked that Major Donovan would know the minute he looked at them that they had consummated their marriage and that, accordingly, he would be furious. Furious enough, Thea secretly hoped, that he would wash his hands of them and send them packing back across the Rio Grande.

But the results of their first meeting were certainly not what either of them had expected.

They arrived at the American Embassy promptly at one and were warmly received by Ambassador and Mrs. Clayton, a proper diplomatic couple, who had them sign the guest book and took them on a tour of the chancery's reception rooms.

Over a lunch of clear soup, chicken patties with tiny green peas, strawberry mousse, and coffee, they told the Claytons about the de Veigas' anniversary fiesta, going into the details about the dinner, the music and the ceremony of the *piñatas* and, in turn, the older couple informed Charles and Thea of the complexities involved in Mexico City's social world.

The finest old families in the city were not particularly sociable to foreigners, even if they *were* French, and were noticeably cool to Americans. That policy was a long-lasting result of the Mexican-American War of 1847-1848 (a war admittedly fought for the purpose of obtaining New Mexico, Arizona, and California, and for which Mexico received fifteen million dollars in payment for the lands), and for the humiliation Mexicans suffered on September 13, 1847, when General Winfield Scott paraded his army before Mexico City's 16th-century cathedral. As for the French; even though their occupation of Mexico had lasted only a short five years, beginning in 1862 with the arrival of the first French troops, ostensibly sent to enforce payment of loans made to the nation, cresting on June 12, 1864, with the arrival of Maximilian and Carlotta, and ending on June 19, 1867, when the Emperor and two of his generals were shot on a hill outside Queretaro; the upper strata of Mexico City society—little affected by those political upheavals—found the French mode of life the best to emulate.

"The British run a close second, of course," the ambassador told them amusedly over coffee. "The men order their clothes from Savile Row, they hire English governesses for the children, and as for afternoon tea—"

"That is a universal custom," Mrs. Clayton finished with a flourish. The ambassador's wife was a bright and charming woman who carried her intelligence well. "Actually, it isn't Americans they hate, it's the United States."

"So we're beginning to understand. We've been reading *El Imparcial*. For a newspaper that's totally Americanized in its layout, it's violently anti-American in its viewpoint," Charles said. "In fact, it looks so much like the *New York Times*, I'm tempted to send Adolph Ochs a copy."

"I think he's enough of a southern gentleman to find it amusing—except that instead of 'all the news that's fit to print,' *El Imparcial*'s motto is 'Mexico for the Mexicans,'" Thea added.

Eventually, their talk turned to that evening's function at the Chinese Club and, after the Claytons informed the de Renilles that they too were invited to partake of Peking duck, the ambassador's wife stood up and excused herself.

"This is my afternoon at the Women's Exchange," she explained. "It's just like the ones in New York and Boston. You must come one afternoon soon, Thea."

"I will as soon as we're completely settled in," Thea promised, and knew that as soon as Mrs. Clayton left, the real reason behind their invitation to lunch would assert itself. Slowly, as this fact dawned, Thea felt her state of relaxation, gained through their meal and conversation, ebb away and be replaced by a cold, hollow feeling.

The ambassador waited a full five minutes.

"This has been a fine opportunity to meet you both, but we *do* have another matter to tend to. If you'll come with me—"

Adjoining the dining room was a small reception room heavy with marble columns and red velvet curtains, and seated on a red velvet loveseat that looked oddly out of place under his bulk was Major John Donovan.

As they approached him, he put aside the issue of *Mundo Ilustrado,* the popular weekly periodical he was reading, and rose instantly to his feet and smiled in greeting.

Over the next half-hour, as they sat and talked, Thea began to wonder if this were the same Major Donovan that they had spoken with beside the lake at Fort Sam Houston. Then he'd been surly to the point of outright rudeness. Today, less than a month later, he was deferential to Ambassador Clayton, and genuinely polite to them. In fact, Thea realized, he was actually verging on charming as they traded stories about the train ride to Mexico City, the bareness of the railway station, and spoke about the customs that governed the diplomatic and foreign communities and the close social ties they shared.

"Because of that closeness, what we want you two to do is going to be that much easier. The foreign colony in the Colonia Juarez district is like a small town. Everyone knows each other, and they all love a honeymoon couple," he finished.

Thea and Charles exchanged glances.

"Are there any precise rules for us to follow?" Charles questioned. "The de Veigas have provided us with letters of introduction, and we already have more invitations than we expected."

"Good!" Donovan's voice was approving. "The main thing is that you behave the same way here as you would in New York and Paris. Accept as many invitations as you can, but only to parties you want to go to. We're not interested in raising suspicions any more than we would want you to do any actual spying."

"Then what exactly is it that you want my husband and me to do?" Thea questioned. "Just listen in, take mental notes, and report them back to you?"

"Essentially, yes. Conversation at parties is a tricky thing, you never know when someone is going to say something important. But I don't want you to force any questions. You can't set yourselves up to be anything but what we arranged."

"And when will we speak with you?" Charles' voice was even, his thoughts well hidden. "With all due respect, Major, if Thea and I are seen too frequently in your company, it can be as much of a problem as our asking questions about topics we shouldn't have any business being interested in."

Major Donovan gave Charles a look of grudging respect. "That's right. We'll only meet once or twice a week in some public place. Do you both ride? Fine. The bridle paths at Chapultepec Park are a good place to begin. Now, what's your schedule so far?"

"The Chinese Club tonight, and the Italian Embassy tomorrow," Charles replied, and gave him a brief run-through of the invitations they'd received, the ones they were accepting, and the few they were declining.

With that much settled, they stood up and shook hands all around.

"Don't look so concerned," Major Donovan told them genially. "We're not expecting great revelations, but a lot of people you'll be meeting can't resist sharing their expertise with an intelligent man, or talking about their important positions with an attractive lady. That's why you had to be married. It's more natural, and there are less problems," he said with a knowing smile. "No gentleman would dream of importuning a newly married woman and, if anyone is stupid enough to try, Charles will be there to protect you from any unwelcome advances!"

"I knew his being polite was too good to last," Thea remarked a few minutes later as they walked out the front door of the embassy.

"Can you imagine me as a strong-arm man?"

"Oh, I don't know. I'd like to think that if some misguided man thought I was interested in more than just casual conversation, a few well chosen words from you would make him see the light!"

"Let's not worry about that now," he said as they crossed the pavement to the curb where the motor car was parked. It was a beautiful October afternoon with the temperature hovering around seventy; too nice a day to do anything serious. "I suppose you want to start your redecorating plans this afternoon?"

"There's nothing I'd like less!" She wrinkled her nose at him. "Let's do something touristy."

"Hernando, we want to visit one of Mexico City's landmarks this afternoon," Charles said as the chauffeur sprang out from behind the wheel to open the door to the tonneau. "What do you recommend?"

"The Alameda, Señor de Renille," he replied promptly. "That is the park opposite your hotel, and this is a beautiful afternoon in which to enjoy it."

Charles looked at his wife. "Does that meet with your approval?"

"A long walk in the park is just what I'd like. I think it'll help us adjust to the city—and to Major Donovan's new attitude toward us. He is a *very* strange man."

"I have to remember never to speak French if I want to say something unkind about him in his hearing. Colonel Forrest told me that, while the major can't *speak* any foreign languages, he understands most of them perfectly. And what do you find so funny?" he demanded as Thea began to laugh.

"Oh, *you*," she gasped. "Did you hear what you just said? You referred to *French* as a foreign language." She sobered suddenly. "I didn't mean it the way it came out."

"But you're very accurate, nonetheless. Until this minute, I never realized that I now *think* in English." He looked shaken. "I don't know how long I've been doing it."

"Both French and English are so closely aligned in your mind that you made the transference without noticing," Thea said gently, taking his hand. "Does it bother you terribly?"

"Not in the least. It's the discovery that surprised me, not the actuality." He grasped her hand even tighter. "I've had so many unpleasant shocks to contend with, that this one hardly counts at all."

"Well, in that case, I've just thought about something we can think about in *any* language. Can you imagine the reaction of our family and friends when they get our telegrams?"

The cable was addressed to the Comtesse Adrian de Renille, and Solange accepted it from one of her maids with a smile of thanks. She was in her bedroom at the dower house where she'd moved following Charles' departure for New York. It was time Guy, Pauline and their children had the *manoir* to themselves, she reasoned. With Charles well once again and learning to make his way in the world, there was no need for them to be so closely attached as a family. She'd settled herself into one of the smaller houses on the estate, and was now comfortably installed among her favorite furniture, pictures and flowers.

Taking a deep breath, Solange surveyed her reflection in her dressing table's mirror and decided that she was well arrayed for that evening's hunt ball in Doucet's peacock-blue chiffon, her pearls glowing against her creamy skin. She then reached for the cable that lay in front of her, not quite able to keep her fingers from trembling.

She read its contents with a growing sense of joy and incredulity, and let out such an exclamation of delight that one of her house-guests for this hunt weekend appeared at her door a moment later.

"Solange." Lady Cecily Benjamin, the Countess of Saltlon, stepped into the room. "I was on my way downstairs and heard you. Is something wrong?"

"No—*no!* Things couldn't be more right." She waved the cable at her younger friend. "Look at this, Cecily. It's so wonderful—"

"—MARRIED MISS THEODOSIA HARPER ON SEPTEMBER 24 IN STRICT INTIMACY BY THE BISHOP OF SAN ANTONIO, TEXAS. PROCEEDING TO MEXICO CITY FOR HONEYMOON AT SANZ HOTEL. LETTER TO FOLLOW. ALLOW YOURSELF TO LOVE—ALLOW FATE TO TAKE ITS COURSE—LIFE IS NOT AS SAD AS YOU JUDGED IT TO BE—"

Cecily finished translating aloud and embraced the comtesse. "How truly marvelous, Solange."

410

"I thought this day might never come. *Incroyable.* Charles is finally married." She consulted the cable again, and a small frown appeared on her beautiful face. "September 24? And this was sent from—where?— Chihuahua. He certainly took his time. And why San Antonio, Texas, of all places? Cecily, do we know any Harpers?"

"Oh, Solange, now is not the time to pick at genealogical roots!" Cecily chided with gentle humor. "But, yes, I *do* know Thea—quite well, in fact. So do Andrew and Janine, I believe. She's a friend of Alix's, and her father is Elston Harper—he and Isaac are rather good friends," she added, referring to her husband, Isaac Benjamin, the Earl of Saltlon who was, at that moment, waiting for them in one of the downstairs salons.

"Ah!" Solange's cry was one of triumph. "How stupid of me to forget. I remember the first time I met her," she said, and related the details to Cecily. "Imagine, after all these years. Is she still pretty?"

"Very—and tall, rather like Alix. Dresses at Poiret and Lucile, also. Tons of cachet. I think Charles has done very well for himself."

"So do I. But why San Antonio?" she persisted, something nagging at her, something she didn't like.

"Don't you remember?"

"Yes—Bruce and Evangeline's daughter Angela married a man from there. How silly of me not to realize it at once. But Charles has been so secretive lately. Until this cable, I hadn't heard from him in weeks. Only a picture postcard from the Exposition in St. Louis. He said he arrived in the city on August 25, the feast day of St. Louis, patron saint of Paris, and considered the coincidence to be a harbinger of good things to come." A new thought dawned. "Cecily, do you suppose—"

"That Thea is *enceinte*, and Charles, both proud and

411

upset as he would be if such were the case, decided that following their marriage a strategic retreat to Mexico for a few months was in order?" Cecily's green-gold eyes became considering. "Will you really mind having a grandchild with a slight hint of *scandale?*"

"For Charles' child, never! If your supposition is correct, it's rather amusing."

"For you and me, possibly, but not for Charles and Thea."

"It is of no matter now. Besides, first babies are always either early or late—it all evens out in the end." She looked at the bisque clock on the mantel. "*Alors*, the time!" Solange exclaimed. "The others are waiting for us, and the carriage must be here by now. I'll take the cable with me. Guy and Andre will be so surprised!"

"We'll drink a toast to them *in absentia*," Cecily said, smoothing out a fold of her green chiffon and gold-shot gown from Poiret, and adjusting a jeweled hairpin in her Titian-red hair. All in all it had been a very good day, she decided. A fine day in the field, and the ball tonight would now have an added surprise.

But as she followed Solange down the stairs, certain peculiarities about Charles' telegram began to prick at her mind. Of course, her first assumption might be right. Judging by Charles' tense withdrawal following his nervous breakdown, Thea had probably had to throw herself at him to get any positive results. Cecily could be quite lenient in these matters. With some men *nothing* worked unless they were staring straight at a scandal. Smart girl, Thea, if she not only did that, but also made certain to get herself right and proper pregnant. In Cecily's opinion there was nothing wrong with Charles de Renille that an adoring wife and new family wouldn't cure. But still. . . .

She and Alix had spoken often this past summer,

catching up on all that had gone on in their lives since they'd seen each other last but, although Thea Harper and Charles de Renille had come up separately, they had never been mentioned as a couple—either present or future. That, in itself, didn't mean anything. They might have met on their own. They might have decided that eloping—leaving their friends and families gaping with surprise—was a funny and romantic thing to do. But why the more than three-week gap in announcing it, and why *Mexico*, of all places, for a honeymoon?

The events, possibilities, and suggestions swirled in her brain. *Thea is a courier for President Roosevelt.* The words formed out of nowhere, a silent voice reminding Cecily of what Silvia de Noyer, her sister-in-law, had once said. It had been just over two years ago that Frederick and Silvia had taken Thea with them to Budapest and, when they returned, she had made that comment.

Cecily pondered the comment. What else had Silvia said? Oh, yes, something about a tiara. Such a silly business, but . . .

Could it be? Well, stranger things certainly happened. And Alix had hinted that Thea *did* work for their government. Would it be so totally unbelievable that Thea and Charles were on some sort of assignment together and had fallen in love after the fact?

Cecily smiled to herself. Governments—*all* governments—could be very foolish at times, she thought. They joined her husband and their friends, Ivor and Millicent Rowland, who had been waiting for them in the salon, put on their wraps, and went out to the carriage for the short trip to the *manoir*. They plan for one contingency and an entirely different one appears. But, after all, isn't that what love is all about? The wondrous occurring when least expected.

Well, however love happens, it happens, and that's all that counts, Cecily determined. Intrigue was for dinner parties, but love went on forever, she decided firmly and, putting aside all ideas of political and diplomatic skullduggery, turned her thoughts to what she and Isaac would give as their wedding present.

Morning sickness was an affliction unknown to Alix Thorpe. She had gone through her first pregnancy in a state of glowing good health. And now, early in her third month, she was repeating that beatific state. But her condition made her tire easily, causing her to sleep later in the morning and to take an afternoon nap on most days, or at least rest quietly for an hour or so.

She was doing just that, relaxing in the master bedroom of their new apartment, her eyes lovingly taking in the spacious dimensions of the room that measured twenty-by-twenty. She had recreated their fourth floor bedroom without losing any of its charm in the added footage and it was just what they wanted—a comfortable, luxurious, and totally private haven.

She was contentedly gazing at the Monet footbridge that hung over the fireplace when the bedroom door opened and Henry came in, his hands full of the afternoon's mail.

"Oh, wonderful, more things to read!" she exclaimed in mock greed, pushing aside the stacks of *Vogue*, *Harper's Bazaar*, *Town & Country* and *Theatre* magazines that she'd been occupying herself with.

"You insatiable woman," Henry teased, depositing the results of the recent mail delivery on the bed table so he could put his arms around her.

"Well, you should know all about that!" she challenged, cuddling against him, not at all minding that this morning there was an extra half-inch around her waistline that hadn't been there yesterday.

"I'd hate to think what would happen if our mail deliveries were reduced to once a day," Henry remarked several minutes later as Alix began to sort through their mail. He paid the rent, all expenses incurred in running the apartment and, except for Doris and Carrie, the servants' salaries; Alix took care of her own clothing bills, the florists' charges, and paid the maids; while together they purchased paintings and furniture.

"Perish the thought!" she warned. "Oh, we have a telegram mixed in with everything else. I wonder who—?" she began, opening the envelope and unfolding the enclosed yellow sheet.

One moment Henry Thorpe was comfortably stretched out on the bed beside his wife, and the next he was being both kissed and pummeled by a laughing Alix.

"And you told me they had nothing in common, couldn't possibly be interested in each other, and were the last possible couple! Well, my dear Lord Thorpe, you were wrong, wrong, *wrong!*"

With considerable difficulty, Henry subdued Alix. "If you take one more swing at me, I may just forget you're having my son. Now, what is this telegram all about—?"

In another second, his mystification vanished, replaced—for one of the few times in his self-possessed life—by speechless surprise. "Are you a witch?" he asked in boundless admiration. "You knew all along—"

"Thank you for the compliment, but no, not quite. I just guessed—no, *felt*—that somehow they might belong together." She put an arm around his neck. "I think they're going to be as happy as we are."

"In that case, Charles must be walking a foot off the ground," Henry said, gathering Alix closer to him.

"And they found each other all by themselves, just the way we did."

"Yes, but we'll have to tell everyone otherwise." His glance fell on the decorative bedside clock. "Do you want to ring up *Town & Country* now? They should be able to get the announcement into next week's edition. And afterwards, I'll speak with Newton about the apartment."

"Oh, all the machinations needed to make it all official," Alix said, stretching like an elegant, languorous Persian cat. "But it's only half-past two, and I think we have a little time left for just us."

"I think so too," Henry agreed with a quiet smile, taking off his suit jacket and tie. "I'm sure Charles and Thea would find nothing wrong in our waiting another hour or two before we saw to it that their marriage was announced in a proper publication and they were made all dull and respectable!"

Angela Browne was deep into the monthly letter she wrote to Mary Anne Magnin, the owner of the finest women's specialty store in San Francisco and her former employer, when Lupe entered the library and placed a small silver tray with a yellow Western Union envelope resting in the center on the smooth wood surface of the Chippendale writing desk. Nela thanked her maid and completed the sentence she was working on. Unlike many women, she did not consider the contents of a telegram to necessarily be bad news, having grown up in a household that believed that cables were a very efficient use of communication. She opened the envelope with no great trepidation.

Her eyes swept the cable and, instantly, her air of faint disinterest vanished.

A feeling of pure joy and delight rippled through her. She reached for the telephone on the desk, barely able to contain her excitement until Central connected her with the store's switchboard and then with her husband's office.

"Nela, I was just getting ready to leave. Is everything all right?"

"It couldn't be better, darling. A telegram just came from Thea and Charles. They did it—it happened—just the way I told you it might," she bubbled happily, and read him the telegram.

There was a long silence, and then Morgan began to laugh.

"You incredible woman," he told her, his voice humming over the wires. "I swear you knew this all along. And to tell you the truth," he went on, "I'm awfully glad we gave Thea and Charles a reception. They probably would have found each other without it, but you were right—we had to do it out of friendship."

"You were a wonderful host."

"And you plan the best parties." He laughed again. "At least now I know what to tell the photographer."

"You heard from him?"

"Just about an hour ago. A very discreet inquiry."

"And people have the nerve to say Texans have no subtlety."

"Oh, we're trying."

"Well, try and get yourself home real fast, lover," she said meaningfully. "We can read the cable together, and then we'll send our own to Thea and Charles in Mexico City."

"Aren't you forgetting something?"

"Now that you mention it, I am. As soon as I hang up with you, I'll ring up the photographer and tell him to send his wedding pictures to the Sanz Hotel in care of Mr. and Mrs. Charles de Renille!"

Charles and Thea spent the remainder of the afternoon strolling arm-in-arm along the well-kept paths of the

417

Alameda. It was a tranquil spot with long stretches of green lawns, beds of exotic flowers, large shade trees, and full-blown palm trees. They admired the handsome fountain that dominated the park's center, and sat on a spotless white bench while a regimental band played sprightly marches.

Thea and Charles agreed that they were reminded of London's Green Park. And, as they left the park and crossed the avenue to reenter the Sanz Hotel, it was probably for the best that they didn't learn, until much later, that the green, graceful, beautiful Alameda Park had, from 1571 to 1812, been the execution sight for the victims of Mexico's Inquisition; the spot selected because the crowd of interested spectators could stand on the steps of the Church of San Diego and have a perfect view of the ensuing *auto-da-fe*.

In the quiet, correct lobby of the Sanz Hotel they separated, Thea to return to their suite, and Charles to Mr. Colton's office to ask for information about the best bank at which to cash part of his letter of credit. It took only a few minutes, and as he was recrossing the lobby, the address of the *Banco Nacional de Mexico* having been provided, he heard his name being called.

"Charles—it *is* you! And in Mexico City, of all places. It's been a long time, *cher*. Much too long—"

In the space of ten seconds, Charles felt his new world turn completely over and, with a sense of intense bewilderment, he regarded the elegant woman who now stood at his side. Her tall, slender figure was shown off to its best advantage by a Worth reception gown of cafe-au-lait-colored taffeta with a row of tiny black velvet buttons down the back. On top of her elaborately arranged golden hair was a hat of matching taffeta trimmed with loops of black velvet ribbon. Her perfume, Jicky, the same as Thea's, drifted around him like an unseen cloud, but

418

instead of putting him into the olfactory swoon that heightened their sensual encounters, Charles now began to feel slightly ill. He looked into rich blue eyes that held more than just pleasure at seeing him again.

"Ophelie."

"Ah, Charles." Her perfect mouth made a perfect *moue*. "All this time goes by and all you can say is 'Ophelie'."

"Well, you *did* take me by surprise. You're the last person I expected to see."

"I return the compliment," she said with a sidelong glance, one gloved hand brushing an imaginary speck of dust from his suit lapel. "But, here we are, together in the halfway house of the world."

"I always thought that was Singapore."

"I've decided it's wherever you want to make it. I'm here in this godforsaken place while Gerard plays with his archaeological friends. What a bore. But now that you're here—" Her fingers brushed against his lapel again. "Incidentally, what *are* you doing here?"

It took Charles a minute to find his voice.

"This is my honeymoon."

"Ah, that poor girl." Ophelie's voice was gentle, but there was—just for a moment—a malicious glint in her eyes. "Who else but you, Charles, would dream of taking his bride to Mexico? Tell me, whom did your maman select for you? The de Brueteil girl, the one with the lisp, or is it Antionette de Crecy? She should be out of the convent school by now."

"You don't know my wife, Ophelie."

"Apparently not." Her voice was icily amused. "*Mon Dieu*, your maman found you an English girl! A proper young miss—or is it a ladyship?—fresh from the schoolroom."

"I found her myself," he said more sharply than he

419

intended. "She's from New York."

"An American!" Ophelie's reaction was somewhere between a chortle and a snort. "And what does your beloved maman say to that?"

"She's thoroughly delighted," Charles said, certain he was lying only for the moment.

"So she would be. Any port in a storm, as they say."

Anger flared in Charles, igniting in his middle like a Fourth of July firecracker, but he strove to keep his voice calm. "I don't speak badly of Gerard, Ophelie, so kindly do not mention my wife, whom you haven't met, in that tone of voice."

"Poor Charles, as intense as ever." She traced a finger playfully across one of his cheekbones. "Voyons, mon cher, do not worry, if your dear bride cannot make you see the lighter side of life, then something else can always be arranged to lighten your mood!"

Little by little, the suite was beginning to take on Thea's personal imprint. But, as Charles crossed the floor of the sitting room and opened the bedroom door he had such a feeling of unreality draped over him that he hardly noticed the first slight changes in the decor, now noticeably lightened with the help of great bouquets of light-colored flowers in simple vases that were placed on some of the decorative tables.

On the threshold of the bedroom he paused, his eyes sweeping the room, the changes finally registering in his brain. Their luggage was unpacked and stored away, and the curtains were looped back to let all the afternoon sunlight in. The Sanz Hotel was built around a patio with an elaborate garden fountain banked with flowers, and each of the hotel's three floors was encircled by an inside gallery.

Thea was rearranging her bottles of Jicky and a variety

of silver-topped crystal bottles and pots that held her tinted face powders, lip colors and other cosmetics on top of the dressing table when she looked up and caught sight of Charles' reflection in the carved-wood framed Louis XVI mirror that hung over the table.

"Are you all right?" she asked, turning to face him. "You look like you've seen a ghost."

"Not quite a ghost." Charles sat down on the edge of the bed, thinking that Thea was right—the blue damask bedspread was the ugliest thing possible and would have to go. "More like a voice from my past."

"From the look of you, I'd say it had to be more than a disembodied spirit. Who is she?"

"How do you know it's a woman?"

"Oh, Charles, I don't think you realize how transparent you are at times," she said, noting with relief that some color had returned to his face, and a smile was beginning to tug at his mouth. "What's her name?"

"Ophelie. Baronne Ophelie de Langlade."

"What a pretty name," Thea allowed and, even as she pressed back a smile, something began to tug at her memory. *There is one guest . . . a Frenchwoman . . . a traidora . . . falsa . . . particular amusements . . .* As she recalled Angelita's warning description, Thea felt her amusement at Charles' condition fade swiftly, replaced by a chill feeling she couldn't shrug off.

"Well, it's nice you ran into a friend from home," she ventured cautiously. "I'll look forward to meeting her."

"Don't be too sure."

Thea's anxiety heightened. "Oh, really? Are all your French friends so utterly charming?"

"I never said she was my friend."

His voice and his look told her, but she had to ask, had to hear his revelation for herself.

"I think we have to get something settled, and I'd like

421

to do it before your *amie* turns up on our doorstep wearing the latest Worth frock, a false smile, and spouting a mouth of two-edged compliments," Thea told him bluntly, unconsciously giving a very apt description of Ophelie. "Just what is she to you?"

"Was," he corrected. "Ophelie de Langlade used to be my mistress."

Chapter Fourteen

October 20-23, 1904

The Mexico City that Thea and Charles arrived in was a study in extreme contrasts. That first night in the capital was a shock to them, and the days that followed provided sight after new sight.

They found the streets of the capital were smoothly paved with asphalt and brightly lit at night by electric street lights while flat-roofed Spanish-style houses resided side-by-side with modern business buildings. Electric street cars clanked past churches crowned with ancient towers and domes—the modern workaday world intruding on the sacred past. Architecture was a mixture of all the Spanish types, ranging from the 16th-century monastery-fortresses in the pseudo-Gothic mode to the neo-classical which followed the lines of Andrea Palladio, to ten and twenty-story buildings built by American companies topped by electric signs advertising such products as Quaker Oats, Singer Sewing Machines, Remington Typewriters and American Cash Registers. Nearly all of those buildings were located on the Calle Cinco de Mayo, transforming the street into a major business avenue where the American, English and Canadian companies had their headquarters, and the spot where English was the dominant language.

The location of the city provided almost ideal year-round weather. Lying in a plain sixty miles long and thirty miles wide, Mexico City was encircled first by cold-looking foothills and then by a series of mountains with volcaniclike tops. Located nearly eight thousand feet above sea level, the thinner air often caused arriving visitors who, unlike Thea and Charles, hadn't had the chance to do their adjusting in another part of the country, to suffer headaches, dizzy spells and shortness of breath, but the climate was even-natured, with the temperatures hovering around seventy degrees nearly every day.

Most of all, Mexico City seemed to have absorbed a major characteristic of the other important cities in the world. Like Madrid and Rome, it was a city of churches which, despite the stringent Reform Laws that outlawed many religious practices of the Catholic Church, flourished and grew; like London, there was a plethora of exclusive, important men's clubs, places where a gentleman could while away a few hours or an entire day, enjoy a well-prepared meal, make business connections at the bar, or, in the case of the Jockey Club, play baccarat for high stakes; the exclusive, structured social world was reminiscent of Paris and Vienna; and like New York, Mexico City was automobile-mad, with Daimlers and Buicks and Oldsmobiles and Delahayes and Cadillacs and Fiats filling the better districts and suburbs, driven by chauffeurs who had to pass an exacting test before they could be licensed.

In short, it was a city where religion covered the primitive, where social distinction cut deep, where old and new never combined but merely coexisted, and where visitors were likely to run into the very last people from their pasts that they expected to see.

Hours later, after a dinner at the Chinese Club which had a membership of nearly four-hundred, Thea still found herself to be wildly amused at the status of Ophelie de Langlade in Charles' life.

"Are there any more like her wandering around?" she wanted to know as they lay stretched across the bed, their formal dinner clothes decorating the carpet. "I know about your actress in Boston, and now there's this Ophelie cat. Tell me about the rest."

Charles' arms tightened skillfully and his mouth came down on hers. "Didn't your mother ever warn you about what happens to too-curious wives?"

"I couldn't care less," she said, slipping one long, slender leg between his equally long, muscular legs. "This is merely what's called good business practice. In other words, I want to know my competition."

"There *is* no competition!"

"Oh, yes, there is, and it started the moment your precious baronne said I was any port in a storm. That trashy, titled bitch!"

"Wouldn't you rather wait until you meet her before you begin using expletives?" Charles' voice was amused. He didn't want any woman but Thea, she was his life, yet the idea of Ophelie, that knowing, demanding witch, thrilled a small part of him in a way he hadn't quite worked out yet.

"Then you agree with me—and don't say no! Oh, Charles—" Thea moved closer against his warm body. "You're a puzzle wrapped up in a secret. Let's see if I have it right—several experiences in general debauchery with a number of elegant and titled older ladies, followed by five years of penance with the Jesuits, then two more years of celibacy ending between the sheets of one of the best suites at the Touraine Hotel, and finishing with me." She ran a finger down his side, over his ribs and hip, and back up again. "How close am I to the facts?"

Charles had never thought of most of his life as anything to laugh about but, as he heard Thea's description of the past ten years of his life, his amusement grew.

"You're dead on target," he told her, "and that's just one more reason why I love you. You put things in their proper perspective. I don't do that very well just now, but the last thing I need is to stay in the past. Don't let me live that way . . ."

"I love you too much to let you destroy yourself that way."

"And I was never in love until you, Thea. That's why entering the Church didn't frighten me," he murmured, pulling the bedclothes closer around them. "I could live without sex, particularly since there was no all-encompassing love out there for me—" He buried his face against her throat. "Experience is an expensive school, but fools aren't educated cheaply."

"If all you had were stolen afternoons with ladies of the *haute noblesse*, I can see your point. What was the first one like?"

"A beautiful marquise for whom I felt a great deal of boyish affection and desire. Then there were a few more of her counterparts, of which Ophelie was the youngest and closest to my own age. Then I went to the Jesuits, then my breakdown, then Tildy—and, at long last, you."

"But what about girls your own age? Didn't you meet them at dinners and balls and such?"

"Oh, Thea, you forget. I'm the youngest son in a titled family and worthy of no matrimonial consideration at all. Girls from families like mine were reserved for Guy or Andre, and girls from newly rich industrial families didn't want me either—a third son is no real step up. In the marriage stakes, I was a pariah, an albatross, a—"

"A wonderful man, and you're all mine!"

"As if I'm ever going to forget," Charles promised as Thea's hands travelled over him, rekindling all the passion they shared.

"Good . . . for both of us," Thea murmured. "And just tell anyone who asks why you married an American that you simply couldn't resist a girl who didn't care what kind of listing she'd have in the *Almanach de Gotha!*"

Dinner at the Chinese Club, the next night's musical evening at the Italian Embassy and the party they attended Saturday night in Tacubaya, a pretty and substantial suburb near Chapultepec Park, at the home of Don Enrico and Dona Luisa de la Garza, Dona Imelda's youngest brother and his wife, were somewhat of a disappointment. Not in terms of food, entertainment or company, but in terms of information that they might give to Major Donovan.

Very simply, nothing of any substance was said. In fact, when they discussed it in the privacy of their suite, both agreed that the conversations they had taken part in were boring, one-sided and totally without any redeeming intellectual features. The men discussed business dealings, the women the intricacies of their social lives, and Thea and Charles, still unfamiliar in their new environment, were reduced to merely smiling, agreeing as much as possible with their new acquaintances, and offering what they hoped were non-controversial, non-offensive opinions.

Instinctively, they knew they were on social trial, and they could not risk offending anyone by acting in a way that any sensitive Mexican might judge as unsuitable.

On Sunday morning, Hernando drove them to the north-central quarter of the city to attend Mass at the Church of San Lorenzo.

The neighborhood wasn't particularly pleasant. The church, erected in 1650 by the Augustinian friars, was showing definite signs of wear, and the tawdry-looking interior with its overuse of gold leaf reminded Thea of churches she'd seen on New York's lower East Side

427

where the Italian and Irish immigrants worshipped, but it was here that Mexico City's English-speaking Catholics gathered at nine every Sunday morning for the service that was conducted in English.

It was one of two church services they attended that morning. Following Mass, Hernando drove them to the fashionable Calle Neuvo Mexico for the eleven o'clock service at Christ Episcopal Church. From his years in England, Charles was more than slightly familiar with the Anglican service. And Thea, elegantly arrayed in a Lucile suit of dove gray linen with a blouse of apricot silk finished with a high ruffle around her neck, framing her face like a flower, a glorious big hat of butter-colored straw with loops of black velvet ribbon held by a gold buckle and a lace draped brim shading her face, sat through the second service as she did with the first—with the attention of a seasoned theatre-goer.

"Will we do this *every* Sunday morning?" Thea asked, more amused than annoyed when they returned to the Sanz, and she was comfortably stretched out on one of the sofas.

"With no Sunday papers to speak of, we have to do *something* together," he countered with a comprehending smile.

"I can think of a few other things."

"I'm sure you can. But seriously, Thea, do you mind church services?"

"Of course not. I believe in being thankful, and I have a lot to give thanks for this morning."

Charles sat down beside her. "Such as?"

"Oh, little things—like a very wonderful husband."

"Now *I'm* the one who's thankful," he said in a soft voice. "But to really answer your question, I think it would cause quite a few problems if we didn't attend either or both services on Sunday. The people we'll be meeting make up a fairly closed community, and—"

"And we have to do more than merely make our presence known," Thea finished. "At least we'll be able to keep our Sunday afternoons and evenings quiet. And tomorrow morning we can really start behaving like tourists."

"I thought you were going to redecorate."

"We'll do that, and see the sights at the same time," Thea replied, a glint of anticipation in her eyes. "Our first stop tomorrow is Mosler, Bowen and Cook to see about a table to put between the sofas and some decent lamps."

"What a purposeful look you have!" Charles teased. "I have an idea that we're not going to see too many sights. In fact, I may just take advantage of one of my new club memberships and vanish for the day."

"Forget it," Thea advised, putting her arms around his neck. "I meant it when I said I wanted all your opinions, and that means looking at furniture with me. Think of it as good practice for our New York apartment."

"If you say so."

"Also," Thea couldn't resist adding, "when your erstwhile mistress finally surfaces, I want to let her know straight off what kind of woman you married!" For a minute, Thea occupied herself with nuzzling at Charles' neck, losing herself in the faint scent of his sandalwood soap blending with the starch from his shirt. She wanted to forget about the parties they had to attend and the sudden presence of Ophelie de Langlade who, Thea knew instinctively, was not a woman to let go of her lovers— past, present, or future—gracefully.

"Are you very unhappy here, darling?"

Thea looked at Charles, her eyes filling with tears. "Just for a minute. Blame it on the altitude."

"I know," he said gently, holding her close. "I love you very much and, as far as I'm concerned, we can leave Mexico City without my having seen anything except the inside of every antique shop and I wouldn't care."

"Charles?"

"Yes, darling?"

"I'm hungry. Absolutely ravenous, if you want the truth."

Charles choked on his laughter. "Room service, or the restaurant?"

"Oh, the restaurant," she decided, swinging her legs off the sofa. "Let me change clothes and freshen my make-up and then we'll go downstairs." She picked up her hat from a side table. "I'm going to use the writing table in the bedroom, why don't you use the one out here for your work?"

"If I have any, I will."

"Good. Since Remington has an office here, shall we buy a typewriter?"

Charles flashed a teasing smile. "A modern machine on an antique desk?"

"It's a reproduction."

"Well, that's different," he agreed as they went into the bedroom. He loved Thea's ability to discover the tongue-in-cheek side of situations, somehow it did more to put things in perspective than any amount of serious discussions could. "If nothing else works, and I can't come up with anything to write," he went on, "I can always make use of the typewriter by pounding out poison-pen letters to Major Donovan!"

The Hotel Iturbide was the gathering spot for the American business community, as well as being the favorite hotel of the tour operators who found the large hotel to be excellent lodging for the groups they led on excursions to the capital and its immediate environs. Although nowhere near as large, it was on the type of Chicago's Palmer House in that neither was tasteful, quiet nor truly luxurious. But it was spotlessly clean, well-furnished and very comfortable and, so far, Major John Donovan was finding it a very suitable place for him to live. He had a spacious single room, and on nights when he was not making his own rounds, he found it a very pleasant spot indeed to read the works of Tolstoy, Chekhov and study his Russian vocabulary and grammar books.

But on this quiet Sunday afternoon, as he stepped off the elevator, he was not bound for his room. And, as he walked down the long hall, he made sure that no maid or porter was loitering about. The door he stopped in front of was five away from his own and, moving faster than most people would have thought possible for a man of his size, he knocked three times on the sturdy mahogany door in the agreed-upon signal, and inserted his duplicate key in the lock.

He waited to speak until he was safely inside.

"Well, you look mighty happy today. Did the doctor have good news for you?"

"The very best. It appears that, in the next two weeks or so, I shall lose several pounds of plaster of Paris." The amused, well-bred British accent was a stark contrast to Donovan's flat western speech. "It *will* be good to get about again."

"Not too much, though. Your government wouldn't like your being spotted straight off."

"No one would recognize me under this bush. I'm fairly safe."

The man stretched out on the bed was in his late thirties, and his pleasant-featured face was mostly obscured by the beard he'd grown for amusement while he was laid up. The Foreign Office career man was used to mistakes and mishaps on assignments—always other people's, of course—but upon arrival in Mexico City in early September *he* had become the victim. All it took was missing the last step as he was getting off the train, and

431

now, weeks later, Basil Summerfield's left leg, from instep to calf, was imprisoned in a bulky, heavy white plaster cast while his badly fractured ankle healed.

Major Donovan pulled up a chair and, for the next half-hour, they discussed a number of topics, ranging from President Roosevelt's campaign for re-election to an editorial in a month-old *London Times* regarding the need for modernizing the British navy. Like many men who have almost nothing in common, they had become great friends, particularly since Basil Summerfield had absolutely no communication with anyone from his own embassy. In fact, the only people who knew he was in Mexico City were Basil's wife, his superior at the Foreign Office, Sir Ernest Garland, and the King of England. The matter that brought him to Mexico was top secret. The Foreign Office had him listed as being on temporary leave of absence, and it had been decided beforehand that he should avoid his fellow countrymen. He could contact the American Embassy if he wished and, when he'd been picked up off the station platform, he was taken to the American Hospital to have his broken ankle set.

"I still can't get used to the Mexican concept that anyone who speaks English here is an American," Basil said, leading their conversation into a more professional turn. "There I was on the station platform, and all the porters were shouting that an American gentleman had suffered an accident and needed an ambulance. In retrospect, I'm very grateful."

"Don't you ever worry that one of the maids or waiters who are used to Americans and can figure out an English accent will give you away? All it takes is a conversation overheard by a third party, a few pesos changing hands, and someone knows who you are and will be busy figuring out what you're doing here."

"I hardly think so," Basil smiled. "Thievery—and that's basically what spying is—is a profession in this

432

country. One sets out to be a thief, or they don't, and a hotel employee wouldn't endanger a good position by dabbling in petty cheating. And, speaking of dabbling, I take it your friends are settled in by now?"

"Very much so. A real touchy pair, if you want my opinion. But you know them, don't you?"

"Not quite. My wife knows the distaff half, and I know the other half's family. No direct contact, although they would know my name."

"We'll leave them in the dark, then," he decided, and then paused for a moment. "They're here for *us*, you know, and they might not find the information you need."

Basil glanced at his cast. "Considering my condition, it's better than nothing. I *do* appreciate this merging of our forces. Tell your ambassador that for me."

"I will and, of course, once you're up and about, if you come across something of use to us . . ."

"It will be passed on immediately." He shifted uncomfortably on the bed. "I want this thing over with so I can go home," Basil said, his glance falling on one of the silver picture frames that decorated the bedside table. "My son is twenty months old, my daughter is less than six months old, and sometimes I think the next time I'll see them James will be at Cambridge and Patricia will be ready for her coming-out. And as for my wife . . ."

Major Donovan didn't really understand the Englishman's sense of off-handed humor, but he smiled at the remarks and assured him that the man he was seeking would show himself soon enough.

"I certainly hope you're right. The other day I came across a remark attributed to President Diaz. It's roughly that every man has his price, and no man his value. Whether or not he said it, there's a certain ring of truth to the statement, and the man I want to find is a very greedy sort who never has enough of anything. If he runs

433

true to form, his price will be very low indeed and, before I know it, he'll be out of hiding."

On this Sunday evening, Ophelie de Langlade was busy planning and plotting—an activity that always gave her a thrill of sheer power. She loved holding people in her sway, seeing them too fascinated by her to break away. Of course, such acts could be dangerous, but a lady, providing she kept a thin veil of discretion and sense of form about her goings-on, could always get away with it.

Ophelie was thirty-two, and she had had ten years of perfecting her technique. Not that it had taken that long, of course—not with a woman like the Marquise Simone de Beauvais for her mother.

The marquise, her daughter remembered, was a *grande amoureuse*, the sort of impeccably groomed, faultlessly chic, almost always titled woman that only France could produce with any success. The woman whose love affairs, whether few or many, inspired a great range of emotions, all necessary when it came to properly conducting those relationships which took place outside of marriage.

When she married the marquis at the tender age of eighteen, Simone knew her responsibilities: to be a pleasant, effective chatelaine at her husband's homes, and to produce a son who would inherit the estate when the time came. In that way, she performed admirably, and she and her husband got on much better than many couples of the *haute noblesse*. Providing that a smooth patina was kept over the marriage, the amusements they found outside of it were forgiven. The marquis and the marquise had their life together and their separate, private lives. The last thing Simone wanted five years after her marriage was another child—least of all a daughter.

Nonetheless, Ophelie was duly born (she was the marquis's child—Simone took no chances on *that*) and turned over to a series of nannies and governesses to be raised. But, by the time the girl reached sixteen, Simone realized that her daughter was fast becoming a beauty, something that would not do at all. The marquise had no wish for competition, least of all from a daughter, and that meant Ophelie had to be married off as quickly and as suitably as possible.

To this matter, Simone turned her most careful consideration.

Far too many of her friends, when faced with beautiful daughters about to be socially launched, had married them off to men many years their seniors. More fools they, Simone thought scathingly. Elderly husbands had an inconvenient habit of dying and leaving behind young brides who, after a year's mourning, blossomed in Paris society as very wealthy and independent women answerable to no one. Well, Simone was not going to risk *that*. No, Ophelie's husband would be quite different. A young and virile man who would see to it that her daughter was suitably occupied as *mere de famille*.

Simone set upon her task with a thoroughness Sherlock Holmes would have approved of. Young Guy de Renille would have done nicely, but he was still at Oxford, and Adrian and Solange were quite reluctant to bind their eldest son to a long engagement and young marriage.

Eventually, she settled on Baron Gerard de Langlade. He was twenty-four, the inheritor of a Normandy *haras* which, if not as large as the de Renille stud farm, was nonetheless substantial. And if he had more of an interest in archaeology than was deemed appropriate for a gentleman, he was wealthy and good-looking and had no immediate family save for a widowed aunt who concurred with Simone—how awful it would be if the de Langlade name died out, and how wonderful it would be for Gerard to have a fine young bride like Ophelie.

And so, four months before her eighteenth birthday, Ophelie de Beauvais walked down the aisle of the Madeleine to become the Baronne de Langlade.

Looking back on it from the vantage point of fourteen years and several thousand miles from France, Ophelie had to admit that her life was really just as she wanted it. Marriage was a necessity. No Frenchwoman had any freedom without it, and any well-bred girl lived a life of such seclusion until her matrimonial prospects could be arranged that, by comparison, English girls in their country schoolrooms lived by relaxed rules, and American girls who, one had to reluctantly admit, got the best educations, ran free like positive savages.

Ophelie had no complaints about Gerard. There was no divorce. He was her husband, and she afforded him the respect of that position. Divorce, according to Ophelie's society, was a useless thing sought by hysterical— generally American—couples. Grand passions generally burned themselves out and were not worth disrupting lives for.

Even as she thought about that, Ophelie had to smile. Her mother had seen to it that she was married almost literally from the schoolroom. No daughter to present to society, no daughter who might, in a few years time, become a social threat. Her mother's plan had covered everything, but she couldn't order up a baby, to be followed on a regular basis by other babies.

They had tried often enough in those first years, but the de Langlades remained childless. Ophelie often thought it would have been nice to present Gerard with one baby, particularly a son and heir. And she was wise enough, no matter how deeply embroiled she was in an *affaire*, to abstain from relations with her lover during the dangerous part of the month. Gerard accepted her volatile, passionate nature, but he would never stand for a child that was not indisputably his.

As their marriage continued Gerard began, slowly but surely, to immerse himself in his first love, archaeology, and as they spent less and less time together, Ophelie took up the time-honored right of wealthy, bored wives—lovers. They were always carefully selected men of equal rank and, for a few months in the spring and summer of 1897, she had captured Charles de Renille.

Now, just over seven years later, Ophelie could still recall every detail of their passion. He had been good—very good—but he had been only twenty-two and, with the intensity that only a serious, scholarly young man could have, he had been willing to cut himself off from love, from her, and submit himself to the yoke of the Church. It hadn't lasted, of course. She had known from the beginning it wouldn't.

Ophelie, in spite of her attitude toward life, wasn't heartless. And when she'd learned, two years earlier, of Charles' return home and heard of his physical and emotional state, she'd been truly shocked. His refusal to see anyone except his immediate family had meant that her meeting with him in the hotel lobby was the first time they'd seen each other since their last afternoon together.

"And in Mexico City, of all places," she said aloud as she reclined against the lace-encrusted satin pillows that decorated her richly carved bed. "Fate *does* move in mysterious ways. Just as I was wondering what my next move would be. Charles . . . so convenient. Whoever would have thought he'd come here? Well, whoever would have thought that *I'd* be here, living in this ghastly country, in a city that makes the most provincial city in France seem exciting by comparison? At least the Sanz is acceptable. It's not the Ritz, but it could be worse—much worse."

Her being in Mexico was mainly her own fault. An involvement *romantique* gone bad. A lover who didn't

437

want to marry the well-connected girl his family had selected as his bride. His people were blaming her and, wisely, Ophelie decided that a trip abroad was in order.

Gerard had participated in many digs in Egypt and Greece without his wife accompanying him, but this time it was going to be different. He was invited to join a dig in Mexico's Oaxaca State in late February, and Ophelie was coming along as far as Mexico City where she would wait for him to complete his expedition.

Thus, the Paris house on the fashionable Avenue Henri Martin was closed, the *haras* was placed under responsible managership, and shortly after the new year of 1904, the Baron and Baronne de Langlade sailed from Bordeaux aboard an older *Transat* liner, the *Xenia*, for New Orleans.

Despite her outside affections, Ophelie had never been a reluctant wife. Gerard might not be the best lover she had ever known, but he was nowhere near the worst, and the two-week voyage was spent mainly in their cabin, in bed, making love with an intensity they had never captured before. And that new feeling remained with them during their stay in New Orleans.

Ophelie disliked the Crescent City intensely. The old-guard Creole society with their opulent houses on Elysian Fields and their derision for "les Americaines" filled her with contempt. She herself disliked Americans on general principle, but what nationality did these people with their airs and graces have but United States citizenship themselves? Damn them all, she thought again and again. The complacent women with their Paris clothes, always conservative, always a year or two out of fashion, and their talk of the trip to France they'd made the previous year, or would make the next year, and their careful, very respectable husbands with their memberships on various Krewes, and their beautiful Octoroon mistresses kept in neat houses on Rampart Street. Far better to spend her days with Gerard, working with him while he did some necessary research at Tulane University, and spending the evening hours with new acquaintances in the "American" Garden District before returning to their suite at the St. Charles Hotel.

They stayed through the celebration of Mardi Gras, and sailed for Vera Cruz the Monday following Ash Wednesday. That had been in February, and now it was October, and here she still was, stuck in Mexico City, having seen Gerard for only one week in all those months.

But she had not been alone all this time. No, for a woman like her there was no need to remain unamused. But now there was Charles, and a wise woman always added up her advantages and moved in the best direction.

With that much certain, Ophelie got up off the bed and walked across the ivory and green patterned Aubusson carpet, her elaborate negligee of peach satin and ecru lace falling into an attractive train behind her.

"How can you fail to succeed?" she asked her reflection, lazily pushing a silver hairpin into her soft golden hair. "Now, first a proper invitation. Charles is probably wondering why you haven't contacted him again. What shall I say? Be sweet and conciliatory, of course, but let him know in what light you still regard him."

She sat down at her decorative little writing table and, after several minutes of careful consideration she took a sheet of her heavy cream stock personal stationery engraved *O de L*, picked up her gold fountain pen and, in her exquisite penmanship, began her missive.

My dear Charles—
    Please forgive my not having been in touch last Thursday. I left almost immediately afterwards to join the French Ambassador's house party at his

retreat in Cuernavaca. Such a charming and picturesque spot. You would have loved it.

But now, here I am again, and we must meet and talk over old and new times. Please set aside tomorrow, Monday, at half-past three, and come to my suite. We shall have a celebratory tea.

Please be assured that this invitation includes your new wife (a new friend is also joining us, so we shall be a proper foursome). I am longing to meet the dear girl. Poor thing—with so serious a husband as you, we must make her life a bit more lively. Until then, I remain your always devoted—

Ophelie

Ophelie put down her pen, carefully blotted the letter, and smiled. There was no doubt about it. At long last, *la vie dans la Ciudad de Majico* was beginning to look up.

Chapter Fifteen

October 24-26, 1904

For Charles, living with Thea had become an experience in the feminine that went far beyond anything he could ever have imagined in the brief affairs he'd been involved in where gratification was the main theme. But his married life was proving to have an all-enveloping attitude that both complimented and increased his own masculinity.

It went far beyond the perfection of her clothes, or her looks, but was made up of a myriad of tiny details. Details that only a woman intent on providing an atmosphere of peace, calm and order could create.

Thea wasn't an overly fussy woman. It was simply that she regarded this—their hotel suite—to be their first home, and it was up to her to see that they were settled in accordingly and not living out of their luggage.

Charles agreed, and saw Thea's plans for their living quarters take shape through eyes that now saw everything she did through a beautiful haze.

Every dress Thea owned was hung on a satin-padded hanger, while her handmade shoes were taken out of her specially constructed shoe trunks and stuffed with pink tissue paper. While in the dresser drawers, tiny bags made out of French ribbon and filled with a blend of patchouli chypre were scattered among the satin brocade cases that held her exquisite, expensive Lucile lingerie and a countless number of silk stockings.

Guerlain's Jicky was her perfume, and she wore enough of it for Charles to feel that he could walk into a crowded room blindfolded and find Thea merely by taking one deep breath. She not only used it in generous amounts, but she also sprayed it around the rooms for added emphasis and, as the days went by, Charles began to find that the fragrance clung lightly to all his clothes.

Flowers were everywhere in the suite: vases of roses and camelias in the sitting room, baskets of gardenias and tea roses in the bedroom, red and white carnations in the dressing room, and violets in the bathroom. Purchased from the Flower Market near the Cathedral by Angelita who went to their stalls every other morning with the list Thea gave her, their suite was transformed into a fragrant garden.

There wasn't a morning since their arrival in Mexico City that Charles didn't wake up knowing that these were the happiest days he'd known in years. Lying beside Thea in a beautiful tangle of sheets and blankets, he found that not even his occasional nightmare mattered very much. Despite the fact that they went to social functions with an ulterior motive, this was their honeymoon—the one chance they would have to be free of almost all responsibility, to concentrate on each other, to plan for their future together.

Thea was determined to make these weeks the foundation of their marriage. To her that meant putting her own definite, unmistakable stamp on the suite. Charles, on Monday morning, October 24, the day of their one month anniversary, already bound to Thea in ties of love, sensuality, devotion, understanding, humor, affection and caring, was finally exposed to the side of his wife he hadn't yet seen—Thea Harper, decorator.

*   *   *

Their first stop that bright, sunny morning was Mosler, Bowen and Cook, Mexico City's premier department store which occupied a prime corner spot on the ultra fashionable shopping district of the Avenue de San Francisco.

They made their rounds in the store together, but Charles soon found himself totally lost under their extensive purchases. In the two and a half hours they spent in the store, floor-walkers sprang to attention and sales clerks rushed to show them merchandise. Thea was no dawdling shopper, she knew exactly what was needed and, by the time they left the store, Charles' head was awash with the variety of silver trays, decorative lamps, bed linen, towels and other necessities that were deemed important to their new life.

"Are we really going to make use of all the things we just purchased?" Charles asked as they ate lunch in the wood-panelled dining room of the American Club.

"I never buy superfluous items, and I have a list of clients who can vouch for me," Thea advised him humorously as they ate the club's specialty of the day, chicken pot pie, accompanied by a sound California chablis. "Do you trust me?"

"Implicitly," he smiled.

"Good . . . then can I lose you for a day? Tomorrow would be best."

"I knew the day would come when you'd decide a husband wasn't a needed accessory for the daylight hours!" he teased her.

"Don't flatter yourself," Thea countered. "This is all for you, and I want you to be good and surprised when I have everything arranged, but it's no good if you're underfoot all day. You can occupy yourself elsewhere—in strictly masculine company, of course!" she added in an oblique reference to Ophelie de Langlade.

"I'm sure the University Club and the Reforma

Athletic Club will welcome my presence. I assume you'll permit me to return for tea?"

"I think so. And speaking of tea . . . Is there any last-minute information I should have for this afternoon—such as watching out for stray claws?"

Charles' eyes narrowed slightly. "It's going to be just as boring as all those other parties we've been to," he said, a clear note of warning in his voice.

"Do you really think so?" she challenged, meeting his gaze. "I'm going there *very* well prepared for the worst!"

Charles felt the back of his neck prickle in warning. Thea was spoiling for a chance to take on Ophelie, sight unseen. It had begun the moment she'd read the note inviting them to tea and seen the words "dear girl." There were any number of comments he could make to her regarding Ophelie, but he wisely decided to say nothing further and turned his attention to his lunch.

Charles can be very naive when he wants to be, Thea thought as she speared a piece of chicken on her fork. He knows all about Ophelie's tactics, but he thinks because he isn't interested she'll politely back off. And he'll keep thinking that until the minute he wakes up in bed with his precious baronne beside him. But I can't say any of those things to him. Even the most intelligent men have blind spots, and I guess Ophelie is Charles'.

"Are you in the mood to go on with our shopping?" Thea asked at last, putting her hand halfway across the table in an unmistakable gesture.

"I'm ready to go anywhere with you," he replied softly, his hand covering hers, their slight rift repaired.

They finished lunch holding hands across the table, oblivious to any looks—both tolerantly amused and slightly shocked—given them by their fellow diners.

"Do you think the American Club is going to survive us?" she said over dessert and coffee.

"I think so. Of course, if we were at the British Club,

we'd be ignored, but the French Club would have sent over a bottle of champagne."

"Ah, romance," Thea smiled. "How would the German Club have treated us, do you think?"

"We don't go to the German Club for lunch."

"Just as well, they don't understand the concept of honeymooners at all."

They were still laughing over each other's silliness when they left the American Club, all discussion about Ophelie temporarily shelved as they completed their shopping tour. The Bodegas Universales was their destination, and Charles and Thea passed a very enjoyable hour wandering the aisles of the extensively stocked store where Mexico City's foreign community purchased their English jams and jellies, American canned goods and boxed cereals, French wines, and assorted liquors.

Julian Levy, the store's proprietor, gave them a guided tour. He worked personally with Charles, making the liquor selections from the list Thea had compiled. It was during this stop in their expedition that Thea resumed the guise she'd adopted during the early days of their marriage—that of casual deference. While they had selected furnishings for the suite, she had been the main decision-maker. Even in male-dominated Mexico, a woman intent on decorating her home was treated with respect and a husband wasn't expected to know much. Now she offered her own opinions, but it was clear that the one making the final choice was Charles.

It was the balance wheel, the mutual admiration of each other, their deferring to one another when the public occasion called for it, that made their private life more equal, Charles knew as Hernando drove them back to the Sanz. He thought: Thea would have no more presented Mr. Levy with her list and single-handedly decided among the brands offered than I would have told the salesmen at Bowen, Mosler and Cook what style of lamp we wanted.

Suddenly, Charles realized he wasn't looking forward to tea at Ophelie's. It was barely three o'clock, six hours before they were due at a dinner party being given by the directors of the Mexican Light and Power Company, the Canadian corporation which supplied almost all the city's superb industrial and private electrical power and, in all truth, what he wanted to do in the intervening hours was to be alone with Thea in the privacy of their bedroom. He wanted to slowly undress her, to undo the tiny buttons of her Paquin tailleur and silk blouse, to unfasten the ribbons and laces of her Lucile lingerie, and to take down her hair before removing his own clothes so they could stretch out across the bed together with nothing between them. He wanted a long afternoon of kissing, touching and whispered renewals of love, with his body pressed into hers. . . .

Reluctantly, he drew away from his thoughts. They had an appointment this afternoon, and that was that. On one level, it was not going to be as sensual or fulfilling as several hours of lovemaking but, on another level, it had all the makings of a first-class French farce. Charles smiled inwardly. Ophelie had made all sorts of comments and observations about Thea. Thea had been blunt when it came to her view of Ophelie, and only one of them was right. He didn't love Ophelie any longer (if he ever had) but, as Hernando drew the motor car up in front of the hotel, Charles felt a twinge of sympathy for the Baronne de Langlade. That very sophisticated, all-knowing lady was in for quite a surprise. All in all, afternoon tea was promising to be a very interesting event for all parties concerned.

"Really, Ophelie, one would think the President of Mexico were coming to tea. Enough of this fussing about.

Come and sit with me until your friends arrive."

Ophelie permitted herself a second to glare briefly at the handsome, blonde-haired man in the well-cut business suit who was relaxing against the many pillows that decorated her deeply cushioned Louis XV sofa that was upholstered in a soft ivory brocade, before returning to the task of making certain her sitting room was in a state of absolute perfection.

She allowed herself a self-satisfied smile as her glance moved over the room. When she'd first arrived, the suite's furnishings had been suitable, even handsome. But Ophelie, suddenly realizing this was now her home until Gerard finished his dig, declared that she couldn't live with such decor, and set about redecorating. The second bedroom—which would be Gerard's when he finally returned—she left mostly intact, but every piece of furniture in the sitting room and her bedroom had been replaced. Fortunately, it was an easy task to find good furniture in Mexico—the city's antique stores were well-stocked with fine French furniture.

The sitting room had been transformed into a proper showcase for her blonde beauty and, obvious to anyone who saw it, this was not a room where a man lived. A delicate ivory and rose Aubusson rug covered the hardwood floor and, arranged in fine groupings around the room that looked out onto the street, were two sofas covered in ivory brocade, an Empire-style bergere upholstered in ivory and pink-striped satin, and a pair of blond beechwood Regence armchairs coolly covered in a white-on-white striped satin took care of half the room, while a piano inlaid with elaborate lacquer-work, its top down so it could hold a variety of heavy silver picture frames displaying lavishly inscribed photographs, took care of the other half. A Louis XV two-drawer marble topped commode with Chinese lacquer work depicting court ladies in a summer pavillion was placed against a wall, and a tulipwood table was placed between the sofas. A Regence mirror framed in blue enamel with carved and gilded flowerhead panels hung over the fireplace, and a newly designed Gubelin clock with delicate art nouveau carvings and a roman numeral dial, flanked by a pair of small but superb Sevres vases with delicate Chinese panels decorated the marble mantel.

A perfect room, Ophelie thought. Charles should be suitably impressed—and his bride suitably unnerved. Judging by Charles' Puritan instincts, he probably picked someone straight out of a log cabin. It's time for him to remember what a proper woman looks like.

Ophelie dressed almost exclusively at Worth's, with occasional forays to Lucile (strange to think that an Englishwoman could create all that beautiful lingerie), buying their most elaborate models. Her jewels were flawless, her hair elaborately styled, she knew the most skillful way in which to use cosmetics, and her perfume was Guerlain's Jicky. It was a style guaranteed to capture a man's attention. It worked in France, in New Orleans (even though it was Gerard who occupied her days and nights), and, most importantly, in Mexico City.

"I think this shall do," she informed Guenther von Basedow, the man who had been her lover for the past six months. "I sent Marie to see to the floor waiter. I want the tea to be here when they arrive."

"I don't think I've ever seen this side of you before, Ophelie," Guenther teased as she sat down beside him. "All these housewifely tasks—arranging the flowers, seeing to our tea, checking to make sure the room is perfectly dusted—reveal a whole new facet of your personality!"

After a flash of irritation, Ophelie began to laugh. "That is also known as being a good hostess which, if you had anything but those dreary fraus at your embassy who can't even arrange a vase of flowers properly, you might know something about!"

"I must admit that only a Frenchwoman can take on so many roles and excel at all of them," he said gallantly as he took one of her long-fingered hands in his, and raised it to his lips for a kiss.

"And only a German gentleman can properly compliment a lady," she responded.

"Between you and me, Ophelie, I think we have begun a new era of Franco-German relations."

For a minute, Guenther von Basedow considered kissing Ophelie, but decided against it. After all these months he knew that his delectable blonde mistress, who had turned out to be so greedy and who enjoyed their secret indulgences to the fullest, hated to have her *maquillage* disturbed. In any event, a key turned in the lock, and Marie, the baronne's maid who had accompanied her mistress from France, entered the sitting room carefully wheeling a two-tiered tea cart.

He waited patiently while both women set out the refreshments. Realistically, the German diplomat knew that his affair with Ophelie was nearing its end. He had no desire to continue with such a relationship once her husband returned, since that was guaranteed to make bad blood all around and, although it might be difficult to replace her, it was not altogether impossible.

For the past several days he had heard tales about her past lover, Charles de Renille, and his unexpected appearance in Mexico City with his American bride. Guenther had listened to her opinions, remarks, and rages with a combination of humor, resignation, and boredom. Ophelie had few women friends, none at all in Mexico and, he reasoned correctly, part of being her lover was listening to what she normally might have passed on to a confidant of her own sex. Watching her now, fussing over the teapot, cups and saucers and the cucumber sandwiches and the jelly roll like a new bride awaiting a visit from a formidable mother-in-law, but really thinking like an eagle about to catch an unsuspecting rabbit in its lair, he was hard put to keep a straight face. Ophelie was a woman who thought she had all the answers and could therefore dominate all situations. But Guenther, long in the world of diplomatic espionage where nothing was as it seemed, had a good idea that this overly confident lady was about to be quite unpleasantly surprised.

"This is all perfectly charming," he said at last, putting on his best diplomat's face. "I'm quite looking forward to this little gathering."

"Yes, I think I've planned it all quite well," she agreed, speaking in an oblique manner because of her maid's presence. "But please, Guenther, do not frighten Charles' diminutive child bride by acting like the big, bad wolf!"

Before he could reply, there was a brief knock at the door and, instead of speaking, he observed Ophelie quietly, waiting for her reaction.

"Marie, show my guests in," she instructed. "Now you will see what I was telling you about," she whispered in his ear, her eyes a shade too bright. "All things do arrange themselves. Ah, Charles . . ." Her voice moved up several tones. "At long last—"

Thea had dressed carefully for this afternoon's encounter, choosing a Lucile afternoon dress of old blue Indian crepe with insets of Irish lace, silk and gold embroidery on the sleeves and around the neck and, the moment she crossed the threshold of the suite and saw their hostess, she knew that every assumption she'd made about Ophelie was correct.

Reclining against the silk cushions in a Worth tea gown of ivory silk mousseline over accordion-pleated yellow chiffon with a crossed Empire yoke of black lace,

Thea thought Ophelie looked like a cat—a very, very surprised cat.

"—I'm so glad you could come this afternoon, and this is your charming . . . young . . . bride . . ."

Never, Thea thought with a thrill of delight, am I ever going to forget the look on the baronne's face. Yes, that's right lady, take a good, long look.

To her credit, Ophelie recovered quickly. Introductions were made and she made a great fuss about settling them on the opposite sofa, pouring out the tea and serving the sandwiches. She was indeed momentarily shocked (this woman was *not* whom she had envisioned Charles marrying), but before Ophelie could set her thoughts in order, Guenther began the conversation.

"It's Miss Harper, isn't it?"

"It was until September 24th," Thea smiled. "Have we met before, Mr. von Basedow? Oh, wait—"

"Just over two years ago in London," he supplied. "At a theatre party given by the Earl and Countess of Saltlon in honor of Admiral and Mrs. Dalton."

"What a perfect memory you have! It was *ZaZa* with Madame Rejane at the Imperial Theatre, and we all had dinner at Rule's first, followed by Grand Marnier souffle and champagne at Saltlon House," Thea recalled triumphantly.

"I return the compliment about memory. How much ground one covers in two short years and a few months."

"How unexpected," Ophelie interposed smoothly. "And here I imagined Charles plucked you straight from the schoolroom."

"Not quite, Madame." Thea looked at her over the rim of her teacup. "I was so pleased when Charles told me such a *dear old friend* of his was staying here," she said, placing unmistakable emphasis on her words.

"And what else did Charles tell you about me?"

"Oh, everything a wife needs to know," Thea

remarked in a honeyed voice, all the time thinking, *plus a few other observations made to me by the maid.* "Of course husbands, or at least *my* husband, can always be counted on to tell the absolute truth at the proper moment!"

For the next few minutes, their conversation became more general in nature, carefully skirting around the touchy subject of past relationships. They discussed the Museum of the National Palace with its beautiful antiques, and the notorious *Volador*—the Thieves Market near the Plaza Mayor—where every morning stolen goods were sold by tawdry, dangerous-looking vendors whom the police knew well enough not to bother. Rare books, silverware, gold items, paintings and rugs were offered for sale—no questions asked.

"An acquaintance of mine purchased a small Murillo for about thirty dollars in American money," Guenther volunteered. "Of course, he doesn't plan to have it hung until he returns home to Berlin."

"I should hope not," Charles murmured, silently thinking it was reprehensible enough to purchase goods known to be stolen, but to talk about having committed a felony— "Apparently it's possible to buy almost anything here."

"Particularly if it came from Maximilian's court." Ophelie gestured at the room. "The Mexicans—even the best families—are a very suspicious lot, and they won't touch *anything* from them. They think it's bad luck. I refurnished this suite for practically nothing."

Despite her misgivings about her hostess, Thea was somewhat impressed. Truth be told, it wasn't entirely to her taste, and she'd certainly never furnish a room like this for a client. Too much Louis XV, too much marquetry work, and the room wasn't large enough to accommodate the elaborately framed mirror which dwarfed the otherwise fine Sevres vases and clashed with the modern clock. And then there were all those huge white Provence roses in the heavy silver vase. Still, she felt compelled to say something positive.

"Please accept my compliments on your efforts Madame, and a bit of my envy. You're so lucky to have a piano. I miss not having one in our suite."

In a way, Thea didn't want to have to take on Ophelie. It was one problem she could live very well without. By sheer instinct, she didn't trust the baronne an inch, but everyone had to have a chance. The remark about the piano was meant as an opening, but Ophelie's response was as clear as a slamming door.

"Why, how nice to hear that you have a special talent! Charles, if you want to take the first step in being a properly devoted husband, you must buy a piano for your bride immediately. Think of how pleasantly it will occupy her time while you are . . . otherwise engaged," she added, looking at him through her lashes.

Charles didn't quite believe what he heard. "I don't think either Thea or I will have much time to play the piano," he said calmly. "We have more invitations than we can count, and our daylight hours are divided between sightseeing expeditions and visits to the antique galleries."

"If Ophelie has left them any stock," Guenther put in humorously.

The baronne rose above such remarks, and turned her attention back to Thea.

"I assure you, I am nowhere near as extravagant as I'm painted. Surely, Theodosia, you understand the need to surround one's self with things one loves."

"Oh, yes," Thea said, not daring to look at Charles. "Being close to what you love is the most important thing in the world."

It went on like that for another hour. Ophelie had never known a defeat like this. Of all the possible brides she had envisioned for Charles, *this* creature had never come to mind. She had to have some flaw, some secret she was hiding. And, once that came to light, Charles' singleminded devotion would become shaky and he would be hers again.

Reassured, she let the conversation drift, and pleasantly discovered that they would all be at the same dinner party that night.

"And that piece of news has to be our swan song for this afternoon," Thea said, making sure her voice held just the right amount of regret at having to leave so soon. "Thank you again for this lovely tea, Madame."

"You must call me Ophelie, my dear Theodosia," she insisted, graciously holding out a hand to her. "I feel these few hours have been a revelation. In fact, I might say that, on sight alone, I'd hardly take you for an American!"

For an endless moment, Thea was silent. All she wanted was to leave this suite as quickly as possible before she was ill. The windows, with typical French distrust of fresh air, were firmly closed, and the atmosphere in the sitting room was thick with the scent of roses and their perfume. She was gathering her forces, planning to verbally squash this woman when Charles spoke, his voice wiping the self-satisfied look from Ophelie's eyes.

"I never understood your dislike of Americans, Ophelie," he said evenly. "I think it may be merely for amusement, rather like smoking cigarettes is for other women. In any case, we've known each other for a long time, but I'd be happy if you'd remember that when you insult my wife you insult me. And, once you've done that, I don't think there's any reason we should know each other any longer. Good afternoon, Ophelie."

"If I were a less even-tempered man, I might be jealous of the intents behind this afternoon's pleasant little

454

gathering," Guenther von Basedow remarked once the de Renilles had left.

"Don't be an idiot. We made an agreement when we began that, when either of us wanted it to be over, the other wouldn't object. Besides," she added nastily, "if all reports are correct, you seem to have acquired a new interest in the person of that young widow who arrived from Rio last month and took one of those charming new houses in the Colonia Juarez."

"What excellent sources you have, Ophelie." Casually, Guenther reached over to the side table closest to him, opened the top of a gold box with blue and white Sevres panels, took out one of his lover's gold-tipped cigarettes, and lit it. After a few puffs, he remarked, "She wasn't quite what you expected, was she?"

"Well, you didn't help the situation any!" she snapped. "Acting as though she were a long-lost friend."

"We've met before, and I saw no reason not to be polite and to recall a pleasant evening." He smiled silkily. "Poor Ophelie, this tea party wasn't the triumph you envisioned. Instead of being an insignificant, tongue-tied chit, Madame de Renille is intelligent, chic, and quite attractive. Apparently your former lover has better taste than you care to give him credit for."

"Did you hear how she spoke to me? That little—"

"Little? I'd say Theodosia is a good three inches taller than you are."

"Amazon, then. I should have known Charles would settle on some oversized witch. Men who've been in seminaries always have odd tastes."

"Is that why you want him back? I thought we had the relationship we both wanted. I admit I've been a little careless lately, and I apologize to you with all my heart. However, I might be jealous if I thought all those unique delights I showed you were going to be used on Charles de Renille."

455

"Don't talk like that!" Ophelie felt an unfamiliar sense of frustration close over her. Nothing this afternoon had gone the way she'd planned. Charles was supposed to be ready to drop into her lap like a ripe plum. Instead—

"Your plans might not work out." There were times Ophelie thought Guenther could read her mind. "Charles might be interested in remaining faithful to Theodosia."

"Whatever for? And why should his wife complain if he *does* stray? There's no divorce, and she'll always be married to Charles. By the time we get back to Paris, I want everything arranged."

"Ah—the French and their arrangements." He put his arms around her. "So you are planning for the future, eh?" His mouth brushed against hers, parted, and touched again, this time crushing her lips beneath his. "My beautiful, beautiful Ophelie, what wondrous times we've made together."

His hands moved over her curves with supreme confidence, and Ophelie felt a familiar heat begin to course through her. He frightened her a little, he always had, but he had also shown her routes to pleasure she never dreamed were possible.

"There is my bed," she murmured as he pushed her deeper into the pillows.

"Soon . . . soon." Guenther's hands were at her breasts, freeing them from the lace of her tea gown. "We have time. Now is the moment for your German, yes? Can you wait for your Frenchman?"

"Yes—" Ophelie's head was swirling. "I can wait— It's you I want— Only you—"

"The next time there's an invitation to have tea with your baronne, I suggest you find another wife to bring along!" Thea announced shortly as they entered their suite. "Hasn't that woman ever heard about the benefits of fresh air?"

In spite of the afternoon's events, Charles was amused. "That's just typical of the French who haven't had the benefits of a healthy country upbringing or a stern British education," he said, sitting down on the arm of the nearest sofa and drawing Thea into his arms, holding her firmly between his thighs.

In that intimate, utterly delightly position, Thea felt her anger and annoyance fade. Charles' head was resting against her shoulder. His hands were at her waist, and all she wanted to do was melt against him and let the world pass by.

"Ophelie wants you back again," she remarked softly, brushing her cheek against his hair.

"Well, I don't want her."

Thea tightened her grasp. "You just remember that!" she warned. "Your baronne isn't going to rest until she has reestablished your long-dead *cinq a sept.*"

Charles raised his head and looked at Thea with a combination of surprise and humor. "How do you know about *cinq a sept?*"

Thea hid a smile. "Like I told you once, I'm not particularly ignorant. In New York, that sort of relationship is called a matinee. A married woman tells her husband she's going to attend a matinee, but she meets her lover instead. Hence the name."

"Yet another aspect of New York life revealed."

"One you're not going to have to worry about." She kissed the top of his head. "What is Ophelie's husband like?"

"Gerard? A very nice fellow. Terribly intelligent, and a superb amateur archaeologist. In fact, Ophelie once told me that Gerard was far more suited for the Church than I ever was."

"Such is life," Thea murmured, tongue-in-cheek. "What do you think he'll say to finding that his wife has taken up with an official of the German Embassy?"

"That's debatable. He and Ophelie pretty much go about their own affairs."

"I'll just bet."

"He may deal with her when he gets back from his dig. Agreeing to have separate lives and causing a scandal are two different things."

"If you say so." Her eyes travelled to the modern ivory and gold clock on the mantelpiece, their first important purchase together. "It's time to get dressed."

Charles craned his neck to look at the clock, and a moment later his grasp tightened meaningfully. "We have time."

"So *you* think. I have a few closetfuls of dresses to go through so I can pick out the perfect gown for tonight. Your precious baronne probably thought I was some little schoolgirl in her first long dress. I gave her quite a shock this afternoon, and tonight I plan to let her know *exactly* who Thea Harper de Renille is!"

Located in an attractive corner of Chapultepec Park, the Reforma Athletic Club was the gathering spot for all athletically inclined gentlemen in Mexico City. The large, handsome clubhouse and carefully tended grounds offered its members the opportunity to play tennis, cricket, field hockey or football (the European game of soccer, not the popular American university game); indoors there was a swimming pool, handball courts and a gymnasium. The perfect place, Charles couldn't help reflecting, as Hernando steered the Columbia skillfully through the tree-shaded gateway to the club, for any man who wanted to work off the previous night's multi-course dinner.

The traditional foods of black beans, hand-ground maize and chili peppers all made into a variety of exotic, pungent-tasting, aromatic meals were almost unknown to Thea and Charles in their month-long stay. These were

e foods of the common people, and any traditional
uisine on the de Veigas' table was in its most refined
rm. And now, in Mexico City, the Gallic influence on
e food they ate was obvious, and Monday night's
nner party in the largest of the private dining rooms at
e popular Cafe de Paris had been no exception to the
le of French-inspired meals.

Thirty couples, all senior officials of the Mexican Light
d Power Company, members of the board, and selected
ests had been served champagne while they dined on
ld walnut soup, fresh boiled abalone with a light chili
uce, a cheese platter, chicken roasted in banana
aves, and a mocha mousse for dessert, accompanied by
iced coffee. The long table had been weighed down with
heavy damask table cloth, silver bowls filled with purple
chids and white roses, gold-banded Limoges china,
avy silver, and multi-faceted glassware—a perfect
tting for the fifteen women seated around the table.

Some of the women had been just passable both in
oks and dress, most had been well turned out in a
nservative way, a few truly chic but, as he reflected
ck on the previous night's festivities, Charles knew
at the only truly special woman there had been Thea.
ot even Ophelie, looking like a porcelain figure come to
e in a Worth's pale rose messaline with a two-tiered
irt and mousseline de soie drapery, had equalled his
ife. Resplendent in a Lucile dinner gown of the palest
scuit-colored voile with a bolero trimmed with sapphire
ue velvet and frills of Alencon lace with a small neck-
ce of sapphires and diamonds around her neck, she had
en seated at the other end of the long table, placed be-
ween Paul Merrill, and the chief of design engineering at
ower and Light.

Seated at the opposite side of the table, several couples
vay from his wife, captured between a wealthy young
razilian widow only recently free of her mourning

period and the lovely, charming Mrs. Frederick Guern
sey, wife of the publisher of the *Mexican Herald*, Charle
observed Thea with love and pride. She could hold he
own in any group, and both men and women wer
captivated by her.

Her charm, he knew, did not lie in manipulating th
people she met, making them think she was the mo
wonderful person in the world. She didn't weave a fals
spell; rather, she met everyone on equal ground.

He also noticed something less pleasant as he tried h
almost forgotten, admittedly mediocre grasp of Po
tuguese on the widow. Obviously the design engineer ha
a great deal to say, but it was also obvious that Paul Me
rill didn't want to give up Thea for too long. There wer
no blatant acts that would cause gossip among the guest
but Charles, himself chafing under the rules of etiquett
that demanded husbands and wives be seated as far awa
from each other as possible at formal dinners, coul
easily recognize the captain's motives.

Now, hours later, as he told Hernando to come back fo
him at half-past three, he couldn't help but admire Thea'
determination once she had put her mind to somethin
Despite the tiring dinner party last night, this was the da
she would redecorate their suite, and the presence of
husband was definitely not needed.

True to his promise of the day before, Charles spent hi
morning at the British Club, exploring their super
library, and eating a traditional English lunch of choppe
lamb steak with chutney dressing in the dining roor
designed to look like those of the fine men's clubs tha
lined Pall Mall, and was now ready to view the athleti
club.

This was his first visit to the Reforma and, as soon a
he presented himself at the main desk just inside th
entrance, the hall porter quickly summoned on the club'
directors and, after an exchange of pleasantries, he wa

given a guided tour. In addition to the facilities he already knew about, there was a small bar and dining room, a lounge, a steam room, a massage room, and a billiard room.

All in all, Charles decided it was a fine male retreat, and he told the director when they returned to the main hall. They shook hands again, and Charles was on his own. The athletic offerings of the club were now his to enjoy, and yet Charles felt oddly disinterested. All he wanted was to be with Thea again, and the hours were crawling by.

Determined to make the best of the remainder of the day, he decided to locate the changing room, and he was halfway down the stairs when a figure hurtled past him at full speed and disappeared among the tall metal lockers. A few seconds later he heard the loud rattle of a locker being opened in a tearing hurry and the sound of a voice swearing in French. Feeling both mystified and amused, Charles continued on his way to locating his own locker. And, after a few false turns, found it was in the same row as his harried, unknown fellow-member who turned out to be a young man sitting on the floor, his arms clutching a black leather portfolio against his chest, an expression of terror and relief mingling on his face.

"Is everything in order?" Charles inquired gently, his curiosity getting the better of him.

"*Oui*, it is all here," the young man replied, turning his head to look at Charles, a sudden recognition dawning in his eyes, his mouth dropping open in astonishment.

Charles' interior surprise equalled his companion's exterior expression. *Ophelie was right, this place is the world's halfway house*, he thought. *One never escapes the people in one's past, they just come back to us at another time.*

It had been just over three years ago when he'd arrived at Le College Saint Michel in Brussels, sent by his

461

superiors to act as a temporary instructor.

In that fateful summer of 1901, a series of anti-clerical laws had been passed and put into effect in France. Written by Premier Rene Waldeck-Rousseau and Emil Combes, the latter a former seminarian, this policy of separating Church and State provided for the systematic elimination of religious orders from France, first by barring religious brothers and priests from teaching in schools, and then by closing the seminaries, beginning with the Jesuits.

Charles' seminary, the largest in northeastern France, had been one of the first affected, and its students were scattered to friendlier territory. He was starting his fifth year as a seminarian then, with the status of a scholastic, deep in the study of philosophy, when the order to leave France came. Under the scrutiny of his superiors, who were debating whether or not he was to be allowed to advance any further, Charles was routed differently from his fellow students.

His illness really began in those warm, early September days. While other far from promising aspirants were sent to the Isle of Jersey in the English Channel, to Maison St. Louis, a former seaside resort now owned by the Jesuits; or to Campion Hall, the Jesuit House of Studies at Oxford, Charles was sent forth to a small seminary in Belgium, and then, a week later, to Le College Saint Michel in Brussels, one of the most exclusive boys' schools on the Continent, run by the Bollandists branch of the Jesuits.

It was a place for him to mark time until the next decision was made. He could work on his study of St. Vincent de Paul in the Bollandists' library, famed in ecclesiastical and secular circles alike for its research into the lives of saints and, as long as he was there, he could help out by teaching English to a group of boys in their final form. Fourteen boys from the finest families in

Belgium, all slated to either inherit titles, be channeled into the army, the Church, or the diplomatic corps following the university. All of whom had somehow managed not only to make no progress whatsoever in this all-important second language, but to mangle the careers of two previous instructor-priests as well.

"It's been a long time, hasn't it?" Charles said to Jean-Christophe de Laulan, one of his former students. "What a pleasure to see you again."

"And you too, . . . sir." Jean-Christophe leaped swiftly to his feet, standing practically at attention in front of the former instructor who had not only captured the admiration of him and his classmates, but had managed to teach them to speak English well enough for five of them to go on to Oxford and Cambridge. "It's been a terrible morning," he explained in a rush. "I never would have pushed by you the way I did, but if this portfolio weren't here, my papa would have banished me to Panama to work on a digging crew as punishment. And if he finds out what I did, he still may!"

"A fate worse than death," Charles quipped, well aware that this young man had no idea of how to address him. Back then, his students had called him Brother. Back then, Jean-Christophe had been a wiry seventeen year old with an unruly mop of bright red hair, who had delighted in aping his instructor's Oxford accent. Today, the accent was still there, but he was nearly twenty, and three inches taller; a sedate young man almost Charles' height, with neatly combed hair that had darkened several shades, and fine brown eyes that looked at him in a combination of admiration and wonderment. "Is your father here on a mission for King Leopold?"

"Papa is the Belgian Minister to Mexico," he said proudly.

"What a fine honor," Charles told him sincerely. "How long have you been in Mexico City?"

"On and off for the past two years. It's like nothing I've ever known before," he told him. "On one hand, it's very cosmopolitan and up-to-date, with all these clubs and the motor cars and all, but on the other—" He shuddered slightly. "There are times I think I can see Montezuma holding court at Tenochtitlan, or the first Spanish settlers establishing their society."

"I know how you feel," Charles comforted. "We've only been here a short time, but there's so much in what you say. It's rather as if the way of life we take for granted doesn't run very deep here."

Still clutching his portfolio, Jean-Christophe sank down on the wood bench that ran between the lockers. "It doesn't. After a while, the atmosphere takes you off your guard, and in *le corps diplomatique* that can be a grave mistake. That's what I did today."

Charles joined him on the bench. "The portfolio?"

"Yes. There's no university system here to speak of, but I take a few courses in music at the conservatory and work as Papa's secretary." The boy looked increasingly miserable. "He trusts me, and I nearly let him down."

"By leaving the case in your locker?"

Jean-Christophe nodded. "I picked up some reports for him at the Foreign Office this morning, and then came here for a set of tennis. I had an advanced class in piano theory at noon, and in the middle of it I realized I left the portfolio behind. First I had to wait for my class to be over, then I couldn't get a cab, and it took two streetcars to get back here." He lowered his voice. "There were a group of attachés from the German Embassy here for a handball tournament this morning, and one can't be too sure . . ."

"I understand," Charles said, knowing exactly what the younger man was thinking.

"But it was here all along, and now I must offer an apology to you . . . sir. I was so involved with this *contretemps* of my own making, I forgot to ask what you are doing in Mexico City."

Charles felt a faint glimmer of amusement. "I'm here on my honeymoon. It's been a long time, with many changes for all of us," he explained gently as Jean-Christophe's mouth opened in surprise.

"Yes, yes, most certainly," he replied, recovering quickly. "When—when we heard of your . . . illness, a special Mass was said for your recovery. The whole school attended."

"I never knew until just now, and I'm deeply touched to know how highly you and your classmates thought of me as a teacher."

"And as a man," Jean-Christophe added, and then fell silent for a moment. "My congratulations sir, to you and your bride."

"Thank you, Jean-Christophe. And would you care to meet my wife by joining us for tea at our hotel this afternoon?"

The boy's serious face brightened. *"Mais oui, certainement*—if there will not be any problems—"

"None that I know of. Now, why don't you ask the hall porter to lock that portfolio in his safe and, while you're doing that, I'll call Thea and let her know I'm bringing an old friend with me. Then, I'll buy you a cold drink to steady your nerves, and we can play a game of billiards until it's time to leave. And, by the way," Charles added as they began to leave the changing room, "you've called me sir three times already and, as far as I'm concerned, that's quite enough. A lot has happened in both our lives since St. Michel's. Wouldn't you rather call me Charles?"

Thea did not install furniture for her clients. It was very simple, she told them. They hired her for advising them in the decoration of their houses and apartments.

She would buy furniture with them, sell them antiques, work out floor plans, and help them in every other way possible, but the actual work of setting up the rooms was left to professional painters, paper-hangers, floor polishers, rug layers, and furniture movers. Hire the best, and there were no problems, she said, and her clients followed. But on this Tuesday afternoon, with the help of Angelita and Concepcion, she was working at arranging all the bits and pieces that went into making this suite their home. The sitting room was complete, the maids were changing the linens on the bed, and Thea was working on the dressing room and bathroom when Charles' call came through.

"You may come back precisely at four," Thea informed him gaily as she heard his greeting, "and I have some wonderful news— We have an apartment! Newton's cable just came."

"That's the best news I've heard today," Charles said, and they briefly discussed the seventh-floor apartment, the letter of agreement that was being forwarded to them, and the lease which Charles would sign when they returned to New York. "Darling, if it wouldn't create a problem for you, I'd like to bring someone back with me for tea. We ran into each other a few minutes ago. His name is Jean-Christophe de Laulan, and his father is the Belgian Minister here." Charles hesitated briefly. "Three years ago, Jean-Christophe was one of my students at St. Michel's."

"Then of course you have to bring him along! I'll order up lots of goodies, and we'll have a fine time," she assured him. And when she returned the receiver to the cradle, Thea stood up purposefully. There was plenty of time in which to finish her work and to be dressed in order to welcome Charles and meet his friend. True, she would have preferred to have her husband to herself this afternoon, but a postponement of an hour or two

466

wouldn't hurt either of them, and would even add a certain touch of heightened pleasure by their being made to wait.

Offhandedly, she wondered about Jean-Christophe. If Ophelie de Langlade was any measure to judge Charles' pre-New York friends by, this afternoon's tea might be no better than yesterday's. Still, she'd heard nothing but praise about the Belgian Minister and his wife. They were both said to be highly principled individuals—and, hopefully, some of their standards had been transmitted to their son.

Smiling, Thea opened the bedroom door. "Angelita, Concepcion . . . how is everything coming? Oh, the bed looks fine. No, I'll arrange the pillows myself, and then I have to order tea. Señor de Renille is bringing a friend back with him, and everything has to be perfect!"

"Thea's been changing some things in our suite," Charles said to Jean-Christophe as he unlocked the door and ushered his former student in. "Darling, we're here—"

Charles' voice ceased abruptly as he stepped over the threshold. This couldn't be the same room he and Thea had walked into just one week earlier!

The sterile, alien air of the sitting room that made them all too aware that they were only a pair of elegant transients had vanished, and Charles' eyes travelled carefully, appreciatively over the transformed area.

The mahogany table with the lapis lazuli legs had been turned into a bar, and from one end to the other, silver trays holding the bottles of liquor they had selected, a cocktail shaker and an ice bucket were carefully arranged on the surface. On the other side of the closed bedroom door, the reproduction of the *bureau plat*, like it or not, had entered the 20th Century; the latest model Remington typewriter now sat in the center of its writing surface. The plain round table around which the four fauteuils were grouped had been transformed into a book table. Now covered by a blue damask cloth, some of their books were arranged around a silver pitcher holding an arrangement of pure white madonna lilies and scarlet poppies, while another round table, this one newly purchased, held all the latest newspapers and periodicals purchased at the Sonora News Company.

"I left all the whodunits and the romances in the bedroom and put all our serious, intellectual books out here to impress all our guests."

Thea's teasing voice brought Charles out of his not-quite-believing state.

"That's a very good idea," he responded, noting how the curtains were tied back to let in the afternoon sunshine, and how beautiful Thea looked leaning back against the new blue and beige silk pillows that adorned both sofas. "Of course, we're going to have to swear Jean-Christophe to absolute secrecy about our true reading habits!"

Thea held out both her hands to the young man who, if anything, looked even more awe-struck by his surroundings than Charles. "Welcome, Jean-Christophe," she said warmly. "I hope you're hungry for tea."

"Famished, madame," he replied quickly, coming forward to bend low over her hands. "I'm honored to meet you."

Charles had a faint feeling of *deja vu* as he watched Jean-Christophe move skillfully back from Thea and take his seat on the opposite sofa. Just as I did on my first day in New York, he thought as he took his place beside Thea.

"Hello, darling."

"Hello, darling," he responded as the newly decorated marble mantel caught his eye. Flanking the clock were a pair of Oriental vases in the palest celadon on stands of carved rosewood, filled with white tea roses and statice—

two grand bouquets that looked as if they might have grown in a garden like that. "Did we buy those vases?"

Thea laughed delightedly. "No, they're our wedding present from the Chinese Minister. I guess I *did* wear you out yesterday afternoon."

"Not *that* badly," he smiled. "I *do* remember buying all the silver things. My wife believes a husband does more than simply pay the bills for redecorating," he explained to Jean-Christophe, who was looking at them with adoring eyes.

"A very wise idea, madame," he said sagely, and Thea and Charles began to laugh.

"Tell Jean-Christophe to call you Thea," Charles advised. "He called me 'sir' three times before I told him it was perfectly all right to call me by my given name."

The last ice had been broken between them and, when Angelita and Concepcion brought in their tea, a strong bond of companionship had already been formed.

Thea had solved the problem of no table between the sofas by purchasing a pair of red and black lacquered trays that had been mounted on wrought iron stands. She directed the maids in dividing the tea things between both tables, and then surveyed the results with an approving eye. There were plates of brown bread and butter, and tiny beaten biscuits stuffed with ham; a three-tiered cake stand held an assortment of petit-fours; and a large round plate displayed a mouth-watering variety of French pastry.

This afternoon, Thea had selected a Lucile afternoon dress of amber taffeta with insets of Cluny lace and ruffled sleeves, making herself a perfect contrast for the predominantly blue and beige tones of the room, as well as for the traditional Imari design of cobalt blue and deep rust with gold trim on the white porcelain background of the cups and saucers and plates of the dessert set they'd purchased.

"We'll feed you, and then you have to look at our wedding pictures," Thea laughingly warned Jean-Christophe as she gestured toward one of the tables flanking the fireplace where a series of simple sterling silver picture frames held their newly arrived wedding pictures.

Jean-Christophe swallowed a beaten biscuit. "When were you married?"

"Just one month ago yesterday in San Antonio," Thea said, skillfully telling her story. "We decided to elope, and to come to Mexico for our honeymoon, but we didn't want to be married without someone we knew there with us. A good friend of mine recently married a man from San Antonio and, when we telegraphed the news, she said her new home was the best place to get married because everyone in Texas loves to go to a party and won't ask too many questions! We had just the kind of wedding we wanted, but I'm afraid that back in New York, we must be an absolute scandal."

"Until the next one comes along," Charles added, marveling at Thea's deft mixing of fact and fallacy. "By Christmas we'll be just one more very respectable couple."

Thea bit back a risque remark and instead asked Jean-Christophe about his life in Mexico City.

Obligingly, he told them about his duties as his father's secretary, and his music courses at the conservatory. But he finally admitted that all he wanted was to be just another university student.

"Papa is quite strict about certain things, you see, and one of them is that we stay together as a family as much as possible," he explained. "I'm an only child, and he and Maman did not want me to be thousands of miles away from them. But, when we arrived here two years ago this past July and found there was no university system to speak of, he allowed me to go to Stanford. Thanks to

Charles, I haven't any trouble with English," he said with a respectful and admiring look at his former teacher. "I completed my freshman year and half my sophomore year when I became Papa's secretary. The man he had was dismissed—sent back to Belgium for some transgression. Papa needed someone he could trust, and asked me to take a year off and help him out."

"How very wonderful of you to do that," Thea praised. "And don't worry about missing a year. I know lots of young men and women who've done that, and they find they have much more interest in their studies when they go back—plus a whole new outlook."

Jean-Christophe looked immensely cheered by Thea's words. She had given him praise and hope that this missed year wouldn't affect him adversely, and now he wanted to return the favor. He looked approvingly around the room, noting the attractive lamps and the art nouveau needlepoint screen in front of the fireplace.

"Charles told me that you were arranging for all your purchases today," he said, polishing off an eclair stuffed with coffee mousse and selecting a portion of genoise cake topped with a realistic-looking pink cream rose flavored with Grand Marnier. "It's so difficult to live among furnishings chosen by other people, but you've made this sitting room your own with no help at all. At the chancery, we live with all the furniture left behind by the other ministers. My maman reads all the American women's magazines," he supplied, "and every so often she threatens Papa that she is going to hire the New York interior decorator, Theodosia Harper, to come to Mexico City and redo the Legation!"

Thea and Charles listened to Jean-Christophe's words and, choking back their laughter, exchanged mirthful glances.

Jean-Christophe was nonplussed. "Have I said something wrong?"

"Of course not," Thea assured him. "But I'm afraid your mother's plans aren't going to work out. You see, *I'm* Theodosia Harper."

"But—oh—" The boy looked stricken. "I'm such an imbecile—I should have realized—"

Charles laughed and placed a serving of chocolate ganache, a rich cake bursting with incredibly dense chocolate cream, on Jean-Christophe's plate. "Eat some chocolate, it will cheer you up—and don't be upset."

"Charles is right—I'm not insulted—and I'm honored by your mother's interest in me as a decorator." Thea helped herself to an equally rich piece of chocolate cake adorned with toasted almonds, and then stood up, crossed the floor to open the bedroom door, and disappeared inside. A moment later she was back. "My card," she said to Jean-Christophe. "Please give it to your mother with my compliments."

He studied the distinctive calling card with its drawing of a Hungarian Vizula holding a basket of flowers in its mouth, and the words engraved beneath the animal that was the hunting dog of Hungary's aristocracy. "Maman will be over the moon," he murmured, putting the card in his billfold.

"Also tell her that, if she likes, I'll be happy to recommend some other interior decorators she might want to consider," Thea said. And then, her curiosity finally getting the better of her, switched topics. "What kind of teacher was my husband, Jean-Christophe?" she asked, oblivious to Charles' groan. "He told me about teaching at St. Michel's, but he hasn't told me *how*."

"We were an ungovernable group when it came to learning English, my friends and myself. The problem was we couldn't stand our instructors, and the Rector didn't realize that a religious habit is no protection to a teacher who isn't liked. When Charles came, he knew just how to treat us. That first morning he walked into

472

the classroom, asked us to introduce ourselves, and then he perched on the desk and said that not one word of French was to be spoken in the next hour and a half. We studied Shakespeare, Pope and Dickens, read the London *Times* and wrote letters to the editor."

"Were any of them published?"

"No, just graded by their overworked teacher by a very dim electric light," Charles put in with wry humor. "A less dedicated—or possibly smarter—teacher would have mailed them off to Great Victoria Street and let the *Times*' esteemed editors decide what to do with them!"

Between the three of them they demolished the tea and, when only the crumbs were left, Thea and Charles showed off their wedding pictures, and let Jean-Christophe browse among their books.

He was eagerly leafing through Charles' autographed copy of *The Naval War of 1812* when he stopped, looked up, and regarded them with grave eyes. "This has been a wonderful afternoon, one of the best I've had in the past nine months outside of my own family." He put the book down and looked squarely at them. "Life here is a lie. A false *gemeinschaft*. We pretend—those of us in the foreign community and the more liberal members of the Mexican upper class—that we all get on famously. But it's all false. Antoine, my father's former secretary, didn't commit some stupid diplomatic mistake, he was passing reports to the German Embassy . . ."

While Jean-Christophe's voice trailed off, Thea closed her right hand around Charles'. Her heart began to pound sickeningly. The polite facade had its first small tear.

"You don't have to tell us this," Charles comforted him.

"I do. You have to know what's going on. Antoine wasn't giving away anything important, or doing it for too long, so he was just sent back to Brussels. Our foreign office will put him in some dead section where he'll be of no interest to anyone. That's how they do it. Lie, evade, and cover-up. We pretend we're all one big family, but it's nothing like that," he ended bitterly. "It varies in degrees, but we all hate each other, and that's the only truth!"

"Poor Jean-Christophe," Thea murmured several minutes later after the Belgian Minister's son had thanked them profusely for their hospitality and left. Now they were standing on the section of the gallery just outside their sitting room, looking down at the flower-banked patio dominated by a large marble fountain. "He must have been carrying that grief inside him for months."

"This day has been a series of shocks for him," Charles said, and related the details of their meeting in the changing-room of the Reforma Athletic Club. "The incident with the portfolio upset him very badly, and he could hardly discuss it with his father."

"Then I'm glad we were here for him," Thea said, putting her arms around Charles' waist and leaning against him. "Do you think he knows about us?"

Charles' arms closed around her. "What makes you say that? Because of what he said about his father's secretary?"

"Yes—because he said all of this *after* he saw the inscription T.R. put in the copy of his book. 'For Charles de Renille, who holds high the qualities of freedom and loyalty,'" she quoted. "You can't blame Jean-Christophe for thinking we just may be something more than typical honeymooners who can't spend more than an hour out of each other's sight!"

Charles drew her closer. "I love you so much."

"And I love you just as much. I love your mind for its clarity, because it knows right from wrong. I love your heart because it's honorable, and your soul for its purity. And I love your body because every time we make love we pledge ourselves all over again."

"There are times when I feel so unworthy of you," Charles whispered. "But right now I think I'm the luckiest man in the world. I was so proud of you last night at the Cafe de Paris, not only because you were the most beautiful woman there, but because you were the most intelligent, honest and charming. And tonight, at the Bolivian Legation—"

Thea gave him a secret smile. "I think I forgot to mention something. This afternoon, just after you called, I rang up the wife of the Bolivian Minister and, apologizing profusely, explained that we had to withdraw from this evening's reception."

"You didn't!" Charles was both startled and delighted at Thea's tactics.

"I most certainly did! I said I was headachy and dizzy—probably a delayed reaction to the altitude—and that you insisted on remaining at my side."

Charles' eyes sparkled with comprehension. "I suppose you have your—or is it our—cure worked out?"

"Mm-hmm." Thea drew him back into the sitting room and, finally out of the sight of any other guests of the hotel who might be taking that moment to enjoy a bit of late afternoon sunshine on the gallery, she kissed Charles deeply and fully on the mouth, not quite taking him by surprise, but still having a moment or two before his own response began, making the room swirl around her.

"Our bedroom," she told him a minute later, her mouth brushing lightly against his ear. "From hotel room to pleasure dome."

"It would be bliss with you on an army cot in a tent."

"I think I've done a little bit better than that." She took his hand. "Come—"

It was like being in a brand new room.

The first thing Charles saw were the two new reading lamps with adjustable necks and subtly pleated satin shades that were placed on the nightstands and surrounded by their favorite books. The second thing he saw was the transformed bed.

The blue damask bedspread that had so irritated Thea had been banished, as had the hotel linen and blankets. Now the mattress and pillows were covered with the most expensive sheets she could find, their fine, snowy whiteness replete with eyelet trim and scalloped borders.

Thea stood quietly beside Charles, letting him take in the sight of six large, square pillows, three on each side, as well as the supplementary arrangement of half a dozen decorative pillows made of satin and lace. A goose-down filled puffed satin comforter—perfect for the cooler nights—was placed on the bed, and a duplicate was neatly folded on the white brocade-covered bench that was placed lengthwise at the foot of the bed. Resting on top of the extra comforter, open and ready as if it were time to get ready to retire for the night, were their nightclothes.

"If you don't say something, I'm going to think that we've become a modern version of the shoemaker and his wife—I can decorate for everyone else, but not me and my husband."

Charles turned to her. "I'm truly speechless. I could never have believed that a room could be turned around with just a few purchases."

"Sometimes that's all it takes," she pointed out. "New linens and comforters, and more pillows for the bed. The extra satin and lace pillows for the chaise lounge—not much at all. And as for the bathroom . . . If you'll come with me—"

Except for a few new framed prints hanging on the walls, and a swirled lead crystal vase filled with red and white carnations, the dressing room was still the same, but the bathroom had undergone the same transformation as the sitting room and bedroom.

Already equipped with excellent fixtures, there was now a thick white rug on the floor. The ledge of the large marble bathtub held bottles of Jicky bath salts, porcelain bowls of Jicky and sandalwood soaps, and large natural sponges. In piles beside the tub were the finest quality, fluffy white bath towels, and hand towels of the same quality hung on the racks that flanked the large marble washstand whose shelf held shell-shaped dishes of cucumber and glycerin soaps and the tortoiseshell box that held Charles' shaving equipment.

Overwhelmed, Charles leaned against the sink. "This is all perfect. Now I know how your clients must feel when their homes are redecorated."

Professionally speaking, Thea knew that was one of the highest compliments Charles could ever give her. She locked her arms around his waist, brushing her cheek against his.

"Wait until we get back to New York," she promised. "Our apartment is going to have everything we love in it. For now, this is just our laboratory to see what works and what doesn't, a place for us to be together with as much comfort as possible." She laughed and pressed herself against him. "Shall we begin our experiment now?"

With one easy movement, Charles swept Thea up in his arms, pausing long enough to kiss her and reignite the spark that was always just under the surface. "There's nothing I'd like better," he said as he carried her back to the bedroom, and the open and inviting bed. "I can't think of anything I'd rather do then spend the evening right here with you while we pretend to the rest of the world that we're too ill to go out!"

In the days when the Aztecs ruled Mexico, Chapultepec Park had served as a fortress, its summit rising nearly two hundred feet above the valley, giving an excellent view of all who approached. In the early years of the 16th century, Montezuma II transformed the fortress into his summer residence, building gardens and fish ponds, an aviary, harem baths, and a hunting lodge. And, less than sixty years before this warm autumn of 1904, it had been the sight of one of the last major battles of the Mexican-American War of 1847-48. But now, in the first decade of the 20th century, Chapultepec was miles of beautiful pathways bounded by magnificent trees—a showplace park that ranked with any of the other major public parks in the great cities of the world.

Within its boundaries, that park contained not only the Reforma Athletic Club, a zoo, a skating ring, and a popular cafe, but an automobile club which was currently under construction. The focal point of the park was Chapultepec Castle. Constructed in 1785 as a viceregal residence, it now served as the warm weather residence of Porfirio Diaz and his charming second wife Carmen and, in the morning hours of the summer months, it was possible to meet the now seventy-four-year-old President of the Republic taking an early morning stroll around the lake. Although it functioned as the official home of a head of state, one wing of the castle was the province of Mexico's military college where young cadets from the country's best families were trained for careers as army officers and wore uniforms patterned after those worn by the aspirants of St. Cyr, France's premier military academy.

Open to the public from half-past five in the morning to seven in the evening, the park was a gathering spot to see and be seen and, on Wednesday morning, a few minutes before nine, Hernando drove the Columbia touring car around the final *glorieta* on the Paseo de la Reforma, turned onto the Avenida del Bosque, and deposited Thea and Charles—both in riding clothes—in front of the stables.

"Hernando will be back in two hours—that should be enough time for what we have to do," Charles said as they went to see about the saddle horses they'd need for that morning's activity. "If we finish early, we'll visit the deer park."

"I'm going to hold you to that no matter how long this takes. After we finish with Major Donovan, I want to spend several peaceful minutes watching the deer graze."

"Just be glad your major had the presence of mind to select the bridle path instead of the Molino del Rey part of the park."

"The old battlefield from the Mexican-American War? That *would* have been more like him."

"Particularly since it's now part of the government factory that makes cartridges for the army," Charles concluded dryly. "Ah, here's the stable manager with our horses. *Buenas dias, señor*—"

Even their upcoming first meeting with Major Donovan couldn't mar the beauty of the late October morning. They had spent the long night in each other's arms, their bodies pressed close together, reveling in the deepness of their love. They had woken in the bright morning sunlight fulfilled and ready to face the day that required them to make their first report.

The drive along the Paseo de la Reforma had been a fine distraction. The entire two and a half mile length, beginning at the statue of Charles IV on his horse and ending at Chapultepec Park, was a flawless expanse of roadway, a double avenue shaded by eucalyptus trees and bordered by the most fashionable houses in the city, almost all erected in the past fifteen years, and almost all built in a style more reminiscent of the finest homes of Paris, not Madrid. At intervals, the avenue widened into circles called *glorietas*. There were six of them, each four hundred feet in diameter, every one of them providing a calm oasis of careful landscaping and well-tended flowers.

"The Paseo de la Reforma is probably one of the few good ideas that Maximilian ever had," Thea remarked as she and Charles, mounted on their rented horses, made their way out of the stable area toward the area of the park known as The Bosque.

"Like most not-too-intelligent men who are suddenly given positions of great power, the Emperor must have had visions of himself riding down the avenue mounted on a splendid white horse with a cheering crowd lining both sides of the road."

"I have an idea that was just the motivation behind it," Thea agreed. "But when it comes to watching someone on a horse, I'd much rather see you than some boring king or emperor. You could ride a dray animal and look as though you were on a thoroughbred. I'm a good rider, but you're superb."

"I'm just like any other man who grows up on a *haras*," Charles smiled as they took their mounts along a bridle path where old cypress trees were hung with Spanish moss, forming a graceful fringe like so much soft lace, "which meant that I was half boy and half horse—a perfect centaur." He touched his heels to the sides of the horse and moved ahead of Thea at a quick gallop. Behind him, he could hear her laughter as she urged her own horse on in their impromptu race. The groves of palms, ferns and old oak trees, the floral borders and new young trees all reminded him of Paris' Bois de Boulogne—a potent remembrance of what had come before in his life, the promise of the future, and the intrusive problems of the present.

John Donovan was waiting for them at the agreed-upon spot and, to their mutual surprise, the major was smiling as he greeted them.

"If all the reports on the society page of the *Mexican Herald* are true, the both of you are all the latest rage in young married couples," he said as they dismounted and joined him at the foot of a bronze statue that had a large bouquet of fresh flowers adorning it.

"They call it *muy simpatica*," Charles said with a dismissing shrug. "I think it means that we smile a lot, don't disagree and know which fork to use at dinner!"

"I really wish we had something to tell you," Thea said, not really telling the truth; if there was no information then they had a legitimate reason to leave. "Most of the people we've met so far don't seem to have—or care to discuss—any conversation out of the mundane."

He raised his eyebrows. "Nothing at all?"

"I was having a fascinating conversation with some-one from Canadian Power and Light the other evening—"

"That would be Mr. Cathcart."

Thea's eyes narrowed, and she threw a look at Charles. "If you're expecting us to inform on people, Major Donovan, you have the wrong couple!"

"Now, Mrs. de Renille, there's no need to get all excited." The major's voice was soothing. "No one is going to reprimand a man for a dinner party conversation. Besides, I doubt if he were telling you anything that isn't common knowledge."

Then why do you want to know about it? Charles thought, but kept silent. This was Thea's event, and she wouldn't appreciate interference on grounds of hus-bandly protection.

"Did Mr. Cathcart mention he'd just come back from Panama?"

"And that he'd been invited to make the trip by John Wallace," Thea added in a careful voice, referring to the man who'd been appointed chief engineer of the Panama Canal.

"And—?"

"And all he said was that he was asked to inspect Ancon and write a report on his views of the modernization process the area will have to undergo. You shouldn't be worried, Mr. Cathcart was *very* enthusiastic about the project."

The major nodded in approval. "Anything else?"

"I might have had a longer conversation if it hadn't been for Captain Merrill. He seems to have forgotten that it isn't polite to monopolize one's partner at dinner to the exclusion of all else."

The irony in Thea's voice was completely lost on the major.

"I asked him to keep an eye on you, since husbands and wives don't sit together at those dinners. A stand in for Mr. de Renille, as it were."

"I'm not in need of a protector, Major, and I certainly don't need a surrogate husband," she said coldly. "Please convey that to Captain Merrill for me."

"As you wish . . . Mrs. de Renille," he said, adding her married name as if it were some unimportant afterthought. "Tell me," he went on casually, "why weren't you two at the Bolivian Legation's reception last night?"

"Thea wasn't feeling well," Charles said as calmly as he could, "and I certainly wasn't going without her. And, if I remember correctly, we are at liberty to pick and choose among our invitations."

"No quarrel with me, Mr. de Renille." Major Donovan made a conciliatory gesture. "Tell me, have you and your . . . wife had any difficulties among the people you've met?" he asked cryptically.

"Why, because they don't like Americans here, and because I'm French—which the Mexicans seem to have a penchant for—you think someone will let their guard down and pass a remark that they wouldn't dare make in front of my wife?"

"That's the general idea. Anything?"

"No." Charles' voice was uncompromising. He certainly wasn't going to pass on any of Jean-Christophe's confidences to the major. "And the Germans don't appear to be doing anything special, either. Their embassy has far too many officers and attachés. They seem to be everywhere, singly and in groups, but none of them are walking around with TNT in their pockets!"

The morning was rich, green and full of promises—more like May than October—but the air between the two men had become threatening. Alarmed, Thea looked from Charles, his tall, well-knit body shown off to its best advantage in his flawless riding clothes, to Donovan, with his rigid and unyielding military carriage, still managing to look somewhat round-shouldered in a kit that looked as if it had come from a Sears, Roebuck's catalog—and not a recent one, either. She had to say something quickly or this meeting was going to turn ugly.

"This is a very secretive city, Major," she offered. "No one tells *anything* and, even then, it may be a lie. It's like being at a Venetian *bal masque*."

Her statement worked and the air of tension eased.

"You're very right, Mrs. de Renille," he allowed in a weary voice. "The social life you and your husband are leading *is* like being at a masked ball but, just remember that no disguise stays on forever!"

"I think it is such a shame that Americans of your quality, Madame de Renille, must have a president like Theodore Roosevelt."

For a second Thea, as she stood in a corner of the ballroom at the Russian Embassy, wasn't sure if she'd heard correctly.

"I'm sorry," she said to the wife of the Austrian Minister, speaking over the strains of the Strauss waltz, "but what did you say?"

"That it is too bad your country has such a blustering

483

bully as its head of state. Why, he wasn't even born in the United States!"

For a long minute, Thea turned her attention to the dancers moving along the highly polished floor. Ophelie, looking quite sure of her charms in Worth's white taffeta gown spangled in silver over an underdress of tucked white mousseline, waltzed by in Charles' arms, and Thea felt a sharp twinge of pure jealousy. She and her partner for this dance, Oliver Gordon, first secretary at the British Embassy, had decided to sit this one out and had joined a group that included a young couple from the Italian Embassy, Guenther von Basedow and Baroness Annalise von Grelheim. They had been making the usual inconsequential small talk under the rock crystal chandeliers, remarking on the embassy's fine oil paintings and tapestries, the rich brocade-upholstered furniture, the room set aside for icons, and the amusing rumor that Imperial Russia never sent its ambassadors off on assignment without a trunk full of Faberge bibelots to be dispensed at the proper parties, when the Austrian baroness dropped her little bombshell. An attractive woman in her early thirties, the whipped cream of Demel's had not yet made a noticeable difference in her figure, and she was well set off in Worth's silvery green satin embroidered in cream floss, but she also had one of those syrupy Viennese voices that Thea always instantly mistrusted—and, with good reason, it now appeared.

"Wherever did you hear such a lie?" Thea finally questioned in a voice so calm it amazed her. "The United States Constitution forbids anyone being President who wasn't born in America."

Annalise looked disbelieving. "I know nothing at all about your constitution, but I *do* know what I read in the newspapers. Kurt was at our legation in Madrid when your country had its little dispute with Spain," she explained to their group, "and a newspaper article stated very clearly that your now-President was born in Haarlem, in Holland, came to the United States, and was a policeman in New York City!"

"Oh, *that* story!" Thea exclaimed contemptuously. "The *Sun* reprinted it, and everyone in New York laughed about it for days! It's an utter and complete lie!"

The others began to laugh, but the baroness flushed and looked daggers at Thea, who smiled back sweetly and brushed an imaginary speck of dust off the plaited gold satin sash of her white chiffon and charmeuse Lucile gown.

"Of course we all knew that story was absolute bosh— particularly when it referred to Harvard as a 'commercial school'," Oliver Gordon said in a jocular voice just as the music ended and Charles and Ophelie joined them. "Even in England we know what store you Americans put in your Harvard University."

After that comment—for which she could have happily kissed the somewhat overweight Oliver—Thea was swamped with questions about Harvard and Theodore Roosevelt and, as she answered each inquiry, she could feel Charles' boundless pride in her.

"Is your father a professor at Harvard?" Pia della Carvelli wanted to know.

"No, he was researching his first book at the Harvard Library the year Theodore Roosevelt was a senior. Daddy was asked to tutor some last-year students in the natural sciences, and the President was one of that group. I was a year old at the time, and we lived just across the Charles River, in Boston, on Joy Street, and the President used to come to our house. I have this faint memory of him tossing me in the air—"

"Now who is lying?" Annalise's voice was triumphantly jeering. "Your beloved President is an old man, well over fifty years old, and you are what—twenty-three, twenty-four?" She gave a uniquely European gesture at their little group. "A teller of tall tales, like all Americans!"

"Really?" Thea thought she was going to choke on her unexploded temper, and only Charles' steady, comprehending gaze kept her from slapping the Austrian baroness. "I'll be twenty-six on November 14th. I was born in 1878. The time I'm referring to was the university year of 1879-1880. President Roosevelt was born on October 27, 1858, making tomorrow his forty-sixth birthday!"

To Thea's amazement, Annalise turned on Guenther von Basedow. "It's your fault, you—you feeder of lies! When we were all in Madrid in 1898, that night you dined with Kurt and me, you showed us that article and swore it was true!"

The German diplomat remained umoved. "My dear Annalise, if I recall correctly, all I said was that, with Americans, one never knew where they came from. Of course, everyone knows that the President is, on his father's side, descended from one of the finest families of New York, and from his mother is attached to an equally aristocratic Georgia family. I'm sure that the fact that the Bullochs were slave owners, and that two of the President's uncles, Confederate officers both, had to flee to England following the Civil War, will have no detrimental effect on the voters next month."

"Herr von Basedow, I congratulate you on your grasp of American history!" Thea said gaily, a cold feeling sweeping over her. Continental Europeans simply didn't make a deep study of American history and Presidents unless they had an ulterior motive in mind. "I hope you're as hopeful for the President's success on the eighth as I am."

"As an interested observer, I certainly am, Madame de Renille. And perhaps later this evening you will favor me with news of how your father's expedition in Egypt's

Valley of the Kings is progressing. Surely we won't have to hold our breaths until Elston Harper's next book appears?"

The ice inside Thea grew colder. "If you're depending on me for inside gossip, I'm afraid you may have to wait. None of my father's letters have caught up to me here. In fact," she went on, keeping her tone light, "you seem to have more first-hand information than I do. I expect you could tell me what cataract my father is on!"

Or have your intelligence system find out, she thought grimly.

"*Ach*, no." He favored her with a friendly smile that did not quite reach his eyes. "My information comes from an uncle who is a professor at Cairo University. He happens to be a great admirer of your esteemed father, and was very pleased to make his acquaintance this past August in that city's Turf Club. Such a charming man, Mr. Harper, my uncle wrote me, *he* would make a fine President!"

"Your country needs a true gentleman to lead it," Ophelie put in in a silky voice. "But, of course, the baser instincts of your fellow citizens will keep that from ever happening. A man of the people, indeed! It is typical of you Americans that President Roosevelt, despite his fairly suitable background, is a blustering bully."

"You've been paying too much attention to *El Imparcial*, Ophelie," Charles said in a quiet, dangerous voice. "You should have the Sonora News Company send you over a few copies of the *New York Times*. They may be two weeks old, but I think your reading habits could do with some contrast."

"Ah, Charles, your bride has made you quite the American, but you know what they say about converts— they *always* behave so queerly!" She gave him a sweeping look. "If we are not careful, you shall lose all your French outlook, and *then* what shall we have?"

"So far, I haven't had any complaints about my outlook—or anything else for that matter."

There was an unmistakable warning note in Charles' voice, and Thea had to bite back a smile as Ophelie made a brief apology. Then, as the baronne made a motion with her shoulders, Thea noticed something that almost made her miss the other woman's reply. Almost, but not quite.

"You see, Charles, you're already becoming belligerent. You must remember that we French always know when it's best to withdraw and protect ourselves rather than stand and fight a losing battle!"

"Oh, you French can certainly protect yourselves—and your belongings," Thea told her hotly, her eyes turning green with anger. "And my government should really thank yours for that little favor. I have it on rather accurate authority that down in Panama the railroad built by France is in poor condition, and the buildings put up by the Compagnie Nouvelle are falling to pieces, but all the abandoned equipment was perfectly stored away. Thanks to France and the care it showed, our engineering crews are overhauling the excavators right now and will be making very good use of them in about six weeks—turning the hole France decided it was best to leave behind into the Panama Canal!"

A damp, chill wind blew along the deserted Paseo de la Reforma and, in the tonneau of the Columbia, Thea moved closer into Charles' arms, her head resting on his shoulder as Hernando drove them back to the Sanz.

"This is so nice," she whispered.

"Did I tell you how proud of you I was at the Embassy?" Charles asked as his cheek brushed against the rich sable that outlined the hood of Thea's black velvet evening coat. When they returned to New York, he decided, he would go to Revillon Feres and order Thea

488

a full-length sable cloak like the one Henry had given Alix. "You told off the Austrian Minister's wife superbly!"

"The whipped cream at Demel's is smarter than she is," Thea murmured and, several moments later, added, "Are you *sure* I didn't embarrass you in front of all your friends?"

"If any of those people were truly my friends, I deserve to be embarrassed—on the grounds of being a very poor judge of character."

"Speaking of characters . . ."

"Major Donovan?"

"The very same. He was right, you realize. The masks certainly slipped off tonight."

"Austrians." Charles shrugged. "Their country is the picture postcard of Europe, but they're smothering under a rigid social order that refuses to change, or accept change in others. They produce mechanical clocks, delicious pastries and abstract intellectuals, but they can't deal with heavy industry, an effective navy or build a canal that another major power couldn't complete."

"In other words, they need someone to be jealous of."

"Rather. And, since Germany is too close, and everyone for one reason or another envies England—"

"The United States makes a convenient whipping post," Thea finished, and began to laugh softly.

"Would you like to let me in on the joke, or is it merely the altitude finally making you light-headed?"

"No, I think I discovered something else tonight, and the key word is *whipping*."

"Would you care to explain further?"

"It's something only another woman would notice," Thea informed Charles seriously. "When Ophelie gave one of her adorable little gestures, I noticed something she was trying very hard to cover up with white face paint and rice powder. There's a nice bruise on her shoulder that hasn't completely healed, and she doesn't want anyone to see her porcelain-white skin marked up. I don't blame her," Thea continued triumphantly. "After all, if I were her, I wouldn't want to let it be known that I let my lover, Guenther von Basedow, beat me!"

Chapter Sixteen

October 27-31, 1904

Early the next afternoon, Thea was examining a selection of gold and porcelain boxes in one of the better antique salons that lined the Avenue de San Francisco, a shop that had a gold-bordered, hand-lettered window sign announcing "English Spoken Here," when the bell attached to the door tinkled to announce the arrival of a new customer, and she looked up to see Ophelie de Langlade, well turned out in a Worth street dress of maroon broadcloth trimmed in velvet, closing the door behind her.

For a long minute, the two women observed each other silently. Ophelie remained with one hand on the doorknob as if she were making up her mind whether or not to leave. And Thea, her magnifying glass clutched in her right hand, felt every inch of her body—elegantly clad in a beige serge Lucile suit with a shaded beige taffeta blouse with fine handmade tucks and bands of bead embroidery—tense in preparation for a confrontation.

"Is Mr. Lopez here?" Ophelie inquired at last in a faintly bored voice, referring to the shop's proprietor. "Unlike some customers, I don't care to deal with his assistants."

"Please don't be concerned, Ophelie," Thea advised, letting herself relax just a bit. "Mr. Lopez is on the premises and should be back shortly." Thea returned to studying the markings on an unusual French 18th century gold box with a hinged cover crafted in the shape of a bottle. "He's up in one of the storerooms."

The baronne nodded, and began to explore the well stocked shop. Vittorio Lopez, the half-Italian, half Spanish owner, prided himself on both the exclusivity of his merchandise and the discernment of his clientele. Culled from the city's leading social, diplomatic, and business families, as well as the occasional tourist who recognized the quality of his stock, his salonlike atmosphere of fine carpets over hardwood floors, mahogany counters, glass topped vitrine tables holding an inexhaustible supply of bibelots, selected pieces of fine furniture, and a small but ever-changing assortment of wall hangings and paintings, had become as much a gathering place for women as the ladies' section of the American Club, the Women's Exchange, and even La Imperial, Mexico City's most fashionable *dulceria*.

Thea was well aware of those facts, and all she could do was hope that Mr. Lopez would return before Ophelie got bored with peering into vitrines and decided that another barbed little conversation was in order.

I'm surprised I haven't run into her here before, she thought. This is just the sort of place Ophelie would patronize on a steady basis. No out-of-the-way places for her. Good . . . she looks interested in that equestrian painting—for her husband or lover?—I hope she stays on the other side of the room. Of course not. No such luck for me . . .

"What an interesting selection," Ophelie remarked coming over to stand by Thea and observe the eight assorted boxes arranged on a velvet pad. "Which of them are you purchasing?"

"All." Thea leaned against the mahogany counter. "The selection here is superb."

"Quite so," Ophelie agreed, "and, speaking of superb, where is Charles?"

"Oh, here and there," Thea remarked evasively. She wasn't at all concerned that Ophelie might bring up last night's little incident. Women like her always brushed social unpleasantness under the carpet. But, at the same time, Thea knew that the baronne's attitude toward her was one of barely veiled hostility, and she had no intention of giving her any advantages. "He said something about visiting the Spanish Club."

"What a very trusting bride you are to let Charles out on his own."

"The last time I looked, my husband was quite capable of crossing the street by himself and remembering the number of our hotel suite. He also," Thea added meaningfully, "isn't the sort to be easily swayed by the first fast talker who comes down the pike."

Ophelie's gaze flickered over Thea, from her black-velvet edged beige felt hat to her perfect suit down to her beige calf shoes with their jet and steel embroidery, and came back up again.

"You do not wear your engagement ring?" she inquired with mock surprise. "My dear Theodosia, it is not that you're afraid of robbery? I assure you, Mexico is quite a safe place."

"I'm sure it is, Ophelie. However, the truth is that I don't have an engagement ring. Charles and I eloped, and there wasn't time to purchase one."

"And you haven't asked Charles—?" Ophelie was truly horrified at both this breach of etiquette and Thea's apparent casualness at the matter.

"I'd never do such a thing."

"No, I suppose you wouldn't. Even if an engagement ring is the most important purchase a man can make."

"Perhaps. But I think there's only one important purchase a man can make for his bride—and Charles has already made it," Thea said, lifting her left hand to the brim of her hat in a casual gesture.

Ophelie pointedly ignored the golden glint of Thea's wedding ring and fanned her face with her gloves.

"Isn't it terribly stuffy in here?"

"No, I think it's perfectly comfortable." Thea peered at Ophelie noting, with more concern than she cared to admit, that the baronne looked rather green. "Could it be something you ate?"

"Guenther took me to the Grambrinus Restaurant for lunch. Their food is superb."

"Italian food?"

"The owner is Italian, but the food is German."

"Then that explains it—you should never eat sauerbraten this early in the day!" Thea said with a laugh just as Mr. Lopez, carrying a bulky object wrapped in burlap, returned to the salon.

"Ah, Baronne de Langlade, what an unexpected surprise! And Madame de Renille, I trust all is in order?"

"Very much, Mr. Lopez. These boxes are just what I had in mind."

The canny antiques dealer took in both women, immediately sensing some sort of rivalry between them—and a potential added profit for him. He had been Ophelie's major source of supply when she had redone her suite, and Thea had proven herself a discerning customer, for both her private and professional lives.

With a few deft twists, he removed the protective covering from his bundle and, on another part of the counter, unrolled an antique Savonnerie rug of a floral design in sapphire, turquoise and plum woven on an ivory field.

Both Thea and Ophelie ran their hands over the smooth, silken surface of the weave and exclaimed over its beauty while Mr. Lopez stood a little to one side, watching their reactions a shade too blandly.

Thea looked obliquely at the fiftyish man with his center-parted brilliantined hair and caught a look in the black eyes that she'd come to know well over the past few years, having seen it frequently in other dealers. The look of a man who planned to play two of his clients against each other and reap all the gains.

Acting as if the rug were of the least possible interest to her, Thea opened the clasp of her Mark Cross black morocco-leather handbag and withdrew another Mark Cross creation, a fitted little leather case called a "housewife" which held spools of black and white silk thread, an assortment of scissors, needles, buttons, and, most important to her, a tape measure. While Ophelie and Mr. Lopez were naming their prices, Thea measured the rug, her plan of action forming.

"—without a doubt, it is genuine Louis XIV," Mr. Lopez was saying. "And it is rumored to have been the personal property of the Empress Carlotta herself!"

"If every piece of furniture, every rug and bibelot I've seen since last March had indeed belonged to the Empress, then she must have needed the entire French fleet to transport them to Mexico!

"And the measurements are *so* awkward," Thea sighed, half to herself.

Ophelie turned on her. "This rug is a perfect oval!"

"Of *course* it is, but it's eight feet three inches long, and six feet three inches across at its widest point and, unless you have a room with approximate measurements—"

"It's for my reception room in Paris."

Thea nodded in understanding. "I'm awful leery of old rugs, myself. This beautiful thing is *at least* one hundred and fifty years old, and has spent the last forty here in Mexico. Now Mr. Lopez has stored it superbly, but the climate makes *so many* inroads on the weave and warp. Frankly, if it were me, I'd *much rather* have one of those new rugs they're weaving at Tientsin in China."

Ophelie didn't give up easily. She questioned Mr. Lopez closely about the Savonnerie's origins, haggled with him for a few minutes, displaying more skill in bargaining than Thea previously would have given her credit for, and ended by gracefully refusing the purchase.

"I hadn't realized the hour was so late. I have to get ready for tea," she said, pulling on her gloves. "I would like to invite you to join me, Theodosia, but I have an invitation in which you could not possibly be included. Not on my part, you understand, but my hostess is *quite* conservative, and new people like Americans—even when they're providentially married to Frenchmen—are rather *arriviste*."

"I wouldn't *dream* of intruding," Thea drawled. "And, as it happens, I have my own invitation for tea this afternoon, so . . ."

They parted politely. Thea watched Ophelie leave the establishment and waited until she was sure her rival was gone before turning back to Mr. Lopez, who was repacking the rug.

"And what do you think you're doing?" Thea questioned with amusement. "When I got here, Mr. Lopez, you assured me that you had a rug put away that I would love to have."

"Yes, madame. But what you said to the baronne . . . You made it clear that you didn't want it for your own . . ."

"I don't. It's for a client, the same one I'm buying these gold and porcelain boxes for. We both know this rug will be in perfect condition a hundred years from now." The dealer and the decorator exchanged trade smiles. "Now, Mr. Lopez, I *do* have an appointment for tea so, if you'll see to it that this rug goes to Mrs. Collier Channing at Four East Sixty-fifth Street, New York City, we can discuss price . . ."

*　　　*　　　*

Of all the invitations Thea had received, the only one that left her feeling nervous was the gracious note from the Baronne Ghiselle de Laulan inviting her to tea on Thursday afternoon.

Even that morning's arrival of Don Renaldo and Dona Imelda in Mexico City, and the Baronne's pleasant insistence that, of course, Señora de Veiga must also come to the Legation, did nothing to ease Thea's nerves.

The more she heard about the Belgian Minister and his wife, the more she became certain that they were people who, no matter how well they adapted to change, never sacrificed their extremely high standards of life. A very small part of Thea worried that, no matter how highly the Baronne de Laulan regarded her as a decorator, there might be reservations about her as Mrs. Charles de Renille.

But, as she and Dona Imelda entered the Belgian Legation, located on the fashionable Calle de Londres, and were taken to the residential section where Ghiselle de Laulan awaited them, Thea instinctively felt her state of nervous tension ease, and it disappeared completely when she saw the slender woman with the dark red hair that was so much like her son's, and the smile that left no doubt as to the sincerity of her welcome.

"Your photograph in *Harper's Bazaar* did you no justice at all!" Ghiselle announced after introductions and pleasantries had been exchanged. She took them across the black and gold Persian Senna rug of wool, woven with silk warp threads that covered the hardwood floor to the elaborate sofas by the fireplace. "Now, it is just the three of us for the moment, although Jean-Christophe will join us when tea arrives."

A fire was glowing warmly in the black and white marble fireplace. And Ghiselle, elegant in Lucile's Gobelin-blue Rajah-silk afternoon dress that was combined with chiffon taffeta and overlaid with burnt ivory

Bruges lace, settled her guests on the plump sofas in a room she cheerfully conceded was far too overcrowded.

"This is our family salon, you see," she explained, "and, unfortunately, the Legation's furnishings are a combination of what was left behind by previous ministerial families, what we brought with us from Brussels, and what we purchased here."

Thea had dressed carefully for this afternoon, selecting a striking Lucile ensemble that combined an afternoon dress of white serge with a coat of heavy white chiffon bordered in serge, buttoned with a row of jade buttons, and tied at the waist with a self belt of chiffon and, as she took off her white kid gloves, she cast an appreciative glance over the drawing room. Not large, it was nonetheless a sunny room whose windows overlooked a small private garden and, Ghiselle told them, many of the objects were things she and her husband had collected at their stays in various European capitals.

"This fabric is from Hungary, isn't it?" Thea asked, running a hand over the sea-green silk fabric that was embroidered in silk floss, lightly jeweled, and which had been fashioned into slipcovers for the sofa. "Do you remember, Dona Imelda, the little shop next door to the chocolaterie we always went to in Budapest, the one that was nothing but bolts and bolts of the most incredible fabrics?"

"The proprietor's name was Kugler, and we bribed him with a box of apricots dipped in milk chocolate," Dona Imelda went on, looking the very picture of urban sophistication in a Paquin afternoon gown of blue taffeta edged in dark blue velvet. "Then—and only then—did he take down all those fabrics he wrapped in black paper and hid on the farthest shelves."

"And he used a long wooden stick with a metal hook on the end," Ghiselle added. "It was always such fun to go there, the year Francois was Minister in Budapest, although I always left after each visit covered in dust!"

"Thea must have purchased twenty different bolts of fabric," Dona Imelda said. "Have you made use of them?"

"Most of my clients have. Do you remember that lovely yellow satin? At this very moment it's livening up a not-too-sunny drawing room on Rittenhouse Square. I've sold some, used others as wedding presents, and kept the one that looks like this. It's in pink and, when Charles and I go home, I'm going to cover a sofa in it for our bedroom."

For the next half-hour, the three women traded remembrances about Budapest, recalling the Hungarian antiquities at the National Museum, the 15th century Italian masters at the National Gallery, the Chinese and Indian bronzes at the Zichy Museum, recalling the dinners eaten at Drechsler's across the street from the Opera House, and afternoon tea at the extravagantly decorated New York Cafe.

They were recalling delectable chocolate cream truffles that melted in the mouth, and chocolate covered cherries with the tang that comes from being aged in Grand Marnier, when Jean-Christophe entered the room, swinging jauntily around the English mahogany writing table with its turquoise-inlaid desk set, and stopped for a moment in front of the six-panel japanned leather screen to observe the *tableau* in front of him. He kissed his mother and reacted with boyish enthusiasm to both Thea and Dona Imelda. But his face clearly showed disappointment that the refreshments had not yet arrived.

"What a greedy boy you are," his mother chided lovingly. "Now sit down, be good and you shall have your tea."

While Jean-Christophe took his place beside his mother on the sofa that was covered in soft green velvet, Ghiselle rang for the maid who appeared promptly, a troubled expression on her placid, middle-aged face.

"Our tea, please, Mathilde."

"*Oui*, Madame, but one thing—" The maid in her black taffeta uniform and white organdy apron and cap crossed the floor to whisper something in her mistress's ear.

The baronne's face became perplexed. "She is here, now? The invitation—*voyons*—show her in, Mathilde . . ." Ghiselle waved a hand in resignation. "The party I invited for tea *tomorrow* has come today instead. Ah, Ophelie, *bienvenue*. Have you made the acquaintance of Imelda de Veiga and Thea de Renille?"

I knew it, Thea thought, caught between despair and laughter. Just as everything is going along smoothly, the Wicked Witch of the West shows up. Frank Baum can write his next Oz book with Ophelie as the villainess. Oh, this afternoon is *not* going to be fun.

Through half-closed lids, Thea watched as Ophelie, resplendent in a Worth reception dress of sapphire blue silk trimmed in quilted chiffon velvet with a deep collar and yoke of lace, paused for a moment in front of a small round table draped in gold damask and weighed down with a number of gold boxes in various shapes and sizes. As she approached the center of the room, Thea noticed that the face under the brim of her blue hat trimmed with dull pink roses was pale and strained.

"Forgive my being late, Ghiselle," she said coolly, slipping off her sable boa, "but there was an unexpected bit of business I had to deal with. Gerard is due back soon, and I wanted to be certain all the communiques he received were in order."

"Surely you don't mean you've been holding his mail for all these months," Ghiselle said, shocked.

"It's mostly boring reports from our solicitors in Paris. Gerard wants to concentrate fully on his dig, and those things would only distract him."

"Still, I cannot imagine being separated from one's husband for months at a time, and being in a strange city besides. You must find it very long at times."

"There are compensations, Señora de Veiga."

As far as you're concerned, there surely are, Thea thought wickedly. All those little diversions you've found. I wonder—is it a riding crop you fancy, or does Guenther do it manually?

Obviously, the arrival of Ophelie de Langlade caused a rift in the afternoon that had started out so pleasantly. But the arrival of Mathilde and another maid with the tea provided an opportune pause.

The marble table between the sofas was covered in a fine linen cloth deeply edged in lace, and silver trays were placed on it. There was a fine French sterling tea set and napkins with lace borders that matched the tablecloth and the china, with its pattern of widely scattered red and blue flowers bordered in gold, was Haviland's graceful Cathay.

Their conversation moved onto neutral topics while they ate.

Ghiselle poured out cups of Earl Grey tea and sliced the small loaves of bread that were made of brioche dough and offered them with fresh butter and strawberry jam. This was followed by covered custard cups filled with vanilla *flan*, large raspberry tarts, and completed with the *piece de resistance*, a *marquise au chocolat*—rich sponge ladyfingers combined with chocolate mousse, topped with whipped cream and generous shavings of chocolate.

They did more than justice to the tea, and all four women indulged Jean-Christophe, insisting he have the crusty ends of the loaves, eat the extra tart and have a fourth slice of the *marquise au chocolat*.

In turn, Jean-Christophe—immediately sensing that there was some sort of extra tension between Thea, whom he liked, and Ophelie, whom he didn't care for at all—told diversionary stories about his piano teacher at the Conservatory who wore a lily in his lapel and carried a silver dish full of coconut candies which he never shared. He also told stories about his time at Stanford and how he knew Dona Imelda's eldest son, Roberto. He also told about being on the rowing crew, how he earned his letter and how his classmates called him "Chris."

He finished his last morsel of cake, obviously reluctant to leave, but he stood up. "Papa is waiting for me," he told the women, kissing each one's hand and embracing his mother. "The only reason I was able to escape was that he has a visitor."

"Anyone we know, *mon cher?*" Ghiselle asked.

Jean-Christophe shook his head. "An Englishman with a cane. I've never seen him before, but Papa was anxious to receive him."

After Jean-Christophe left, Dona Imelda turned to Ghiselle. "What a conscientious young man," she said warmly.

"Yes, his father and I are quite proud of him." Ghiselle refilled their tea cups. "We'll miss Jean-Christophe when he goes back to the university in January. But a year away from his studies is quite enough. Stanford was a wonderful experience for him. The American university system is *so* healthy for young men; some of our universities in Europe could take a leaf from their counterparts."

Ophelie certainly doesn't look pleased about *that*, Thea thought with secret delight. Right now, she'd love to say something appropriate to a Continental sophisticate, but she can't make a remark and still be expected to be received by the Belgian Legation.

Even as she enjoyed her rival's discomfiture at having to keep silent in order to remain in what was left of Ghiselle's good graces toward her, a new thought dawned in Thea, and she felt a feeling of horror go through her. Could it be that Ophelie was some sort of German agent, having become one out of boredom or through sexual blackmail? A shallow woman, one who never thought beyond her own pleasure and position was always an easy mark. . . .

But then, what do you call yourself? she thought severely. But, before Thea could divide apples by oranges in an attempt to reach an answer, she heard Ghiselle de Laulan's voice, and the question that brought her back to the present.

"My dear Thea, you must tell us how you redecorated the White House!"

"I'm very much afraid *Harper's Bazaar* exaggerated a bit when they interviewed me for their 'Women of Interest' column." Thea laughed. "I redid the ladies retiring room, and helped Mrs. Roosevelt, Alice and Ethel arrange their rooms but, as for any of the rooms in the official quarter. . . ."

Thea loved to talk about her business. Regardless of the fact that her first client had been the White House, her first clients had wanted more than just a recommendation by the President, and if her work hadn't been any good she wouldn't have had a firm for very long. But now, as she told these stories, Thea was suddenly aware of being on very shaky ground—particularly since, in her other meetings with Ophelie, she had never let on that she was anything other than Charles' bride.

"Did you purchase that rug after I left Lopez's?" Ophelie inquired with the first real smile Thea could recall seeing.

"Of course I did. I have a client who's going to be very appreciative of my find."

The baronne inclined her head in a gracious bow of concession. "Then I don't mind losing the rug to you. You should have a proper swan song."

Thea was nonplussed. "Excuse me?"

"Swan song for your client. Interior decorators are an American necessity, but we have no need for them in France. Besides which, Charles would never permit you to open a firm in Paris, fail with it, and therefore shame him and his family!"

"I would *never* dream of bringing disgrace on any of the de Renilles and, if Charles and I were going to make our home in Paris, I might have doubts as to having a decorating firm there. But, since that won't be our home—"

"You won't be living in Paris?" Ophelie's voice was indignant.

"That's hardly a crime," Ghiselle murmured. "And their future domicile is of no concern to anyone but Thea and Charles."

Ophelie's eyes were blazing at Thea. "You've tricked him into living in America!"

"If you know my husband as well as you claim, Ophelie, you'd know that no one tricks Charles," Thea shot back. "And, as for living in America, we'll be living in New York. There are those of us who think that may be two different things!"

Thea's attempt at humor went straight over Ophelie's head.

"How did you force it on him?"

"It's Charles' signature on our apartment lease, not mine."

"And you think that by keeping Charles in New York, he will allow you to keep on with your . . . your amusement?" Her mouth curved upward in a smile of contempt. "Your family might have permitted you to arrange the houses of strangers, but Charles' opinion of your continuing to do *that* will be no different than if you wanted to walk the streets!"

Pure rage filled Thea, and she would have loved to

reach out and put her hands around Ophelie's throat, forever silencing that false, mocking voice. A red film seemed to drop over her vision, and the only reality was Dona Imelda pressing her cool hand over hers.

"I'm shocked to hear you speak like that, Ophelie!" Dona Imelda's voice rang out clearly. "Charles is not as censorious as you remember him—if he ever was at all. He is quite proud of Thea and her profession, and never more so than when my husband and I gave her the commission to decorate the town house in New York that we've purchased."

This pronouncement was followed by a long minute of silence which Ghiselle finally broke, her voice quiet and firm, like that of a headmistress of a fine girls' school.

"Ophelie, I think the time has come for you to leave. I can forgive your misreading my invitation and coming today instead of tomorrow, but I cannot forgive your insulting my guest in my home. If you go now, we shall forget that the last few minutes ever took place."

For several minutes after Ophelie left, they sat quietly together.

"I can't thank both of you enough," Thea said at last. "Those were a very difficult few minutes."

"It's amazing how unattractive even the most beautiful of women become when they're jealous," Ghiselle replied. "One makes allowances so that no more of their unpleasant tendencies will come out."

"We were in the same antiques shop this afternoon, and Ophelie told me that her hostess for tea this afternoon was terribly conservative and didn't receive new people like Americans."

"What a horrid thing to say." Ghiselle looked shocked. "She is obviously very jealous of you over Charles. Women like her can never imagine that a man might not care for them. Do not let her near Charles," she warned.

"Oh, then I would scratch her eyes out!" Thea said, and finally began to laugh over the incident. She clasped Dona Imelda's hand. "And thank you with all my heart for saying what you did about the town house."

"And why not?" Dona Imelda replied lightly, leaning over to lightly kiss her cheek. "I meant every word of it. Renaldo and I have discussed this matter at some length. The house is on East 67th Street—number twelve—but we haven't done anything with it. I've kept an eye on your development as a decorator. I never wanted anyone but you to do it, but you had to grow to the task of twenty-three rooms and a carte blanche budget."

Thea was touched almost beyond words. "I'm so honored, I can't say anything without sounding like an idiot. . . ."

"There's no need to cry. Oh, my dear, did you really think I thought so little of your ability that I simply made up a tale in order to silence a *corazon duro* like Ophelie de Langlade?"

Thea was an expert list maker. At times she was sure it was the only way she kept her busy life running smoothly, providing her with a concise agenda of people she had to see, things she had to buy and places she had to go. And, on this Monday morning, the final day of October, the day before the forty-eight hour religious holiday of All Saints' and All Souls' Day, she was seated at her writing desk in the bedroom, covering sheet after sheet of paper with her ideas for both their present life in Mexico City and their future together in New York.

"Do you have any stationery left?" Charles inquired teasingly as he came out of the dressing room, pulling on his suit jacket. Since the arrival of the de Veigas four days earlier, Charles had spent the business hours of each day with Don Renaldo at his offices in the modern building that also housed the Mexican Light and Power Company in the Calle Cinco de Mayo. Today they would not be meeting, but Thea suspected that more had transpired in the past few days than he would tell her about, and she thought it best not to question him too closely.

"Oh, a few pieces here and there," she said lightly. She wanted Charles to confide in her on his own. *Nothing* would let her turn into one of *those* wives, women who couldn't let their husbands take a walk around the block without conducting a major interrogation on their return. "I've been making some preliminary plans. We're not going to be in Mexico City much longer, and I want our departure to run smoothly. We also have fifteen empty rooms waiting for us in New York—and that includes a drawing room/library that measures twenty by forty-eight. I'm writing to the rug buyer at Sloane's—he's the sweetest man—to let him know what sort of floor covering we'll need."

Charles smiled. "Are we going to have a *pendaison de la cremaillere?*"

"Of course we're going to have a house warming! In fact, I've had a wonderful idea. Why don't we give a buffet, but serve only desserts and champagne! We'll have mousses, tortes, ice cream and—"

"And we'll all eat ourselves ill." Charles' smile deepened. "It's a wonderful idea. I love it," he said, his gaze moving adoringly over Thea, wearing a Chinese robe of cyclamen pink silk quilted damask embroidered with butterflies and blossoms in woven silk and set off by deep cuffs of white satin. "Are you going out today?"

"No, I'm going to be very lazy this morning. After I finish my lists, I plan to relax with a silly romantic novel until it's time to go to lunch with Dona Imelda."

"You sound very industrious to me."

"I think I may very well be. Dona Imelda said that, since we're eating in their suite, we might as well go over the floor plans."

Thea had told Charles of her commission as soon as she'd returned from that disquieting tea party at the Belgian Legation. He'd been very pleased for her, at this new affirmation of her talent, but now, days later, Thea began to speculate that she was the cause of her husband's somewhat distracted air.

Could Ophelie have been right? Thea wondered. Could Charles have been expecting her to close down her business regardless of the fact they'd be living in New York? Perhaps they'd both taken too much for granted over the past few weeks, and they could use the next weeks to smooth out the usual early marital difficulties.

Thea looked down at the papers spread over her writing desk. Over the past few days, Ophelie de Langlade had precluded John Donovan as the person she liked least.

Ophelie had appeared for a concert at the German Club on Thursday evening as if nothing had happened five hours earlier. It was at the Casino Aleman, a splendidly outfitted building replete with a beer hall, bowling alley, gymnasium, library, ballroom and string of reception rooms that the baronne had made her feelings for Charles quite clear. And, during the evening's concert, she stayed close to his side, the combined charms of Haydn, Schumann and Schubert apparently only a faint diversion.

Not that she'd been ignored, Thea recalled. Why was it some men could never accept no for an answer? Paul had been at her side all evening long. They'd entered the club, greeted the German Embassy's First Secretary and his wife, who were hosting the evening's chamber music concert, and were separated as all married couples were at social events. That was the last time she stood beside Charles until the final *auf wiedersehens* were offered shortly after midnight.

Friday night at the Japanese Legation, and Saturday

night at the Cercle Francais, Mexico City's French Club, had been no better. Charles was occupied with Ophelie, and she was cornered by Paul, and Sunday afternoon had been the worst of all.

Chapultepec Park was the city's Sunday afternoon gathering place, Major Donovan told them, and no one seeing them at the Castle would take any special notice. They would simply look as if they'd met by accident.

They had entered the Castle through huge gates guarded by full-sized bronze figures of soldiers at attention, and had spent the next hour wandering hand-in-hand around the terrace floor, seeing the hand-carved Spanish chairs in the first small salon, and the blue and gold satin brocade that covered the walls of the *Recamara Azul* and showed off the room's fine antique furniture and the silver engraved with the mark of Maximilian, as well as a reception room which had once been Carlotta's boudoir.

In the next reception room, where a suite of fine French furniture upholstered in a Gobelin tapestry was the main sight, Thea and Charles joined up with Major Donovan and, while they discussed the necessary events, the beautiful dining room, whose walls were carved Alstian oak, and the justly famous *Salon des Embajadores,* where pink and gold upholstered Louis XV-style furniture was the focal point, provided excellent cover for them as they walked. The guards who moved discreetly about, making sure that the tourists did not try to touch the paintings or penetrate into the private apartments of President and Mrs. Diaz, did not pay attention to the attractive young couple who seemed to be having such a fine conversation with the middle-aged man they'd met.

They attracted no special interest from anyone and, just as Thea felt most calm about the whole afternoon, as they stood on the great terrace where the sweeping view stretched for miles, another couple joined them, ending the afternoon's security and peace.

"You look as if you've drifted a thousand miles away."

Charles' voice brought her back to the present, and she blinked at him, feeling as though she were coming out of a trance.

"I was thinking about the past few days—yesterday afternoon in particular."

"Are you still harping on the appearance of Guenther von Basedow and Ophelie?" Charles inquired in a tone of voice Thea had never heard him use—a tone of cold imperiousness. "I hardly think they were following us. Everyone goes to Chapultepec on Sunday, and they're no exception."

"So I gather," Thea replied, her voice becoming tinged with acid. "Until this moment, I never realized that one might give up several delightful hours with a riding crop and chiffon scarves in order to wander through rooms of furniture and tapestries. According to your Ophelie, Frenchwomen have no need to study other people's interiors!"

"She is not *my* Ophelie!" Charles had been seated on the edge of the bed, separated from Thea by about five feet but, as he spoke, he stood up, an expression of anger suffusing his face, and she quickly realized that the writing table was no protection from a husband whose bad temper had been triggered.

"Do you enjoy maligning Ophelie?" he inquired at last, his voice icy.

"About as much as she enjoys castigating me—which is rather a lot!"

"What harm has she ever done you?" he inquired in honest wonderment. "I admit our first tea together was hardly an event of great warmth but, since then, she hasn't spoken a word about you to me."

"Then what *have* you two been discussing the past few nights?"

"France . . . Normandy, things we both know. At least we have common ground between us. I might ask what topics of conversation you and your devoted captain find to discuss. A man you didn't even know two months ago!"

"He wants to show me the city."

"Is that a new version of showing off one's etchings?"

"It may be. But, at this point, I think I can protect myself against a line better than you can!"

The air was electric with emotion between them, all the carefully structured atmosphere of sensuality that surrounded their bedroom was covered by the vilest of emotions—sexual mistrust and jealousy.

"Just what is it you're trying to insinuate?" Charles' voice was grim.

"That your darling former mistress is playing you a tune, you're about to dance it and, if you don't look out when the music ends, the bed you wake up in won't be this one!"

"Is that all you have on your mind?"

Thea rose slowly from her chair and came over to stand by Charles. "So far, I haven't heard you complaining. Or do you close your eyes and play a wife/mistress switch?"

Charles felt his face flush. "That's disgusting!"

"Facts of life sometimes are. It gives you a thrill, doesn't it, Charlie, to have Ophelie fawning over you, whispering to you, just like the old days?"

"Ophelie behaves like a perfect lady—behavior you might take a lesson from!"

For a moment, Thea stared at him in disbelief. "You are enjoying it—you and your cheap piece of French pastry. But let me tell you that if you get into her bed, don't come back to this one. I'll know it if you do. I'll smell that bitch on you!"

"You both wear the same perfume," Charles began, and stopped, acutely aware he'd said too much and now

511

had no idea of how to get free.

"I know how you look when it's over, and you can't wash that off!"

"Are you crazy?"

"Not as much as you are if you think you're going to have a fling and get away with it." Thea looked squarely at Charles, honestly not certain if she wanted to kiss him or punch him. "Or is *thinking* the key word here?"

The moment the words were out of her mouth, Thea knew she'd hit home. Charles went pale, an icy mask of control sliding over his features.

"I think it would do you a great deal of good to remember that you're my wife, and behave toward *my* old friends with the same courtesy I give *yours*," he told her with quiet rage. "Kindly keep your outlandish fantasies about Ophelie to yourself, or I'll have to make sure that you do!"

Thea's eyes widened into great pools of fury. "Just go ahead and try, and we'll see who ends up black and blue! You're mine—all mine—and I'm not sharing."

"And I'm leaving," he said briefly, coldly.

"Good . . . and don't come back until you decide to stop playing games."

"Well, don't hold your breath, as they say," Charles snapped and, swinging around, he stalked out of the room, the door banging shut behind him.

As soon as she heard the sitting room door slam, Thea slumped down on the bed and let the tears she'd been holding back come.

Oh, what have I done this time? she thought as she cried. Suppose he goes straight to Ophelie? Suppose he leaves me? It was all his pride—he was amused that Ophelie still wants him—he doesn't see her duplicity, but he wouldn't have fallen into her bed. . . .

Thea threw herself across the bed and let her emotions have free rein. The past few days had been awful. She was

512

nervous all the time, tired in the mornings and, as angry as she was at Charles, all she wanted was for him to come back so they could make love. Confused, she sat up and found a handkerchief in the night table drawer. All her emotions were in a turmoil and, as her hands brushed against her breasts, a tremor of disbelief went through her.

She had purposely put all thoughts of this happening out of her mind, but now the reality invaded.

Her tender, slightly swollen breasts meant nothing in themselves but, added to all the other problems that had suddenly been plaguing her, and now her sudden fit of jealousy. . . .

It's too soon—you're only eight days late, she thought. It could be the air, the altitude or just the adjustment to being married.

Her mind ran through a litany of excuses and possibilities, but Thea already knew the real answer. She got up off the bed warm with the certainty that she was pregnant with Charles' child.

Charles strode through the Sanz's lobby and onto the street in such a white heat of righteous indignation that he literally had no idea of where he was going.

His beautiful, adoring, sensuous wife, who made his life such a joy, had suddenly turned into a vicious-tongued bitch who made her threats very clear, and the transformation left him very shaken—and very angry.

Unfavorably, he compared Thea to Ophelie; not in a sexual sense, but in terms of having shared a familiar life. Being with Ophelie brought France back to him in a thousand different ways—all of which had nothing to do with the feeling he had for Thea, and never would.

Why can't she understand that a few minutes with Ophelie isn't going to threaten our marriage or our love? he thought. Why does Thea insist on imagining that I'm dividing my time between two beds?

Charles' stride matched his temper, and the pedestrians that crowded Mexico City's sidewalks during the daylight hours gave him a wide berth. One look at his furious, set face and the vendors who spent their days offering passers-by lottery tickets, bunches of flowers, and sad-eyed puppies of uncertain pedigree, thought better of pressing their wares on him.

Charles was still seething as he turned onto the Avenue de San Francisco. But, as the curio stores gave way to the more exclusive shops, his anger began to fade, and was replaced by a more long-lasting feeling—shame at his actions.

How could I have insinuated that Thea needed to take lessons in how to behave from Ophelie? he wondered painfully as he stopped and looked into a window of a shop where fine linens were sold.

What a fool you are, he told his reflection in the plate glass. You've never been happier in your life, yet all you want to do is play the boulevardier. Worse than that, you've been forgetting your responsibility, not only to your marriage, but to your promise to President Roosevelt. It's this city— A crazy place— I can't wait until we get out of here—

He stood for a few more minutes, looking at the variety of tablecloths displayed in the window without really seeing them. He had to make it up to Thea, but common sense told him that now was not the time to return to their suite. He also knew he had to bring a present back with him—but what?

He hadn't bought even the smallest of trinkets for Thea since they were married, and a feeling of shame at his oversight filled him. One of the first things he'd said to Thea was that he didn't want her to think she was marrying a cheap Frenchman, but that was exactly what he was acting like.

In his mind's eye, he could see Thea at parties, her elegant clothes set off by her fine jewelry—the exquisite triple strand of her family pearls, her modern rose quartz and diamond pendant, as well as other assorted pieces that she'd informed him were present from her father, or inherited from her mother.

And nothing from him except her wedding ring.

Galvanized into action, he turned from the window and continued along the avenue to La Perla, the jewelry salon of the Diener brothers which, Don Renaldo had discreetly informed him, was a fine establishment if he wanted to make a purchase that involved precious stones.

To his immense surprise, the salesman he presented himself to was expecting him.

"Señor de Veiga was in the other day and mentioned your name. He said that you might be paying a call on us, and asked that we extend every courtesy toward you," he was politely informed as he was led across the taupe-carpeted room with its glass and wood counters to a velvet-curtained alcove decorated with a small table and velvet-upholstered chairs. "Señor de Veiga also instructed that we are to place at your disposal a selection of unset stones that he keeps with us in the event you are interested in a special gift for your wife."

A wave of gratitude for Don Renaldo rose in Charles. The older man had arranged this in such a way that he didn't feel obligated to either accept out of relief that someone else had made the decision for him, or refuse out of pride.

"My wife and I eloped, and there was no time to buy an engagement ring," Charles lied to the salesman, recalling that fateful morning at Henry Hertzberg's in San Antonio. "I want to surprise her with a proper ring on her birthday. It's the fourteenth and, if I select the stone and the setting now, can it be ready in time?"

"Most assuredly, sir," the salesman reassured him.

515

"Now, if you'll just wait a few moments—"

Fortunately, Charles recalled Thea's ring size, and the selection of the stone and its setting went smoothly. It was only when the proceedings were complete that Charles became aware that this engagement ring in no way made up for the contretemps of a few hours before. He could not go back to Thea empty-handed.

"I'm also interested in something I can give my wife now," Charles began, choosing his words carefully, wondering if he looked as foolish as he felt. "Nothing . . . nothing terribly important. A bagatelle. A bangle to surprise her with. A trinket."

"Of course, sir," the salesman said, politely ignoring Charles' stumbling explanations. "I think we have some excellent pieces, one of which I'm sure will please you."

Excusing himself, the salesman left the alcove and returned to the main salon. Taking a black velvet-lined tray, he unlocked the vitrine where the finest jewelry La Perla sold was kept, and selected ten pieces to arrange on the tray. He wasn't at all impressed by Mr. de Renille's show of off-handedness. Five years of employment by the Diener brothers who, all things considered, ran a rather tight ship, weren't for nothing. You couldn't work here and not learn to spot a young husband who'd just had his first fight with his bride and was ripe to salve his conscience with an expensive piece of jewelry.

Thea awaited Charles' return with a full-blown case of butterflies.

Of course he might not be coming back, she told her reflection in the dressing table mirror as she put the finishing touches on her *maquillage*. Right now he might even be with Ophelie, in her bed, in her arms, agreeing with her that he made a horrible mistake in marrying me!

If it hadn't been for Dona Imelda, she might have actually begun to believe any story that her overactive

516

imagination could come up with, Thea acknowledged. Normally, she would have hesitated before confiding in the older, conservative woman but, when she arrived in the de Veiga suite for lunch, Dona Imelda's warm approach to her had melted the careful air of reserve she kept up, lest the wealthy Mexican woman consider her in some way unsuitable. Discussions about floor plans, fabric swatches and paint colors were put aside in favor of a heart-to-heart talk about men in general and husbands in particular.

Now, at nearly four in the afternoon, she had followed Dona Imelda's advice to put on her prettiest tea gown, but the rest was up to Charles.

I'm not going to tell him I think I may be pregnant, Thea decided. It's the wrong time, I'm not really sure, and I *won't* use my condition—confirmed or otherwise—as some sort of hold over Charles. He doesn't deserve treatment like that, and it isn't the sort of marriage I want—

The sound of the sitting room door being opened brought Thea out of her thoughts and, with a pounding heart, she rose quickly from the dressing table bench and stood where Charles could see her when he opened the door.

It was the longest minute of her life.

The door opened in slow caution, and then she and Charles were facing each other silently. The afternoon had turned unusually cold and windy. He looked tired and chilled—and very, very wary.

"Charles," she began, and stopped, unable to go on.

His eyes travelled over her, viewing her slender, full-bosomed figure in the Lucile tea gown of flower-trimmed flesh-colored satin with a tunic of ruffled lace and a blue satin bodice studded with tiny pearls much like a hungry man looking at a banquet he wasn't sure he'd be allowed to partake of. Suddenly, he remembered what his father

517

had told him about marital disagreements and what a man had to do when he was in the right and his wife was being difficult over nothing. He followed his father's advice, and the next minute he had Thea in his arms.

"I'm sorry," he whispered, burying his face in her hair as Thea clasped her arms around him, holding him close. "It was all my fault— I was amusing my masculine vanity— There's no one for me but you—"

Thea pulled back to look at Charles' face. "I thought you were never coming back. Or worse, you were going to come back out of duty, because it's your responsibility, and that I was some sort of mistake."

"Mistake?" Charles repeated. "The only mistake is mine. I know Ophelie is a greedy and discontented woman, but I was willing to overlook that because she's a countrywoman of mine. I was wrong in that. I don't want to make love to her, I don't want to *talk* to her. I love you."

Thea blinked back her tears. "Our first fight." She pressed herself against him. "I don't want Paul, and you don't want Ophelie. But where have you been all afternoon?" she asked, concerned.

"Walking all over the city, going in and out of churches, killing time," he confessed. "I don't even remember where I ate lunch."

"My poor darling. What a day you've had . . . you must be chilled to the bone."

"Not if you keep doing *that*," he said as Thea finished kissing him. "Don't you want to continue warming me up?" he asked when she made no further move to caress him.

"What you said— That I had nothing else on my mind— I love making advances on you, but if you don't want them—"

"I love nothing better," he said, and then there was no more need for words.

518

In its way, this kiss was as unforgettable as the first one they shared but, on this afternoon, they could take their time, trading long kisses and slow caresses, sharing every tender moment together.

The bed was soft beneath them, and Thea could feel Charles' mouth moving along the side of her neck while his hands moved to undo her tea gown. She felt herself grow warm with desire and, suddenly, their clothes became elaborate garments designed specifically for the purpose of keeping them apart.

"Why do women have to wear such complicated clothes?" Charles inquired thickly as his fingers were stymied by the unfamiliar fastenings at her waist.

"So that we can give rich men who've always had everything a few problems," Thea quipped, moving slightly so that Charles could have a better grasp at the tiny hooks and eyes that were eluding him.

"You're wrapped up like a present," he groaned in a combination of humor and delayed desire, his fingers tangled in the satin and lace. "A Christmas present. The best present I've ever had, and the only one worth having."

The tiny, intricate fastenings gave way, and then she was finally naked under his touch, every inch of her longing for his love. His bare skin pressed against hers, his cool flesh warming and expanding under her stroking fingers as she urged him on.

His kisses moved from her mouth to her throat and then down to her breasts. Thea felt her nipples growing hard as his tongue moved in exquisite motions over first one and then the other.

Her own excitement was blending with an overwhelming need. For a moment they strained together and then, with one fluid motion, they were one. She met his thrusting body, welcoming him deep inside her, glorying in their soaring flight of love.

It seemed to Thea that hours had passed as she lay contentedly in Charles' arms, her head on his shoulder, their bodies close together. She was drifting in her own world when she felt his body move away from hers and, through half-closed eyelids, she saw his strong bare back bend over the side of the bed to reach among the clothes scattered over the floor.

Her eyes were closed when, a minute later, she felt something cold go around her wrist, and the sound of a clasp being fastened. Curious, she raised her arm, opened her eyes, and her feeling of lassitude vanished.

"A diamond bracelet! Oh, Charles—"

He propped himself up on an elbow. "Don't you like it?"

"Of course I do! But I wasn't expecting—"

"That's the general idea behind a surprise present."

Thea looked at Charles, his long body stretched out beside her, half-covered by the sheet, and she reached out to him.

"I've always wanted to wear nothing but a sheet and a diamond bracelet!"

"It becomes you," he said, pressing a trail of kisses along her arm, from her shoulder to the top of her wrist where the glittering bracelet rested. "I never knew I could want to buy something so much until I saw it on the jeweler's tray. I still had all of my $1500 win from the Kentucky Derby, and I couldn't think of another person that I wanted to spend it on."

"What did you tell the salesman?"

"That I wanted a bangle for my wife," Charles said, laughing. "He must have seen me coming a mile away."

"Well, I don't care. I'm so thrilled . . ."

His eyes moved over the long, curving line of her body under the sheet that was discreetly tucked around her.

"Would you care to thank me properly?"

"I think that could be arranged." Thea's voice was

520

softly provocative. "This morning, when you walked out, all I wanted was for you to come back so we could make love. I love you and want you all the time."

He gathered her close against him. "So do I. There are days I wish we never had to get out of bed."

Thea bent her head to deposit a series of kisses along the strong, satinlike skin of his shoulder. "This—our love—is so important, and so glorious, that sometimes I'm afraid one day it'll disappear in smoke."

"No, never. This is our honeymoon and we're supposed to be like this. Later on—"

"What about later on?" Thea looked sharply at him. "Nothing is ever going to change the way I feel about you."

"I feel the same way. But I'm told things even out, simmer down, the fires go cool," he said as they slid back against the pillows. Charles' mouth and hands began to investigate the soft, tender undersides of her breasts.

"Oh, you're impossible—and wonderful. I want to hold you so close and belong only to you."

"Always?" he asked as her breasts swelled into his hands.

"Yes," she gasped. "Even if our lovemaking *does* become less important to us."

Charles looked surprised. "When are you planning on that happening?"

"Oh—" Thea moved against him in an unmistakable signal. "Maybe around the time of our golden wedding anniversary!"

Chapter Seventeen

October 31, 1904

September 24.—Miss Theodosia Harper, daughter of Mr. Elston Harper and the late Mrs. Harper, to Mr. Charles de Renille, third son of the late Count Adrian de Renille of Lisieux, France; at the Cathedral of San Fernando, San Antonio, Texas.

Jane Miles' exclamation of surprise echoed off the walls of her oyster white and pale pink Regency sitting room and brought her husband, who'd been in his own dressing room which opened off the opposite end of their bedroom, rushing in to see what was wrong.

"Are you all right?" he questioned, concerned, as he stepped over the threshold to see his wife holding the latest issue of *Town & Country* in her hands, an expression of amazement on her face. "I heard you scream. In fact, I think all of Sheridan Circle must have heard you. What's going on?"

Jane waved the magazine at her husband. "It's right here in black and white. Come and see for yourself. Thea's married!"

Hugh Miles, for not the first time in his career, silently blessed his military training for keeping his expression free of surprise as he took the periodical from his wife's hands, scanned the page devoted to marriage announcements, and read the first listing, easily noticeable because of its September date.

Well, well, he thought, smiling inwardly. This *is* unplanned, but not really unexpected. Two fine young people like that. An obvious attraction. I can't tell Jane, of course, and I wonder what I can say to T.R. Oh, well, all in a day's work . . .

"Why this is fine news!" he said warmly, putting on a bright smile. "Why do you look so glum?"

"Oh, this is awful, just dreadful," she groaned, her blue crepe morning dress rustling as she paced over the oyster white carpet.

The colonel was thoroughly mystified. "I thought you'd be delighted."

"Delighted?" Jane stopped pacing. "Oh, Hugh, really! This means that Thea was engaged all the time she was in St. Louis. In fact, she was in the process of eloping!"

Colonel Miles took a deep breath. "That was hardly any of our concern. Thea's a grown woman."

"She could have told us she was engaged," Jane fretted. "It would have made things so much easier, and I wouldn't have told Paul. Oh, I've made such a fool of myself."

"With Captain Merrill? Jane—" The colonel's voice became clouded. "I repeatedly told you *not* to meddle!"

"I—I couldn't help it. I told him Thea was really very fond of him, and that when they were in Mexico he should press his suit."

The colonel tossed *Town & Country* on his wife's writing table where it landed with a thud among the rest of her morning mail. There was no use getting angry, he told himself.

"Well, what's done is done." He spoke with a calmness he certainly didn't feel. "Paul is a gentleman, and so is Charles. I'm sure there won't be any compromising situations. Now, Jane . . ."

Colonel Miles spent the next half-hour comforting his wife and then it was time to leave for his weekly meeting with the Secretary of the Army.

In spite of his irritation at his wife's actions, as he left their four-story stone mansion built of brick and Bowling Green granite in a style of modified Roman Renaissance, he found himself becoming both amused and delighted at the morning's unexpected news.

Good for Thea and Charles, he thought as he got into his waiting Oldsmobile and told the chauffeur he was ready to start for Army Headquarters. I like to see young people who know their own minds and, when I think about it, I'd much rather see Thea married to Charles de Renille than Paul Merrill. They'll want to leave Mexico soon, of course. Too bad, they're doing a fine job. I'd better send a letter off to Donovan telling him he's not to create any impediment if they want to come home now.

As the motor car turned down Massachusetts Avenue leaving Sheridan Circle behind, Hugh Miles began to smile. Up and down the Eastern seaboard this morning, people would be opening up the latest issue of *Town & Country*, and a good number of them would recognize the names of Theodosia Harper and Charles de Renille.

More business for Tiffany's in the form of wedding presents, he thought. Ambassador and Mrs. Jusserand are going to be pleased but, if I had my choice of one place I could be today, it would be in the White House when Theodore Roosevelt hears the news!

"Theodore—Theodore, I have to speak with you!"

Theodore Roosevelt stepped out of the elevator and into the White House's family quarters ready, after a long morning's work in the Oval Office, for a pleasant family lunch when he heard his wife's clear voice and her compelling tone—one she rarely used. Taking a deep breath, he went into her sitting room with less enthusiasm than usual.

"Good afternoon, my dear," he said, kissing her. "Is this something important, or can it wait until after our meal?"

"Absolutely not," Edith Roosevelt said firmly, returning her husband's kiss and settling him down beside her on the sofa. "This is of the utmost importance."

"If it's about Alice," he began, wondering what exploit his oldest child was up to now. America's own "princess" achieved almost as much space in the press as her father.

"It's *not* about Alice. In fact, she is as annoyed with you as I am. And so is Ethel, and Belle."

"Well, if you, both our daughters and your secretary Miss Hagner, are taking exception with me, I must have done something awful. The only problem is, I can't recall anything!"

"How could you possibly forget to tell us that Thea was getting married?" she inquired, and placed *Town & Country* in her husband's hands.

The President scanned the announcement, hiding his surprise with great skill. "Well," he said at last.

"Well, indeed!" his wife retorted. "You can't tell me that she never mentioned a word about it to you on the train ride to St. Louis!"

"She didn't, as a matter of fact," Theodore Roosevelt said blandly. "Thea's a very discreet girl."

"It's an elopement, of course. But they seem to be all the rage lately."

"Oh, now, Edith," he said in a comforting voice, putting his arms around his wife. "It's not that bad. I'm sure Thea and Charles knew what they were doing. Some young couples *don't* want all the fuss of a big wedding."

"I know that. It's just that I thought you knew all along."

"I can't keep a secret *that* well!" he exclaimed, amused, and stood up. "Now that that's settled, I'll get ready for lunch, and we'll discuss our wedding present to them. Silver, do you think, my dear?"

"No, they'll be sinking under the weight of it from all the other presents they'll receive. Since this isn't an official gift, we have more leeway. Something in porcelain would be nice."

Theodore Roosevelt nodded in agreement. "My calendar isn't too busy this afternoon. Why don't we take an hour and go to the Mendelsohn Galleries?"

It wasn't until he was alone in the privacy of the Presidential bathroom, washing his hands, that Theodore Roosevelt permitted himself an ear-to-ear smile.

None of this had been planned with this end in mind, but he was far from displeased. Human nature worked in very mysterious ways.

Such fine young people deserve every happiness, he decided, reaching for a towel.

Everything's going splendidly, he thought. My re-election, the assignment in Mexico, and now this. We'll have to invite them to the White House when they come home. Too bad this is an event I can't talk too knowledgeably about. I wonder if Jules has heard. Has Hugh? Probably, knowing Jane.

Theodore Roosevelt started for the family dining room feeling delighted. It wasn't every day that the President of the United States found out that he had been an inadvertent, albeit very successful, matchmaker.

Chapter Eighteen

November 1-4, 1904

All Saints' Day and All Souls' Day are the holiest days in Mexico. For these two days the entire country devotes itself to the religious festival with a total dedication and commitment that no manner of Reform Laws can quell.

In addition to the Masses attended by the faithful (and even by those who weren't, since there was nothing else to do in the city on those days), certain traditions abounded in this most strict of all countries. Some of these traditions, Thea and Charles agreed, were in turn touching, amusing, and outright repulsive. On the streets, vendors sold caricatures of well-known politicians that were printed on brightly colored paper and accompanied by funny verses; a special bread was sold in the bakeries; florists sold *cempasuchiles*, a beautiful flower resembling the marigold, to take to the cemeteries; and, least appealing of all, little skulls made of sugar candy were sold in dulcineras throughout the city.

Both days moved forward in a set pattern, but the holiness of the forty-eight hour period was, for the most part, lost on Thea. It was not out of any latent Protestant prejudice at having to sit through elaborate and solemn Catholic services but, rather, that her mind projected itself past the two day holy festival.

Neither Tuesday's Mass at the Cathedral, the oldest Christian church in North America, with its 426-foot long Doric facade and rich interior which was undergoing renovation, nor Wednesday's Mass For the Commemoration of the Faithful Departed at the now familiar Church of San Lorenzo, had Thea's full attention. She made a good pretense of following the service, knowing how much it meant to Charles, particularly Wednesday's Mass, since it was a link to the father he loved so much, but another matter claimed priority.

Thea was pushing the hours until Thursday. Thursday was Charles' birthday. And on Thursday, she wanted to give him the most precious gift of all—the news that she was going to have their baby.

In those first confused hours after she realized that she might be pregnant, Thea knew that her first responsibility was to get herself to a doctor.

Realistically, she knew that, at this point, even if she had conceived, an examination would confirm nothing. But her instinct told her that this was the right thing to do and, after a few exploratory telephone calls, she ascertained that the American Hospital was the place for her to go, and Dr. Winston Benning, the eminent Boston gynecologist, was the physician to see.

To Thea's surprise, Dona Imelda insisted on coming along with her.

"This is not a visit to be made alone," she told Thea on Monday afternoon. "You are in a strange country, about to see an unknown—although I'm certain very superb—doctor and, if your news is disappointing, you should not be without comfort when you leave."

Thea had been deeply touched by Dona Imelda's concern and now, on Thursday morning, as Hernando drove them to the American Hospital, she found her affection for the older woman deepening. Instead of talking to her about maternity and family, she tactfully asked her questions about her plans for Charles' birthday celebration.

"Did you know that today is also the Feast of Saint Hubert?" Thea said as Hernando skillfully moved the Columbia touring car in front of a smaller, far less impressive-looking Fiat. "He's the patron saint of Normandy, and every year there's a very famous Mass said at the cathedral in Lisieux, with a special chorus of ten in the choir. Charles told me they dress in hunters' pink, and play the *Obyre-Tindare* on hunters' horns."

"How very beautiful it sounds, and so very fitting since Saint Hubert is the patron saint of hunters," Dona Imelda remarked. "I take it Charles misses his home and family very much today."

Thea nodded. "He told me that, if we were in New York, and only engaged instead of married, he would have gone back to France to see his family and attend the Mass with them for one last time. He's more homesick today than he'll tell me, Dona Imelda, and I'm very grateful the French Embassy came through the way it did. The ambassador invited Charles to a special service he's sponsoring, followed by a luncheon at the French Club."

"In other words, Charles has a suitable distraction for today and, by tonight, you shall hopefully have some very compensating news for him."

"A very special birthday present," Thea said as they reached their destination.

The American Hospital turned out to be a large, modern building with a highly efficient staff and both women were promptly shown into Dr. Benning's office where a uniformed nurse greeted them.

The doctor's waiting room was a pleasant surprise, decorated with white wicker furniture covered with bright chintzes, vases full of fresh flowers, and tables holding an assortment of women's magazines.

"How very refreshing," Dona Imelda said as she sat down in an armchair whose soft green and white cushions contrasted pleasantly with her Paquin suit of sage green serge trimmed with black satin braid and set off by a white satin blouse.

"All of the sudden, I'm very, very nervous," Thea said, unable to sit down. Her Poiret suit of dark blue serge trimmed in bands of plaited braid outlined in narrow gold braid, with a yellow silk blouse with lace frills at the neck and wrists, had been chosen to give her courage, but it wasn't helping, and her heels clicked on the hardwood floor as she paced back and forth.

"Thea, it's all going to be fine—you know you're doing the right thing today," Dona Imelda said soothingly.

"Ever since the first time Charles and I made love, I forced myself *not* to think about having a baby," Thea said frankly, finally sitting down in the chair next to Dona Imelda's. "I wanted it to happen, but now I'm down to *this*, and I'm very scared."

"Mrs. de Renille, the doctor will see you now."

Thea looked from the nurse's polite, smiling face to Dona Imelda's encouraging one and, her heart pounding, she rose, crossed the floor to where the nurse was waiting and, taking a deep breath, allowed herself to be shown into the doctor's office.

She'd already learned that Dr. Winston Benning was a highly esteemed Boston gynecologist attached to both New England Women's and Children's Hospital and Massachusetts General, and had been invited by the board of Mexico City's American Hospital to spend a year south of the border both in private practice at the hospital and instructing at the medical college. He had an impressive resume, but it was no indication as to the personality of the doctor himself, and Thea felt she was quite justified in being nervous—a feeling that vanished as soon as she saw the reserved-looking man in his early fifties rise from his chair to greet her as she was shown in.

"When you made this appointment, you mentioned to my nurse that you think you may have started a baby," Dr. Benning said a few minutes later as they sat in opposite corners of his leather sofa that was placed under the windows of his book-lined consulting room. "Do you have an idea of how far along you might be?"

"Not very far, I'm afraid," Thea admitted, relaxing under both the doctor's calm, Boston-accented voice, and his unstuffy manner. "I'm eleven days late, as of today. I know an examination won't be conclusive, but at least I can make sure I'm in good order. And," she added, "today is my husband's birthday."

"And you'd be appreciative if I could help you in giving him a very special present," Dr. Benning concluded with a warm smile. "Well, we'll see if that's possible in a few minutes, but first, a few questions. How old are you, Mrs. de Renille?"

"Twenty-five. Twenty-six on the 14th."

"And your husband?"

"He's thirty today."

"The date of your wedding was—?"

"September 24th."

"And your last cycle was on—"

Thea supplied the answers to all Dr. Benning's questions, and waited while the doctor made a few notes on a pad.

"From the dates you've given me, I'd say there's a good chance that you have conceived," he said with an encouraging smile. "And I'm glad you're aware of the necessity of an examination. I take it you have your own doctor back in New York?"

"Dr. Emily Stern on 16th Street," she supplied, not expecting Dr. Benning to show any recognition. But, to her surprise, he looked delighted.

531

"This is fine. I knew Dr. Stern when she was Emily Allister. In fact, I was her supervising physician during her intern's year and for the first year of her gynecological residency. I also delivered her first son," he added with a twinkle in his light blue eyes. "I'm glad to find you're in such good hands. Now, for the next step—"

There was a well-equipped dressing room and a maid to help Thea out of her clothes and into an examining gown. And, almost before she realized it, she was in the examining room where Dr. Benning and his nurse were waiting for her.

The pelvic examination was skillfully conducted, with Dr. Benning proving to be an extremely considerate physician. Now she knew where Emily had learned her tender manner toward her patients, Thea thought as she answered the additional questions put to her. It was so much like her yearly examinations in New York, that the reasons behind her being there finally slid into their proper perspective.

"I think I may have some good news for you, Mrs. de Renille," Dr. Benning said several minutes later when Thea was dressed again and they were back in his consulting room. "As we discussed, all your preliminary symptoms could be caused by the changes in your life— this altitude certainly doesn't help matters—but the internal examination *did* show that your cervix is in a position that either indicates your monthly cycle is about to begin—or that you're in the very early stages of pregnancy. I also believe that an intelligent woman can come up with the right answer long before the doctor can."

Thea thought for a long minute, absorbing the doctor's words, and then she looked across at him with a smile of certainty. "I've never been late," she told him. "Not once in twelve years, not for any reason."

"Well, then," Winston Benning's smile matched Thea's. "I think you should now go back to your hotel and tell your husband that he may very well be a father this coming June."

Thea had planned every detail of Charles' birthday celebration with the greatest of care, beginning early in the day.

On their breakfast tray she placed his first present, a small enamel box with a finely detailed rendering of a handsome thoroughbred horse on the lid and, resting beside the box, a perfect white Malmaison carnation to wear in his buttonhole. Taking into account that he would be back from the Mass and the luncheon party that followed before she returned from the doctor, Thea arranged his next presents in the dressing room. Another Malmaison carnation—this time red instead of white— was placed in its own bud vase, and arranged alongside it was an ebony walking stick with a gold top, a magnifying glass with a French Sevres and bronze *dore* handle, and a set of mother-of-pearl cuff links and shirt studs set in fine old gold—every item found during her travels through the city's antique shops.

"I still can't find the words to tell you what all of these birthday presents mean to me," Charles said hours later as they dressed for dinner.

"You're only thirty once," Thea told him as she came into the dressing room so that he could hook up her Poiret gown of white chiffon and lace with a narrow green velvet belt. "I want today to be special for you."

For a moment, Charles was silent as he concentrated on the tiny, very stiff hooks and eyes.

"I'm sorry if I was out of sorts last night and this morning," he said finally in a quiet, reflective voice. "I've been distant and distracted—and thinking far too much about myself."

"You've earned a day off," Thea said, turning and putting her arms around his shoulders. "But tonight is all for you. Every bit of it. I want to make this the best birthday you've ever had!"

"It already is," he assured her as Thea helped him fasten a stubborn cuff link. "I want to do everything for you, but every so often I'm finding out that it's very nice to be the one who's pampered."

"That's something I'm going to have a lot of fun doing. And now, before I devote myself to you for the rest of the evening," Thea added as Charles pulled her close for a kiss, "what do you say to fastening my necklace?"

A minute later, Charles fastened her small diamond and emerald necklace and, as soon as Thea put on the green and white striped silk Directoire coat edged in white satin that was part of her gown, making its provocative cut more respectable for dining in a restaurant, and Charles put on the jacket to his dinner suit, they were ready to leave.

It was half-past seven, and the lobby was filled with men and women in formal clothes either enjoying a pre-dinner drink in one of the lobby's alcoves, entering the restaurant, coming in or going out of the main entrance. Charles and Thea joined the throng and were making their way toward the exit when the man standing at the registration desk, surrounded by a small mountain of luggage, caught their attention.

The man's obviously expensive suit was badly rumpled, his hand-made shoes were scuffed and dusty and, as they drew closer, it became apparent that the Sanz's latest guest was badly in need of a shave.

"Another addition to our cheery band of expatriates," Charles murmured to Thea but, before she could reply, the man in question completed the registration forms, capped his fountain pen, looked up, caught Charles' eye, and instant recognition passed between them.

"Charles. Charles de Renille. What a surprise to see you again!"

"Gerard de Langlade." Both men shook hands warmly. "We thought you were still down in Oaxaca."

"I've done all I could down there," he said with a self-disparaging gesture, pushing his thick blonde hair impatiently out of his eyes. "Amateurs like me are always welcome on digs—up to a point, that is—and I was in danger of wearing out mine. The dig site is run under the joint auspices of the Sorbonne, Cambridge, and Harvard and, since I'm not a professor at any of those august institutions, I began to feel rather left out," he finished with an apologetic smile as his gaze moved to Thea. "Forgive me, madame, but archaeology is my greatest interest and, once I begin to talk about it, I forget all else."

Possibly if you paid more attention to your wife, she wouldn't have to amuse herself by being beaten by her German lover, Thea thought nastily, but she had to admit there was something about Gerard de Langlade that she liked. Unlike his wife, he had a friendly manner, a good face, and blue-green eyes that held no hint of duplicity.

"Welcome to Mexico City, in any case," Charles was saying. "It's time you caught up on a few changes—in my life at least. Thea darling, this is Baron Gerard de Langlade. Gerard—" Charles' voice was filled with love and pride. "—I want to present my wife, Thea. We're here on our honeymoon."

Gerard's strained, exhausted look faded instantly at Charles' words and, after he kissed Thea and shook his friend's hand in congratulations, the three retired to a nearby alcove.

"Am I keeping you from some function?" Gerard inquired as they sat down in comfortable Empire-style bergeres which were upholstered in a red and gray striped silk.

"No, we're early for our dinner reservation," Charles assured him, signaling for a waiter to bring a round of aperitifs.

"But are *we* keeping *you?* I know if I hadn't seen Charles in eight months, I'd want him to come to me as quickly as possible," Thea couldn't resist saying, skillfully avoiding Charles' warning look.

Gerard's smile was a bit grim around the edges. "I think Ophelie can manage without me in her life for a few minutes more. Actually, it hasn't been that long since we've seen each other. She came down to Oaxaca in September. Didn't she mention that? No? Typical of my wife lately, unfortunately. The National Stud of France was interested in acquiring one of my horses, and they sent papers I had to sign," he explained as the waiter came with a tray of drinks. "The papers were sent to me here at the Sanz, and I wired Ophelie to convey them personally," he finished rather shortly, and began sipping his cocktail, giving the de Renilles absolutely no indication of how that reunion had gone.

"We want to hear more about your dig," Charles said shortly afterwards, glancing at a nearby clock, "but now we *do* have to go."

"It's Charles' birthday today," Thea put in with a loving glance. "We're celebrating privately at dinner tonight and—"

"And if I keep you any longer, the restaurant will give your table away," Gerard said, eyes twinkling with understanding and amusement. "*Heureux anniversaire*, Charles. Happy birthday," he said as they stood up and moved back to the center of the lobby. "You both deserve an excellent celebration tonight. And I have an idea that, even if you're late, your reception at the restaurant will probably be a great deal warmer than the one I'll receive upstairs," he finished in a voice of amused irony.

*   *   *

"Poor Gerard," Thea remarked, half sympathetically, half amused, some forty minutes later as they sat at their secluded table at Sylvian's. "He didn't sound terribly thrilled at seeing Ophelie again. I imagine that, at this moment, in spite of indoor plumbing and a nice bed, he's rather missing the nice, quiet, very masculine atmosphere of the dig site."

"Once, a very long time ago, Ophelie said that it was Gerard, not me, who was better suited for the Church," Charles told her.

"I don't know him well enough to compare your personalities, but I think that being exposed to the baronne for too long a time can make an otherwise normal man develop all sorts of tendencies," Thea said airily.

"In other words—" Charles challenged, already suspecting what Thea's theory was.

"I'm lucky you didn't become a Trappist."

"My father once suggested that if I really wanted to do something useful, I should join the Carthusian Friars at the Monastery of La Grande Chartreuse and help them make their liqueur," Charles said, a small pain entering his heart at the memory and then, aware his own secrets had no place in their conversation, he moved to change the subject. "But that was all a very long time ago, and there are certain things that are much more important in our lives." His hand reached out to cover hers. "This is the best birthday I can remember, and you've planned it all to perfection."

Sylvian's was Mexico City's finest restaurant. Devoted to the fine cuisine of France, its menu made no concession to the Mexican cuisine, and its spacious interior was faintly reminiscent of Maxim's, with small shaded lamps on the tables, glass panels, and musicians who would play music for dancing promptly at ten.

A week earlier, Thea had paid a visit to the restaurant,

and, working with the maître d', selected the table, the food, and the wine. The management had been more than pleased to help her plan a birthday dinner for her husband and, so far, everything was going just the way she wanted.

Together they waited as the sommelier cut away the metal at the neck of the bottle of Moet et Chandon 1895 that had been chilling in the silver ice bucket beside their table, deftly extracted the cork, and poured a small amount of the golden liquid into a tulip-shaped glass for Charles to taste and approve.

"You have excellent taste in champagne," Charles said softly after he nodded at the wine steward to fill their glasses. "And in husbands as well," he added, his eyes dancing like twin topazes.

"I like to think so," she agreed, her heart filling with love for Charles, and the anticipation of the news she would give him in a few hours. She lifted her champagne glass. "To my husband on his birthday. For the man who has all my love, now and always."

The look on Charles' face was one of such unabashed love, need and desire that it was all Thea could do not to put her arms around him right there. He had never looked at her like this in public before; he was always loving but unfailingly correct, saving his more passionate side for when they were alone together.

He raised his own glass to Thea's, and they touched rims. *"Toujours a toi,"* he told her tenderly. "Forever thine. I think that if I died right here, it would be with the certainty that I'd found the greatest love of my life—the one I thought didn't exist for me."

For a few indescribably tender minutes they sat side by side, holding hands, their gazes locked together in total understanding. If it was up to them, they might have stayed that way indefinitely, except that the maître d', deciding that even such devoted lovers as the de Renilles needed sustenance, signalled to his waiters to begin serving their meal.

As much in love as they were, Thea and Charles were both young and healthy enough to do superb justice to their dinner and, obligingly, they began their meal with goose liver paté in a pastry crust, billi-bi soup made according to Maxim's famous recipe. It was only when the plates held only the scant remains of the lobster in herb-scented cream sauce that they once again became aware that they were not the only two patrons in the restaurant.

"The entire restaurant's probably talking about us by now," Charles said, amused.

"I certainly hope so. And I hope they're all green with jealousy!"

Charles began to laugh. "Oh, Thea, sometimes you are so—"

"Bitchy. Go ahead and say it. It's rather a compliment, I think. Besides, you know perfectly well that, if you had a wife who was all fluttering eyelashes and sweet-as-sugar remarks, you'd be ready to choke her in six months!"

Charles tried unsuccessfully to hide his smile. "Can't I keep *any* secrets from you?"

"Any number of them, no doubt. But none that matter."

The arrival of Charles' birthday cake not only halted their loving banter, but caught the attention of all the other diners as well. Thea had had to fight for this cake. A proper birthday cake, the management had insisted, was a *paté a genoise*, a *gateau symbolique*, richly adorned with butter cream swirls, shells and rosebuds and, since it was for a Frenchman, the frosting should be chestnut or mocha or—at the very least—praline. But not for her husband, Thea insisted. A birthday cake had to be a happy thing; chocolate, with the appropriate number of candles for the honoree to make a wish on and blow out.

It had taken quite a bit of wrangling but, in the end, Thea—with one or two compromises—had won and, as she saw Charles' face light up with all the power of the cake's flickering candles, she was glad she'd kept to her own ideals.

"Thirty-one candles," Charles said after a quick count.

"One to grow on," she offered informatively. "Blow out the candles quickly, darling, or I'll be tempted to sing 'Happy Birthday'—and don't forget to make a wish!"

Charles blew out all the candles in one try, and he leaned back with an expression of mock exhaustion. "Is this the purpose of American birthday parties? To wear out the celebrant with wine, rich food and a cake like this? Incidentally, how did you get the pastry chef to agree to a cake with two layers and candles and keeping the shells and rosebuds along the edge only—and in chocolate?" Charles inquired as they removed the tapers and he cut the first slice of dark sweet chocolate butter cream frosted *gateau* to reveal the double layer of *genoise*.

"Oh, a little bit of blackmail applied here and there works wonders," Thea said, adopting an airy tone. "I said that if they couldn't see their way clear to carry out my idea, I'd order up a big, gooey cake from the Women's Exchange!"

"You shouldn't terrify the management of a fine restaurant like that," Charles teased, reaching for the bottle of champagne. "This time for you," he said, refilling their glasses. "And my sympathies to any maitre d' who doesn't fall in with your plans—"

They were still in an almost silly mood when they left the restaurant an hour later. The champagne and excellent food had cast its spell on them, and it was one Thea was suddenly reluctant to break.

"Do you know who I feel sorry for tonight?" she inquired as they entered the sitting room of their suite.

"Guenther von Basedow."

Charles looked faintly nonplussed. "Why *him* of all people?"

"Because he was there at Sylvian's, all alone at his table, waiting for the dinner companion who never arrived."

"Ophelie?"

"None other. And, right now, I'm sort of hoping Gerard beat her when he got up to their suite and found her all ready for a night on the town with her lover!"

Charles gave a short laugh. "If everything you've been telling me is true, she probably rather enjoyed it. And, speaking of enjoyment . . ."

Thea went first into the bedroom, casting a careful, almost professional eye over the bed that Angelita had turned down for them. Her heart was beginning to beat faster in anticipation. She slipped off the hip-length coat, draped it over the closest chair, and then settled on the bed, leaning back against the pillows.

Should I wait? she wondered, her emotions in turmoil. It *is* too soon. If I'm wrong, Charles will be so disappointed, but if I'm right and I don't tell him tonight, I'll always regret it.

"Would you care for another birthday present?" Thea said, putting aside all her doubts and acting quickly before she lost her nerve. Charles entered the room and closed the door behind him.

He sat down beside her. "I don't know if I can take the excitement of one more surprise."

"Well, you're going to have to," Thea announced, putting her arms around his shoulders and kissing him. "It's the best birthday present I could ever give you," she said, drawing back so she could look at his face and see his response. "We're going to have a baby."

For an endless moment, the world seemed to suspend itself between them and Thea, who had been expecting

541

an outpouring of joy, began to become alarmed.

"Charles . . ."

"I don't believe it."

"Well, you have almost nine months to adjust," she said, deciding to treat the matter lightly.

"Are you certain?" His voice was doubtful.

"Not entirely—it's too soon. But I *know*, I feel it. . . ." Quickly, Thea told him about her visit to Dr. Benning. "Charles, I thought you'd be happy—"

Charles ran his hands through his hair. "It doesn't make any sense . . . I can't believe . . . I was told . . . When I was recovering, all the doctors who came—" He reached out and took her hands. "One of them told me I could never father a child; that my high fevers had ruined any chance of that."

Thea would have done anything to wipe the look of anguish from his face. She thought: I'd love to get my hands on that doctor. How does a presumably responsible physician ruin a man like that?

"Charles—my own darling—do you believe that doctor now? Did you ever?"

He looked at her through a haze of pain. "I refused to let myself think we could make a child together, that's why I never said a word to you about it all these weeks. I thought it would be difficult enough in the months, in the years, ahead when nothing would happen—"

"That damn doctor, I'd like to choke him!" Thea exploded. "What did that idiot tell you?"

For the first time since she told him the news, Charles began to smile. "He was elderly, English and very highly esteemed and, after he examined me, he said that while future relations would be possible—should I care to undertake them—that I must not think in terms of procreation. He said—" He stopped, the pain replaced by something very much like amusement. "He said my sap would have no strength, that my high fevers had

542

destroyed the potency of my seed."

Thea wanted to take Charles in her arms, to comfort him, to wipe away his pain but, as she heard his words, she began to laugh.

"Procreate . . . your *sap* . . . no strength . . . potency of your seed. . . ."

She was laughing endlessly and, a minute later, Charles joined in and the bedroom rang with their merriment.

"There is no way a doctor can make an absolute judgment like that," she said finally when they were both calm again and stretched out across the bed still in their evening clothes.

"I didn't have any choice but to believe him," Charles pointed out. "Besides, I was in such poor shape physically that I couldn't imagine making love, being married or any other situation where I'd have to give all of myself."

"I never had any doubts," Thea said, leaning over him, brushing back his thick silky hair. "After we made love the first time and I figured out that the days were right, I knew I was going to have your—our—baby."

"De Renille wives always have their first baby nine months and two weeks after their wedding day."

She looked into his sparkling eyes. "I think we're going to manage a somewhat better margin of respectability than that."

"What did you mean by the days being right?"

Thea smiled knowingly. "I think we can save your introduction into the intricacies of basic female biology for another time."

Charles sat up, pulling Thea along with him. "Are we really going to have a baby?" he asked, and Thea's last doubt that she might possibly have spoken too soon vanished.

"Yes, we are. Sometime in July, I think, just before the

weather gets really hot. And, if everything's all right, I can even have the baby at home the way Alix did Isabelle. Do you think your mother will want to come over?"

"Definitely—it will be a moment of glory for her," he said, but a concerned look was in his eyes. "Thea, I've just realized I don't know a thing about being a father!"

"You'll learn—and you'll be a wonderful one, just like your father was to you and your brothers."

It was as if her words had been a sponge passing over Charles' face, so swiftly was every bit of happiness and anticipation removed from Charles' face. Suddenly the anguish was back again, and his eyes were filling with tears.

Shocked, Thea cast about frantically for something to say, but her mind was a blank. Instinctively, she reached out to Charles, but he shook her off.

"A wonderful father," he rasped out. "My father was that, and I loved him." Hot tears were starting to slide down his face. "If I can be half as good as he was, I'll be content. But all the time our child is growing up, I'll wonder if he'll do to me what I did to my father."

"Charles—" Thea was dizzy with shock and surprise. "I don't understand. I want to help you, but you have to trust me, to let me in," she pleaded, tears beginning to burn at her eyes. Something was wrong—terribly, terribly wrong.

"Understand," he choked. "How can I make the woman I love understand that, by my own stupid actions, I helped to kill my own father?"

Thea had never seen a grown man cry before. When her mother had died, she knew her father had wept, but he had done it privately, and she'd seen only the ravages the tears left, not the act itself. But now she watched helplessly as Charles, overcome by his last outburst, buried his face in the bed and began to cry, all his

544

emotions laid bare before her.

I think I knew this all along, she thought, pulling Charles' head into her lap. There was some secret hidden so deep within him that it couldn't come out, not until it was triggered by something so unexpected . . . This has something to do with his dreams . . . He never talks about his father as easily as he does the rest of his family . . . All this pain and misery locked inside him for so long . . .

Thea forced herself to cut off her disjointed thoughts. They weren't going to help Charles. Half-baked theories weren't what were needed now. The only thing for her to do was play it by ear.

Gradually, the intensity of his sobs lessened and, a few minutes later, trailed off in a series of hiccups.

"Do you know you're married to a liar?" he asked at last in a thick voice filled with self-hate. "I lied to my father, I lied to my mother and brothers, I lied to you and, worst of all, I lied to myself. I wasn't released from my vows because of my breakdown. The truth is, they simply didn't want me any longer. I was about to be thrown out when I collapsed."

I never even suspected it might have been like that for him, Thea thought. Charles keeps his secrets so well that they finally began to eat away at him. I want to help him, but I can't, not just yet. This is his own torment, and he has to walk through it alone.

"But why?" Her voice was low and compassionate. "A prize scholar from a fine family—"

"Who had no business being allowed into the Jesuits, or any other Order! I faked my way in and managed to fool everyone for a while, but no one is stupid forever and, somewhere along the line, my superiors finally realized that. I was under inspection when the orders to leave France came, and we were scattered. Where I was posted was the key. Not to Jersey, or to England, but to Belgium, to a small seminary that was more of a clearing house for failed seminarians than a house of studies. If they hadn't needed an English instructor at St. Michel's, I probably would have been released within a month of my arrival. The Society is able to dismiss candidates almost up until the time of ordination, there's always a canonical law that can be cut to fit—''

Sitting on the bed, Thea was receiving a crash course in Jesuit by-laws but, so far, none of it was connecting to what Charles had told her about his father. He was ridding himself of a nightmare too long suppressed, and he had to do it his own way.

"I didn't have a well day from the moment I crossed the border from France to Belgium. I wasn't lucky enough to fall apart all at once. I went through it slowly, one painful symptom after the other. But I was teaching, proving that I could *do* something, and I was proud of my students and my efforts. And then, about a week before the Christmas holiday began, my father came to see me.

"I hadn't seen him since August of 1897 and, suddenly, it was December of 1901, I was in the Rector's study, and the man who'd once told me that I was no longer his son was holding me in his arms.

"But he didn't look like the father I remembered. That August day, his hair had been as black as mine is now, but the next time I saw him it was snow white. He was only in his fifties, Thea, but he looked seventy—frail and tired. But I didn't care, it meant so much to see him again. We talked for about a half-hour, and then I took him to meet my students. We all ate our midday meal together, speaking only in English.''

He's getting paler every minute, Thea thought with growing apprehension. He won't be able to go on like this much longer. But this is his way—all his—and I can only listen and be here for him . . .

"He could barely eat," Charles' voice continued, "and I couldn't either. And, when the meal was finally over, we walked in the garden and talked to each other for the first time in years."

Thea could imagine how it had been: the father and son walking in the frozen garden of what was considered to be one of the finest boys' schools on the European continent. She could see them reconciled after years of strain and silence, but still apart in terms of pride.

"He wanted me to come home with him, to leave right away. I don't know if he knew what was happening to me, but he said the world was full of runaways and one seminarian wasn't going to make too much of a difference. We were in the courtyard, standing in front of the carriage he'd hired. Father said all I had to do was get in with him and we'd drive away. No one would stop us and, later on, everything could be arranged."

Thea knew what "everything" meant.

"Do you mean your father would have bought your release from the Church? That enough money would have smoothed over your walking out cold?"

"As they say, money talks. And, when you bring it down to the lowest common denominator, Rome is no different from any other organization."

"But you didn't go with your father," Thea said carefully. "You stayed behind."

"I couldn't tell him, Thea." Charles' voice was tight with remembered pain. "I couldn't find the words to tell him that I was going to be dismissed, and that I'd be home by summer. We stood there, two very ill men, neither of us able to surmount our pride. I couldn't admit I'd failed, that he'd been right about me all along, and my father couldn't tell me he was dying."

For a minute, Thea couldn't breathe. Once again, time was suspended between them.

"In the end, he left alone. I stood at the gate, watching the carriage disappear into the Brussels traffic. Ten days later, my father was dead and, when they told me, I died also. Little by little, my body began to malfunction. And, finally, it just gave out, helped along by the knowledge that, if it hadn't been for me, my father might have lived a little while longer and have had his youngest son at his bedside when he died."

Thea was the one crying now, the wetness streaking her eye black. Her heart ached for Charles, for how he'd suffered. But, even as her emotions cried out for him, her cool, analytic mind was shifting gears, throwing off unanswered questions.

"Charles. . . ." She spoke cautiously. "What did your father die of?"

"Pneumonia, brought on by prolonged exposure to the elements—and probably aided by the journey from Normandy to Brussels and back again."

"But you said he was dying and wouldn't tell you. Charles, he couldn't have been dying of pneumonia when he got to Brussels."

Suddenly, Thea wasn't confused any more. The facts were there in front of her, waiting for Charles' confirmation.

"He—he had a disease of the blood." Charles' body went rigid and unyielding. "Leukemia—"

At the sound of that awful word, some great tension snapped in Thea, and relief flooded through her body. "You couldn't have changed anything," she began, but Charles held her off.

"Not about his eventual death, no. Because of his disease, that was inevitable. But he would have lived longer if he hadn't come to Brussels. Or if I'd just come home with him . . ."

His words trailed off, and they held each other for a very long time. Charles was worn out. He had opened his heart to her, told his secrets, and now his battered emotions were paying the price.

"I wouldn't blame you if you never felt the same toward me again," Charles said at last as they lay back against the pillows. "You gave me the most wonderful news a man can possibly hope for, and I reward you by crying like a ten year old, and then I tell you about my father . . . A secret I should have kept to my grave."

"I love you," Thea said, cupping his face in her hands. "And I guess I'm going to have to go on saying it until it sinks in. You've suffered terribly, but nothing you went through is worse than what you insist on inflicting upon yourself. You didn't help kill your father, unintentionally or otherwise."

An expression of pain creased his face. "My father died of pneumonia, not from his disease."

"That's how it frequently happens."

Charles looked nonplussed. "Don't try to make excuses for me, Thea. My pride, my miserable, obstinate pride—"

"Charles, listen to me! Leukemia is an insidious disease. It destroys from within, and its victims eventually lose their resistance to illness—even a simple cold can be deadly."

"How do you know this?" Charles demanded.

"You can't have a close friend go all through medical school and not learn a lot of technical details. Alix has told me all sorts of things. The way your father died. . . . Charles, it saved him from all the pain and disintegration that comes at the end. He knew the danger of travelling in cold weather—I'm sure of it—but he loved you enough to risk that because he wanted to see you again. Please, darling, take that gesture your father made to you and *don't* blame yourself for what happened afterwards."

"When I was home again, ill, almost destroyed, and I found out the details behind my father's illness, I felt sole responsibility for it. It haunted me—"

"The dreams?"

He nodded. "No one escapes punishment for their transgressions."

"I think you've paid more than enough. Why don't you stop flagellating yourself over your father? I don't think he'd want that from you. You've been so busy inflicting pain on yourself that you forgot all about mourning for him."

"I have an idea that I finally began to do that about an hour ago," Charles replied, taking Thea gently in his arms. "I feel awful—and better—than I have in the past two years."

Thea smiled. "I'd better get you some aspirin or you'll have a splitting headache by morning."

"I already do," he admitted ruefully, and Thea slipped quickly out of his arms.

She was back in a minute with two white tablets and a glass of water. "Take this," she instructed, "and then we'll get ready for bed."

"This hasn't been the night you expected, has it?" Charles said after he took the aspirins and drained the glass. "I even ruined your dress."

Thea looked down at her gown, now badly creased and tear-stained, and smiled. She remembered how Paul Poiret himself had done the final fitting, and how he'd exclaimed over her figure and her face.

"It doesn't matter," she told him truthfully. "It can be cleaned, or I can order a replacement. And, in case you haven't figured it out yet, you're more important to me than any dress I own!"

They got ready for bed, helping each other out of their clothes, but saying little until Thea had straightened the bed, fluffed the pillows and they were ready to get under the covers.

"I love you," Charles said as they lay back against the pillows, "and I love our baby. And tonight," he went on, his hands slipping lightly under the rich lace top of her pale gray satin nightgown so he could gently cup her breasts, "I'm the luckiest man in the world!"

"Wait until July," Thea promised with a smile, as her own hands went under the collar of his nightshirt to caress his shoulders and back. "Wait until you see our daughter. We're going to have a beautiful baby."

Charles laughed. "I don't doubt that for a second, but I'm afraid it's going to be a boy. There are simply no girls in the de Renille family. The babies are always male."

Thea smiled a secret, knowing smile and shook her head. "It's going to be a girl—just you wait and see."

Charles switched off the bedside lamp and pulled the puffed silk comforters over them, a feeling of deep contentment washing over him as Thea nestled close against him. It was after four in the morning and Charles knew that, for as long as he lived, he would never forget this night; not only for the promise of their future together, but for the peace he'd found about his past.

Thea had been right: he had never mourned for his father; the self-reproach had been easier. But now he was finally facing the truth that his father might have died at the same time even if he hadn't come to Brussels. All it would have taken for the results to be the same was a freezing cold morning in the stable yard—a few hours with his horses rather than his son.

Charles' temples were still pounding and his throat felt raw but, as he held Thea in his arms, he had the feeling that his life—despite whatever hurdles of buried emotions he still had to face—was finally and completely returned to him. In fact, come July, he wouldn't be at all surprised if their baby turned out to be a girl after all.

Chapter Nineteen

November 7-24, 1904

On the west side of the Plaza Mayor, near the National Palace that was the official residence of President Diaz, even though he did not live there, preferring to make his winter domicile at his far more modest house in the Cadena, was the Monte de Pledad, founded in 1775 as the National Pawnshop of Mexico.

Based on the French Montes de Piele, it functions for those in need of cash to obtain funds by legally pawning personal property and thereby avoiding usurers. All levels of Mexican society made use of this system. The money loaned, on all manner of goods except livestock, ranged from a few pennies to thousands of dollars. For the poor it was a convenient way to stretch their meagre earnings. For the once wealthy with fortunes that hadn't kept up with a changing world, it was the route to a box at the opera. And, for Mexico City's foreign community, the National Pawnshop provided a place for them to dispose of household belongings that they had acquired during their stay and didn't want to take home—a fine fast way to pick up extra cash.

The Monte de Pledad opens its doors every afternoon for the sale of unredeemed pledges to the general public. And, once through the arched doorway and cool patio into the huge *almonte*—salesroom, the prospective buyer is greeted by the sight of a seemingly endless number of stalls. Each offering an array of jewelry, assorted bibelots, chandeliers, fine carpets, saddles, sewing machines, carriages, and now, in this new age of technology, the occasional motor car.

Since their arrival in Mexico City, Thea, accompanied by Charles, had made a weekly visit to the pawnshop. She had quickly developed favorites among those vendors who ran the better stalls. And, on this Monday afternoon, the day before Election Day, Thea felt that she finally struck paydirt—both for herself and her clients.

At Charles' favorite stall, where the vendor dealt exclusively in fine books, they had found an edition of *The Great Modern Painters* that had been published by Goupil et Cie. in Paris in 1884. The four volume work, printed on papier Japon, each volume bound in blue morocco with gilt-stamped spines, would be the perfect Christmas present for Alix and Henry, they decided.

Leaving her husband among the books, Thea went on to a carpet vendor where she found a Persian Senna rug of red and gold wool woven with silk warp threads and, after that purchase was concluded, she paid a visit to her favorite stall, the one run by Señor Mendoza, who greeted her with a happy smile.

"A bonanza, Señora de Renille," he said sotto voce, escorting her into his stall. "Some important clients have decided not to redeem their pledges, and you have the first opportunity to see the merchandise. *Con permiso—*"

Thea was long used to dealers who promised her goods which never lived up to expectation, and she took all such statements with a grain of salt. But there *were* rare instances when the advance word held, and this was one of those times.

There were a pair of triangular Faberge picture frames of red enamel banded in gold, a modern Cartier clock of blue and white enamel accented with silver with a white enamel face on an agate base and, the one item Thea had hoped to find but never really believed she would until they were back in New York, a French Directoire fruitwood dining table, fifty-five inches wide with four leaves that extended its length to one hundred and eighteen inches.

"I want my husband to see this," Thea said a few minutes later, putting away her tape measure. "I think it's perfect for our new dining room, but we'll see. No chairs?"

"Alas, no, señora. But look at the grain—"

"Can you tell me something about the previous owner?" she asked, not at all distracted by his selling technique.

"*No es costumbre,* señora. It is not our custom. But it comes from a fine home, and I will see to it that it is shipped to you in New York."

Thea had learned a long time ago that one of the best ways to fend off a dealer when a purchase hadn't been cemented was simply to smile a lot and say nothing.

So much had changed since Thursday night, she reflected, taking a step back to view the table. The last barrier between them was down, the final secret shared, and Charles' pain was out in the open—the first step in finally putting it behind him.

Nothing can stop us now, Thea thought triumphantly as she examined the table's legs. Neither of us are paying dues on debts that we paid a long time ago.

"Why don't you let me sweep you up in my arms and take you away from here? There's Cuernavaca, Guadalajara or even the floating gardens at Xochimilco. Now, what do you say to my suggestions?"

"Go away, Paul, before Charles comes back and there's a scene," Thea said, meeting Paul Merrill's gaze with an uncompromising look.

It had been like this at every party, Paul Merrill

following her, staying at her side, whispering half-humorous, half-suggestive comments in her ear. He sent her flowers every morning, and notes that Thea read and burned immediately afterwards, causing Charles to tease that she must be keeping secrets.

Now she watched as his gaze took her in from head to foot, admiring her Lucile afternoon suit of blue chiffon broadcloth with a shirred girdle and undersleeves of matching taffeta and a blouse of Irish lace. With an unpleasant feeling coursing through her, Thea realized that this was the same way Charles looked at her.

Instinctively, Thea moved to the far end of the stall, and Paul followed her, pretending a great interest in a Rose Canton teapot while they talked.

"Will you please leave me alone?" she said quietly, firmly.

"Why? I meant what I said that night at the de Veigas. I want to marry you."

"I *am* married, and it's to the man I love. Now and forever."

He smiled patiently. "I told you once, you don't have to pretend."

"I'm not pretending, dammit!" Thea snapped.

"Look, I can understand what you feel for Charles. He's a good fellow. Loyalty is a wonderful virtue, but you don't have to overdo it."

"I've never given up being amazed at how some perfectly intelligent men can be so backward," Thea said with far more coolness than she felt, her eyes scanning the salesroom before coming back to Paul. "Have you seen Charles?"

"You don't have to sound like I hit him over the head and dropped him in some back alley. He's fine."

"Good. I want him to see this table."

"There aren't any chairs."

Thea took a deep breath. "Oh, that won't matter too

555

much. Benjamin Altman sent us a congratulatory cable and asked what we wanted for a wedding present. A dozen chairs will do nicely, I think. Or even just two, one for either end, we can get the rest at Sloane's. Paul, is Charles still at Señor Garcia's stall?"

With great interest, Paul studied a wall hanging woven in shades of green, rose and cream and, bearing a metal tag that read *remante de prendas el dia 25 del corriente mes*, meaning that it was being held for the auction sale that the Monte de Pledad held on the 25th of every month. Thea hated auctions.

"He's out on the patio with my superior officer," Paul said with deliberate slowness. He was loathe to lose Thea's company and, although he knew he'd blundered badly at the Hacienda de Veiga, nothing he said seemed to make up for it. Apparently, her loyalty knew no depths when it came to that Frenchman. "He said to tell you he'd wait for you there."

"Well, thanks a lot," Thea snapped. With Major Donovan's consent, they had decided to move their meetings out of Chapultepec Park to more central surroundings. "If I hadn't asked, you would have kept me here for the rest of the afternoon," she said angrily, grabbing her black lizard handbag off the Blue Willow plate it had been resting on and, after picking up the plate and checking its markings, took it as well, and quickly made her way to the front of the stall.

Señor Mendoza was busily employed with a new customer, a rather well set up man with a neatly trimmed ginger-colored beard that exactly matched the color of his hair, and a cane resting on the table beside him. As Thea joined them, he lifted his eyes from the tray of fine jewelry he was studying and, when they made contact, she had the strangest feeling that he'd not only heard every word she and Paul exchanged but knew exactly what was going on between them.

"Señor Mendoza, please see to the lady. I believe she's in somewhat of a hurry."

His well-bred British accent unnerved her for a second.

Do I know this man? she thought. He's very familiar, but . . .

Quickly, she snapped her attention back to the dealer.

"I'm afraid I've just learned that my husband has met an acquaintance of ours, and they've gone out to the patio. I promise to bring him back with me before we leave, so don't sell the table to anyone else."

"Of course not, Señora de Renille. Do you also wish the plate?"

"Yes, please," she said, handed it to him, and then turned to the man beside her. "Thank you for allowing me to interrupt your consultation."

"Not at all. I am more than happy to gain a few more minutes to make up my mind. A present for my wife," he explained, gesturing at the tray. "Could I possibly impose—?"

Thea smiled at the Englishman. "I'm pleased to be of help. Now, let's see. . . ." Her hand hovered over the jewelry. "This," she said, selecting a large Florentine cameo set with diamonds. "Every woman loves a cameo."

"Exactly," he said with a sigh of relief. "And, since I've been away from home since August, I should also take—"

"The pearl bracelet with the diamond clasp and, if your wife is fond of Rose Canton ware, there's a charming teapot in the back," she finished, unable to resist laughing. "Have a happy trip back to England."

"That was very nice of you," Paul remarked as they left the salesroom.

"I love to help people buy things. Besides, even though half the aristocracy of Mexico City is pawning their

557

jewelry here, it doesn't make it Tiffany's or Asprey's or Cartier. Señor Mendoza is scrupulously honest, but I wouldn't buy any really important jewelry from him, bargain or not."

She kept a step or two ahead of Paul on the way to the patio but, as they stepped into the sunlight, he grasped her elbow firmly. It was a gesture Thea particularly hated, and she felt her temper flare white hot as she tried to shake herself loose. But Paul's fingers were like iron and, smiling blandly, he steered her toward a group of wrought iron benches placed under shade trees.

"Here we are," he announced cheerfully and, unseen, his fingers tightened once more and then let go. "Will there be anything else, sir?" he inquired of Major Donovan.

Thea's face was a mask of pure, murderous fury. The same feeling Charles now had in his heart for Captain Merrill. Until the last few moments he hadn't paid much attention to Thea's complaints about the attaché. Where he came from, women complained about a lack of male attention, not a surfeit.

Now I know differently, he thought. He held Thea as if she were a piece of property—his property. It's a demeaning thing, not only for the woman but for the man . . . shows him off as a bully and a braggart. Well, in my own way, I'm just as guilty, but I can repay that now. . . .

"Paul, do you care for golf?" Charles inquired as Thea sat down beside him in a swish of rich material. "I thought that if you did, we might play together."

"I'd like that. My membership just came through at San Pedro. Would you care to join me tomorrow morning?"

"I was going to suggest the very same thing. Will eleven suit you?"

"That's fine." He turned back to Donovan. "Sir?"

"No, that's all, Captain. See you later at the embassy." He gave the younger officer's back a considering look. "That young man is going to go far," he announced when Paul was out of earshot.

"As what, a strong-arm man or a bouncer?" Thea inquired nastily.

"Oh, Paul's just . . . well, what you ladies call effective. He doesn't let his opportunities go by. He's just seeing to his future."

"Call him off, Major." Thea's voice was cold. "I don't like his hovering around me."

"For all the two of you have been doing the past five days or so, you shouldn't have any cause to complain."

"And we're not going to be doing much more," Charles said calmly. "We're here to tell you we're leaving."

Surprise quickly replaced complacency on Donovan's face. "You're not finished!"

"Frankly, I don't think we ever got started. Face it, Major," Charles continued, forcing himself to be calm, telling himself a scene wasn't going to work, that even though the only person near them—a thin-faced, thirtyish man who only gave them a single glance—was now buried in *El Imparcial*, one didn't make a fuss in public. "We don't like doing this, we don't like Mexico, and we want to go home."

"Well," he drawled, "I can't stop you from going, but I can sure put a monkey wrench in your lives once you're both back across the Rio Grande. In case you don't know, Mr. de Renille, in the United States, annulments, to have any legality, are civil, not religious. The Archbishop of San Antonio can't set you free again, only the state of Texas can do that, and a word here and there can see that it's never granted. Of course, you can always go for divorce, but you two wouldn't like that, all public and messy—"

Seated side by side on the bench, Thea and Charles

exchanged looks, Donovan's threat—real enough to *him*—was their signal. They were free.

"Is there something that makes you think we want an annulment?" Charles questioned in a quietly dangerous voice.

"You're crazy, both of you," Donovan said scathingly. "Country club loons, and I'm stuck with them."

"Crazy?" Thea echoed. She didn't care if he called her crazy, in a way it was almost a compliment. But for Charles it was a slur, and she wouldn't stand for it. "Do you want to know what I think is crazy, Major Donovan? This city, that's what. There's a population of nearly half a million here, of which only six thousand are English-speaking foreigners, but they run it all—and hate each other in the process. Sure, the Americans, the British and the Canadians all get along, belong to each other's clubs and socialize together, but most of the time they're like survivors of some shipwreck who ended up in some very luxurious outpost where no one's particularly happy, but no one wants to leave. You all enjoy the exclusive clubs, the servants that come cheap, the round of dinner parties and the exotic flowers that cost pennies, that way it's easier to pretend that this isn't the land of *pan o palo*, bread or the club, according to its leader."

"Mrs. de Renille, please." Major Donovan looked frantically around him. Insane, both of them. They wanted out? Fine. He'd be glad to wash his hands of them.

"It's all based on money, isn't it?" Thea went on before he could continue. "Our government has 750 million dollars invested in this country, and England about 500 million. Germany, France, and Russia also have large sums of money sunk into Mexico, but do you know what we've discovered, Major? Only Germany seems to know what they're doing. I don't think the Panama Canal is ever going to be half as vulnerable to German influence as Mexico is right now. Look around you. German ships are clogging the port at Vera Cruz, the Germans practically run the banking industry and, whatever trade the United States doesn't control, they do. Their salesmen speak fluent Spanish, and their catalogues are printed in Spanish, showing goods designed *specifically* for the Mexican market, with all the prices given in Mexican currency. And, to inject a social note, they know whom to marry. Lots of nice German-Mexican marriages around; the children are generally ghastly looking, but it's a good hedge against the future. Hard to side with the United States in a time of crisis when some of your family are German citizens."

"I think you've said quite enough, Mrs. de Renille."

"Really? I'm only doing what was asked of me—reporting back things I've heard," Thea responded with poison sweetness.

He stood up, looming tall over them. "As far as I'm concerned, you can leave right this minute, but both of you make too good an impression at those parties."

"The French Embassy's ball is next week, the German Embassy's ball several days after that," Charles said. "We'll stay through those functions, give you a final report, and then leave. Is that agreeable to you?"

"Fine with me," Major Donovan said curtly, and turned to go. "I'll see you soon."

"One thing before you go, Major. Do you read *Town & Country?*"

"The society magazine? Not often, Mrs. de Renille."

"Well, why don't you see if the Sonora News Company has the October 29th issue yet? If you read it carefully, you might find a certain announcement very enlightening."

"You were perfect," Charles said a minute later when they were alone together, their only company the silent man still seated nearby, still buried in his newspaper. "I don't think he's ever going to recover from your reading

561

him the facts."

"Yes, but it was you who let him know we couldn't be persuaded to stay on, no matter what kind of impression we made." She tucked an arm through his. "Do we *really* have to stay until after the German Embassy's ball?"

"I don't want to any more than you do, but it's important that we do. We'll put a proper finish on our assignment instead of just packing up and running."

"I understand how important it is for you to tie off all loose ends, and we'll be leaving before we know it," Thea said, resting her head on his shoulder, oblivious to the flow of people going in and out of the Monte de Pledad, as well as to the man near them who had now exchanged *El Imparcial* for the *Mexican Herald*. "I have some good news, though. I've found our dining room table. There aren't any chairs to go with it, but we can buy them later. Shall we have a look?"

They bought the dining room table, and then left the National Pawnshop, walking to the nearby Portal de los Mercanderes where twenty-seven graceful arches and exposed brick walls provided a background for the colorful posters announcing bullfights, theatrical events and upcoming lottery drawings. Nestled among the curio shops and dulcineras that lined the walk was a small printer's shop, barely big enough to fit both Thea and Charles.

"Where did you find *this* spot?" Charles asked, amused, as they approached the worn wooden counter that ran the width of the shop, effectively cutting it in half.

"Mrs. Clayton. She swears by this hole in the wall. They do all the invitations for the American Embassy."

A small, elderly man appeared from the dark depths of the store's back room, and his face lit up when he saw Thea. "Ah, Señora de Renille, your cards are ready. My finest effort," he said, reaching under the counter and coming up with a small, square box.

"This is a surprise for you," Thea told Charles as she lifted the lid. Packed tightly inside were at least a hundred three by five cards of the finest white stock with matching envelopes. "I decided it was close to the time we'd need them," she said, extracting a card and handing it to him.

"It's too bad we didn't come here first," Charles said as he began to laugh. "If we'd given one to Major Donovan, I think he finally would have understood us."

"He might even give us a wedding present."

"Don't be *too* hopeful," he warned, still laughing.

With that, Charles paid the bill the stationer presented, and he and Thea went off to celebrate at a nearby ice cream shop. The box wasn't heavy and the cards, with beautiful black engraving, read:

Mr. and Mrs. Charles de Renille
will be at home
after the twentieth of December
at 667 Madison Avenue

At eleven in the morning, the San Pedro Golf Links were a green and peaceful oasis, a perfect place for two men to enjoy a round of golf and some good conversation before a pleasant lunch at the clubhouse. Located in the suburb of Mixcoac, the newly completed road made the trip from Mexico City a short one and, not too long after their arrival, Charles and Paul had changed into gray flannel and plaid shirts—the latest in golf clothes for men. They signed for their equipment, acquired caddies, and were on the fairway by eleven twenty.

Charles hated golf. To him, the idea of spending time at a game that consisted of hitting a small white ball with a club in an attempt to land it in a hole a number of yards away was a monumental waste of time. But he wanted a chance to talk to Paul without interruption, meaning that a game of tennis or handball was out. And, since he didn't want their conversation to be overheard, lunch or a drink at one of the clubs was not feasible.

"I've never been out this way during the daylight hours, it's really very attractive," Paul said as they approached the third hole, their caddies following at a respectful distance. "Do you know this area?"

"We've been out to Tacubaya for parties, and to the *Jardin de Propagacion* to see the plants and flowers."

"You've been very fortunate in your invitations. It isn't easy to establish the right kind of social life here. I don't think there's an embassy or business concern that hasn't had to order people back because they've gotten involved with the wrong sort."

"Like the Belgian Minister's former secretary?"

Paul gave him a surprised look. "So you heard about that. Fortunately, de Laulan kept a pretty tight lid on the situation. He's a good man, and when the story began to make the rounds it was far enough in the past so that it wasn't a hot topic any longer. Ambassador Clayton told me about it, but from whom did you hear it?"

"Jean-Christophe de Laulan. He was a pupil of mine a long time ago." A long time, Charles thought. Not quite three years. In my time, a century.

"Do you miss it?" Paul asked, and Charles knew instantly what was being referred to.

"I miss teaching, but I don't miss being with the Jesuits."

"Pity. I thought it might have made it easier if you did. That way, you wouldn't feel left out after the annulment."

"There's not going to be an annulment," Charles said decisively, cutting off the rest of Paul's statement. "Thea and I are together for always."

"You can't hold Thea in a sham marriage against her

564

will!" Paul exclaimed, his eyes bright with indignation. "I want to marry her, and she wants me. We were together in St. Louis."

"The only thing you and Thea did in St. Louis was indulge in a mild flirtation in which you were encouraged by Mrs. Miles. It's a situation I'm not the least jealous of. Thea didn't love you then, and she doesn't love you now. She loves me, and I love her."

"You liar! It's a fake marriage!"

"That turned very real," Charles said quietly. "Women are so much more honest than men, no matter what anyone says. We fell in love almost from the moment we met. But while Thea faced up to it, I did my best to deny it and to ask myself what she'd want with someone like me. I saw both of you on the patio the night of the de Veigas' ball. I should thank you for making the advances that you did. It finally opened the floodgates for us."

"Do you really expect me to believe any of this?"

"I hope that you do, and I also hope you'll believe that if you ever again touch Thea the way you did yesterday, I'll wrap a golf club around you."

Paul considered him quietly for a few moments. "I want you to know that I never make passes at another man's wife," he said at last. "It's only that Thea and I got on so well and then, when Donovan started harping on the two of you . . . He *still* hasn't figured it out!" It was a statement, not a question.

"We may have to end up by drawing him a picture."

"That oaf. What he told me. . . ." Paul stopped, and held out his hand. "I'm sorry, truly. He told me that you two were strictly companions, putting on a good show, and that I should go ahead with my courtship because you didn't—or couldn't—care."

It was a warm day for November, even for Mexico, but Charles felt an icy rage sweep through him. He stayed rooted to the spot, his eyes fixed downward on the carefully manicured grass.

"He thinks I'm a useless remittance man who isn't any better than he has to be. I violate his sense of propriety," Charles said in a tightly controlled voice.

"I should have seen through him at once. He really doesn't think any better of me," Paul said. "This is all partially my fault so, if you want to take a swing at me, I'll understand."

"I don't want to hit you, Paul. You're as much a victim of the good major as Thea and I are. He simply didn't want us down here, he doesn't want amateurs mucking up his game, and I can't say I really blame him. We haven't accomplished that much."

"Possibly you weren't supposed to."

"What?"

"Look, how much can you really have expected to find out here?" Paul inquired without expecting an answer. "The President had very high hopes, but he doesn't realize that down here *everyone* talks, and most of the time it's pure drivel."

"Then we haven't helped a bit."

"On the contrary, you and Thea have picked up quite a bit of information; mainly that our government isn't very greatly loved. That's a help, believe me. But, if there's some great chunk of information out there that might prove to be crucial in the years ahead, you haven't come across it."

"Why are you telling me this? You could cause a lot of trouble for yourself."

"That's not likely unless you talk, and you don't seem to be the type. Besides," he added cynically, "I'm being transferred. I got my marching orders this morning."

"I'm sorry." Charles didn't know what else to say.

"Don't be." Paul smiled. "My place of exile is rather nice. I'm being sent to London."

"As you said, it's not Elba."

"Charles, don't worry, I'll be out of your lives within the week. The army either can't make up its mind, or they want everything done yesterday. In any case, I'm just sorry I was too stubborn to listen to Thea. The three of us could have had a nice friendship."

"I think that's something that can be salvaged," Charles pointed out. "After all, we're all survivors of Major Donovan. When you come home on leave next year, we'll expect you to visit us in New York."

They played the next hole, completed their shots, and then looked at each other.

"You're the worst player I've ever seen," Paul said frankly.

"I hate golf," Charles replied emphatically. "But this is the only way I could think of for us to talk in relative private. Since we've settled a lot between us, what do you say to forgetting this game right now and having lunch?"

"That's the best idea I've heard in a long time. What do you say to a *Cerveza de Milwaukee?*"

Charles tore their score cards in half. "Let's go. Right now, a cold glass of beer sounds better than a hole-in-one!"

Ophelie de Langlade was not a happy woman. In the past month nothing seemed to be going right. Charles and Guenther and Gerard. Her former lover, her present lover, and her husband. Their faces, voices, and personalities swirled around in her head until she felt ill.

It was finished with Guenther, almost as abruptly as it had begun. All she had to show for the past months was a variety of semi-healed bruises, and a catalogue of new techniques she'd probably never be able to use again.

Gerard's arrival had been unexpected to say the least, turning up in their suite just as she was about to leave to meet Guenther for dinner. Even as she'd moved forward to welcome Gerard, her thoughts had immediately centered on the man sitting at Sylvian's, waiting for her and, hours later, in her husband's arms, he still commanded her attention as she wondered what had transpired while he waited for her at their table. Had he ended up dining alone, or had he left and gone to pay a call on her replacement, the young Brazilian widow whose husband was rumored to have expired under such mysterious circumstances as to necessitate her leaving Rio when her year of mourning was over?

It wasn't fair. None of it was fair, Ophelie fumed over and over again until, in her mind, there was only one culprit—Charles de Renille. If it weren't for Charles, she could have ended her relationship with Guenther two weeks ago, concluding their unique pleasures in a graceful manner rather than in an abrupt termination. And if she and Charles had then become lovers, Gerard would not be taking so much for granted, assuming that their week together in Oaxaca had meant a new turn in their marriage.

Ophelie shifted slightly in the chair she occupied in one of the lobby's alcoves—the one which gave her a clear view of the comings and goings of the hotel's guests—and grimaced slightly. This morning when Gerard had rung up the de Renille suite to invite Charles to lunch with him and one of the directors of Mexico's National Museum, only to learn from Thea that Charles had already left to play golf and have lunch at the San Pedro Golf Links, an idea had formed, and she was now waiting to carry it out.

Men were so easy. Creatures who could be swayed by women with so little effort it was pathetically laughable. An amusement—that's what she would now have with Charles. She would show him that no man, no matter how faithful he was to his wife, was immune to a bit of properly applied charm.

As she waited, her mind drifted back to the week she'd spent with Gerard in Oaxaca. Even as the Mexican Southern Railway had transported her smoothly southward, Ophelie had carefully planned her reunion with the husband she hadn't seen since March. His last letters had let her know, in no uncertain terms, that he'd heard about her latest *amour*. Fortunately, Guenther was, at that time, not one to leave unnecessary reminders of their passion on her body. And, once she reached Oaxaca, was reunited with Gerard, and they repaired to the surprisingly modern and comfortable Chavez Hotel, it hadn't been too difficult to convince him that the rumors he'd been hearing were just so many tall tales.

Just as she was recalling the passionate hours they'd shared, Ophelie caught sight of Charles as he came into the hotel lobby. *A la fin des fins,* she thought, and stood up, her Worth afternoon dress of copper-brown taffeta with a yoke and collar of silk Cluny lace rustling as she moved to intercept him.

"Charles, I've been waiting forever for you! Surely golf cannot be that interesting a game," she stated archly.

Charles gave her a weary smile. "No, Ophelie, it isn't. But it can be very informative."

"You're not making any sense, but all men have a tendency to do that." She smiled appealingly at him. "Now, come with me. Gerard has been wanting to see you all day," she told him, deftly amending the truth to suit her purposes.

"I'm tired, Ophelie. Please give Gerard my regrets and tell him we can have lunch tomorrow if he likes."

It took all of her famous powers of persuasion but, in the end, Charles came with her. He was strangely docile, as if he had come to some great personal crossroad to which he was still adjusting, but his quietude vanished

569

when they reached her suite and he found it unoccupied.

"What is this, Ophelie, one of your amusing little tricks? If it is, as far as I'm concerned, you can forget any idea you've thought up."

"Charles—" She uttered his name in a way no man ever resisted.

"God, but I'm stupid," Charles said, angrily running his hands through his hair. "Thea warned me about you, but I wasn't having any of it." He regarded her coldly. "Why, Ophelie? Why must you set out to entrap every man who catches your attention?"

She shrugged expressively. "What else is there for a woman to occupy her time with? One can spend only so much time at Worth's. After all, not all of us have the skills of your dear bride." With a slow, sinuous movement, Ophelie came toward Charles as he stood stiffly by the door, and she put her arms around him.

Charles looked coldly at her. "You're the sort of Frenchwoman, Ophelie, who gives other Frenchwomen a bad name. I only wonder what took me so long to realize it."

"Ooh—" Ophelie's eyes filled with tears. "You horrid beast," she cried at him. "Don't you have any feeling at all left for me?"

How did I get myself into this? Charles thought as he watched Ophelie rush into her bedroom. How? Because Thea's right—I'm blind about Ophelie, she knows it, and plays all her tricks on me.

For a minute, Charles was tempted to walk out of the suite, but he could hear Ophelie sobbing and, reluctantly, he went toward her bedroom.

She was stretched out face down across her bed, crying into a large lace-edged handkerchief, and Charles sat down beside her. This was wrong, he knew it, but he was a product of his upbringing, and one did not leave a woman weeping unless one were a total, unfeeling cad.

"Of course I care, Ophelie," Charles said quietly. "We've known each other for a long time, and I can't ignore that, but—"

He got no further. As Ophelie turned to him, Charles cursed himself for his mistake. No person about to have a crying fit was going to take the time to find a handkerchief, only someone playing at crying was at luxury to do that.

You're in it this time, he thought. Let's see if you can get out of it without being more of a fool than you already are.

"I knew you cared," Ophelie crowed. "I knew it! Now, my dear, sweet Charles, we can talk about us."

"There is no *us*." His voice was uncompromising, but Ophelie only leaned back against the pillows and laughed.

"Something can always be arranged. You are too good, *cher*, to waste on your American. You don't belong among the barbarians in New York. Come back to France. Come and live where you belong."

Charles could see their reflection in the French oval mirror framed in silver gilt that hung over her dressing table, and he saw them for what they were—a man and a woman who had once been on intimate terms, parted from each other, met again, and were strangers.

His gaze slid to the surface of her dressing table, the surface decorated with a silver-gilt toilet service, bottles of Jicky, assorted gold and silver boxes. Charles quickly lost count of all the items, but one thing became crystal clear. Life in France would be like living permanently in this room—perfectly luxurious, undeniably correct, and totally suffocating. Already he could feel the strictures closing in around him, heavy like the air in this room, and he felt as if he were about to choke.

"I'm going to live where I belong," he told her finally, "and, if I'm going to be among barbarians as you think then, quite possibly, they're the people I should be with.

Their society gave me back my life, the one I was born to encouraged me to destroy myself. From where I sit, there is no debate as to where I go. Make your peace with Gerard, Ophelie, or run after von Basedow, or find a new male body to amuse yourself with, because I'm not interested."

As her brain absorbed his words, her confident smile faded. This wasn't the way it was supposed to work out. *She* was supposed to do the rejecting, not Charles. *He* was the one who was to be cajoled and enticed, brought to the brink and then tossed aside. It had simply never occurred to her that Charles would be unmovable, not out of any great moral stand, but because he didn't want her.

"No one treats Ophelie de Langlade like this!" she cried, a strange anger filling her.

"Really?" Charles looked disinterested. "I thought I was behaving rather well, but possibly that isn't how you like to be treated. Thea has quite a few theories about that," he added casually, getting to his feet and starting for the door.

"I haven't finished with you, Charles."

"No, but I'm done with you."

"I'll get you. No man walks out on *me*. You'll be sorry for this."

With one hand on the doorknob, Charles turned slowly and regarded his former lover. At that moment, whatever lingering feelings of affection he had for her vanished. She was no longer a grand lady, only a slightly dishevelled and rather angry woman. She had always been a fantasy figure to him, a fairy queen rather than a real person, he realized. But now he truly saw her for the spoiled and demanding woman she was.

"Good afternoon, Ophelie," he said pleasantly. "Please remember to give my best regards to Gerard if you care to mention this afternoon to him. I'm sure he'll understand why I decided this was not the time for me to pay a prolonged visit. But, if you'll take my advice, you won't concoct any interesting tales. Thea is waiting for me, and I'm sure you want to do something to your face before Gerard comes back and sees that you've been acting like a spoiled child who has just discovered the world doesn't revolve around her alone."

Thea sat at the writing table in the bedroom working on her latest group of thank you letters. She had honestly not been expecting any wedding presents from those they met in Mexico City but, on the day the vases arrived from the Chinese Minister, Thea decided that if almost perfect strangers were generous enough to send them presents, she owed them an immediate thank you note.

So far their "take"—as Thea jokingly referred to their gifts—had been more than generous. The Japanese Minister had sent vases, a matching pair made of white porcelain painted with rich blue irises; the Italian Ambassador gave a small 16th Century marble figure of a cherub, a perfect ornament for the coming holiday season; Ambassador and Mrs. Clayton gave them a beautiful hand-drawn linen tablecloth with two dozen matching napkins; but the Russian Ambassador had been the most lavish, presenting them with a fourteen-piece gilded porcelain tea set from Faberge.

Thea had spent this Election Day attending a ladies' luncheon at the British Embassy, going shopping at the Women's Exchange and returning to the suite, fully expecting to find Charles already there. He wasn't waiting for her, but two more wedding gifts were and, pausing only long enough to take off her hat and put aside her gloves and handbag, she opened the latest offerings and set to work on the notes without changing out of her Poiret afternoon dress of biscuit-colored peau-de-crepe trimmed in silk soutache and finished with a chiffon velvet belt. She was signing the last letter when she heard a key turn in the lock of the drawing room door and, a moment later, Charles came into their bedroom, weariness mingling with relief on his face.

"You look exhausted," Thea said as she got up to kiss him, putting her arms around his waist and bracing herself against his diaphragm. "Was it very bad with Paul?"

"I swear I'm never going to set foot on a golf course again," he said, kissing her back, his arms closing tight and warm around her. "I'm convinced the only reason men play golf is because they have ugly wives they want to spend a long time away from."

"Were you playing at the country club all day?"

"We never even finished our game," Charles laughed. "We concluded our conversation and decided that a sandwich and a glass of cold beer sounded like a lot more fun than hitting that white ball."

"I knew I married a very smart man. I take it you didn't have to hit Paul with your nine iron?"

"Not at all," Charles said as he sat down on the bed, pulling Thea long with him. "He wants you to know how very contrite he is about this whole misunderstanding."

"Misunderstanding!" Thea exclaimed. "That's the understatement of the year!"

"More than you know," he said, and told her about their conversation.

"I'm not even going to waste my breath on the machinations that go on in the mind of our good major," Thea decided when Charles finished. "But what did you and Paul talk about all this time?"

"The usual things. President Roosevelt, today's election, the New York Giants, the Army-Navy Game and the Exposition at St. Louis." He gave Thea an amused look. "Why didn't you tell me Paul bought you one of those ice cream cornucopias?"

"You never asked." She gave him a considering look.

"I should be as mad as hell at you. I had visions of you and Paul coming to blows on the green and being thrown out of the golf club in disgrace. Instead, you spend your time in the clubhouse having a buddy-buddy conversation!"

"Maybe we'll do that the next time," Charles promised, leaning over to kiss her.

"You've been gone a long time, though. I know male conversation goes on forever but. . . ." Thea let her voice trail off and waited.

"I was with Ophelie."

For a long minute, Thea remained quiet. "There are a number of ways to take that statement." Thea forced herself to speak with an archness she didn't feel. A lead weight was taking hold in the pit of her stomach. Contrary to everything she said, Thea couldn't tell if Charles had made love to Ophelie or not. She only knew that he would tell her the truth, and the wait for his reply was torture.

"She didn't seduce me," Charles said with a faint smile. "In fact, I don't think she wanted to."

"That's a switch. Then what did she want? And, while we're at it, how did you end up there in the first place?"

Charles related his meeting with Ophelie in the lobby. "She wanted to show me how vulnerable I still was to her by enticing me and then rejecting me. She almost had me fooled at first. You were right, Thea. I *was* seeing her through some sort of haze. Nostalgia is a dangerous sport, and I think Ophelie was counting too much on my having once idolized her." His face took on a wry expression. "I never knew I could feel so out of place as I did when I sat on her bed."

Thea gave him one significant look through her lashes. "I should certainly hope so!" she said, and broke through Charles' last wall of reserve.

"Not like that!" he said, and began laughing. "I don't

575

hate her and, even better, I don't hate myself for momentarily having bought her fake crying fit. There was *nothing*, only that I didn't belong with her, or anything she represented, and that my home is with you."

"Oh, Charles—" Thea couldn't say anything else, only hold onto him as her emotions spun out of control, past fear and lingering suspicion into certainty and joy. "This makes our whole miserable assignment worth it. But you liked my being jealous, didn't you?" she couldn't resist adding.

"I'd hate to think you didn't care enough to make the effort," Charles admitted, "or that you were complacent enough to think I'd never look."

"Oh, you'll look. I'd worry if you didn't. But just as long as you remember that you have a *very* possessive wife."

"Just the one I want," he said but, instead of the kiss Thea was expecting, he stood up. "We have a social obligation tonight," he reminded her. "As long as we're leaving next week, we might as well do it all properly."

"You're right," Thea admitted as she stood up, still not ready to give up on fitting in a tryst before they left for the American Club. "Do you want to see our latest loot?"

"More like the spoils of war," Charles couldn't resist saying.

"Just look on it as good preparation for New York and several hundred boxes from Tiffany's."

"If you say so." Charles looked doubtfully into one of the boxes on the writing table. "I know it's Meissen, but what do we use it for?"

"Charles, you cannot convince me that you can't recognize a candy dish," Thea said, choking on her laughter as she showed him the figure of a cherub holding out a fluted plate. "It's really rather nice of Guenther von Basedow to send this to us. Better this than the souvenirs he probably gave Ophelie. I wonder what she told Gerard about her stray bruises?"

"Your mind has some very nasty turns," Charles said, but he was smiling as he moved to the next box and parted the layers of white tissue paper. "Now *this* is beautiful."

"From the de Laulans," Thea said tenderly as she and Charles admired the present; two perfectly formed, long-necked birds made of fine white porcelain with gold bands around their necks and their feathers were shaped to create a low vase.

"Swans," Charles said.

"A goose and a gander," Thea corrected. "A much more symbolic gesture. In Oriental legend, the goose and the gander are partners for life and mate only with each other." Her arms slipped around him. "Just like us. And, as long as we're speaking of mating. . . ."

Charles' only reply was a soft groan as Thea let one hand travel lightly over one of his hips, her fingers tracing circles as they moved down to explore a muscular thigh. He closed his eyes, enjoying the first wave of sensation, letting it wash away the tenseness that remained from his encounter with Ophelie.

"Do you know how I knew you weren't with Ophelie— at least not willingly?" she purred in his ear. "From the way you looked when you came in." It wasn't strictly true, Thea acknowledged, but this wasn't a moment for utter accuracy. "I know how you look when it's over. You're like a big black and white cat that's been given a bowl of cream and stroked all over. Now the baronne might have had a go at you but, if it were her idea, you wouldn't look the way you do with me at all."

"If you go on like this, we're never going to leave the suite until it's time for us to go home," Charles said thickly, his senses swimming. His feeling of weariness vanished under her touch and her voice, and now all he wanted was Thea. Every inch of her was his. He moved his hands along her curves, molding her body against his frame.

"The bathroom," Thea gasped, her fingers weaving into his hair.

"What . . . ?" Charles was momentarily distracted from kissing Thea's neck as he unhooked her dress.

"In the bathroom," she insisted. "The bathtub . . . it's big and marble and made for us . . ."

Laughter began to bubble up between them, lightening the intense web of passion forming around them.

"You never suggested . . ."

"Neither did you . . ."

"I was afraid you'd think I was some sort of decadent Frenchman . . ."

"We owe it to each other," Thea laughed, urging him toward the bathroom, "because, in a few hours, we're going to have to go to the American Club and celebrate the President's re-election. Good Reform Democrat that I am, when the returns come in and I have to cheer on the Republican incumbent, I want to be sure I have something very, very wonderful to think about!"

It was after one in the morning before Thea and Charles left the American Club. The Election Night party, which had begun at eight, was still in full swing five hours later, the club members and their guests celebrating Theodore Roosevelt's landslide—although not yet official—victory.

The party had floated along on a steady stream of good California champagne and a generous buffet that included cream of chestnut soup, celery and nut salad in tomato cups, chafing dishes of beef stroganoff with rice breasts of chicken in cream sauce, lobster Newburg platters of shrimp salad and chicken salad, and dessert that included Lady Baltimore cake and three flavors o ice cream.

A direct telephone line to the *Mexican Herald* had been established and, every time the new election results were announced, the numbers were listed on a blackboard and wildly cheered.

"Someday the Democrats will have a first rate candidate, and *then* wait and see the election results," Thea promised as they crossed the pavement to the waiting automobile.

"Yes, but hopefully, when that day comes, we'll be in our own home," Charles remarked, as much as admitting for the first time that he too was not fond of Mexico City. "The Sanz," he told the waiting chauffeur, who knew their destination but liked to have the proprieties observed.

"At once, señor," Hernando responded, although he threw a questioning look at the brightly lit facade of the American Club. This was the first time in his weeks of being the driver for the de Renilles that the young couple were not among the last guests to leave. "Was the fiesta in honor of your President not to your liking?"

"No, it was very much to our liking," Charles smiled. "President Roosevelt has won a great victory tonight, but we're too tired to stay until the last vote is counted."

Hernando gave them such a smile of delight that, as he drove them back to the hotel, Thea and Charles decided that he must have made a bet with one of the other chauffeurs who was also in line outside the club, and now stood to collect a windfall.

They were still reviewing the election night party a short time later when the car's engine began to rattle alarmingly, and Hernando pulled the Columbia over to the curb.

"*Que tal*, Hernando?" Charles asked, concerned, as the chauffeur's head remained hidden under the motor car's open hood. "How goes it?"

"Not well, señor," he said, coming back to the tonneau where they sat. "I was having problems with the auto when I drove you back from Mixcoac this afternoon. The mechanic at the garage didn't have an opportunity to look at it, and I hoped it might last out tonight." He gave an expressive shrug. "I've done everything I can, but nothing works, please be patient and I'll find you a cab . . . first class, of course," he added.

"No, thank you, don't bother," Charles said. "We can't be more than five minutes from the Sanz. We'll walk."

Hernando's protestations were vehement. It was not proper for a lady and gentleman to return to their hotel on foot at such a late hour; but Thea loved the idea, and together they set off down the Avenue de San Francisco, leaving Hernando with the auto.

"Do you mind?" Charles asked as they strolled down the deserted street arm-in-arm. "It seemed such a waste of time to wait for a cab to come along when this way is so much faster."

"I totally agree," Thea said. "And it's also a chance to walk off the party. That's the bad thing about political gatherings—all those smoke-filled rooms."

"Under those circumstances, I think that our going back to the hotel like this is a fine idea, but is it really all right for you?" Charles' face became concerned. "I was so caught up in my own solution that I didn't think to ask. I know you're not certain, but—"

"I *am* certain, and there's nothing to worry about. I'm healthy as a horse."

"Well, even at the *haras*, our brood mares are treated with the greatest of consideration."

"Brood mare!" Thea tried to sound indignant, but laughter was bubbling up inside her. "Is that what I am now that I'm going to have a baby?"

"What would you say to my calling you a slightly

pregnant mermaid?" Charles asked tenderly. "You're not the only one who had some very pleasant recollections tonight."

They stopped under a street lamp and Thea clasped her arms around Charles' neck. "Did anyone ever tell you how sweet you are when you're almost totally submerged? Very, very appealing, in fact," she whispered, brushing her lips across one cheek until she reached his mouth, warm and eager for her kiss.

The street, always crowded with people in the daylight hours, was completely deserted, and there were no witnesses to their embrace, an embrace Thea knew she would never have inaugurated unless their privacy was almost total.

"What a spell you weave over me," Charles said softly as they reluctantly released each other and resumed their walk.

"That spell works both ways."

"And it even extends to a bit of semi-public love." Charles' voice was teasing.

"It's our honeymoon," Thea countered humorously. "We have to try everything once."

It was well after midnight, and the avenue that was Mexico City's most fashionable gathering spot was a deserted stretch of sidewalk and, as they went along, Thea began to develop the prickling sensation that they were being followed. Street crime was not too common in Mexico City but, as a New Yorker, Thea knew that if you thought someone was following you, they probably were, and the motive was robbery.

"Someone is trailing us," Thea whispered a few steps later.

"I know," Charles responded quietly.

Instinctively, they quickened their pace, and from behind them came the unmistakable sound of measured, cautious footfalls picking up speed.

"I feel like we're in some Sherlock Holmes story," Thea said. "All that's missing is the fog."

"Now we can use a cab," Charles said briefly, his eyes scanning the avenue in a fruitless search for a vehicle.

After one quick look behind them, neither bothered again. Although the street itself was well-lit, the dark, deserted doorways provided ample cover.

"If the worst happens, I'll give them my diamond bracelet and you'll hand over your billfold, and that will be that," Thea said, trying to keep the panic out of her voice at the thought of having to come face-to-face with a thief. Then the terror inside her took another turn, one that was absolutely farfetched but still within the realm of possibility.

"What makes you so sure it's our money and jewelry he wants?" Charles remarked suddenly, fueling Thea's new fantasy. The Alameda was coming into view, which meant that they were only a short distance from the Sanz. If the person following them was intent on some sort of harm, he had to act soon.

"A single candle in the night," Charles said unexpectedly, and Thea saw a figure moving toward them, carrying a brightly lit lantern.

It was a member of Mexico City's Metropolitan Police making his rounds. Known as *serenos* because of the lanterns they carry, their job, at least in the better districts, was a fairly easy one since nearly all the windows sported heavy iron bars, and extremely heavy doors created a barrier that couldn't be breached by a stick of dynamite. Unlike the mounted police Thea and Charles had seen in Chihuahua, the capital city's police were a uniformly courteous group, friendly to tourists and the *sereno* who approached them was no exception.

He was inquisitive as to who they were, sympathetic about their disabled motor car, concerned that they were undertaking this walk unaccompanied, and insisted o scorting them back to their hotel—an offer Thea and Charles accepted with alacrity.

"For a few minutes, I thought we were never going to see the Sanz again," Thea said as Charles unlocked the door to their suite ten minutes later.

"I thought that, as a New Yorker, you were impervious to little things like street thieves," Charles responded as they stepped over the threshold.

"Oh, it wasn't the idea of being held up that bothered me, but I had visions of us being abducted, taken to the basement of the German Embassy, and tortured for all our information!"

"Unfortunately, that was also my vision," Charles admitted, leaning back against the closed door, a grim expression on his face. "It's frightening to think about. And then there's always the question of *how* and *why*. As careful as we've been, someone's picked up on us and, no matter how we make fun of them, Germans *aren't* stupid." He looked at Thea who was moving about the sitting room with a strange expression on her face, and then abruptly ran into the bedroom. "Thea . . . is something wrong?"

"Charles, come in here, please," her voice floated back to him, and he walked into the bedroom to find Thea seated on the edge of the bed, a glazed expression on her face.

"Someone's been through our suite," she said in a stilled voice. "I knew it as soon as we came in."

Charles glanced around the bedroom. As far as he could tell, this chamber, like the sitting room, was in its usual perfect condition. The bed was turned down for the night, the lamps were giving off soft light, their nightclothes were laid out; everything looked normal.

"I don't see . . . Are you sure Angelita or one of the other maids didn't move something around?"

Thea gave him an even look. "Why would the maid

rearrange all our newspapers and magazines? When w[e]
left, the newspapers were arranged by date, the mo[st]
recent first, and the magazines were in alphabetic[al]
order. They're not now. And then there's my writin[g]
table—" Thea had to take a deep breath befo[re]
continuing. Her heart was racing, her hands were icy an[d]
why did she have the feeling Charles didn't believe he[r?]
It didn't seem possible that Charles, who was so sensiti[ve]
to their needs and feelings, was oblivious to the[ir]
surroundings.

She was still turning that problem over in her min[d]
when she felt the bed take Charles' weight, and the ne[xt]
moment his arms were around her. Instinctively, The[a]
put her head on his shoulder.

"Don't you see?" she asked at last.

"Because the magazines and newspapers are out [of]
order? They might have been knocked to the floor by on[e]
of the maids, and put back without thinking."

"It's possible," she allowed. "Both Angelita an[d]
Concepcion read English, and it's possible they we[re]
taking a few minutes to look through our magazines. [I]
don't care if they were. But I can't see either maid sittin[g]
down at my writing table and reading through my clie[nt]
books."

Now Charles was startled. Thea's client books, tw[o]
black-leather-covered notebooks were a matter of dee[p]
professional importance to her. Both were alphabetical[ly]
arranged; one as an address book, and the other was [a]
client by client listing, describing what business she an[d]
her client had contracted.

"I had them in the center of the writing table, one o[n]
top of the other, with the writing book first. They're [in]
reverse order now." Thea began trembling. "Charle[s,]
don't you see, someone came into this suite, technical[ly]
our *home*, and went through our belongings. As far as I'[m]
concerned, that's worse than being robbed."

"Are you sure nothing's missing? What about your jewelry? A ten-year-old could pick the lock on the wall safe."

"Oh, Charles." Thea drew out of his embrace and looked up at him, a faint glimmer of amusement in her eyes. "I thought you'd noticed weeks ago and were too much of a gentleman to say anything . . ." She broke off, laughter bubbling up in spite of her bad fright.

"Thea," Charles said, recognition dawning, "are you telling me that your jewelry is fake?"

"Every last piece—except for your bracelet, of course," she smiled, holding up her wrist. "Didn't you notice?"

"Lapidary is not among my talents," Charles pointed out. "Are they paste?"

"No, just very good copies, my family pearls in particular. It's safer to leave the real pieces in the bank when I travel."

Charles kissed her. "I not only have a brave wife, but a smart one as well."

"Brave?" She shook her head. "No, just very angry that Ophelie got in here somehow and spent a pleasant evening browsing through our personal things. I wonder if she tried on any of my dresses." Thea looked intently at Charles. "Aren't you going to argue with me about how I can be so sure it was Ophelie who was here?"

"No, because I think you're right. Just as I think her coming here had nothing to do with our being followed tonight. Ophelie is angry and jealous, but she isn't doing favors for the German Embassy."

Thea leaned back on the bed, pulling Charles with her. "If you say so, I'll give her the benefit of the doubt. But I still hate it. It's like someone watching while we make love."

Charles let his hand travel gracefully up Thea's side, ending at the curve of her breast. "Would you like me to check the closets before I go any further?"

"You forgot about looking under the bed."

"What about the terrace?"

"If Ophelie's dumb enough to be out there, she deserves to freeze," Thea quipped. But, somewhere deep inside her, a cold rock of fear remained, and she clung to Charles in the hope that their passion would melt the terror remaining in her.

Something had changed in their lives tonight, Thea knew. They had been lulled by the civility of their life in Mexico City, by the idea that nothing wrong could ever happen to them here. Her father had once told her that the more perfect the illusion, the colder the truth when it was revealed. It was true, all too true, and tonight the feeling of security they enjoyed had been shattered.

"The President isn't going to run again!"

The amazement in Charles' voice was overwhelming, and Thea looked up in astonishment. "What did you say?"

"President Roosevelt announced that he had no intention of seeking another term. It's here in the paper."

Thea eyed his newspaper doubtfully. "That's *El Heraldo*, they could be making it up. Do any of the others have it?"

Together, they checked through *El Diario*, *La Patria* and *El Imparcial*, saving the English-language *Mexican Herald* for last. But they all carried the same statement that Theodore Roosevelt had made.

"On the fourth of March next I shall have served three and a half years, and this three and a half constitutes my first term. The wise custom which limits the President to two terms regards the substance and not the form. Under no circum-

586

stances will I be a candidate for or accept another nomination."

Thea groaned painfully and threw the *Mexican Herald* across the room. It was Wednesday afternoon, the day after the election, and Thea and Charles had only recovered from the night before a scant hour earlier. As usual, their bedroom was filled with flowers, mail, newspapers and breakfast trays, but now a cloud of depression fell over them.

"The stupid things that honorable and intelligent men do," Thea said at last, her voice disbelieving.

"It may not be as bad as it sounds. No one is going to take his statement seriously, and he'll change his mind."

"No, he won't," Thea said bleakly. "Right now, he could probably kick himself for this statement, but he'll never take it back. I always thought T.R. was too smart to ever back himself into a corner, but I was wrong."

"I can't pretend to understand American politics. To confide an awful truth, I can barely make out French politics, but I can tell you this: Theodore Roosevelt is not the last decent, intelligent and far-seeing man of government. There will be others to take his place. Maybe not right away, but eventually."

"I certainly hope so. The Democrats haven't got anyone promising on the horizon; they just have a penchant for digging up William Jennings Bryan from whatever rock he's hiding under. And as for the Republican Party—" Thea's voice became scathing. "With Mark Hanna as power-broker, all we have to look forward to is that fat pig, William Howard Taft. It's over, Charles. All the promise, all the possibilities, all the horizons Theodore Roosevelt might have created and molded in the United States are gone, wiped out by three sentences."

"When people make grave mistakes, they generally do

587

it in a very straightforward manner," Charles pointed out gently as Thea slid her arms around him. "But, somehow, we always manage to get on with our lives. I think we only have to worry when people stop falling in love. And this," he said with a rueful smile, comes from a man who, six months ago, was convinced he had no future."

"As long as we're together, we have a wonderful future," Thea said, running her hands over his hair. "We trust, we share and we give—"

Charles' mouth closed skillfully over Thea's. "Speaking of giving," he smiled a minute later, "I think now is the moment for one of your birthday presents."

Thea gave him an amused look. "Only *one?*"

"Don't be greedy," Charles responded with a smile and another kiss. "Today's Wednesday, your birthday's Monday—you can wait for the rest. Now, close your eyes."

Thea did so, hearing Charles move from the bedroom to the dressing room and back again. Despite the diamond bracelet, Thea really had no idea as to how Charles' taste ran when it came to presents.

"Open your eyes."

Thea saw the small black velvet box that could contain only one thing, and her heart overflowed with love. "Oh, Charles. . . ."

"I want to see your face when you open the box, and I want to put it on your finger." Charles' eyes were like two incredibly rich, warm topazes. "I've had it for a few days, but I couldn't wait any longer for your birthday."

On a bed of white satin rested a four-carat pigeon's-blood ruby surrounded by sixteen small diamonds set in fine old gold.

"A ruby is fire and divine love, the Holy Spirit, creative power, and royalty," Charles explained in a hushed voice. "In the Crusades, the ruby was a love token. 'Wisdom is more precious than rubies' comes from that time—a very appropriate expression for us, but I thought you'd like a ruby anyway."

"A few weeks ago, Ophelie tried to get a rise out of me by asking why I didn't have an engagement ring. I told her you'd already given me the most important ring I could have," she said, reaching for his hands. "I love you, and this is so perfect and so unexpected, I could cry. Put it on for me. . . ."

It fit perfectly, sliding into place over her wedding band as if it had been designed in advance.

"When we were preparing to leave Hacienda de Veiga, Don Renaldo mentioned that if I were interested in purchasing an engagement ring for you, he had several unset stones in the vault at the Diener Brothers shop, and if there was one I liked, it was at my disposal. If he hadn't given me that potent hint," Charles concluded shamefacedly, "you still wouldn't have this ring."

"Oh, I don't know," Thea said. "Someday you'd walk past Tiffany's and get the general idea. I'd be patient."

"Too patient."

"Not about everything. I'd still be a much happier woman if we went home tonight instead of next week."

Charles bent his head for a moment and, when he looked at her again, his face was grave. "I know you want to leave. *I* want to leave. But we can't go yet. There are times I wish we'd never come to Mexico City, but we have to fulfill as much of the promise we made to President Roosevelt as possible. We have to do it properly, from beginning to end, and now we almost have. We found each other—no one could stop that from happening— and I finally let go of my ghost. We've laid the foundation of our life together, and soon we'll start living it. One week from today, Thea, we'll be going home."

It was an accepted social fact that the French Embassy's gala was the most important and looked-forward-to event on the season's calendar of diplomatic receptions, dinners and balls. Here, the music would make dancing more graceful, the food would be more sublime, the favors have more cachet, and the candle-light softer and more becoming for the women guests who always seemed to be more beautiful and certainly better gowned than at other functions of equal importance.

British functions had the best conversation, the Americans played the latest dance tunes, and the Russians gave the best favors, but only the French could supply both elegance and the sense of being somewhere special.

Located in a Paseo de la Reforma mansion that looked as if it had been transplanted from the Avenue du Bois, Paris' most exclusive street, the French Embassy on Saturday evening, November 12th, was ablaze with light, and a seemingly endless stream of motor cars and carriages left their occupants at the foot of a long red carpet that extended from the edge of the sidewalk to the main entrance.

"I think every woman here must be wearing her best and most expensive ball gown," Thea whispered to Charles as they made their way through a series of formal salons replete with bronze and crystal chandeliers, fine marble mantels, gilt-framed mirrors, and marquetry-panelled rooms filled with Louis XV and Louis XVI furniture.

"But none of them come close to you," Charles whispered back, appreciatively noting her Lucile gown that combined two shades of soft peach chiffon over satin, the skirt embroidered with diamant. "Do you have any dresses you haven't worn yet?"

"Oh, two or three," Thea smiled. "But why don't you let me have my fun? By January or February, none of them are going to fit!"

"At least it'll keep us from having to go to functions like this," Charles remarked as they approached the ballroom, were announced by the butler, and greeted the French ambassador and his wife, an aristocratic-looking couple who seemed younger than their years, and who warmly welcomed them.

As Thea looked around her she recognized that, although her gown was one of the most fashionable of those being shown off in the white and gold ballroom, her jewelry was far more modest. She wore only the diamond bracelet Charles had given her, the fake version of her mother's triple strand of pearls with a diamond flower clasp, and an equally false small tiara of diamonds and pearls.

She doubted if any of the other women had had their jewelry copied. Certainly not Dona Imelda, exquisite in a Paquin gown of dusky blue tulle over blue satin with tulle shoulder straps and a gold ribbon outlining the decolletage, a perfect background for her elaborate parure of turquoise and diamonds. Ghiselle de Laulan's diamonds, that so perfectly complemented her Lucile gown of silvery gray tulle over rose tissue silk trimmed in silver paillettes, couldn't be anything but genuine. Thea saw any number of exquisitely turned-out women, but none quite reached the height of complicated chic that Ophelie de Langlade achieved.

Seated alone on a six-and-a-half foot long Louis XV winged-back *canape* of carved beechwood upholstered in gold silk, she looked like a Fragonard or Boucher painting brought up to date. She wore a complicated Worth creation of pompadour satin with white mousseline over heavy cream and gold satin brocade. Perfectly cut blue-white diamonds added to the picture of incredible richness—diamonds in her golden hair, diamonds at her ear lobes, around her throat, and encircling her wrists.

"A perfect frost, isn't she?" whispered the scathing

591

English voice of Jean Gordon, wife of the British attaché who had been with Thea during her first social run-in with the Austrian Minister's wife and Ophelie at the Russian Embassy. "Dead white, too. Not a bit healthy-looking," she went on, smoothing a fold of her Doucet gown of jade green mousseline belted in silver gauze.

"It's all that white face paint," Thea whispered back, but she had to agree that Ophelie didn't look at all well.

Still, Thea reasoned silently, the Baronne de Langlade's health was not her concern but, in a way, she was actually beginning to feel sorry for her. How awful to lead a life bounded by Worth's on one side and Cartier on the other, with no wide grasp of interests, no women friends, and the prime amusement being various affairs conducted while keeping a civil face on one's marriage.

What an awful way to live, Thea thought. How do you go on year after year with no responsibility outside of being sure that you don't get pregnant by your latest lover? How lucky I am to have the kind of life I do . . . how lucky I am to have Charles. . . .

For Ophelie, this gala night was a new experience in misery. Guenther had used her for his own pleasure and then tossed her aside like a used newspaper and, since his return, Gerard had been civil but totally unreachable. It was only Charles who gave her a faint glimmer of her old fight. In just a short time, there would be a crack in Charles' comfortable new world, she thought with an inward smile.

At first, when she'd bribed the hotel porter to let her into the de Renilles' suite on the pretext of retrieving a personal object left behind, she had wondered if this were the right thing to do. But, once alone in the deserted rooms the thrill was almost like making love with a new man for the first time.

She'd browsed through the sitting room—nothing of any interest there—but, in the bedroom, to use the ghastly American expression, she had struck paydirt. Sitting at the bedroom's writing table, leafing through Thea's notebooks, it had all come back to her.

New Orleans.

Why *hadn't* she recalled it before? Mrs. Clayton Poole and her newly redecorated house in the Garden District. How she had spent hours talking about her fashionable New York decorator, Ophelie recalled.

The dancing began, but Ophelie sat most of them out, letting the men come to her, sit beside her, flirt with her. They all came. From the French Ambassador on down. And, eventually, Charles crossed the shining hardwood dance floor and sat beside her.

"Not dancing, Ophelie?" Charles didn't particularly want to be here, engaging in this conversation. He thought about Ophelie entering their suite and looking through their most private possessions and it revolted him, but he knew that it would look very strange indeed if he didn't pay his social respects to her. As he inhaled Ophelie's perfume, he could almost hear Thea saying what did it matter what a group of people they'd most likely never see again had to say about what he did or didn't do. But Charles' response to the demands of the social rules he'd been raised by was too ingrained to ignore. "I haven't seen Gerard yet tonight," he said.

Ophelie shrugged in response. "We came in together, greeted the ambassadorial couple, then he found one of his archaeological friends and disappeared into one of the salons for a long discussion in which I play no part." She smiled bitterly. "That's one of the things I like about you, Charles. No matter how much you hate events like the one tonight, you're dutiful to the end." She motioned languidly with one hand. "Of course, Thea appears to be enjoying herself."

"Yes," Charles agreed as he looked at Thea, who stood several feet away in the middle of an admiring group.

"Is that all you can say?"

"It seems to be sufficient to answer your question."

"True. But how strange not to see Thea's devoted American army captain hovering nearby."

"Captain Merrill has been reassigned to the American Embassy in London. He left the day before yesterday to take up his new post."

"How she must miss her cavalier. I know *I* would in her place." Ophelie's far-sighted gaze became observant. "How remarkably ripe and blooming Thea looks these days," she went on. "Why, she's positively glowing."

"There's an excellent reason for Thea to be ripe, blooming and glowing, as you put it," Charles said with a smile and pride he couldn't keep out of his voice. "She's going to have a baby, and I hope you have no great objection to that, Ophelie, because it happens to be mine!"

"How can you be so sure?"

Her words, spoken under the music, were unintelligible to those near them, but to Charles she might as well have been shouting at the top of her lungs. He regarded her with horror.

"What did you say?"

"You heard me, *mon cher* Charles, you heard," she crowed softly. "When we were in New Orleans we met a charming woman named Mrs. Poole. I admired her home, and she told me all about her interior decorator, Thea Harper. Perfectly thrilled with her work, of course, and then she gave me the *most* interesting gossip."

"Very well, Ophelie, what are you trying to say?" Charles' voice was hard.

"Only what Mrs. Poole told me. That your perfect bride was—or may still be—the mistress of a man named Philip Leslie. He's a banker and, apparently, their affair is the talk of New York," she said, her voice scaling triumphantly upward. "No wonder Thea responded so

594

swiftly to your suit, and insisted on an elopement. The child she's carrying was probably conceived in her lover's bed!"

For the first time in her life, Ophelie de Langlade tasted utter and complete defeat. Her words, which were supposed to provide a *coup de grace* for Charles, reverberated around her and, in a split second, she realized that the only person she'd hurt in repeating Mrs. Poole's gossip was herself.

The wife of the British Ambassador, and the wife of the American Ambassador, both of whom were standing nearby, threw her scathing looks. Don Renaldo de Veiga and Baron Francois de Laulan, a tall, dignified man with steel gray hair and the rosette of the Order of Leopold in his buttonhole, stopped their own conversation to look at her in disbelief.

But Charles was the worst of all.

He said nothing, and his topaz-colored eyes took her in, lingering over every inch, making her feel like a specimen captured for laboratory observation. He heard every incriminating word she said. Words, whether true or not, which were guaranteed to cause doubts and everlasting marital problems. And then, after countless moments of waiting for an explosion that never came, he began to laugh. At her. And as his rich, honest laughter rang out, Ophelie could feel the steel walls of her own trap closing in around her.

"*Me?* Philip Leslie's mistress?" Thea stopped undressing long enough to stare at Charles in astonishment. "So *that's* what you were laughing at!"

"It was that or, for the first time in my life, with centuries of the de Renille blood in my veins and ingrained honor to live up to, I would have hit a woman."

It was nearly three in the morning, and Charles and Thea were in their dressing room, getting ready for bed.

Charles' clothes were already draped neatly over a wooden stand and, wrapped in his dressing gown, he reclined in the wing chair, watching Thea as she stood before her open closet doors, removing the remainder of her formal regalia.

"Now *that* would have been a different diversion for an Embassy ball." Thea kicked off her peach satin shoes with their embroidered rhinestone inset and unhooked her pale peach-colored silk stockings. "It might start a new trend. But it should take place before the supper dance, I think. That way all the guests will have a sure fire topic of conversation during the ten course meal!"

"What an awful imagination you have," Charles said, but his eyes were laughing.

"Not only me," Thea said. "My God, when I came back from New Orleans, the only things I brought with me—besides my very substantial fee—were recipes for yam souffle, pecan pie and turkey stuffing made out of oysters and pecans. Now I find that my former client thinks she hired the *femme fatale* of decorators and can't wait to tell her friends about it. Do you think it'll be good for business?"

"Wouldn't you rather have your clients whispering about what a good looking husband you have?" Charles asked, amused.

"Oh, any woman can get a husband, no one likes to gossip about that," Thea countered humorously. "It's only fun to make up tales about an unmarried woman and all the married men she's supposedly busy seducing."

"Is that how those stories get started?"

"Charles, there are women in this world who have too much money, too much time on their hands, and aren't overburdened with either brains or good old common sense." Thea removed her final garments and slipped a nightgown of pink crepe de chine touched with fine antique lace over her head. "To set the story straight

596

Philip was involved with my business to begin with," she explained, coming over to sit in Charles' lap. "I had trouble renting office space and Daddy was in South America, so I needed help."

"And Philip came to your aid." It was a statement, not a question.

"He co-signed the lease with me and promised that, if I had any problems—the monetary kind—he'd help me out because he didn't want me ruining my trust funds. I was a little slow getting started, but I never needed that help. Philip saw to the business end of it and, while I spent the summer of 1902 in Europe, Kezia saw to the painters and floor polishers, and helped me in a dozen different ways. They're close friends and I love them. But, as for Philip and me having some sort of intimate relationship—" Thea smiled and nestled closer to Charles. "You found out the answer to that the first time we made love. And as for thinking that I could debase a friendship like that—"

"You never could," Charles said, his arms closing tighter around Thea while his mouth moved along the side of her neck.

"Poor Mrs. Poole," Thea said, gasping a little at Charles' nuzzling gestures. "She's going to be terribly upset when she gets my letter informing her that she's no longer my client."

Charles paused in his preliminaries to look quizzically at Thea. "You're actually going to do that?"

"Of course I am! Oh, darling, how could I ever keep a client who thinks I prefer sharing a man with another woman as opposed to having one all to myself!"

In every person's life, there is a narrow, invisible line that separates right from wrong and, although there are those who operate more skillfully than others, the danger of stepping too far eventually affects even them. Tonight,

Ophelie de Langlade was miserably aware that she, who had successfully skirted that unseen boundary for so long, had finally fallen over the side of the precipice.

Worse than the disapproval and shock of the other guests, even worse than Charles' laughter, had been Gerard's reaction. Total, utter silence.

He knew, she was sure of that. When a woman commits the *gaffe* of destroying herself in public, word gets around very quickly. And who better to run and tell the story to than the husband?

The rest of the night had been agony. The seven course dinner served on silver plate and accompanied by vintage champagne had been torture for her. Laced so tightly she could barely breathe, Ophelie sat through the meal, tasting only a few bites from each offering. The remainder of the evening had somehow played itself out and, now, as she entered her bedroom, all Ophelie wished was that this entire episode would turn out to be nothing more than a bad dream.

Marie was in the process of helping her undress when Gerard walked into the bedroom. Never in all the years they'd been married had he ever come into her chamber without arranging for his visit before hand.

"I've come to tell you that I want you to be ready to leave Mexico at the end of the month," he said quietly and without preamble after telling Marie her ministrations were no longer required.

"I'd be happy to leave tomorrow morning," she replied, and it was the truth.

"I'm sure you would be," he replied, "but my business isn't completed as yet. Besides," he added, his gaze travelling over her elaborately decorated bedroom, "I'm sure it will take you at least that long to pack."

He turned to leave and, in the few steps it took him to reach the door, Ophelie realized that a solid, impenetrable wall had sprung up between them, and she moved to try and make a breach in it.

"Gerard . . . don't you want to talk?"

"About what?" he asked, turning to face her. "I really don't see that we have anything to discuss, Ophelie. You're my wife, that doesn't change, but it seems that we have no real necessity to communicate—at least at this time. I will always honor you in public, but as for our private life—"

"*What* private life? I'm only the person you come home to between expeditions!" Ophelie exploded, rushing across the room to place herself between him and the door. "Don't you *dare* leave me! No one turns around and walks out on *me!*"

"Like Guenther von Basedow?" he questioned cruelly. "Don't look so surprised *ma cherie,* of course I knew what was going on. More so than usual, in fact. You didn't play it too subtly this time, did you, my dear? Everyone knew what you were doing, and just waiting for the inevitable to happen. He didn't even wait to become bored with you. I knew where you were going the night I returned, and when you didn't join him, he was through with you."

Drawing a deep breath after his recitation, Gerard studied his wife. She was undeniably beautiful, even now, with tears streaking her face paint. Her remarkable, elaborate gown that had made her look like a member of the court at Versailles was removed, as was her jewelry, and she was clad only in her lacy Lucile lingerie and mercilessly tightened stays, her full breasts rising and falling with her emotions. He loved her, he supposed, but tonight her reprehensible behavior left him cold.

"Why a German, Ophelie?" he asked at last. "Why von Basedow?"

"He was here, he was convenient." She shrugged expressively. "It has nothing to do with us."

"It never does. But where does Charles enter into your little *tableaux?*"

"Charles is the cause of all of this," she hissed, reduced to rage again. "He always was something of a Puritan, and that American wife of his is as jealous and possessive as they come. She does not understand our French ways."

Gerard's hands grasped her shoulders. "Our ways," he repeated. "Over the past few days I've come to the conclusion that our ways—if indeed they *do* exist outside of your imagination—are not the best ways to conduct one's life. And tonight you gave me all the confirmation I needed." His fingers tightened around her soft skin. "Our marriage is going to be very different from now on."

"Gerard, you're hurting me." She struggled ineffectively for a moment before asking, "What do you mean by *different?*"

"To begin with, this was my last expedition. Oh, I'll still read all the journals, and keep up on the latest finds, but no more digs. And no more Paris for you. We're going to live in Normandy for more than just a few months of the year," he went on, watching shocked disbelief replace anger on her face. "I'm going to see that the *haras* is worthy of the de Langlade name again and, more importantly, I want to see if we can have a child together. It's not too late."

"And how long do you expect our little experiment to last?"

"Until there's proof beyond a doubt that you can' have a child."

"But—but I'm barely thirty-two. That could be ter years!"

"Or more. By that time, possibly no one will ever remember about your little affair in Mexico City, or how you tried to impugn the honor of another woman."

Ophelie's mind was reeling, but she knew her husban was right about one thing. It would take several othe major scandals to blow away her own mistakes.

"I suppose you want to begin my punishment tonight?"

"Punishment?" He released her. "You didn't think it was punishment on the *Xenia,* or in New Orleans, or in Oaxaca. But no, not tonight." Gerard took a step backwards. "I have the desire for you, Ophelie, but not the conscience. My body wants you, but my mind says no, not after your performance at our embassy tonight," he said as he opened the bedroom door. "The passion is present, but every time I think of your actions my spirit is repulsed. Good-night, Ophelie."

There are probably three dozen places I'd rather be tonight, particularly considering Charles' idea but, on the other hand, it might turn out to be *very* different, Thea thought as she stood in the upper gallery that encircled the main reception hall of the German Embassy.

Tonight, Monday, November 14th, was her birthday. And, since Saturday, enough had changed in their lives to make this night more bearable.

Even without Charles saying a word on the subject, Thea knew that his temporary inability to write—or, more specifically, to find a subject to write about—weighed heavily on him. But on Sunday afternoon the wall around his imagination had fallen away and, all that afternoon, and almost all day Monday, the suite had been filled with the sound of steadily clicking typewriter keys.

Just a few hours before she'd been putting on her make-up, deciding that twenty-six didn't look too bad after all, when Charles came into the bedroom, put a thick sheaf of papers on the dressing table, and went into the bathroom to get ready. While his bath ran, Thea began to read the neatly typed pages and, except for pausing to apply mascara and spray on more perfume, didn't stop until she reached the last page.

There were three articles, each twenty pages long, dealing with places they'd visited in Mexico City.

"Sunday at the National Palace" related the day they spent touring the confines of El Palacio Nacional whose 675-foot facade occupied all of the east side of the Plaza Mayor. Cards of admission to the President's winter residence were granted only for Sundays, and Charles went step-by-step through their visit the week before. "Past Splendor" told of the exhibit of the belongings of Carlotta and Maximilian at the Museo Nacional de Mexico where 250 pieces of silverplate crafted by Christofle, numerous photographs, the saddle Maximilian was using at the time of his capture, an assortment of swords, Carlotta's marble bathtub, and other assorted objects of *le confort moderne* were all that remained of the life lived by that ill-fated imperial couple. The third piece, "The House of Tiles," related the history of the building that housed the Jockey Club. Built in the 1700s by the Count del Valle, the handsome mansion had earned its name of *Casa de Los Azulejos* from the blue and white porcelain tiles imported from China which covered the exterior. It was as much guided tour as article, describing the sumptuous interior and grand staircase of the most select of all the clubs in Mexico's capital.

Thea was reading the last page when Charles came out of the dressing room, fully dressed except for his tail coat.

Thea held out the pages to him. "This is the best birthday present you could give me. They're all wonderful."

Charles looked quietly pleased. "I wasn't sure—"

"Well, I am."

"It's been so long since I wrote something on my own that I'd begun to think all I could do was translations of other people's work," Charles admitted, pulling up a chair so he could sit close to Thea. "Do you think I should show these to Dick North?"

"Definitely. He'll know the best magazines for them. I'm so thrilled—five or six more and you'll have a book!"

"One article at a time, please!" Charles laughed. "But that's Dick's idea, too. He wants me to write my idea on the back of his calling card—"

"A la David Belasco."

"Exactly. Except when Dick told me that, I really didn't have any idea who David Belasco was!"

"Well, now you do, and these articles are a perfect swan song to our stay in Mexico City."

For a long second, Charles was very silent, regarding her out of eyes that grew dark with seriousness.

"I've been thinking that we might try another sort of swan song."

"How do you mean?"

"Thea, we were asked to come here, brought together for a purpose: to see if we could discover if the German Embassy was planning to start any problems. We really haven't done very well." Charles pointed out honestly. "All we really have is a lot of party gossip that could have taken place in any world capital, and the not-too-surprising news that a lot of people don't care for the United States Government."

"And don't forget what they think about T.R.," Thea added, a prickly feeling rushing over her skin. "But we know all of that. What's your idea, Charles?"

"That we should be a little more . . . investigative tonight than we've been before."

Thea sat quietly, letting his words sink in. "It's bad enough being a snoop, having come here with an ulterior motive, but I won't be a spy."

"I will." Charles' voice was even. "That day Paul and I played golf together, he mentioned that there might be some large chunk of information floating around out there, but that no one had come across it."

"Then what do you have in mind?" she asked, her nerves standing on end.

"We both know what embassy balls are like," Charles said, his eyes lighting up. "Too many people are invited, everyone wanders around, and no one can keep track of anyone else. I can get into Guenther's office, look around, and be out again before I'm missed."

"This is like some boys' adventure story for you, isn't it?" Thea demanded, exasperated. "And how are you going to locate his office? I don't imagine his name's on the door."

"I don't think so either. But I *did* run into Guenther a few weeks ago at the Jockey Club's bar, and the topic of conversation turned to you—"

"Me?"

"He'd heard that you were a decorator, and jokingly mentioned that his office could use one. It seems he has a pair of marble busts of Maximilian and Carlotta that are the ugliest things imaginable."

"What a waste of good marble," Thea remarked dryly.

"I'll let you know when I see them."

"I don't think I'll ever understand how intelligent, adult men like to go back to their childhoods!" Thea exploded. "Suppose all of his papers are locked in a safe? What then?"

"Very simple." Charles stood up and lifted from the presentation case on the dressing table a necklace designed with a deep turquoise opal surrounded by twenty-six sapphires and fastened it around Thea's neck. "Remember, I'm one of three brothers, and we grew up stuffed on the classics. Therefore, our favorite pastime was playing Wild West bank robbers," Charles said humorously. "We used to practice on my father's safe and, as frequently happens, the three of us became rather first-rate amateur cracksmen."

Now, several hours later, as she leaned against the black and white Carrara marble that formed the gallery handrail, Thea was beginning to wonder what Charles was up to. Supper had ended an hour before and, in the flow that spread from the ballroom to the reception rooms on both the main floor and the second floor of the Paseo de la Reforma mansion, she and Charles had made their way up the main staircase. When they reached the gallery, they separated, Thea remaining where she was, and Charles disappearing down one of the long hallways.

I guess I should be grateful Charles isn't one of those men who grow up regretting they didn't run away with the circus when they were ten, take a raft down the Mississippi, or never got over being cut from the football squad in their freshman year at college, she thought. All my husband wants to do is play at being a spy for one night. Compared to some tales I've heard, that's not too bad.

Except that he could get caught being in the wrong place at the wrong time, her inner voice insisted.

As Charles had predicted, the gala tonight *was* overcrowded. As she kept her position near the top of the stairs, the candles on the massive crystal chandelier with the emerald green lantern hanging inside glinting off her necklace and engagement ring and throwing shadows on her Lucile gown, Thea began to realize that she had met nearly everyone here tonight at some time during their stay in Mexico.

There were more people arriving now, men and women who were invited after supper for the dancing. All large balls had not quite top drawer people who weren't included in all the festivities and, as Thea picked them out, she wished Dona Imelda or Ghiselle de Laulan were here with her so they could exchange opinions. But the de Veigas had returned to the hacienda on Sunday afternoon, and the Belgian Minister and his wife hadn't been invited. Fending for herself, Thea studied the guests, but quickly averted her eyes from a cavernous-looking man with shifty eyes who was observing her with equal intensity.

I know him from someplace, but where? she thought. What an awful dress suit he's wearing . . . good tailor but in bad condition . . . the way Daddy's clothes looked when he came back from Brazil two years ago . . . the tropics. . . .

"At Germany's Embassy, we permit no beautiful ladies to stand alone." Guenther von Basedow slipped into place beside Thea. "And where is your husband?"

Ransacking your office, Thea thought, but out loud she said, "That's a very good question. But when your embassy insists on being *so* hospitable— Well, it does become difficult to locate a loved one."

Guenther's smile was a bit indulgent. "My ambassador believes in large gatherings. Personally, they are not my favorite form of entertainment, but since I have no say in the social arrangements . . ." He let his sentence trail off with a light shrug.

Thea gave him an understanding smile. She and Charles had agreed before hand that, during the time he would be occupied, she was to keep an eye on Guenther von Basedow's movements and, if she thought he might be going to his office, move in and keep him busy.

She had been keeping him under casual observance, but she never imagined it was going to be this easy.

"I hope we'll have the pleasure of your company for some time to come," he was saying.

"I'm afraid not," Thea responded with a bright smile. "We'll be leaving for home in a few days."

Better not to be too specific, she thought. You never know . . .

"There's so much for us to do back in New York," she went on quickly. "I'm sure that, as a bachelor, you've never thought of what goes into setting up a new home."

"No, I very much regret to say I haven't."

"Regret?" Thea was determined to spin this conversation out as long as possible. "That's not a word I'd connect with you."

"If you saw my office, you'd understand. It seems to be the repository for furniture no one else wants."

"Not Belter, I hope."

"Biedermeier."

"Almost as bad." Thea couldn't believe they were having this conversation. "How do you stand it day after day?"

"As long as I don't look at the marble impressions of the late Emperor and Empress, it's somewhat bearable. Of course, I'll be travelling a bit now, so my office won't be as important as it is now."

"Then let me wish you a pleasant journey in advance."

He raised his eyebrows slightly. "As long as I watch out for flying insects, I should find it very enlightening. I'm going to Panama."

For an endless minute, the only sound Thea was aware of was a rushing in her ears. Weeks of idiotic parties filled with inane chatter and tonight, technically their last night in Mexico City, involved in a conversation only to gain time for Charles, she was on the edge of finding what she had been sent for.

Isn't it ironic? she asked herself. But be careful with Guenther, he didn't get where he is by giving information away.

"Wait a few years until the beach area at Ancon becomes the resort they're planning," she said, deliberately keeping her voice light.

"I'm afraid that the hotel at Colon shall have to do for me," he said. And, for a few minutes, they discussed the latest newspaper interview with Colonel William Crawford Gorgas, who was not only an authority on tropical diseases, but also the natural successor to the late Walter Reed since the latter's untimely death from appendicitis in 1902.

"How tragic it would be if the colonel-doctor succumbs to the same disease which he is dedicating himself to bring under control."

Thea knew she was being led but, in the interest of gaining time, she played up. "Dr. Gorgas has had yellow fever," she supplied informatively. "So has his wife. In fact, the disease brought them together about twenty years ago in Texas. She was desperately ill, and he was the only doctor in the area who'd already survived yellow fever. He was called in on the case, even though the prognosis was very dim. But she lived and, during her recovery, they fell in love and were married when she recovered."

"What an excellent omen for his project."

"Absolutely," Thea agreed. All she could wonder was what Charles might have found and what was taking him so damn long.

Charles had located Guenther's office without any difficulty. As in all embassies, the protocol in assigning who worked where was strict. The ambassador came first, then the chargé d'affaires, and then the first secretary and, once Charles had established their locations, he set about finding the working place of Guenther von Basedow. He moved casually down the long, thickly carpeted corridor that ran from the ambassador's suite back to the central gallery where Thea was waiting for him.

Ideally, Charles would have liked to take swifter action but, well aware that what he was doing was, technically, a form of breaking and entering, he made himself move slowly, as if he had nothing more in mind than studying the unimpressive and poorly executed paintings that lined both walls.

It's good to have an alibi in case someone comes along, he reminded himself. *Mon Dieu,* but these paintings are botch jobs . . . I didn't think even Germans had such poor taste . . . fourth office away from the ambassador's . . . more important than he lets on . . . they don't even lock their doors . . . this is it . . . complete with Maximilian and Carlotta on the mantelpiece. . . .

Charles' disjointed thoughts ceased as he stepped quickly inside, closed the door behind him, and switched on the light, his eyes sweeping over the room. He restrained himself from turning the lock. If he was unlucky enough to have someone walk in while he was here, he could always come up with a plausible tale, but there was no way to explain away a locked door.

Thea was right all along, he told himself as he sat down behind the desk. This is living out a boyhood fantasy—a chance at being a combination Raffles and Jesse James. Get this over with or, in another few minutes, you'll begin thinking you're some sort of government agent.

Guenther von Basedow's desk turned out to be a large, rather unimpressive affair of dark walnut with elaborately carved sides. A heavy leather writing surface nearly covered the entire top, and a bronze and crystal desk set and a telephone were the only decorations. It was up-to-date and sensible—and completely unlocked.

Charles felt his heart sink to his feet as he slid open the first drawer. Nothing. Nothing at all. Schedules, lists of meetings, an appointment book, a folder containing a series of letters suggesting ways to strengthen the German business community in Mexico so that those selling similar products for rival companies would cease to regard each other as competition and band together to show other nations how Germans could act in unison.

All for the Fatherland, of course, Charles thought scathingly, moving on to the next drawer, keeping an eye on the long case clock in the corner. Ten minutes gone. Five more, and that's it. There's nothing in this drawer either. No wonder von Basedow was able to spend so much time with Ophelie. The man does absolutely no work . . .

He almost missed the letter. Two pages long and carefully handwritten on stationery engraved with the crest of the German Embassy. It had been placed between another handwritten report that was of no interest to him. It was only as he flipped through the pages and saw the descrepancy that he noticed the concealed letter.

Although, like most Frenchmen of his age and class, raised on tales of the Franco-Prussian War, preferring never to admit that he knew even one word of the language of his nation's hereditary enemy, Charles spoke excellent German. He also read it with only slightly less ease than he did English, and the letter he scanned sent his blood running cold.

Without thinking twice about the implications of his act, he folded the letter in thirds, slipped it into an envelope, and put it in the inside pocket of his tail coat.

We want you to try and discover if they're planning trouble now or will wait.

The President's words rose in his memory as Charles switched off the light and left the office. He had the answer, the one they thought wasn't there, and now he had to find Thea. With this bit of information tucked away in his pocket, their welcome at the German Embassy had suddenly worn itself out.

Of course Guenther's trip to Panama is official, Thea thought, disgusted with herself for her vivid, overactive imagination. A nice two week excursion so attachés from six embassies and legations can see the work on the canal begin. They'll be guided every step of the way but, as soon as Guenther said Panama, you imagined him setting off with dynamite and blasting caps in his suitcase. Great scenario, Thea, it sure helps to liven up the dull truth.

She was still in conversation with Guenther when a man making his way carefully up the staircase caught her eye. Like every other man in the embassy tonight—except for those arrayed in full-dress military splendor, he wore a full-dress suit, a fashion that made men who were similar in age, type, and build look alike. But, even if the walking stick he used didn't identify him, his ginger-colored hair and beard did.

It was the Englishman she'd met at the Monte de Pledad, Thea realized with a small start of recognition. The one she'd helped select jewelry for his wife.

Funny, I thought he must have gone back to England by now, she thought, leaning slightly over the railing to get a better look at him.

"Someone you know?" Guenther inquired, following Thea's gaze, a cold glint of recognition suddenly appearing in his eyes—a look Thea didn't like at all.

"No, not really," she said carefully, pulling back, and then the tightness around her heart eased.

Charles. Coming toward her from one of the long corridors. Above the crush of men and women, all talking away in at least four different languages, his topaz gaze locked into her green one, sending a clear signal to her.

"Guenther, this has been a fascinating conversation, and I wish we could continue, but I've finally sighted Charles, and—"

"Husbands *do* make certain demands," he allowed, gracefully bending over her hand. "Thank you for a very pleasant time."

As she moved easily around the groups of men and women, Thea could feel her heartbeat quicken with anticipation and relief. She could not imagine what Charles had discoverd, if anything. All she was sure of was that, once they walked out of the German Embassy

611

they were free, finished forever with the machinations of one government against another.

The marble staircase with the deep red carpeting over it loomed up in front of her and Thea threw a quick glance over her shoulder to see where Charles was.

The vice-president of American Cash Register always has a lot to say, Thea thought, amused, as she saw the portly, middle-aged man buttonhole Charles. Now I just have to get past my friend from the National Pawnshop. Let's hope he's not in a talkative mood. Well . . . not with me, at least. He seems to have quite a few things to say to that funny-eyed fellow with the moldy suit, though. *Why* do I think I've met both of them before . . . ?

". . . did you really think we'd never find you?" the red-haired man was saying. "After all, there's a great deal of truth in the saying 'trash comes up to its own level'."

"So the Foreign Office sends its own garbage collector—like the turkey buzzards of Vera Cruz—"

"Oh, insults won't send me away. Now, come along like a good guest. There's no protection for you here, and we have some things to discuss—"

Their conversation was growing louder, and snatches of it floated past Thea.

It's none of your business, she told herself. Just go downstairs and wait for Charles—

Her right foot was in mid-air, about to take the first step, when the man in the worn dress suit stepped away from his adversary and dashed toward the stairs.

It took only a second, and all that was necessary was a slight nudge at her shoulder. It was little more than a grazing motion, something that, had she been standing still, wouldn't have had any effect on her.

But Thea wasn't standing still. She didn't even have the advantage of seeing him coming. All Thea knew was that suddenly there was nothing solid beneath her fee

nd that her body was pitching backwards, stretching out
ull-length against the red carpeting with the hard, cold
aarble beneath it, and there wasn't even time for her to
ry out in astonishment and pain as her head made
ontact with the stairs and the black spots forming in
ront of her eyes spread into overwhelming darkness.

"Mr. de Renille?"
"Yes." Charles lifted his head from his hands and
ooked up to see a tall, reserved-looking man, a doctor's
oat over his dinner clothes, standing in front of him.
"I'm Winston Benning, Mrs. de Renille's physician,"
e said in a voice that Charles, frantic with fear as he was,
dentified immediately as pure Back Bay Boston. "I've
ome to tell you that your wife is going to be fine."

For the past forty-five minutes, Charles had been
eated in the waiting room of the American Hospital,
uffering the worst mental and emotional tortures he had
ver known. The turmoil he'd undergone during his
lness was suddenly nothing compared to the horror of
eeing the person he loved most in the world slip down
alf the length of the grand staircase, her slender body
oming to a halt on the landing, her rich green chiffon
own spreading over the carpet.

The next few minutes were utter pandemonium as
hat seemed to be every guest at the German Embassy
rowded close to see what had happened. Both the
mbassador and Guenther von Basedow had wanted to
all the ambulance from the German Hospital insisting,
n the tones Germans always seemed to adopt when
xtolling their country's accomplishments, that it had
ne best doctors and the best service, until Charles was
eady to commit mayhem on both of them.

Pushing all delicacy aside, he briefly informed them
hat Thea was pregnant, her doctor was at the American
Iospital, and would they kindly see to summoning their

ambulance before his wife miscarried on the Germa
Embassy's grand staircase.

Thea had been unconscious through the entir
discussion, the wait for the ambulance, and th
frightening ride through the deserted streets ending a
the American Hospital's emergency entrance where th
doctor on call was waiting. Dr. Benning was on his wa
and, as Thea was taken into an examining room, sh
began to regain consciousness, slightly dizzy and achin
from the fall, but totally aware of her surroundings an
of Charles. Finally, a kind but efficient nurse bustled hir
out to the waiting room just as Dr. Benning arrived, s
that he actually didn't meet the gynecologist until h
appeared in front of him.

Charles rose unsteadily to his feet. "I want you t
know that, if there's any difficulty, any choice to make
it's Thea I care about. I can live without a child, but
can't live without my wife."

Dr. Benning regarded Charles solemnly. "There's n
chance of that happening, Mr. de Renille. You're marrie
to a strong, healthy American girl, not a fragile Europea
flower," he told him with an encouraging smile.

The hard, cold knot of fear that had formed in Charles
chest slowly began to dissolve. "May I see her now?"

"No," Dr. Benning said in a gentle voice, "not righ
now. Your wife *did* take quite a bump on the head, and
want to make sure there's no concussion. Also, despit
what I said, the first three months are the mos
dangerous, so Mrs. de Renille is going to have to be th
guest of the American Hospital for several days."

"She isn't going to care for that."

"No, I imagine very few people enjoy an unexpecte
sojourn in a hospital room."

"Particularly since we were going home on Wednes
day."

"Hmm." Dr. Benning smiled slightly. "This is no plac

614

to talk. Come with me to my office. Now," he continued a minute later when they were in his consulting room, "shall we have a drink? I think you could do with one."

"Thank you," Charles said as he sank down on the leather sofa. Right now, he felt as if *he* had fallen down the stairs. And, grateful as he was for the doctor's offer, the idea of sherry, port or madeira, all that a proper Boston physician would serve, wasn't very appealing and. . . .

"Scotch or bourbon, Mr. de Renille?"

Charles recovered quickly. "Bourbon, Dr. Benning," he replied, and watched as the older man took a bottle of Old Forrester from a locked cabinet and poured two drinks into Waterford glasses. "I wasn't expecting—"

He put one of the glasses in Charles' hand. "Obviously there were a number of things you weren't expecting tonight."

"I'm not much of a drinker."

"Neither am I. However, this is strictly medicinal. I gave Mrs. de Renille a sedative, and this is yours. Drink up."

The bourbon began to spread its warmth through Charles, and a few minutes later he and Dr. Benning were talking about Bailey's ice cream sundaes where the hot fudge drips over the side of the silver dish and onto the tray below when a sharp knocking on the door interrupted them.

"Come in," the doctor called, and a second later Major Donovan entered the consulting room. The two older men regarded each other, neither wavering an inch, and finally Winston Benning spoke first.

"May I help you?" he inquired in a formal, frozen Boston voice.

As in everything else, Thea has excellent taste in doctors, Charles thought with pride. No one intimidates or gets past this man.

"I'm a friend of the de Renilles," the major said a shade too glibly. "I heard about the accident and came to see if Mrs. de Renille was all right."

"Thea's asleep now," Charles said, aware that the code of ethics physicians were sworn to prevented Dr. Benning from speaking about a patient's condition to someone who was not a member of the family. "She'll be fine, but she has to stay here a few days for observation, to make sure she doesn't have a concussion, and that she won't miscarry—"

"*Miscarry*," Donovan interrupted. "She—she's—"

"Pregnant," Charles supplied, his voice icy.

"Well, well." A knowing smirk played across his mouth. "Merrill's a faster worker than I gave him credit for. I guess that now—"

The rest of the sentence never made it out of his mouth as Charles sprang off the sofa in one long movement and like a deadly panther after its prey, was on John Donovan in a split second. The major had a good twenty pounds on him, but Charles moved swiftly, grasping Donovan by his lapels and literally slamming him against the wall of books, cursing him in both French and English, using words he wasn't even sure he remembered.

Again and again Charles slammed Donovan against the books, his body making continual contact with the leather-bound volumes, until Dr. Benning literally had to pull them apart.

"Enough!" he said sharply, stepping between them. "Now what the hell is going on, and who is this Merrill?"

"An attaché at the Embassy who has just been reassigned. He's a friend of Thea's and mine," Charles explained, stretching the truth but too angry to care. "Unfortunately, Major Donovan has the idea that the captain is my wife's lover.

"It's *my* baby that Thea's having," he said, swinging savagely on the major. "*Mine!*"

The color ebbed out of John Donovan's face. "Do you know what the penalty is for striking an officer of the United States Army? How would you like to explain yourself in front of a board of inquiry, you crazy fool?"

"I'd like nothing better," Charles snapped. "I'd love to explain to your superior officers how you tried to taint the reputations of three people. I don't care about my own, but I *do* care about my wife and, strangely enough, I wouldn't want to see Paul Merrill hurt by your machinations. He's an officer and a gentleman. The only misstep he made was becoming attracted to Thea before she was married and, later, listening to whatever tales you wove about us. I can forgive his falling instantly in love with Thea, because that's what happened to me. Only, in my case, those feelings were returned. I'm sure a board of inquiry would find that to be a very interesting testimony."

Major Donovan rubbed the back of his neck. "That's not why we sent you here," he glowered. "Love has nothing to do with your assignment!"

"The day that falling in love can be cut to fit any situation is the day I give up on our civilization. But I don't suppose that means anything to you," Charles said scathingly. "You couldn't understand what happened between Thea and me. You have no love in you—not for another person."

At Charles' words, all the glowering bombast in Donovan seemed to die, and a tragic look came into his eyes. "Do you think that because I don't have a great name and fortune behind me, that I have no idea what it is to love someone?" he questioned in an unexpectedly sad voice. "I don't blame you for thinking like you do. You have no way of knowing about my personal life— about the fact that I was married, or that I have a five-year-old son."

Charles was shocked. "I just assumed—"

617

Donovan waved a hand in dismissal. "The way I assumed you were safe because—" His eyes slid to Dr. Benning, relaxing on the sofa, only his sharp eyes betraying the fact that he was observing them. "—because of what you'd been through. That was in the beginning. Later on, I guess I knew, but the other way was easier. Easier not to acknowledge what had happened between you two, not to imagine—" He broke off and took several deep breaths before continuing. "I—I never expected to get married, but when I was back east one year I met Margaret. She—she'd been a professor at Bryn Mawr and going west to Arizona, to Fort Huchacha, was a great adventure to her. We had a fine life together and then, when our boy was almost a year old, she developed a bad cold, then pneumonia, and then she was gone."

Charles was riveted. "And your son?"

"He's with his grandparents in New Haven, Connecticut. It's the best place for him. They're well-to-do people, and they love him. I see him once a year when I'm on leave," he added.

"How very sad for you," Charles said, his words conveying all, leaving little more to be said.

Major Donovan left a few minutes later and Charles sat down on the leather sofa. He picked up his abandoned glass and drained the remains in one quick gulp. This time there was no relaxing warmth from the bourbon, only a dull burning.

"This has been quite a night for you, hasn't it?"

Charles jumped at the sound of the quiet voice. For a minute he'd forgotten about Winston Benning seated at the other end of the sofa.

"Yes," he said at last. "Things are never what we assume them to be."

"I'm at an age where the sense of duty that the young feel astounds me." His voice was tinged with wonderment. "You and your wife must both have extraordinary

618

feelings of responsibility to submit to an arrangement that didn't take either of your personalities into consideration at all."

For the first time since his dinner at the White House, Charles was beyond keeping the secret. He didn't care if Winston Benning was Kaiser Wilhelm's personal agent. He was tired of secrets, half-truths and outright lies. He had passed through too much to ever live that way again, and he told the doctor the entire story.

"I thought as much," was his only comment.

"When—when we fell in love, Thea didn't want to come here," Charles said miserably. "In a way, what happened tonight was my fault. If I'd listened to her—"

"You can't go back," the doctor said. "And don't create problems you can't solve. That's no way to build a happy and lasting marriage. Listen to me, Charles, there's nothing more you can do here tonight. Go back to your hotel, get some sleep, and come back tomorrow. Thea will need her personal belongings, and she'll want *you*, her husband, not a self-incriminating idiot. Come on—"

Outside the hospital, Hernando was waiting with the motor car, having followed the ambulance from the German Embassy. After reassuring the concerned chauffeur that all was well, Charles was driven back to the Sanz and, less than fifteen minutes later, he was in their suite.

For a minute, his gaze settled on the dressing table, on the presents other than the necklace he'd given Thea for her birthday—the gold mesh evening bag with the emerald clasp, the powder compact that combined pink-gold and silver in a pattern of trellised leaves studded with small rubies, and the silver *minaudiere* designed by Van Cleef and Arpels and ordered from Asprey's by La Perla for a special client who then refused it. Charles had then purchased the sterling silver box with its gold and ruby clasp, certain that Thea would love its modern design and neatly fitted interior—and then he looked away, his heart aching. This room *was* Thea and, being in here alone, about to face their first night apart since they were married, was going to be more lonely and painful than he ever could have imagined.

In the dressing room, Charles stripped to the skin, leaving his clothes where they fell and, in the bathroom, he showered, making the water as hot as he could bear, then as cold, standing beneath the steady stream until the last vestiges of the past six hours were gone. But soap and water couldn't wash away the event he'd instigated—the event that, albeit inadvertently, led to Thea's mishap. She'd been in the wrong place at the wrong time and it was his fault.

He took his culpability in the incident seriously, but it wasn't until he re-entered the dressing room and saw his tail coat abandoned on the floor that Charles remembered that, in the rush of events, he'd forgotten all about giving John Donovan the letter he'd taken from Guenther von Basedow's desk.

"I think you've brought half of my belongings to me," Thea said late the next morning, leaning forward to wrap her arms around Charles as he sat beside her on the bed while two hospital maids were busy unpacking the suitcases; the contents of her dressing case were already arranged on the room's simple vanity table. "Thank you so much. I know it's silly, but having all of this here makes me feel better—"

"You look radiant," Charles said sincerely. Thea had already changed into a nightgown of white crepe de chine with insertions of Swiss lace, pinned her hair up in a loose knot, and applied a few strategic dabs of Jicky. "I feel as if I've been beaten up in a dark alley."

"Oh, I'm sore too," Thea reassured him. "And I have a small bump on my head to remind me of last night." She

620

tightened her hold on him. "When I woke up this morning . . . for a minute I was so afraid that I'd miscarried—"

"But you didn't, and you're not going to," Charles said soothingly, placing her back against the pillows.

"This means we can't go home tomorrow. I know I have to be careful and make sure all is going well, but I *am* disappointed."

"So am I. But it's better this way," he said softly, saving more intimate endearments until after the maids left.

In a short time, the room was transformed. Thea had been given the best room the American Hospital offered but, even with its attractive chintz draperies and cushions, it was cool and impersonal. But not any longer. Now the bare surfaces were covered with books and flower arrangements, and her own satin and lace pillows adorned the bed.

"Have you ever considered taking up the decoration of hospital rooms?" Charles teased her.

"In a manner of speaking, I have," she told him with a new gleam of anticipation in her eyes. "Not hospitals, although they could use it, but hotels. Specifically, all the new luxury hotels in New York. I've been thinking about this for the past week," she continued. "Now that I'm having a baby, I want to make some changes without giving up my business or just depending on clients like the de Veigas. Without morning sickness, my figure isn't going to last very long. I'll be showing by January, and by April I'll have to stop work entirely."

Charles smiled. "I can see why. A new client might find your grandly carrying on when you're six months along a bit unsettling."

"That's *their* problem. But no more out-of-town clients. I hated it anyway. Half the time they weren't sure if I were visiting royalty or a superior servant," Thea recalled, laughing. "But as far as new business is concerned, I'm going to look to the hotels. Do you think it's a good idea, darling?"

"I think it's the best one I've ever heard. And, if you need any further proof, just remember our suite at the Sanz the first time we saw it!"

For several minutes they involved themselves in the discussion of New York City's new luxury hotels. If the St. Regis, the Gotham, and the new Astor were any indication, more would follow. And with Thea's reputation already so firmly established, she wouldn't have any difficulty in convincing the new managements that she should have contracts to decorate several of the suites.

They were still making plans when a nurse came in with Thea's lunch tray and reminded them that she had to take it easy for today.

"I'll leave you now, darling, but I'll be back later. The Sanz's kitchen is doing something special for your dinner. They'll send over enough for two, and we'll share it."

They exchanged another kiss, and Charles was across the room, hand on the doorknob, when Thea's voice stopped him.

"Charles—sweetheart—one thing before you go. You don't have to tell me if you'd rather not, but what did you find in Guenther von Basedow's office last night?"

He recrossed the floor, and sat down again on the edge of the bed, a dull, rushing sound echoing in his ears.

"How do you know I found anything at all?" Charles asked cautiously.

Thea met his eyes without blinking. "From the look on your face when you came into the gallery. I knew you came up with something. That's why I was in such a rush to get to the stairs." She smiled regretfully. "If I'd been a little more careful, I wouldn't be here now.

Rotten timing."

"You don't know the meaning of the word."

"But what did you find?" Thea insisted, putting aside her luncheon tray. "Was it a report?"

"Only this," he replied, and handed her the letter kept in his inside jacket pocket. "One letter—more of a proposal, really—with rather deadly implications."

Thea read the letter through once, then again, her mind rapidly translating the German to English, absorbing the words. Finally, she handed it back to Charles.

"Quite an idea," she said. "Don't blow up the Panama Canal, don't incite a civil war, don't even try to make a pact with Mexico—at least not yet. Just agitate the working crews."

"Better than dynamite," Charles said in a quiet voice tinged with bitterness. "I gather they really think the canal can be built this time. If they thought John Wallace would have to abandon the project in disgrace the way Ferdinand Lesseps and the Compagnie Nouvelle did, this letter—even in its rough form—wouldn't exist."

"What a compliment. And for a rough idea, it's rather well thought out. And easy enough to carry out if this concept is adopted," she added. "Imagine . . . convince the German-American workers that their true duty lies in aiding the country that they immigrated from; implant the idea in the Irish-American crews that Germany and Ireland have a twin destiny; and agitate among the black and native workers, who always get the worst of everything."

Thea handed the letter back to Charles, her heart filled with fear, not only for the future, but for her husband's act of courage.

"Do you think Guenther has missed this yet?" she said finally. "Last night he told me that he's making some sort of officially sponsored trip down to Panama, and if he decides to look over his . . . shall we say *notes*—"

She deliberately left her sentence unfinished, and Charles' expression became wry.

"I have no doubt that he's already discovered that it's missing. But as for knowing who opened his desk—" Charles smiled briefly. "No German operative has begun to follow me yet. Nonetheless, I'd better see to passing it on."

"I think that would be a good idea," Thea agreed. "But do you want to hand it over to Major Donovan, or keep it for Colonel Miles?"

"I haven't decided yet," he said honestly. "Technically, I've stolen this. And, for all I know, the correct procedure when that happens is to arrange the secret return of the document and pretend it never took place. But that's enough speculation for now," Charles said, and leaned over to kiss Thea. "I want you to have lunch and then rest. This is going to take a lot of thought before there's any action. I didn't resort to theft to have this letter treated as though it were nothing more important than a lost pair of gloves."

Over the next week, Thea's room at the American Hospital became a gathering spot for the women she'd met during their weeks in Mexico City.

The news of her accident at the German Embassy had travelled along the grapevine and, by Wednesday afternoon, when Dr. Benning said she could receive visitors, a stream of female friends and acquaintances came to call, bearing flowers, presents and all the latest gossip.

Ghiselle de Laulan was the first to arrive, followed closely by Mrs. Clayton, and Lady Duff, the wife of the British Ambassador. Dona Luisa de la Garza, Dona Imelda's sister-in-law came on a regular basis, bringing along her daughter Victoria, both laden with flowers from their garden and food from their kitchen. Jean

Gordon was another welcome visitor, providing Thea with an hour of such good conversation that both women regretted that they hadn't had the opportunity to become better friends, and they parted with the promise that the Gordons would stop in New York on their way back to England next year. The wife of the French Ambassador paid a visit, as did the wife of the Bolivian Minister. Even the German Ambassadress and Annalise von Grelheim paid courtesy calls and sent flowers. But on this Monday afternoon, November 21st, exactly one week after her accident, the last person Thea expected walked into her room—Ophelie.

As usual, both women silently considered one another. Ophelie was faultlessly turned out in a Worth tailored suit of two shades of gray-striped cheviot with an open, hip-length coat, a high-necked blouse of Irish lace, a red cloth waistcoat, and a full gray fox boa. Thea reclined against her pillows in a Lucile tea gown of flower-trimmed flesh-colored satin with a tunic of ruffled lace and a blue satin bodice.

"Would you care to sit down?" Thea said, breaking the silence, noting that the Baronne de Langlade was the only one of her visitors to arrive empty-handed.

"Yes . . . thank you," Ophelie murmured, sitting down in a wicker armchair, pushing her rich fur boa over the back. "I didn't expect to find you . . . well . . ."

"Looking as if I had no business being in a hospital?" Thea suggested with a smile. "Actually, I'm just here for observation, to make sure there aren't any serious after-effects from my fall. I'm pregnant," she explained.

"All de Renille brides conceive practically on their wedding nights."

"So Charles has told me. Frankly, I don't care about the others, family tradition or any of it. This is *our* child, and no one else has any part in it!"

The implication in Thea's words was clear, but Ophelie

chose to ignore it. "Do you believe in birth control?" she inquired idly.

"Of course I do. So does every other right thinking woman."

"Charles might have a thing or two to say about that."

"Oh, we have a tacit agreement on the subject. I don't mention any techniques I know, and therefore it's not a trouble to his conscience. Besides, I think Charles may secretly agree with me, only he hasn't worked it all out yet. Now, shall we have some tea?"

Thea honestly didn't know what to make of either Ophelie's visit or her apparent attempts to conduct a normal conversation, but the suggestion of refreshments seemed to be the best route to take.

"Are you expecting other visitors this afternoon?" Ophelie asked then the maid arrived with a large pot of tea and a plate of butter cookies.

"No, I don't think so. For about a week, my room was a rather chic place to come, but most people don't like to pay extended hospital visits. Besides, I'll be released in another day or so."

"You'll be going back to New York?"

"I expect so," Thea said evasively, pouring out the tea. She still didn't like Ophelie, and had no intention of providing her with an opening.

Ophelie looked over Thea's room with careful eyes, noting the extravagant bouquets of flowers and gift baskets. She saw the needlepoint Thea was working on, the books and magazines she was reading, and a small object on the night table caught her attention.

"What a strange little thing," she exclaimed, indicating a wooden baby shoe last covered with small metal *milagros*, that was set among Thea's belongings.

"Yes, isn't it," Thea agreed. "It's a present from Angelita, my maid at the hotel. The metal figures are charms that the Mexicans use when praying for a medical

626

miracle. Not that I was in any danger but, when Charles brought it to me, he said it also brings good luck."

Ophelie seemed to have no direct response to her comment, and for the next several minutes both women confined their conversation to neutral ground. Like most women of their upbringing, they acted as if the past weeks of unpleasantness, ending with Ophelie's savage lie the night of the French Embassy gala, had simply never happened. They were not friends now and were never going to be. Therefore, the only necessity was that they be civil and polite when they met in the same circles. Their conversation centered mainly on clothes, discussing Worth versus Poiret, and Lucile versus Paquin, and in the end deciding that if there was one designer who would leave a great mark on 20th Century women's fashion, he—or more likely she—hadn't made their appearance yet.

"Is Charles coming to see you?" Ophelie asked rather unexpectedly, glancing at Thea's bedside clock. "I really don't want to see him."

"That's rather a change, isn't it?"

"All right, I had that coming," Ophelie replied, drawing a deep breath as if her stays were too tightly laced. "But I really can't face him."

"He won't be here for at least another hour. When my room became the fashionable gathering spot, we decided that he would come first thing in the morning, we would have breakfast together, he would leave and come back around five. The Sanz's kitchen has been doing our dinner, so we have our evening meal together, and he stays until it's time for me to go to bed."

"How very pleasant for you," Ophelie murmured without rancor.

"Ophelie, please don't worry. I'm sure Charles doesn't hold too much against you. He knows you've been under a bad strain—"

"You mean Guenther," she interrupted. "Odd how even a few weeks can provide a whole new perspective on one's life." She looked straight at Thea. "Guenther used to beat me," she said almost carelessly.

"I know," Thea replied, equally nonchalant, as if they were discussing a new perfume. "I saw one of your bruises. *Blanc d'Argent* doesn't cover all that well."

Ophelie shrugged. "It wasn't like that, not at first. But a few months ago he told me—well, you can imagine what. He said he always kept one woman for those activities, and another for the more usual. But, with Mexico being such a rigid Catholic country, there wasn't much of a selection—"

"*Selection?*" Thea laughed. "That's the first time I've heard sado-masochism described as though it were a shopping expedition."

"Is that what they call it—sado-masochism? I'd always wondered what the alienists' term would be. In any case, He didn't force me. I agreed quite readily. Some of it was even rather thrilling but, as time went on, he wasn't careful any more and . . ." She shuddered slightly.

"You found out it wasn't your cup of tea after all," Thea suggested.

"That's as good an expression as any. Once you start that sort of a relationship with a man, there's no going back. But we had an agreement that when either of us decided it was over, that was it."

"Is that why you wanted Charles? So you'd have an excuse?"

"Yes—and that's the first time I've ever admitted it—even to myself. But then Gerard came back and Guenther pulled out. For the first time, *two* men had rejected me."

"And having your husband isn't good enough?"

Ophelie shifted again, an expression of such discomfort on her face that Thea actually felt sympathetic toward her.

"Would you like me to ring for a maid to loosen your stays?" she offered.

"Then how am I supposed to fit back into my clothes again? I'm laced as tight as I can bear it, and yet my skirt barely came together at the waist—" She took yet another deep breath in an effort to gain momentary relief from the merciless stiffening that constricted her. "You don't understand about Gerard and me," she said, switching back to their main topic of conversation.

"Apparently not, but I really can't see deliberately setting out to be unfaithful for no good reason at all. And don't tell me that's how it's always done!" she added snappishly.

"No, it isn't. But since Gerard is so interested in his archaeology, and I can't have a child—"

"I'm sorry. That news must have been very painful for you."

"News?" she said blankly. "No, I've simply never been able to conceive. I don't need a doctor for that. You see, it's me, not Gerard. I've always been very careful about that."

"But you really don't know one way or the other. You've never been examined—?"

"A waste of time for me. Of course, now that Gerard has made his intentions quite clear—we are going back to the *haras* for a very long time. I'm down to my true test as a possible brood mare. I don't think I'm going to be as successful as you are."

"Well, why don't you see a specialist and find out for certain? There's nothing to lose—"

They were still discussing the matter when the door opened and Dr. Benning came in, his usually reserved face wreathed in a bright smile.

"I have some very good news for you," he said after greetings were exchanged. "We're releasing you tomorrow, Thea."

"At last! I can't tell you how happy I am."

"Your face says it all," he said, smiling. "Now, if there's nothing else—"

"Dr. Benning, before you go, this is Baronne de Langlade, and she's not certain if she's able to have a baby or not. Possibly you could be of some help to her."

"In a strictly medical sense, of course," he said humorously, and then began to question Ophelie with the usual preliminaries. "Would you care to come with me to my office, Madame la Baronne?" he questioned. "My calendar is clear, and my nurse is still on duty. A pelvic checkup shouldn't take too long."

Ophelie was somewhat shaken by this turn of events but, after a few protestations, she gave in and prepared to accompany Dr. Benning to his office. She picked up her boa and handbag and unexpectedly bent over and kissed Thea lightly on the cheek.

"I don't think this will change anything," she whispered in her ear, "but you *are* right about one thing, I should be better informed than I am. I've avoided this for far too long. However it turns out, I just want to say thank you."

Charles had acquired the letter on a Monday night and now, just eight hours short of one week, he still had it in his possession. With a combination of ingrained caution and natural reluctance at having to see Major Donovan again, he had put off telling him about the potential firebomb he had taken out of Guenther von Basedow's desk.

Every hour I hold on to it, it becomes more dangerous, Charles thought as he got ready to visit Thea at the hospital. They've missed it by now, I'm sure of it, and someone is going to remember seeing me wandering where I had no business.

Quickly, Charles gathered together the pages he'd

spent the afternoon typing. With Thea's afternoons taken up by the ladies of Mexico City's upper strata, he had been using that time to write, doing more articles about the sights of the capital.

In the bedroom, he dropped the typed pages on the writing desk, now bare of Thea's ornaments. And, after another bout of reluctance, he lifted the telephone receiver and asked the switchboard for the American Embassy.

A minute later, John Donovan was on the line.

"Will this take long?" he asked gruffly. "With Captain Merrill gone, I'm swimming in paperwork."

"Then I'm afraid I'm going to add one more piece to it," Charles said, and told the major what he was holding.

The response at the other end was explosive.

"What did you say you had?"

"A letter written by an attaché—if that's the title you care to use—at the Germany Embassy proposing several ways the work crews at the Panama Canal can be disrupted without any blame to an outside power," Charles repeated.

"So you're the one," Donovan said, his voice grudgingly appreciative. "The word on the grapevine is that the Kaiser's boys have lost something important and are offering a reward for it."

"Well, I don't need any money, and I certainly have no need for this letter."

"Then why the hell did you take it?"

"Because I was trying to be of help, to find an answer to the questions we came here with. If you're not interested, I'll just put a match to it and—"

"You'll do no such thing! God, the problems *you've* caused. All right, first thing tomorrow morning, meet me at Chapultepec Park."

"That's fine with me. About half-past seven?"

"Good. Do you know the memorial to the cadets of the

1847 war? I'll meet you there—and don't be late!"

The connection was broken, and Charles returned the receiver to the cradle. Poor man, he thought with an involuntary wave of sympathy that surprised him. No wonder Thea and I thought he had no personal life, much less a wife who died and a son who's farmed out to grandparents. I suppose he mistrusts everyone and everything because of that. Either that, or he regards himself as some sort of moral guardian.

With the sort of mental shrug that all Frenchmen use to dismiss eccentric behavior in others, Charles set about getting ready to see Thea. He hated spending so much time alone in the suite, it only made their separation harder to bear.

But not after tomorrow. By this time tomorrow, he knew, he and Thea would be together again, and he would have had his last encounter with Major Donovan.

It was only seven-twenty when Charles guided his rented mount around the central *glorieta* from which all paths in Chapultepec Park began and onto the path that would take him to his meeting with Major Donovan. Thea was being released from the hospital this afternoon, and the sooner this last part of their stay in Mexico City was concluded, the happier he'd be.

In a way, their meeting spot was significant. Erected in 1881 by the Military College Association, the Monument to the Memory of the Cadets honored those young men who fell in the Battle of Molino del Rey against the American Army. It was a heartrending reminder that the relationship between the United States and Mexico would always have that unlawful, expansionist war as a permanent rift in what should be a peaceful and progressive relationship.

Charles could see the outline of the monument through the thick foliage. It was a clear, crisp morning and, as he came even closer, he could see the major's horse tethered to a tree. Skillfully, he reined his own horse, dismounted, and went to find John Donovan.

But the last thing Charles expected to see was that the major was already at the monument—sprawled face down in the bushes, blood slowly trickling over one ear.

Charles saw immediately, from the look of the wound, that all it had taken was a single, strong, swift blow to take immediate effect. He was still breathing, still alive, but not for much longer if help was not brought at once.

In three steps, Charles was at his horse, mounting it. John Donovan wasn't an adversary any longer, he was an injured man in need of aid.

He was halfway down the bridle path back to the central *glorieta* when he saw one of the park's gardeners coming toward him on foot, holding a flower arrangement to place on the monument

"*Muy urgente!* There's an emergency!" he shouted, his voice sharp and authoritative. "A North American gentleman has been injured and is in need of aid. An ambulance is needed, and the police!"

Not, Charles thought as he urged his horse on, that the man who did this is waiting around for anyone to find him.

Home. . . . I'm going home.

That was the thought Thea woke with and, although it might not be exactly correct, she had no idea how long they'd be staying on at the Sanz—she was getting out of the hospital, and that was what mattered.

Charles had brought so many of her things to the hospital that packing was going to take almost as much time as it would if she was back at the hotel. And, by nine, with her breakfast tray finished, Thea set to work. She was busy filling a suitcase with lingerie cases when she heard the door open, and expecting to see the maid, Thea glanced up to see Charles, still in his riding gear, his face pale and drawn.

"What happened?" she breathed, and the next instant she was in his arms. "You look as though you just escaped from a madman."

"I may have just avoided that fate, but Major Donovan didn't," he said, and related the morning's incident, watching as Thea's eyes widened in disbelief and horror. "He's here now, I came with him in the ambulance, and I've been waiting until the doctors finished. . . ."

"Is he alive?"

"By some miracle, yes. But with a fractured skull."

Still holding each other, they sat down on the edge of the bed.

"That damn letter!" Charles' voice was bitterly reproachful. "It's like Pandora's Box. But at least now I know where I stand; they know it's gone."

"Do you suppose that Major Donovan was the one who tipped them off?" Thea ventured.

"In military intelligence, it's perfectly possible." He pushed his hair out of his eyes. "Whatever happened, it's up to me now."

A cold tremor of fear ran through Thea. "Charles, please don't do anything foolish."

"I won't, but I have no intention of allowing this letter to be returned to the Germans. It violates everything I was brought up to believe in, as well as everything I promised President Roosevelt."

"I know," Thea said quietly, "and I wouldn't want you to betray any of those principles. Now—what can I do?"

Charles looked at the bedside clock. "I'll be back here at four. Will you be ready to leave?"

"Have I let you down yet?"

"No, and I don't think you ever will," he said tenderly, standing up. "I'll be back before you even miss me."

"I've missed you enough this past week to last the rest

of my life." Thea stood up and put her arms around his neck. "Take care, and I'll be waiting for you."

Charles was almost to the hospital's entrance when he heard a familiar voice call him, and he turned to see Dr. Benning coming toward him.

"Do you have any further word on Major Donovan?" he asked a second later.

"Fractured skulls aren't precisely my main line of work," Winston Benning replied a shade dryly. "But I have spoken to the surgeon on his case. It's too early to tell, of course but, provided the major can survive the next seventy-two hours, he has a good chance. But what a rotten line of work," he added with an off-handed look at Charles.

"I'll be glad to see the last of it," Charles admitted. "But I was raised to always do my duty and see things through to the end and, because of that, right now I feel as if Henry V were addressing me personally: 'He who hath no stomach for this fight, let him depart. . . .'"

"Ah, Shakespeare," Dr. Benning smiled. "As I've gotten older I've found the Bard of Avon has apt words for nearly every situation. But *Henry V* doesn't apply to you, Charles. In your case, it's *Macbeth*. Think about that. But, in the meantime—" He held out his hand. "I don't expect to see you and Thea again until we're both on the other side of the Rio Grande. Godspeed to both of you."

It was just one more twist of fate that Winston Benning should refer to *Macbeth*, Charles thought as he was driven back to the Sanz. That was the first Shakespearean play he'd assigned to his students at St. Michel's. He knew the play inside out, and there was only one line that the doctor could have been referring to:

Stand not upon the order of your going, but go at once.

Charles was so lost in his plans that, when he stepped

inside the suite, he didn't see Jean-Christophe sitting on one of the sofas, his head buried in the *Atlantic Monthly*.

"I hope you don't mind," he said, getting rapidly to his feet, "but I have some wonderful news I want to share with you, and the managing-director was good enough to let me in."

Charles smiled faintly. "I'd like to hear some good news for a change."

"Has something happened to Thea?" the boy asked in alarm. "Maman said—"

"No, Thea's fine," he said, quickly reassuring him. "But that's about the only thing that is right. Let's sit down, and then you can tell me your news."

"The cable came last night from the Foreign Office in Brussels. We'd been expecting it, but not quite so soon," Jean-Christophe explained cryptically. "The official news will be announced tomorrow—Papa has been appointed the Belgian Minister to Washington, beginning the first of next year!" he finished proudly.

Charles, in spite of the problems he was facing, felt the boy's keen anticipation and responded in kind.

"All my congratulations—and Thea's too, of course. Are your parents looking forward to this?"

"They're ecstatic. Maman will have a new chancery to decorate without having to work around what was left behind, Papa will have the most prestigious appointment he could hope for and, since he will soon have another secretary, I can go back to the university. Papa is insisting I complete my sophomore year at Georgetown, but for next year I can see about going to one of the other great schools, possibly Yale or Princeton—"

Jean-Christophe's excited voice ran on in Charles' brain, and a sudden light pierced through the darkness. Either by his own design, or by accident, Major Donovan had been caught in the middle of this mess about the letter, and Charles knew the next time the net fell, i

636

wouldn't be on the wrong person. Even now he might be followed. He had to temporarily get rid of the letter, pass it into safer hands.

"I have a favor to ask of you, Jean-Christophe, and please don't say yes out of any regard you have for me or Thea," he said carefully. "As you may have guessed, our honeymoon is something more than just the usual journey of a newly married couple. We were asked to come here by President Roosevelt with a specific purpose in mind," he went on, dropping the other facts as if they'd never existed in the first place, finally realizing that, as far as he and Thea were concerned, they no longer mattered. "But to cut a long story short, I came across a piece of valuable information that someone wants to get back very badly indeed. Earlier this morning, one man nearly lost his life over it."

If Charles was trying to warn Jean-Christophe off, it wasn't working. Like all carefully sheltered young men, he longed to do something dangerous and deadly, and yet be patriotic at the same time. He listened to Charles' story and knew his moment had come.

"What can I do?" he asked as soon as Charles finished.

"First, I want you to go to the Colonia Station and buy two Pullman tickets for Thea and me on the five o'clock train to Laredo. I think there's a possibility I'm being followed."

Jean-Christophe's earnest expression was replaced by a smile. This was better than the penny dreadfuls he'd read while at Stanford.

"Of course I'll do that! In fact, I think you and Thea should have two compartments. It's not only more space, but if you are being followed, and your *Boche* spy follows you on the train, he won't know which compartment to enter first," he explained in a truly serious voice.

"Thank you," Charles replied, hiding a smile. "I hadn't thought of that possibility, and your idea is very good."

"I'll go immediately for the tickets and bring them back here. But now for the other thing—the really important one—"

"You don't have to undertake this if you'd rather not. This isn't a lark, Jean-Christophe," he warned, and then told him the entire story.

"Of course I'll take the letter!" he exclaimed. "How could I do otherwise?"

Charles glanced at the clock on the mantelpiece. There was so much to do between now and four and, although the last thing he wanted to do was involve Jean-Christophe in a potentially dangerous situation, the circumstances demanded he take the chance.

"If the train runs on time, Thea and I should get across the border on Thursday. As soon as I think it's safe, I'll cable you what to do next. But if," he began, and hesitated for a moment, "if anything happens, I want you to keep the letter, and when you reach Washington, give it directly to President Roosevelt."

Gerard came into Ophelie's bedroom carrying a glass of champagne into which a spoonful of strawberry syrup had been stirred.

"This is for you, *cherie*," he announced, sitting down on the bed. "My mother believed that this remedy was the best available."

Ophelie looked doubtfully at the tulip-shaped glass. "What a terrible thing to do to champagne."

"Don't worry, it's not vintage." He leaned over to kiss her lightly. "I've never known you to refuse champagne."

"No, but three in the afternoon is more suggestive of tea, not Veuve Clicquot!"

Despite her protests, Ophelie took the glass and began to sip its contents. It had been like this since she returned

638

from the American Hospital yesterday and given Gerard her astounding news. It had swept away all the barriers between them. Now Gerard treated her like porcelain. But there was still caution under his elation and, as she rested against her pillows, Ophelie asked a chancy question.

"Do you have any doubts? Most men would, you know."

"I'm not most men, and I'm not worried at all," he assured her, his hands moving gently along the golden waves of her hair that flowed over her shoulders. "Everything comes in its own time, and that week in Oaxaca was ours."

"This means no more of your running off on archaeological expeditions," she teased.

"I've already given them up," he reminded her.

"But I thought that now you might have changed your mind."

"Why should I? Now I have more reason than ever to stay with you. Besides, the last months have given me all the intrigue I can handle for a while and—"

"Intrigue?" Ophelie interrupted. "On a dig with a lot of musty old archaeologists?"

"You really don't know?" Gerard asked in wonderment. "I thought you must have known all along. Ophelie, didn't it occur to you what a dig run under the joint auspices of the Sorbonne, Oxford, and Harvard really is?"

Suddenly, she was filled with amazement. "Is that why you were so worried about Guenther and me?"

"That was one of the reasons."

"Then you were all spies?"

"Not at all. The majority were all eminent men, with only a few agents slipped in. But we were all warned to keep an eye on visitors passing through. As you saw, Oaxaca is rather strategically situated for anyone going to or coming from Central America, and we collected our share of tourists—so called."

"Anyone interesting?"

"Yes and no. I'm afraid that, as an agent, I'm rather a loss," he said regretfully. "But there were two German engineers—very delightful fellows on their way back from Panama. They said there was no doubt that, with the latest technological advances, the Americans could build the canal, but it might be a very drawn out task considering the varied groups that would be down there. . . ." Gerard's voice trailed off, and they were both silent for several minutes.

"What a sickening business. Of course, I used to think it would be terribly exciting—like a lot of other things," Ophelie said.

"That's understandable. But it's not a profession for dabblers like Charles and me—"

"*Charles?*"

"Are you really *that* innocent?" he questioned, not unkindly. "Charles and Thea are in it all the way." Gerard got up and stood looking down at Ophelie with an adoring expression. "I want you to rest now, darling. I have some letters to take care of, but we'll have the whole night together—"

Gerard waited until he was certain Ophelie had fallen asleep before he left their suite and went down one floor to the de Renilles' rooms. He had to speak with Charles, give him information he should have passed on earlier. But, when he reached the suite, the doors were wide open and the only occupant was one of the maids.

"It's Angelita, isn't it?" he asked politely as a cold wave of apprehension passed over him. "Is Señor de Renille here?"

Angelita put down her feather duster. "No, señor, they've left. Gone back to the United States. Señora de Renille was supposed to come back from the hospital thi afternoon. But this morning, Señor de Renille had me pack up the rest of their clothes, thanked me for my service, and said they were going home tonight," she told him truthfully. In her eyes, he was as trustworthy as his wife was false.

Belatedly, Gerard saw how bare the suite was, stripped of all the de Renilles' personal possessions. He moved quickly, thanking Angelita profusely and handing her a generous tip.

Out in the corridor, he raced for the stairs; there was no time to spare for the lift. He had to get to his phone and call the Iturbide Hotel. Pray God that his friend was there, not out on some other wild goose chase.

Be there, he thought silently, taking the stairs two at a time. For once let something go right. Let me be of aid to Charles and Thea before it's too late. . . .

"Of course I'm hoping that, in your rush to get us on this train, you remembered what to pack," Thea said teasingly as they relaxed following a good dinner in the dining car in one of their two connecting staterooms on the Mexico City to Laredo train.

"How could I make any mistakes with the lists you made?" Charles smiled, leaning his head back against the rich blue plush upholstery. "They told me exactly what we'd need on the train, what was to be sent to the baggage car, what had to be shipped to New York, and what to leave behind." He folded his arms behind his head. "We'll probably be getting trunks and packages for the next three months."

"Oh, probably," Thea agreed. "But I don't care. We're on our way back across the border, and that's all that matters."

It was now nine at night and, in the past five hours, their life had been turned around in a way Thea still couldn't quite believe. She had been counting the hours

641

until this day and, when it had finally arrived, it hadn't been the way she'd expected.

Thea had been ready when Charles walked into her room promptly at four. There had been the nurses to thank, the maids to tip, flower arrangements to distribute among the other patients, and the good-luck charm to leave at Major Donovan's bedside, but twenty minutes later they were free to walk out of the American Hospital and go back to the Sanz—or so Thea had thought. Hernando was waiting with the motor car and, once they were under way, Charles confided his plans and, by the time he had finished explaining, they were at the Colonia Station.

So far, it had all been ridiculously easy, Thea realized now, hours later. No one was expecting them to simply pack up and leave, and the element of surprise was on their side. It didn't even appear that they were being followed. They had merely gotten out of the motor car, given Hernando a very fond farewell, proceeded through the stark, unattractive terminal, past the open gate, and onto the waiting train with nothing in their wake except several porters with their luggage.

"How nice of Jean-Christophe to think of taking two compartments," Thea said, as Mexico's varied and sometimes frightening landscape, now hidden by the dark cover of night, flashed by them. "It gives us so much more room."

"I'm afraid Jean-Christophe was thinking in terms of protection," Charles replied with a smile. "He said that if we were being followed, and the agent saw we had two compartments, he wouldn't be sure which one we were in."

"That sounds like a plot out of a penny dreadful," Thea laughed. "It's a good thing he'll be going back to college in January. A few more of those ghastly books with their purple tales of intrigue, not to mention the atmosphere in Mexico City, and he'd never be able to concentrate on literature, history and philosophy again!"

"I think that may be why his father is going to keep him at Georgetown for the spring semester. A reintroduction to the tough Jesuit educational system before he can go skylarking off to Yale or Princeton."

"Poor boy," Thea murmured, but her eyes were sparkling. "But enough of Jean-Christophe. I know we have all this space," she said, running her fingers over the fine wood grain of the panelling, "but I don't think that's any reason for us to be so far apart."

They were sitting directly across from each other.

"Is it . . . is it all right?" Charles asked, anxiety mingling with desire. "I wasn't sure what Dr. Benning might have told you—"

"Only that we can't swing from the chandeliers. But other than that, we have months and months and, as long as we omit gymnastics—"

Charles laughed and held out his arms to her. "Come here," he said and, for a few minutes, Thea sat across him. Together they slowly and lovingly rediscovered each other, kissing, touching and holding until she slipped out of his grasp and stood up.

"If you'll unhook me, we can both be a lot more comfortable," Thea promised, turning her back to him. "Particularly if we go next door. When we were going in to dinner, I asked the porter to make up the other compartment."

"You think of everything," Charles said, and his fingers were at the fastening of her Lucile day dress of pale tan wool and four rows of white chiffon frills on the sleeves.

Thea slipped out of the dress, placed it neatly on the seat, took off her beige calfskin shoes ornamented with beige grosgrain bows, put them beside the dress, and turned back to Charles.

643

"Five minutes," she said, and opened the connecting door.

In the other compartment, the lights had been turned on and their personal belongings scattered about, but here, in the second room, Thea found only the quiet, well-ordered air that staterooms on trains acquire when they're newly prepared for the night with fresh, crisp bed linen, warm blankets and only the comforting blue glow of the night light to provide illumination.

It was just enough light to see by and, by the time Thea finished undressing, her eyes had adjusted well enough so that she could remove her maquillage in the washing cubicle, put on a pink silk nightgown with insets of beige lace, and slip into bed without having to turn on a supplementary light.

Warmly covered by the blankets, she luxuriated in the cool feel of the sheets, and tried to hear what Charles might be doing in the next compartment, but the sounds of the train wheels on the track and the high-pitched hoot of the whistle drowned out all other noises.

Suddenly, Jean-Christophe's precautions didn't sound so amusing. Someone could be in there, hitting Charles over the head and looking for the letter and I'd never hear a thing, she realized with a sharp jolt of fear. All the danger she and Charles were now in dawned on Thea, and her heart began to pound in fright. Until they crossed the border on Thursday, anything was possible.

The connecting door clicked open and Charles, in pajamas and dressing gown, came over to her, sitting down on the bed with his usual easy grace.

"I'd almost forgotten how beautiful you are in bed," he whispered, bending over to press his mouth against the hollow at the base of her throat.

At his touch, her fears quieted and a delicious warmth began to spread through her. Her hands curved over his shoulders, holding on to him. "Until you came in, I was imagining the worst things," Thea whispered.

"I know." Charles raised his head. "We're still not out of danger and, every time I try to get us out of it, we fall in deeper. I'd have given anything to trade places with you for the past week. It should have been me down those stairs, not you."

"It's over," Thea whispered, comforting him. "I'm still having our baby, and we're finally on our way home. We've done what was expected of us, and we have nothing to look back on in shame."

Charles slipped off his dressing gown, lifted the covers, and slid in beside her. Slowly, he gathered Thea into his arms, and they lay together, silently reacquainting themselves with the closeness and warmth that the past week had deprived them of.

"*Pajamas?*" Thea asked in amusement a short time later. "You haven't worn them in months. In fact, I don't know how you ever came to buy them in the first place. You're simply not the pajama sort."

"I'm not, and they are quite a bother to get rid of in a hurry, but how I came to buy them is a story in itself. I was wandering through Brooks Brothers, about to go out to Cove House, trying to adjust to the idea of what I was getting into. Finally it dawned on me that I was walking through the store like a zombie, so I ended up buying a half a dozen pair of pajamas that I didn't need or want in order to make a graceful exit. When it turned out that no provisions had been made for separate bedrooms, they seemed to be a very wise purchase. Then, of course, not now," he added.

"Then why are you wearing them now?"

"Propriety."

"Funny." Thea's fingers were on the buttons of the pajama jacket. "Whatever am I going to do with you?"

"Just what you've been doing all along," he said as the last button came undone and her fingers trailed lightly

645

down the length of his chest. "Look how far we've both come since September. I think we're managing just fine," he finished thickly, his mouth finding hers, and then all the problems they'd left behind, and all the problems they were taking with them, faded into temporary unimportance.

From Mexico City to Tolucca to San Luis Potosi to Saltillo, the National Railways of Mexico train made its steady way north to the Rio Grande and Laredo. All Tuesday night and all day Wednesday, the scenery encompassed almost all of what Mexico's countryside had to offer. From snow-capped peaks to deep valleys to dry plains studded with the gigantic cactus plants that had held such a repulsive fascination for them on their trip down only six weeks before.

Now, at shortly after nine on Thursday morning, the train was gathering speed as it pulled out of Monterey. Only 167 miles from the border, this small and bustling city nestled in the fertile valley of the Santa Catarina River, like Oaxaca to the south and Chihuahua in the northwest, had a substantial American population. Under other circumstances, Thea and Charles might have broken their journey in this picturesque spot, taking a day or two to stay at the Hotel Continental and explore the single-towered cathedral and the newly completed Palacio de Gobierno. But these were not normal circumstances, short side trips were not on their schedule, and their only aim was to get to the other side of the Rio Grande and safety.

"Charles, do you really think that Major Donovan was going to return the letter you took?" Thea asked as they returned to their compartment following a breakfast neither could really enjoy. Why, Thea wondered miserably, had the last hours of this trip, instead of relaxing them, made them more tense?

646

"Unfortunately, I keep coming back to the same conclusion," Charles said regretfully as they sat down. "He was livid when I told him, and he must have decided that the best method was simply to get out of it. The man who assaulted him must have been an intermediary of some sort—a German agent would have either left him alone or killed him, no halfway jobs with them."

"As long as we haven't put the de Laulans in any danger—"

"Please—" Charles' expression became deeply troubled. "I don't like what I did, but it was the only possible solution I could come up with. I couldn't risk bringing it with us, the hotel safe wasn't any better and, if I mailed it, it could have been intercepted. Jean-Christophe was the best on a list of very poor choices. Funny, I hadn't even considered him until I got back to our suite and found him there, then it all fell into place."

"Then it was the right thing to do," Thea said reassuringly. "I'm sure that right now the letter is safe in the Belgian Legation, waiting for your cable of instructions."

"You're probably right, and I'm worrying over nothing," Charles replied, putting an arm around Thea's waist. "But I think that, after today, my life as a secret agent is over. Do you mind?"

"Not in the least," Thea said emphatically, resting her head on his shoulder. "And, since my exotic career as a personal courier to the President has reached its conclusion, we can consider this a mutual retirement." She cuddled closer. "It's getting later, isn't it?"

"Every minute."

"Oh, be serious!"

"I am." Charles checked his watch. "Nearly ten."

"Then it's time to get ready," Thea said, wondering why she didn't feel more enthusiastic. "Dress and makeup and all sorts of things men never have to worry about. While I do all those things, you can relax and read *The Monterey News*," she went on, referring to the English language newspaper Charles had purchased from a vendor who'd come on board during the Monterey stop. "But we *do* have one thing to decide."

"What's that?"

"Well," Thea said, injecting a light tone in her voice, "do we have an early lunch on the train, or a late one in Laredo?"

Gradually, the dry valleys dotted with cactus gave way to desolate plains studded with sorry-looking bushes and patches of yellowish grass, and then the train was rushing into the National Railways of Mexico Station at Nuevo Laredo, and the customs inspectors were coming on board.

It was Pullman passengers first, and those who held day coach tickets afterwards but, even so, they were prepared for a long wait. This wasn't their trip down in the de Veigas' private car. No special privileges here, they reminded each other. But, as almost everything else in Mexico, this final encounter was also not what they expected, and their luggage was checked over in the most cursory of fashions.

"*Adios, señor y señora, vaya usted con Dios,*" the courtly old customs inspector wished them as he left a few minutes later, and then a short time after that, the train was under way again, gathering more and more speed until it was going full throttle over the long steel bridge that spanned the Rio Grande and, still speeding, came into the Laredo station on a scream of brakes.

"It's over," Thea said in a voice of quiet amazement. "Our great adventure has come to an end."

"It's all so normal," Charles said as they left the train and entered the International and Great Northern Railway Station. "Look, porters are tending to luggage

648

people are waiting for their trains and a news kiosk is selling newspapers and chocolate bars. We've been thinking that we're so important and in such potential danger that half the German Embassy is after us, then we get to Laredo and see we're just two more travellers. If I suddenly got up on one of the benches in the waiting room and shouted that I'd taken a secret document from the German Embassy in Mexico City, that one man was nearly killed in an attempt to recover it, and that we had to leave because we were in great danger, no one would care."

"I wouldn't go quite so far in saying no one would care, but I *do* agree with you about everything else. This train station is just what we need—a good, strong dose of reality to put our lives back in perspective." Thea felt herself moving into a celebratory mood, and she was glad she'd changed into Lucile's cafe-au-lait taffeta suit with a four-flounce skirt trimmed in dark velvet ribbon and a blouse of soft cream lace under the bolero top. It might be a little formal to wear in a train station, but her old ebullience was returning, and she figured Laredo could do with a dash of haute couture.

"The station manager next?" Thea asked as they stopped at the kiosk to purchase that morning's *San Antonio Express*, two day old *St. Louis Globe-Democrat* and *Chicago Tribune* and, most valued of all, a three day old *New York Times*.

"That's our first stop, and then on to the hotel."

"Good, all of the sudden I'm absolutely famished!"

During dinner last night, they made their schedule. Today, Thursday, they would spend in Laredo, and on Friday morning would take the train to San Antonio, the six-hour journey bringing them there in time for tea. They would spend the weekend with Nela and Morgan, tell them all their adventures, and call on the Archbishop before catching Monday afternoon's Katy to St. Louis.

649

Another night's rest, this time at the Jefferson Hotel, was in order before they could board the Washington bound train.

The station manager was every bit as helpful as they knew he would be, placing his office at their disposal, ordering up their train tickets for San Antonio, personally telegraphing his opposite number in that city to prepare and have waiting their Katy tickets, and sending his office boy to the Western Union desk with the telegraph blanks they'd filled out—messages to Nela and Morgan in San Antonio, and Alix and Henry in New York; room requests at the Jefferson Hotel and Washington's Shoreham. Charles had sent the telegram reserving a suite at the St. Regis from Mexico City.

"We might not need that Washington hotel reservation," Thea pointed out a half hour later as they settled into their room at Laredo's Hotel Hamilton overlooking Jarvis Plaza. They'd already placed their order with room service for hot soup and sandwiches, a half bottle of white wine, and a pot of coffee—Thea remarking that, since dinner was early today, they were better off with a light lunch. Charles concurred and ordered accordingly, although he couldn't see why this Thursday dinner should be at a different time. "The Mileses may want us to house guest."

"Does that disturb you?"

"Not really. They have a stunning house—almost a mansion—on Sheridan Circle. But Jane is a bit of a—let's say meddler. She may ask you a lot of questions."

"Then I'll answer them." Charles laughed and sat down beside her on the overstuffed sofa, his arm stretching out along the back. "I'm different than I used to be, and I'll survive a day or two at the Mileses'. It will just be another new experience."

"Well, if it's new experiences you're after, we can make a side trip to Baltimore," Thea offered.

"Is there something of special interest there?"

"No, just Henry's cousin and his new wife."

Charles gave her a puzzled look. "Henry's cousin is the Earl of Vickford."

"The very same, but he's living in Baltimore now."

Somewhere in the depths of Charles' mind, a faint memory stirred. "Wasn't there some sort of scandal—that he was living in sin with some Irish girl?"

"According to Henry, it was quite a scandal in England about a year and a half ago when word got around that Anthony Thorpe was keeping his mistress in his family home. There's more, of course, but that's all Henry will say. Alix says he's absolutely silent on the rest of the details."

"I imagine so. After all, Tony committed the unpardonable sin of being found out," Charles said sympathetically.

"It isn't as if Helena weren't from a good family—her grandfather's a marquis—but people *do* love a scandal and, even though they did get married almost immediately afterwards, the best thing seemed to be for them to leave England until it all blows over—or until there's another great calumny."

"But why Baltimore?"

"For the same reason you went to New York—no one knows them there. And Baltimore society being what it is, no one cares. To them, Tony's a recently remarried widower with two young sons from his first marriage and a new wife who writes romance novels."

"Then we'll definitely have to pay them a visit," Charles said, laughing. "After all, there's nothing better than a newly married couple to provide inspiration."

"Oh, now you're getting the hang of it," Thea said, managing to kiss him as she laughed.

"I thought I already had the knack," Charles challenged, his hands going around her waist, his mouth closing over hers.

They were still laughing and cuddling on the sofa when Charles heard a sound behind them. "Room service," he said, turning. "We've been waiting for you. . . ."

His voice didn't trail off, it stopped cold, and Thea looked over Charles' shoulder toward the door, her blood chilling in her veins.

It wasn't the waiter from room service, it was the man from the top of the stairs at the German Embassy. The man who—accidentally or otherwise—had pushed her down the stairs. Now he stood just inside their room, observing them with a contemptuous expression in his pale, shifty eyes, a disdainful twist to his mouth—and with a gun in his hand.

"Who the hell are you?" Charles asked a moment later in an even voice that didn't betray the sudden rush of shock and surprise at the fact that he and Thea, instead of being safe, were now hostages. Even as he spoke, all his cool logic rose to the surface, and he moved slightly so that his body was shielding Thea's.

"Oh, let's just say I'm someone who has been watching both of you with a great deal of interest. Now I know I'm not the person you've been expecting—he's not the sort who ever handles this end of it. But on the other hand I've been looking forward to finally making your acquaintance, Mr. de Renille," he said, his British accent rather ragged around the edges. His gaze shifted to encompass Thea. "You don't remember me, do you, Mrs. de Renille?"

"How nice—you're holding a gun on us, and you expect me to play parlor games," Thea remarked with icy incredulity, still not quite believing she and Charles were in this situation.

"As long as we're your hostages, you might use whatever remains of your good manners and introduce yourself," Charles said in a dangerous voice.

"I thought your wife might save me the trouble of these tiresome social duties but, like most women, it's obvious she retains no memory of a person if they're of no use to her."

Charles' hand pressed down on Thea's, both for reassurance, and to silently signal her to let his derogatory remark pass.

"—we met briefly in London two years ago," he went on.

"You're Arthur Coburn," Thea said, and suddenly it all came flooding back to her—the gossip about the Foreign Office official who was so interested in his superior's wife, and the hushed-up scandal of what had happened late one Friday night in June at Tantley Hall, the Buckinghamshire home of the Earl and Countess of Saltlon. She knew the truth behind the rumors from Alix, who had them direct from Cecily Saltlon but, in those late June-early July days of 1902, just back from Budapest, Dresden and Amsterdam, and about to return to New York to open her business, all the intrigue about how the British Foreign Office was coping with the fact that some of its bright young men were rather chummy with certain individuals from Berlin, had gone straight over her head.

Until now.

"Thank you for remembering, Miss Harper. Correction—Madame de Renille," he said with a gallantry that Thea recognized as false. "And now that our pleasantries have been concluded. . . . The letter please, Mr. de Renille."

Charles looked past the ominous barrel of the Smith and Wesson revolver to the thin-faced, narrow-mouthed man in the suit that had once been a fine piece of Savile Row workmanship, but now showed the debilitating effect the tropics had on clothes. He was a nondescript entity, perfect for the shadow world of espionage because he was so unmemorable. Here was a weak man with any number of faults and bad tendencies ready to be exploited by another person, Charles decided.

When a weak man gets power, he becomes a bully, Charles remembered from somewhere, and centuries of de Renille breeding rose up in him.

"Why should I? I haven't come this far with it to hand it over to you."

"This gun should convince you to do otherwise," Arthur replied grimly, pointing it directly at Charles' heart.

"The Hamilton is a rather small hotel," Charles said conversationally. "Shoot us and you'll never make it to the lobby. Texans as a group might not care too much about foreign matters, but cold-blooded murder is quite another situation."

"I don't want to hurt either of you," Arthur Coburn declared, his hand holding the gun not wavering, "but I've come close to murder once and, after that, the act ceases to be frightening."

"Then you attacked Major Donovan," Thea said. To her own amazement, she felt oddly calm and, like Charles, she was determined to keep their captor talking as long as possible.

A smile played around his thin lips. "It was all an accident, of course. I didn't plan to hurt him any more than I meant to push you down the stairs at the German Embassy. In your case, the mishap provided the distraction I needed to escape but, as for your major, I didn't mean to hit him on the head as hard as I did, but he was such a *fractious* man—"

"Was he going to give you the letter?"

"Of course he was, my dear Mr. de Renille!" He gave an unpleasant laugh. "Naturally, you saw yourself as doing some sort of monumental good deed when you took

654

the letter. No—don't tell me how. You amateurs always think you're so clever. But it doesn't work like that at all. Whenever an embassy let us say *loses* an important document, they simply let it be known on the grapevine that they want it returned—no questions asked."

"And all is forgiven," Charles muttered.

"Ra-ther," Coburn seconded and, for a moment, Thea felt that this whole incident had taken on the tinge of a debate between two British university graduates.

"Did you really think I would have given Donovan the letter if I'd seen you standing beside him?"

"Oh, no. I was going to stay further along the bridle path and keep well out of sight until you were gone. I decided to introduce myself beforehand. That was a mistake. Your major didn't take to me, told me to get out of his sight, that he didn't want to have to lay eyes on me one more time than he had to."

"Is that why you hit him?"

"He started by saying that he didn't want to deal with intermediaries, wanted to know why someone from the German Embassy wasn't there. He pounced on me, then started to shout, and I had to keep him quiet, so I used this—" He indicated the revolver with his free hand. "I honestly didn't mean to hit him so hard."

"You said that before."

"And I said something else before. The letter. I'm going to be very well paid for giving it back to its rightful owner."

Throughout this entire incident, Charles had been on the lookout for an opening, and now he had it. Arthur Coburn wasn't a traitor in the normal sense of the word. Obviously, for all he cared, England and Germany could tear each other to pieces and the United States could have a civil war on its hands from the disruptions among the canal crews as long as he collected the money he got for selling stolen information. And as Charles heard his stream of complaints of how poorly the Germans paid for the information he'd given them, he observed their room. The Hamilton's manager had described it as one of the hotel's "select" rooms with an area arranged as a small sitting room, the bed set into an alcove and the bathroom and dressing room beyond that. The alcove was a place of safety, but they were trapped on the sofa. Then Charles saw that the door had remained partially open. When he'd stepped into the room, Arthur had pushed it with his foot, but it hadn't closed all the way.

If only someone would pass in the hall, he thought, and wondered about their room service waiter. No, we don't need another person involved—no innocent bystander hurt by accident. I can get us out of this if only he doesn't actually want to read the letter before leaving—

"Guenther could get more money for me if he wanted," Arthur went on, "they fall all over him at the embassy. He's their fair-haired boy, but I wonder what they'd say if they knew about some of his private proclivities. Guenther likes his women very, very willing, you see. Very willing for all sorts of things that I can't mention in front of a lady," he finished with a mock bow at Thea.

"So you're going to ransom the letter," Thea hazarded. To her own surprise, her fright suddenly lessened. The sight of the revolver chilled her to the bone but, somewhere deep inside her, she knew he wasn't going to shoot them. "What are you going to do? Offer it to the American Embassy, tell them that they can now have, for a sizable fee, what was almost theirs for free?"

"The ultimate irony," he agreed. "Your major, who is no gentleman, developed the instincts of one at the wrong time. How he went on that the United States government doesn't open other people's mail. But, in forty-eight hours, I'm going to auction off this letter to

656

the highest bidder—Berlin or Washington—and then never have to worry about money again. I can go to—" He broke off and looked squarely at Charles. "The letter—and believe me, this is the last time I intend to ask. Give it to me, and I'll go. After all, who is going to believe your story? No one at all," he smirked, and held out his free hand.

Out of the corner of his eye, Charles saw what he hadn't quite let himself believe would happen. He knew he was approaching the apex of the moment as the nearly closed door began to open wider and wider.

Carefully, he opened his suit jacket and held out one side to show the envelope in the inside pocket. If he could only get Arthur to bend over—

"Give it to me," Coburn snapped, and Charles' heart sunk. It wasn't going to be easy this way. Shifting so that his body completely blocked Thea's, he held out the envelope bearing the crest of the German Embassy.

Charles had sealed the envelope shut, and there was no way Arthur Coburn could open it with the gun in one hand. He looked in anger from the envelope to Charles and back again, but he had no more time to waste and, with his precious treasure, he began to move backwards.

"Thank you for your hospitality," he began, a smile twisting on his lips. Then he reached for a doorknob that wasn't there.

It was over as unexpectedly as it had begun. The tall, ginger-haired man Thea knew from the Monte de Pledad stepped over the threshold and, moving as stealthily as a cat despite his slight limp, came up behind Arthur Coburn and dropped an arm over his chest, effectively pinning his arms. Coburn still held the gun, but Charles sprang forward to pull the revolver out of his hand and, for a moment, the three men were locked in a very uneven struggle.

Charles was hampered by the Smith and Wesson he

now held and, seeing this, Thea jumped off the sofa, took the revolver from her husband's hand, and moved a few steps back to take aim.

Thea hated guns but she knew how to use one and, on Arthur Coburn, who was putting up more of a fight than she would have imagined he was capable of, she would have no hesitation about using it. Or so she thought.

It was almost unbelievable but he had broken away from both men trying to restrain him and, with one wild dash, he made toward the door that was now wide open. In a second he was over the threshold and out of sight.

Quietly, Thea watched as Charles retrieved the envelope from the floor, and the ginger-haired Englishman picked up the walking stick he'd propped against the wall. She placed the Smith and Wesson revolver on an end table.

"I guess I'm not as cold-blooded as I think I am," Thea said, putting her arms around Charles. "I had a chance to shoot at him and I didn't . . . or couldn't."

"I'm glad you didn't, Mrs. de Renille. I know you have good reason to want to put a hole in Arthur Coburn—certainly he's skittish enough to have done the same to you and Mr. de Renille. I might have been very tempted to do the same thing myself," he admitted, and then smiled slightly. "I've just realized we've never been properly introduced. I'm Basil Summerfield, and you may not know me, but—"

"But if your wife is Lady Anne Summerfield, I may know *her*," Thea interjected.

"Then we are at least on familiar ground."

"I'm glad that we all have some social contact in common," Charles put in as he and Basil shook hands, "but aren't you concerned that your quarry got away?"

"He doesn't have the letter."

"And neither do I," Charles grinned. "It's the envelope I took from the German Embassy, but the pages inside are blank. At this moment, the real letter is safe in the Belgian Legation."

"I think we'd all better sit down and tell our individual stories," Thea advised. "Whatever happened to our room service order, do you think?"

"It should be here momentarily," Basil said. "Your waiter came along just as I was about to make my move. I told him to wait until we had this whole incident settled, and then bring enough food for three. I'm afraid I've taken the liberty of inviting myself to have lunch with you."

"*We?*" Charles asked, pointedly ignoring the rest of Basil's remarks as they sat down. "Thea and I thought you were alone out there."

"When I came through the doorway, yes, but outside, stationed at either end so there was no chance of his getting away, were several Texas Rangers. I daresay Arthur's about to receive his first taste of American justice via the Laredo jail. That'll keep him until—" He broke off and smiled brightly. "Ah, here's our lunch. I took the additional liberty of substituting a bottle of champagne for your white wine."

There was a pleasant pause as the waiter served the cream of tomato soup, set out the chicken salad sandwiches, and opened and poured the champagne. Charles signed the check, waving away Basil's suggestion that this should be on the British Foreign Office, and the waiter left, leaving behind his trolley with their coffee and dessert on it.

"You must let me buy you dinner tonight," Basil insisted as they ate.

"Your offer is accepted—provided you tell us as much about your mission as possible," Charles said.

"Absolutely," Thea put in. "All of this might be normal to you, but to us the idea that we're sitting and eating a nice meal when only twenty minutes ago a man was holding a gun on us is an experience in the absurd that I can live without."

"Believe it or not, I feel the same way," Basil smiled, "only I've been at this cat and mouse game longer than either of you. I had quite a task avoiding you in London this summer, Mrs. de Renille."

"It's Thea. And why did you have to avoid me?"

"So that I wouldn't be identifiable to you, should our paths cross in Mexico City. We knew that President Roosevelt had used you as a courier and was going to do so again. At the time, it was simply a precaution. I had no idea that our paths would cross quite as closely as they did."

"You were on the train to Laredo with us?" Charles inquired.

"As was Arthur. He was following you and I was following him."

"In order to watch over us." Charles shook his head. "It's an act vaudeville wouldn't touch with a barge pole."

"Very farcical, I agree. But let me start at the beginning, which, oddly enough, is two summers ago. I handle rather sensitive documents in my position at the Foreign Office and, through a series of incidents I needn't go into, I gradually became aware that Arthur Coburn, who was one of my subordinates at the time, was passing information—some of it classified, some of it not—to Guenther von Basedow at the German Embassy in London. I had what I thought was a foolproof plan to put an end to him. Arthur is a heavy gambler, and not a winning one either, and he has a taste for very pretty, very expensive women. I confided my problem to my wife, and Anne volunteered to be of aid—"

Thea's mind flew back to the coronation summer, to her arrival in London, to the parties she'd attended where the lovely Lady Anne Summerfield was always escorted by Arthur Coburn, never by her husband who was always said to be "busy at the Foreign Office."

"It was very brave of your wife to help you as she did," Thea told Basil. "It caused quite a bit of gossip."

"Even more so when Anne found out that she was finally going to have a baby. It was ours, of course. Arthur never got *that* close to her," he explained, more for Charles' benefit than Thea's. "Fortunately, we had enough to end Guenther von Basedow's operations in England, and we reassigned Arthur to South America."

"Is that always how it's done?" Charles questioned, wishing he didn't have this feeling of bitterness washing through him. Espionage, when run by gentlemen, was hampered by the rules gentlemen always lived by. "No scandal at any cost?"

"Unfortunately. We transferred him to Brazil. We thought he couldn't do much harm in Rio but we were wrong. Last January, we got word that he had simply walked into the Embassy one morning, turned in his notice, and disappeared. For three months, there was nothing, and then reports began to come in that Coburn was turning up at some of our more remote outposts, offering to help out with translations, picking the brains of senior officials, and then moving on."

"But how did he come to Mexico City?" Charles wanted to know.

"By rail through Central America," Basil replied almost whimsically. "We can definitely place him at Colon on May 4, the day the Compagnie Nouvelle transferred the canal works from France to the United States. Whatever else he is, Arthur isn't stupid, and he must have kept his eyes and ears open while he was there, picking up all sorts of information that he knew would prove useful to him at a later date. He must have found out that his old partner-in-crime was in Mexico City, and off he went. Guenther von Basedow is some sort of secret agent for the Kaiser and, wherever he's assigned, you can be sure he's either taking some sort of mischief with him, or planning trouble for some later date."

"They probably kept in touch somehow," Charles pointed out. "But if Arthur had changed his center of interest from his own country to the United States, how do *you* fit into it? Or were you on his trail from the South American incidents?"

Basil nodded and rubbed his beard. "We were running around in circles, but once we knew he had settled in Mexico City, my superior, Sir Ernest Garland, sent me over. In fact, except for Ernest and my wife, no one knows where I am. I never established any contact with my own embassy in Mexico City," he told them, and then related the events of his arrival in the capital. "Your Major Donovan was a great help to me."

"*Him?*" Thea interrupted incredulously. "He was going to return the letter!"

"That's exactly how we wanted it played," Basil smiled. "I'd been trying in pin Arthur for weeks, but I have both of you to thank for bringing him out in the open."

"Our afternoon at the Monte de Pledad," Charles said, remembering the man on the patio. "He overheard our conversation."

"I think he might have had his eye on you before that day. You're both young, wealthy, attractive, and deeply in love—not the sort people ignore."

"Now I know who was following us on Election Night!" Thea exclaimed. "I suppose he disabled our motor car also. Or don't you know about that?"

"Oh, I knew, and even though it's of little comfort to you now, you and Charles weren't in any danger. We've been keeping a rather close eye on you."

"But what happened at Chapultepec Park?" Charles insisted. "If you and Major Donovan had it all planned out, how did he end up with a fractured skull?"

"By playing his part a bit too well. He was supposed to grouse about Arthur, but I expect he chewed on the scenery and inadvertently caused his own predicament," Basil said, and then told them the rest of the story. How Gerard de Langlade, who was an old friend of

Basil's, and whose archaeological expedition included men who had interests other than simply uncovering ancient artifacts, had called him at the Iturbide Hotel to tell him that the de Renilles were leaving on the five o'clock train.

"I made it with about ten minutes to spare and, when I found that Arthur was also on board, I sent a cable from Saltillo, asking that I be met in Laredo by the Texas Rangers."

"But what happens now?" Thea asked, surprised by the net of protection that had been stretched around them, impressed by Basil's abilities, proud of Charles' actions this afternoon, and very, very glad that it was now over.

"Well, he *has* been arrested—for breaking and entering and threatening two American citizens with a loaded gun. I'm sorry I had to stretch the truth a bit about your citizenship, Charles, but I was sure you'd understand under the circumstances."

"Don't think twice about it," Charles said reassuringly. "As long as he's behind bars and we won't have to look at him again."

"Never fear. You *will* have to sign a complaint against him, but that can wait until tomorrow morning. You won't have to wait around for a trial, though. We have people in Washington who'll be coming to collect him. Extradition and things like that," he said in a vague voice from which Thea and Charles could tell that, from then on, the matter had nothing to do with them.

"So this is it," Charles said. "For a while, Thea and I were worried that we really hadn't been of any service, hadn't fulfilled the promise we'd made."

"Oh, no," Basil protested, "never feel like that! You care, you try and you believe. That counts for more than anyone will ever admit to."

"Are you glad this is over, Basil?" Thea questioned with a touch of amusement. "Or, on those days at the

Foreign Office, when it's nothing but boring meetings and over-written reports, are you going to miss the past weeks?"

"Not the broken ankle," Basil replied as he and Charles traded comprehending looks. "But, if you mean the way of life out of *Boys' Own Adventure*, no, I won't, not really. My home and my family mean more to me than skulking through Mexico City in my bearded disguise. It *was* fun—on and off, but not as a way of life, and every real man knows that."

"Thea equates our playing secret agents as a subset of wanting to run away with the circus when we were ten."

"She's probably right," Basil observed with a smile. "And now I think the time has come for me to finally get rid of my last disguise. The hotel barber awaits me. And then I'll visit the jail to make sure all is going well there. Now, what time is dinner?"

"Five," Thea said emphatically as Basil groaned.

"That's barbaric!"

"Not today. It's a very special meal."

"At five o'clock?"

"Just for today," Thea said, all her natural ebullience returning. "Really, Basil, are you going to sit there and tell me you have no idea how important this Thursday is?"

"Be careful," Charles warned with a deep smile. "I think we both messed up on an important American celebration."

"Oh, there's my brilliant French husband." Thea tucked her arm through Charles', and beamed across at an amused Basil seated in the armchair, sipping a cup of coffee. "There *is* a celebration today and, considering what we've all been through in the past seventy-two hours, our dinner is going to be *very* appropriate. After all, today is Thanksgiving!"

Chapter Twenty

All in all, their house warming had been an enormous success, Thea decided as she surveyed the dining room table with a pleased smile. Only four short hours earlier, the French Directoire table that they'd purchased at the Monte de Pledad, both its leaves firmly in place, had been raced with a snowy damask cloth and a centerpiece that was a Flora Danica soup tureen—their wedding present from the Roosevelts—filled with red and white Rubrum lies and statice. But now, shortly before midnight, only crumbs remained from the buffet, proving beyond a doubt that when forty well-dressed, well-educated men and women are faced with a table of extravagant desserts, they immediately turn into street urchins let loose in a candy store.

She had lovingly arranged the desserts around the table so that the guests wouldn't have any trouble reaching them. But even in her wildest flights of fancy, Thea couldn't have imagined their friends' eventual action.

The *buche de Noel*, the richly frosted and decorated chocolate logs that no French Christmas was complete without, had gone over so well that the two extra cakes, baked just in case, had been devoured as well. The marquise au chocolat, made according to Ghiselle de

Laulan's recipe, had proved equally popular, as had the cold apricot souffle. Large crystal bowls that only a short time before had been heaped with chocolate and lemon mousse and whipped cream were now scraped clean, as were the Limoges custard cups that had held the *pots d' creme au cafe*. They had decided no party was complete without ice cream, and Dean's, the city's popular caterer had sent over two young men who'd spent the evening turning out a rich vanilla ice cream that the guests had immediately doused in Grand Marnier custard sauce.

But now the party was over, and all that was left was an uncountable pile of dessert plates, silver ice cream dishes, forks, spoons, and crumpled-up napkins. The once-pristine tablecloth was dotted with samples of every confection and several damp splotches made by the champagne.

Even with the beautifully arranged table reduced to crumbs and dirty dishes, the dining room was perfect, Thea concluded as she let her gaze move over the finely proportioned eighteen by twenty foot room. In here, as in the rest of the apartment, the walls were lacquered ivory white, a perfect backdrop for the rooms she and Charles were furnishing with such love and care. In fact, so far this was the only room that was completely ready with its Persian rug woven in old ivory, rose, and yellow, laid on the floor, curtains of soft rose silk at the windows that overlooked 62nd Street, and a small rock crystal chandelier suspended from the ceiling. The fruitwood chairs with rose silk seats looked as if they had come with the table. At Sloane's they had found two satinwood side tables for contrast, and a fine Impressionist painting of a summer garden finished the room.

Enough for tonight, Thea told herself firmly. Tomorrow morning the maids will come back, and I can send the tablecloth over to Alix, and she'll have Mrs. Land take the stains out. Go and find Charles.

There were two sets of French doors in the dining room and, after Thea switched off the lights, she went through the pair that led to the small, square hallway rather than the drawing room. Her Lucile gown of pale pink chiffon with a skirt of three tiered ruffles edged in deep pink narrow ribbons rustled softly as she glanced into the reception room that served to divide the apartment, separating the drawing room/library and the dining room from the bedrooms. For a minute she stood on the threshold, imagining the room from her guests' view as they'd come off the elevator, into the semi-private hall, and through the front door hung with a Della Robbia wreath.

The reception room was small, glossy, and almost jewel-box-like with the inlaid parquet floor rubbed to a high gloss, a reproduction Baltimore Hepplewhite sofa covered in a dramatic-looking black chintz splashed with pink peonies placed against one wall, while another was the backdrop for a two-drawer beechwood bombe chest with a silver bowl filled with red carnations and holly on the top and a mirror framed in black and gold enamel hung above it.

"Do you want to know what I've just realized?" Thea said a moment later as she stepped into the combination drawing room/library that was a full forty-eight feet long and twenty feet wide, and looked at Charles who sat at a Louis XV carved giltwood and marquetry gaming table with cabriole legs ending in hoofed feet. It was in this room that their friends, between forays at the dessert table, had gathered to eat and drink champagne and, for a change of pace, pluck gold-foil wrapped marrons glaces—ordered via Maison Glass from Debauve and Gallais—that they'd placed in Lalique crystal ash trays and set on various end tables. "That we've just finished opening up all our wedding presents and, on Sunday morning, it's Christmas and we can start all over again!"

"Please," Charles groaned in mock dismay. "I've just about recovered from that stockpile of presents waiting for us when we got to the St. Regis."

"Oh, look who's complaining. I'm the one with writer's cramp!"

"Well, it doesn't show. Why don't you come over here and keep me company and we can review our forces. Everyone's gone," he told her. "I've paid and tipped the men from Dean's, tipped the servants we borrowed from our friends, and sent Mrs. MacKay home," Charles finished, referring in the last instance to their new cook the only help they'd hired so far and who, like Alix's Mrs Wiley who had recommended her, was employed on a daily basis. "We're alone at last."

"Sometimes the best part of the party is just after your friends have gone home," Thea said as she walked across their wool pile Chinese rug of blue and cream. Woven in Tientsin, the pattern included roundels with stags and cranes which represent longevity, and scattered butter flies, the symbol of great age. The rug buyer that Thea depended on at Sloane's hadn't failed them. And, when it had been laid the length of the room, they had been astounded by its beauty. A beauty no less dimmed because of the furniture now resting on it. "Is this all that's left of our dessert feast?" Thea asked, amused, as she sat down opposite Charles. "Half a dozen pet fours?"

"And this bottle of the Moet," Charles added indicating the bottle resting on the silver tray along with the small cakes.

"No more marrons glaces? The boxes in the kitchen are empty."

"There *have* to be some left. If you check the ash tray I'll find two clean glasses, and then we can relax together."

"Charles, before you go—" Thea's voice took on

very concerned tone. "Did it *really* work for us tonight, or is it just that our friends accepted a house warming in an apartment that isn't finished yet because we stuffed them with sweets?"

Charles shook his head and took her hands in his. "Why are you worried now?" he laughed, looking at her from across the gaming table. "I think we inadvertently became the party of the holiday season, and we'll probably have to do it every year. I can't remember the last time I saw so many people having such a good time."

"Well, you're right about that," Thea admitted, her belated case of hostess' apprehension easing. "This is the first time I can remember that Dick North, unless he's at the dinner table, stopped chain-smoking at a party."

"Consider that your vindication, then," Charles said. "I'm off to search down two unused champagne glasses."

"Try the last case in the dining room pantry in the Tiffany box," Thea advised. "One of my clients sent us a dozen champagne glasses. I didn't think we'd need them tonight, so I just put them away."

While Charles went for the glasses, Thea took the tray holding the bottle of champagne and the petit fours and moved from her chair beside the gaming table to one of the sofas. With the practiced ease of a woman who knows her own home down to the last dinner napkin, she checked the Lalique ash trays, rescuing the remaining marrons glaces from among the discarded gold-foil wrappers and, turning off all the lights except the one by the sofa they would be using, she sat down to wait for Charles.

Exactly one month ago, they had been on the Laredo train, and tonight they were in their own home. In a way, it was still incredible and unbelievable but, in a deeper and more important way, the life they wanted to build and share was moving in the right direction.

Originally, she and Charles had planned to give this

party in January or February, but Thea had wanted to entertain during the pre-Christmas season pointing out that, if they waited until the apartment was totally complete, their house warming would take place *next* Christmas.

Kicking off her pink satin shoes, Thea reclined on the sofa's soft ice-blue silk damask upholstery and admired the Childe Hassam landscape that Alix and Henry had given them as their wedding present. They'd hung the soft painting by the noted American Impressionist in an honored place and, as she looked at it, Thea relaxed, not tired any longer, not even introspective, just very, very happy.

Thea and Charles had returned to New York on December 6th, and had gone straight to the St. Regis Hotel, living there for the next fifteen days in an elegant fifth floor suite replete with Louis XVI furniture covered in beige silks and rose satins, an impressive tapestry hanging from the wall of the sitting room, a working marble fireplace with a bronze Venetian clock on the mantel, a bed draped in cloth of gold, and silver-mounted bath equipment in the marble-walled bathroom. Rudolph Haan, the St. Regis' proprietor, had personally welcomed them when they arrived at the hotel from the Congressional Limited; Chef Emil Bailly had wanted to know if there were any dishes to be specially prepared; and whenever they dined in, headwaiter Elie Herbomez gave them the best table in the restaurant with its ornamental bronze ceiling.

If Charles had been surprised to find the apartment already painted the exact shade they wanted and the floors polished to a high gloss, just waiting for the rugs to be laid and the furniture moved in, and amazed at how quickly they were actually able to move from the St. Regis into 667 Madison Avenue, he was absolutely speechless at the amount of wedding present

670

they received.

Besides the paintings, mirrors, porcelain and glass given them by their friends and family, there had been the presents from a wide range of acquaintances. Nearly always silver, and almost all coming from Tiffany's, they included ivory-handled chafing dishes, wine buckets, ash trays, water pitchers, mustard pots, picture frames, grape scissors, clocks, and chocolate pots.

In between the little dinner parties given for them, and the nights they dined alone, there had been new shows to catch up on. On their very first night back in New York they had gone with Henry and Alix to the opening of the comic musical *It Happened In Nordland* at Lew Fields' Theatre, they had also found time to see *Humpty Dumpty* at the New Amsterdam Theatre, and to take in Ethel Barrymore's thrilling performance in *Sunday* at the Hudson Theatre.

"What *are* you smiling about?" Charles inquired with an amused smile as he returned with two tulip-shaped champagne glasses that he promptly filled with champagne. "You look thoroughly pleased with yourself."

"I am," she said, accepting one of the glasses. "And now, a toast. To you—and to *Century Magazine* for having the wisdom and good sense to buy all your articles and ask for three more besides!"

Charles laughed and kissed her. "I honestly never thought my articles would ever be accepted by such a prestigious magazine," he admitted, "but, as long as we're making toasts, I think we should drink to the officer of Morgan's Bank who's being transferred to Paris, and is renting the house my Uncle Pierre left me. Now, I'm the first to admit the rents demanded on the Avenue Montaigne are high, but what he'll be paying us is straight to the sky."

"Which means that, by New York standards, it's a reasonable fee. But he and his family will be happy, and we're happy, and," Thea said carefully, curling up beside Charles, putting an arm around his middle, "that if we sit here toasting all the good luck we've had, we'll be here until dawn."

"In that case, we can enjoy the remains of our party—a lone bottle of champagne, six petit fours, and ten marrons glaces."

"Now we know the price of being a successful host and hostess," Thea smiled as they nibbled at the last of the treats. "But, unless the telephone rings, it's just us until tomorrow morning."

"Seven or eight hours to relax and recoup."

"Really?" Thea tried to pretend surprise. "I was thinking more along the lines of pleasure and passion."

In the soft light, Charles' eyes darkened slightly, a sign Thea knew as a clear signal that he felt as she did. With a soft laugh, she kissed him under one ear, and was rewarded as he pulled her across his lap, his arms closing tightly around her.

"I didn't want to overtire you," he whispered, his face buried in her hair.

"I'm never tired of you . . . I want you all the time . . . it's even more intense than it was in the beginning, if that's possible . . . a side effect of pregnancy . . ."

"Better than morning sickness."

"Oh—much," she gasped, and then, "Yes, again, just like that," as his hands swept over her sensitive breasts to her waist, and then repeated the motion in the opposite direction.

She arched against him, her fingers weaving into his hair as she found his warm mouth, his desire increasing as she pressed closer and closer against him, their clothes becoming very unwelcome barriers to fulfillment.

"Do yourself," Thea whispered as Charles' hand paused at the tiny hooks and eyes. "I can get m own dress off—''

A minute later, their clothes were discarded on the sofa, and Charles gently lowered Thea onto the soft wool of the carpet, his hands and mouth moving adoringly over every inch of her. Fully dressed, Thea didn't look at all pregnant, but nude the first changes that her body would eventually undergo had made their appearances, and the new firmness of her bosom and the increased roundness of her natural curves increased the erotic sensations of their lovemaking.

Closing her eyes, Thea abandoned herself to Charles, drawing her fingers down his spine to the sensitive small of his back, tracing circles around each vertebra as he pressed into her.

With the deep, rich pile of the carpet beneath her, and Charles' possessive body above her, Thea lost all track of time and sense of place. The luxury apartment building that was their home ceased to be real, as did their own apartment, and even the room they were in with its large Christmas tree of green balsam decorated with treasured ornaments, peppermint canes and strings of popcorn and topped by a Lalique glass figure of *Pere Noel* that Solange had sent them, seemed to vanish. Charles' soft hair brushing against the side of her face, his mouth at the side of her throat, his body intimately against hers, and his pulsing, welcome invasion were the only realities. She was his and he was hers and, as their world soared around them, spinning them into a web of pleasure and sensation, it was the ultimate reaffirmation of their love.

There was no fire in the marble fireplace tonight and, between the faint hiss of steam coming from the radiator and the heat generated by their bodies, one wasn't necessary as they lay side by side, completed and content.

Charles was on his back, his swirling senses slowly returning to normal. They belonged together so perfectly and yet, each time together was a revelation, he thought.

He was aware of Thea's body alongside his, aware of her ripening perfection, glad that she had told him about her pregnancy as soon as she suspected so that he could see every change that took place in her from the first.

Next Christmas, he thought as his peripheral vision registered Thea sitting up and reaching past him, their baby would be five months old and they would hold it up to the tree so it could touch the ornaments and—

A cold stream of liquid being poured over his belly brought him rudely out of his pleasant thoughts of impending fatherhood and he yelped in surprise. Thea had ever so carefully poured her champagne into his navel and now she bent over him, licking up the golden liquid and laughing at the same time.

"I've wanted to do that for so long," she said, resting her cheek against his champagne-streaked skin.

"And I want to do this," he said, pulling her up to him for a kiss.

"You're wonderful," she said, smoothing back his hair.

"So are you, but there are times I think that, if I try to tell you how happy you make me, I'll cry for joy."

Together they sat up, leaning back against the sofa, cuddling close together as they looked out the wide windows framed by blue silk curtains.

"It's snowing," Thea said, entwining her legs with his. "And sometimes I think that, if I try to tell you what our life together means to me, I'll sound so inane you'll wonder why you ever fell in love with me in the first place."

"Oh, no," Charles' eyes glowed with love. "Never that. But how did I ever get so lucky as to find you?"

"We're made for each other—in every way. So why don't you just relax and enjoy it?"

"As long as you promise not to pour champagne on me again."

"No such promise, lover." Thea's eyes took in every inch of him. "One of these days, I'm going to pour a whole bottle of champagne over you and kiss it all off . . . but I'm not going to tell you when!"

"I'll risk that—as long as it's not after a party like the one we just gave!"

"Oh, we'll get used to entertaining—I hope. Look at Alix. Henry swears that their guests are under instructions to eat the food, get on with each other, and pull their own weight in the conversation—or else!"

"That's the only way to do it," Charles said, recalling his own first night at the Thorpes' dinner table.

"I agree, but we still have the adjustment to make. It's one thing to be a guest and quite another to find that, once you're married, all your friends expect you to reciprocate in style!"

"And you do it grandly," Charles assured her. "I can just imagine what you'll do with a full scale dinner party."

"But not quite yet," Thea laughed, with a glance at her still-flat stomach. "Oh, we'll give intimate dinners for eight or ten friends, but nothing overpowering until next fall. I know—we'll give one in honor of your mother, but tonight's party served as our last attempt at en masse entertaining until then."

"'This night we held an old accustomed feast, where to we have invited many a guest such as we love,'" Charles quoted. "Your Dr. Benning told me Shakespeare has words for every occasion."

"He was right. We did have only people we love here tonight. I wish Daddy were back from Egypt. I know you would have been so proud if some of your family were here, but everyone we invited means something to us. No invitations out of obligation from us."

"I loved being host in our own home, welcoming our friends, and knowing that we're welcome in their homes in return—"

"Our home," Thea said softly, caressing his face. "It's almost like saying our love. Every time you say it, my heart spills over with joy."

Charles' eyes searched her face. "That feeling works both ways. It's as if I've been searching for this place in time all my life. France is my heritage and my background, and the home of my family whom I love with all my heart but, when I became a man, it ceased to be *my* home. I wandered for years and then, when I thought I'd lost it all, I came to New York. I had to find myself again and, when I did that, I was ready to find you. You're my home, Thea, the only one I'll ever want."

Outside, the snow was falling in thick flakes and, by dawn, Madison Avenue, along with the rest of the city, would be a solid blanket of perfect white. But, in the building on the corner of 61st Street, in the only apartment still showing light, Thea Harper de Renille moved closer into her husband's arms.

"Welcome home, Charles, my darling, my love, welcome home."

Epilogue

667 Madison Avenue
New York
July, 1905

Life has taught us that love does not consist in gazing at each other but in looking outward together in the same direction.

Antoine De Saint-Exupery

July 31, 1905

"Are there *really* fifteen rooms in this apartment, Thea?" Solange de Renille questioned as she relaxed on a small sofa covered in the pink jewelled fabric that Thea had purchased in Budapest three summers ago.

"Of course there are," Thea assured her mother-in-law from her lacquer-white four-poster bed draped in rose-pink China silk. The bedroom Thea and Charles shared was all cream and pink, with fine white silk muslin curtains lined in the same material as the bed hangings; mostly white furniture, either painted or of beechwood; and great bouquets of soft flowers, mainly pink and white peonies, in crystal vases. Over the fireplace hung the painting Solange had given them, an appealing Mary Cassatt landscape. "But in this building they count every single space as a room. That's why Alix's twenty rooms seem more like thirty," she explained, understanding Solange's perplexity at New York apartments. "At the Dakota, they don't include reception rooms, pantries and major coat closets in the count!"

Solange had been in New York for a month, arriving on the *La Savoie* with fifteen trunks of clothes guaranteed to see her through the summer and into the colder weather, jewelry—both heirloom and new—for Thea, paintings, presents from Baccarat and Lalique, and tons of baby things from Au Nain Bleu and Fairyland for the arrival she had come to witness.

She had come down the gangplank on a clear summer

afternoon when even the docks of Manhattan look beautiful, and run straight into her son's arms, all her aristocratic demeanor vanishing when she saw his beloved face. Mr. Cullen was waiting to see her through customs and, once that formality was completed, Charles had escorted her out of the French Line pier and out to the street where his new Oldsmobile touring car, with the chauffeur standing beside it, was waiting to drive them back to Madison Avenue.

Thea was in the final weeks of her pregnancy and Solange, sensitive to the difficulties of a young woman having her first baby, even one as aware and up-to-date as Thea, strove to make this endless period of waiting easier for her by being the perfect mother-in-law, with compliments and praise instead of questions and complaints.

In all truth, Solange found very little to disturb her. She loved Thea on sight, recognizing at once that her youngest son's wife couldn't be any more perfect for him than if she'd chosen the young woman herself. She was pleased with their home as well, finding 667 Madison Avenue with its porte-cochere entrance, limestone facing, and carved figures decorating the second floor to be a proper domicile for the *jeune maries*. The apartment, with its high-ceilinged rooms and classic plaster moldings, pleased Solange aesthetically, and she truly admired Thea's skill as a decorator. Any qualms she felt about the apartment being on the seventh floor, and the fact that, until the baby came and a nurse would be installed, Charles and Thea's servants—a cook and two maids—came on a daily basis, Solange kept to herself. This was not Paris, this was New York, and it was not her life, it was theirs.

She also endorsed Charles' having spent the winter working as a French instructor at the Dwight School, praised his articles about Mexico that Doubleday, Page

680

was going to publish in book form after having achieved success in the *Century Magazine*, and urged him to take on a translation of a novella by the late Emile Zola that had recently come to light.

And so Solange had rather taken to life in New York, calling on old friends, making new acquaintances, visiting the shops and museums, going to the Dakota to see Henry and Alix and admire their son who had been born at the very end of March.

Naturally, she'd been eager to be on hand when the baby was born and, six days earlier, on July 25, it had taken all the combined persuasive efforts of Alix, Henry, Thea and Charles to convince Solange to spend a night on the town with the Thorpes. Dinner at Sherry's, followed by Fay Templeton's new show, *Lifting The Lid*, at the New Amsterdam Theatre was tempting, she admitted, but it was important to be at the apartment if and when . . . not that she intended to interfere with Emily Stern or the nurses, but—

In the end, she'd gone with Henry and Alix, not only to dinner and the play, but to a late supper at the Beaux Arts Cafe as well and, as soon as she returned to the apartment, she knew something was different. There was a new feeling that hadn't been there a few hours before, and all she needed was one look at Charles' shining, transfigured face as he came into the reception room—

"How do you feel, Thea, really?" Solange insisted.

"Slender again," Thea laughed. "Truly, *la belle mere*, I can't tell you how nice it is to have a waistline again!"

"Oh, I remember. I was in your condition three times," Solange pointed out, also laughing. "But new mothers like you and Alix have it so much easier—a skillful dressmaker to do normal-looking clothes for you, a doctor who treats you intelligently, whiffs of ether all long, and not having to spend weeks in bed afterwards."

"Emily believes in her patients getting out of bed

twenty-four or forty-eight hours after they have their babies as long as everything went well and, since I delivered in less than three hours—" Thea leaned back against the pillows. "It was like being on an express train. I couldn't believe it was over that quickly."

"You and Alix both."

"She was lucky this time again—Robert was born in just over an hour."

"So now you and your best friends all have babies. It's so much nicer like that, I think," Solange said. "What did Angela and Morgan name their baby?"

"Michael, after Morgan's father, and Regina and Ian named their little girl Chloe."

"What a pretty name," Solange said just as Charles came into the bedroom, carrying the afternoon mail.

"Having a good talk?" he asked, crossing the Savonnerie rug of rose, cream, and soft blue to sit beside Thea on the bed.

"We've been having a wonderful time talking about the usual things—like how wonderful you are—"

"And what you should do next," Solange added.

"Is this what's known as a daughter-in-law and mother-in-law getting on splendidly—and deciding between them what the husband and son should do with his professional life."

"Of course we were," Solange replied tartly. "You have a wife and a child to look after."

"I'll teach, I'll write and I'll translate."

"Richard North told me you would make a fine literary agent for European authors seeking American publishers."

"I don't know if that's such a compliment, Maman Dick thinks literary agents are the invention of the devil Of course, I can always let my wife support me," Charle said with a smile and a wink at Thea, but the comtesse saw the gesture and only laughed.

"You can't fool me, Charles. No matter what fun you make, I know how serious you are on the inside."

"That's better than the other way around," her son replied. "Oh, another thing, we just had a call from Tiffany's. Tomorrow they'll be delivering a present for ur baby from the Roosevelts."

"How nice," Solange replied. "But have either of you een the President since last November?"

"He had breakfast here on St. Patrick's Day. Didn't we ll you?" Thea asked.

"Well, there have been a few more important things appening," Solange smiled. "Isn't there a parade in ew York on St. Patrick's Day?"

"There certainly is, and the President took part in it is year, and then he had a big family wedding to go to. is niece Eleanor married her cousin Franklin, and T.R. ave the bride away. Early in the morning was the only me he could come and see us."

"Thea fed the President like a trencherman," Charles elated. "Broiled grapefruit with brown sugar, scrambled ggs with caviar, raisin pumpernickel bread with butter, nd lots of coffee."

"A very elegant meal for a trencherman, but perfect r a head of state," Solange smiled and took the mail that hea held out to her—letters from France, and the latest sue of *Scribners* which had a serial she was following. Did he enjoy it?"

"Oh, he loved the food, and he thanked us again and gain for going to Mexico City, and I think he was elighted that he had been an inadvertent matchmaker r us," Thea related. They had already told Solange the ll story behind their meeting, marriage, and stay in lexico.

"How was his family wedding?" the comtesse asked, aking for granted the fact that the de Renilles would ave been invited.

"Ask Charles. He and Henry went together since Al and I were rather out of commission by March 17. Wh. was it Henry said about the wedding, darling?"

"That the bridal couple would end up magnificently just fade away into the Social Register."

"Ah, well, time will tell," Solange said as she opene one of her letters and glanced at the pages. "Anoth baby—twins in fact—for Gerard and Ophelie!"

"What!"

Thea and Charles spoke at the same time, the astonishment obvious.

"Didn't you know? I assumed that you had since all you were in Mexico together—"

"We didn't know a thing," Thea exclaimed. "Opheli must have been further along than I was, and she was s sure she couldn't have a baby . . ." Quickly, Thea tol them both about Ophelie's visit to her room at th American Hospital. "Dr. Benning's examination result must have been very surprising to her."

"She must have been twice as surprised to deliver twi girls," Solange pointed out. "Pauline says the one ha Ophelie's eyes, the other Gerard's, so they can tell the apart."

"Among other things," Thea murmured to Charles who choked back his laughter, and announced it was tim to feed the baby.

"Charles is a wonderful father," Solange remarked a soon as Charles left the room. "But then, with the bab you produced, how could he fail to be."

"And I'm glad that you could share this time with us."

"Share, but not intrude on," Solange said as Charle returned carrying his infant daughter. "Ah, c'est un ange," she whispered, taking a look at her grand daughter. "Absolute perfection." She patted Charles cheek. "I'm off to my room to read the latest installmen of *The House of Mirth.* I know no good shall come to Mrs. Wharton's Lily Bart, but still I read on."

She left, and Charles sat down on the bed, holding the baby so that he and Thea could look down at the pink and cream form that was their six day old daughter. As they gazed at her, thick-lashed lids fluttered open to reveal Charles' topaz eyes with just a hint of green; the baby's soft, glossy hair promised to be a duplicate of Thea's.

Never, Thea thought, would she forget Charles' face when he saw their baby for the first time. It had been a combination of joy, disbelief and utter adoration for both of them, and five minutes later they had the perfect name that had eluded them over the months.

"Tatiana," Charles had said, "after Shakespeare's Queen of the Fairies." And the name fit perfectly.

"We've done pretty well, haven't we?" Thea asked as Charles transferred Tatiana to her arms. "Last year at this time we didn't even know each other, and now we have our baby, our home and each other."

"That's better than doing pretty well—it's superb work," Charles said as he gently undid the satin ribbon that held together the top of her pink crepe de chine nightgown and bent over to tenderly kiss one breast before guiding it to the infant's rosebud mouth.

Tatiana nursed hungrily, and Charles watched in fascination. "She's like a porcelain doll come to life," he whispered. "A perfect beauty, just like her mother."

"Oh, Charles—" For a moment, Thea was at a loss for words. "I haven't had a chance to tell you this in the past week, but all this winter, as I was getting bigger and bigger, you never made me feel that I was on some sort of pedestal, or that I was in my pregnancy alone."

"I think that I learned a great deal about giving and sharing while we were in Mexico," Charles replied. "And I never wanted you to worry that I saw you as some sort of brood mare, or that I was put off by you."

"You joked about it, though—the brood mare business."

"What else can you expect from a man who grew up on a stud farm?" Charles' eyes began to twinkle. "You know what they say, the early learning always sticks no matter what."

Thea smiled. "I certainly hope it does. Oh—look who's finished. Our gourmet in training."

"And a very selective one at that. Only the best for our Tatiana," Charles said quickly, kissing them both before they set about the task of burping her, and making sure her fine lawn gown was smooth and clean before cradling her gently, watching as she went back to sleep.

"I think I'm still getting used to her," Thea whispered.

"So am I. But there's also this great feeling of calm. That we're going to manage at being parents very well."

"I told you that nine months ago."

"And you were right, but remember that I don't do things the easy way."

"No, only the right way. Or it comes out right in the end, and that's what counts," Thea said, and they both thought about last November, Mexico City and Laredo, and of Basil Summerfield who had risked more than they had to capture Arthur Coburn, now in British protective custody; and Major Donovan, now recovered and a staff officer at a Massachusetts installation so he could be near his son; and the de Laulans who were established in Washington, and Jean-Christophe who would go to Princeton in the fall; and the de Veigas whom they would see in September when the older couple planned to come to New York.

People who, for better or worse, had crossed their path, the majority of whom would always go on and triumph because their principles and beliefs would guide them to always identify right from wrong.

"I was just thinking how far we've come together."

"So was I. And I don't think we've done badly at all," Charles said, and Thea knew the great satisfaction, happiness and contentment that lay behind his simple words because she felt the same emotions in herself.

Together, they delightedly watched Tatiana sleep and, quietly, Charles began to sing a song he had learned in his own nursery days:

> Sur le pont d'Avignon,
> L'on y danse,
> L'on y danse—